英文文法全書

WORLD TALK: DANCING WITH ENGLISH
A BOOK OF COMPREHENSIVE GRAMMAR

Dennis Le Boeuf
景黎明

彩色二版

UNIT 1

句子

Sentences

UNIT 2

名詞

Nouns

UNIT 3

代名詞

Pronouns

冠詞

Articles

5

形容詞

Adjectives

6

副詞

Adverbs

7 關係詞與形容詞子句和名詞子句

Relatives in Adjective Clauses and Noun Clauses

連接詞與並列句和從屬子句

Conjunctions, Compound Sentences, and Dependent Clauses (Adverbial Clauses and Noun Clauses)

UNIT 9

介系詞

Prepositions

UNIT 10

動詞

Verbs

UNIT 11

時態

Tenses

UNIT 12

主動語態與被動語態

The Active Voice and the Passive Voice

UNIT 13

直接引語與間接引語

Direct Speech and Indirect Speech

UNIT 14

語氣

Mood

UNIT 15

句子的結構

Sentence Structure

UNIT 16

分詞、不定式和動名詞

Participles, Infinitives, and Gerunds

UNIT 17 標點符號

Punctuation

UNIT 18

首字母大寫

Capitalization

UNIT 19

平行結構

Parallel Structure

UNIT 20

分詞片語和垂懸結構

Participial Phrases and the Dangling Construction

UNIT 21

重疊詞和累贅修飾語

Doublet Phrases and Unnecessary Modifiers

UNIT 22

主詞和述語一致

Subject-Verb Agreement

附錄

索引

問題一 如何才能有效地學好道地的英語，避免洋涇濱英語？

在過去，人們學習英語時主要是著重在學習英文文法，但人們後來意識到，就算把文法規則都背上了，卻仍然無法在真實的世界中和英語人士交流。於是，外語教育開始強調英語的聽與說訓練，這種「交流法」對 ESL（English as a Second Language）學生來說，特別能產生效果。所謂 ESL 學生，是指生活在英語系國家，但不是以英語為母語的學生。他們幾乎每天有 16 個小時接觸標準地道的英語，在與母語人士溝通的過程中，如果講錯、寫錯了，母語人士的老師會糾正他們，或者他們也可以從旁人不解的表情中意識到的錯誤。

然而，這種方式對 EFL（English as a Foreign Language）學生來說，成效就不彰了，所謂 EFL 學生，是指在非英語系國家中學習英語的學生。原因很簡單：學生們彼此互相交流的，不過是蹩腳的英語。例如：

一個學生大聲地用英語說：「My home has a car.」
另一位學生不甘示弱地跟著說：「My home has two cars.」

很快地，每個學生都用這個錯誤的英語句型「My home has . . .」大聲喊叫，而沒有意識到自己講的英語是錯誤的。

還有，在某座小學裡，學生都會說：「I like to play balls.」

這句話可窘大了，但是學生們渾然不覺！ EFL 學生如果講錯了，很少能得到有效的糾正，結果就學了錯誤的英語而不自知，以致於日後講出來、寫出來的都是洋涇濱英語。我們來看一下下面的英語辨析：

✗ "Our home has three cars," said sweet little Dee.
✔ "We have three cars," said sweet little Dee.
✔ "My family has three cars," said sweet little Dee.
「我們家有三輛小汽車。」可愛的小蒂說。

ⴑ have 是用來表示「擁有;佔有」,表示所屬關係。

ⴑ Our home 不能擁有汽車,但人(people)就可以擁有汽車。

上面的例子是華人學生常犯的錯誤。中文說「我們家有三輛汽車」,如果要使用動詞 have 來表達這句話,那麼「我們家」就要用「we」或「my family」來表達,因為只有「人」才能擁有汽車,「home」不是人,無法擁有汽車。

坊間還有一種學習方法,強調「大聲喊出英語」,喊得越大聲,你的英語就會越好,並認為這是學好英語的唯一最佳方法。如果鼓勵學生大膽講英語,這是可以的,不過,倒不會因為聲音喊得大聲了,英語就可以學得漂亮。我們在美國認識一個亞洲來的研究生,他的專業表現很優秀,也可以用英語滔滔不絕地講上幾個小時,只是遺憾的是,美語人士只能尷尬地微笑望著他,因為他們聽不懂這位老兄的英語。

學習語言,是為了溝通,如果你練習了一口蹩腳的英語,那麼你講得再大聲、再流利,母語人士還是聽不懂你說的話、看不懂你寫的英語。

加州大學著名的語言教育教授 Stephen Krashen 博士,他在《閱讀的力量》一書中表示:任何一門語言的掌握,是來自於「輸入」,而不是來自「輸出」;是來自「理解」,而不是來自「生產」。顯然,EFL 學生首先需要**大量輸入正確的英語**,盡量減少錯誤的輸入。「聽」和「讀」,是輸入;「說」和「寫」,是輸出。

要學習好漂亮、道地的英語,首先,要大量地聽標準英語、大量地閱讀簡易有趣的現代英文書籍。聽和讀同時進行,效果最好。

通過大量地聽和閱,掌握了一些標準的句型和一定的字彙量,然後再練習輸出(說和寫)。在練習輸出的過程中,還要不斷地加強輸入(聽和讀)。

學習文法,也要結合大量地閱讀。閱讀有趣的英語內容,這對 EFL 學生來說是很好的練習,這也就是為什麼我們盡全力要讓本書成為一本有趣的文法書。

我們也盡量要讓本書不同於其他的文法學習書。本書詳細闡述各種基礎或進階的文法規則和慣用法,並且廣泛運用各種領域的題材來編寫有趣的例句,還包括英式和美式英語的許多重要區別。此外，書中的例句也運用大量的押韻，讓你閱讀起來可以琅琅上口。在學習例句的同時，你也可以試一試，看看句尾的字與句中哪些字押韻，讓你的英語學習變得更饒富趣味。

書中也編寫了一些有趣的故事。我們努力寫出栩栩如生、趣味盎然的句子，有日常生活中的詼諧快樂的句子，也有文學式寫作的句子，這樣讀者就會覺得這本書不單單是在談枯燥的文法規則，而是一本趣味書籍。

這本書還有一個特色：書中包含了很多的人名。英文的人名，是外語教育中很重要的一個部分，但卻常被忽視了。很多文法書的例句大都使用代名詞 he, she, we, I，這樣的寫法雖然比較簡單，卻顯得枯燥，不太真實。在現實生活中，人們在談話或寫作時，常常會提及人名。讀到有人名的例句時，你會感覺到真實性。總之，這是一本鼓勵 EFL 學生趣味閱讀，和英語文法「翩翩起舞」的一個嘗試。

我們衷心盼望，EFL 的老師和學生會覺得本書好用又有趣。你可以把這本書當作工具書來使用，這是一本豐富的綜合性文法書，凡是你需要掌握的文法規則，本書都囊括了，甚至也包括了一些具挑戰性或爭議性的文法規則。認真學習這本書，可以幫助你在英語考試中獲得高分。如果你是英文老師，這本書將可以幫助你的學生奠定最厚實的英文文法基礎。你也可以把本書當作一本閱讀材料，欣賞書中的栩栩如生的句子、詼諧的內容、趣味的韻腳，還有各式各樣的故事性內容。這是本書與一般的文法書特別不同的地方。

問題二 亞洲學生和母語人士溝通時，最大的困難是什麼？

在美國大學教國際學生時，我們發現，這些學生所面臨的最大的困難，是字彙量有限，因而導致閱讀速度緩慢。這些學生在踏進美國之前，未大量閱讀英語，因此閱讀速度很慢，每晚都得熬夜完成老師交付的閱讀課業。同樣一份閱讀作業，美國學生可能只需要三個小時就可以讀完，亞洲學生卻可能要花上十個小時才能完成。

有一次，我們驚訝地發現，來自亞洲的研究生，連閱讀小學四年級程度的小說都有困難。當時，我們要學生在週末時閱讀一本叫做《甜河谷姊妹》（*Sweet Valley Twins*）的小說。這本小說，美國大學生大概只要一、兩個小時的時間就可以讀完，然而，優秀的亞洲學生卻花了七、八個小時才看完，對他們來說，裡面的生字很多。然而，這本書事實上是為美國小學四年級的學生所寫的趣味故事書。

有限的閱讀量，導致有限的字彙量；有限的字彙量，又導致聽力理解和閱讀理解的困難。而字彙的匱乏，導致不知道如何恰當地表達自己，也連帶地造成了在說和寫方面的困難。

許多在 TOEFL 考試中拿高分的學生，卻在閱讀、寫作、聽、說各方面都面臨了很大的困難，尤其是閱讀，這也是美國的亞洲學生所面臨的很大困境。為什麼聰明勤奮的亞洲學生到了美國大學之後，在大量閱讀和寫作方面的課業要求上，感到苦惱呢？為什麼在托福考試中拿高分的亞洲大學生和研究生，卻不知道美國小學四年級學生所使用的字彙呢？

美國四年級的小學生（九歲），他們所掌握的字彙量是 29,300，而托福的字彙測驗量卻只有 14,000 字。在亞洲，這有限的 14,000 字彙量，是 EFL 教學的目標。

更不幸的是，這些勤奮聰明的亞洲學生來到美國之後，要和他們競爭的同學，並不是九歲的美國小學生，而是美國的大學生或研究生。而美國大學二年級的學生，他們平均的字彙量是十二萬字！

亞洲托福高材生的字彙量	14,000
美國四年級小學生的字彙量	29,300
美國大學二年級生的字彙量	120,000

在一些亞洲國家，中學畢業生的字彙量是 1,000 到 2,000 個字，高中畢業生則是 8,000 字。這樣的字彙量足夠嗎？在美國，五歲孩子的平均字彙量是 9,600，六歲的孩子是 14,700，八歲的孩子是 26,300，九歲的孩子是 29,300，十歲的孩子是 34,300，而二十歲的大學生是 120,000。顯然，在亞洲，如果希望學生能夠在 20 歲時掌握到 120,000 個英語字彙，那麼 EFL 教育需要從一開始就朝重視閱讀的方向發展。

問題三 英美人士是如何精通英語的？

在美國，優秀的學生平均每天閱讀 2 小時 12 分，約閱讀 25,000 字的字彙量，並且每天聆聽 15,000 至 35,000 個英文單字。

美國的中小學常會舉辦閱讀比賽。有一年，一所小學為了鼓勵七歲的學生閱讀，便以招待去主題樂園玩為獎品：凡是在一年內閱讀 800 本趣味書籍的二年級學生，都可以獲得免費一日遊。那一年，有一個七歲的男孩讀了 1,643 本書。後來，這個小男孩在 19 歲時就獲得了物理博士。這所學校的美國老師明白這個基本的道理：任何語言中的佼佼者，都是通過大量閱讀趣味書籍而誕生的。

在亞洲，是否有學校鼓勵這種趣味閱讀競賽？我們何不也嘗試一下？如果我們不鼓勵學生們從小就大量閱讀英語，又如何能期待他們熟練地掌握這門世界語言呢？

問題四 對於如何學習英語的研究結論，是什麼？

許多學者對人們如何有效學習英語，進行過大量研究。加州大學的 Stephen Krashen 博士對這類研究進行了仔細分析。Krashen 博士出版過許多關於如何學習英語的書，不論是對母語人士或非母語人士來說，Krashen 博士都是公認的著名專家。Krashen 博士做出的總結是：**趣味閱讀**，能有效地提高閱讀理解能力、寫作技巧能力、擴大字彙量、提高拼寫能力、更有效地運用文法，並且擴大知識面。

學校需要為 EFL 學生提供豐富的趣味英語書籍，否則語言教學不可能有所突破，EFL 學生在與英語國家的學生競爭，或是在進行國際商貿時，將繼續處於不利的地位。

總結

有趣而高品質的輸入，可以減少英文的錯誤，也就是說——大量聽標準英文來提高口語能力，大量閱讀趣味簡易書籍來提高文法和寫作程度。**你閱讀得愈多，你的語言能力就愈強**。

本書就是基於這個理論而完成的——學習英語要基於大量的趣味閱讀。在這本書裡，你可以找到你需要的文法規則，你會閱讀到許多押韻的趣味例句（這些都是道地的英語），也會學到許多人名。閱讀這本厚厚的趣味文法書，你在拼寫、英文文法、閱讀理解、寫作技巧、字彙量等各方面，都將士別三日，令人刮目相看！

本書特色

誰敢說文法不重要？文法是語言的解讀器，缺少文法，在英語的世界裡寸步難行。本書的專業美籍作者，在美國、中國、臺灣有多年豐富的教學經驗，對英語文法有深入的研究，嘔心瀝血地編寫了這本豐富完備的綜合性文法書，內容涵蓋所需要的文法項目。本書具有下列特色：

完整詳盡的文法知識：本書從基礎的文法到進階的文法要項說明、比較，地毯式地蒐羅所有英文文法，不管是中學生、大學生、社會人士或是老師，不論是自修、教學，或是要準備全民英檢、學測、高普考，還是托福、多益等留學考試，本書都是絕對必備的英文文法工具書！

文字圖解分析：本書利用格線、箭頭指引等圖解方式，解說一目了然！

豐富的表格整理與對照：將文法項目以表格方式呈現，強化條目之間的比較效果。

正誤用法比較：以正誤用法來分析文法的用法，點出學生常犯的文法錯誤。

豐富趣味的例句：例句類型包羅萬象，充滿想像力，有玩笑話、日常對話、童話等，內容涵蓋天文、經濟、歷史等範疇，提升學習效果。例句中常採用押韻的字彙與人名，朗讀起來韻味十足，饒富樂趣。

補充說明與延伸學習：書中不時穿插「Note」和「Diving Deep Into English」，前者是補充說明，後者是延伸學習，可參照內容學習，亦可單獨查閱！

文法、字彙一網打盡：除了羅列完備的文法，本書大量的字彙舉例、用字遣詞多變化的例句，可以幫助你吸收英文單字。

英美用法比較：本書以美式英語文法為主，引導讀者學習最標準的美式英語，輔以相關英式英語的用法比較，讓讀者得以瞭解差異 。

運用大量的英語姓名：市面上一般的書籍，往往以 he/she/it 等作為例句的主角，不然就是全書都採用 John、Mary 這些簡易常用的人名，使得學生對於實際生活中接觸到的外籍人士姓名，覺得陌生拗口，唸不出來。本書例句大量使用不同的英文人名，句子多變化，更能強化讀者對英文姓名的認識。

忠於發音之人名翻譯：您是否曾經依據中文翻譯，猜測某個人名的英文發音，卻發現兩者相差甚遠呢？本書採取與發音相近的翻譯，減少讀者被翻譯誤導，而唸錯姓名的機會。況且，許多人名與句中的某個字是押韻的，可以幫助練習語感。

實用的附錄：本書共編寫七篇附錄，提供時態變化、常用詞彙等資訊，讀者可與內文參照閱讀，也可單獨背誦。

文法術語索引：我們將書中出現的文法術語，分別編排中文與英文索引，不但各類文法術語一目了然，搜尋專有名詞相關用法更是便捷！

穿插彩色插圖：幫助理解、記憶，學習兼具效率與趣味。

學習方式

從頭開始讀起：本書依照國外學童學習文法的最佳學習步驟編排，入門讀者可從頭依序學習，由簡而深，學習完整的文法知識。

隨時查詢文法：本書編排詳盡的目錄、索引，設計清楚易見的書眉，因此除了逐條閱讀，本書亦是隨時查詢文法要項的工具書。即使已經學過文法，你還是需要一本這樣完善的參考書，隨時查閱。

獨立內容學習：清楚明顯的「Note」與「Diving Deep Into English」的補充說明格式，除了搭配上下文閱讀，亦適合單獨翻閱學習。

檢索方式

由目錄檢索：層次分明、豐富的目錄，是查詢各大文法要點的第一道入口！

由索引搜尋：本書分列中、英文專有名詞的索引，詳列各項文法術語的說明頁數，包括〈Diving Deep Into English〉的索引。

詳盡交叉參照：文中依照內容需要，補充可參照的相關條目與頁碼，例如「參見第 1 頁〈Unit 1 句子〉」，參照最便利！

本書結構與使用圖解

單元：依文法主題分為 22 個 Unit，Unit 下再細分 Part。

Note：補充説明，配合上下文參照閱讀。

有些文法學家將**行為動詞及其後面的受詞和狀語**，統稱為述語（以下綠色字）。

- My dog found a big bone.
  我的狗找到了一根大骨頭。

Diving Deep Into English：延伸學習，補充説明與前述主題相關的重要文法常識，主題明確，亦適合單獨學習及查閱（書末附有索引）。

Diving Deep Into English　魚（fish）的單複數

fish 的複數形有兩種：fish 和 fishes。

1. 指同種類的魚，或泛指的魚：無論單數還是複數，都用 fish。
2. 指多種不同種類的魚：fish 或 fishes 兩種複數形式皆可（但以 fish 較常見）。

those fish

several kinds of fish
several kinds of fishes

文字圖解說明：使用色彩、線條的圖解方式，幫助理解文法。

- She is one of the most interesting women (that) I have ever met.
  她是我見過最有趣的女子了。　↑ 受詞
- Is there anything (that) I can do for you? 我能為你做些什麼？（that：受詞）
- Is this all that is left? 就剩這些嗎？（that：主詞）

插畫圖解說明：以輕鬆可愛的插圖方式呈現，幫助理解文法，提高學習效率。

詳盡的交叉參照：提供相關文法的參照頁碼及標題，有助一次釐清文法觀念。

b 在**連綴動詞**（be、appear 等）或用作連綴動詞的**感官動詞**（look、sound 等）後面，要用形容詞 good，不用副詞 well。參見275頁〈6 連綴動詞 + 形容詞；行為動詞 + 副詞〉。

使用符號說明

✗ 錯誤用法

✓ 正確用法

American	美式英語
British	英式英語
Mainly American	主要為美式用語
Mainly British	主要為英式用語
Common	常用語
Less common	較不常用語
Not common	不常用語
Formal	正式用語
More formal	更正式用語
Very formal	非常正式用語
Informal	口語用語

Casual	非正式用語
Awkward	笨拙的用法
Unnatural	不自然的用法
Natural	自然的用法
Proper	適當的用法
Not proper	不適當的用法
Positive	原級
Comparative	比較級
Superlative	最高級
Redundant	累贅、多餘的用語
Not standard	不標準的用語
Acceptable	可接受的用語
Better	較佳的用語
Idiomatic	慣用語
Grammatically correct	文法正確
Definite	明確的用語
Less definite	較不明確的用語
Direct speech	直接引述
Indirect speech	間接引述
Affirmative	肯定句
Interrogative	疑問句
Negative	否定句
Passive	被動語態
Active	主動語態
Statement	陳述句
Question	疑問句
Careful	謹慎的用法
Not careful	不謹慎的用法
Clear	清楚的用法
Not clear	不清楚的用法

UNIT 01 句子

Sentences

句子的定義

句子（Sentences）

1 句子由一組詞構成，表達一個完整的概念。一個句子包含兩個主要成分：**主詞**和**述語**。也就是說，一個句子必須要有**主詞**和**述語動詞**。

句子 → **主詞** + **述語**

← 述語動詞用來說明主詞所做的動作，或主詞所處的狀態。

- She wrote **a funny story.** 她寫了一個有趣的故事。
- Margo will fly **over Chicago.** 瑪歌將從芝加哥上空飛過。
- NASA hired **Amy Shaw.** 美國國家航空暨太空總署雇用了艾咪・蕭。

2 句子還可包括**主詞補語**、**受詞**、**狀語**（用來修飾動詞、形容詞、另一個副詞或整個句子）、**定語**（用來修飾名詞或代名詞）等句子成分。

3 一組詞如果沒有主詞和述語動詞，就不是一個句子，不過在口語中回答問題時，有時會用**省略句**作簡略回答。省略句裡有可能只有主詞。

Who is going with me, you or Sue?

Sue.

↑ 口語中，可以使用省略句作簡略回答，省略句裡可以只有主詞（Sue）。

2 主詞（Subjects）

1 **主詞**是述語動詞所描述的人、動物、地點或事物，一般置於句首，但在 there be 結構、倒裝句和許多疑問句中，主詞位於動詞後面。主詞可以是一個字、一個片語，或是一個子句，例如：

主詞是一個字	Wendy	溫蒂
主詞是一個片語	lovely Wendy	可愛的溫蒂
主詞是一個子句	those who want to go	那些想去的人

2 依形式而言，主詞可分為以下兩種：

簡單主詞	man 人　we 我們	← 一個名詞或代名詞。
完全主詞	the angry old man 憤怒的老人	← 一個名詞或代名詞，及其修飾語。

3 就數量而言，主詞還可分為以下兩種：

單一主詞	Wendy	溫蒂
複合主詞	Wendy and Lily	溫蒂和莉莉

- **The boy jumped over the fence.**
  那男孩跳過柵欄。
  ↑ 誰跳過柵欄？是那男孩。主詞是 The boy。
- **She will give me her cellphone number.**
  她要把她的手機號碼給我。
  ↑ 誰會給我手機號碼？是她。句子的主詞是 She。
- **I will sell my grandma's antique car.**
  我要把奶奶的古董車給賣了。
  ↑ 誰要賣車？是我。句子的主詞是 I。
- **My little dog Scot kicked the ball to Paul.**
  我的小狗史考特把球踢給保羅。
  ↑ 誰踢球？是我的小狗史考特。片語 My little dog Scot 是句子的主詞。

3 述語（Predicates）

1 **述語**用來描述主詞的**行為**或**狀態**，以動詞擔任，一般置於主詞之後。可分為以下兩種：

簡單述語	walk, are walking, have walked, will have walked 走	← 只有單一述語動詞，或是一個述語動詞加上助動詞。
完全述語	walked fast to the beach 快速地走向海灘	← 包括述語動詞，以及修飾這個動詞的一切詞彙，如副詞、副詞片語等。

2 述語動詞可以是一個「單一動詞」或「複合動詞」，例如：

單一動詞	walked 走	← 只有一個動詞。
複合動詞	walked and talked 邊走邊講	← 由 walked 和 talked 兩個動詞組成。

- **She** danced. 她跳了舞。 → 簡單述語（單一動詞）
- **Bing** is hunting. 賓在打獵。
  ↑ 簡單述語（助動詞＋述語動詞；單一動詞）
- **Ann** ran and ran. 安跑了又跑。 → 複合動詞
- **The balloon** is flying high in the blue sky.
  氣球在蔚藍的天空中高高飛翔。 → 完全述語

Diving Deep Into English 1 句子結構圖解分析

簡單主詞　單一述語動詞

❶ Wendy Peach walked.
溫蒂．皮奇　散過步了。

完全主詞　完全述語

❷ Lovely Wendy Peach walked quickly to the beach.
可愛的溫蒂．皮奇　迅速地走向海灘。

複合主詞　複合述語動詞

❸ Tom and I walked and talked.
湯姆和我　邊走邊聊。

簡單主詞　完全述語

❹ Kay will learn to ride a horse today.
凱　今天要學習騎馬。

完全主詞　簡單述語（助動詞 can ＋述語動詞 wink）

❺ The pink doll can wink.
這個粉紅色的洋娃娃　會眨眼睛。

複合主詞　簡單述語（助動詞 can ＋述語動詞 swim）

❻ Jim and I can swim.
吉姆和我　會游泳。

簡單主詞　完全述語

❼ Kay is swimming with her dog Ray.
凱　正在和她的狗雷一起游泳。

4 主詞補語（Subject Complements）

主詞補語是出現在**連綴動詞**（連綴動詞用來描述狀態，如：be、seem、appear、look、become 等）後面的名詞、形容詞、片語（介系詞片語、不定式片語、動名詞片語）或子句，用來補充說明主詞的特質、狀態。

- Henry is hungry. → 主詞補語為形容詞。
  亨利　餓了。
- Her cottage is by Deer Lake. → 主詞補語為介系詞片語。
  她的別墅　在鹿湖附近。
- The clown is upside-down. → 主詞補語為形容詞。
  小丑　倒立。

- Scot's two sisters are (both) astronauts. → 主詞補語為名詞。
  史考特的兩個姐姐 （都）是太空人。

- Mom is on the phone. → 主詞補語為介系詞片語。
  媽媽 在打電話。

有些文法學家把**連綴動詞及之後所有的詞**，都看作述語（以下綠色字）。

- He is greedy. 他很貪婪。
- Dwight became famous overnight.
  杜威特一夕之間成了名。

5 受詞（Objects）

受詞是直接或間接**接受動詞動作**的名詞、代名詞、片語（名詞片語、動名詞片語、不定式片語）或子句；跟在**介系詞後面**的名詞、代名詞、片語或子句，也是受詞。

↓ 名詞片語作受詞。

- Bess made her own wedding dress.
  貝絲縫製了她自己的結婚禮服。

- Jake ate all the cheesecake.
  傑克吃了所有的起司蛋糕。

- My dog found a big bone.
  我的狗找到了一根大骨頭。

- I like to believe that people in the long run are going to do more to promote peace than our governments.
  (President Dwight David Eisenhower)
  我願意相信，在促進和平方面，人民比政府的貢獻終究會更大。
  ↑ 不定式 to believe 作動詞 like 的受詞，that 引導的子句作不定式動詞 to believe 的受詞。

有些文法學家將**行為動詞及其後面的受詞和狀語**，統稱為述語（以下綠色字）。

- My dog found a big bone.
  我的狗找到了一根大骨頭。
- He went on talking about his new jeep until I fell asleep.
  他繼續談著他的新吉普車，直到我睡著。
  ↳ 主詞是 He。述語動詞 went on 說明主詞在做什麼。動名詞片語 talking about his new jeep 是動詞 went on 的受詞，until I fell asleep 是時間副詞子句。

6 狀語（Adverbials）

狀語用來區別或限制事物的動作、形態、性質，由**副詞**、**片語**（介系詞片語、分詞片語、不定式片語）或**子句**擔任。

1 **副詞**（adverb）：副詞是用來修飾動詞、形容詞、另一個副詞或整個句子的詞，用來告訴我們事件發生的**時間**、**地點**、**方式**等，在句中作**狀語**。例如：

- cheerfully 愉快地
- however 然而
- never 永不
- often 時常
- quickly 快速地
- quietly 安靜地
- really 真正地
- yesterday 昨天
- widely 廣泛地

- **Mary is** very naughty. 瑪麗很淘氣。
  ↳ 副詞 very 修飾形容詞 naughty。

- **Dwight** snored very loudly **last night.**
  杜威特昨晚打呼的聲音很大。
  ↳ 副詞 loudly 用來修飾動詞 snored。
  ↳ 副詞 very 則用來修飾另一個副詞 loudly。
- **Amy** cheerfully sent **a text message to Lily.**
  艾咪愉快地發了一個手機簡訊給莉莉。
  ↳ 副詞 cheerfully 修飾動詞 sent。

- Jean is reading quietly in his cabin. 琴正在小屋裡安靜地閱讀。
  ↳ 副詞 quietly 修飾動詞 is reading。

- However Jim did his magic tricks, it was very clever of him.
  吉姆不管變什麼魔術把戲，他都很機敏。
  ↳ 副詞 However 修飾子句 Jim did his magic tricks。

2 **副詞片語**（adverbial phrase）：副詞片語是具有和副詞相同功能的片語，在句中作**狀語**，表示**條件**、**原因**、**目的**、**程度**和**方式**等。這些副詞片語可以放在句首、句尾、句中，或其所修飾的成分前面。

- My cat is sleeping on the cot with Scot. 我的貓和史考特在吊床上睡覺。
  ↳ 兩個介系詞片語 on the cot 和 with Scot
  是副詞片語，修飾動詞 is sleeping。

- Owing to her grin, she will certainly win. 就衝著她這個微笑，她贏定了。
  ↳ 介系詞片語 Owing to her grin 是句中的
  原因副詞片語（又稱原因狀語）；副詞 certainly 修飾動詞 will win。

- Steve is snoring in a tent. 史蒂夫在帳篷裡打鼾。
  ↳ 介系詞片語 in a tent 是句中的地點副詞片語（又稱地點狀語）。

- Kate has been in Nigeria since 2008.
  凱特從 2008 年開始就在奈及利亞了。
  ↳ 介系詞片語 in Nigeria（地點）和 since 2008（時間）是副詞片語，
  作狀語，修飾動詞 has been。

- Encouraged by her previous success, Trish tried to catch more fish.
  受到前次成功的激勵，翠西努力去釣更多的魚。
  ↳ 前面的 Encouraged 這組字是分詞片語，在句中作原因狀語。

- To show politeness, we should use the three magic expressions, “Please,” “Thank you,” and “Excuse me.”
  為表示禮貌，我們應該使用這三個神奇的用語：請、謝謝、對不起。
  ↳ 句首的 To show politeness 是不定式片語，
  在句中作目的狀語，修飾後面的整個句子。

Thank you.
Please.
Excuse me.

- **Erica and Trish are going to America** to study business English.
  艾芮卡和翠西要去美國攻讀商務英文。
  ↑ 句尾的不定式片語 to study business English 作目的狀語，修飾動詞 are going。

- Since the hurricane destroyed our home, **we've been staying at the high school.**
  自從颶風毀壞了我們的家，我們就一直住在那所高中裡。
  ↑ since 引導副詞子句，表示時間，在句中作時間狀語。

- With the help of Sue, **we finally got to Honolulu.**
  在蘇的幫助下，我們終於到達了檀香山。
  ↑ 介系詞片語作狀語。

- **Did he win the marathon** by a narrow margin?
  他在馬拉松賽跑中險勝嗎？
  ↑ 介系詞片語作狀語。
  » 參見 257 頁〈Unit 6 副詞〉。

7 定語（Attributives）

定語用來修飾**名詞**和**代名詞**，可由形容詞、代名詞、名詞、數詞（如 three, the third）、不定式片語、介系詞片語、分詞或子句來擔任。片語和子句作定語時，要置於所修飾的字後面。

- **Lily is a** pretty **and** witty **girl.**
  莉莉是一個既美麗又機智的女子。
  ↑ 形容詞作定語，修飾名詞 girl。

- **What are you going to do during** your **vacation in July?**
  你七月放假時打算做什麼？ → 代名詞作定語，修飾名詞 vacation。

- **Is your husband a** bus **driver?**
  你的丈夫是公車司機嗎？
  ↑ 名詞作定語，修飾名詞 driver。

- **Bess has no wish** to move back to the U.S. 貝絲一點都不想搬回美國。
  ↑ 不定式片語作定語，修飾名詞 wish。

- Who is that weird guy with a long beard?
  那個留著長鬍子的怪咖是誰？
  ↳ 形容詞 weird 作定語，修飾名詞 guy。
  ↳ 介系詞片語 with a long beard 作定語，修飾名詞 guy。

- Is that crying boy called Roy?
  正在大哭的那個男孩叫羅伊嗎？
  ↳ 現在分詞作定語，修飾名詞 boy。

- After Ann won the 100-meter sprint, her father had a satisfied look on his face. 安在百米衝刺中獲勝後，她的父親臉上露出滿足的神情。
  ↳ 過去分詞作定語，修飾名詞 look。
  » 參見 715 頁〈Unit 15 句子的結構〉。

- I lent her a book that is easy and fun to read.
  我借給她一本讀起來輕鬆又有趣的書。
  ↳ that 引導的子句作定語，修飾名詞 book。
  » 參見 715 頁〈Unit 15 句子的結構〉。

This book is easy and fun to read.
這本書好讀又有趣。

除了極少數的副詞（如：here, there）外，副詞通常不修飾名詞，不作定語。here、there 等副詞作定語，要置於所修飾的名詞後面。

- the basketball players over there 在那邊的那些籃球運動員
- the computers here 這裡的電腦

8 受詞補語（Object Complements）

受詞補語通常由名詞、代名詞、形容詞或片語擔任，位於受詞後，對受詞進行補充說明。

- Sue is going to paint her bedroom door red.
  蘇打算把她臥室的門漆成紅色。
  ↳ 形容詞作受詞補語。

- We appointed Tom treasurer. 我們任命湯姆為出納。
  ↳ 名詞作受詞補語。

句子的種類

1 **肯定句**：用來陳述事實，並對事實進行肯定，而不是否定或提問。
肯定句以**句號（.）**結尾。

- **I'm glad that he quit smoking and drinking.**
我很高興他戒了菸和酒。

2 **否定句**：如果在動詞前面加上否定詞，例如 not、never、rarely、hardly，那麼這個動詞或句子就帶有否定意義，構成**否定句**。否定句也以**句號（.）**結尾。

- **I do not want to kiss Scot, because he smokes a lot.**
我不想親史考特，因為他是個大菸槍。

» 參見 666 頁〈2 否定陳述句〉。

3 **疑問句**：用來提問，以**問號（?）**結尾。

- **Do you want the last piece of cherry pie?**
你想要最後一塊櫻桃派嗎？
- **Why did she take college classes while still in high school?**
為什麼她還在念高中就修了大學的課程？
- **Did the three blind mice run away when the farmer's wife waved her big knife?**
當農夫的妻子揮起她的大刀時，那三隻瞎眼老鼠跑走了嗎？

» 參見 669 頁〈Part 2 疑問句〉。

4 **感嘆句**：用來表達驚訝、懷疑、生氣、煩惱和歡樂等感情，以**驚嘆號（!）**結尾。

- **What a beautiful day to play!**
  真是一個適合玩樂的好天氣啊！
- **Isn't Bart strong and smart!**
  巴特真是又強壯又聰明！
  ↑ 注意 這句不是疑問句。
  » 參見 684 頁〈Part 4 感嘆句〉。

5 **祈使句**：用來表達命令、強烈的要求或告誡，通常以**句號（.）**結尾，但如果是一個**強烈命令**，也可以用**驚嘆號（!）**結尾，在這種情況下，這個命令句既是祈使句也是感嘆句。祈使句的主詞是第二人稱 **you**，但通常主詞 you 會被省略。

- **Please ask Tom to call Mom.**
  請叫湯姆打電話給媽媽。
- **Watch your step.** 留心腳下。
- **Go away, Kay!** 走開，凱！
- **Don't feed the animals.** 請勿餵食動物。
- **Ben, never do that again.** 班，不要再做那種事了。
  ↑ 祈使句的句首可以加一個人名，強調主詞。
- **Dee, don't mess with me!** 蒂，別惹我！
- **Stop it!** 住手！
- **Nick, be quick!** 尼克，快一點！
  » 參見 687 頁〈Part 5 祈使語氣〉。

UNIT

02 名詞

Nouns

名詞的定義

1 何謂名詞？

名詞是用來表示人、事、物、地點、行為、感情等的字或片語，例如：

- Mark jogs along a path in Central Park. 馬克在中央公園裡的小路上慢跑。
  ⤷ Mark 是人的名字，path 是物的名稱，Central Park 是地點的名稱，三者都是名詞。

2 人物（People）

- adult 成人
- baby 嬰兒
- female 女人
- fool 傻瓜
- hero 英雄
- heroine 女英雄
- pilot 飛行員
- princess 公主
- youth 青年

Diving Deep Into English 2 人物名詞的常見拼法

❶ 以 -er 結尾的人物名詞

- banker 銀行家
- buyer 買方
- customer 顧客
- driver 司機
- lawyer 律師
- manager 經理
- painter 畫家
- police officer 警官
- reporter 記者
- seller 賣方
- teenager 青少年
- writer 作家

❷ 以 -or 結尾的人物名詞

- actor 演員
- collector 收藏家
- conductor 指揮
- director 導演
- doctor 醫生
- editor 編輯
- inventor 發明家
- neighbor 鄰居
- visitor 參觀者

❸ 以 -ist 結尾的人物名詞

- artist 藝術家
- dentist 牙醫
- pianist 鋼琴家
- scientist 科學家
- tourist 觀光客
- typist 打字員

❹ 以 -ian 結尾的人物名詞

- historian 歷史學家
- librarian 圖書館員
- musician 音樂家
- politician 政治家

3 無生命的事物（Inanimate Things）

1 服裝鞋帽 Clothing and Things You Wear

- belt 腰帶
- hat 帽子
- ice skates 溜冰鞋
- jacket 夾克
- pants 褲子
- shoes 鞋
- swimming suit 泳衣
- T-shirt T恤
- underwear 內衣（總稱）

2 傢俱 Furniture

- bed 床
- bookcase 書櫥
- chair 椅子
- chest 五斗櫃
- closet 衣櫥
- couch 長沙發
- desk 書桌
- lamp 燈
- sofa 沙發

3 餐具 Eating Objects

- bowl 碗
- cup 杯子
- fork 叉子
- jar 罐子
- lid 蓋子
- pan 平底鍋
- plate 盤子
- pot 壺；鍋
- spoon 湯匙

4 交通工具 Means of Transportation

- airplane (plane) 飛機
- bicycle (bike) 自行車
- boat 船
- bus 公車
- car 汽車
- helicopter 直升機
- jeep 吉普車
- motorcycle 摩托車
- ship 船
- taxi 計程車
- train 火車
- truck 貨車

5 食品和飲料 Food and Drinks

- bread 麵包
- beef 牛肉
- bean 豆子
- carrot 胡蘿蔔
- cheese 起司
- chocolate 巧克力
- corn 玉米
- egg 蛋
- eggplant 茄子
- fish 魚
- French fries 薯條
- hamburger 漢堡
- ice cream 冰淇淋
- juice 果汁
- meat 肉
- milk 牛奶
- milkshake 奶昔
- nut 堅果
- pea 碗豆
- peanut 花生
- popcorn 爆米花
- potato 馬鈴薯
- rice 米
- salt 鹽
- soda 汽水
- soup 湯
- tomato 番茄
- vegetable 蔬菜
- water 水
- wheat 小麥

6 水果 Fruit

- apple 蘋果
- banana 香蕉
- blueberry 藍莓
- cherry 櫻桃
- coconut 椰子
- grape 葡萄
- lemon 檸檬
- mango 芒果
- orange 柳丁
- peach 桃子
- pear 梨子
- pineapple 鳳梨
- strawberry 草莓
- tangerine 橘子
- watermelon 西瓜

7 植物 Plants

- bush 灌木
- flower 花
- grass 草
- maple 楓樹
- pine 松樹
- rose 玫瑰
- tree 樹
- violet 紫羅蘭

8 自然與天體 Sky and Space Things

- cloud 雲
- comet 彗星
- Jupiter 木星
- lightning 閃電
- Mars 火星
- Mercury 水星
- moon 月亮
- Neptune 海王星
- Pluto 冥王星
- rain 雨
- rainbow 彩虹
- Saturn 土星
- snow 雪
- star 星星
- sun 太陽
- thunder 雷電
- Uranus 天王星
- Venus 金星

9 地球上的物體 Earth Things

- dirt 泥土
- dust 灰塵
- field 田地
- hill 山丘
- mountain 山
- river 河流
- rock 岩石
- soil 土壤
- stone 石頭
- stream 小河
- valley 山谷
- water 水

10 娛樂 Entertainment

- baseball 棒球
- band 樂團
- DVD 數字影音光碟
- game 遊戲
- Internet 網路
- movie 電影
- ping-pong 桌球
- radio 廣播
- television 電視

11 書寫工具 Writing Items

- blackboard 黑板
- computer 電腦
- crayon 蠟筆
- keyboard 鍵盤
- monitor 顯示器
- paper 紙
- pen 筆
- pencil 鉛筆
- whiteboard 白板

12 讀物 Things to Read

- article 文章
- book 書
- electronic book 電子書
- email 電子郵件
- letter 信件
- magazine 雜誌
- newspaper 報紙
- sign 標誌

13 房間和建築 Rooms and Buildings

- apartment 公寓
- bathroom 洗手間
- cabin 小屋
- cottage 別墅；農舍
- church 教堂
- library 圖書館
- house 房子
- kitchen 廚房
- sauna 桑拿
- shower 淋浴間
- skyscraper 摩天大樓
- study 書房

4 生物（Living Things）

1 動物、鳥、昆蟲 Animals, Birds, and Insects

- ant 螞蟻
- bat 蝙蝠
- bear 熊
- bee 蜜蜂
- butterfly 蝴蝶
- camel 駱駝

- cat 貓
- chick 小雞
- chicken 雞
- cockroach 蟑螂
- cow 母牛
- deer 鹿
- dinosaur 恐龍
- dog 狗
- donkey 驢
- dragon 龍
- dragonfly 蜻蜓
- duck 鴨子
- eagle 老鷹
- elephant 大象
- fly 蒼蠅
- fox 狐狸
- frog 青蛙
- giraffe 長頸鹿
- goat 山羊
- goose 母鵝
- hen 母雞
- horse 馬
- kangaroo 袋鼠
- kitten 小貓
- lamb 小羊
- leopard 豹
- lion 獅子
- lizard 蜥蜴
- monkey 猴子
- monster 怪獸
- mosquito 蚊子
- mouse 老鼠
- owl 貓頭鷹
- ox 牛
- panda 熊貓
- parrot 鸚鵡
- peacock 孔雀
- penguin 企鵝
- pet 寵物
- pig 豬
- pigeon 鴿子
- polar bear 北極熊
- rabbit 兔子
- raccoon 浣熊
- rat 鼠
- reindeer 馴鹿
- sheep 綿羊
- snail 蝸牛
- snake 蛇
- spider 蜘蛛
- squirrel 松鼠
- swan 天鵝
- tiger 老虎
- turkey 火雞
- turtle 烏龜
- wolf 狼
- zebra 斑馬

2 魚類和水中生物 Fishes and Other Water Creatures

- alligator 短吻鱷
- carp 鯉魚
- crab 螃蟹
- crocodile 鱷魚
- dolphin 海豚
- goldfish 金魚
- lobster 龍蝦
- octopus 章魚
- oyster 牡蠣
- prawn 明蝦
- sea horse 海馬
- seal 海豹
- shark 鯊魚
- starfish 海星
- whale 鯨

5 情感（Feelings）

- anger 怒氣
- anxiety 焦慮
- hatred 憎恨
- joy 愉悅
- kindness 仁慈
- love 愛
- lust 欲望
- respect 尊敬
- sadness 悲傷

6 地點（Places）

1 普通地點名詞 Common Nouns for Places

- airport 機場
- bank 銀行
- bookstore 書店
- church 教堂
- cinema 電影院
- department store 百貨商店
- factory 工廠
- farm 農場
- gymnasium (gym) 健身房
- hospital 醫院
- hotel 旅館
- mall 購物中心
- museum 博物館
- nursery 托兒所
- theater 劇院；電影院

2 專有地點名詞 Proper Nouns for Places

a 國家（Countries）

- America 美國
- Australia 澳洲
- Britain 英國
- China 中國
- Egypt 埃及
- France 法國
- Germany 德國
- India 印度
- Japan 日本
- Malaysia 馬來西亞
- Russia 俄羅斯
- Singapore 新加坡

b 州／省（States/Provinces）

- California 加州
- Florida 佛羅里達
- Michigan 密西根
- Quebec 魁北克（加拿大的十省之一）

c 世界主要城市（Cities of the World）

- Athens 雅典
- Bangkok 曼谷
- Beijing 北京
- Berlin 柏林
- Chicago 芝加哥
- London 倫敦
- Los Angeles 洛杉磯
- New York 紐約
- Paris 巴黎
- Rome 羅馬
- Seoul 首爾
- Tokyo 東京

名詞的種類

1 普通名詞（Common Nouns）

1 普通名詞是普通的名稱，不是特定的人、事、物或地點的名字。

- mom 媽媽
- merchant 商人
- equipment 設備
- dad 爸爸
- boss 老闆
- idea 主意

・**Dwight and the girls play basketball every night.**
杜威特和那些女孩每天晚上都打籃球。

ㄊ girls、basketball、night 不特指任何人或任何事物，所以是普通名詞。
ㄊ 複數名詞在字尾要加 -s（參見 35 頁〈Part 4 名詞的單複數形式〉）。

2 **單數可數的普通名詞要加冠詞**：普通名詞既可以是**單數**，也可以是**複數**。當普通名詞用作單數時，前面需要一個**冠詞**（a/an 或 the）。

・**My newborn baby is a girl.** 我剛出生的寶寶是個女孩。

» 參見 137 頁〈Unit 4 冠詞〉

2 專有名詞（Proper Nouns）

1 專有名詞是指**特定的人、事、物或地點**的名稱，其首字母必須**大寫**。

- Buckingham Palace 白金漢宮
- Disney World 迪士尼世界
- Hong Kong 香港
- Michigan State University 密西根州立大學
- Madrid 馬德里
- Sunday 星期天
- January 一月
- Dennis 丹尼斯

・**When did you marry Larry?** 你是什麼時候嫁給賴瑞的？
・**We got married just before Nancy and May graduated from Liverpool High School.** 我們是在南西和梅從利物浦高中畢業前夕結婚的。

- Nancy and May are in a romantic play at Northern Michigan University. 南西和梅在北密西根大學的一齣浪漫劇裡有演出。
- **The romantic play called *Love Will Stay* was written by May.** 那部叫做《愛情不滅》的浪漫劇是梅寫的。

  ㄴ 上述四個例句中，Larry、Nancy 和 May 為特定人物的名稱，藍字部分為特定地點的名稱，Love Will Stay 是戲劇名（書名、戲劇名在句中通常用斜體或是加底線），這些都是專有名詞。

NOTE

專有名詞中的**冠詞**和部分**較短的介系詞**（三個字或三個字以下），不需要大寫。

- The states and territories of the United States of America appear below in alphabetical order.
  美國的州和領地依字母順序排列如下。
  ㄴ 冠詞 the 和介系詞 of 不大寫。

2 專有名詞通常不與 the 連用。

✗ Is Ann from the Japan?

✓ Is Ann from Japan? 安是日本人嗎？

NOTE

有些專有名詞要與定冠詞 the 連用。比如，某些含有普通名詞的地名、組織名、國家名（參見 160 頁〈14 要加 the 的專有名詞〉）。

- the Atlantic Ocean 大西洋（大洋名）
- the United Nations 聯合國（組織名）
- the United States 美利堅合眾國（國家名）

3 抽象名詞（Abstract Nouns）

1 抽象名詞不用來指具體的人、事或物，而是用來表達**品質**、**觀念**、**感情**等抽象概念的名稱。換言之，代表觀念、感情或是**無法觸摸到的**東西的字，就是抽象名詞（能觸摸到的，就是具體名詞，例如 chair、dog、fish 等）。

- ability 能力
- anger 生氣
- attention 注意力
- beauty 美
- charm 魅力
- cruelty 殘酷
- danger 危險
- death 死亡
- doubt 懷疑
- equality 平等
- faith 信任
- fear 恐懼
- freedom 自由
- happiness 幸福
- hatred 憎恨
- joy 歡樂
- liberty 自由
- literacy 讀寫能力
- love 愛
- loyalty 忠誠
- sadness 悲傷
- truth 事實
- wealth 財富
- wisdom 智慧

・**In 1775 Patrick Henry said, "Give me liberty or give me death."**
1775 年，派翠克・亨利說：「不自由，毋寧死。」
↑ liberty、death 是一種無形的概念，屬抽象名詞。

・**To everyone's joy, they got married last week.**
大家都很高興，因為他們上星期結婚了。
↑ joy 表達的是一種感情，所以是抽象名詞。

We got married.
我們結婚了。

2 抽象名詞與冠詞的搭配

a 抽象名詞前通常**不加冠詞**（the/a/an）：大部分抽象名詞為**不可數名詞**，不與冠詞連用，也沒有複數形。

- beauty 美
- danger 危險
- hatred 憎恨
- love 愛
- truth 真理
- wisdom 智慧

・**Are they in love?** 他們在談戀愛嗎？

・**Wisdom is better than strength.** 智慧勝過力量。
↑ 參見 174 頁〈4 有些抽象名詞，不加冠詞〉和 32 頁〈2 不可數名詞〉。

b 抽象名詞後面有**修飾語**時，前面就要加 the。

» 參見 174 頁〈4 有些抽象名詞，不加冠詞〉。

・**The anger that separated Mary from Larry was scary.**
造成瑪麗和賴瑞分手的那股憤怒很可怕。
↑ 抽象名詞 anger 被形容詞子句 that separated Mary from Larry 修飾。

・**The boiling anger between Mary and Larry was cooled by Father Gary.** 蓋瑞神父平息了瑪麗和賴瑞之間的盛怒。
↑ 抽象名詞 anger 被介系詞片語 between Mary and Larry 修飾。

c 當抽象名詞之前有**形容詞**時，就可以加不定冠詞 a/an。

- **Jim has a passionate love for Kim.** 吉姆熱戀著金姆。

d 有些抽象名詞是**可數名詞**，有複數形式。當可數的抽象名詞用作**單數**時，就要和冠詞（a, an, the）連用。參見 31 頁〈1 可數名詞〉。這類的抽象名詞如下：

- decision 決定
- idea 主意
- lie 謊話
- feeling 感覺
- intention 意圖
- thought 想法

- **I think she told a lie.** 我認為她撒了謊。

3 抽象名詞的常見字尾

a 以 -ness 結尾的抽象名詞（大多只需在同根形容詞後面加上 -ness）

- dark → darkness 黑暗
- happy → happiness 幸福 → 把 y 改成 i，在後面加上 -ness。
- ill → illness 身體不適
- kind → kindness 仁慈
- lonely → loneliness 寂寞 → 把 y 改成 i，在後面加上 -ness。
- mad → madness 瘋狂
- rich → richness 富有
- sad → sadness 悲傷
- shy → shyness 害羞
- sick → sickness 疾病
- weak → weakness 虛弱
- willing → willingness 樂意

b 以 -ion 結尾的抽象名詞

- confusion 混亂
- decision 決定
- formation 構成
- creation 創造
- education 教育
- repetition 重複

c 以 -y、-ty 或 -ity 結尾的抽象名詞

- ability 能力
- loyalty 忠誠
- quality 品質
- beauty 美
- modesty 謙虛
- quantity 數量
- honesty 誠實
- novelty 新穎
- reality 現實
- jealousy 嫉妒
- poverty 貧窮
- responsibility 責任

4 集合名詞（Collective Nouns）

1 集合名詞是指**團體**或**集體**的名稱，例如：

- army 軍隊
- class 班級
- crowd 人群
- audience 觀眾
- committee 委員會
- team 隊；組

2 「**數目的一部分**」和「**錢的總和**」也被視為集合名詞，例如：

- one-third 三分之一
- five thousand dollars 5,000 美金

・ **A jury will judge him.** 陪審團要審判他。

↳ jury 是團體的名稱，所以是集合名詞。

・ **One-third of the staff at Bird High School joined the Health Hub Club.**
柏德高中三分之一的教職員工加入了健身中心俱樂部。

↳ One-third 是數目的一部分，所以是集合名詞；staff、Club 是團體名稱，也是集合名詞。參見 912 頁〈附錄 3 集合名詞表〉。

3 集合名詞是**可數名詞**，所以也有**複數形式**：

- class → classes（班級）
- company → companies（公司）
- family → families（家庭）
- government → governments（政府）
- herd → herds（牧群）
- team → teams（隊伍）

4 集合名詞作主詞時，既可以接單數動詞，也可以接複數動詞。如果集合名詞指的是一個**整體**，那麼就接**單數動詞**；如果集合名詞強調的是團體裡的**單個成員**，那麼就接**複數動詞**（尤其是在英式英語裡）。

・ **The Beatles was my favorite music group.**
披頭四是我最喜歡的樂團。 →整體

・ **The Beatles were some of the most famous singers in history.**
披頭四樂隊的成員名列史上最著名的歌手之中。 →團隊裡的個體

5 不過，集合名詞接**單數動詞**的情況較多。

- **It is a lot of fun, because our women's soccer team is winning.**
  真快樂，因為我們的女足隊要贏了。
  ↑ 足球 美式 soccer 英式 football
- **Sue thinks her family is going to move to Honolulu.**
  蘇認為她家要搬到檀香山了。
- **The jury is reaching its decision about Nancy Lee.**
  陪審團快要對南西·李做出判決了。 → 注意 用單數 its，而不是複數 their。
- **The Chicago Band is going to Disneyland.**
  芝加哥樂團要去迪士尼樂園。
- **The Women's Club is collecting money for the city library.**
  婦女俱樂部在為市圖書館募捐。
- **"A million dollars is a lot of money!" screamed Jenny.**
  珍妮尖叫著說：「一百萬美金是很多錢耶！」
- **The water company is raising its rates.** 自來水公司要漲價了。
- **The American government is trying to help Nigeria with its pollution problems.** 美國政府在幫助奈及利亞解決其污染問題。

6 集合名詞應當搭配單數動詞還是複數動詞，英美用法不一。在**美式英語**裡，family、committee、union、staff、government 和 team 這些集合名詞後面，通常都用**單數**動詞。然而，在**英式英語**中，這些集合名詞卻常被視為**複數**，因此常與複數動詞和複數代名詞（they、them 等）連用。不過，在英式英語裡，如果把這類集合名詞看作一個**整體單位**，而不是一群人時，就要用**單數動詞**和**單數代名詞**。例如：

| 美式 | **Dan's family is having a discussion about his college plans.**
| 美式/英式 | **Dan's family members are having a discussion about his college plans.**
| 英式 | **Dan's family is/are having a discussion about his college plans.**
丹一家人正在討論丹上大學的計畫。

美式 Our football team has a lot of experience.

美式／英式 Our football team members have a lot of experience.

美式 我們的美式足球隊經驗豐富。

英式 我們的足球隊經驗豐富。

英式 Our football team has/have a lot of experience. 我們的足球隊經驗豐富。

↳ football 在英式英語中指「足球」，在美式英語中意為「美式足球」（又稱美式橄欖球）。

» 參見 891 頁〈2 集合名詞〉和 893 頁〈3 外來語複數名詞〉。

football/soccer 足球

American football 美式足球／美式橄欖球

7 以下三個集合名詞的後面，一律接**複數動詞**：

- police 警方
- people 人民
- cattle 牛

✕ In Greece, the police is looking for a terrorist.

✓ In Greece, the police are looking for a terrorist.
希臘警方在搜尋一個恐怖分子。

8 與定冠詞 the 連用、當作集合名詞的形容詞（如：the poor, the old）時，總是接**複數動詞**。

- The rich are getting much richer, the poor are still poor, and the middle class is going nowhere.
富人變得更加富有，窮人依然貧窮，而中產階級卻沒有任何進展。
↳ 集合名詞 the rich（= rich people）、the poor（poor people）作主詞，述語動詞用複數形式；集合名詞 the middle class 要與單數動詞搭配。

9 表達數目的集合名詞，是單數還是複數？表達**數字**的片語通常被看作**整體**，所以是**單數**；但如果被看作是**一組個體單位**，那就是**複數**。

- Ten dollars is not enough to buy two tickets for the play *Liz Practices Zen*. 10 美元不夠買兩張《莉茲打禪》的戲票。 ← 指一個總數。
- About forty thousand dollars have been spent tutoring my son.
我兒子的補習費已經花了我大約四萬美金。 ← 指一些個體單位。

- One-fourth of the faculty of Rice University is going to be at the graduation ceremony.
  萊斯大學有四分之一的教職員工將出席畢業典禮。 ← 指一個整體單位。

- One-fourth of the faculty members of Rice University are immigrants. 有四分之一的萊斯大學教職員工是移民。
  ↑ 指一群被視為個體的人。

- Four plus seven is eleven. 4 加 7 等於 11。
  ↑ 指一個總數。
  ↑ 注意 用 plus 時，一定要用單數動詞。

- Four and seven are/is eleven. 4 加 7 等於 11。
  ↑ 指一些個體單位。
  ↑ 注意 加法用 and 時，如果看成並列主詞，述語動詞要用複數；如果將主詞看作表示整體意義的數學運算，也可用單數述語動詞。

- Two years is a long time for me to wait for Amy to get out of the army. 等艾咪從軍隊退伍，還要等兩年，這對我來說可是一段漫長的時光。
  ↑ 指一個整體單位（一段時間）。

- Two years have passed since I last saw Lulu.
  自從我最後一次見到露露，已經過了兩年了。
  ↑ 指一些個體單位（一年、兩年）。
  » 參見 890 頁〈1 表總數的數字〉。

5 複合名詞（Compound Nouns (Noun + Noun)）

1 複合名詞的三種構成方式

a 由兩個或兩個以上的名詞構成，形式上為兩個或三個字，意義上為一個字。

- apple juice 蘋果汁
- mountain climber 登山者
- income tax 所得稅
- World Chess Championship 世界西洋棋錦標賽

- All the members of the women's basketball team like to eat ice cream. 這支女籃隊的隊員都喜歡吃冰淇淋。
  ↑ ice cream 由兩個名詞構成，basketball team 由三個名詞構成（basket + ball + team），但意義上都指一個字。

· **She likes chocolate milk, but I like milk chocolate.**
她喜歡巧克力牛奶，而我喜歡牛奶巧克力。
⮤ chocolate milk：含有巧克力的牛奶；milk chocolate：含有牛奶的巧克力。

b 由兩個名詞組成一個字，沒有連字號。（這些複合名詞因為已經很普遍，所以由兩個字演變為一個字。）

- airline 航線
- boyfriend 男朋友
- rainbow 彩虹
- armchair 扶手椅
- earthquake 地震
- schoolchild 學童
- background 背景
- bathroom 浴室
- newspaper 報紙

c 由兩個或兩個以上的名詞組成一個字，帶有連字號。

- father-in-law 岳父；公公
- job-hopper 常換工作的人

» 參見 916 頁〈附錄 4 複合名詞表〉。

1 有些複合名詞由「**V-ing + 名詞**」構成，此 V-ing 形式通常說明後面的名詞功能。

- living room 客廳
- turning point 轉捩點
- drinking water 飲用水

2 有些複合名詞由「**名詞 + V-ing**」形式構成。

- filmmaking 電影製作
- sunbathing 日光浴
- lifesaving 救生術

3 有些複合名詞由「**動詞 + 副詞**」或「**副詞 + 動詞**」構成。

- breakout 證券的突然漲價
- input 輸入
- outlet 出口
- downpour 傾盆大雨
- make-up 化妝
- push-up 伏地起身

4 有些複合名詞由「**副詞 + 名詞**」構成。

- bystander 旁觀者
- downstairs 樓下
- underground 地鐵；地下組織

5 有些複合名詞由「**名詞 + 動詞**」構成。

- sunrise 日出
- sunset 日落
- waterfall 瀑布

6 有些複合名詞由「**形容詞 + 名詞**」構成。

- full moon 滿月
- upper class 上層階級
- wastebasket 廢紙簍

2 常運用複合名詞構詞的情況

a 在「名詞 + 名詞」中，第一個名詞通常要用單數。

① 第一個名詞起**形容詞**的作用，所以即使這個名詞有複數的意思，也通常用**單數**。例如：

✗ It was a five-hours trip by boat from the coast to the island.
✓ It was a five-hour trip by boat from the coast to the island.
乘船從海岸到島嶼的行程，花了五個小時。
↳ 即使 five-hour 含有複數意義，也要用單數。
↳ 又例如：a two-hour meeting（一場兩小時的會議）。

② 複合名詞的複數形，只需要把**第二個名詞**變成複數形式。參見 43 頁〈5 複合名詞的複數形式〉（如：a hotel receptionist → two hotel receptionists）。

- Working as hotel receptionists sounded interesting to Ann and Dan. 安和丹認為當飯店接待員很有趣。

有些複合名詞中的第一個名詞要用複數形式。

1 以複數形式出現的名詞（customs 海關、savings 儲蓄）：

- a customs officer → two customs officers 海關官員
- a savings account → two savings accounts 儲蓄存款戶頭

2 涉及一種以上的項目或行為：

- the building materials industry 建築材料工業
- the foreign languages department 外語系

b 描述東西的「**材料**」時，常用複合名詞（名詞 + 名詞）的結構。

- Chicken soup is soup with chicken in it. 雞湯是裡面有雞肉的湯。
- Cotton shirts are shirts made of cotton. 棉襯衫是棉花做的襯衫。
- A silver fork is a fork made of silver. 銀叉是銀製的叉子。

c 「**動詞 + -er**」所構成的名詞，常與另外一個名詞連用，以複合名詞（名詞 + 名詞）的方式出現。

- My brother Sam is a taxi driver.
  我的兄弟山姆是一個計程車司機。

- Kay bought a hair dryer and vacuum cleaner yesterday.
  凱昨天買了吹風機和吸塵器。

3 **「名詞 + 名詞」與所有格（s' 或 's）結構的比較**：如果第一個名詞擁有第二個名詞，或經歷了第二個名詞所描述的事件，或與第二個名詞有關聯，就用所有格形式（s' or 's），否則就要用「名詞 + 名詞」結構，例如：

✗ Did you buy a new shoe's brush?

✓ Did you buy a new shoe brush?

你買了一把新鞋刷子嗎？

↑ 鞋不可能擁有刷子，也不可能經歷刷子，鞋與刷子之間也沒有人際關係，因此這句應該用「名詞 + 名詞」結構（複合名詞）。

- My dog's name is Fame. 我的狗狗叫做費姆。
  ↑ 擁有：狗擁有一個名字。
- Peg's accident last month broke both of her legs.
  佩格上個月的事故，讓她兩隻腿都骨折了。
  ↑ 經歷：佩格經歷了一場事故。
- Are two of Jerry's ex-girlfriends now his wife Mary's secretaries?
  傑瑞的兩個前女友，現在都成了他妻子瑪麗的祕書？
  ↑ 人際關係。

» 名詞的所有格形式，參見 50 頁〈Part 5 名詞的所有格〉。

» 複合名詞，參見 208 頁〈5 作形容詞用的名詞（構成複合名詞）〉。

可數名詞與不可數名詞

1 可數名詞（Countable Nouns）

1 大多數名詞都是**可數名詞**，之所以稱為可數名詞，是因為這些名詞所指的人、動物或事物**可以計數**。

2 可數名詞有**單數**和**複數**之分，複數名詞要用**複數形式**（字尾加 -s），單數可數名詞**可與 a 或 an 連用**。

3 可數名詞前面可以用**數詞**（one、two、three 等）。

- an apple → two apples 蘋果
- a pilot → two pilots 飛行員
- a computer → two computers 電腦
- a snake → two snakes 蛇
- a doctor → two doctors 醫生
- a teacher → two teachers 老師
- a lion → two lions 獅子
- one tiger → two tigers 老虎

✕ Is she really great singer?
✓ Is she really a great singer? 她真的是一名優秀的歌唱家嗎？
↳ 單數可數名詞不能獨立使用，前面必須有 a/an/the/my 等。

✕ She likes a peach.
✓ She likes peaches. 她喜歡吃桃子。
↳ 複數可數名詞可以獨立使用，泛指時，不需要 a/an/the/my 等修飾。
↳ 注意 習慣上不說「She likes a peach.」，而要用複數名詞「She likes peaches.」。

2 不可數名詞（Uncountable Nouns）

1 **不可數名詞**指沒有複數形式（字尾不可加 -s）、不能和不定冠詞 a/an 或數詞連用的名詞。之所以稱為不可數名詞，是因為**無法計數**。不可數名詞有時也稱作 **mass noun**（包括**物質名詞**和**抽象名詞**）。參見 920 頁〈附錄 5 不可數名詞表〉。

- air 空氣
- blood 血
- bread 麵包
- clothing 衣服
- courage 膽量
- dust 灰塵
- homework 家庭作業
- honesty 誠實
- jam 果醬
- mail 郵件
- meat 肉
- milk 牛奶
- money 錢
- pork 豬肉
- progress 進展
- rice 米
- sleep 睡覺
- steam 蒸汽
- steel 鋼鐵
- tea 茶
- wood 木材
- woodwork 木製品
- zeal 熱心

✗ Does Mom have a lot of butters?

✓ Does Mom have a lot of butter? 媽媽有很多奶油嗎？

↑ 不可數名詞沒有複數形式。

・Kay eats bread every day. 凱每天都要吃麵包。

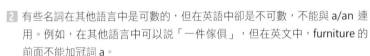

↑ 不可數名詞可以獨立使用（沒有 the/my/some 等）。

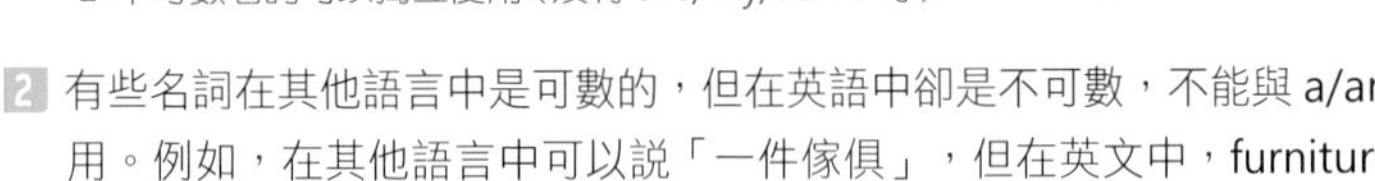

2 有些名詞在其他語言中是可數的，但在英語中卻是不可數，不能與 a/an 連用。例如，在其他語言中可以說「一件傢俱」，但在英文中，furniture 的前面不能加冠詞 a。

- advice 忠告
- baggage 行李
- bread 麵包
- chalk 粉筆
- furniture 傢俱
- hair 頭髮
- information 資訊
- knowledge 知識
- luck 幸運
- luggage 行李
- news 新聞
- work 工作

3 不可數名詞不能與數詞連用，也沒有複數形式。

✓ excellent English 流暢的英文	✗ two excellent Englishes	
✓ bread 麵包	✗ a/one bread	✗ two breads

✔ homework 家庭作業	✘ a/one homework	✘ two homeworks
✔ milk 牛奶	✘ a/one milk	✘ two milks
✔ money 錢	✘ a/one money	✘ two moneys
✔ progress 進展	✘ a/one progress	✘ two progresses
✔ water 水	✘ a/one water	✘ two waters
✔ weather 天氣	✘ a/one weather	✘ two weathers

4 當不可數名詞在句中作主詞時，**述語動詞**應該用**單數**。

- **Information about how to stop bleeding is important to everyone.**
  如何止血的報導，對每個人來說都是重要的。
- **His hair is too long.** 他的頭髮太長了。
- **The news was depressing.** 這則新聞很令人沮喪。

5 如何表達某些不可數名詞的數量？在某些不可數名詞前，可以用 a piece of 等片語表達數量概念。 參見 142 頁〈Diving Deep Into English 24〉。

- **Would you like a piece of cheese?** 你要不要來一片起司？
- **Does Jenny have a jar of honey?** 珍妮有一罐蜂蜜嗎？

3 作可數或作不可數時，意義有所不同的名詞

1 有些名詞既可以作可數名詞，也可以作不可數名詞，但意思不同。

不可數 **Does she like coffee?** 她喜歡喝咖啡嗎？

可數 **"Two coffees, please," said Louise.** 露易絲說：「請給我兩杯咖啡。」

ℓ two coffees = two cups of coffee（容器）

ℓ 在口語中，tea、beer、juice 等飲料，表示 a cup of、a glass of 等的意思時，可以用作可數名詞。

不可數 **Is Scot an English teacher with experience and good sense?**
史考特是一位有經驗、有見地的英語老師嗎？ → 經驗

可數 **Last night I had a rather odd experience.**
昨晚我遭遇了一場很古怪的經歷。 → 經歷、閱歷

不可數 Time flies when you're having fun in the sun!
每當你在陽光下玩得很開心時，時間就過得很快。 → 時間

可數 Did Sue read you that book full of rhymes ten times?
那本充滿押韻的書，蘇已經給你讀過十遍了嗎？ → 次、回

不可數 She makes beautiful jewelry out of glass, silver, and gold.
她用玻璃、銀子和金子製作出美麗的首飾。 → 玻璃

可數 Would you like a glass of orange juice?
你要不要來杯柳橙汁？ → 玻璃杯

2 還有些名詞表示「**整體物質**」時，是**不可數名詞**；表示「**某物質的一例**」時，是**可數名詞**。

- made of stone 石頭做成的 → a small stone in my shoe 鞋裡有塊小石頭
- with long black hair 長長的黑髮 → a hair in my soup 我湯裡有一根頭髮

4 可數與不可數名詞常用的限定詞：some 和 any

1 some 和 any 既可以修飾**複數名詞**，也可以修飾**不可數名詞**，
參見117頁〈6 any和some：代名詞或限定詞〉：① some：常用於**肯定句**中。
② any：常用在**疑問句**和**否定句**中。

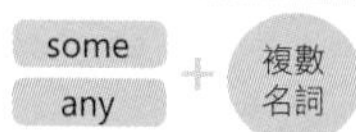

- Paul Powers bought me some flowers. 保羅．鮑爾斯買了一些花給我。
  ↑ some + 複數名詞（flowers）
- Did they have any complaints about the air show?
  他們對飛行表演有沒有什麼不滿？
  ↑ any + 複數名詞（complaints）
- Are there any tickets available for that ballet? 那場芭蕾舞還有票嗎？
  ↑ Are there + any + 複數名詞（tickets）

some
any
+ 不可數
名詞

- She would like some black tea.
  她想喝點紅茶。
  ↑ some + 不可數名詞（tea）
- He didn't get any money from me.
  他沒有從我這裡得到過一毛錢。
  ↑ any + 不可數名詞（money）
- Is there any apple juice left from the party? 聚會上的蘋果汁有剩嗎？
  ↑ Is there + any + 不可數名詞（apple juice）

名詞的單複數形式

1 單複數名詞的定義

1 可數名詞有單、複數形式之分。

2 **單數名詞**（名詞的單數形式）：指的是一個人、一隻動物、一樣東西或一個地方，例如：

- man 人
- dog 狗
- cellphone 手機
- bedroom 臥室

3 **複數名詞**：用以表示人、動物、事物或地方的數量不只一個，字尾通常有別於單數名詞，例如：

- cherry → cherries 櫻桃
- kiss → kisses 親吻
- student → students 學生
- woman → women 婦女

2 規則（Regular）名詞的複數形式

規則一 **大部分單數名詞 → 字尾 + -s**

- book → books 書
- brother → brothers 兄弟
- cat → cats 貓
- chair → chairs 椅子
- door → doors 門
- egg → eggs 蛋
- face → faces 臉
- floor → floors 地板
- girl → girls 女孩
- rock → rocks 岩石
- snake → snakes 蛇
- weekend → weekends 週末

・It rains cats and dogs. 下著傾盆大雨。

規則二 字尾為 -s、-x、-z、-sh、-ch 的名詞 → 字尾 + -es

- address → addresses 地址
- bench → benches 長凳
- boss → bosses 老闆
- box → boxes 盒子
- branch → branches 樹枝
- brush → brushes 刷子
- bus → buses 公車
- bush → bushes 灌木
- church → churches 教堂
- class → classes 班級
- crash → crashes 相撞事故
- cross → crosses 十字架
- dish → dishes 盤子；菜餚
- dress → dresses 洋裝
- fox → foxes 狐狸
- glass → glasses 玻璃杯
- kiss → kisses 親吻
- lunch → lunches 午餐
- match → matches 火柴；比賽
- peach → peaches 桃子
- quiz → quizzes 測驗
  ↑ 須先重複字尾 z，再加 -es。
- sandwich → sandwiches 三明治
- tax → taxes 稅
- watch → watches 手錶
- wish → wishes 願望
- witch → witches 女巫

I give my baby Ken many kisses on his rosy cheeks every day.

我每天都要親吻我的寶貝肯的粉紅臉頰很多次。

NOTE

一般而言，以 -s、-x、-z、-sh 或 -ch 結尾的名詞要加 -es 構成複數， 但也有例外。stomach 和 monarch 雖以 -ch 結尾，但只需要加上 -s 來表示複數，因為這兩個名詞的 -ch 發音是 /k/ 而非 /tʃ/，所以複數形式的變化和以 -k 結尾的名詞一樣。

- stomach → stomachs 胃
- monarch → monarchs 君主

規則三 名詞字尾為子音 + -y → 去 y 加 -ies

- baby → babies 嬰兒
- berry → berries 莓果
- candy → candies 糖果
- cherry → cherries 櫻桃
- city → cities 城市
- copy → copies 複製品
- country → countries 國家
- diary → diaries 日記
- family → families 家庭
- glory → glories 可誇耀的事
- jelly → jellies 果凍
- lady → ladies 淑女
- library → libraries 圖書館
- lily → lilies 百合花
- reality → realities 事實
- spy → spies 間諜
- story → stories 故事
- variety → varieties 品種；種類

He told me lots of funny stories about Aunt Annie.
他給我講了許多關於安妮姨媽的有趣故事。

規則三不適用於**專有名詞**，專有名詞即使以「子音 + -y」結尾，其複數形式也只加 -s，不可去 y 加 -ies。例如以下兩個人名：

✔ two Marys ✘ two Maries
✔ three Larrys ✘ three Larries

規則四 名詞字尾為「母音 + -y (-ay, -ey, -oy, -uy)」 → 字尾 + -s

- bay → bays 灣
- birthday → birthdays 生日
- day → days 日子
- delay → delays 延遲
- display → displays 展示
- doorway → doorways 出入口
- essay → essays 論文
- highway → highways 公路
- holiday → holidays 假日
- play → plays 戲劇
- ray → rays 光線
- runway → runways 跑道
- stay → stays 支撐物
- tray → trays 托盤
- way → ways 路
- X-ray → X-rays X 光

字尾 -ey

- chimney → chimneys 煙囪
- donkey → donkeys 驢
- journey → journeys 旅程
- key → keys 鑰匙
- kidney → kidneys 腎臟
- monkey → monkeys 猴子
- survey → surveys 調查
- turkey → turkeys 火雞
- valley → valleys 山谷

字尾 -oy/-uy

- boy → boys 男孩
- guy → guys 傢伙
- joy → joys 樂事
- toy → toys 玩具

Mars

There are many deep valleys on Mars.
火星上有許多深深的低凹處。

1 以 -quy 結尾的名詞，仍須將 y 改成 i，再加 -es：

- soliloquy → soliloquies 獨白

2 為何 gallery 的複數是 galleries，galley 的複數卻是 galleys？

gallery（畫廊） → 以子音加 -y 結尾，需要把 y 變成 i，再加 -es（galleries）。

galley（單層甲板大帆船） → 以母音加 -y 結尾，因此只加 -s 就可構成複數（galleys）。

規則五 名詞字尾為 -f、-fe → 去 f/fe，加 -ves

- calf → calves 小牛
- half → halves 一半
- knife → knives 刀子
- leaf → leaves 葉子
- life → lives 性命
- loaf → loaves 塊狀麵包
- self → selves 自己
- shelf → shelves 架子
- thief → thieves 小偷
- wife → wives 妻子
- wolf → wolves 狼

We can save lives if we don't play with knives.
如果我們不玩刀子，就可以保命。

Diving Deep Into English 3 名詞字尾為 -f/-fe 的多種複數變化

❶ 一般而言，以 -f 或 -fe 結尾的名詞，複數形式是去 f/fe，再加 -ves。然而也有例外，有些直接加上 -s 即構成複數。例如：

- belief → beliefs 信仰
- brief → briefs 概要
- chief → chiefs 首領
- giraffe → giraffes 長頸鹿
  - giraffe 有兩種複數形式：
    - giraffes（加 -s）
    - giraffe（單複數同形）
- gulf → gulfs 海灣
- handkerchief → handkerchiefs 手帕
- proof → proofs 證據
- roof → roofs 屋頂
- safe → safes 保險箱

❷ 有些以 -f 結尾的名詞的複數，可加 -s，也可去 f 加 -ves。

- dwarf 侏儒；矮人 → dwarfs → dwarves
- hoof 蹄 → hoofs → hooves
- scarf 圍巾 → scarfs → scarves

❸ 以 -ff 結尾的名詞，通常加上 -s 構成複數：

- cliff → cliffs 懸崖
- tariff → tariffs 關稅表；價格表

規則六 名詞字尾為「子音 + -o」→ 字尾 + -es

- cargo → cargoes 貨物
- echo → echoes 回聲
- hero → heroes 英雄
- tomato → tomatoes 番茄
- potato → potatoes 馬鈴薯

✗ Could you please buy some potatos and tomatos from the supermarket?

✓ Could you please buy some potatoes and tomatoes from the supermarket?
請去超市買一些馬鈴薯和番茄，好嗎？

Diving Deep Into English 4 名詞字尾為 -o 的多種複數變化

❶ 字尾為「**子音 + -o**」的名詞，變複數時通常加 **-es**，但有些字雖然以子音加 -o 結尾，其複數形式卻只加 -s，不加 -es。

- hello → hellos 哈囉；喂
- hippo → hippos 河馬
- kilo → kilos 公斤
- memo → memos 備忘錄
- piano → pianos 鋼琴
- photo → photos 照片
- solo → solos 獨唱
- yo-yo → yo-yos 溜溜球

❷ 還有一些以子音加 -o 結尾的名詞，既可以加 -es 構成複數，也可以加 **-s** 構成複數。

- buffalo 水牛
  → buffalos
  → buffaloes
- mosquito 蚊子
  → mosquitos
  → mosquitoes
- volcano 火山
  → volcanos
  → volcanoes
- mango 芒果
  → mangos
  → mangoes
- tornado 龍捲風
  → tornados
  → tornadoes
- zero 零
  → zeros
  → zeroes

規則七 名詞字尾為「母音 + -o」→ 字尾 + -s

- kangaroo → kangaroos 袋鼠
  ↳ kangaroo 有兩種複數形式：
  - kangaroos（加 -s）
  - kangaroo（單複數同形）
- radio → radios 收音機
- studio → studios 工作室
- video → videos 錄影帶
- zoo → zoos 動物園

- **Maybe those two kangaroo/kangaroos over there by the tree escaped from a zoo.**
  那邊靠樹的兩隻袋鼠也許是從動物園逃跑出來的。

3 不規則（Irregular）名詞的複數形式

有一些名詞在構成複數時是沒有規則的，請讀者仔細學習下面的不規則名詞，這些常常會被用錯：

- Ben and Glen are short bald men. 班和葛倫是兩個禿頭的矮個子男人。
- There are four children in the TV den. 有四個小孩在電視房裡。

1 單複數不同形

- child → children 小孩
- foot → feet 腳
- goose → geese 鵝
- man → men 男人
- mouse → mice 老鼠
- ox → oxen 牛
- tooth → teeth 牙齒
- woman → women 女人

man 的複數是 men，human 的複數卻是 humans。

- Ruth has a loose tooth. 露絲有一顆牙齒鬆了。
- My baby has two new teeth. 我的嬰兒長了兩顆新牙齒。

- Sometimes John acts like a child. 約翰有時候舉動像個小孩。
- When did you tell the children to chase the hen?
  你是什麼時候叫那些孩子去追趕那隻母雞的？

- Dan is a very tall man. 丹是一個身材很高的男人。
- The two men are running around in circles, chasing a hen.
  那兩個男人在兜著圈子跑，追趕一隻母雞。

- Is that a fox near your ox? 在你的牛旁邊是一隻狐狸嗎？
- She is riding a wagon pulled by two oxen. 她搭乘兩頭牛拉的牛車。

- A goose was sleeping by the peaceful pond. Then three geese landed nearby, and there was no more peace.
  一隻母鵝在平靜的池塘邊睡覺，接著三隻母鵝在附近降落，從此便不得安寧。

- A louse lived alone on a little mouse. One day two mice came to visit and gave the little mouse two lice. How many lice does the little mouse have? 一隻蝨子獨自居住在一隻小老鼠的身上，有一天，兩隻老鼠登門拜訪，帶給這隻小老鼠兩隻蝨子。這隻小老鼠有多少蝨子了？

2 單複數同形

- one aircraft → two aircraft 飛機
- one bison → two bison 野牛
- one deer → two deer 鹿
- one fish → two fish 魚
- one goldfish → two goldfish 金魚
- one moose → two moose 麋鹿
- one sheep → two sheep 綿羊
- one species → two species 種類

・A sheep is in front of my jeep. 我的吉普車前面有一頭綿羊。

・Ann has two sheep in her jeep. 安的吉普車裡有兩隻綿羊。

・Is the polar bear an endangered species? 北極熊是瀕臨絕種的動物嗎？

・Are humans and monkeys two closely related species?
人和猴子是兩種緊密相關的物種嗎？

單複數同形名詞還包括一些表示民族的名詞，如：

- a Chinese → two Chinese
- a Vietnamese → two Vietnamese

Diving Deep Into English 5 魚（fish）的單複數

fish 的複數形有兩種：fish 和 fishes。

① 指同種類的魚，或泛指的魚：無論單數還是複數，都用 fish。

② 指多種不同種類的魚：fish 或 fishes 兩種複數形式皆可（但以 fish 較常見）。

several kinds of fish
several kinds of fishes
幾種種類的魚

・Scot cooked a skinny fish in the pot, and I ate the two fish that were hot! 史考特在鍋裡煮了隻瘦巴巴的魚，而我把那兩隻已經熱了的魚吃了。

・I cooked a fish and put it on a big dish. My wish was to put many kinds of fish/fishes on that big dish. 我煮了一隻魚，並把它放在一個大盤子上。我希望能在那個大盤子上放各式各樣的魚。

4 單位數量詞的複數形式

1 dozen（一打）、hundred（一百）、thousand（一千）這類明確指出數量的名詞，在變複數形式時不需要在字尾加 -s。

- a dozen roses（12 朵玫瑰花）→ two dozen roses（24 朵玫瑰花）
- a hundred balloons（一百個氣球）→ two hundred balloons（兩百個氣球）
- a thousand dollars（一千美元）→ two thousand dollars（兩千美元）

- **"I'm going to the store to buy a dozen eggs," said Pam.**
  "Could you also buy two dozen large chocolate chip cookies?" asked Sue.
  潘姆說：「我要去商店買一打雞蛋。」
  蘇問道：「再買兩打大巧克力薄餅，好嗎？」

2 用來形容「**大量的**」，而非明確指出數量時，則可加上 -s，並接 of 片語。

- dozens of roses 幾十朵玫瑰花
- hundreds of balloons 數以百計的氣球
- thousands of dollars 數千美元

- **Kay wants to hold on to hundreds of balloons so that she can fly away.**
  凱想抓著數以百計的氣球飛走。

5 複合名詞（Compound Nouns）的複數形式

1 複合名詞的複數形式比較複雜，通常是把複合名詞中的基本名詞（即此名詞中的主要成分）變成複數，例如：

- airport bus → airport buses 機場公車
- birdhouse → birdhouses 鳥舍
- book review → book reviews 書評
- bookstore → bookstores 書店
- car door → car doors 車門
- chophouse → chophouses 牛排館
- housewife → housewives 家庭主婦
- spoonful → spoonfuls 一匙的量
- daughter-in-law → daughters-in-law 媳婦

- looker-on → lookers-on 旁觀者
- man-of-war → men-of-war 軍艦
- passer-by → passers-by 行人；路人
- runner-up → runners-up 亞軍
- son-in-law → sons-in-law 女婿

- **Will the attorneys general that are sky-diving with the brigadier generals be arriving soon on Raccoon Hill?**
  那些與準將們一起進行特技跳傘的首席檢察官，很快就要到達浣熊山了嗎？
  ↳ attorney general 中，attorney（律師）是基本名詞，而 brigadier general 中，general（將軍）是基本名詞。

- **During the shoot-out yesterday, the five bank robbers were killed, but the three passersby and both of the deputy sheriffs were not wounded.** 在昨天的槍戰過程中，那五名銀行搶劫犯被擊斃，而三位路人和兩名副警長都沒有受傷。

2 一些複合名詞沒有明顯的基本字，通常在最後一個字上加上複數字尾。

- higher-up → higher-ups（大人物；上級）
- go-between → go-betweens（中間人）
- good-for-nothing → good-for-nothings（無用之人）
- grown-up → grown-ups（成年人）

3 複合名詞「**woman/man + 名詞**」變成複數時，前後兩個名詞都要用複數形。

- woman doctor → women doctors（女醫生）
- man servant → men servants（男僕）

4 有些以 man 和 woman 結尾的複合名詞，變成複數時與 man 和 woman 的變化形式相同。

- policewoman → policewomen（女員警）
- gentleman → gentlemen（紳士）
- postman → postmen（郵差）

- **If we love our country, we should also love our countrymen.**
  (President Ronald Reagan, 1911–2004) 如果我們熱愛祖國，也應該熱愛我們的同胞。

6 外來名詞的複數形式

還有一些外來名詞有特殊的複數形式：

1 -is → -es

- analysis → analyses 分析
- basis → bases 基礎
- crisis → crises 危機
- oasis → oases 沙漠中的綠洲

2 -on → -a

- criterion → criteria/criterions 標準
- phenomenon → phenomena 現象

3 -x → -ces

- index → indices 索引（寫成 indexes 也可以）
- appendix → appendices 附錄（寫成 appendixes 也可以）

4 -us → -i

- alumnus → alumni 校友
- focus → foci/focuses 焦點
- fungus → fungi/funguses 菌類
- radius → radii/radiuses 半徑
- stimulus → stimuli 刺激物
- syllabus → syllabi 教學大綱

5 -um → -a

- memorandum → memoranda/memorandums 備忘錄
- referendum → referenda/referendums 公投

7 人名的複數形式

1 無論是名字還是姓，一般來說，人名的複數形式都是加 -s；只有字尾是 -s、-sh、-ch、-x 或 -z 時，才加 -es。

2 即使人名是以 -y 結尾，也只加 -s 構成複數，不要改變為 -ies，也就是：**不能改變人名原來的拼寫**。

✗ **In Mary's school, there are two Sherries and six Charles.**

✓ **In Mary's school, there are two Sherrys and six Charleses.**
瑪麗的學校裡有兩個叫雪麗的，六個叫查理斯的。

名字	• Fred → two Freds • Mona → five Monas • James → two Jameses • Fritz → three Fritzes
姓氏	• Brown → the Browns（the Brown family 布朗家） • Cory → the Corys （the Cory family 柯瑞家）
家人	• Wayne, Jane, and Zane Erickson → the Ericksons（家庭成員有三個）
夫妻	• Mr. and Mrs. Goodman → the Goodmans（已婚夫婦，不用 the Goodmen） • Mr. and Mrs. Wolf → the Wolfs（已婚夫婦，不用 the Wolves）

8 永遠以複數形式出現的名詞

1 只以複數形式出現的名詞有哪些？

以下這些名詞永遠只以**複數形式**出現，它們在意義上都是**單數**的，然而有些只搭配**單數動詞**，有些只搭配**複數動詞**，請詳見第 2、3 條說明。

- belongings 財產
- briefs 短內褲
- clothes 衣服
- earnings 收入
- economics 經濟學
- glasses 眼鏡

↑ 美式用 glasses，英式用 spectacles。

- jeans 牛仔褲
- mathematics 數學
- news 新聞
- pants 褲子
- physics 物理學
- politics 政治
- remains 遺跡
- riches 財富
- scissors 剪刀
- shorts 寬鬆運動短褲
- socks 襪子
- spectacles 眼鏡
- sunglasses 太陽鏡
- thanks 感謝
- tights 緊身褲
- trousers 長褲

2 形式為複數、意義為單數的不可數名詞

有些名詞形式上看起來是複數，實際上卻是**不可數名詞**，作主詞時，後面應該接**單數動詞**。這些名詞通常是表示**學科**、**遊戲**、**運動**或**疾病**的名詞。

- aerobics 有氧運動
- athletics 體育運動
- billiards 撞球
- checkers 西洋跳棋
- civics 公民學
- dominoes 骨牌遊戲
- economics 經濟學
- mathematics 數學
- measles 麻疹
- mumps 腮腺炎
- news 新聞
- optics 光學
- physics 物理學
- politics 政治／政治學

- The news is sad and makes us mad. 這則悲傷的消息使我們很憤怒。
- Politics is very complicated. 政治很複雜。

mathematics 的縮寫有兩種：

美式 math

英式 maths

Diving Deep Into English 6　economics、statistics 和 politics 可作單數，也可作複數

❶ 這些字有時也具有**複數意義**：

- **Mary's politics are wild, because she's still a child.**
  瑪麗的政治觀念很荒唐，因為她還只是一個孩子。
  ↑ 指政治態度、立場、觀念。

❷ 判斷這類詞彙是單數還是複數的祕訣是：

1. 如果把這些以 -ics 結尾的名詞，看成是**一般的**、**泛指的**字，例如「一門學科」，那麼就是**單數**的。
2. 如果把這些以 -ics 結尾的名詞，看成是**特定的**、**限定的**字，例如「某人的信仰」，那麼就是**複數**的。

- **Statistics isn't a difficult subject for me.** ← 指學科。
  對我來說，統計學並不是一門很難的學科。
- **That company's statistics are often misleading.** ← 指一組數據。
  那家公司的統計資料經常會誤導人。

3 形式為複數、意義為單數的複數名詞

a 一些名詞在意義上是單數，卻具有複數形式，而且總是與**複數動詞**連用。仔細看看這些物件的組成，多半具有「**一雙**」、「**一對**」的意味，像褲子一定是兩個褲管，剪刀由兩個刀片組成，很好辨認。

- glasses (= spectacles) 眼鏡
- gloves 手套
- handcuffs 手銬
- jeans 牛仔褲
- pants 長褲
- scissors 剪刀
- shorts 寬鬆運動短褲
- tights 緊身褲
- trousers 長褲

✕ **My aunt's pink pants was made in France.**

✓ **My aunt's pink pants were made in France.**

我姑媽的粉紅色褲子是法國製的。

- **Her new scissors are sharp enough to cut leather.**
  她的新剪刀鋒利得可以剪皮革。
- **"Where are my glasses?" "Your glasses are next to the TV."**
  「我的眼鏡在哪裡？」「你的眼鏡在電視旁邊。」
- **Are my green jeans in the washing machine?**
  我的綠色牛仔褲在洗衣機裡面嗎？

b 要表達這類名詞的**數量**時，要用「a pair of」、「two pairs of」等片語來修飾。a pair 、this pair 作主詞時，要用**單數動詞**（如下面第二個例句）。

✕ **She left her three new blue jeans at the zoo.**

↑ 不能用數字修飾 jeans。

✓ **She left her three pairs of new blue jeans at the zoo.**

她把三件新藍色牛仔褲忘在動物園裡了。

- **There is a pair of scissors somewhere near that pear.**
  在那顆梨子的旁邊有一把剪刀。

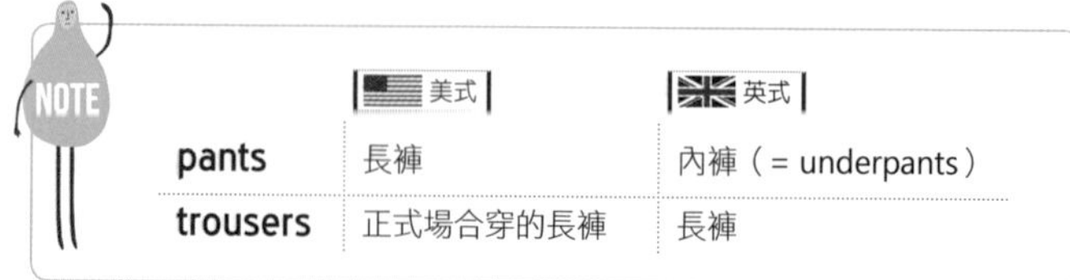

NOTE

	美式	英式
pants	長褲	內褲（= underpants）
trousers	正式場合穿的長褲	長褲

4 表示單一物品的複數名詞

有些名詞表示單一物品（亦即意義為單數），卻永遠用複數形式。這種名詞作主詞時，**述語動詞**要用**複數**。

- arms 武器
- belongings 財物
- customs (= tariffs) 關稅
- earnings 收益；薪水
- fireworks 煙火
- funds 存款
- goods 商品；貨物
- greens 蔬菜
- grounds 建造物周圍的土地；庭院
- lodgings 住宿屋
- looks 面容
- manners 禮貌
- oats 燕麥
- odds 機會；可能性
- outskirts 郊區
- quarters 軍營；住處
- regards 問候
- remains 遺跡
- riches 財富
- savings 存款；積蓄
- stairs 樓梯
- surroundings 環境
- terms 條件
- thanks 感謝
- whereabouts 行蹤
- winnings 贏得的錢

- **Kitty understood that her company's earnings were pretty good.**
  姬蒂了解到她公司的收益很不錯。

- **On the ground next to that collapsed house, the remains of two dogs were found.**
  在倒塌的房子旁的空地上，找到了兩隻狗的遺骸。

5 形式為複數、單複數同形的名詞

crossroads 十字路口	a crossroads	→ two crossroads
means 手段、方法	every possible means	→ all possible means
species 種類	a species	→ many species
series 系列	a series	→ three series

- **That Internet advertisement is an effective means for finding potential buyers of our new jet.**
  那則網路廣告是開發我們新噴射機的潛在客戶的有效方法。
  ↑ means 單複數同形，用作單數時，要用單數動詞。

名詞的所有格

1 所有格的定義

1 **所有格**是一個字，或看作是字的形式，用以表示某人或某物的**附屬關係**。**名詞的所有格**代表物主的身分或所有權，以所有格符號「'」來表示，或用 **of 結構**（如：the top of the mountain）來表示。在這個單元裡，我們會討論名詞的所有格（在 Unit 3，會討論代名詞的所有格，例如 his、my、their、whose 等）。

- Dan's 丹的
- Dwight's 杜威特的
- cat's 貓的
- its 它的
- lady's 女士的
- men's 男士們的
- my 我的
- whose 誰的
- the girls' 女孩們的

・**Brooke took** John's **book.** 布魯克拿了約翰的書。
↑ 單數名詞的所有格形式，要用「's」。

2 所有格的構成

規則一 不以 -s 結尾的單數名詞 → 字尾加「's」

不以 -s 結尾單數名詞（包括名字），其所有格形式是在名詞的最後一個字母後面加上所有格符號「'」，再加上 s，即「**'s**」。

- John's plane 約翰的飛機
- my aunt's cottage 我阿姨的別墅
- Singapore's economy 新加坡的經濟
- Mary's little lamb 瑪麗的小羊
- Ms. Mona Marsh's mushrooms 夢娜・馬西女士的蘑菇
- Jane's hippo 珍的河馬
- the witch's broom 女巫的掃帚

- **Were that man's pants made in France?**
  那個人的褲子是法國製的嗎？
  ↳ 不以 -s 結尾的單數名詞，所有格符號「'」應放在 s 前面，即「's」。

- **My neighbor's telescope is aimed at the star-filled sky.**
  我鄰居的望遠鏡瞄準了星光燦爛的天空。
  ↳ 在 neighbor 後面加上「's」，表示「是誰的望遠鏡」（鄰居的望遠鏡）。

規則二 以 -s 結尾的單數名詞 → 字尾加「's」

以 -s 結尾單數名詞（包括名字），也是加「**'s**」。

- Dennis's sweet wife 丹尼斯溫柔可愛的妻子
- Dr. Seuss's books 蘇斯博士的書
- Dickens's novels 狄更斯的小說
- the boss's naughty boy 老闆的調皮兒子
- the princess's golden ball 公主的金球
- the witness's reply 證人的回答

- **The princess's golden ball fell into a well.**
  公主的金球掉進井裡頭了。

- **Mr. Dickens's voice sounds like a sick chicken's.**
  狄更斯先生的聲音聽起來像隻病雞。
  ↳ Dickens's：以 -s 結尾的單數專有名詞，加「's」表示所有。
  （有人也用 Dickens'，不過不常見。）
  ↳ chicken's：單數普通名詞，加「's」表示所有，後面省略 voice (= chicken's voice)。

以 -s 結尾的專有名詞或單數名詞加了「's」後，會增加一個音節；如果增加的這個音節會造成發音困難，可以只加「'」。

- for goodness' sake 看在老天爺的份上
- Los Angeles' freeways 洛杉磯的高速公路
- Mr. Jones' car (= Mr. Jones's car) 鐘斯先生的汽車

規則三 以 -s 結尾的單數古人名、外來人名 → 字尾加「'」

有些以 -s 結尾的單數名詞，尤其是一些比較古老或外來的人名，通常只加所有格符號「'」。

- Socrates' philosophy 蘇格拉底的哲學
- Jesus' life 耶穌的一生
- Moses' flight from Egypt 摩西的逃離埃及

規則四 規則複數名詞（以 -s 或 -es 結尾）→ 字尾加「'」

以 -s 或 -es 結尾的複數名詞，其所有格形式只需要在名詞後面加所有格符號「'」，不加 -s。

- my parents' donkey 我父母的驢子
- the teachers' room 教師室
- the witches' brooms 女巫的掃帚
- my sisters' chicks 我姐妹們的小雞

✗ **The Smiths's friends love to listen to myths.**

✓ **The Smiths' friends love to listen to myths.**

史密斯家的朋友們喜歡聽神話故事。

↳ Smiths 是 Smith 的複數形，在 Smiths 後面加所有格符號「'」，構成所有格形式。

↳ The Smiths = The Smith family

↳ The Smiths' friends = The Smith family's friends

- **The nurses' faces are red because of his curses.**

  那些護士被他罵得臉都紅了。

  ↳ 在以 -s 結尾的複數名詞 nurses 後面只加所有格符號「'」，就構成所有格形式。

規則五 不規則複數名詞（不以 -s 結尾）→ 字尾加「's」

不以 -s 結尾的不規則複數名詞，所有格形式是在名詞後面加上「**'s**」。注意所有格符號「'」要放在 s 前面。

- a children's book 兒童書
- women's magazines 婦女雜誌
- a men's changing room 男更衣室
- people's health 人民的健康

- **The children's toys are tiny plastic girls and boys.**
  這些孩子們的玩具是一些塑膠製的迷你女孩和男孩。
  ↳ children 是不以 -s 結尾的不規則複數名詞，加「's」構成所有格形式。

- **"Where is the women's room?" asked Claire.**
  克萊兒問：「女廁在哪裡？」
  ↳ women 是 woman 的複數形式，加「's」構成所有格形式。

規則變化

單數	複數	複數所有格
girl（女孩）	→ girls	→ girls'
bird（鳥）	→ birds	→ birds'
boss（老闆）	→ bosses	→ bosses'
hero（英雄）	→ heroes	→ heroes'
Mr. and Mrs. Blare（布雷爾夫婦）	→ the Blares	→ the Blares'
Mrs. and Mr. Fox（福克斯夫婦）	→ the Foxes	→ the Foxes'

不規則變化

child（小孩）→ children → children's

daughter-in-law（媳婦）→ daughters-in-law → daughters-in-law's
editor-in-chief（總編）→ editors-in-chief → editors-in-chief's
↳ 如何避免 daughters-in-law's 這種笨拙的所有格用法？
參見 54 頁〈3 所有格「's」和「of + 名詞」在意義上相同〉。

字母和年代的複數形式 + 's

在字母和年代後面加「**'s**」，就構成了字母或年代的複數形式。

- Pam's parents will soon know that she only received C's on her final exams. Bad news travels fast.
  潘的父媽很快就會知道她的期末考只得到了 C。壞消息總是傳得很快。

- Jim lived in London during the 1990's.
  = Jim lived in London during the 1990s.
  吉姆二十世紀九十年代時住在倫敦。
  ↳ 年代的複數形式也可以只加 -s。

3 所有格「's」和「of + 名詞」在意義上相同

1 of 也可以表示所有權，用 of 時，不需要再用所有格符號「'」。有些名詞使用所有格「's」或「of + 名詞」結構，在意義上沒有什麼不同，**可以互換**。

- the beauty of Bali = Bali's beauty 峇里島的美麗 → 指自然現象。
- the policy of our school = our school's policy 我們學校的政策
- the brooms of the witches = the witches' brooms 女巫的掃帚
- the philosophy of Socrates = Socrates' philosophy 蘇格拉底的哲學
- the speech of the President = the President's speech 總統的演說
  ↑ 指主題或話題。
- the length of the train = the train's length 火車的長度 → 指物體的性質。
  ↑ 注意 指人的特質時，例如 Sue's kindness，通常用 's 所有格。

2 一些**複合名詞**複數形式的所有格，如 brothers-in-law's（姐夫）、editors-in-chief's（主編）、daughters-in-law's（媳婦），看起來很笨拙，為了避免這種笨拙的所有格用法，最好用「of + 名詞」的結構來表示所屬關係。

Awkward **my two brothers-in-law's parents**
Better **the parents of my two brothers-in-law** 我兩個姊夫的父母

4 所有格「's」和「of + 名詞」結構的不同用法

1 **人名**和**動物名**通常在後面加上「**'s**」或「'」構成所有格，表示所屬關係、個人或職業關係、人的特質。

- Susan's new electric car 蘇珊的新電動汽車
- the dog's tail 那隻狗的尾巴
- Mary's illness 瑪麗的病
- my children's toys 我孩子們的玩具
- Tom's stupidity 湯姆的愚蠢
- Amy's new boss 艾咪的新老闆

2 一般說來，**無生命的事物**不用「's」構成所有格，而用「**of + 名詞**」的結構來表示所屬關係。

✗ the mountain's bottom
✓ the bottom of the mountain（山腳）

✗ the page's top
✓ the top of the page（這一頁的上方）

✗ *Sweet Valley High*'s main characters
✓ the main characters of *Sweet Valley High*（《甜蜜高谷》這本書的主要角色）

✗ the book's cover
✓ the cover of the book（書的封面 = the book cover）

- **Nancy looked through Amy's window and saw the blue sea.**
  南西從艾咪的窗戶望出去，看見了藍色的大海。 → 指人

- **Did the RN see the sea from the window of the kitchen?**
  = Did the RN see the sea from the kitchen window? → 指物
  那位護理師從廚房的窗戶望出去，看見大海了嗎？
  ↑ RN 是 registered nurse 的縮寫，意思是「註冊護士」。

- **Are there any toy rockets in Jean's pockets?** → 指人
  琴的口袋裡有玩具火箭嗎？

- **Are there any toy rockets in the pockets of Jean's jeans?** → 指物
  琴的牛仔褲口袋裡有玩具火箭嗎？ → of + 物（jeans）；人（Jean） + 's。

有些無生命的事物，也可以用**複合名詞**的方式表達所屬關係。

- the book cover 書本的封面
- the bathroom door 浴室的門
- the kitchen window 廚房的窗戶

3 談論**某個過程**或**某些固定的稱號**時，也用「of + 名詞」。

- the destruction of the forest 森林的破壞
- the Princess of Wales 威爾斯王妃

4 「**of+ 名詞**」用於較長或複雜的片語，可以指物，也可以指人。

- **The cheers of the students sitting in the last row were quite loud and wild when they were told they had won the book reading contest.** 在得知贏得書本閱讀大賽後，坐在最後一排的學生，他們的歡呼聲很熱烈，震耳欲聾。

  ↳ 名詞 students 後面由現在分詞片語 sitting in the last row 限定。

- **The terrible Sichuan earthquake of May 12, 2008 resulted in the deaths of more than 80,000 people.**
  2008 年五月 **12** 日發生的可怕的四川大地震，造成了八萬多人罹難。

  ↳ 「of + 名詞」也用於特定的日期（May 12, 2008）。
  ↳ 句中的第二個 of 後面是一個較長的名詞片語。

5 不過，許多涉及**時間**、**測量**、**國家**、**政府**的片語以及**擬人化**的片語，雖是無生命的事物，卻習慣用「**'s**」或「**'**」構成所有格形式。

- two weeks' salary 兩個星期的薪資
- an hour's work 一個小時的工作
- this week's class meeting 本週的班級會議
- today's newspaper 今天的報紙
- New Year's resolutions 新年的決心
- tonight's Channel 6 news program 今晚第六頻道的新聞節目

美式 **She's away on her three-week vacation.**
英式 **She's away on her three weeks' vacation.**
她正在外地度她為期三週的假期。

擬人法

- for heaven's sake 看在老天爺的份上
- the company's future 公司的未來
- the sun's rays 太陽的光線
- for goodness' sake 看在老天爺的份上

the sun's rays

測量

- a thousand dollars' worth 一千美元的價值
- a stone's throw 丟一顆石頭的距離（很近，一箭之遙）

- ten cents' worth 十美分的價值
- at arm's length 一個手臂的長度距離

國家政府
- Canada's main export 加拿大的主要出口品
- the French government's new foreign policy 法國政府的新外交政策

5 所有格可單獨使用

1 當上下文的文意清楚時，所有格（名詞 + 's，或以 -s 結尾的規則複數名詞 + '）可單獨使用，省略所有格後面的名詞，以避免重複。

- **Claire's hair is dark, but her daughter's is fair.**
  = Claire's hair is dark, but her daughter's hair is fair.
  克萊兒的頭髮是黑的，但她女兒的頭髮卻是金色的。

2 帶有所有格符號的所有格形式，常用來指某人的**辦公室**、**工作室**或**商店**，此時所有格後面的 office（辦公室）、shop（商店）、store（商店）等字可以省略。

- **He stole some bread from the baker's.** 他從麵包店偷了一些麵包。
- **Did she vomit at the doctor's?** 她在醫生的診所嘔吐了嗎？
- **Does Mrs. Harbor's poodle like to go to the barber's?**
  哈伯夫人的貴賓狗喜歡去理髮店嗎？

3 人名的所有格形式可用來指**某人的家**，多半是指朋友的家。此時，所有格後面的 home、house 等可以省略。

- **Please call and find out if Lee is still at Nancy's.**
  請打電話看看李是否還在南西家？
- **Ann's friends are going to give her a birthday party this Saturday night at Dan's.** 這個星期六晚上，安的朋友們要在丹的家為她舉辦生日派對。

6 所有格可修飾另一個所有格

1 一個所有格可以修飾另一個所有格，即兩個所有格「**'s**」連用。

- Jane's lawyer's petition 珍的律師的訴狀

2 但這種結構比較拗口，應盡量避免，在這種情況下最好改變句子的措辭，使用 of 片語來表示所有格。

- the petition of Jane's lawyer 珍的律師的訴狀

Awkward **My son's teacher's husband asked, "Who wants to volunteer to help with the picnic?"**

Better **The husband of my son's teacher asked, "Who wants to volunteer to help with the picnic?"**
我兒子的師丈問：「誰願意幫忙安排野餐？」

Awkward **Roy's children's toys were stolen by some boys.**

Better **The toys of Roy's children were stolen by some boys.**
羅伊的小孩的玩具被一些男孩偷走了。

7 專有名詞的所有格，不與 the、a、an 連用

1 專有名詞的所有格，不能與冠詞 the 或 a/an 連用。

2 帶有「's」或「'」字尾的專有名詞所有格，可以取代定冠詞 the。

3 在所有格形式中，不能遺漏所有格符號「**'s**」。

✗（多了冠詞）	✗（少了 's）	✓
a Mary's turtle	→ Mary turtle	→ Mary's turtle 瑪麗的烏龜
the Britain's climate	→ Britain climate	→ Britain's climate 英國的氣候
the Canada's economy	→ Canada economy	→ Canada's economy 加拿大的經濟

- **Are those Roy's toys?** 那些是羅伊的玩具嗎？
  - ↳ Roy's toys = the toys that belong to Roy
  - ↳ 專有名詞所有格 (Roy's) 不與 the 連用，「's toys」相當於「the toys」。

- **Is that Mary's motorcycle standing next to Gary's?**
  蓋瑞摩托車旁邊的那輛摩托車是瑪麗的嗎？
  - ↳ 專有名詞所有格 (Mary's, Gary's) 不與 the 或 a 連用。

- **Toronto's weekend weather isn't getting any better and will probably get wetter.** 多倫多這週末的天氣不會變好，可能會變得更多雨。
  - ↳ 用名詞所有格 Toronto's 修飾 weather。
  - = **The Toronto weekend weather isn't getting any better and will probably get wetter.**
    - ↳ 定冠詞 the 修飾名詞 weather，專有名詞 Toronto 後不再用所有格形式。
  - = **This weekend's weather in Toronto isn't getting any better and will probably get wetter.**
    - ↳ 表示時間的詞 weekend 可以用所有格形式。這是常見的說法。
  - = **The weather in Toronto this weekend isn't getting any better and will probably get wetter.**
    - ↳ 這也是常見的說法。

8 複數姓氏的所有格前面要與 the 連用

複數姓氏的所有格前面要與 the 連用。

- the Benches' friends 班奇家的朋友們
- the Blooms' travel trailer 布盧姆家的旅行掛車
- the Flowers' poodle 弗勞爾家的貴賓狗

- **The Browns' house is at the end of this street.**
  布朗的房子在這條街的街尾。
  - ↳ The Browns (the + 複數姓氏) = The Brown family
  - ↳ 名詞 house 由名詞所有格 Browns' 修飾，而 The 實際上修飾的是被省略的名詞 family，亦即，The Browns 中的 The 與專有名詞 Browns 無關，而是用來限定普通名詞 family。

9 普通名詞的所有格與 the 連用

普通名詞的所有格，要與 the 連用。比較下面例句：

- **Is Jane's cat fat?** 珍的貓胖不胖？
  - ⤷ Jane's cat = the cat that belongs to Jane
  - ⤷ 專有名詞所有格（Jane's）不與 the 連用。
- **Is that the doctor's cat?** 那是那位醫生的貓嗎？
  - ⤷ the doctor's cat = the cat that belongs to the doctor
  - ⤷ 普通名詞的所有格就可以加上 the。
  - ⤷ 定冠詞 the 修飾普通名詞 doctor；「's cat」取代了 the cat。
- **Is that Jenny's money or the boy's money?**
  那是珍妮的錢，還是那個男孩的錢？
  - ⤷ Jenny's money = the money that belongs to Jenny
  - ⤷ the boy's money = the money that belongs to the boy

Diving Deep Into English 7 「女子籃球隊」要怎麼說？

ⓐ the girl basketball team
ⓑ the girls basketball team
ⓒ the girls' basketball team

「女子籃球隊」要怎麼說？上述三種說法，何者正確？

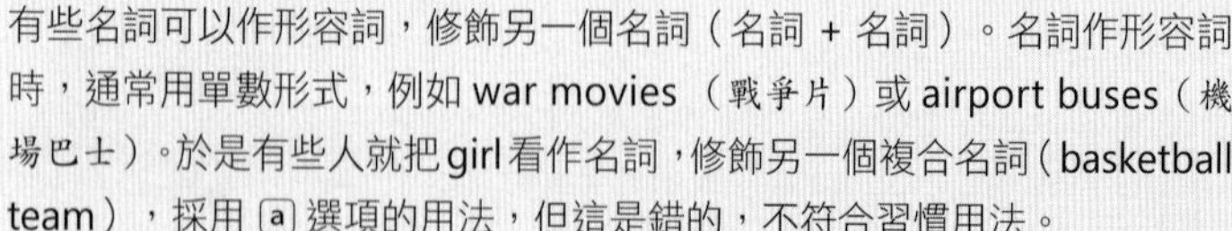

有些名詞可以作形容詞，修飾另一個名詞（名詞 + 名詞）。名詞作形容詞時，通常用單數形式，例如 war movies （戰爭片）或 airport buses（機場巴士）。於是有些人就把 girl 看作名詞，修飾另一個複合名詞（basketball team），採用 ⓐ 選項的用法，但這是錯的，不符合習慣用法。

若是使用複數名詞 women，我們不會說 the women basketball team，而是用所有格形式 the women's basketball team。同理，「女子籃球隊」應該用複數所有格形式 ⓒ 才是正確的，這就是慣用法。很多文法規則都有例外，有時不能硬套文法規則，而應遵守習慣表達法。

10 節慶名稱的所有格用法

1 單數名詞的所有格形式

- New Year's Day 新年
- Father's Day 父親節
- Mother's Day 母親節
- Valentine's Day 情人節

2 複數名詞的所有格形式

- April Fools' Day 愚人節
- Presidents' Day 總統日
- All Saints' Day 萬聖節

3 無所有格

- Christmas Day 聖誕節
- Columbus Day 哥倫布日
- Independence Day（美國）獨立紀念日
- Labor Day 勞動節
- Martin Luther King Day 馬丁·路德紀念日
- Memorial Day 陣亡將士紀念日
- Thanksgiving Day 感恩節

有些節日名稱只用**名詞複數形式**，而不用複數所有格形式。

- Veterans Day 美國退伍軍人節（11 月 11 號）
- United Nations Day 聯合國日（10 月 24 日）

11 其他名詞的所有格用法

- teacher's pet 老師寵愛的學生
- driver's license 駕照
-  dog's life 狗的生活
- traveler's check 旅行支票
- visitor's permit 訪客許可證

- teachers' room 教師室
- workers' unemployment benefits 勞工的失業救濟金
- women's movement 女性運動

12 成對名詞的所有格

1 聯合物主 → 最後一個名詞 + 's 或 + '

以 and 連接的兩個名詞，如果兩個人**共同擁有某物**，這兩個人就看成一個整體（聯合物主），只需要在**最後那個名詞**後面加「's」或「'」。

✗ Del's and Molly's date **was ruined when Sally's angry ex-boyfriend Mark showed up and began to yell.**

✓ Del and Sally's date **was ruined when Sally's angry ex-boyfriend Mark showed up and began to yell.**
莎莉的前男友馬克怒氣沖沖地在戴爾和莎莉約會時出現，開始大喊大叫，戴爾和莎莉的約會就這樣被破壞了。
↑ 兩個人（Del and Sally）共同擁有某物（date）。

・**I saw Kay at** Dennis and Jane's apartment **on Saturday.**
星期六我看見凱在丹尼斯和珍的公寓裡。 → Dennis 和 Jane 一起住的公寓。

2 獨立物主 → 每個名詞都 + 's 或 + '

如果以 and 連接的兩個人**分別擁有某物**（獨立所有權），而不是共同擁有，則**每一個人的名字都要加**「's」或「'」。

✗ **Were** the Lakes **and** the Browns' houses **damaged during the two earthquakes?**

✓ **Were** the Lakes' and the Browns' houses **damaged during the two earthquakes?**
雷克家的房子和布朗家的房子在那兩次地震期間被震毀了嗎？

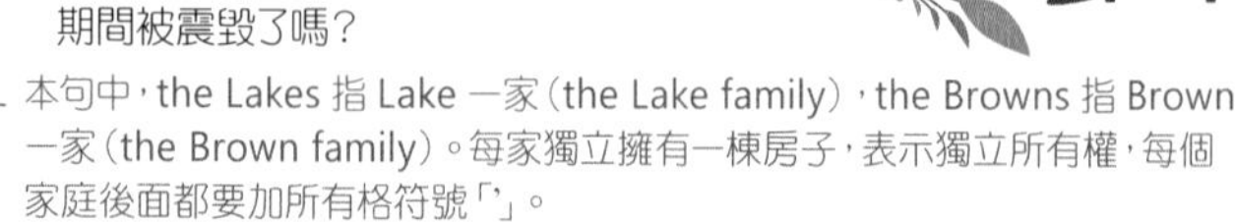
↑ 本句中，the Lakes 指 Lake 一家（the Lake family），the Browns 指 Brown 一家（the Brown family）。每家獨立擁有一棟房子，表示獨立所有權，每個家庭後面都要加所有格符號「'」。

・Ann's and John's pocket computers **were both made by a company called Swans and Amazons.** 安的口袋型電腦和約翰的口袋型電腦都是一家叫做「天鵝和亞馬遜」的公司製造的。

- Claire's and Adam's clothes **always clash, because hers are sleek and sexy and his have a lot of pockets and are great for spending time outdoors.** 克萊兒和亞當的衣服總是不協調，因為克萊兒的衣著時髦又性感，而亞當的衣服卻有一大堆口袋，適合戶外穿。

13 of 所有格 + 's 所有格（雙重所有格）

1 「of 所有格 + 's 所有格」，這種結構叫「**雙重所有格**」。

- **Look at that cute puppy** of **Sue**'s.
  瞧瞧蘇那隻可愛的小狗。

2 當 any、some、all、this、that、these、those 等字，與名詞所有格同時修飾一個名詞時，要用上述的雙重所有格。

✗ All Dr. Seuss's **books are interesting and funny.**
✓ **All** of **Dr. Seuss**'s **books are interesting and funny.**
= **All books** of **Dr. Seuss**'s **are interesting and funny.**
休斯博士寫的所有書，都非常有趣。

3 「of 所有格」與雙重所有格的區別

a 當所修飾的名詞是 picture、painting、photograph、statue 等時：

1. 使用**雙重所有格**：指創作者或某人的收藏物。
2. 使用 **of 所有格**：指某人的肖像畫、玉照或雕像等。

- **This is a picture** of **Jane**'s.
  這是珍畫的（或收藏的）一幅畫。

- **This is a picture** of **Jane.**
  這是一幅珍的肖像畫。

b 當所修飾的名詞是 friend、cousin、uncle 等時，在英式英語裡，「of 所有格」和「雙重所有格」所強調的重點不同。

- **Tom is a friend of my husband's.**
  湯姆是我先生的一位朋友。
  ↑ 雙重所有格：英式用法，強調我丈夫的朋友不只有一個。美式比較少用此結構。

- **Tom is a friend of my husband.**
  = Tom is my husband's friend.
  湯姆是我先生的朋友。
  ↑ of 所有格：英式用法，強調兩者之間的朋友關係。
  ↑ 注意 美式用「's」所有格（my husband's friend），強調「兩者之間的朋友關係」；用 of 所有格（a friend of my husband）或用「one of」結構（one of my husband's friends），強調朋友不只有一個。

14 's 所有格 + of 所有格

描述同一片語中不同名詞之間的多種關係時，通常用「's 所有格」來表示**來源**、**所有者**或**製造者**，用「of 所有格」來表示**主題**或**話題**。

→ 表示所屬關係（屬於 National Gallery）
→ 表示主題（以 King Charles 為主題）

- **the National Gallery's portrait of King Charles**
  國立美術館的查理士國王肖像畫

→ 表示創作者（Jane Smith 所畫的）
→ 表示主題（以 President Washington 為主題）

- **Jane Smith's portrait of President Washington**
  珍·史密斯所繪製的華盛頓總統肖像畫

UNIT

03 代名詞

Pronouns

代名詞的定義

代名詞是用來代替名詞的詞， 可以分為以下幾大類：

1 **指示代名詞**：指明某個特定的人或物。

- this
- that
- these
- those

2 **人稱代名詞**：有人稱區別的代名詞。

- I
- he
- we
- it

3 **所有格代名詞**：所有格代名詞又分為所有格形容詞／所有格限定詞，和獨立所有格代名詞。

- your
- my
- mine
- hers

4 **疑問代名詞**：用來詢問何人、何物、何事。

- who
- what
- which

5 **反身代名詞**：用於反身用法的複合人稱代名詞。

- myself
- yourself
- herself

6 **相互代名詞**：表示相互關係的代名詞。

- each other
- one another

7 **不定代名詞**：不具體指明是某人或某物。

- each
- everyone
- few

- **Jake's English exam was a disaster, because he made too many spelling mistakes.** 傑克的英語考試糟糕透了，因為他犯了太多的拼寫錯誤。
  ↳ many 是不定代名詞。

» 關係代名詞的用法，參見 301 頁〈Unit 7 關係詞與形容詞子句和名詞子句〉。

指示代名詞

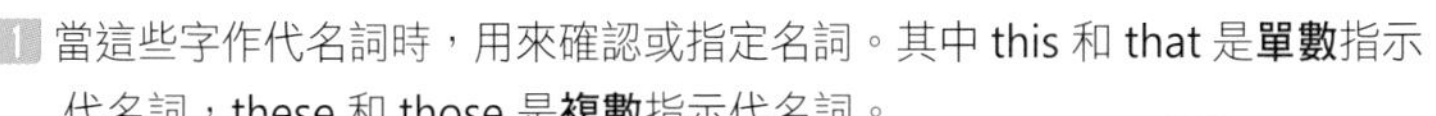

1 當這些字作代名詞時，用來確認或指定名詞。其中 this 和 that 是**單數**指示代名詞，these 和 those 是**複數**指示代名詞。

- **That is my friend Bart, and he is very smart.**
  那是我的朋友巴特，他很聰明。
  ↥ That 是指示代名詞，用來指代單數名詞（Bart）。
- **She will never forget this.** 她將永遠不會忘記這件事。
  ↥ this 是指示代名詞，指一次最近的經歷。
- **Those are my shoes.** 那些是我的鞋。
  ↥ Those 是指示代名詞，用來指代複數名詞（shoes）。

2 這些指示代名詞無論是單數形式還是複數形式，當作主詞時，既可以用來指**物**（things），也可以用來指**人**（people）。

- **This is my sister Liz.** 這是我的姐姐莉茲。 → This 指人（Liz）。
- **Is that her fur hat?** 那是她的毛皮帽嗎？ → that 指東西（fur hat）。
- **These are Mat's cats.** 這些是麥特的貓。 → These 指動物（cats）。
- **Those are Mike's mother and brother.** 那些人是邁克的母親和哥哥。
  ↥ Those 指人（mother and brother）。

3 this、that（單數）和 these、those（複數），也可以用來表示「以下所述」或「以上所述」。

- "I can't believe what I heard about mayor Eve Player."
  "Really? Well, you might want to watch this.
  It's a podcast from the Bright Knight
  News Website."「我不相信伊芙·皮雷爾市長的那些傳聞。」
  「是嗎？那你也許會想看這個，這是《光明騎士新聞網站》的錄影。」
  ↥ this 指「以下所述」(what is about to follow)，即下面一句所要說的東西。
  Andrew is going to quit school and get married to Sue. I think that's not wise. 安德魯打算輟學去和蘇結婚。我覺得那樣不太明智。
  ↥ that 在這裡指「以上所述」，指前句剛提及過的事情。

2 作指示形容詞用的 this、that、these、those

1 這些字也作**限定詞**，也就是**指示形容詞**，修飾跟在其後的名詞。（一些文法學家認為限定詞是形容詞的一種類型。）限定詞的定義和用法，參見138頁〈Part 1 冠詞和限定詞〉。

2 this 和 that 後面接**單數**名詞，these 和 those 後面接**複數**名詞。

- Would you like this piece of cheese? 你想吃這片起司嗎？
- Would you like these two pieces of cheese? 你想吃這兩片起司嗎？

3 this 和 these 表示「**這裡**」，即在我們附近的東西；
that 和 those 表示「**那裡**」，即不在我們附近的東西。

- **Louise, could you bring that plate of cheese to me, please?**
  露易絲，請把那盤起司拿給我好嗎？
  ↳ plate 不在說話者的身旁，應該用 that。

- **This tall tower wasn't built in an hour.** 這座高塔決非是短時間內蓋好的。
  ↳ This 是指示形容詞，指出是哪一座高塔（which tall tower）。
  這裡指靠近說話者的這座高塔，說話者也許正站在塔樓上。

- **These raspberry pancakes are Jake's.**
  這些覆盆子煎餅是傑克的。
  ↳ These 是指示形容詞，指出是哪些覆盆子煎餅（which raspberry pancakes）。這裡指靠近說話者的覆盆子煎餅。

raspberry pancakes

- **Those blueberry pancakes are for you and Jerry.** 那些藍莓煎餅是給你和傑瑞的。
  ↳ Those 是指示形容詞，指出是哪些藍莓煎餅（which blueberry pancakes）。這裡指不在說話者附近的藍莓煎餅。

blueberry pancakes

4 this 和 these 常用來指**剛發生、正在發生**或**即將發生的事**；
that 和 those 指**過去發生的事**或**已經完成的事**。

✗ **This vacation with Kate was great!**

✓ **That vacation with Kate was great** → 假期已經結束，用 That 和過去式 was。
與凱特共度的那個假期真是太棒了！

✓ **This vacation with Henry is wonderful!** → 假期進行中，用 This 和現在式 is。
與亨利共度的這個假期真是太棒了！

- **Are you enjoying these choral singers?**
  你喜歡這些合唱歌手嗎？ → 正在進行

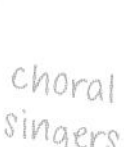

choral singers

- **Those smelly toes of yours made Rose hold her nose.**
  你的那些臭腳趾害得蘿絲捏住她的鼻子。 → 過去事件

- **Was that lecture about song writing very long?** → 過去事件
  那場關於歌曲創作的演講很長嗎？
  » 參見 207 頁〈4 指示形容詞 / 指示限定詞〉。

Diving Deep Into English 8 電話用語中的 this 和 that

在接來電時，詢問對方是誰有以下方法：

英式 Who is that? 您哪位？

美式 Who is this?

美式 Whom am I speaking to?

美式 To whom am I speaking?

在某些表達中，this（這麼；這樣地）或 that（那麼；那樣地；非常），可用來替代副詞 so，作狀語，以強化其後的形容詞或副詞。

- Scot always sells a lot of ice cream when the weather is this hot.
  天氣像這樣熱時，史考特通常會賣出很多冰淇淋。
  ↑ to this extent

- We can't plan that far ahead.
  我們沒辦法計畫那麼久之後的事。
  ↑ to that extent
- Kate never stayed out that late.
  凱特從來沒有那麼晚不回家。
  ↑ that = very（用於否定句）
- I didn't like the movie that much.
  我不是那麼喜歡那部電影。
  ↑ that = very（用於否定句）

人稱代名詞

1 人稱代名詞的意義與作用

1 **人稱代名詞**（I、you、him、it、we、them 等）是用來代替**名詞**的詞，可以指人或物。當沒有必要使用或重複名詞時，就可以用人稱代名詞來代替。

- I 我
- you 你；你們
- him 他
- her 她
- we 我們
- they 他們
- me 我
- he 他
- she 她
- it 它
- us 我們
- them 他們

✗ **Tell Sally I miss Sally.**

✓ **Tell Sally I miss her.** 請轉告莎莉，說我想她。

↑ 用人稱代名詞 her 來避免重複 Sally。

✗ **Jane's father asked Jane to remind Jane's father to pick up Jim at the gym.**

✓ **Jane's father asked her to remind him to pick up Jim at the gym.**

珍的父親要她提醒他到體育館去接吉姆。

↑ 沒有必要重複 Jane 和 Jane's father。

✗ **Paul had a bad fall yesterday. Paul broke a ski and hurt his left knee.**

✓ **Paul had a bad fall yesterday. He broke a ski and hurt his left knee.**

昨天保羅重重地摔了一跤，摔破了一個滑雪板，還傷了左膝。

↑ 沒有必要重複 Paul。

- **Mom said she did not know Tom.** 媽媽說她不認識湯姆。

  ↑ 沒有必要重複 Mom。

- **The police caught Del with the stolen fur and put him in jail.**

  警方逮捕了戴爾，在他身上搜出被偷的毛皮，並拘留了他。

  ↑ 沒有必要重複 Del。

2 「人稱代名詞」這個文法術語可能會使人產生迷惑，誤以為這些代名詞只能用來指**人**，實際上，一些人稱代名詞也可以用來指**物**或**動物**，如：she、her、he、him、it、they、them。

- She is a very fast car. 那輛車跑得很快。→ 指物。
- They are cute puppies, aren't they?
  牠們是很可愛的小狗狗，不是嗎？→ 指動物。

3 此外，one 也可以作代名詞，代替上下文中的名詞（參見 77 頁〈5 代名詞 one 和 ones〉）；還可以作不定代名詞，表示「任何人」（參見 134 頁〈15 one 一個；任何人〉）。

4 who 和 whom 則是**疑問人稱代名詞**（參見 89 頁〈Part 5 疑問代名詞〉）。

2 不要用人稱代名詞重複主詞

如果句子已經有了一個主詞，就不要再用人稱代名詞去重複句中的主詞。

✗ New York City it needs a lot of clean water every day.
✓ New York City needs a lot of clean water every day.
紐約市每天都需要大量的純淨水。

✗ Monkeys they don't live in Antarctica.
✓ Monkeys don't live in Antarctica. 南極洲沒有猴子。

✗ A museum in Toronto it wants my antique cars.
✓ A museum in Toronto wants my antique cars.
多倫多的一家博物館想要我的古董車。

3 人稱代名詞的三種形式：主格、受格、所有格

1 **人稱代名詞的三種格**

a **主格代名詞**：在句中作主詞。

b **受格代名詞**：在句中作受詞，包括作介系詞的受詞。受格代名詞不是動作的執行者，而是動作的接受者。

C 所有格代名詞：用來表示物品的主人是誰，常用來回答「誰的？」（Whose?）這類的問題。在 Part 4 中將針對所有格代名詞作進一步說明。

	主格	受格	所有格：所有格限定詞	所有格：獨立所有格代名詞
第一人稱	I	me	my	mine
	we	us	our	ours
第二人稱	you	you	your	yours
第三人稱	he	him	his	his
	she	her	her	hers
	it	it	its	—
	they	them	their	theirs
疑問人稱代名詞	who	whom	whose	—

⤷ 從上表可以看出，人稱代名詞有三個人稱，每個人稱又分為單數和複數（其中第二人稱單複數同形），第三人稱單數還有陽性、陰性和中性之分。

主格	受格	所有格限定詞	獨立所有格代名詞
I like Jane.	Jane likes me.	It's my house.	It's mine.
We like Jane.	Jane likes us.	It's our house.	It's ours.
You like Jane.	Jane likes you.	It's your house.	It's yours.
He knows Jane.	Jane knows him.	It's his house.	It's his.
She knows Jane.	Jane knows her.	It's her house.	It's hers.
They know Jane.	Jane knows them.	It's their house.	It's theirs.
It is a dog.	Jane likes it.	Its tail is short.	—

2 代名詞與其所替代的詞必須同「格」

受格代名詞不可用來作主詞，反之，也不可以用主格代名詞來作受詞。在介系詞後面，要用受格代名詞。

✗ Amy cried, "Please help I."

✗ Amy cried, "Please help mine/my!"

✔ Amy cried, "Please help me!" 艾咪喊著：「請幫幫我！」

⤷ me 是動詞 help 的受詞，所以要用受格代名詞；不可用主格代名詞 I 作受詞，當然也不能用所有格形式（mine, my）作受詞。

- I like cats that eat rats. 我喜歡會吃老鼠的貓。
  ↑ I 是句子的主詞（主格），不可用受格代名詞 Me 或所有格代名詞 My/Mine 作主詞。

- He loves Bess. 他喜歡貝絲。 → He 是句子的主詞。

✗ Why is prim Kim with he?
✓ Why is prim Kim with him? 為什麼拘謹的金姆會和他在一起？
↑ 介系詞 with 後面要用受格 him。

- This coat is for her, and it's made out of artificial fur.
  這件人造毛大衣是給她的。 → 介系詞 for 後面要用受格 her。

4 代名詞 it

1 it 可用來指人，確認人的身分。

✗ Hello. I'm Amy Smith.
✓ Hello. This is Amy Smith.
✓ Hello. It's Amy Smith. 喂，我是艾咪‧史密斯。

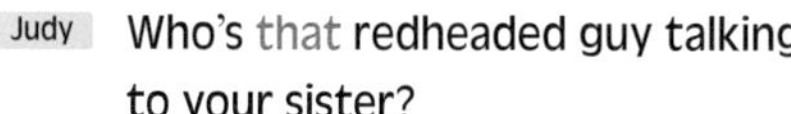

Judy	Who's that redheaded guy talking to your sister?	跟你妹妹說話的那個紅髮小夥子是誰？
Larry	It's Gary. (= That's Gary.)	是蓋瑞。

Dan	Ann, you've got a phone call.	安，你的電話。
Ann	Find out who it is, and tell the caller I'm snoring on the couch.	看看是誰打來的，跟他說我正在沙發上打鼾。
Dan	No, you talk to whoever is on the phone yourself.	我才不要，你自己去跟來電的人說。

2 it 也可以用來指 nothing、everything 和 all。

Annie and her medical team did all they could, but it was not enough to save Danny. 安妮和她的醫療小組盡了一切努力，但還是無法挽救丹尼。

- Everything is all right with Paul, isn't it? 保羅一切安好，對嗎？

3 it 可作**主詞**，常用在表示**時間**、**天氣**、**氣溫**、**距離**及**目前形勢**的片語中。

- **"What time is it?" "It's 9 p.m."**「現在幾點？」「晚上九點。」
- **"What day is it?" inquired Kay. "It's Monday again," answered Ben.**
  「今天星期幾?」凱問。「又是星期一了。」班回答。
- **It's my mom's birthday.** 今天是我媽媽的生日。
- **It has snowed for two days.** 已經下了兩天的雪了。
- **It's forty degrees below zero, and my knees are cold.** 今天零下 40 度，我的膝蓋好冷呃。
- **It's about six blocks from here to the docks.**
  這裡距離碼頭約六個街區。

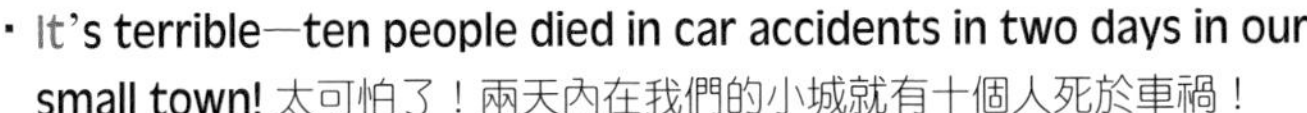

- **It's terrible—ten people died in car accidents in two days in our small town!** 太可怕了！兩天內在我們的小城就有十個人死於車禍！

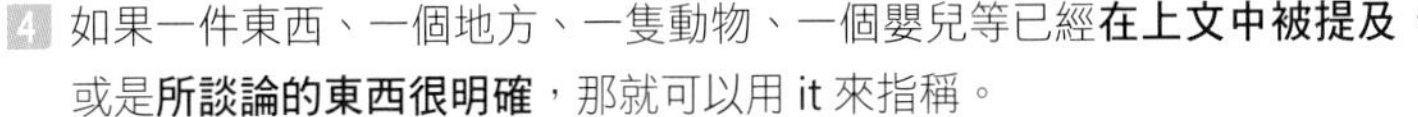

4 如果一件東西、一個地方、一隻動物、一個嬰兒等已經**在上文中被提及**，或是**所談論的東西很明確**，那就可以用 it 來指稱。

- **I love Houghton, Michigan, but it's awfully snowy.**
  我喜歡密西根州的霍頓城，但那裡總是在下雪。
- **When your colt grows a little bigger, you need to let it run in the field.** 當你的小馬長大一點時，你就得讓牠在原野上奔跑。
- **"Is it a boy or girl?" asked Roy.**「是男孩還是女孩？」羅伊問。
  ↳ 用 it，表示不知其性別。
- **"What is the spy movie about?" "It's a story about glory."**
  「那部間諜片演些什麼?」「演一個關於榮耀的故事。」
- **My country owes me nothing. It gave me, as it gives every boy and girl, a chance. It gave me schooling, independence of action, opportunity for service and honor.** (President Herbert Hoover)
  我的國家對我有恩。它給了我機會，就像給每一個孩子機會一樣。
  它讓我受教育，讓我獨立行動，給我為國效力和獲得榮譽的機會。
  ↳ it 在這裡指地方（my country）。

5 it 作**形式主詞**，實際主詞是句尾的不定式、名詞子句或動名詞片語 。

- It's hard to fail, but it is worse never to have tried to succeed.
  (President Theodore Roosevelt)
  失敗雖難以讓人忍受，但更糟的是從來都沒有做過成功的嘗試。
  ⌊ 兩個獨立子句裡的 it 都是形式主詞，實際主詞是不定式片語（to fail 和 never to have tried to succeed）。

- It is reported that the U.S. President is going to visit Shanghai in July. 報導說，美國總統七月份會訪問上海。
  ⌊ it 是形式主詞，實際主詞是 that 引導的名詞子句。

- It was nice talking to you. 跟你聊天很愉快。
  ⌊ it 是形式主詞，實際主詞是動名詞片語。

6 it 作形式主詞，用於**強調**句型：「it is/was + 被強調的部分 + who/that 子句」。被強調的部分可以是主詞、副詞或受詞等，但不能用來強調動詞。

- It's your mom that wants to speak to you.
  是你媽媽想跟你講話。
  ⌊ 強調主詞。

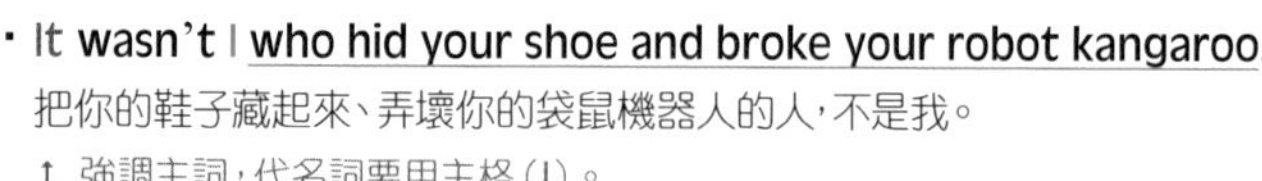

- It wasn't I who hid your shoe and broke your robot kangaroo.
  把你的鞋子藏起來、弄壞你的袋鼠機器人的人，不是我。
  ⌊ 強調主詞，代名詞要用主格（I）。

比較

- It's the principal that/who wants to speak to you and Matt.
  是校長要跟你和麥特談話。
  ⌊ it 用於強調句型：「it is + 被強調部分 + that/who 子句」，that 引導的子句不是限定修飾 the principal（校長只有一個，不需要限定性子句來修飾），而是強調句型中的形容詞子句。

- That's the teacher who wanted to speak to you and Matt
  想跟你和麥特談話的就是那位老師。
  ⌊ who wanted to speak to you and Matt 是限定性形容詞子句，修飾先行詞 the teacher。這句不是強調句型，不能用 it。

5 代名詞 one 和 ones

1 **one** 用來代替上文已經提及的某個名詞，以避免重複那個名詞。one 的複數形式是 ones。

- **"Is this your car?" "No, mine is the red one by the tree."** → one = car
  「這是你的車子嗎？」「那不是我的車，我的車是紅色的，在那棵樹旁邊。」

- **She often turns small problems into big ones.** → ones = problems
  她常把小問題變成大問題。

2 one 只能代替**可數名詞**，不能用來代替不可數名詞。

✗ **I asked for some orange juice, not apple one.**
✓ **I asked for some orange juice, not apple juice.**
我要的是柳橙汁，不是蘋果汁。
↑ juice 是不可數名詞，不能用 one 來代替，需要重複 juice。

- **If you need money for the trip to Australia, I can lend you some.**
  如果你的澳洲之行需要錢，我可以借你一些。
  ↑ money 是不可數名詞，不能用 one/ones 來代替，這裡的 some = some money。

3 ones 不能單獨使用，必須跟一些附加的內容一起使用（如：big ones, the ones on the bookshelf, which ones），而 some 可以單獨使用。

✗ **"Mom, I want some jellybeans." "OK, let's go and buy ones."**
✓ **"Mom, I want some jellybeans." "OK, let's go and buy some."**
「媽媽，我想要雷根糖。」「好吧，我們去買一些。」

- **Lulu has 12 jellybeans in her pocket: 8 green ones and 4 red ones.**
  露露的口袋裡有十二個豆形糖果：八個綠色的，四個紅色的。

Dan	**Please pass me the two new towels I bought yesterday.**	請把我昨天買的那兩條毛巾遞給我。
Ann	**Which ones?**	哪兩條？
Dan	**The blue ones on the shelf.**	架子上的那兩條。

» one 作不定代名詞的用法，參見 134 頁〈15 one 一個；任何人〉。

6 人稱代名詞構成複合主詞或複合受詞的用法

1 「複合」意味著一個以上。人稱代名詞與其他詞彙（名詞或人稱代名詞）構成**複合主詞**時，必須用**主格**形式，後面所接的動詞要用**複數動詞**。

- You and he need **to talk about greed.**
  你和他需要談談貪婪這個問題。
  ⮡ You and he 是複合主詞，應該接複數動詞 need。

- Jill and I **will swim back to the beach and get dry.** 潔兒和我要游回海灘，然後把身子擦乾。
  ⮡ Jill and I 是複合主詞，要用主格代名詞 I。

- **Both** he and I are **interested in buying the same antique car.**
  他和我都想買同一輛古董車。
  ⮡ Both he and I 是複合主詞，用主格代名詞 he 和 I，用複數動詞 are。

2 人稱代名詞與其他詞彙構成**複合受詞**時，必須用**受格**形式。無論是在動詞還是介系詞後面的複合受詞，都要用人稱代名詞的受格形式。

✗ **She showed** Mike and I **a black cat and asked us if we wanted to adopt it.**

✓ **She showed** Mike and me **a black cat and asked us if we wanted to adopt it.**
她給邁克和我看了一隻黑貓，並問我們是否願意收養。

⮡ Mike and me 是動詞 showed 的複合受詞，複合受詞要用受格代名詞 me。

- **Dee loves to create trouble for** you and me.
  蒂喜歡給我們兩個人製造麻煩。
  ⮡ you and me 是介系詞 for 的複合受詞，不能用主格代名詞 I。

- **Between** you and me, **Mary is going to break up with her boyfriend Jerry.**
  不要告訴別人喔，瑪麗準備和男朋友傑瑞分手。
  ⮡ Between 是介系詞，後面接受格代名詞（me），不接主格代名詞（I）。
  ⮡ between you and me 是慣用語，意思是「你我私下說說就好，不要告訴別人」。

7 人稱代名詞的排列順序（you and I）

談及「我和你」時，英文要把 you 放在前面，說成「you and I」。出於禮貌，人們通常最後提及自己（I、me）。

- you and I → you and me 你和我
- she and I → she and me 她和我
- Mary and I → Mary and me 瑪麗和我

▪ Why don't you and I go out tonight and count the stars in the sky?
你和我今晚何不出去數一數天上的星星呢？

▪ Nancy made chocolate shakes for Mary and me.
南西為我和瑪麗做了巧克力奶昔。

▪ Sue and I are moving to Honolulu.
蘇和我要搬到檀香山。

常成對使用的代名詞

- he and she → him and her 他和她
- he and we → him and us 他和我們
- he and I → him and me 他和我
- she and I → her and me 她和我
- she and they → her and them 她和他們
- we and they → us and them 我們和他們
- they and I → them and me 他們和我

如果名詞和**並非指說話者**的代名詞一起連用，則代名詞通常放在前面（例如：she and Larry）。

▪ Let her and her husband work out their problems.
讓她和她丈夫去解決他們的問題吧。→ 代名詞 her 放在名詞前面。

8 動詞「to be」的後面，要用主格代名詞

1 一般來說，動詞 to be 的後面要接**人稱代名詞的主格**（I、he、she、we、they 等）作主詞補語（例如：This is he/she.）。這類動詞有：

- is
- shall/will be
- have/has been
- should/would be
- had been
- shall/will have been
- may/might be
- was
- should/would have been
- may/might have been
- can/could be
- must/ought to be
- could have been
- must/ought to have been

電話上 On the phone

Ann	**Hello! May I speak to Dan please?**	你好！請問丹在嗎？
Dan	**This is he (speaking).**	我就是。

↑ 當你拿起電話，對方說要找你，正確的回答是「This is he.」「This is she.」。
↑ 也可以直接說出你的名字，這種用法更自然，即：This is Dan (speaking).

一般來說，to be 後面都要用主格代名詞，但在**電話用語**中，**第一人稱**通常用「It's me.」。在這種情境裡也可以用主格「It is I.」，不過使用主格的說法會顯得很拘謹。

Gary	Hello!	喂！
Mary	Hello! Is this Gary?	喂！是蓋瑞嗎？
Gary	Yes, this is Gary.	是，我就是。
Mary	Hi! It's me, Mary.	嗨！是我，瑪麗。
Gary	Hi, Mary! How are you?	嗨，瑪麗！你好嗎？

2 句型「**it is/was + that/who**」是強調句型，被強調的部分放在動詞 to be 後面，如果被強調的部分是主詞，人稱代名詞要用主格。

- **It wasn't I who told this lie.** 這個謊言不是我說的。
- **Was it she who gave a cookie to Ben again?** 是她又給了班　塊餅乾的嗎？
- **You have to admit that it is they who wanted to stay.**
  你得承認，是他們想留下來的。

NOTE

如果被強調的部分是**受詞**，人稱代名詞就要用**受格**。

- It is him that Louise wants to please. 露易絲想討好的人就是他。

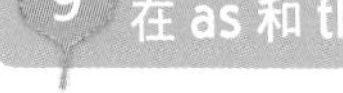

9 在 as 和 than 的後面，要用主格代名詞，還是受格代名詞？

1 口語用受格代名詞

- **She is almost as tall as me.** 她幾乎和我一樣高。
- **My three younger sisters can run faster than me.** 我的三個妹妹跑得比我快。

2 正式語用「主格代名詞 + 動詞」

- **My sister Pam is almost as tall as I am.** 我妹妹潘姆和我差不多高。
- **Dan can run faster than I can.** 丹跑得比我快。
- **Lulu writes better than I do.** 露露的文筆比我好。

3 **使用正式語用法，可以消除歧義**：as 和 than 的口語用法（即接受格代名詞），有時容易引起歧義，例如：

Not clear **Lee loves ice cream more than me.**

↑ 這句話的意思究竟是「李愛吃冰淇淋勝過於愛我」，還是「李比我更愛吃冰淇淋」？兩種句意都有可能。為避免歧義，可將句子作如下修改：

Clear **Lee loves ice cream more than he loves me.** 李愛冰淇淋勝過於愛我。

Clear **Lee loves ice cream more than I do.** 李比我更愛冰淇淋。

» 參見 240 頁〈Part 8 比較級的用法〉。

10 except 和 but 的後面，要用受格代名詞

1 except（除了……之外）的後面要接**受格**代名詞。

✗ **Everybody except she was afraid to touch the dead rat's fur.**

✓ **Everybody except her was afraid to touch the dead rat's fur.**
除了她，大家都不敢摸那隻死老鼠的毛。

↑ except 在這裡是介系詞，後面要接受格代名詞 her，不要用主格形式 she。

- No one in our class knows how to ski except you and me.
  我們班上除了你和我以外，沒有別人會滑雪。
  ↥ 介系詞 except 後面接受格代名詞 me。

2 but 也可以表示「除了……之外」，意義等同於 except，用於 nothing、everybody、nobody、all 等字的後面。但 but 後面要用主格還是受格代名詞，文法學家看法不一。請看這兩個例句：

- No one saw Annie but I.
  ↥ 有些人認為，but 在此是連接詞，應該接主格代名詞 I。
  （這句是否正確，請見下面第三條。）
- No one saw Annie but me. 除了我以外，沒有別人看見安妮。
  ↥ 也有許多文法學家把這裡的 but 看作介系詞，因此當 but 片語出現在句尾時，用受格代名詞 me 是完全正確的。

3 應該把 but 看作**介系詞**，其意義和用法相當於介系詞 except，後面接受格代名詞。

✗ Everybody but I am afraid to touch that big spider.
↥ 假如把 but 看作連接詞，那麼動詞的人稱和單複數，就要和 but 後面的名詞或代名詞一致，這樣便會出現上述的錯誤。
↥ 主詞 Everybody 須接單數第三人稱動詞 is，而連接詞後面的第一人稱主詞 I 則須接動詞 am，如此就不能搭配在一起，因此 but 在這裡應該是介系詞。

✓ Everybody but me is afraid to touch that big spider .
✓ Everybody is afraid to touch that big spider but me.
除了我以外，大家都不敢摸那個大蜘蛛。
↥ 這裡的 but 是介系詞，單數動詞（is）與單數主詞（Everybody）一致。
↥ 可以把介系詞片語 but me 移動到句尾。

- All of the girls but/except you and her have gone to swim in the creek.
  除了你和她，其他的女孩都去小溪那邊游泳了。
- No one but me wants to visit Lily.
  = No one wants to visit Lily but me.
  除了我，沒人想去拜訪莉莉。

11 受格代名詞的口語用法

在**口語**中，常用代名詞的**受格**形式當作主詞（尤其是受格代名詞 me），簡短作答，或者用在動詞 to be 後面。

Ann	Who broke the window?		是誰打破了窗戶？
Dan	① Him. (= It was him.)	→ 口語	是他。
	② He did.	→ 正式語	

- "Who's there?" "Me. (= It's me.)" 「是誰在那裡？」「是我。」
  - ↥ 這裡要用「Me.」或「It's me.」，比「It is I.」更常見。
  - ↥ 在簡短回答中，人稱代名詞單獨使用時，習慣上要用受格。
- "I'm hungry and tired." "Me too." 「我又餓又累。」「我也是。」 → 口語
- "Is there anyone who wants to play tennis with Liz?" "Definitely not me."「有誰想和莉茲打網球的嗎？」「那絕對不是我。」

12 省略人稱代名詞的受格

如果受詞在同一個句子裡已經出現，則人稱代名詞的受格不能用於不定式片語或形容詞子句。

✗ Those strawberries look ripe enough to eat them.

✔ Those strawberries look ripe enough to eat.
那些草莓看起來已經熟了，可以吃了。

↥ Those strawberries 是句子的主詞，又是不定式動詞 eat 的受詞，因此不能在不定式裡用受格 them。

✗ She is the new ballet dancer I told you about her yesterday.

✔ She is the new ballet dancer (whom) I told you about yesterday.
她就是我昨天告訴你的那位新來的芭蕾舞舞者。

↥ the new ballet dancer 是句子的主詞補語，又是形容詞子句中介系詞 about 的受詞。因此，不能在 about 後面用受格 her。但可以用關係代名詞 whom 來引導子句，whom 是 about 的受詞，可省略。

所有格代名詞

1 所有格限定詞（Possessive Determiners）

1 人稱代名詞有專有的所有格形式，如 my、its、one's 等，這些**所有格代名詞**置於名詞或名詞片語前面，作限定詞（形容詞）用，因此也稱為**所有格限定詞**或**所有格形容詞**或**形容詞性物主代名詞**。參見 207 頁〈3 所有格形容詞 / 所有格限定詞〉。

單數

人稱代名詞	所有格限定詞
I 我	my 我的
you 你	your 你的
he 他	his 他的
she 她	her 她的
it 它；牠	its 它的；牠的

人稱代名詞	所有格限定詞
we 我們	our 我們的
you 你們	your 你們的
they 他們	their 他們的

2 不可以用受格代名詞或主格代名詞，來代替所有格代名詞。

✗ May I use you phone?

✓ May I use your phone? 我可以用一下你的電話嗎？

↳ your 表示所屬，不可用主格或受格代名詞（you）來代替所有格形式（your）。

- What did my wife buy? 我太太買了些什麼東西？
  ↳ my 是所有格形式。（誰的妻子？我的妻子。）
  ↳ 不可用受格代名詞（me）或主格代名詞（I）來代替所有格形式（my）。
- While swimming around in the pail, my toy whale is waving its tail.
  我的玩具鯨一邊搖著尾巴，一邊繞著桶子游泳。
- The students like to hike with their English teacher, Mr. Mike Blare.
  學生喜歡跟他們的英文老師邁克·布雷爾先生一起去遠足。

3 不可以在動名詞（-ing 形式）前面使用受格代名詞或主格代名詞（動名詞具有名詞的性質，因此要用形容詞修飾）。

- Bing has developed good health and endurance because of his daily jogging and swimming. 賓每天都慢跑和游泳，練得很健康，體力很好。
  ↥ 在 -ing 形式（jogging and swimming）前要用所有格形式，不可用受格代名詞（him）或主格代名詞（he）。

Informal Dan insisted on me taking a week off and going to Japan.

Formal Dan insisted on my taking a week off and going to Japan.

丹堅持要我去日本度假一個星期。

↥ 非正式語中，在一些片語動詞（如 insist on）的後面，有時可以在 -ing 形式前使用受格形式，但在考試、商務信函等正式語中，要用**所有格形式**，不要使用受格。

4 所有格形式不會因所接的名詞是單數或複數而改變形式。

- Our friends are going on a trip to Australia. 我們的朋友們要去澳洲旅行。
- Our friend is going on a trip to Australia. 我們的朋友要去澳洲旅行。

2 獨立所有格代名詞（Substitutional Possessive Pronouns）

1 獨立所有格代名詞的定義和用法

a 除了起形容詞作用的所有格代名詞（又稱「所有格形容詞」或「所有格限定詞」）外，還有一種所有格代名詞，叫做**獨立所有格代名詞**或稱**名詞性物主代名詞**。

單數
- mine 我的
- his 他的
- yours 你的
- hers 她的

複數
- ours 我們的
- theirs 他們的
- yours 你們的

b 獨立所有格代名詞可以指**單數**名詞或**複數**名詞；可以作動詞的主詞、受詞或補語，也可作介系詞的受詞。獨立所有格代名詞的**主格和受格同形**。

c 獨立所有格代名詞後面不可以接名詞。

d its 通常只用作限定詞，後面接名詞，不作獨立所有格代名詞。

✗ Jan often writes email to a friend of her in Japan.

✗ Jan often writes email to a friend of hers friends in Japan.

↑ 獨立所有格代名詞後面不可以接名詞。

✓ Jan often writes email to a friend of hers in Japan.

簡常常給她在日本的一個朋友寫電子郵件。

↑ hers 是 she 的獨立所有格代名詞，當作介系詞 of 的受詞。

↑ hers = her friends（用來指代複數名詞）。

↑ 「of + 獨立所有格代名詞」構成雙重所有格，在此處表部分概念（朋友之一）。

- **My puppy is outside, and hers is inside.** 我的小狗在戶外，她的小狗在室內。

  ↑ hers 作主詞；hers = her puppy（用來指代單數名詞）。

- **Dan often phones a friend of his in Iran.** 丹常打電話給他在伊朗的一個朋友。

  ↑ his 是 he 的獨立所有格形式，作介系詞 of 的受詞（a friend of his = one of his friends）。注意 his 既是 he 的獨立所有格形式，也是 he 的所有格限定詞形式。

- **That airplane piloted by Dan's girlfriend, Liz, must be his.**

  丹的女友莉茲駕駛的飛機，想必是丹的飛機。

  ↑ 獨立所有格代名詞 his，作主詞補語；his = his airplane（用來指代單數名詞）。

- **Paul stretched out his hands to grab mine.** 保羅伸手抓住我的手。

  ↑ mine 作動詞的受詞；mine = my hands（用來指代複數名詞）。

2 獨立所有格代名詞和所有格限定詞的區別

a 所有格限定詞／所有格形容詞

- my
- your
- his
- her
- its
- their
- our

b 獨立所有格代名詞

- mine
- yours
- his
- hers
- theirs
- ours

所有格限定詞 用在名詞前面	獨立所有格代名詞 單獨使用	
• my swine 我的豬	mine 我的	• This swine is mine. 這頭豬是我的。 • These swine are mine. 這些豬是我的。 ↑ swine 單複數同形
• your boar(s) 你的公豬	yours 你的	• That boar is yours. 那頭公豬是你的。 • Those boars of yours are outdoors. 你的那些公豬在外面。

his sports car(s) 他的跑車	his 他的	· Is that sports car his? 那輛跑車是他的嗎？ · Are those sports cars his? 那些跑車是他的嗎？
his problem(s) 他的問題	his 他的	· That is my problem, not his. 那是我的問題，不是他的。 · Those are my problems, not his. 那些是我的問題，不是他的。
her furs 她的毛皮衣	hers 她的	· Those furs are hers. 那些毛皮衣是她的。
our flower(s) 我們的花	ours 我們的	· Are these glass flowers really ours? 這些玻璃花真的是我們的嗎？
their teddy bear(s) 他們的玩具熊	theirs 他們的	· These teddy bears are Claire's, not theirs. 這些玩具熊是克萊兒的，不是他們的。

· Did you see Dee and Del in their nice new RV? Theirs (= Their RV) is really reliable, but ours (= our RV) is so old that it runs mostly on our prayers.

你見過蒂和戴爾坐他們漂亮的新露營車嗎？他們露營車的性能很穩定，而我們的已經破舊不堪了，大多數的時候得靠我們的禱告來運轉。

↳ RV 在美國很普遍，是供旅行時用的活動房屋式旅遊車，裡面有臥室、廚房、洗手間。

· These dogs of mine used to work for the police department.
= My dogs used to work for the police department. 我的狗為警方工作過。

↳ 「of + 獨立所有格代名詞」在此處加強語氣。

· Those dogs of yours can be trained to help blind people.
= Your dogs can be trained to help blind people.
你的狗可以訓練來幫助盲人。

· These two strong dogs of ours can pull a sled.
= Our two strong dogs can pull a sled. 我們兩隻強壯的狗能夠拉雪橇。

· Those dogs of theirs are trained to catch criminals.
= Their dogs are trained to catch criminals.
他們的狗受過訓練，能夠追捕罪犯。

3 成對代名詞的所有格

如果不是使用「人名 + 's」來表示**兩個物主**（比如：Jane's and Mike's），而是使用**代名詞的所有格限定詞**（your、my、our、his 等），則不要將兩個所有格限定詞一起連用（如 your and my），而要把物品（如下面第一個例句中的 cellphone）**放在兩個所有格限定詞之間**，再把後一個所有格限定詞改成**獨立所有格代名詞**（mine、yours、hers 等），這樣聽起來比較自然。

成對代名詞的所有格 → 所有格限定詞 + 名詞 + and + 獨立所有格代名詞

Awkward Your and my **cellphones were made by the same company.**
Natural Your **cellphone** and mine **were made by the same company.**
你的手機和我的手機是同一家公司製造的。

Awkward Their and our **cottages were designed by Claire Flowers.**
Natural Their **cottage** and ours **were designed by Claire Flowers.**
他們和我們的別墅都是克萊兒·弗勞爾斯設計的。

Awkward His and my **signatures were on the new label designed by Mabel.**
Natural His **signature** and mine **were on the new label designed by Mabel.**
美博設計的新商標上有他的簽名，也有我的簽名。

Diving Deep Into English 9 文法學家對所有格代名詞的認定不一

❶ 有些文法學家把 my、mine、your、yours、his、her、hers、its、our、ours、their、theirs 統稱為**所有格代名詞**。

❷ 有些文法學家把 my、your、his、her、its、our、their 稱為**所有格形容詞**、**所有格限定詞**或**形容詞性物主代名詞**，因為這些字用在名詞前面來限定名詞；而把 mine、yours、his、hers、ours、theirs 稱為**所有格代名詞**、**獨立所有格代名詞**或**名詞性物主代名詞**，因為這些字不用在名詞前面，而是單獨使用。但無論你怎麼稱呼這些字，它們都是用來表示物主的身分（ownership）。

疑問代名詞

1 疑問代名詞的定義

1 疑問代名詞是用來提問的代名詞，可分為指**人**和指**物**（動物和無生命的事物）兩種，列表如下：

指人
- who
- whom
- whoever
- whomever
- whose

指物
- which
- whichever
- what
- whatever

↳ 與 of 引導的片語連用時，which 可以指人（例如 which of you）。

- Who asked the question: "Which of you has a house in Honolulu?"
  是誰問這個問題的：「你們有誰在檀香山有房子？」
  ↳ Who 和 Which of you 指人。

2 疑問代名詞一般放在**句首**，置於動詞前面。也可以放在**介系詞**後面。

- What are the duties of an animal trainer? 馴獸師的職責是什麼？
  ↳ 疑問詞（主詞補語）+ 連綴動詞 + 主詞
  ↳ 這句的 What 是主詞補語，但依然要置於句首，放在連綴動詞 are 的前面。
- What did you do yesterday? 你昨天做了什麼？
  ↳ 疑問詞（受詞）+ 助動詞 + 主詞 + 主動詞
  ↳ 這句的 What 是動詞 do 的受詞，但依然要放在句首，位在助動詞 did 的前面。

More formal　To whom did Lulu give the dictionary?

Less formal　Whom did Lulu give the dictionary to? 露露把字典給了誰？

↳ 介系詞 to 可以放在句首（非常正式），也可以放在句尾。

2 who 和 what

1 who（作主詞）指**人**。（Who is = Who's）

- **Who ate all of my stew?** 誰把我的燉肉吃光了？ → Who 指人，用來提問。
- **Who's that?** 那是誰？

2 what（作主詞）指**動物**或**無生命的事物**。（What is = What's）

- **"What is making that loud noise?" "It's a big bear."**
  「那個吵鬧聲是什麼造成的？」「是一頭大熊。」 → What 指動物，用來提問。
- **What's your goal in life?** 你的人生目標是什麼？ → What 指事物，用來提問。

3 who 作主詞時，如果是簡單現在式，後面要跟動詞的單數形式，即使知道回答可能是複數形式。

✗ **Who want a cup of milk tea?**
✓ **Who wants a cup of milk tea?** 誰想要來一杯奶茶？
↑ 對一組人提問。雖然想要奶茶的人可能會有數個，但是動詞還是要用單數。

4 疑問代名詞 what 和 who 作**主詞**（或主詞的一部分）時，應**放在動詞的前面**，且通常不與助動詞 do/does/did 連用。

✗ **Who did say those bad words about Sue?**
✓ **Who said those bad words about Sue?** 是誰說了蘇的那些壞話的？

✗ **What did happen to Kay yesterday?**
✓ **What happened to Kay yesterday?** 凱昨天發生了什麼事？

- **Who knows what happened besides Andrew?**
  除了安德魯，還有誰知道發生了什麼事？
- **Who will help the ship's crew?** 有誰願意幫助那艘船的船員？

5 疑問代名詞 what 和 who 作**受詞**時，要與助動詞 do/does/did 連用。

✗ **What you said just now?**
✓ **What did you say just now?** 你剛才說什麼？

↳ What 是動詞 say 的受詞，要用助動詞 did。
↳ 助動詞 did 放在疑問詞 What 之後、主詞 you 之前。

- Who did you tell **about the bell that fell into the well?**
= Whom did you tell **about the bell that fell into the well?**
你對誰提過那個掉進井裡的鐘？
↳ Who 作動詞 tell 的受詞，是口語用法。
» 參見本頁下面第二點〈2 who 的口語用法與 whom 的書面用法之比較〉。

3 who 和 whom

1 who 和 whom 的正式用法：who 和 whom 只能作疑問代名詞，不能作限定詞。一般而言，who 作主詞，whom 作受詞。

- Who saw **Kay and Lulu today?** 今天有誰看到了凱和露露？
↳ 句型為「Who（主詞）+ 述語動詞」。Who 是主詞，不需要助動詞 do/does/did。
- Whom did you see **riding on Mark's motor scooter?**
你看到了誰騎在馬克的摩托車上？
↳ 句型為「Whom（受詞）+ 助動詞 + 主詞 + 述語動詞」。
↳ Whom 是動詞 see 的受詞，要用助動詞 did；
助動詞 did 放在疑問詞 Whom 之後、主詞 you 之前。
- With whom did you dance **in the movie *Zoom*?**
你在電影《急速上升》裡跟誰跳了舞？ → 介系詞後面一定要用受格 whom。

2 who 的口語用法與 whom 的書面用法之比較

a 在英語口語中，疑問代名詞 who 可以作主詞，也可以作受詞，而 whom 只能作受詞。

- Who **is marrying Sue?** 誰要娶蘇？ → Who 是句子的主詞，Whom 不能作主詞。

Informal Who **did the police arrest?**
Formal Whom **did the police arrest?** 警方逮捕了誰？
↳ Who 作動詞 arrest 的受詞，是口語用法。
↳ Whom 作動詞 arrest 的受詞，是書面用法。

Informal Who did Ms. Bloom talk to just now about that sick cow?

Formal Whom did Ms. Bloom talk to just now about that sick cow?

Very formal To whom did Ms. Bloom talk just now about that sick cow?

剛才布盧姆女士在跟誰談論關於那隻病牛的事？

↑ 當介系詞 to 放在動詞後面時，句首可以用 Who（口語）或 Whom（正式語）當受詞。

↑ 當介系詞 To 放在句首時，介系詞後面就只能接 whom 作受詞，不能接 who，這種用法非常正式。（參見下面的 b 項目）。

b 介系詞位於句首，後面接疑問代名詞作受詞時，一定要用 whom，不能用 who。

Very formal For whom did Mr. Powers buy those flowers?

Formal/Informal Whom/Who did Mr. Powers buy those flowers for?

鮑爾斯先生買那些鮮花給誰？

Very formal With whom did you talk in the chat room?

Formal/Informal Whom/Who did you talk with in the chat room?

你在聊天室裡跟誰交談？

Very formal To whom did Sue give her hotel's revenue?

Formal/Informal Whom/Who did Sue give her hotel's revenue to?

蘇把她飯店的收入給誰了？

4 what 和 which

1 用作疑問代名詞

a what 的意思是「什麼」，用於指**動物**或**事物**，不能用來指人。which 的意思是「哪一個／哪一些」，用於指**動物**或**事物**。

- **What did he say?** 他說了什麼？ → What 用來指事物，意思是「什麼」。
- **Which is prettier—Gary's guitar or the one I bought for Rich?**
  哪一個比較漂亮——蓋瑞的吉他，還是我買給瑞奇的那把吉他？
  ↑ 疑問代名詞 Which 指物，意思是「哪一個」。

- **Which is cuter—my poodle or your poodle?**
  哪一個比較可愛——我的貴賓狗，還是你的貴賓狗？
  ↳ 疑問代名詞 Which 指動物，意思是「哪一隻」。

b which 的後面如果接有 of，也可以用於指**人**（如 which of them）。

- **Which of you lied to me?** 你們之中哪一個對我撒了謊？
  ↳ 疑問代名詞 Which 後面接介系詞 of，可以指人。

c which 可以與 of 連用，what 不能與 of 連用。

✗ **What of the three magazines has the article about Rich?**
✓ **Which of the three magazines has the article about Rich?**
這三本雜誌，哪本上面有關於瑞奇的文章？
↳ 疑問代名詞 Which 指物，後面跟了介系詞 of。

疑問代名詞 which 後面接有 of 時，才能指「人」。
✗ Which is the faster runner—Lulu or Sue?
✓ Who is the faster runner—Lulu or Sue?
誰跑得快一些——露露還是蘇？

2 用作疑問限定詞

which 和 what 可以修飾**人**或**物**（what 作限定詞，主要修飾物，只偶爾可以用來修飾人）。如果供選擇的事物或人物比較**具體且數量較少**，就用 which；如果供選擇的事物或人物**數量不確定**，就用 what。

- **What color are Sue's new shoes?** 蘇的新鞋是什麼顏色？
  ↳ What 用於提問時，並沒有限定顏色讓對方選擇，選擇的顏色數目未知，對方需要從泛指的各種顏色中選出一種顏色。

- **Which color do you prefer—red, green, or blue?**
  你比較喜歡哪一種顏色：紅色、綠色，還是藍色？
  ↳ Which 問句中給出三種顏色，讓你從這個限定的範圍內做出選擇。

- **What subject is she studying at the University of Michigan?**
  她在密西根大學裡修哪門學科？
  ↳ What 修飾事物，所指稱的學科數目未知。

- What leader would allow such a disaster to happen?
  是什麼樣的領導人會讓這樣的悲劇發生？
  ↳ What 作限定詞時，可以修飾人（leader），所指稱的人數目未知。
- Which girl—Lulu or Sue—does Mike like?
  邁克喜歡哪一個女孩——露露還是蘇？
  ↳ Which 修飾人，供選擇的範圍是一小群特定的人（兩個女孩）。
- I like all these skirts. Which one do you think I should buy?
  這些裙子我都喜歡。你認為我應該買哪一件？
  ↳ one 前面要用 Which，不用 What。
  » 參見 212 頁〈Diving Deep Into English 36〉。

5 疑問所有格代名詞 whose

whose 是**疑問所有格代名詞**，是 who 的所有格，用來指**人**，意思是「誰的」，可以作代名詞或限定詞。當它修飾名詞作限定詞時，有時又被稱為**疑問形容詞**或**疑問限定詞**。

- "Whose purse is next to the phone?" "It's mine."
  「電話旁的錢包是誰的？」「是我的。」
  ↳ Whose 在這裡作限定詞，修飾名詞 purse。
- That cute bamboo shoe doesn't fit Lulu's foot, so whose is it?
  那隻可愛的竹鞋不合露露的腳，那會是誰的呢？
  ↳ whose 在這裡作代名詞。
- Whose puppy can sit quietly on a mitt?
  誰的小狗能夠靜靜地坐在隔熱手套上？
  ↳ Whose 為限定詞，修飾名詞 puppy。
  ↳ mitt 指「隔熱手套」、「棒球手套」、「拳擊手套」等連指手套。

mitt
隔熱手套

- Whose son is that?
  那是誰的兒子？
  ↳ Whose 為限定詞，修飾名詞 son。
  » 參見 211 頁〈7 疑問形容詞 / 疑問限定詞〉。

容易誤用的所有格及相關縮略形式

1 所有格 its：區別於 it's

1 將 it's 和 its 混淆，是書面英語中最常見的錯誤。it's 是 it is 或 it has 的縮寫。

2 its（牠的；它的）相當於 of it，是**所有格**形式，與 my、his、her、our 一樣，用來表示物主身分或所有權，是一個所有格限定詞，後面接名詞。

3 當分不清該用 its 還是 it's 時，可以試著用 his 來取代句中的 its，如果句子有意義，就用所有格 its；如果句子變得毫無意義，就要用縮寫形式 it's。

- **Pat has a lazy cat. Its name is Ocean, and it always moves in slow motion.** 派特有隻名叫「海洋」的懶惰貓，牠總是行動遲緩。
  - Its 是所有格限定詞，修飾名詞 name。Its name 相當於 His name。
  - 如果用所有格代名詞 His 代替句中的 Its，句子仍具意義（His name is Ocean）。
- **It's the best gift Scot's wife has ever received in her life. It's a pretty yacht from Scot!**
  這是史考特的太太這一生中收到的最好禮物，那是史考特送的一艘漂亮遊艇。
  - 如果用所有格代名詞 His 代替句中 It's，就成 His the best gift 和 His a pretty yacht，句子變得不知所云。因此可斷定不能用所有格形式 Its，要用縮寫形式 It's。
- **It's my duty and pleasure to promote Malaysia for its exotic beauty.**
  宣傳馬來西亞奇特的美，既是我的職責，也是我的榮幸。
  - It's 是 It is 的縮寫形式（It is my duty . . . ）；its 是所有格限定詞，修飾名詞 beauty。
- **The dance company had its monthly meeting today in France. It's trying to devise new dances that will make artistic advances.**
  今天舞蹈公司在法國召開每月一次的會議，公司正致力於設計新舞蹈來推動藝術發展。
  - 第一句 its 是所有格限定詞，修飾名詞 meeting；
    第二句 it's 是縮寫形式（It's trying = It is trying）。

2 所有格 their：區別於 they're 或 there

1 their 是 they 的所有格，表示物主身分或所有權，用作所有格限定詞，修飾名詞。

- **Their dogs like to fight all night.**
  他們的狗喜歡整夜打架。
  ↑ Their 是所有格限定詞，修飾名詞 dogs。

- **Did Coco and Mark go with their friends Jane and John to Yellowstone National Park?**
  可可和馬克跟他們的朋友珍和約翰一起去過黃石國家公園嗎？
  ↑ their 是所有格限定詞，修飾名詞 friends。

2 they're 是 they are 的縮寫，要有一個縮略符號「'」來代替被省略的字母。

- **They're the best soccer players in Budapest.**
  他們是布達佩斯最優秀的足球運動員。
  ↑ They're 是 They are 的縮寫。

3 there 是地點副詞，不能用來表示物主身分，也不用來修飾名詞。

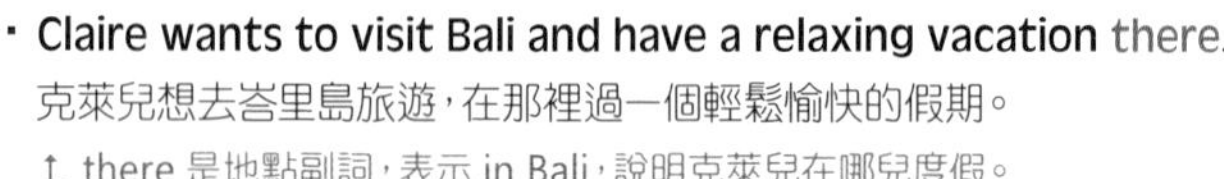

- **Claire wants to visit Bali and have a relaxing vacation there.**
  克萊兒想去峇里島旅遊，在那裡過一個輕鬆愉快的假期。
  ↑ there 是地點副詞，表示 in Bali，說明克萊兒在哪兒度假。

3 所有格 your：區別於 you're

your 是 you 的所有格形式，表示物主身分；you're 是 you are 的縮寫形式。

- **You said that you couldn't believe your ears.**
  你說，你不能相信自己的耳朵。 → your 是所有格，修飾名詞 ears。

- **I don't understand what you're talking about.** 我不懂你在說什麼。
  ↑ you're 是 you are 的縮寫。

4 所有格 whose：區別於 who's

1 whose 是 who 的所有格，表示物主身分或所有權，是修飾名詞的**所有格限定詞**，用在疑問句中。（註：whose 作關係代名詞時，意思是 of whom/which「某人的、某物的」，引導形容詞子句，參見 317 頁〈1 whose 限定詞〉。）

2 who's 是 who is 或 who has 的縮寫，必須有縮略符號「'」，代替省略的字母。

- **Whose basketball team is front-page news?** 誰的籃球隊成了頭版新聞？
  ↳ 所有格限定詞 Whose 修飾名詞 basketball team。
- **Whose toy UFO was flying around Joe?** 圍著喬飛的玩具飛碟是誰的？
  ↳ 所有格限定詞 Whose 修飾名詞 toy UFO。
- **Who's good at singing the blues?** 誰擅長唱藍調？
  ↳ Who's good = Who is good
- **"Whose girlfriend is Liz Blare?" "According to *Who's in the News*, Liz is Bart Smith's sweetheart."**「莉茲．布雷爾是誰的女朋友？」「根據《新聞人物》，莉茲是巴特．史密斯的心上人。」
  ↳ 所有格限定詞 Whose 修飾名詞 girlfriend；Who's = Who is
- **"Whose jeep is that, and who's going to drive it out of that deep puddle?" "That's my jeep, and Jim is going to drive it out of the puddle."**「那是誰的吉普車，誰要把那輛吉普車從那個深水坑裡開出來？」「那是我的吉普車，吉姆要把它從那個深水坑裡開出來。」
  ↳ 所有格限定詞 Whose 修飾名詞 jeep； who's = who is

Diving Deep Into English 10 發音雷同的所有格代名詞與縮寫詞

有些所有格代名詞和一些縮寫詞的發音相似，請注意分辨。

所有格代名詞	縮寫詞
its	it's = it is/it has
their	they're = they are there're = there are
your	you're = you are
whose	who's = who is

反身代名詞和相互代名詞

1 myself 和 me 的誤用情形

我們常在需要用 me 的地方誤用了 I 或 myself。請記住：主格代名詞 I 不能作動詞或介系詞的受詞，myself 不作主詞，也不能隨便作受詞（myself 作受詞的用法參見 99 頁〈2 反身代名詞的用法〉），在**動詞**或**介系詞**後面要用受格代名詞 me。

✕ Is this ice cream for Lee and myself?
✕ Is this ice cream for Lee and I?
✔ Is this ice cream for Lee and me?
這冰淇淋是給李和我的嗎？
↳ me 是介系詞 for 的受詞。

✕ Last night Jane and myself had a long walk in the rain.
✕ Last night Jane and me had a long walk in the rain.
✔ Last night Jane and I had a long walk in the rain.
昨天晚上，珍和我在雨中走了很長的路。
↳ I 是複合主詞的一部分，要用主格。

- Please give me the key. 請把鑰匙給我。
  ↳ me 是動詞 give 的受詞。不能說成 give myself 或 give I。
- Some people like her can eat tiny amounts of food and not lose an ounce.
  一些像她這樣的人，即使只吃一點點東西，體重也不會稍微減輕。
  ↳ her 是介系詞 like 的受詞，不能說成 like she 或 like herself。

2 反身代名詞的用法

1 反身代名詞的形式和意義

a **反身代名詞**用以引起對自己的注意，以 -self（單數）或 -selves（複數）結尾，也叫做**反射代名詞**（mirror pronoun）。

b 反身代名詞 myself、yourself 等，不能取代 I、me、she、her 等人稱代名詞。當**主詞和受詞指相同的人或物**時，就用反身代名詞來避免重複；反身代名詞也可用於表示**強調**，因此也稱為**增強語氣的代名詞**（intensive pronoun）。

- myself 我自己
- yourself 你自己
- himself/herself/itself 他自己
- ourselves 我們自己
- yourselves 你們自己
- themselves 他們自己

2 用來指代主詞（反身）

a 反身代名詞用來指代主詞，這時主詞和受詞指**同一個人或物**。

- **He blamed himself for the argument with Sue.** 他因與蘇爭吵而自責。
  ↑ 句子的主詞（He）和受詞（himself）是同一個人，要用反身代名詞。

  比較 **He can't blame me for his bad choice.**
  不能因他自己的錯誤選擇而責怪我。
  ↑ 句子的主詞（He）和受詞（me）不是同一個人，不要用反身代名詞。

- **Amy dried herself after she came out of the lake.**
  艾咪從湖裡爬起來後，把自己的身體擦乾。

dry herself 把她自己擦乾

- **Be careful getting the knife off the shelf, and don't cut yourself.**
  把刀從架子上拿下來時要小心，不要割到自己。
  ↑ yourself 與祈使句被省略的主詞 you 一致。

- **I am going to the toyshop to get myself a small robot.**
  我要去玩具店替自己買一個小機器人。

- These women taught themselves how to fix their cars. 這些婦女教會了自己如何修車。
- Claire admired herself in the mirror while brushing her hair. 克萊兒一邊梳頭，一邊欣賞鏡中的自己。

admire herself
自我欣賞

b 句子的**主詞**和**受詞**指的是**同一個人或事物**，在緊跟動詞的介系詞後面用反身代名詞。

- Sam always talks about himself. 山姆總是在談論自己。
- Sam loves nobody but himself. 山姆誰也不愛，只愛自己。
- Claire is proud not only of herself but also of her future husband, Scot. 克萊兒不僅自豪，而且也為她的未婚夫史考特感到驕傲。
- Something is wrong with Sally, because she is always talking to herself. 莎莉有點毛病，她老是自言自語。
- Say hello to your parents, and take care of yourself.
  向你父母問好，你自己也好好保重。
  ⮤ yourself 與祈使句被省略的主詞 you 一致。
  ⮤ 類似的「動詞 + 介系詞」，還包括 be ashamed of, believe in, care about, look after, look at 等。

Take care of yourself!
好好保重喔！

在表示**地點**或**位置**的介系詞後面用人稱代名詞，不用反身代名詞。

- Jim came out of the train station and saw garbage all around him. 吉姆走出火車站，看到身旁滿是垃圾。 → him 用來指代 Jim。
- Jim sat on the bench and put his backpack next to him.
  吉姆在長椅上坐下來，然後把背包放在身邊。
- Take an umbrella with you. It might rain. 帶上雨傘，可能會下雨。
  ⮤ 在 bring/take something with . . . 後面不用反身代名詞。

3 **加強語氣**：反身代名詞也可作**同位語**，用來表示**強調**，意思是「親自，本人，本身」。

- I myself built this robot.
  = I built this robot, not anybody else.
  我親自製造了這個機器人。

- The cottage itself is nice, but the yard is too small. 別墅本身還不錯，但院子太小了。

- The students themselves created the Blue Moon Website.
  學生們自己設計了「藍色月亮網站」。

- Nancy built this cottage herself.
  = Nancy herself built this cottage.
  南西親自修建了這間房子。

- Only Clive himself can decide what he is going to do with his life.
  只有克萊夫本人可以決定該如何對待自己的人生。

- I want to speak to the president himself, not his secretary.
  我想跟董事長本人談，而不是跟他的祕書談話。

4 指句中的其他成分：反身代名詞除了指句子的主詞外，也可以指其他成分。

- Jenny says that she loves me for myself, not for my money.
  珍妮說她愛的是我這個人，不是我的錢。
  ↳ 句子前面已經提及了講話者（me），然後用反身代名詞 myself 來作介系詞 for 的受詞，用來指代講話者，而不是用來指代主詞 she。

3 反身代名詞的慣用語

1 by oneself 獨自；沒有伴

- by myself
- by himself
- by ourselves
- by herself
- by yourself

- I can't carry this big box by myself. 我不能獨自扛起這個大箱子。
  ↳ without help 獨自；沒有幫助

- Lily likes to spend time by herself. 莉莉喜歡獨自一人消磨時光。
  ↳ without company; alone 獨自；沒有伴

・ **My husband and I want to explore that cave by ourselves.**
我先生和我想自個兒去探索那個洞穴。
ㄴ without company; alone 獨自；沒有伴

2 反身代名詞的其他慣用語

- be oneself 正常的健康狀況；正常的情緒
- behave yourself 規矩點
- keep it to yourself 不讓人知道
- talk to oneself 自言自語

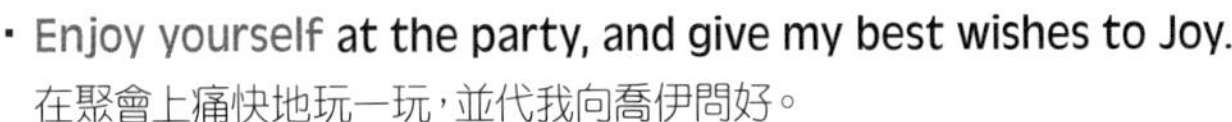

・ **Enjoy yourself at the party, and give my best wishes to Joy.**
在聚會上痛快地玩一玩，並代我向喬伊問好。
ㄴ Enjoy yourself. = Have fun. 好好地玩。

・ **On the long table was the sign "Help yourself."**
在長桌上有一個牌子，上面寫著：「請自行取用。」
ㄴ Help yourself. = Take whatever you want. 自行取用。

Help yourself.
請自行取用。

・ **By the swimming pool, I saw another sign "Make yourself at home."**
我在游泳池旁看見另一個牌子，上面寫著：「請當在自己家一樣。」
ㄴ Make yourself at home. = Enjoy this home as if it were yours.
（把這裡當自己家。）

4 含代名詞的複合主詞的反身代名詞

主詞是含代名詞的複合主詞時，該用哪一個反身代名詞呢？複合代名詞裡只要有第一人稱（I 或 we），就要用 ourselves；如果複合代名詞裡有第二人稱（you）而沒有第一人稱，就要用 yourselves。

・ **You, Ann, and I always get ourselves into trouble by listening to Dan.**
我、你還有安，因為聽丹的話而常常給自己惹上麻煩。
ㄴ 複合主詞含第一人稱 I，反身代名詞應該用 ourselves。

・ **You and Lulu deceived Mom and yourselves as well.**
你和露露欺騙了媽媽，也欺騙了你們自己。
ㄴ 複合主詞裡有第二人稱 You，而沒有第一人稱 I 或 we，
因此反身代名詞應該用 yourselves。

5 相互代名詞的用法（each other 和 one another）

1 each other 和 one another 是相互代名詞，是「彼此」、「互相」的意思：

- 用來指兩個人或物時 → 用 each other
- 用來指兩個以上的人或物時 → 用 one another

2 不過，在口語中，現在也常用 each other 來指兩個以上的事物，但決不能用 one another 來指兩個。

- **Sue and my brother love each other.**
  蘇和我哥哥互相愛慕。
  ↑ 指兩個人，不能用 one another。

- **My Grandmother Bloom and her friends, Lily, Amy, and Ann, all help one another/each other.**
  我的布盧姆奶奶和她的朋友們，莉莉、艾咪和安，大家都彼此互相幫助。
  ↑ 兩個人以上用 one another，在口語中也可以用 each other。

3 相互代名詞也可以有所有格形式。

swimming fins 蛙鞋

- **The twins often borrowed each other's swimming fins.** 這對雙胞胎常常互借彼此的蛙鞋。
- **Should teachers have students correct one another's/each other's papers?** 老師應該讓學生修改彼此的論文嗎？

6 -selves 與 each other 的比較

- **We stood side by side in front of the mirror and looked at ourselves.**
  我們肩並肩地站在鏡子前，望著鏡中的自己。

- **Dan looked at me, and I looked at Dan. We looked at each other for a few seconds and then started to laugh.**
  丹看著我，我看著丹。我們相互看著對方幾秒鐘，然後開始笑了起來。

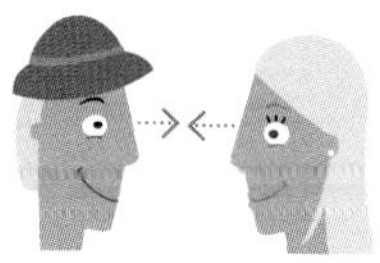

不定代名詞

1 不定代名詞的定義（兼談不定限定詞）

1 **不定代名詞**或**不定限定詞**泛指（不具體的）人、地點、事物，即指某個含糊的或未知的人或物。例如：

- all 全部
- either 兩者之一
- neither 兩者都不
- some 一些
- another 另一個
- every 每一個
- no one 沒有人
- somebody 某人
- any 任何一個
- everybody 每個人
- nobody 沒有人
- someone 某人
- anybody 任何人
- everything 每件事
- none 無一
- something 某件事
- anything 任何事
- few 一些
- one 一個；任何一個
- such 這樣的人／事物
- both 兩者
- many 很多（可數）
- other 他者；另一方
- each 各個；每個
- much 很多（不可數）
- several 幾個；數個
- little 一點

2 上面這些字裡，有些既可以作**不定代名詞**，也可以作**不定形容詞／不定限定詞**，請看下面的例子。

- All was quiet in the school.
  = Everything was quiet in the school. 學校裡一片寂靜。
  - All 是不定代名詞，作句子的主詞，指事物，接單數動詞（was）。
  - 不過，在現代英語中，不常用後面不跟名詞的 all 來表示 everyone 或 everything。
- All our classmates are tired from the long hike around the lake.
  繞著湖遠足後，我們所有的同學都感到很累。
  - All 是形容詞／限定詞，修飾名詞 classmates。
- Both of you have taken an oath. 你們兩個都發過誓。
  - Both 是不定代名詞，作句子的主詞。

take an oath 發誓

- Both men are interested in economic growth.
  這兩個男人都對經濟發展感興趣。 →Both 是形容詞／限定詞，修飾名詞 men。

- One of our teachers is from Japan. 我們有一個老師是日本人。
  ↳ One 是不定代名詞，作句子的主詞。

- One student was sick today and missed the English exam.
  一個學生今天生病了，錯過了英語考試。
  ↳ One 是形容詞／限定詞，修飾名詞 student。

- Many students watched the basketball game; some cheered for one team, and some cheered for both teams.
  許多學生觀看了那場籃球賽；他們當中有些為其中一支隊伍喝彩，有些則同時為兩支隊伍喝彩。
  ↳ Many 是形容詞／限定詞，修飾名詞 students；one 是形容詞／限定詞，修飾名詞 team；some 是不定代名詞，作句子的主詞；both 是形容詞／限定詞，修飾名詞 teams。

2 與不定代名詞搭配的人稱代名詞及動詞的單複數

1 單數不定代名詞（與單數人稱代名詞及單數動詞連用）

人稱代名詞應該與其先行詞（即其所指代的詞）一致，當不定代名詞作先行詞時，人稱代名詞要與不定代名詞的數一致。下列不定代名詞作先行詞時，要搭配**單數動詞**、**單數人稱代名詞**和**單數所有格代名詞**（he、she、it、his、her、its）：

- another 另一個
- anything 任何事
- anybody/anyone 任何人
- each 每個
- something 某事
- somebody/someone 某人
- either 兩者中之任一個
- everything 每件事
- everybody/everyone 每一個人
- every 每個（只作限定詞）
- nothing 無事
- nobody/no one 無人
- one 一人；一事
- neither 兩者中無一個

- Is anything wrong with Liz? 莉茲怎麼了嗎？
- Nothing has happened to him. 他沒有遇到任何事情。
- Is anybody hurt? 有人受傷嗎？

Informal Everyone is looking forward to their vacation in the sun.

Formal Everyone is looking forward to his or her vacation in the sun.
人人都盼望著過一個陽光明媚的假期。

Ꝉ 單數不定代名詞（Everyone）+ 單數動詞（is）+ 單數所有格代名詞（his or her）；正式用語中（包括考試），不要用複數所有格代名詞 their 來指代單數不定代名詞 everyone。

Informal Each of the girls is wearing their best dress.

Formal Each of the girls is wearing her best dress.
每個女孩都穿著自己最漂亮的洋裝。

Ꝉ 單數不定代名詞（Each）+ 單數動詞（is）+ 單數所有格代名詞（her）；正式用語中（包括考試），不要用複數所有格代名詞 their 來指代單數不定代名詞 each。

Informal One may not become fluent in English unless they read 25,000 English words every day.

Formal One may not become fluent in English unless he or she reads 25,000 English words every day. → 美式英語

Formal One may not become fluent in English unless one reads 25,000 English words every day. → 英式英語
想要練就流利的英語，就得每天閱讀 25,000 個英文單字。

Ꝉ 單數不定代名詞 One 要與單數動詞 reads 和單數人稱代名詞「he or she」或「one」搭配，正式用語中（包括考試）不能用複數動詞 read 和複數人稱代名詞 they。

在日常生活中，有人（包括英美人士）會用複數詞來搭配 everyone、each、one。但這種用法不標準。在考試、正式的文體或商務英語中，一定要遵守文法規則，用標準的英語。

2 複數不定代名詞（與複數人稱代名詞及複數動詞連用）

有些不定代名詞永遠指複數意義的人或物，因此要搭配**複數人稱代名詞**（they、them）和**複數所有格代名詞**（their）及**複數動詞**。

● both 兩者 ● few 一些 ● many 許多 ● other 其他 ● several 幾個

- Both of the new students had Claire cut their hair.
  這兩個新生都找了克萊兒幫他們剪頭髮。
  ↳ Both 是複數，應該搭配複數所有格代名詞 their。

- Few of the students still have their parents picking them up after school. 學生中很少有人放學後仍然讓他們的父母來接他們。
  ↳ Few 是複數，應該搭配複數動詞 have、複數所有格 their 和人稱代名詞 them。

- Many of the reporters did their best to report on Hurricane Jane. 許多記者使出渾身解數去報導颶風珍。

- Several of the band members sang their songs at the county fair.
  樂隊裡有好幾個成員在縣裡的市集上唱歌。

3 可以是單數也可以是複數的 all、most、some

all、most 和 some 可以是單數，也可以是複數，當它們與**複數名詞**（cats、dogs、coins 等）連用時，就是複數；當它們與**不可數名詞**（water、sand、anger 等）連用時，就是單數。

- Some of the differences between us are that you like to hum, sit, and knit and I like to chew gum, walk, and talk. 我們之間的一些差別是，你喜歡哼歌、坐著、編織，而我喜歡嚼口香糖、走路、說話。
  ↳ differences 是複數名詞，因此 Some 應該接複數動詞 are。

- Some of the milk is spilling on the tablecloth. 一些牛奶灑到了桌布上。
  ↳ milk 是不可數名詞，因此 Some 應該接單數動詞 is。

- All/Most of her art is about nature.
  她所有的／多數的藝術品都跟大自然有關。
  ↳ All/Most + of + 不可數名詞（art）+ 單數動詞（is）

- All/Most of those nice cats have caught mice.
  那些可愛的貓全都／大都抓到了老鼠。
  ↳ All/Most + of + 複數名詞（cats）+ 複數動詞（have caught）

3 all：一切，全體；所有的（代名詞或限定詞）

1 all 可以作**主詞**，後面常接 that 引導的形容詞子句，意思相當於 everything 或 the only thing，此時主要動詞要用**單數**形式。當主詞 all 指 everybody、all the people 時，動詞用**複數**。

- All that begins well ends well. 凡事有好的開始，就會有好的結束。
  - ↳ All 是代名詞，意思是 everything，作主詞時，接單數動詞 ends。
- All (that) he talked about was sports. 他談論的全是和運動有關的話題。
  - ↳ All 用在子句前，作整個句子的主詞，要接單數動詞 was。
- I hope all are healthy and happy. 我希望大家都健康、幸福。
  - ↳ = I hope everybody is healthy and happy.
  - ↳ all = all the people，後面接複數動詞 are。
  - ↳ 現代英語更常用 everyone/everybody。

2 all 可以作動詞的**受詞**，也可以出現在動詞 to be 後面作**補語**。all 放在主句動詞的後面，子句前。

- Gus has done all (that) he can to help us. 加斯盡力幫助了我們。
  - ↳ all 用在形容詞子句（that he can to help us）前，作動詞 has done 的受詞。
- That is all she wanted to talk about. 她想談的就是這些了。
  - ↳ all 用在動詞 is 後面作補語，形容詞子句 she wanted to talk about 修飾 all。

3 all 可以和介系詞 of 連用。

- All of you are invited to my birthday party this Saturday night.
  你們全都受到了邀請，來參加我這週六晚上要舉行的慶生會。
  - ↳ All of + 複數代名詞（you）+ 複數動詞（are）
- All (of) her sisters and brothers were at the airport to see her off. 她所有的兄弟姐妹都在機場給她送行。
  - ↳ All (of) + 複數名詞（her sisters and brothers）+ 複數動詞（were）；有時 all 之後加不加 of 均可。
  - » 參見 110 頁〈Diving Deep Into English 11〉。

4 all 可以放在主詞或受詞後面。有的文法學家認為，這種用法中的 all 是**限定詞**，另一些文法學家認為是**代名詞**。

- These apartments all belong to Paul Long. 這些公寓住宅都屬於保羅・龍。
  ↳ all 用在句子的主詞 These apartments 後面，句子主詞是複數，動詞也應該用複數 belong。These apartments all . . . = All of these apartments . . .
- Paul has said farewell to us all. 保羅已經跟我們大家告別了。
  ↳ all 接在句子的受詞 us 代名詞後面。us all = all of us

5 all 可以用在情態動詞或助動詞後面。

- You can all go to play baseball. 你們都可以去打棒球。
  ↳ all 放在情態助動詞 can 後面。You can all go . . . = All of you can go . . .
- The small statues made out of gold had all been sold.
  = All of the small statues made out of gold had been sold.
  那些用金子製造的小雕像已銷售一空。
  ↳ all 放在助動詞 had 後面。

6 如果意思是**否定**，不用 all 作主詞，而往往用 not all 作主詞（即，用 not all 來表示否定，而不用 all . . . not），意思是「並非所有」。

Unclear All of the departments did not file a report.
↳ 這個句子有兩種意思：一，有些部門沒有（即，不是所有的部門）把報告歸檔。二，沒有一個部門把報告歸檔。書面和口語都應避免這種引起歧義的句子。

Clear Not all of the departments filed a report.
不是所有的部門都提交了報告。
↳ 要表示「並非所有」的意思，最好改用這個句子。

Clear All of the departments failed to file a report.
所有的部門都沒有提交報告。

Clear None of the departments filed a report. 沒有一個部門提交了報告。
↳ 要表示「沒有一個」，可以改用上面最後兩個句子。

7 all 除了作代名詞，還可以作形容詞／限定詞。比較下面兩個句子：

- All she needs is a little honey in her tea.
  她所需要的只不過是在茶裡加一點蜂蜜而已。
  ↳ All 是代名詞，作句子的主詞，接單數動詞 is。
  ↳ she needs 是省略了 that 的形容詞子句，修飾 All。

- All the children love the brilliant colors of leaves in the fall.
  所有這些孩子都喜歡秋天五顏六色的樹葉。
  ↳ All 在這裡是限定詞，修飾名詞 children。
  ↳ 句子的主詞是 children，因此動詞用複數形式 love。
  » 限定詞的定義參見 138 頁〈Part 1 冠詞和限定詞〉。

Diving Deep Into English 11 all 與 all of 的比較

❶ **all（不加 of）**：用於「名詞」或「形容詞 + 名詞」前時，all 後面不接 of。

- All flowers are beautiful. 所有的花兒都美麗。 →All + 名詞（flowers）
- All little girls are as pretty as pearls. 所有的小女孩都像珍珠一樣漂亮。
  ↳ All + 形容詞（little）+ 名詞（girls）

❷ **all (of)（加不加 of 都可以）**：當 all 用在 the、my/your、this/that 等字的前面時，可以加 of，也可以不加。

- All (of) my email pals love to read novels written by Judy Blume.
  我所有的 email 筆友都喜歡閱讀 Judy Blume 寫的小說。
- Did you eat all (of) the chicken? 你把所有的雞肉都吃光了嗎？

❸ **all of（一定要加 of）**：all 在 it、us、you、them 前面時，須用 of。

- Dee has invited all of us to her beach party.
  蒂邀請我們所有人參加她的海灘聚會。
- No, I did not eat all of it. 沒有，我沒有把它吃完。

❹ 比較「all . . .」與「all (of) the . . .」

- All children should receive the appropriate vaccinations.
  所有兒童都應該接受適當的接種。 → 泛指所有的孩子。
- All (of) the children in our town have received the appropriate vaccinations. 我們鎮上的所有兒童都已經接受過適當的接種。
  ↳ 特指我們鎮上的孩子。參見 115 頁〈Diving Deep Into English 15〉。

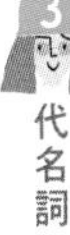

4 both：兩者都（代名詞或限定詞）

1 both 指兩個人或東西，作主詞或修飾主詞時，要用複數動詞。

- **Both are going far away.** 兩個都要走很遠。
  - Both 是代名詞，在句子裡作主詞。當 both 作句子的主詞時，要用複數動詞（are）。
- **Today both Lily and Sue were late for geography class.**
  今天的地理課，莉莉和蘇都遲到了。
  - both 是限定詞，修飾名詞 Lily and Sue，要用複數動詞（were）。

2 **both 和介系詞 of 連用。**

- **Both of them are trying to catch the thief who stole the gem.**
  他們兩個都在試圖去抓偷寶石的賊。
  - Both 是代名詞，後面接 of：「Both of + 複數代名詞（them）+ 複數動詞（are）」。
  - both 和 us/you/them 之間一定要加 of。

» 參見 112 頁〈Diving Deep Into English 12〉。

3 **both 也可以放在主詞或受詞後面**。有的文法學家認為這種用法中的 both 是**限定詞**，有的認為是**代名詞**。

- **Those two agents both have multiple talents.**
  那兩個代理商都多才多藝。
  - both 放在句子主詞 Those two agents 後面。
  - Those two agents both . . . = Both of those two agents . . .
- **I like them both.** 他們兩個我都喜歡。
  - both 放在句子的受詞 them（代名詞）的後面。 them both = both of them

4 **both 放在助動詞或 be 動詞後面。**

- **They will both be happy if you give them some chocolate.**
  如果你給他們一些巧克力，他們兩個都會很高興。
  - both 放在助動詞 (will) 後面。
- **Our twin daughters are both great athletes.**
  我們的兩個雙胞胎女兒都是優秀的運動員。
  - both 放在 be 動詞（are）後面。

5 both 既是**代名詞**，也是**限定詞**。

- Both women **have decided to make Rome their home.**
  兩位女士都決定要在羅馬定居了。
  ↑ Both 是限定詞，修飾名詞 women。

- Both her daughters **love otters.**
  ↑ Both 是限定詞，修飾 her daughters。
  = Both of her daughters **love otters.**
  她的兩個女兒都喜歡水獺。
  ↑ Both 是代名詞，後面接 of + 複數名詞。

» 限定詞的定義參見 138 頁〈Part 1 冠詞和限定詞〉。

Otters
水獺

Diving Deep Into English 12 both 與 both of 的比較

❶ both（不加 of）：用於名詞或「形容詞 + 名詞」前時，both 後面不接 of。

- Both birds **sang loudly.** 兩隻小鳥高聲歌唱。 →Both + 名詞（birds）

❷ both (of)（加不加 of 都可以）：當 both 用在 the、my/your、these/those 等字的前面時，可以加 of，也可以不加 of。

- Both of these **houses are made of stone.**
  = Both these **houses are made of stone.** 這兩幢房子都是用石頭建造的。
  ↑ 還可省略 these/of these 等，只用 both（如：Both houses are made of stone.）。

- Both of her **parents are dentists.**
  = Both her **parents are dentists.** 她的父母都是牙醫。
  ↑ 「both + of」的結構後面一定要加「the/these/those/my/your/Mary's + 複數名詞」（比如，不能說：both of students，必須說 both of the students, both of these students, both of my students 等）。

比較 由 and 連接的複合名詞前只能用 both，不用 both of。如：只能說 both your aunt and uncle，不能說 both of your aunt and uncle。

❸ both of（一定要加 of）：both 在 it、us、you、them 前面時，後面要接 of。

- Both of us **ride the yellow school bus.** 我們兩個都達乘黃色的校車。

Diving Deep Into English 13 both 與 all 的不同之處

❶ both 指兩個人或物，all 指兩個以上的人或物。

❷ both 作句子的主詞時，用複數動詞；all 作句子的主詞時，如果意思是 everything、the whole thing、the only thing，用單數動詞；如果意思是 everyone、every one 就要用複數動詞。

- **Both of the identical twins were quiet in the hall.** 那對同卵雙胞胎在大廳裡都很安靜。
  ↳ Both 作句子的主詞，動詞用複數 were。
- **All was quiet in the hall.** 大廳裡一片寂靜。
  ↳ All 作句子的主詞，在這裡指 everything，動詞用單數 was。
- **All of the students were quiet in the hall.**
  所有的學生都安靜地待在大廳裡。
  ↳ All 作代名詞，是句子的主詞，在這裡指 every one of the students，與複數動詞 were 連用。

5 each：每個；每，各自的（代名詞或限定詞）

1 each 用來指一個團體（兩個或兩個以上的人或物）裡面所有的人或物，**強調分別看待每個個體**。

2 each（作限定詞用）+ 單數名詞 + 單數動詞：
each 作限定詞時，後面接單數名詞和單數動詞。

- **Each new day is a new chance to learn and play.**
  新的每一天，都是一個新的學習和玩耍的機會。

3 each（作代名詞）+ 單數動詞（ + 單數代名詞）：each 作代名詞來當句子的主詞時，後面接單數動詞和單數所有格代名詞。

- **Each has his or her own cellphone.** 每個人都有自己的手機。

4 each of + 複數名詞／代名詞 + 單數動詞 +（單數代名詞）→ 正式文體
each of + 複數名詞／代名詞 + 複數動詞 +（複數代名詞）→ 非正式文體

each of + 複數名詞／複數代名詞作主詞時，要接單數動詞和單數所有格代名詞。

- Each of the girls has her own set of pearls.
  這群女孩中每一個人都有自己的一套珍珠。
  ↑ 有些人會用複數動詞 have 和複數所有格代名詞 their，去搭配單數不定代名詞 each，但這種用法不合規範，考試時要按照文法規則，用單數動詞和單數代名詞。
  ↑ 注意 與 all of 的用法相同，each of 後面也一定要用「the/these/my 等 + 名詞」。

5 複數主詞 + each + 複數動詞（ + 複數代名詞）：each 放在複數主詞（複合主詞）後面，要用複數動詞和複數代名詞。

- Mary and Joe each have their own thoughts about being friends with Larry. 關於與賴瑞交朋友一事，瑪麗和喬各有主張。

Diving Deep Into English 14 each、both、all 的比較

❶ each、both、all 可以作**限定詞**。

- "Each turtle is different," explained Mike.
  邁克解釋說：「每一隻烏龜都不一樣。」 →Each（限定詞）+ 單數名詞 + 單數動詞
- "Both turtles are green," said Jean. 琴說：「這兩隻烏龜都是綠色的。」
  ↑ Both（限定詞）+ 複數名詞 + 複數動詞
- "All turtles are cute," declared Paul.
  保羅聲稱：「所有的烏龜都很可愛。」 → All（限定詞）+ 複數名詞 + 複數動詞

❷ 「each/both/all + of + us/you/them」可以在句中作**主詞**。

- Each of us has made some bad mistakes.
  我們每個人都犯過一些嚴重的錯誤。 → Each of us + 單數動詞（has）
- Both of us have made some bad mistakes.
  我們兩個人都犯過一些嚴重的錯誤。 → Both of us + 複數動詞（have）
- All of us have made some bad mistakes.
  我們大家都犯過一些嚴重錯誤。 → All of us + 複數動詞（have）

❸ 「each/both/all + of + us/you/them」可以在句中作**受詞**。

- I want each of you to help clean up the beach.
  我要你們每一個人都幫忙清理海灘。

- **I want** both of you **to take an oath.** 我要你們兩個都發誓。
- **I want** all of you **to clean the hall.** 我要你們所有的人都去打掃大廳。

❹ each/both/all 可以放在主格代名詞（they, we, you）後面。

- They each think **the same about the importance of reading.** 他們每個人對閱讀的重要性的看法一致。
- They both think **the same about the importance of reading.** 他們兩人對閱讀的重要性的看法一致。
- They all think **the same about the importance of reading.** 他們大家對閱讀的重要性的看法一致。
  ↑ 上面三句的主詞都是 They，都用複數動詞 think。

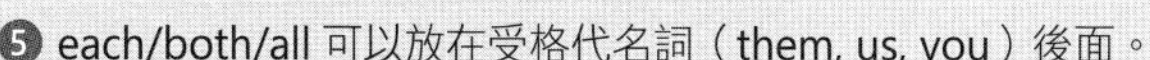

❺ each/both/all 可以放在受格代名詞（them, us, you）後面。

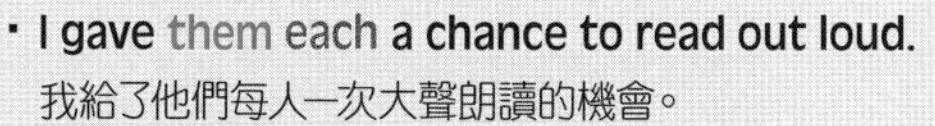

- **I gave** them each **a chance to read out loud.**
  我給了他們每人一次大聲朗讀的機會。

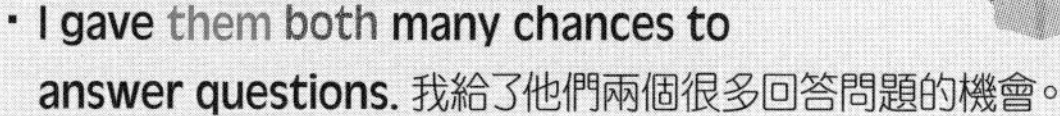

- **I gave** them both **many chances to answer questions.** 我給了他們兩個很多回答問題的機會。
- **I gave** them all **many chances to learn the biology vocabulary.**
  我給了他們所有的人很多學習生物學詞彙的機會。

Diving Deep Into English 15 each 與 every 的比較

❶ 作限定詞時，every 和 each 都與**單數名詞**連用。接在 every 和 each 後面的名詞主詞都應該與**單數動詞**連用。在很多情況下，every 和 each 作為限定詞在意義上沒有多大的區別，可以互換。

- Every day/Each day **is different.** 每一天都不同。
  ↑ Every/Each + 單數名詞 + 單數動詞
- **Jim looks older** every time/each time **I see him.**
  我每次看見吉姆，他都好像老了一點兒。

❷ 如果要把一些人或一些東西**個別對待**（一次一個），最好用 each（特指：指每一個人或物）；反之，如果我們是**集體對待**（一個團體），最好用 every（泛指：指大家），every 在意義上比 each 更接近 all。

- **Dr. Rice gave every patient the same advice.**
  = Dr. Rice gave all patients the same advice.
  賴斯醫生給所有病人同樣的建議。 → 指一個團體，強調總體概念。
- **Each patient has unique healthcare needs.**
  每一個病人都有獨特的醫療照顧需求。 → 強調個體性。
- **Grandma Pool has four granddaughters, and today each granddaughter (= each) received a prize at school.**
  普爾奶奶有四個孫女，今天，每個孫女都在學校裡收到了一個獎品。
  ↑ 這裡特指具體的四個孫女，因此用 each granddaughter，而不用 every granddaughter。也可以只用代名詞 each 作主詞。
- **Every child wants to play every day.**
  每一個小孩子都希望每天都能玩耍。 → 這裡是泛指所有的孩子。

❸ each 可以指**兩個或兩個以上**的人或東西；every 指**三個或三個以上**的人或東西。也就是說，指兩個人或東西時，不用 every。

- **There are many new peach trees on each side of the avenue.**
  = There are many new peach trees on both sides of the avenue.
  在大道的兩旁有很多新種的桃樹。
  ↑ 指兩旁，不能用 every，要用 each。both 雖指兩個，但後面要接複數名詞（both sides of the avenue）。
- **There are many oak trees on every/each side of the town square.** 在市鎮廣場的每一邊都有很多橡樹。
  ↑ 指兩邊以上（廣場的四邊）。

❹ 表示某事發生的**頻率**，要用 every，不能用 each。

- **"How often do you surf the Internet?" "Almost every day."**
  「你多久上網一次？」「幾乎每天都要上網。」
- **There is a bus going downtown every ten minutes.**
  每十分鐘就有一輛公車開往市中心。

❺ each 作代名詞，可以用「each of (the/these/my . . .)」或「each of us/them」結構；every 只能作限定詞，不能作代名詞，因此後面不能直接接 of，但可以用 every one of 結構。

- **She carefully read each of the sentences.**
  她仔細地讀了每一個句子。
  → **She has read every one of my books.**
  她讀過我所有的書。

- **Each of us is unique.**
  我們每一個人都是獨特的。
  → **Every one of us is special.**
  我們每一個人都是特別的。

almost、nearly 後面要用 every，不能用 each。
- nearly/almost every German student
  幾乎每一個德國學生

6 any 和 some：代名詞或限定詞

1 我們用 some 和 any 來修飾**不可數名詞**和**複數名詞**，不用 a/an。some 和 any 可以作**限定詞**，也可以作**代名詞**。

» 參見 34 頁〈4 可數與不可數名詞常用的限定詞：some 和 any〉。

代名詞		限定詞	
some of the students 一些學生	→	some students	複數名詞
some of the milk 一些牛奶	→	some milk	不可數名詞
any of my books 我的任何書	→	any books	複數名詞
any of his help 他的任何幫助	→	any help	不可數名詞

- **In the basket, there are some kittens playing with a pair of mittens.** 籃子裡有幾隻小貓在玩一雙連指手套。
  ↳ there are + some + 複數名詞（kittens）

- **There is still some milk in the bottle.**
  瓶子裡還有一些牛奶。
  ↳ There is + some + 不可數名詞（milk）

- Gus likes to do things on his own; he doesn't want any help from us.
  加斯做事情喜歡自己一個人來；他不想要我們的任何幫助。
  ↳ any + 不可數名詞（help）
- Are there any tickets available for us to see Kay dance in the ballet? 我們想觀看凱的芭蕾舞表演，還能買到票嗎？
  ↳ any + 複數名詞（tickets）
  ↳ 在否定句和疑問句中，如果 any 修飾的是可數名詞，要用**複數名詞**（如：any mistakes, any questions, any tickets）。

2 any（一點、一些、絲毫）和 some（一些）常常是相對的，any 用在**疑問句**和**否定句**中，some 常用在**肯定句**中。

- Let me give you some advice. 讓我給你一些建議吧。 → 肯定句中用 some。
- Jenny made hardly any mistakes in her thank-you note to Denny.
  珍妮寫給丹尼的感謝信裡幾乎沒有任何錯誤。
  ↳ 句中有具有否定含意的詞 hardly，應該用 any。
- There isn't any apple juice left. 沒有蘋果汁了。 → 否定句
- Do you know any of her American pals?
  你認識她的任何一個美國朋友嗎？ → 疑問句
- I can't go out with you to the movies tonight. I have some homework to do. 我今晚不能跟你去看電影。我有一些家庭作業要做。 → 肯定句
- Danny said, "I need some blue blankets for tomorrow. Do you have any I could borrow?"
  Kenny replied, "Sorry, I don't have any."
  丹尼說：「我明天需要一些藍色的毯子，你有沒有可以借給我的？」
  肯尼回答：「對不起，我沒有。」
- She finished the writing assignment without any help from me.
  她獨立完成了寫作作業，我並沒有給予任何幫助。
  ↳ 這雖不是否定句的句型，但 any 要與具有否定含意的 without 連用。

3 表示**請求**、**邀請**、**提供**的問句中，如果期待對方給予肯定的回答，那麼在**疑問句**中也可以用 some。

- Could I have some plum juice? 我可以喝點梅子汁嗎？ → 請求
- Would you like some bubble gum? 你想不想吃泡泡糖？ → 提供

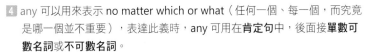

4 any 可以用來表示 no matter which or what（任何一個、每一個，而究竟是哪一個並不重要），表達此義時，any 可用在**肯定句**中，後面接**單數可數名詞**或**不可數名詞**。

- **Any doctor will tell you that smoking leaves a brain unfit for healthy thinking.** 任何一個醫生都會告訴你，抽菸會使得頭腦不能健全地思考。

- **Let every nation know, whether it wishes us well or ill, that we shall pay any price, bear any burden, meet any hardship, support any friend, oppose any foe to assure the survival and the success of liberty.** (President John Fitzgerald Kennedy)
  讓每一個友邦和敵國都知道，我們將不惜付出任何代價，承擔任何重擔，迎戰任何艱難，支持一切朋友，反對一切敵人，以確保自由的生存與勝利。
  ↑ 在肯定句中，any 要與單數可數名詞用在一起（如 any price, any friend）。

- **Sue inquired, "When is the best time to visit you?"**
  Mike answered, "It doesn't matter—any time you like."
  蘇問：「什麼時候來看你最好？」邁克回答：「任何時間都可以，你想來就來。」
  ↑ 這裡的 any 接不可數名詞 time。

7 以 -body、-one 或 -thing 結尾的複合不定代名詞

1 somebody、someone、something、somewhere 與 anybody、anyone、anything、anywhere 之間的區別，和 some 與 any 之間的區別是一樣的。參見 117 頁〈6 any 和 some：代名詞或限定詞〉。

① somebody 和 someone 的意思是相同的，anybody 和 anyone 的意思也是相同的。

② somewhere 和 anywhere 是**副詞**，其餘的字是**不定代名詞**。

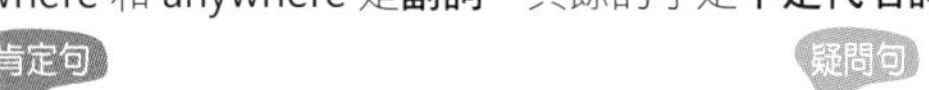

- **Somebody called while you were out.** 你不在時，有人打電話來。 → **Is there anyone at home?** 有人在家嗎？

肯定句 否定句

- **I've got something important to tell you.** 我有重要的事情要告訴你。 → **Sue didn't say anything bad about you.** 蘇沒有講過任何你的壞話。

- I'm sure I've seen him somewhere before.
  我確定以前在哪裡見過他。

→ Have you seen Claire anywhere?
  你在什麼地方看見克萊兒了嗎？

- If Claire continues to be lazy, she will never go anywhere. 如果克萊兒繼續懶惰下去，她將一事無成。
  ↥ anywhere 與否定副詞 never 連用。

2 something 通常用於肯定句，但可以用於表示**提供**或**請求**的疑問句中，**期待對方作肯定回答**時，也可以用 something。

- Would you like something to drink? 你想喝點什麼嗎？ → 提供
- May I have something to eat? 我可以吃點什麼嗎？ → 請求
- What's wrong with you? Do you have something in your eye?
  你怎麼呢？眼睛裡有什麼東西嗎？ → 期待對方作肯定回答

3 anybody、anything、anywhere 通常用於否定句及疑問句。用於**肯定句**時則表示「**無論任何人、事物、地點都無所謂**」。

- "Where should I park my bike?" "Anywhere outside this square."
  「我應該把我的自行車停在哪裡？」「這個廣場外的任何地方都可以。」
- She thinks anybody can learn to fly a jet.
  她認為任何人都能學會駕駛噴射機。
- Bing is so thirsty that he could drink almost anything. 賓口渴到什麼都可以喝下去。

4 if 引導的子句裡用 any、anybody、anything、anywhere。

- I'm sorry if I have caused you any trouble.
  如果我給你惹了麻煩，請原諒。
- Please let me know if you need anything. 如果你需要什麼，請讓我知道。
- If anyone calls, please tell the caller I'll be back at 3 p.m.
  如果有人來電，請告訴對方我下午三點會回來。

修飾這些不定代名詞的形容詞，要放在其後。

- someone important 某號重要人物
- anywhere quiet 任何安靜的地方
- anything interesting 任何有趣的事情

- There is something wrong with Kay today. 凱今天不對勁。
- There is nothing wrong with Kay today. 凱今天沒有不對勁。
  = There isn't anything wrong with Kay today.
  凱今天沒有任何的不對勁。
  ↑ 肯定句用 something，否定句用 nothing 或否定詞 not + anything。

Diving Deep Into English 16 everyone 與 every one、anyone 與 any one 的比較

❶ everyone = everybody（指人）：當不好分辨一個句子究竟應該用 everyone 還是 every one 時，可以用替換法進行判斷。如果可以用 everybody 來替換，那麼就應該用 everyone，因為 everyone 和 everybody 的意思相同。**everyone 後面不能接 of**。

❷ every one = each one = each single one（指人或物）：不能用 everybody 來替換的，就應該用 every one，**every one 後面常接 of**，相當於 each one 或 each single one。

- **Everyone wants to have fun in the sun.**
  大家都想在陽光下盡情地玩一玩。 → Everyone = Everybody
- **Every one of us wants to have fun in the sun.**
  我們每一個人都想在陽光下盡情地玩一玩。
  ↑ Every one of us 表示團體裡的每一個人。
- **Everyone (= Everybody) wanted to talk to the new English teacher.** 人人都想跟新來的英文老師聊天。
- **Every one of the cabins in this park was built by my grandson.**
  這個公園裡的每一個小屋都是我的孫子蓋的。 → 指物
- **Claire has four girls, and every one of them loves to wear pearls.** 克萊兒有四個女兒，每一個都喜歡戴珍珠。 → 指人

❸ anyone (= anybody) 和 any one of 的用法與 everyone 和 every one of 一樣。

- There wasn't anyone (= anybody) in my class that wanted to swim today. 今天我的班上沒有任何人想游泳。
- If any one of you wants to sing at the party, that would be great. 你們誰想在聚會上唱歌，那就很棒了。

8 nobody (= no one), nothing, nowhere, no, none

1 這些否定意義的詞既可置於句首，又可單獨使用。（no 是**限定詞**，nowhere 是**副詞**，其餘的是**代名詞**。）

- Nobody (= No one) seemed to understand me. 似乎沒有人理解我。
- "What did you say?" "Nothing." 「你說什麼？」「什麼也沒有說。」
- Few of my classmates wanted to go camping on Saturday, and none wanted to go mountain climbing. 我的同學中很少有幾個人想星期六去野營，更沒有任何人想去爬山。
- No smoking! 禁止吸菸！ → no 在這裡是限定詞，指「不許、不要」。
- "Where did Kay go yesterday?" "Nowhere. She stayed at home." 「凱昨天去了哪裡？」「哪裡也沒有去。她待在家裡。」
  ↑ Nowhere 在這裡是副詞（nowhere = not anywhere）。

2 這些否定詞也可放在動詞之後，尤其是 be 動詞和 have/has/had 之後。

- There is nobody at home. 家裡一個人也沒有。
- He had nothing important to say. 他沒有什麼重要的事要說。

3 anyone、anybody、anything 常與否定詞 never、not 連用，而 nobody、never、nowhere、no 等字本身就具有否定意味，句中只要用一個否定詞就可以了，即要避免雙重否定。

● no = not any ● nothing = not anything ● nobody = not anybody

✗ She never said nothing about her divorce.
✓ She never said anything about her divorce.
✓ She said nothing about her divorce. 她對她離婚的事隻字未提。

✗ Claire is not nowhere to be seen.
✓ Claire is nowhere to be seen. 到處都看不見克萊兒。

✗ I don't want to sing for nobody right now.
✓ I don't want to sing for anybody right now. 我現在不想為任何人唱歌。
ㄴ 否定意義的動詞（isn't, didn't, can't）不與 no、nothing、nobody 等連用。

9 none of

1 none of + 複數名詞／複數代名詞 + 複數動詞 美式

美式英語認為 none 的意思更接近 not any (of them)，所以在「none of + 複數名詞／複數代名詞」的結構中是複數，應該接**複數動詞**。

- None of them were called Adam. 他們之中沒有人叫亞當。
- None of us speak French. 我們之中沒有人說法語。

2 none of + 複數名詞／複數代名詞 + 單數動詞 英式正式
none of + 複數名詞／複數代名詞 + 複數動詞 英式口語

在**英式英語**中，none of 和複數名詞或代名詞連用時，動詞可以單數，也可以複數。正式文體中用單數，因為英國人認為實際主詞是 none，而 none 的意義是 no one（沒有一個）或 not one（沒有任何一個），所以動詞要用單數，但在非正式文體中，英國人追隨美式英語的用法，常用複數動詞。

British formal None of those answers is correct. 那些回答都不正確。

British informal None of these tall young women play basketball.
這些高個子的年輕女子竟然沒有一個是打籃球的。

3 也許再過幾年，「**女王英語**」（Queen's English，即英式英語）在正式文體中也會改用「**山姆大叔的英語**」（Uncle Sam's English，即美式英語）形式：「None of those answers are correct」；而「None of those answers is correct」也就可能從文法書中消失。換言之，這不是英式英語和美式英語的區別，而是傳統文法和現代文法的區別。

1 almost + none of + 複數名詞 + 複數動詞

當「none of + 複數名詞」被 almost 修飾時，動詞要用複數。

- Almost none of the workers are shirkers.
  這些工人中幾乎沒有人偷懶。 → 不能用單數 is。

2 none but + 複數名詞 + 複數動詞

none 後面接「but + 複數名詞」時，動詞要用複數。

- None but his most loyal friends believe his story about Mary.
  除了他最忠誠的朋友，沒有人相信他所說的關於瑪麗的故事。
  ↑ 不能用 believes。

3 none of + 不可數名詞／單數代名詞（it）+ 單數動詞

none of 和不可數名詞或單數代名詞 it 連用時，就只能用單數動詞。

- None of the political news is of any interest to Liz.
  沒有一條政治新聞讓莉茲感興趣。
- He told us a story about Sue, but none of it was true.
  他告訴我們一個關於蘇的故事，但那故事沒有一點真實性。

4 簡而言之，當 none 作 none of them 講時，就是複數；
當 none 作 none of it 講時，就是單數。

Diving Deep Into English 17 none 與 no 的比較

❶ no 是**限定詞**，與名詞連用，而 none 是**不定代名詞**，不與名詞連用。

- **She has no friends in her school.**
  = She doesn't have any friends in her school.
  她在學校裡一個朋友也沒有。 → no = not any
- **His recovery from cancer was no small miracle.**
  他的癌症痊癒了，真是一個大奇蹟。 → no = not a
- **I left three apple pies in the fridge, but now there are none.**
  我在冰箱裡留了三個蘋果派，但現在一個也沒有了。

❷ none 後面常接 of（none of），no 後面不能接 of。

- none of them/us/you/it
- none of my friends
- none of his money

Diving Deep Into English 18 none與no one的比較

❶ none 的意思是 not any，指「人」或「物」，後面可以接 of。
none 作主詞，根據意思可接**單數**或**複數**動詞。

❷ no one 就等於 nobody，指「人」，後面不能接 of。
no one 作主詞時，要接**單數**動詞。

- **None of Amy's friends went to see if she had won.**
  艾咪的朋友中沒有一個去看她是否贏了。 → none 後面可以接 of。

- **Paul wanted a toy blowgun, but there were none in the mall.**
  保羅想要一個玩具吹箭筒，但這家購物中心一個也沒有。
  ℓ there were none = there weren't any blowguns
  ℓ none 用來指代複數名詞，動詞用複數（were）。

- **No one went to see if Amy had won.**
  沒有人去看艾咪是否贏了。 → no one 後面不能接 of。

- **No one steals a stale bun. = Nobody steals a stale bun.**
  沒有人會偷一個不新鮮的麵包。 → no one 作主詞，要用單數動詞（steals）。

✗ **The dinner started at six, and not one of the chocolate milk was left when Kate arrived at eight.**

✓ **The dinner started at six, and none of the chocolate milk was left when Kate arrived at eight.**
晚餐六點就開始，凱八點才來，這時巧克力牛奶都喝完了。
ℓ not one of 後面要接複數名詞，如：not one of the boxes、not one of the girls。不可數名詞（chocolate milk）要與 none of 搭配。
ℓ none 用來指代不可數名詞，表示「一點也沒有」，動詞用單數（was）。

10 neither 和 neither of

1. neither 用來指兩個人、事物、行為或觀念，表示「**兩者都不**」。

2. **neither + 單數動詞**

neither 作**代名詞**擔任句子的主詞時，neither 被視為**單數**，後接單數動詞。

- "Did you like Roy's two robotic toys?"
  "Neither was as much fun as his computer game called 'Fuzz.'"
  「你喜歡羅伊的兩個玩具機器人嗎?」
  「他的兩個玩具機器人都沒有他那個叫〈模糊〉的電腦遊戲好玩。」

3 neither + 單數名詞 + 單數動詞

neither 作**限定詞**用時，後面接單數名詞和單數動詞。

- Neither student is prudent. 這兩個學生做事都不謹慎。

4 neither of + 複數名詞 + 複數動詞〔非正式〕
neither of + 複數名詞 + 單數動詞〔正式用語〕

「neither of + 複數名詞」這個結構在句中作主詞時，非正式用語用複數動詞，正式用語中要用單數動詞。（商務英文或考試中，要用正式用語。）

Informal Neither of her cats were willing to purr.
Formal Neither of her cats was willing to purr.
她的兩隻貓沒有一個願意發出滿足的喵嗚聲。

Informal Neither of the skirts fit me.
Formal Neither of the skirts fits me. 那兩件裙子都不適合我穿。

Diving Deep Into English 19 neither 與 none 的比較

❶ 談及**兩個**人、事物、行為、觀念時，要用 neither（兩者皆非）。

❷ 當談及**兩個以上**的人或東西（一群人或一組東西中的成員）時，要用 none（全部皆非）。none 是 all 的反義詞，只能作代名詞。

- The two detectives smiled, but neither understood the clue.
  這兩個偵探笑了，但實際上他倆都沒有理解這條線索。 → 兩個

- Neither of the twin sisters would listen to their mother.
  這對雙胞胎姐妹都不聽她們母親的話。 → 兩個

- None of my classmates trust/trusts Andrew.
  我的同班同學都不信任安德魯。 → 兩個以上

Diving Deep Into English 20 both、neither、either 的比較

❶ both（作限定詞）指「兩者都」（= one and the other），後面接**複數**名詞。但在否定句中，則要用 neither，而不用 both。

❷ neither（作限定詞）指「兩者都不；兩者之中沒有一個」（= not either, not one or the other），後面接**單數**名詞。否定句中用 neither，不用 both。

❸ either（作限定詞）指「兩者之中的任何一個」，尤其是指「兩者之間無論哪一個」（= one or the other），後面接**單數**名詞。

✗ Both swimsuits do not fit her.
✔ Neither swimsuit fits her. 兩件游泳衣都不適合她穿。
↳ 在否定句中，要用 Neither，而不用 Both。

- "Is Ray free to play soccer on Saturday or Sunday?"
  "Ray's mom said he's free on either day/both days."
  「星期六或星期天雷有空踢足球嗎？」
  「雷的媽媽說這兩天雷都有空。」
  ↳ either（= one or the other）指「兩者之中的任何一個」，後面要接單數名詞。

- "Which day is better for you, Monday or Tuesday?"
  哪一天你比較方便，星期一還是星期二？
  "Either day is OK for me." 任何一天都可以。 → 肯定
  "Both days are OK for me." 這兩天都可以。 → 肯定
  "Neither day is OK for me." 這兩天都不合適。 → 否定

❹ 作代名詞的 both、either、neither 與 of 連用時的句型如下：

- both of + 複數名詞 + 複數動詞
- either of + 複數名詞 + 單數動詞 → 正式
  either of + 複數名詞 + 複數動詞 → 非正式／少見（避免用複數動詞）
- neither of + 複數名詞 + 單數動詞 → 正式用語
  neither of + 複數名詞 + 複數動詞 → 非正式（考試中避免使用複數動詞）

- Do both of the Bench twins speak French?
  班奇家的雙胞胎都會說法語嗎？

- Does either of the Bench twins speak French?
  班奇家的雙胞胎有沒有其中一個會說法語？

- That's too bad. Neither of the Bench twins speaks/speak French.
  太遺憾了，班奇家的雙胞胎沒有一個會說法語。
  ↥ 正式用語、商務英語、考試要用單數動詞搭配「neither of + 複數名詞」。

✗ Both of his parents did not want Jim to pay the rent.
✓ Neither of his parents wanted Jim to pay the rent.
吉姆的父母都不想要他付房租。 → 否定句中要用 Neither，不用 Both。

11 another：限定詞或代名詞

1. another 可以作**限定詞**，也可以作**代名詞**，如果後面接有名詞，another 就是限定詞；否則就是代名詞。

2. another 是一個字，不能寫成 an other。another 指前面已經提及過的那一類人或東西中「又一個、再一個」，後面通常接**單數可數名詞**，不接複數名詞，也不接不可數名詞。

- another cup of tea 又一杯茶
- another rocket 另一個火箭

cherry pie

- Why did you buy another cherry pie?
  你為何又買了一個櫻桃派？
  ↥ another 是一個字，後面要接單數可數名詞（cherry pie）。

✗ May I have another bread?
✓ May I have another piece of bread? 我可以再吃一片麵包嗎？
↥ another 後面通常不能接不可數名詞（bread）。

3. 但當 another 指人或物的具體數量時，就可以與數字及複數名詞連用了。

another + 數字（two, three 等）+ 複數名詞

- I hope Kay stays here for another ten days.
  我希望凱在這裡再待十天。

12 other：限定詞或代名詞

1 other 可以用作**限定詞**或**代名詞**。與名詞連用時，other 是限定詞；其他情況下是代名詞。

2 other 可以**特指**一組（兩個或兩個以上）人或物中的其他（一個或多個）成員。作這種意義時，other 常常與 the、her、his 連用（如：the other . . ., his other . . .）。

- **Sue is looking for her other shoe.**
  蘇在尋找她的另一隻鞋。
  ↳ 限定詞，特指兩者中的另一個。

- **He swam from one side of the wide river to the other side.** 他從寬廣大河的一邊遊到另一邊。
  ↳ 限定詞，特指對面。

- **President John Adams believed that there were two kinds of education. He noted, "One should teach us how to make a living and the other how to live."**
  約翰·亞當斯總統認為教育有兩大類，他說：「一種是要教我們如何謀生，另一種是要教我們如何生活。」
  ↳ one 可以與 the other 連用，表示「兩者中的一個和另一個」。

3 **泛指**用「others」（代名詞）或「other + 複數名詞」（限定詞），意思是「其他人或物」；**特指**用「the others」（代名詞）或「the other + 複數名詞」（限定詞），意思是「剩下的」。

- **A capacity and taste for reading gives access to whatever has already been discovered by others. It is the key, or one of the keys, to the already solved problems.** (President Abraham Lincoln)
  讀書的能力和愛好，使我們有機會瞭解別人所發現的一切。那是一把（或其中一把）開啟已被破解的疑難問題的鑰匙。
  ↳ 代名詞，泛指別人。

- One of the mothers wiggled and giggled, and then so did the others.
  其中一位媽媽扭著身子咯咯笑起來，接著其他媽媽也跟著這樣做。
  ↑ 代名詞，特指（一組人中）其餘的人。

- Sam's mom said, "My son doesn't like to play with other kids.
  山姆的媽媽說：「他不喜歡跟別的孩子玩耍。」 → 限定詞，泛指別人。

- Sue sighed with relief after the other kids began to talk to her.
  其他孩子開始跟她說話後，蘇如釋重負地嘆了口氣。
  ↑ 限定詞，特指（一組人中）其餘的人。

4 other 可以表示「另外的，外加的」，指已提到或已知的人或物中額外的部分，與**數字**連用，句型為「two/five/ten/hundred 等 + other + 名詞」。

- In addition to Lulu, three other girls have asked to play the computer game called "Pearls."
  除了露露之外，還有三個女孩也要求玩名叫「珍珠」的電腦遊戲。 → 另外的

5 **any other 的用法**

a any other + 複數名詞 （用於疑問句）

- Are there any other questions? 有其他問題嗎？ → 疑問句

b any other + 單數可數名詞 （用於陳述句）

- Neither believe nor reject anything, because any other person has rejected or believed it. Heaven has given you a mind for judging truth and error. Use it. (President Thomas Jefferson)
  不要因為別人相信或否定了什麼，你也就跟著去相信或否定。
  上帝已賜予你一個用來判斷真理和謬誤的頭腦。多動腦筋。 → 陳述句

c any other + 單數可數名詞 （用於比較級）

- Can Penny Bridge swim faster than any other female student at her college?
  潘妮．布里奇能游得比大學裡其他的女生都快嗎？ → 比較級

13 many、much、a lot of (= lots of)、plenty of：限定詞或代名詞

1 many 和 much 可作限定詞（形容詞），也可作代名詞，如果後面接有名詞，就是**限定詞**（形容詞），否則就是**代名詞**。

2 much 修飾**不可數名詞**，many 修飾**複數名詞**。

3 a lot of 和 plenty of 與**不可數名詞**和**複數名詞連用**。

不可數名詞	複數名詞
● much time 許多時間	● many hours 許多小時
● much of the milk 許多牛奶	● many of the cows 許多頭牛
● a lot of time/lots of time 許多時間	● a lot of hours/lots of hours 許多小時
● plenty of money 許多錢	● plenty of eggs 許多蛋

↑ plenty = more than enough，指比足夠的分量還多。

- **Mary didn't have many friends until she met Bess, Sue, and Jerry.**
  在認識貝絲、蘇和傑瑞之前，瑪麗沒有幾個朋友。 → many 修飾可數名詞。

- **Don't let too much sun destroy your skin.**
  不要讓過量的日曬傷害你的皮膚。 → much 修飾不可數名詞。

4 **疑問句**和**否定句**中用 many、much 和 a lot (of)。**肯定句**中不可用 much，但可以用 many，不過在口語中 plenty (of) 或 a lot (of) 更常見。

- **"How much money do you have with you?" asked Jenny.**
  "I've got plenty for both of us to use on the trip," replied Gus.
  「你身上有多少錢？」 珍妮問。
  「我帶的錢足夠我們兩個旅途中用。」加斯回答。
  ↑ 不能說 「I've got much.」，much 不用於肯定句。這句的 plenty 是代名詞。

- **"Do you have many American friends?" asked Jenny.**
  "No, I don't have many American friends, but I do have a lot of British friends," replied Trish.
  「你有很多美國朋友嗎？」珍妮問。
  「沒有，我沒有很多美國朋友，但我有很多英國朋友。」翠西說。
  ↑ many 用在疑問句和否定句中，a lot of 用在肯定句中。
  ↑ 也可以說 I do have many British friends。

・Be quick with your rhyme, because we don't have much time.
趕快寫你的押韻詩吧，我們沒有多少時間了。 → much 用在否定句中。

5 much 或 many 可以用在肯定句中的 as、so、too 的後面。

・Dan is going to stay in Bali as many days as he can.
丹要在峇里島盡可能多待些日子。

・Kay and I have so much work to do today. 凱和我今天有太多的工作要做。

・Ann still has too much homework to do and too many new words to teach Dan. 安還有太多的家庭作業要做和太多的新單字要教丹。

6 注意 too 與**形容詞**和**副詞**連用，而 too much 和 too many 則與**名詞**連用。

✗ That milk is too much old. → too much 後面不能接形容詞（old）。
✓ That milk is too old. → too + 形容詞（old）。
✓ That milk is much too old. → much 在這裡是副詞，用來表示程度。
那牛奶太不新鮮了。

・Coco often drives too fast and has had two bad accidents.
可可開車常常很快，已經出過兩次嚴重的車禍。
↑ too + 副詞。

・Kay asked too many questions today. 凱今天問的問題太多了。
↑ too many + 複數名詞（questions）。

・There is too much traffic on Highway 75 today. 今天 75 號公路上很塞。
↑ too much + 不可數名詞（traffic）。

14 few、a few、little、a little：限定詞或代名詞

1 a few、few、a little、little 可以作**代名詞**，後面接 of 片語，也可以作**限定詞**，修飾名詞。

代名詞
- a few of us 我們當中的一些人
- few of us 我們當中幾乎沒有人
- a little of my time 我的一些時間
- little of my time 我的那一點點時間（否定含意，指幾乎沒有）

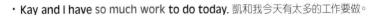

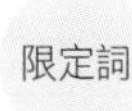

限定詞
- a few students 一些學生
- few students 幾乎沒有學生
- a little time 一些時間
- little time 幾乎沒有時間

2 a little、little 通常修飾**不可數名詞**，而 a few、few 則修飾**複數**名詞或**複數**代名詞。

- **Be patient. I'll be ready in a few minutes.** 耐心點，我再幾分鐘就好了。
- **If you are hungry, I've got a little tea, two potatoes, and a few tomatoes.** 如果你餓了，我有一點兒茶、兩顆馬鈴薯和幾個番茄。

3 little 和 few 具有**否定**含意，表示「幾乎不，幾乎沒有」；而 a few 和 a little 卻具有**肯定**含意，表示「有一些」，意思接近於 some。

- **Trish knows little English.** 翠西不太懂英語。
- **Trish knows a little English.** 翠西懂一點兒英語。

- **He has little influence with his wife when she is angry.**
  當他的夫人生氣時，他幾乎控制不了她。 → 否定含意
- **Would you like a little honey?**
  你想不想吃一點兒蜂蜜？ → 肯定含意（a little honey = some honey）

- **Jim is a strange guy, and few people like him.**
  吉姆是一個古怪的傢伙，沒有幾個人喜歡他。

- **Jim is a strange guy, but a few people like him.**
  吉姆雖是一個古怪的傢伙，但還是有些人喜歡他。
  ↑ a few people = some people

- **Few of us can speak English as fluently as Gus.**
  我們之中沒有幾個人能像加斯那樣流利地說英文。 → 否定含意
- **A few of us can speak Chinese fluently.**
  我們之中有幾個人能講流利的中文。 → 肯定含意（A few of us = Some of us）

- **Coco is a strange woman, but she has quite a few friends in Tokyo.**
  可可雖然是一個古怪的女人，但在東京卻有許多朋友。
  ↑ quite a few 是一個習慣用語，意思是「相當多」，等於 a lot of。

15 one（一個；任何人）：代名詞或限定詞

1 不定代名詞 one 的句型為：**one of + 複數名詞／複數代名詞 + 單數動詞**

- "One of my friends is dying," cried Ming.
  敏哭道：「我的一個朋友快死了。」
- One of us has to stay here. 我們當中有一個人要留在這裡。
  ↑ 主詞是單數不定代名詞 one，要用單數動詞。

比較 one 作限定詞的用法：

1 one + 單數名詞 + 單數動詞

- One swallow does not make a summer. 一燕不成夏。
  ↑ 主詞是單數名詞 swallow。

2 one or more + 複數名詞 + 複數動詞

- One or more cars are parked illegally on Clay Street every day. 每天都有一輛或更多的汽車非法停在克萊大街上。
  ↑ 主詞是複數名詞 cars。

3 one or two + 複數名詞 + 複數動詞

- One or two students from her school have won scholarships from Yale University. 她學校的一、兩個學生（幾個學生）獲得了耶魯大學的獎學金。
  ↑ 主詞是複數名詞 students。

4 one and + 分數 + 複數名詞 + 複數動詞

- One and a half years have passed since I last studied English with Trish.
  = A year and a half has passed since I last studied English with Trish. 從我上次跟翠西一起學英文之後，已經過了一年半。
  ↑ 由不定冠詞 a/an 引導（a/an + 單數名詞 + 分數），要用單數動詞。

5 one and + 分數 + 複數名詞 + 單數動詞（視為一個整體）

- One and a half cups of coffee is enough for me.
  一杯半的咖啡足夠我喝了。→ 一個整體

2 one 也可用來泛指「任何人」，這種意義的 one 應該和哪些代名詞搭配？請看下面例句。

Sexist Whichever ocean one looks at, he will find some pollution.

Mainly American Whichever ocean one looks at, he or she will find some pollution.

Mainly British Whichever ocean one looks at, one will find some pollution.

Informal Whichever ocean one looks at, they will find some pollution.

American/British Whichever ocean you look at, you will find some pollution.

無論你觀看哪一個海洋，都會發現有些污染。

a **英式英語**：不定代名詞 one 後面接 one/one's/oneself（如上面第三句）。

b **美式英語**：不定代名詞 one 作主詞時，如果後面需要重複這個 one，從前常用 he, him, his 和 himself 等來代替（如上面第一句），以避免重複彆扭的詞 one。但近年來為了避免性別歧視（sexist）語言，就改成 he or she 和 his or her（如上面第二句）。也有人用特殊的形式 he/she 和 his/her。

c **口語／非正式語**：有些人用複數代名詞 they、them、their 來搭配單數不定代名詞 one。這種用法受到許多文法學家、編輯和作家反對，因為文法規則規定，**單數不定代名詞**（one、everybody、anybody、each 等）要搭配**單數動詞**和**單數人稱代名詞**或**單數所有格代名詞**。因此在商務信函、學術報告、考試中，要遵守文法規則，使用正式用語。類似上面的第四句，在考試中務必避免。

d 重複 one 或用 he、he or she、he/she 等，都顯得笨拙、不自然。用複數代名詞 they、their，又不符合文法規則。

e 無論是在口語還是在正式的文體中，用 one 來泛指「任何人」都顯得很不自然。因此越來越多的人選擇使用 you 或 we，這樣可以避免性別歧視語言，也避免了彆扭的 one 和笨拙的「he or she」等，而且還可以避免用複數 they、their 搭配單數不定代名詞 one，而且在文法上也完全正確（如上面最後一句）。

Diving Deep Into English 21 同一字作限定詞與代名詞的區別

❶ 限定詞 + 名詞：通常泛指人或物。

- Most Americans like to eat toast.
大多數美國人都喜歡吃烤麵包。 → 泛指

- I want to buy some rings. 我想買一些戒指。 → 泛指

❷ 代名詞 + of + the/these/my + 名詞：
一般用來特指某群人或某一組事物。

- Most of the people at the party are watching the movie *Ghost*.
聚會上大多數的人正在看那部名叫《鬼》的影片。 → 特指

- Some of my rings are missing. 我的一些戒指找不到了。 → 特指

	代名詞 + of + 名詞（特指）	限定詞 + 名詞（泛指）
用於 the 前面	● some of the people here 這裡的一些人 ● most of the students in my class 我班上的大多數學生	● some people 一些人 ● most students 大多數學生
用於 this、that、these、those 等前面	● too many of these old computers 太多這些舊電腦 ● any of those books 任何的那些書	● too many old computers 太多舊電腦 ● any books 任何書
用於 my、his 等前面	● a few of my rings 我的一些耳環 ● most of his money 他大部分的錢	● a few rings 一些耳環 ● most money 大部分的錢
用於 it、us、them 等前	● all of us 我們所有人 ● most of them 他們大多數人 ● some of it 它的一些	● all people 所有人 ● most cars 大部分的車子 ● some milk 一些牛奶

UNIT

04 冠詞

Articles

冠詞和限定詞

1 冠詞（Articles）

冠詞可分為兩種：**不定冠詞**（a/an）與**定冠詞**（the），作用類似於形容詞，用來修飾名詞，因此一些文法學家也把這三個字歸為**限定詞**。

- **Lady Gaga is an excellent entertainer.** 女神卡卡是一位出色的表演者。
  ↳ 不定冠詞 an 修飾名詞 entertainer，起限定的作用。
- **I can't find the salt.** 我找不到鹽。→ 定冠詞 the 修飾名詞 salt，起限定的作用。

2 限定詞（Determiners）

限定詞（例如：this、that、these、those、my、your、his、its、their、our、some、a few、many、much、a little、plenty、a、an、the）其實是一種**特殊的形容詞**，放在名詞前面起修飾作用。限定詞主要分為兩組：

第一組

● 冠詞	a/an, the
● 所有格代名詞	my, your, his, her, its, our, their, one's, whose
● 指示詞	this, these, that, those
● 疑問詞	what, whatever, which, whichever

第二組 不定限定詞、數量詞

- some, any, no
- each, every, either, neither
- much, many, more, most, a little, less, least, a few, fewer, fewest, enough, several
- all, both, half
- one, two, three, etc.

» 參見 65 頁〈Unit 3 代名詞〉。

不定冠詞 a 和 an

1 a/an 的定義

不定冠詞 a/an 用於**非特指**的可數名詞前面，表示談論的是一個人或一個東西。

- **He has got a big mouth and an evil eye.**
  他嘴大話多，眼神惡毒。
  ↑ a big mouth 在這裡的含意是「太多嘴了」。

- **Ann told us a story about a tall lady married to a short man.**
  安給我們講了一個高大女子嫁給了一個矮個子男人的故事。
  ↑ one story; one tall lady; one short man

2 a/an 修飾單數可數名詞

可數名詞用作單數時，不能單獨使用，應有 a/an 來修飾，或由其他限定詞（the、my、his、that 等）來修飾。

✗ My mom is dentist.
✓ My mom is a dentist.
我媽媽是牙醫。

- **"A hospital is a place where sick people are cared for," explained Claire.**
  克萊兒解釋說：「醫院是照顧病人的地方。」

Diving Deep Into English 22 是 a truck, a jeep, and a car 還是 a truck, jeep, and car？

❶ 系列單數可數名詞構成平行結構時，可以把冠詞只放在第一個項目前，也可以在每個項目前重複使用冠詞。

- **I saw a truck, (a) jeep, and (a) car stuck in the deep mud.**
  我看到一輛卡車、吉普車和汽車，陷進了深泥坑裡。

❷ 但如果有的項目要用 a，而有的要用 an，就得重複不定冠詞。

- **She saw an enormous toad and a huge snake on the road.**
  她看見路上有一隻巨大的蟾蜍和一隻巨大的蛇。

❸ 如果指同一個人的不同職位，不能重複不定冠詞。

- **Tom is an American writer and artist.** 湯姆是一個美國作家及藝術家。

3 a/an 和 one 的區別

1 a/an 和 one 都表示「一個」，有時可以互換。

- **Please wait for a/one minute.** 請等一分鐘。
- **She weighs a/one hundred and ten pounds.** 她的體重 110 磅。

2 如果要**強調數量**（談論的是一個人或一件事，而非兩個或更多），用 one，不用 a/an。

- **Do you want one pear or two?** 你想要一個梨還是兩個梨？
- **Only one passenger was injured when the bus hit the wall.**
  當公車撞到牆上時，只有一名乘客受了傷。

3 表達「在某一類物品中任意一個」的意思時，用 a/an，不用 one。

- **Would you like a cup of coffee or tea?** 你想要一杯咖啡還是茶？
  ↑ 並非強調數量，不用 one cup of coffee or tea。

4 在**數字**或**數量**表達方式中，用 a/an，不用 one。

- twice a year 一年兩次
- a few 一些
- half an hour 半小時
- a huge number of students 很多學生

5 a/an 表示「每一，每」，相當於 per。這種情況不用 one。

✗ travel at 100 kilometers one hour

✓ travel at 100 kilometers an hour 以每小時 100 公里的速度行進

↑ an hour = per hour

4 a/an 不修飾不可數名詞

不可數名詞前面不能用 a/an。

- Sugar is sweet, but meat is what I like to eat.
  糖是很甜沒錯，但我愛吃的是肉。
  ↑ sugar 和 meat 都是不可數名詞，前面不需要不定冠詞 a 或 an。

✗ That's a great news about Kate!

✗ Those are great news about Kate!

✓ That's great news about Kate!

✓ That's a piece of great news about Kate! 那是一則和凱特有關的好消息！

↑ news（新聞；消息）雖然看起來像是複數名詞，實際上卻是不可數名詞，前面不能用不定冠詞 a 或 an，也不與複數動詞連用。

✗ It's such a wonderful weather!

✓ It's such wonderful weather! 今天的天氣真好呀！

↑ weather（天氣）是不可數名詞，前面不能用不定冠詞 a 或 an。

Diving Deep Into English 23 可數名詞與不可數名詞

❶ **可數名詞**（可以數的人或事物的名稱）：可以是單數，也可以是複數。

- arrow 箭 → an arrow → two arrows
- boy 男孩 → one boy → two boys
- computer 電腦 → a computer → three/many computers

❷ **不可數名詞**（不可以數的事物的名稱）：只能是單數，不能和不定冠詞 a/an 連用。可以說 bread，但不能說 a bread、two breads。

- blood 血
- lightning 閃電
- money 錢
- water 水
- bread 麵包
- love 愛
- rice 米
- wood 木頭

» 參見 31 頁〈Part 3 可數名詞與不可數名詞〉。

❶ a piece of/two pieces of + 不可數名詞

一些不可數名詞與 a piece of（一張）、a bit of（一點點）、an item of（一項）、a drop of（一滴）等片語連用後，就具有可數的性質，有單數和複數形式。這類字變複數時，不可數名詞本身不變，只把**量詞**（piece、jar 等）變為複數。

- a bar of chocolate　two bars of chocolate　一／兩塊巧克力
- a bar of soap　two bars of soap　一／兩塊肥皂
- a bolt of lightning　two bolts of lightning　一／兩道閃電
- a clap of thunder　two claps of thunder　一／兩聲雷鳴
- a drop of water　two drops of water　一／兩滴水
- a drop of blood　two drops of blood　一／兩滴血
- an ear of corn　two ears of corn　一／兩穗玉米
- a glass of milk　two glasses of milk　一／兩杯牛奶
- a grain of rice　two grains of rice　一／兩粒米
- a jar of jam　two jars of jam　一／兩罐果醬
- a jar of honey　two jars of honey　一／兩罐蜂蜜
- a bag of sugar　two bags of sugar　一／兩袋糖
- a piece of advice　two pieces of advice　一／兩則忠告
- a piece/loaf of bread　two pieces/loaves of bread　一／兩塊麵包
- a piece of chalk　two pieces of chalk　一／兩支粉筆
- a piece of cheese　two pieces of cheese　一／兩片起司
- a piece of cloth　two pieces of cloth　一／兩塊布
- a piece of equipment　two pieces of equipment　一／兩個設備
- a piece of furniture　two pieces of furniture　一／兩件家具
- a piece of information　two pieces of information　一／兩則消息
- a piece of jewelry　two pieces of jewelry　一／兩個珠寶
- a piece of luggage　two pieces of luggage　一／兩件行李
- a piece of mail　two pieces of mail　一／兩封郵件
- a piece of music　two pieces of music　一／兩段音樂

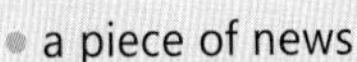

- a piece of news　　two pieces of news　　一／兩則新聞
- a piece of paper　　two pieces of paper　　一／兩張紙
- a piece of toast　　two pieces of toast　　一／兩片烤麵包
- an article of clothing　　two articles of clothing　　一／兩件衣服

· **There is not a drop of cranberry juice left in the bottle.**
瓶子裡一滴小紅莓汁都不剩了。
↑ juice（汁）是不可數名詞，不能加不定冠詞，但可以用 a drop of cranberry juice, a glass of cranberry juice 等。

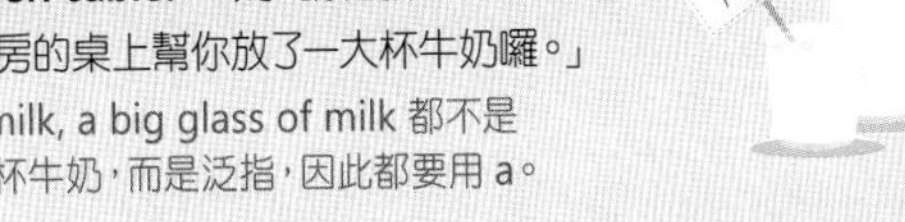

· **"Mom, I'd like a glass of milk, please."**
"I already put a big glass of milk for you on the kitchen table."「媽，請給我一杯牛奶。」
「我已經在廚房的桌上幫你放了一大杯牛奶囉。」
↑ a glass of milk, a big glass of milk 都不是特指的哪一杯牛奶，而是泛指，因此都要用 a。

❷ cloth, clothes, clothing

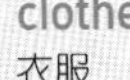

cloth 布	不可數名詞	指做衣服、窗簾等的布料，或擦洗東西的布。「一塊布」不是 a cloth，而是： ● *a piece of cloth* 一塊布
clothes 衣服	總以複數形式出現，沒有單數形式	指衣服，「一件衣服」不能說 a clothe 或 a clothes，而是要用以下的表達方式： ● *something to wear* 穿的衣物 ● *an article of clothing* 一件衣服 ● *a dress* 一件洋裝 ● a *suit* 一套西裝
clothing 衣服 （總稱）	不可數名詞	「衣服」的總稱，也可以指特定場合的衣服，比如 outdoor clothing（戶外服）。如果要表示單數的意思，要用以下的表達方法： ● *a piece of clothing* 一件衣物 ● *an item of clothing* 一件衣物 ● *an article of clothing* 一件衣物

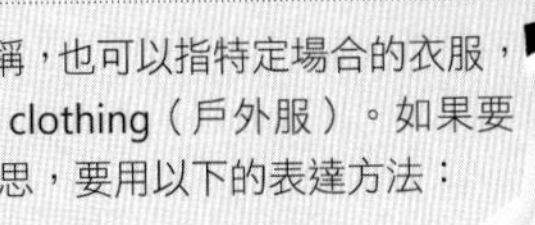

wedding clothing
婚禮服

5 a 或 an 的基本使用原則

1 a 與**子音開頭**的字連用：a + 子音開頭的字、首字母縮寫詞、數字、字母

- a boy 一個男孩
- a monkey 一隻猴子
- a puppy 一隻小狗
- a crab 一隻螃蟹
- a nose 一個鼻子
- a zebra 一匹斑馬

- a BS degree 理學士學位 → a + 子音開頭的首字母縮寫詞
- a CBS news broadcast 哥倫比亞廣播公司的新聞節目
  → a + 子音開頭的首字母縮寫詞
- a GM car 一輛通用汽車公司的車 → a + 子音開頭的首字母縮寫詞
- a + 1, 2, 3, 4, 5, 6, 7, 9, 10, 12（8 和 11 要用 an） → a + 子音開頭的數字
- a + b, c, d, g, j, k, p, q, t, u, v, w, y, z → a + 子音開頭的字母

2 an 與**母音開頭**的字連用：an + 以字母 a、e、i、o、u 開頭的字

以母音發音開始的字，前面要用 an。字母 a、e、i、o、u 通常發母音，不過也有以下情況：

① 字母 u 也有發子音 /ju/（稱為長音 u）的情況，不要在長音 u 前面用 an（參見 145 頁 Diving Deep Into English 25）。例如：

- a university 一所大學

② 字母 o 也有發子音 /w/ 的情況，這時前面也要用 a，不用 an，例如：a one-way street（參見 146 頁 Diving Deep Into English 26）。

a
- an accident 一場意外
- an afternoon nap 一個午覺
- an aunt 一位阿姨
- an apple 一個蘋果

e
- an eagle 一隻老鷹
- an elephant 一頭大象
- an expected result 一個預料中的結果
- an ear 一隻耳朵
- an empty bottle 一個空瓶
- an egg 一個雞蛋

i
- an ice-cream cone 一個冰淇淋筒
- an indoor party 一場室內宴會
- an input 一個輸入指令
- an invitation 一個邀請

o
- an oil leak 一次石油外洩
- an only child 一個獨生子女
- an orange 一顆柳丁
- an outcome 一個結局

u
- an umbrella 一把雨傘
- an unexpected result 一個意外的結局
- an unusual imagination 一種不尋常的幻想
- an upstairs bathroom 一間樓上的洗手間

Diving Deep Into English 25 以母音字母 u 開頭的字，前面到底該用 a 還是 an？

❶ a + 發子音的 u 開頭的字：如果一個字的首字母是母音字母 u（或 eu），但其發音卻以子音發音「ju」開始，那麼這個字前面要用 a。

- a useful machine 一台有用的機器
- a union meeting 一場工會會議
- a European 一個歐洲人
- a uniform 一件制服
- a UFO 一架不明飛行物
  - UFO = Unidentified Flying Object
- a U-boat 一艘潛水艇
- a unit 一個單元
- a university 一所大學
- a unicorn
- a UCLA student 一個加州大學洛杉磯分校的學生
  - UCLA = University of California at Los Angeles
- a UNICEF employee 一名聯合國兒童基金會的員工
  - UNICEF= United Nations International Children's Emergency Fund
  - 此單位已改名為 United Nations Children's Fund，但原縮略形式仍沿用。

❷ an + 發母音的 u 開頭的字：

某些字的 u 是母音發音，不定冠詞要用 an。

- an ugly mood 一個壞心情
- an uncertain future 一個不確定的未來
- an uncle 一位叔叔
- an urge 一股衝動

Diving Deep Into English 26 以母音字母 o 開頭的字，前面到底該用 a 還是 an？

❶ **a + 發子音的 o 開頭的字**：如果一個字的首字母是母音字母 o，但其發音卻以子音發音「w」開始，那麼這個字前面要用 a。

- a one-day trip 一個一天的行程
- a once-in-a-lifetime event 一個千載難逢的事件

❷ **an + 發母音的 o 開頭的字**：許多字的首字母 o 是母音發音，要用 an。

- an object 一個物體
- an opening 一個空地／一個空缺
- an oak 一棵橡樹
- an oath 一個誓言

3 **an + 不發音的 h**：以不發音的 h 開始的字，第一個音節是**母音**，因此前面要用 an（參見 147 頁 Diving Deep Into English 27）。這類字不多，常見的有：

- heir [ɛr] 繼承人
- honest [ˋɑnɪst] 誠實的
- hour [ˋaʊr] 小時
- heirloom [ˋɛrlum] 祖產
- honor [ˋɑnɚ] 榮耀
- hourly [ˋaʊrlɪ] 每小時的
- honesty [ˋɑnɪstɪ] 誠實
- honorable [ˋɑnərəbḷ] 榮譽的

不發音的 h
- *an honest [ˋɑnɪst] effort* 一份真誠的努力
- *an hour [ˋaʊr]* 一小時

發音的 h
- *a historic [hɪsˋtɔrɪk] event* 一個歷史事件
- *a hot [hɑt] sun* 一個艷陽

4 **an + 以 f、h、l、m、n、r、s、x 開頭的縮寫詞**：這八個字母雖然是子音字母，但實際上是以母音發音開始，因此要用 an，例如：

- an FBI [ɛf bi aɪ] agent 一位聯邦調查局特務
- an MBA [ɛm bi e] degree 一個工商管理碩士學位
- an RN [ɑr ɛn] 一名註冊護士
- an X-ray [ˋɛksˋre] machine 一台 X 光機器

比較
- a NATO [ˋneto] diplomat 一名北約外交官
- a FIFA [ˋfɪfɑ] official 一名國際足聯官員

↳ NATO 和 FIFA 雖然是縮寫詞，卻以單字的拼音方式發音，而不是以字母的方式發音。

Diving Deep Into English 27 h 開頭的字，到底該用 a 還是 an？

❶ 以 h 開始的字前面通常用 a，例如：

- a history book 一本歷史書
- a hotel 一家旅館
- a hive 一個蜂窩
- a honeycomb 一個蜂房

❷ 但如果這個字是以**母音發音**開始（h 不發音），就要用 an，例如：

- **Gus and I waited an hour for our bus.**
  加斯和我等了一個小時的公車。

Diving Deep Into English 28 是 an herb，還是 a herb?

❶ 單字 herb（草藥）在美式英語裡，h 不發音 [ɜb]，以不發音 h 開始的字，前面要用 an。

❷ 而在英式英語裡，herb 的 h 要發音 [hɜb]。

American **She used an herb to make the tea.**
British **She used a herb to make the tea.**
她用一個草藥泡茶。

5 an + 母音開頭的數字：以母音發音開頭的數字，前面冠詞要用 an。

- an 8-hour day 八小時的一天 → 指 8 小時工作制
- an 18-year-old basketball player 一位 18 歲的籃球運動員
- an 85 mph wind 一陣時速 85 英里的風
- an 11 a.m. meeting 一場早上 11 點的會議

6 依發音決定該用 a，還是用 an

1 **a + 子音開始的字**：當一個字一開始的發音是子音時，不定冠詞用 a。

2 **an + 母音開始的字**：當一個字一開始的發音是母音時，不定冠詞用 an。

3 總結：一個字的前面要用 a 還是 an，取決於字的**發音**（而非拼寫），關鍵在於這個字的**第一個音**是**母音**發音還是**子音**發音（而非首字母的拼寫是母音字母還是子音字母）。也因為如此，正確的發音是正確使用英語的關鍵之一。

4 對比：

alligator

以子音發音開始的字	以母音發音開始的字
a crocodile 一隻（亞、非）鱷魚	an alligator 一隻美洲鱷
a bed 一張床	an elevator 一個電梯
a Federal Bureau of Investigation agent 一位 FBI 探員	an FBI agent 一位 FBI 探員
a UFO 一架幽浮	an Unidentified Flying Object 一架幽浮
a unicorn 一隻獨角獸	an umbrella 一支雨傘
a hungry baby 一個饑餓的寶寶	an honorable man 一個可敬的人
a hat 一頂帽子	an heir 一位繼承者
a report 一份報告	an RV 一輛 RV 休旅車
a mall 一個賣場	an MA degree 一個碩士學位
a one-horned deer 一隻獨角鹿	an orange 一顆柳橙
a five-course meal 含五道菜的一份餐點	an eight-course dinner 一個八道菜的晚餐

定冠詞 the

定冠詞 the（這個／那個；這些／那些）用於特指的、已提及過的名詞前面，可以修飾單數或複數可數名詞，也可以修飾不可數名詞。

1 the 用於再次提及的名詞前面

1 單數可數名詞：在談話或書寫中首次提及一個人或物時，常用不定冠詞 a/an 來修飾；隨後再次提及時，就要改用定冠詞 the。

- **Jerry used to have a dog and a hog. However, after he had received complaints from his neighbors about the noise and smell, he sold the dog and ate the hog.** 傑瑞曾經養過一隻狗和一頭豬，不過，他聽到鄰居抱怨吵鬧聲和臭味後，就賣了那隻狗，吃了那頭豬。
  ↑ 第一次提及一個 dog 和一個 hog，要用不定冠詞 a；再次提及時，就要用 the。

- **A nice mouse in a rice box had a lonely louse. One day seven mice came to the rice box and gave the nice mouse eleven lice.**
  米箱裡有一隻可愛的老鼠，牠有一隻孤伶伶的蝨子。有一天，七隻老鼠到米箱來拜訪，帶給這隻可愛的老鼠 11 隻蝨子。

2 複數名詞：第一次提及一些事物時，用複數名詞就行了，不用加冠詞；隨後提及這些特定的事物時，就要在複數名詞前加定冠詞 the。

✗ The bees are the insects.
✓ Bees are insects. 蜜蜂是昆蟲。
↑ 非特指的複數名詞，不用 the。

- **"Steve's tree has a lot of red leaves!" exclaimed Scot. "But the red leaves are falling off the tree," said Ted.**

史考特感嘆道：「史蒂夫的樹有好多紅葉子呀！」
「可是那些紅葉子都從樹上掉落了。」泰德說。

⮤ 第一次提及紅葉，用複數 red leaves；再次提及就需要在前面加 the，指前面提及過的紅葉。第一次提及 tree 時，用了所有格限定詞 Steve's 來限定 tree；再次提及時就用 the 取代 Steve's，以避免重複。

3 **不可數名詞**：初次提及不可數名詞時，不能有冠詞修飾；隨後提及時，就可以加定冠詞 the。

- **Mrs. Power brought me some bread and milk, but the bread was stale and the milk tasted sour.**
  鮑爾斯太太帶了一些麵包和牛奶給我，可是那些麵包壞了，牛奶也酸掉了。
  ⮤ 麵包和牛奶是不可數名詞，初次提及時，可以用 some 來修飾，隨後再次提及時，就用 the 來修飾。

2 the 用於已知的事物或周圍情況

1 特指談話雙方都知道的、特定的人或物，或者從周圍環境可以清楚判斷出所指的是具體的哪個人或物時，就要用 the。the 通常暗示「你知道我談的是哪一個（些）」。例如，我們在房間裡談論 the floor、the door、the ceiling、the carpet 等。

- **"Remember to lock the door," said Sue.** 「記得鎖門。」蘇說。
  ⮤ 聽者知道說的是哪一道門（指所在房間的門）。
- **May I use the phone?** 我可以用一下電話嗎？
  ⮤ 在這個疑問句裡，聽者知道 the phone 指的就是 your phone。
- **She is going to the station to pick up her husband.**
  她要去車站接她老公。（the station in that town）
  ⮤ 類似的還有：(go to) the bank, the post office, the airport 等。
- **Please pass me the salt and butter.** 請把鹽和奶油遞給我。
  ⮤ salt 和 butter 可以共用一個 the。

- **Del whispered, "The bread is stale."** 戴爾耳語道：「這麵包不新鮮。」
  ⮤ 不可數名詞通常不用冠詞，但如果是指某個明確的東西，即聽者知道我們談及的是什麼，不可數名詞前面可以用定冠詞 the，如上面的 the salt, the butter, the bread。

- Mom made the beds. 媽媽把床鋪好了。
- Joe's dad washed the windows.
  喬的爸爸清洗了窗戶。
  ⮤ 複數名詞前通常不用冠詞，如果指的是明確的人或物，或聽者知道我們談及的是什麼，複數名詞前就可用定冠詞，如上面的 the beds, the windows。

3 獨一無二的人或物，要加 the

當這個名詞是獨一無二的人或物時，就要加 the。

- the Devil 撒旦
- the earth/Earth 人類／地球
- the Great Wall 萬里長城
- the international market 國際市場
- the International Space Station 國際太空站
- the king 國王
- the London Eye 倫敦之眼
- the moon 月亮
- the North Pole 北極
- the planets 行星
- the Pope 羅馬教皇
- the president 總統；董事長
- the sky 天空
- the solar system 太陽系
- the South Pole 南極
- the stars 星星
- the sun 太陽
- the Taj Mahal 泰姬瑪哈陵
- the United Nations 聯合國
- the universe 宇宙
- the world 世界

» the Great Wall、the Taj Mahal、the United Nations 等，參見 160 頁〈14 要加 the 的專有名詞〉。

- Is the moon bright tonight?
  今晚的月兒亮不亮？
- "Does the Moon orbit the Earth and the Earth orbit the Sun?" asked my six-year-old brother.
  「月亮繞著地球轉，地球繞著太陽轉嗎？」我六歲大的弟弟問。
  ⮤ 當從天文的角度來談 moon、earth 和 sun 時，這幾個字通常大寫。
- Is the U.S. President going to visit India in July?
  美國總統七月要訪問印度嗎？
  ⮤ president 指「總統」時，要大寫。指「總裁」、「董事長」時，不用大寫。

1 Earth（地球）也有不加冠詞的用法，特別是片語 on earth/Earth。另外，earth 指「泥土」、「陸地」、「人間」時，不要冠詞。

- Who is the tallest woman on earth?
  誰是地球上／世界上最高的女子？

2 上面提及的一些獨一無二的事物，有時可以用 a/an，比較下面例句：

- The sun is hidden behind a cloud. 太陽被一朵雲彩遮住了。
- Is it hard to have fun under a hot sun?
  在火辣辣的太陽下要玩得開心很難嗎？
  ↑ 如果太陽前有一個形容詞，就可以加 a/an。

4 泛指下列事物，要加 the

- the atmosphere 大氣
- the environment 環境
- the climate 氣候
- the weather 天氣
- the sky 天空
- the ground 地面
- the human race 人類
- the sea 大海
- the future 未來
- the past 過去
- the wind 風
- the public 公眾

- The sky suddenly turned dark. 天空突然變得昏暗起來。
  ↑ The sky 也可以看成是獨一無二的事物。
- She loves swimming in the sea. 她喜歡在海裡游泳。

表示這些事物的**某個實例**時，用 a/an。比較下面例句：

- I could hear the wind howling outside.
  我聽見外面的風在咆哮。 → 泛指
- There's a cold wind blowing from the north.
  從北方吹來一股冷風。 → 實例

- Do you know what will happen to me in the future?
  你知道我未來會有什麼遭遇嗎？ → 未來（泛指）
- I hope you have a great future.
  我希望你有一個遠大的前程。 → 前途（實例）

5 形容詞最高級與序數詞，要加 the

在形容詞最高級（oldest、most、best 等）、序數詞（first、second 等），及 only、sole、same、last、next 和 following 等字前面，要加定冠詞 the。

- **Mary lives on the second floor.** 瑪麗住在二樓。
- **Are you the fastest 100-meter sprinter in your school?**
  你是學校最快的一百公尺短跑選手嗎？
- **They have the same name.** 他們的名字一樣。
- **The next message she received was coded text.**
  她收到的下一條消息是密碼文字。

- **You are the only person on earth I've told this story to.**
  這件事我只跟你說過。 → on earth 在這裡指「人間」。

1 second 前面也可以用不定冠詞 a，表示「又一」。

- OK, I'll give you a second chance. 好吧，我再給你一次機會。

2 表示未來式的時間片語「next Friday/week/month/year」等（= the Friday, week, month, year, etc., that comes after this one），next 前**不加定冠詞**，意思是「下星期五／下週／下個月／明年」，與 last Friday/week/month/year（上星期五／上週／上個月／去年）意思相反。例如：

- Next month I am going on a business trip to Bali.
  我下個月要去峇里島出差。

6 「名詞 + of」的介系詞片語，要加 the

the 常與「名詞 + of」形式的介系詞片語連用，**特指**某人或某物，例如：

- the death of the mayor 市長之死
- the beauty of the actress 女演員的美

- the beginning of the tax year 納稅年度的開始
- the end of the year 年底
- the leader of the gang 幫派老大
- the population of the country 該國的人口
- the president of our club 我們俱樂部的會長
- the price of (the) rice 米的價錢
- the sound of gunfire 炮火聲
- the top of the page 這一頁的開頭

the leader of the gang
幫派老大

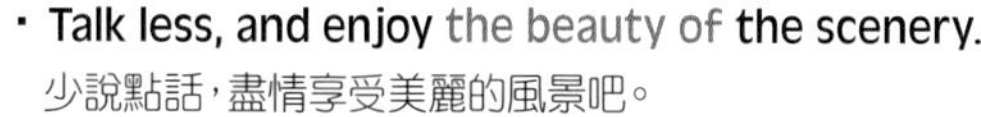

- **Talk less, and enjoy the beauty of the scenery.**
  少說點話，盡情享受美麗的風景吧。

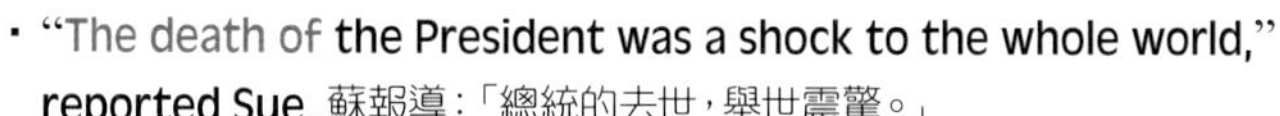

- **"The death of the President was a shock to the whole world," reported Sue.** 蘇報導：「總統的去世，舉世震驚。」

比較下面例句：

- She's a friend of mine. 她是我的一個朋友。　→ 泛指

7 名詞由介系詞片語、分詞片語、子句修飾，要加 the

1 介系詞片語或分詞片語作定語，要置於所修飾的名詞後面，稱為「後置定語」，該名詞（如：NASA conference, young man）前面要用 the。

- **I asked Mary whether she would be attending the NASA conference at 9 a.m. the next day.** 我問瑪麗是否會參加第二天上午九點的太空總署會議。

- **Do you know the young man sitting next to Sue?**
  坐在蘇旁邊的那個年輕男子，你認識嗎？

2 形容詞子句作定語，也要置於所修飾的名詞之後。如果是限定性子句，所修飾的名詞前要用 the。

- **Why don't you tell Dwight the story that you told me last night?**
  你怎麼不跟杜威特講你昨天晚上跟我說的那個故事？
  ↑ 例句中的 that 引導一個限定性形容詞子句，修飾名詞 story。

8 類指的用法，要加 the

1 **the + 形容詞 = 複數名詞**：我們可以在某些形容詞前面加 the 構成複數名詞，指**某一大類的人**或**某一民族**。這類形容詞與 the 結合時，具有**複數**名詞的意義，在句中作主詞時，述語動詞要用**複數**形式。

- the Chinese = the Chinese people 中國人
- the rich = the rich people 富人

- Wise young people always show respect for the old (= the old people). 聰明的年輕人總是會尊重老人。
- The foolish tell lies to the wise. 蠢人對智者撒謊。
  ⮑「the + 形容詞」(the foolish = the foolish people) + 複數動詞 (tell)
- Amy cried as the wounded were being carried into our clinic. 當傷者被抬進我們的診所時，艾咪哭了。
- Bart has found out that the young at heart are always fun to be around. 巴特發現，跟內心充滿朝氣的人在一起總是很愉快。
- The Spanish use a lot of wind power. 西班牙人使用大量的風力發電。

- the aged 老人
- the blind 盲人
- the brave 勇者
- the dead 死者
- the deaf 聾人
- the disabled 身障人士
- the educated 受過教育的人
- the elderly 上了年紀的人
- the free 自由人
- the handicapped 殘疾人
- the homeless 無家可歸的人
- the hungry 飢餓的人
- the injured 傷者
- the oppressed 受迫害的人
- the poor 窮人
- the powerful 掌權者
- the rich 富人
- the sick 病人
- the starving 飢餓者
- the strong 強者
- the uneducated 未受過教育的人
- the unemployed 失業者
- the unknown 無名小卒
- the living 活著的人
- the needy 窮人
- the old 老人
- the wealthy 有錢人
- the wounded 傷患
- the young 年輕人

2 **the + 單數可數名詞（類指）**：定冠詞 the 常與一些**單數可數名詞**連用，表示**類指**（generic）。這種情況在討論科技問題、發明創造時很常見。也可以用完全不加冠詞的複數形式，意思上沒有不同。與連綴動詞 be 連用時，也可以用「a/an + 單數可數名詞」表示某一類的其中一個。

- **She loves living in the age of the computer.** → 類指（generic reference）
  = She loves living in the age of computers. → 泛指（computers in general）
  她喜歡生活在這個電腦的時代裡。
  ↥ the computer 不是指某台電腦，而是泛指整個類屬，所以這句不用 a computer。

- **The cellphone has changed our lives.** → 類指（generic reference）
  = Cellphones have changed our lives. → 泛指（cellphones in general）
  手機改變了我們的生活。 → 這句不能用 a cellphone。

- **Are space elevators the cheapest means of transportation into space?**
  = Is a space elevator the cheapest means of transportation into space?
  = Is the space elevator the cheapest means of transportation into space?
  太空電梯是進入太空最便宜的交通方式嗎？
  ↥ means 意思是「手段」、「方法」，單複數同形。

9 樂器要加 the

談到某人演奏某種樂器，或某人演奏某種樂器的能力時，通常要用 the。

- **She can play the drum, and I can play the guitar.** 他會拉小提琴，我會彈吉他。

play the drum
打鼓

- **Kim is cute when she plays the flute.**
  金姆吹長笛的樣子很可愛。

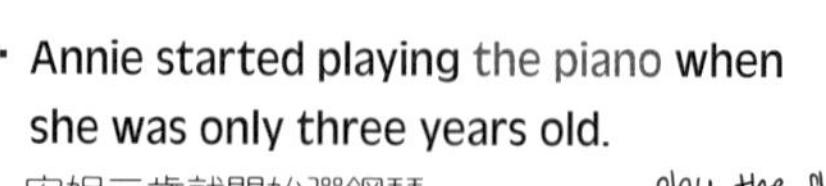

- **Annie started playing the piano when she was only three years old.**
  安妮三歲就開始彈鋼琴。

注意 美國人也常省略 the，用 play piano、play violin、play guitar 等，這在口語中是可以接受的，但是在正式文體中不要省略 the。

10 特定的日期和時間段或特定的歷史事件，要加 the

- the 1990s 20 世紀 90 年代
- the twenty-third century 23 世紀
- the eighties 80 年代
- the Treaty of Versailles 凡爾賽條約
- the Iron Age 鐵器時代
- the Tang Dynasty 唐代

・Mary was born on the first day of the 21st century and wants to live into the 22nd century. 瑪麗生於 21 世紀的第一天，想活到 22 世紀。

11 相對的地理名詞，要加 the

在用 country（鄉村）、sea、seaside、town、coast 和 mountains 這類相對的地理詞語時，即使不特指哪一個海、哪一座山，一般也要用 the。

・I'm going to the country this weekend to see Nancy Wu.
這週末我要去鄉下探望南茜·吳。 → the country = the countryside

・They take most of their vacations on the coast.
他們的假期大都是在沿海地區度過。

・Ray commutes from the suburbs to the city every workday. 每個工作日雷都要從郊區通勤到城裡。

・She prefers the mountains to the sea.
她喜歡山勝過於喜歡海。

commute 通勤

1 但在一些固定詞語裡，sea 前不要 the/a。

- at sea (= in a boat or ship on the sea) 在海上
- go to sea (= become a sailor) 當水手；當船員
- lost at sea (= died at sea or died in the sea) 死於大海

2 比較下面例句：

・He has spent most of his life at sea. 他在海上度過了大半生。

・She wants to live by the sea. 她想在海邊居住。

12 人體部位的名詞，要加 the

表示**人體部位**的名詞出現在表示「**接觸、打擊、疼痛或傷患**」（beat, take, bite, pat, pain, wound）等字的後面時，常用 the，而且這類人體部位的名詞要用**單數**。「the + 人體部位的名詞」，置於介系詞後面，作**介系詞的受詞**。

- pat somebody on the shoulder 拍某人的肩
- a sharp pain in the chest 胸部劇烈疼痛

・**She took me by the arm, and we walked slowly back to the farm.**
她挽著我的手臂，我們慢慢走回農場。

・**With a stick, he beat the wolf on the head.**
他一棍子打在狼的頭上。

・**Did the dog bite Peg on the leg?**
那狗咬了佩格的腿嗎？

・**When I talked to your dad, I tried hard to look him in the eye.**
當我跟你爸爸說話時，我盡量直視他。

談及**某人自己的身體部位**時，通常用**代名詞所有格**形式，而不用 the。「代名詞所有格 + 人體部位的名詞」，在句中作**動詞的受詞**。

・Sam was ready to dive, and Kim turned her head to look at him. 山姆準備好了要跳水，金姆轉過頭去看他。
↳ 不說 turned the head。

・Did you twist your ankle in that hole?
你是在那個洞裡扭傷了腳踝嗎？
↳ 不說 twist the ankle。

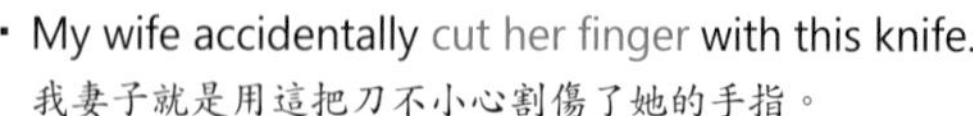

・My wife accidentally cut her finger with this knife.
我妻子就是用這把刀不小心割傷了她的手指。
↳ 不說 cut the finger。

・How did Peg break her leg? 佩格是怎麼骨折的？
↳ 不說 break the leg。

13 與 the 連用的慣用語

- at the same time 同時
- at the sight of 一看見……
- at/in the beginning 一開始
- at/in the end 最後
- by the month 按月計算
- by the pound 按磅計算
  ↑ by + the + 計量單位名詞(按……計算)
- by the way 順便說說
- go to the ballet 看芭蕾舞
- go to the movies 看電影
- go to the opera 看歌劇
- go to the theater 看戲;看電影
- in the afternoon 下午
- in the country/countryside 在鄉間
- in the day/daytime 白天
- in the distance 在遠處
- in the east 在東邊
- in the evening 晚上
- in the middle of 在……當中
- in the morning 早上
- in the north 在北邊
- in the way 妨礙地
- news on the Internet 網上新聞
- news on the radio 電臺新聞
- on the air 在播送中
- on the contrary 正相反
- on the left 在左邊
- on the one hand 一方面
  ↑ 口語中可省略 the,說成 on one hand。
- on the other hand 另一方面
- on the right 在右邊
- on the way 在路上
- the other day 前幾天
- tell the truth 說實話

- Kay bought a new radio yesterday. 昨天凱買了一台新收音機。
- I heard the news on the radio. 我從收音機廣播裡聽到了這則消息。

- Is there a theater in this small town? 這座小城市有劇院嗎? → 一棟建築物
- Amy hasn't been to the theater on Tenth Street for ages.
  艾咪好久沒有去十街的那家劇院了。 → 某個特定的劇院
- Dwight goes to the movie theater/the cinema almost every Saturday night. 杜威特幾乎每一個星期六晚上都要去電影院看電影。
  ↑ 泛指電影院(表示「去看電影」)
  ↑ 在泛指 movie theater (= cinema)、opera、theater 時,用 the。

- *Carmen* is a well-known opera. 《卡門》是一部有名的歌劇。 → 一場歌劇

- She goes to the opera at least once a month.
  她每月至少要去歌劇院看一次歌劇。 → 泛指歌劇院（表示「去看歌劇」）
- I enjoy opera. 我喜歡歌劇。 → 歌劇藝術（表示某種藝術形式）

14 要加 the 的專有名詞

1 地理名稱，要加 the：在下面這些名稱前，應該用 the。

①	河川	• the Nile 尼羅河 • the Amazon 亞馬遜河 • the Yellowstone River 黃石河
②	運河	• the Suez Canal 蘇伊士運河 • the Panama Canal 巴拿馬運河
③	流域 / 盆地	• the Amazon Basin 亞馬遜河流域 • the Thames Basin 泰晤士河流域
④	丘陵	• the Black Hills 黑崗
⑤	山脈 複數形式	• the Himalayas 喜馬拉雅山脈 • the Andes 安地斯山脈 • the Rocky Mountains 洛磯山脈 • the Alps 阿爾卑斯山脈 ↳ 注意 如果不是山脈，是山峰（mount），就不用 the。例如：Mount Everest（聖母峰）。
⑥	沙漠	• the Sahara (Desert) 撒哈拉沙漠 • the Gobi Desert 戈壁沙漠
⑦	海	• the Mediterranean (Sea) 地中海 • the South China Sea 南海
⑧	大洋	• the Pacific Ocean 太平洋 • the Atlantic Ocean 大西洋
⑨	海灣	• the Persian Gulf 波斯灣 • the Gulf of Mexico 墨西哥海灣
⑩	海峽	• the English Channel 英吉利海峽 • the Taiwan Straits 臺灣海峽 • the Straits of Gibraltar 直布羅陀海峽

11	群島 複數形式	● the Hawaiian Islands 夏威夷群島 ● the British Isles 不列顛群島 ● the West Indies 西印度群島 ● the Florida Keys 佛羅里達群島 ↳ 注意 如果不是群島，就不要 the。例如：Hispaniola Island 伊斯帕尼奧拉島（屬西印度群島，即海地島 Haiti）。

- **Have you ever canoed on the Mississippi River?**
  你有没有在密西西比河上划過獨木舟？
- **Is Mont Blanc the highest mountain in the Alps?**
  白朗峰是阿爾卑斯山脈的最高峰嗎？ → 山峰，不用 the；山脈，要用 the。

2 複數形式的名稱（國名、姓氏、隊名），要加 the：除了山脈和群島，其他複數形式的專有名詞（如：國名、姓氏、隊名），也要用 the。

1	國名	● the Bahamas 巴哈馬（位於西印度群島） ● the Netherlands 荷蘭 ● the Philippines 菲律賓 ● the United States (of America) 美國
2	姓氏	● the Browns 布朗家 ● the Wilsons 威爾森家
3	隊名	● the Miami Dolphins 邁阿密海豚隊（美式足球隊）

- **Kay's sister has been hiking and camping with the Johnsons for ten days.** 凱的妹妹跟詹森一家徒步旅行和野營已經十天了。
  ↳ the Johnsons 指 Johnson 一家（the Johnson family）。
  ↳ the + 複數姓氏：表示某一家人。
- **Dwight had a great time at the Browns' last night.** 昨晚杜威特在布朗家過得很快活。
  ↳ 這裡的 the + 複數姓所有格形式（the Browns'），表示省略了 home、house 或 apartment 等。
  ↳ 注意 複數姓氏前必須要 the，無論這個複數姓是所有格形式還是一般形式，都不能刪除 the。

相對於姓氏用法，如果是用名字，就不要 the。比例用法：

- at Mary's 在瑪麗家
- at Mike's 在邁克家

▪ I had a great afternoon at Annie's.
我在安妮家過了一個非常愉快的下午。

3 大型建築物名稱要加 the：飯店、博物館、紀念館（碑）、劇院、畫廊等供大眾使用的建築物，以及橋樑、塔、金字塔、雕像等大型建築物的名稱前面，要有 the。

① 飯店／餐館
- the Holiday Inn 假日酒店
- the Hilton Hotel 希爾頓飯店

② 博物館／美術館
- the Science Museum 科學館
- the British Museum 大英博物館
- the National Gallery 國家美術館（倫敦）
- the Lincoln Memorial 林肯紀念館

③ 劇院／影院
- the Globe Theater 環球劇院
- the Kennedy Center for the Performing Arts 甘迺迪表演藝術中心

比較
- the Whitehall 懷特豪爾劇院 → 劇院名要用 the。
- Whitehall 倫敦官府大道 → 街名不用 the。

④ 大橋
- the Golden Gate Bridge 金門大橋

⑤ 塔樓
- the Eiffel Tower 埃菲爾鐵塔
- the Tower of London 倫敦塔

⑥ 其他建築
- the Empire State Building 帝國大廈
- the Forbidden City 紫禁城
- the Great Pyramid 吉薩大金字塔
- the Great Wall 萬里長城
- the Statue of Liberty 自由女神像
- the Taj Mahal 泰姬瑪哈陵
- the Town Hall 市政廳
- the White House 白宮

NOTE

1 以**人名所有格形式**呈現的建築物（商店、餐館、飯店等）名稱，不要加 the。

- Dennis's Hotel 丹尼斯飯店
- McDonald's 麥當勞
- St. John's Church 聖約翰教堂
- St. Paul's Cathedral 聖保羅大教堂

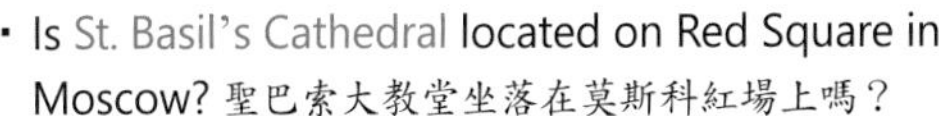

• Is St. Basil's Cathedral located on Red Square in Moscow? 聖巴索大教堂坐落在莫斯科紅場上嗎？

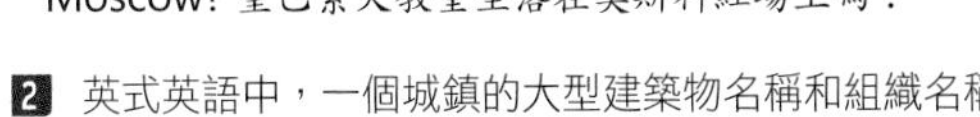

2 英式英語中，一個城鎮的大型建築物名稱和組織名稱前，有時不用 the。但同樣的情況下，美式英語常用 the。

英式
- Canterbury Cathedral 坎特伯雷大教堂
- Bristol Zoo 布里斯托爾動物園
- Manchester City Council 曼徹斯特市議會

美式
- the Presbyterian Church 基督教長老會
- the San Diego Zoo 聖地牙哥動物園
- the Detroit City Council 底特律市議會

4 船名和火車名，要加 the。

- the Queen Mary 瑪莉皇后號
- the Titanic 鐵達尼號
- the Golden Arrow 黄金之箭
- the Orient Express 東方特快車

5 報紙名稱，要加 the。

- The Times 泰晤士報
- The Washington Post 華盛頓郵報
- The New York Times 紐約時報
- the Financial Times 金融時報

⌊ 如果報刊名稱本身就含有定冠詞 the，需要大寫 The。

6 世界上的大區域名稱，要加 the。

- the West 西方
- the Far East 遠東
- the Middle East 中東
- the East 東方

7 政府部門、政治機構、著名的組織、銀行等名稱前，要加 the。

1 政府部門或政府機構的名稱前，通常要 the（包括縮寫名稱）：

- the CIA (the Central Intelligence Agency)（美國）中央情報局
- the FBI（美國）聯邦調查局
- the French Embassy 法國大使館
- the House of Commons 下議院
- the House of Representatives 眾議院
- the Labor Party 工黨
- the Library of Congress 國會圖書館
- the Ministry of Education 教育部
- the Senate 參議院
- the Supreme Court〔美〕聯邦或大多數州的最高法院
- the U.S. Department of State 美國國務院
- the U.S. Justice Department 美國司法部
- the White House 白宮
- the New York City Police Department (the NYCPD) 紐約市警察局

・ **She is working for** the Ministry of Education. 她在教育部工作。

2 著名組織的名稱前，要加 the（包括縮寫名稱）：

- the BBC (the British Broadcasting Corporation) 英國廣播公司
- the VOA (the Voice of America) 美國之音
- the Red Cross 紅十字會
- the United Nations (the UN) 聯合國
- the World Trade Organization (the WTO) 世貿組織

・ The BBC **reported on the huge wind farm in the North Sea.**
英國廣播公司對北海的超大風力發電廠做了報導。

3 銀行的名稱前，通常要 the：

- the Industrial and Commercial Bank of China 中國工商銀行
- the Development Bank of Singapore 新加坡發展銀行
- the Toronto-Dominion Bank 多倫多道明銀行

比較 銀行如果是以創辦人的名字而命名，則不加 the，而在名字後面加 's 或 s。

- Lloyds Bank 羅意德銀行
- Barclays Bank 柏克萊銀行

1 任何以 of 片語構成的地名、建築名，都要加 the。例如：

- the Bank of England 英格蘭銀行
- the Gulf of Mexico 墨西哥灣
- the Houses of Parliament 國會大廈
- the Tower of London 倫敦塔
- the Museum of Modern Art 現代藝術博物館
- the University of London 倫敦大學
- the Statue of Liberty 自由女神
- the Rock of Gibraltar 直布羅陀巨巖

2 例外：

- Bank of America 美國銀行
- Bank of China 中國銀行

15 公司名稱是否要加 the？

1 如果公司名稱裡含有 company 這個字，就要用 the；反之，如果沒有，就不用 the。

- General Motors 通用汽車
- Kodak 柯達公司
- Sony 索尼公司
- British Airways 英國航空公司
- the General Electric Company = General Electric 美國通用電氣公司

- **She thinks the General Electric Company is good at developing new technology.** 她認為美國通用電氣公司對發展新科技很在行。

2 公司名稱是**縮寫形式**，不用 the。

- ABC 美國廣播公司
- GE 美國通用電氣公司
- CBS 哥倫比亞廣播公司
- IBM 國際商務機器公司
- CNN 美國有線電視新聞網
- ICI 英國帝國化學工業公司
- NBC 美國全國廣播公司
- KLM 荷蘭航空公司

- **ABC showed a movie about living under the sea.**
美國廣播公司放了一部關於在海底生活的影片。

3 注意 公司名稱的縮寫形式，與政府部門、政治機構的縮寫詞有區別：

① 公司名稱的縮寫形式，都不用 the。

② 政府部門、政治機構的縮寫詞如果**不讀成一個字，就要用** the（如：the CIA）；**讀成一個字**，就**不加 the**（如：NATO）。

- We stood under a huge wind turbine made by General Electric.
  ↑ 公司名稱若省略了 company，不用 the。
  = We stood under a huge wind turbine made by the General Electric Company.
  ↑ 公司名稱包含了 Company，要用 the。
  = We stood under a huge wind turbine made by GE.
  ↑ 公司名稱的縮寫形式，不用 the。
  我們站在一個由美國通用電器公司生產的巨大的風力發電機下面。

- I will go on a long vacation, and after that I'll go to work for the Federal Bureau of Investigation.
  = I will go on a long vacation, and after that I'll go to work for the FBI.
  我要度一個長假，然後就去美國聯邦調查局工作。
  ↑ 政府部門的縮寫詞，不讀成一個字，要用 the。

- Is the headquarters of the North Atlantic Treaty Organization in Brussels, Belgium? → 政治機構名稱前要用 the。
  = Is the headquarters of NATO in Brussels, Belgium?
  北大西洋公約組織的總部是在比利時布魯塞爾嗎？
  ↑ 政治機構的縮寫詞讀成一個字，就不加 the。
  ↑ headquarters 指所在地（location）時，可以接單數動詞，也可以接複數動詞，但美式英語通常用單數。。

零冠詞

1 一些專有名詞不加冠詞

1 一些地點名稱不加冠詞。

許多地點名稱是由兩個詞構成，而第一個詞往往是人名（Kennedy）或地名（Canterbury），所以這些名稱前面一般不加 the。例如：

1 機場（地名／人名 + Airport）

- Oxford Airport 牛津機場
- John F. Kennedy International Airport 約翰．甘迺迪國際機場
- Vancouver International Airport 溫哥華國際機場

2 教堂（地名 + Cathedral/Abbey/Monastery）

- Canterbury Cathedral 坎特伯里大教堂
- Westminster Abbey 威斯特敏斯特寺院（西敏寺）
- Zen Mountain Monastery 禪宗山修道院（宗教名 + Monastery）

例外 如果用 of 連接的教堂名稱，就要用 the，例如：

- the Abbey of Cluny 克倫尼修道院
- the Monastery of Koya-San 高野山僧院

比較 「地名（形容詞）+ Church」前，常用 the，例如：

- the Roman Catholic Church 羅馬天主教會
- the Atammayatarama Buddhist Monastery 阿塔瑪雅他拉瑪佛教寺

3 湖泊（地名 + Lake；Lake + 地名）

- Deer Lake 鹿湖
- Lake Michigan 密西根湖

例外 如果是複數 Lakes，或「兩個以上的字 + Lake」，就需要 the，例如：

- the Great Lakes 北美五大湖
- the Great Salt Lake 大鹽湖

④ 公園（地名／人名 + Park）

- Disney World 迪士尼世界
- New York Central Park 紐約中央公園
- Hyde Park 海德公園
- Yellowstone National Park 黃石國家公園

⑤ 大學院校（地名 + University/College/Institute）

- Cambridge University 劍橋大學
- Louisiana College 路易斯安那學院

例外 如果用 of 連接的大學名稱，就要用 the，例如：

- the University of London 倫敦大學
- the Industrial Institute of Madrid 馬德里工業學院

⑥ 火車站（地名 + Station）

- Oxford Station 牛津車站
- Glasgow Central Station 格拉斯哥中央車站
- Saigon Railway Station 西貢火車站
- Vancouver Train Station 溫哥華火車站

例外 許多美國人會在「地名 + Station」前面，加上 the，例如：

- the Taipei Railway Station 臺北火車站

⑦ 街道、路、廣場（地名／序數詞／人名 + Street/Avenue/Road/Square）

- Tenth Street 第十街道
- Fifth Avenue 第五大街
- Washington Street 華盛頓街
- County Road 510 第 510 郡道
- Wall Street 華爾街
- Times Square（美國紐約）時代廣場

例外 the High Street 高街

⑧ 山峰（Mount + 地名）

- Mount Qomolangma 珠穆朗瑪峰
- Mount Kenya 肯亞山

⑨ 城鎮（Cities/Towns）

- Bangkok 曼谷
- Taipei 臺北
- New York 紐約
- Cairo 開羅

⑩ 州、省（States/Provinces）

- Florida 佛羅里達
- British Columbia（加拿大）不列顛哥倫比亞省

⑪ 洲（Continents）

- Africa 非洲
- Asia 亞洲
- North America 北美洲
- Antarctica 南極洲
- Europe 歐洲
- South America 南美洲
- Australia 澳洲

例外 如果洲名包含 continent 這個字，就需要 the。這時的 the 不是修飾大洲名稱，而是修飾 continent 這個字。其寫法變成「**the + 地名（形容詞）+ Continent**」，例如：

- the African Continent 非洲大陸
- the Australian Continent 澳洲大陸
- the Asian Continent 亞洲大陸
- the European Continent 歐洲大陸
- the North American Continent 北美洲大陸
- the Antarctic Continent 南極洲大陸
- the South American Continent 南美洲大陸

⑫ 國家（Countries）

- America 美國
- Germany 德國
- Japan 日本
- Great Britain 大不列顛
- New Zealand 紐西蘭
- South Africa 南非

例外 帶有 Republic、Kingdom 等字的國家名之前，以及**複數形式**的國家名之前，要加 the，例如：

- the United Kingdom (= the UK) 英聯合王國
- the Netherlands 荷蘭
- the Dominican Republic 多明尼加共和國
- the United States of America (= the USA) 美利堅合眾國

» 參見 161 頁〈2 複數形式的名稱（國名、姓氏、隊名），要加 the〉。

⑬ 海灣（地名 ＋ Bay/Harbor）

- San Francisco Bay 三藩市灣
- Pearl Harbor 珍珠港

例外 如果用 of 連接的海灣名稱，就要用 the，例如：

- the Bay of Bengal 孟加拉灣
- the Bay of Fundy 芬地灣

- **Hi, I'm Dan, and I'm from** Japan. 你好，我是丹，來自日本。
- **Have you ever swum in** Lake Michigan? 你曾在密西根湖遊過泳嗎？
- **Kay and I want to go to** Disney World **this coming May.**
凱和我今年五月想去迪士尼世界。

2 人名、語言、節日名稱不加冠詞。

- John 約翰
- Dennis 丹尼斯
- English 英文
- French 法文
- New Year's Day 元旦
- Father's Day 父親節
- Christmas Day 聖誕節
- National Day 國慶日

例外 the Fourth of July（美國獨立紀念日）需要用 the，例如：

- I will fly to Rome on the 4th of July.
  我要在 7 月 4 號美國獨立紀念日時飛往羅馬。

例外 中國傳統節日通常要加定冠詞 the，如：

- the Spring Festival 春節
- the Dragon Boat Festival 端午節

the Dragon Boat Festival
端午節

- **Can Trish read and write in Polish?** 翠西能讀寫波蘭文嗎？
- **My son Steve is looking forward to New Year's Eve.**
  我的兒子史蒂夫期待新年除夕的到來。
- **"Is New Year's Day celebrated on January 1 all over the world?" asked little Kay.** 小凱問：「全世界都是在一月一號慶祝新年嗎？」

NOTE

1 比較 French（法語）與 the French（法國人）

- I'm studying French. 我在學法語。→ 這裡的 French 指的是語言。
- The French are designing a new spacecraft to transport people from the Moon to Neptune.
  法國人在設計一艘新的太空船，要把人從月球載到海王星去。
  ↑ The French 指的是民族。

2 New Year（新年）要用 the：

- We want to have a party to celebrate the New Year.
  我們想舉行一次聚會來慶祝新年。
  ↑ 慶祝新年：英式用法中，the 可加、可不加。
- Get rid of your worries and fears, and start fresh in the New Year! 拋掉你的憂慮和恐懼，在新的一年開始新的生活。
  ↑ 指第二年開始，是特指，要有 the。

Diving Deep Into English 29 人名要使用冠詞的情況

❶ 與**形容詞**連用，描述某個人或某人的工作時，可以加 the：

- the American writer Ernest Miller Hemingway
  美國作家歐尼斯特．米勒．海明威
- the late Jerry Bloom 已故的傑瑞．布盧姆

❷ 當兩個名字相同，而想指明所談論的是哪一個人時，可以加 the：

- **That's the Sue Smith I dated in college.**
  那位就是在大學時代跟我約會過的蘇·史密斯。

❸ 複數姓氏前面要加 the（參見 161 頁〈2 複數形式的名稱（國名、姓氏、隊名）要加 the〉：

- **The Browns sold their house today.**
  今天布朗家把他們的房子賣了。

❹ 在你**不認識的人**的名字前面，可以用 a/an，比較下面的例句：

- **There's a Ms. Sue Powers on the phone, and she wants to talk to you.**
  一位叫蘇·鮑爾斯的女士打電話來，說要找你。
  ↳ 意謂著說話者以前沒有聽說過 Ms. Sue Powers。
- **Sue Powers is on the phone, and she wants to talk to you.** 蘇·鮑爾斯打電話來，要找你。
  ↳ 意謂著說話者認識 Sue Powers。

3 月份和星期名稱前，不加冠詞。

- January 一月
- May 五月
- September 九月
- Sunday 星期天
- Monday 星期一
- Thursday 星期四

- **Remember that Peter will visit you in September.**
  要記得彼德九月會去找你。

若月份和星期名稱的前面有**形容詞**修飾，可以用 a/an。若這些名稱後面有**介系詞片語**或**形容詞子句**修飾，就可用定冠詞 the。

- Are you going fishing with Kay on Saturday?
  = Are you going fishing with Kay this Saturday?
  你星期六要和凱一起去釣魚嗎？ → 指下一個星期六。
- Kay and I first met on a wet Saturday in May.
  凱和我初次見面是在五月一個多雨的星期六。
  ↑ 指某個星期六，不是哪個特定的星期六（星期的名稱前有形容詞修飾）。
- She arrived early in the morning on the Saturday of my high school graduation. 她是在我高中畢業典禮的那個星期六一大早到達的。
  ↑ 確切說明是哪個星期六（星期的名稱後有介系詞片語修飾）。
- One day, in a very hot June, Kay and I sang a tune and got married at noon. 一個炎熱六月的某天中午，凱和我先唱了一曲，然後就結婚了。
  ↑ 月份的名稱前有形容詞修飾。

4 太空船（spacecraft）前不要冠詞。

- Challenger 挑戰者號
- Apollo 13 阿波羅十三號

2 三餐、體育運動、學科，不加冠詞

1	三餐	• breakfast 早餐 • dinner 晚餐	• lunch 午餐 • supper 晚餐
2	運動	• basketball 籃球 • baseball 棒球	• soccer 足球 • volleyball 排球
3	學科	• education 教育學 • economics 經濟學	• math 數學 • physics 物理學

- **Is basketball a popular game with young people in St. Paul?**
  在聖保羅市，年輕人流行打籃球嗎？
- **Does Kay play soccer after breakfast every day?**
  凱每天吃完早餐都要踢足球嗎？
- **Are Sue and you going to study kung fu?** 蘇和你要學中國功夫嗎？

- I don't like philosophy, biology, and psychology.
  我不喜歡哲學、生物學和心理學。

比較：如果學科後面有以 of 引導的**介系詞片語**或**形容詞子句**作為修飾語時，就要用冠詞 the，例如：

- the philosophy of science 科學原理
- the philosophy of mathematics 數學原理

- Are you interested in the philosophy of Plato?
  你對柏拉圖的哲學感興趣嗎？ → 特指

Diving Deep Into English 30 三餐與冠詞的連用

❶ **泛指**一天的幾頓餐，不用冠詞 the。

- **Dee, breakfast is ready.** 蒂，早餐準備好了。 → 泛指
- **What are we going to have for dinner?** 我們晚餐吃什麼？ → 泛指

❷ **特指**某人提供的具體一餐時，通常要用 the。

- **Thank you very much for the dinner.** 非常感謝你的晚餐。 → 特指
- **I really enjoyed the lunch Dee made for me.**
  蒂幫我做的那頓午餐真的很好吃。 → 特指

❸ 三餐前面有**形容詞**修飾，說明是「怎麼樣的一餐」時，可用不定冠詞 a。句型：a + 形容詞 + 三餐

- a relaxed lunch 一頓輕鬆的午餐
- a wonderful dinner 一頓美好的晚餐
- a French breakfast 一頓法式早餐
- a late breakfast 一頓晚吃的早餐

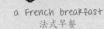

a French breakfast
法式早餐

❹ 表示為**某特別事件**而辦的**正式晚餐**或**午餐**，可用 a dinner 或 a lunch。

- **We're going to have a dinner to welcome Coco back to Chicago.**
  我們要舉行一次晚宴，歡迎可可回到芝加哥。

3 在「名詞 + 基數詞」結構前面，不加冠詞

- Platform 4 第四月台
- Section 2 第二段
- Room 258 第 258 號房
- page 50 第 50 頁
  ↑ size 和 page 要小寫。
- Gate 7 七號門
- size 44 尺寸 44 號

- **Our train leaves from** Platform 4. 我們的火車在四號月臺發車。
- **Do you have these shoes in** size 42? 這雙鞋有 42 號的嗎？

4 許多抽象名詞，不加冠詞

- anger 憤怒
- attention 注意力
- hatred 憎恨
- liberty 自由
- love 愛
- nature 自然
- space 太空
- society 社會
- strength 力量
- virtue 美德
- warmth 溫暖
- wisdom 智慧

- **I'll mention a simple fact: Children need** love **and** attention.
  我要提及一個簡單的事實：孩子需要愛和關心。

如果抽象名詞後面有 of 引導的**介系詞片語**或**形容詞子句**作修飾語，就要有 the。參見 21 頁〈3 抽象名詞〉。

- Ann began to sob while begging on her knees, but she could not appease the anger of the mob.
  安跪著求情時哭了起來，可是她還是無法平息暴民的憤怒。
  ↑ 抽象名詞 anger 被 of 引導的介系詞片語（of the mob）修飾，所以前面要加 the。

5 （泛指）不可數名詞和複數名詞，不加冠詞

泛指某些事物和人（不可數名詞和複數名詞）時，不加冠詞。

- **Bart loves** art. 巴特喜歡藝術。
- **Mom loves** coffee, **and Dad loves** tea. 媽媽喜歡喝咖啡，爸爸喜歡喝茶。
- **We cannot be in a good mood without** food.
  沒得吃的話，我們的心情也好不起來。

- She wants to be a mermaid, wearing jewelry and swimming freely in the sea. 她想當一隻美人魚，戴著珠寶首飾在海裡自由自在地游泳。
- She's afraid of dogs. 她怕狗。 → 這裡的狗是泛指。

Diving Deep Into English 31 （特指）不可數名詞和複數名詞加 the

❶ 當不可數名詞和複數名詞後面有**介系詞片語**或**形容詞子句**修飾時，要用 the，這個不可數名詞或複數名詞就具有**特定**的意義。比較：

- Does Nick like music? 尼克喜歡音樂嗎？ → 泛指
- Sid loves the music of Madrid. 席德喜歡馬德里的音樂。
  ↑ 特定地點的音樂；music 由 of 引導的介系詞片語修飾。
- My grandma loves the music from the 1930s.
  我奶奶喜歡 20 世紀 30 年代的音樂。
  ↑ 特定時段的音樂；music 由 from 引導的介系詞片語修飾。
- The music Eve played on New Year's Eve sounded terrific to Steve. 史蒂夫覺得伊芙在新年除夕演奏的音樂美妙極了。
  ↑ 特定人物演奏的音樂；music 由形容詞子句修飾。

- Can sugar make Pat fat? 糖會使派特發福嗎？ → 泛指
- The sugar Pat ate last year made her fat.
  派特去年吃的糖害她發福了。 → 特指

- People love money and honey. 人都愛錢和蜂蜜。 → 泛指
- The people at the Bunny Inn love money and honey.
  兔子酒店的人喜歡錢和蜂蜜。 → 特指

- She loves flowers. 她愛花。 → 泛指花朵
- The flowers you sent me are very beautiful.
  你寄給我的花真漂亮。 → 特定的花朵

❷ 當不可數名詞和複數名詞指**特定**的、在聽話者心目中**明確**的人或物時，要加 the。

- Children love to play. 兒童喜歡玩耍。 → 泛指所有的兒童。

- I took the children to the science museum today.
  今天我帶孩子去了科學博物館。　→ 特指的一群孩子，也許是說話者的孩子。

- "Where's the sugar and where's the ham?" asked Uncle Sam.
  「糖和火腿在哪裡？」山姆大叔問。
- Pam ate all the sugar and all the ham. 潘姆把所有的糖和火腿都吃光了。

❸ 泛指和特指之間的區別有時並不明顯。比較下面例句：

- Nick enjoys listening to modern music, but I like to listen to classical music. 尼克喜歡聽現代音樂，而我卻喜歡聽古典音樂。
  ↳ modern music、classical music，雖不是指所有的音樂，但仍然是泛指（可稱「半泛指」），不能與 the 連用。
- The music played by Nick today made Amy sick.
  尼克今天演奏的音樂使艾咪想吐。　→ 特指

- Life has changed a lot in the last 20 years.
  最近的二十年來，生活改變了很多。　→ 泛指
- It's hard to imagine life two hundred years from today.
  很難想像 200 年後的生活。　→ 半泛指
- Amy is learning a lot about the life of her Aunt Lily.
  艾咪對她姑媽莉莉的生平瞭解了很多。　→ 特定人的生平

泛指
- She likes coffee. 她喜歡咖啡。
- I enjoy working with people. 我喜歡我的工作與人打交道。

半泛指
- She likes strong black coffee. 她喜歡濃烈的黑咖啡。
- I enjoy working with friendly and lively people.
  我喜歡跟友善、活躍的人一起工作。

特指
- She liked the coffee you made yesterday.
  她喜歡你昨天煮的咖啡。
- I enjoyed the friendly and lively people I worked with yesterday. 我喜歡昨天跟我一起工作的那些友善、活躍的人們。

Diving Deep Into English 32 society、nature、space、industry、business，加不加冠詞？

當 society、nature、space、industry、business 具有**泛指**的意義時，不要冠詞。但當這些字具有**特指**的、**具體**的意義時，就要用冠詞 the。

- **Do you want to be respected by polite society?**
  你希望受到上流社會的尊重嗎？
  ⤷ society 在這裡是不可數名詞，不要冠詞，泛指「我們生活在其中的這個社會」。

- **She loves the variety found in the film society.** 她喜歡電影界的多樣化。
  ⤷ society 在這裡是可數名詞，意思是「社團、協會」，要用定冠詞指特定的社團、協會，例如：the local history society（地方史協會）。

比較
- an industrial society 一個工業社會
- a multicultural society 一個融合多元文化的社會
  ⤷ society 在這裡是可數名詞，指的是一種特殊的社會形態。

- **Nature does not provide everything for the king.**
  大自然並沒有為國王提供一切。
  ⤷ Nature 在這裡是不可數名詞，不要冠詞，意思是「大自然、自然界」，包括所有的生物以及陸地和海洋。

- **The violent nature of a tornado makes me afraid.**
  龍捲風狂暴的特性使我很害怕。
  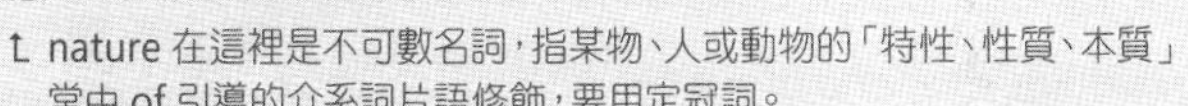
  ⤷ nature 在這裡是不可數名詞，指某物、人或動物的「特性、性質、本質」；常由 of 引導的介系詞片語修飾，要用定冠詞。

- **Humans had just taken another step in exploring space.** 人類朝太空探索又邁進了一步。
  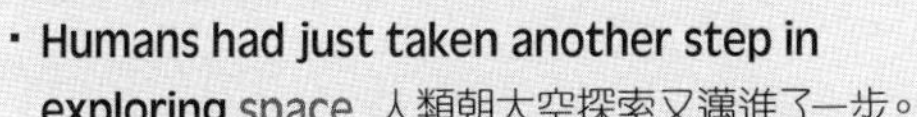
  ⤷ space 在這裡是不可數名詞，不要冠詞，意思是「宇宙、太空」。例如：
  - humanity's grand adventure into space 人類偉大的太空冒險
  - live in space 在太空中生活

to explore space

- **The firecrackers sounded very loud in the confined space.**
  鞭炮在這狹窄的地方顯得很響亮。
  ⤷ space 在這裡是不可數名詞，指特定的空間，而不是太空。

- **Overall, industry has not done well during the last eight months, but the entertainment industry has done great.**
  大體上這八個月以來，工業進展不太好，但娛樂業的發展卻非常好。
  ↳ 泛指 industry 時，不用 the。特指某個行業時，需要用 the。例如：
  - the automobile industry 汽車業
  - the real estate industry 不動產業

- **My daughter is going to college to study business.**
  我女兒要上大學攻讀商務。 → 泛指

- **I believe that the space transportation business will continue to grow in the future.**
  我相信太空運輸業未來會繼續發展。 → 特定的行業

6 所有格形式的人名和專有名詞，或有其他限定詞修飾的名詞，不加冠詞

1 所有格形式的人名和專有名詞不加 the 或 a/an，因為所有格形式本來就屬於限定詞，再用冠詞作限定就重複了。

- Mary's computer 瑪麗的電腦
- Shakespeare's plays 莎士比亞寫的戲劇

- **I borrowed Jim's car and drove to Kim's.**
  我跟吉姆借車，開去金姆家。
  ↳ 人名 Jim、Kim 的所有格（Jim's, Kim's）前面不能用 a 或 the。

- **Are any of Russia's factories producing this type of electric car?**
  有沒有任何一家俄國工廠在生產這類的電動汽車？
  ↳ 專有名詞 Russia 的所有格（Russia's）前面不能用 the。

姓氏的複數前需要用 the，無論是所有格形式還是一般形式。

- the Browns = the Brown family 布朗一家
- the Browns' friends = the Brown family's friends 布朗一家的朋友

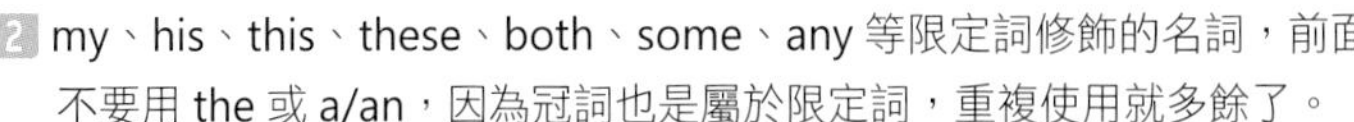

2 my、his、this、these、both、some、any 等限定詞修飾的名詞，前面不要用 the 或 a/an，因為冠詞也是屬於限定詞，重複使用就多餘了。

- **I don't want to hear any excuses.** 我不想聽到任何藉口。
  ↳ 限定詞 any 前面不能有 the 或 an/a。
- **Both Ann and Dan are on the Internet.** 安和丹都在上網。
  ↳ 限定詞 both 前面不能有 the。
- **Kay doesn't have any melons today.** 凱今天沒有甜瓜了。
  ↳ 複數名詞 melons 前面有限定詞 any，不要再用 the。

7 季節名稱，不加冠詞

1 季節名稱前通常不用 the。若表示某個**特定**的春天、冬天等，才加 the。

- spring 春
- summer 夏
- fall (autumn) 秋
- winter 冬

- **When spring comes, birds sing and plum flowers blossom.**
  春天來了，鳥兒歌唱，梅花開放。 → 泛指春天
- **That small asteroid called Kate might hit the Earth in the spring of 2038.** 那個叫凱特的小行星可能會在 2038 年的春天擊中地球。 → 特指的春天

2 與介系詞 in 連用，作**泛指**用時，英式季節名稱前可以加 the，也可以不加 the，而美式常用 the。作**特指**用時，必須用 the。唯獨 fall（秋天）與 in 連用時，一定要加 the。

- in (the) spring 在春天
- in (the) summer 在夏天
- in the fall 在秋天
- in (the) winter 在冬天

- **She loves to go sailing in (the) summer.** 她喜歡在夏天航海。 → 泛指
- **In (the) winter, we usually go to visit Aunt Ann in Japan.**
  冬天時，我們通常去日本拜訪安姑姑。 → 泛指
  ↳ 注意 美式無論泛指或特指都常用 the。
- **Is Paul going back to Moscow in the fall?** 保羅秋天要回莫斯科嗎？
  ↳ in the fall 是固定片語。

- "My baby will be born in the summer," explained Jill.
  潔兒解釋說：「我的孩子將在夏天出生。」
  ↑ 特指下一個夏天。

3 用於 it is 或 it was 等之後，季節名稱前通常不加 the。

- It will soon be winter again! 冬天又要來臨了！

4 表示某個有特色的季節或節日時，用 a/an。

- That was a summer/a Christmas Day I'll never forget.
  那是一個我永遠也不會忘記的夏天／聖誕節。

8 獨一無二的職位，不加冠詞

表示獨一無二的職位名詞，用於動詞 be、become、appoint、elect、make 等後面，不加冠詞。

- Brenda Beam was selected to be captain of the women's volleyball team. 布蘭達·畢姆被選為女子排球隊的隊長。
- Why was Jill Nation elected president of that corporation?
  為什麼吉爾·奈遜被推選為那家企業的總裁？

9 不加冠詞的慣用語

1 **普通可數名詞在一些慣用語中不用冠詞。**

a 談論以某種交通方式旅行，不要 the。下面的名詞與 by 連用，不加冠詞。

- by air 搭飛機／走空運
  ↑ air 是不可數名詞
- by bike 騎自行車
- by boat 搭小船
- by bus 搭公車
- by car 搭小汽車
- by ferry 搭渡船
- by sea 用海運
  ↑ sea 是不可數名詞
- by ship 搭船
- by subway 搭地鐵
- by tram 搭電車
- by train 搭火車
- by taxi/by cab 搭計程車

- Does Gus go to work on foot or by bus? 加斯走路還是搭公車去上班？
  ↑ 注意 走路是 on foot，不能用 by foot。

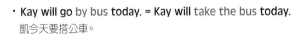

・**Kay will go by bus today. = Kay will take the bus today.**
凱今天要搭公車。

b school、university、class、church、prison、jail 如果表示一種**抽象意義**（表「功能」、「目的」）時，在下面片語裡，不加冠詞。

- go to college 上大學
- be in college 在大學裡（讀書）
- go to school 上學
- be in school/at school 在學校（讀書）
- go to church 上教堂（做禮拜）
- be in church/at church 在教堂（做禮拜）
- go to jail/prison 進牢房／監獄
- be in jail/prison 在牢裡／在監獄裡（坐牢）
- go to class 去上課
- be in class 在課堂上

・**My daughter Kay is in school today.**
= My daughter Kay is at school today.
= My daughter Kay is studying in school today.
我女兒凱今天在學校讀書。

抽象意義 **Amy's brother is in prison for robbery.** 艾咪的兄弟因搶劫入獄。
⤴ Amy's brother is a prisoner.（表「功能」，不加 the。）

具體場所 **Amy went to the prison to visit her brother.**
艾咪去監獄探望她的兄弟。
⤴ Amy went as a visitor, not a prisoner.（表「地點」，要加 the。）

抽象意義 **Does Henry leave school by 4 p.m.?** 亨利下午四點放學嗎？
⤴ Henry is a student.

具體場所 **Henry's mother went to the school to talk to the principal yesterday.** 昨天亨利的母親去學校跟校長談話。
⤴ Henry's mother is not a student.

抽象意義 **Trish is at college studying English.** 翠西在大學裡學習英文。

建築物 **They are building a college in our neighborhood.**
他們正在我們的街坊修建一所大學。

抽象意義 **Kay goes to church almost every Sunday.**
凱幾乎每個禮拜天都上教堂做禮拜。 → to a religious service

具體場所 **He's going to the church to clean its parking lot.**
他要去教堂打掃停車場。 → not a religious service

c work、bed 和 home 在下面片語裡，前面不要冠詞。

- go to work 上班
- go to bed 上床睡覺
- go home 回家
- be at work 在工作／start work 開始工作
- be in bed 在床上
- be at home 在家

· **It's time to go to bed now.** 睡覺的時間到了。 → 具有抽象意義

· **Ms. Bend plans to stay in bed late on the weekend.**
本德小姐計畫這個週末要睡懶覺。 → 具有抽象意義

stay in bed
在床上睡覺

· **Kay sat down on the bed and began to pray.**
凱在床上坐下來，開始祈禱。
↑ 指具體的傢俱（a particular piece of furniture）

· **Your dog is under the bed.** 你的狗狗在床下。 → 具體地點

under the bed
在床下

· **Kay leaves home for work at 7:30 a.m. every weekday.**
凱週一到週五都是早上七點半出門上班。 → 具有抽象意義

· **Is Dirk at home or is he at work?**
德克在家還是在上班？ → 具有抽象意義

d 一些表時間（midnight、midday、noon、night）的慣用語及其他慣用語裡，前面不要冠詞。

- around midnight 午夜時分
- at midday/at noon 在正午
- at night 在夜裡
- from morning till night 從早到晚
- by accident 偶然地、碰巧
- by night 晚間
- by day 白天
- by noon 到中午
- by mistake 錯誤地
- out of job 失業
  ↑ 注意：美式用 out of a job 或 out of work 來表示「失業」。

· **Dwight traveled mostly by night.**
杜威特多半選在夜間上路。

· **Dwight said it might be very cold at midnight.** 杜威特說半夜可能會很冷。

比較
The dog barked all through the night. 狗叫了通宵。

2 一些固定的成對片語，省略冠詞（兩個相同的名詞或兩個相對的名詞）。

- arm in arm 手挽著手
- cheek to cheek 臉貼著臉
- day after day 日復一日
- day and night 日日夜夜
- face to face 面對面
- from head to toe 從頭到腳
- from top to bottom 從上到下
- hand in hand 手牽手
- heart and soul 全心全意
- inch by inch 逐漸地
- on land and sea 在陸地和海上
- see eye to eye with 意見一致
- shoulder to shoulder 並肩地
- side by side 肩並肩
- year after year 年復一年

- We were walking arm in arm around the farm.
我們手挽著手地繞著農場散步。

- Kay is studying the same old subject in the same old way day after day. 日復一日，凱老是用同一個老方法研究同一門老科目。

- Ann is walking hand in hand with her boyfriend Dan.
安與她男友丹手牽手走在一起。

Diving Deep Into English 33 名詞加不加 the，意義不同

小心！即使學會了關於這三個冠詞（a, an, the）的所有規則，在很多情況下仍然很難選擇正確的冠詞。下列兩句都是正確的，只不過意思不同。

- Icy roads are dangerous. 被冰蓋住的路很危險。 → 泛指
- The icy roads are dangerous. 那些被冰蓋住的路很危險。 → 特指

請記住，在英式英語和美式英語中 the 的用法有區別，這加深了 the 的使用難度。例如：

美式	英式
the Taipei Railway Station 臺北火車站	Taipei Railway Station 臺北火車站
the Alma Park Zoo 阿爾馬動物園	Bristol Zoo 布里斯托動物園
the Miami City Council 邁阿密市議會	Manchester City Council 曼徹斯特市議會
celebrate the New Year 慶祝新年	celebrate (the) New Year 慶祝新年（可要也可不要 the）
play piano（不正式） play the piano（正式）彈鋼琴	play the piano 彈鋼琴
go to the hospital （特指或泛指）去醫院	go to hospital（泛指）去醫院看病 go to the hospital 去某特定醫院（通常還會說明去醫院做什麼，如 go to the hospital to see the doctor/visit a friend）

英式 **Ann had a high fever and went to hospital with Dan.**

美式 / 英式 **Ann had a high fever and went to a hospital with Dan.**

美式 / 英式 **Ann had a high fever and went to the hospital with Dan.**

安發高燒，與丹一起去了醫院。

在英式英語中，go to hospital（不加冠詞）是一個固定片語，但美國人認為這種說法是錯的。同樣道理，英式用 in hospital 或 in the hospital，美式只用 in the hospital。

在上面第二句的 a hospital 是泛指醫院，可以翻譯成「去了一家醫院」。第三句中的 the hospital 是特指的一家醫院，說話者和聽話者都明白是哪一家醫院。不過，美國人通常用 go to the hospital 表示「去醫院」，無論是特指還是泛指，很少用 go to a hospital。

UNIT 05 形容詞

Adjectives

Part
1
Definition of
Adjectives

何謂形容詞

1 形容詞是用來形容人或物（名詞或代名詞）的描述性詞彙，對名詞或代名詞進行補充説明，起描繪、修飾、限定的作用。

- beautiful flowers 美麗的花朵
- big eyes 大眼睛
- green trees 綠樹
- hungry children 饑餓的孩子
- poor people 窮人
- quiet places 安靜的地方

- She is smart. 她很聰明。
- He is polite. 他懂禮貌。

  ↑ 形容詞可以置於名詞前，也可以置於 be 動詞後面。

  » 參見 187 頁〈Part 2 形容詞的位置〉。

welcome!
He is polite.
他客客氣氣的。

2 冠詞 a/an 或 the 可以被看作限定詞，也可以視為一種特殊的形容詞，因為它們也修飾名詞。所有格（如 our、Jane's）也是限定詞，或是一種特殊的形容詞。

» 冠詞的用法參見 137 頁〈Unit 4 冠詞〉。

- the intelligent mother 這位聰明的母親
- the brave firefighter 這名勇敢的消防員
- a solid commitment 一個堅定的承諾
- a month's vacation 一個月的假期
- a two-month-old baby 一個兩個月大的嬰兒
- the happiest child 最幸福的孩子
- the unhappiest family 最不幸的家庭
- the richest man/woman 最富有的男人／女人

firefighter
消防員

形容詞的位置

1 形容詞用於名詞前面，或連綴動詞後面

形容詞用於所描述的名詞前面，或是放在連綴動詞的後面。

a 形容詞 + 名詞（定語位置）	b 連綴動詞（be 動詞、look、become、feel、seem）+ 形容詞（主詞補語位置）
• Art is a smart guy. 亞特是個聰明人。	• Art is smart. 亞特很聰明。
• He is going out with a rich woman tonight. 他今晚要跟一個有錢的女人約會。	• Mitch is rich. 米奇很富有。
• He is a sly guy. 他是一個奸詐的傢伙。	• The guy is sly. 這傢伙很奸詐。
• "It looks like a very short skirt when you sit," said Mike.「你坐下的時候，裙子看起來就很短。」邁克說。	• "My skirt is a bit too short, isn't it?" asked Liz.「我的裙子是不是有點太短了？」莉茲問。
• Roy is a quiet boy. 羅伊是一個文靜的男孩。	• Roy often remains quiet when playing with a toy. 羅伊玩玩具時通常很安靜。 ↑ remain 指「保持」時，是連綴動詞。

2 一些形容詞只用於連綴動詞之後

1 有些以 **a- 開頭的形容詞**只用在**連綴動詞的後面**，不能用在名詞前。
這類以 a- 開頭的形容詞並不太多，最常見的有：

- afraid 害怕的
- alight 燃燒著的
- alike 相像的
- aware 察覺的
- alive 活著的
- alone 單獨的
- ashamed 羞愧的
- asleep 睡著的

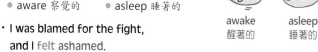

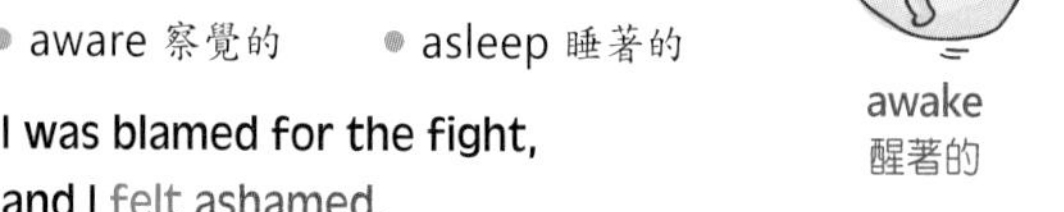

- **I was blamed for the fight, and I felt ashamed.**
  這場打鬥是我引起的，我覺得羞愧。

- **Clair Week's identical twins look very much alike, with the same long, thick black hair, the same dark brown eyes framed by long dark lashes, and the same dimples in their cheeks.**
  克蕾兒·維克的同卵雙胞胎長得好像，一樣長度的粗黑髮，一樣的深棕色眼眸和長長的黑睫毛，臉頰上還有一樣的酒窩。

  ↳ 以 a- 開頭的形容詞，通常置於連綴動詞後，這類形容詞前面有時還可以用 very much 修飾（又如：(be) very much afraid, (be) very much alone）。

2 一些描述**健康**和**情緒**的形容詞只用在**連綴動詞的後面**，不用在名詞前。

- content 滿足的
- fine 健康的
- glad 高興的
- ill 生病的
- pleased 滿意的
- ready 樂意的；準備好的
- sorry 感到難過（抱歉）的
- sure 確定的
- upset 苦惱的
- unsure 不確定的
- unwell 不舒服的
- well 健康的

- **I am glad Bob found a good job.**
  我很高興鮑勃找到了一個好工作。

- **I am sure that sooner or later Mr. Dale will end up in jail.**
  我確定戴爾先生遲早會進牢房。

上表中的一些表示「**健康、情緒**」的形容詞，如果置於**名詞**之前，具有不同的含意。比較下面例子：

- glad tidings 好消息
- an ill wind 倒楣；失此得彼
- a ready tongue 口齒伶俐
- a sorry state 可悲的處境
- a sure way 可靠的方法
- an upset stomach 腸胃不舒服

- Kay feels fine today. 凱今天身體感覺不錯。 → 表健康
- It is a fine day today. 今天天氣好。 → 不表健康
- I am sorry that I lost my tempter just now. 我剛才發了脾氣，我感到很抱歉。 → 表情緒
- She was in a sorry state when she became sick and had no money. 她又病又窮，處境可憐。 → 不表情緒

3 有些只置於連綴動詞後面的形容詞，具有可用於名詞之前的**對等形容詞**。

只用於連綴動詞之後	alive	afraid	alike	asleep	ill
可用於名詞之前	live/living	frightened	similar	sleeping	sick

- **There was a live fish on Trish's dish.** 翠西的盤子上有一隻活魚。
- **The fish on Trish's dish was still alive.** 翠西盤子上的魚還是活的。
  ↳ 名詞前用 live，不用 alive，alive 只用於連綴動詞後。

- **Bing saw a frightened little girl on the top of the burning building.** 賓看見在燃燒的大樓頂上有一個受到驚嚇的小女孩。
  ↳ 名詞前不能用 afraid，要用 frightened，afraid 只用於連綴動詞後。
- **The little girl is afraid.** 那個小女孩很害怕。

- **She took good care of her sick mother.** 她悉心照顧生了病的母親。
- **Her mother was ill/sick, and she took good care of her.** 她母親生病了，她悉心照顧她。
  ↳ ill（生病的）只用於連綴動詞後，sick 可以用於連綴動詞後或名詞前。
  ↳ 當 ill 用在名詞前時，意思是「壞的、不吉祥的、邪惡的」，比如：ill news（壞消息）。

3 只用在名詞前的形容詞

1 **類別形容詞**（描述事物類別）：闡明人或事物所屬的**特定類別**，這類形容詞沒有比較級和最高級。

- atomic 原子能的
- chemical 化學的
- nuclear 原子的
- industrial 工業的
- medical 醫學的
- physical 物理學的

- chief 主要的
- principal 首要的
- main 最重要的
- entire 全部的
- whole 全部的
- only 唯一的

- outdoor 戶外的
- local 當地的
- national 全國性的
- social 社會上的
- northern 北方的
- British 英國的

- live 活的；實況轉播的
- female 女的
- elder 年齡較大的
- eventual 最後的
- former 從前的
- lone 孤單的

- nuclear power plant 核電廠
- social problems 社會問題
- an entire week 整整一星期
- a lone star 孤伶伶的一顆星

- **Trish has some live fish.** 翠西有些活魚。
  ↑ 形容詞 live 只能用在所描述的名詞前，不能用在連綴動詞 to be 後。
- **My elder/older brother Scot owns a yacht.**
  我哥哥史考特擁有一艘遊艇。
  ↑ 英式英語用 elder brother，美式英語用 older brother。

- **Scot is three years older than me.**
  史考特比我大三歲。
  ↑ elder 只能用在所描述的名詞前，不能用在連綴動詞 to be 後，因此這句不能用 elder。older 卻可以用在名詞前，也可以用在連綴動詞後。

2 **強調**用的形容詞：

- absolute 完全的
- mere 僅僅的
- sheer 純粹的
- utter 絕對的
- an absolute lie 十足的謊言
- sheer nonsense 純粹胡說八道
- a mere thought of 一想到……
- an utter refusal 斷然拒絕

- **I have made an utter fool of myself.**
  我的所作所為十足就是個傻子。

4 形容詞置於 something 等字的後面

1 形容詞應該放在下面這些不定代名詞以及類似的字之後：

- anywhere 任何地方
- something 某事
- anybody 任何人
- somewhere 某處
- everything 每件事
- somebody 某人
- anything 任何事
- nothing 微不足道的事

2 比較以下的用法：

形容詞置於不定代名詞後面	形容詞置於名詞前面
• anything interesting 任何有趣的事	• interesting news 有趣的消息
• nothing frightening 沒什麼好害怕的	• a frightening sight 可怕的景象
• something horrible 某件可怕的事	• a horrible story 一個可怕的故事
• somewhere quiet 某個安靜的地方	• a quiet place 一個安靜的地方
• somebody dirty and disgusting 某個骯髒又可憎的人	• a dirty and disgusting man 一個骯髒又可憎的男人
• anyone capable 任何能幹的人	• a capable manager 一個能幹的經理

- **Let's find** somewhere quiet **to walk and talk.**
  = Let's find a quiet place **to walk and talk.** 我們找個安靜的地方邊走邊談。

- **Did** anything interesting **happen?** 有沒有發生什麼有趣的事情？
- **Did you hear** any interesting news**?** 你有沒有聽到什麼有趣的消息？

- **There is** something frightening **about lightning.** 閃電有點可怕。
- **A flash of light from a nearby bolt of lightning is** a frightening sight**.**
  從附近的一道閃電傳來的閃光，是個很可怕的景象。

- **Has** something horrible **happened to Mabel?** 美博發生了什麼可怕的事嗎？
- **Have you told Mary** your horrible story**?** 你告訴瑪麗你那個可怕的故事了嗎？

- **Is there** anyone capable **of leading the business?**
  有沒有人有能力領導這個企業？
- **Is she** a capable manager**?** 她是一個能幹的經理嗎？

5 形容詞用於測量名詞後面

- six feet tall 六英尺高
- two kilometers long 兩公里長
- twenty-three meters high 23 米高
- two feet deep 兩英尺深
- eight years old 八歲

・My brother is six feet tall, and so is my mother.
我哥哥身高六英尺，我媽媽身高也是六英尺。（6 英尺約等於 183 公分）

・My house in Miami is twenty-three meters high.
我在邁阿密的房子有 23 米高。

・Sally's sailboat is eight years old.
莎莉的帆船已有八年的船齡了。

sailboat
帆船

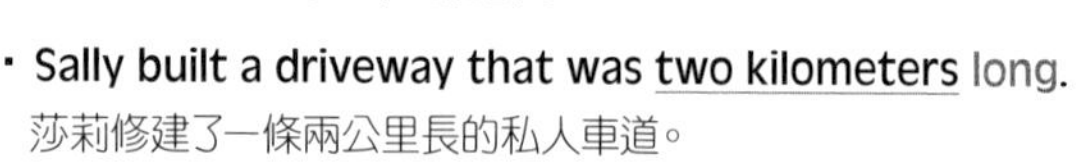

・Sally built a driveway that was two kilometers long.
莎莉修建了一條兩公里長的私人車道。

・My jeep went through a creek that was two feet deep.
我的吉普車開過一條兩英尺深的小溪。

6 動詞 + 受詞 + 形容詞

形容詞還有一種位置，是放在「動詞（尤其是使役動詞）+ 受詞 + 形容詞」結構的受詞後面，作受詞的補語。

- make me upset 讓我苦惱
- keep the door open 讓門開著
- leave me alone 不要打擾我

Keep the window open.
讓窗戶開著。

・Eddie, please get the limousine ready. 艾迪，請將豪華大轎車準備好。
↑ 使役動詞（get）+ 受詞（the limousine）+ 形容詞（ready）

・Your sad message made Dad mad. 你那令人悲傷的消息讓爸爸很生氣。

・Coco painted her house yellow. 可可把她的房子漆成黃色的。

・Bess thinks your colorful dress wonderful. 英式
= Bess thinks that your colorful dress is wonderful.
貝絲覺得你那件五顏六色的洋裝很好看。

7 放在名詞後面，作定語的形容詞

1 一些形容詞用在名詞後面當作定語，通常是慣用的片語，這些片語也可以看作複合名詞，例如：

- Attorney General 首席檢察官
- court martial 軍事法庭
- Secretary General 總書記
- Poet Laureate 桂冠詩人

2 形容詞最高級或 the first/last/next/only + 名詞 + 形容詞

當某個名詞置於**形容詞最高級**或 first、last、next、only 等字的後面，一些作主詞補語的形容詞（如 available, imaginable, possible, suitable, alive）等可以緊跟在名詞之後作定語，相當於形容詞子句（即定語子句）。

・**Does the oldest man alive live in Nagasaki?**
世界上最老的男子住在長崎嗎？
↳ the oldest man alive = the oldest man who is alive

・**Del knows the only way possible up Mount Bell.**
= Del knows the only possible way up Mount Bell.
戴爾知道唯一一條可以上貝爾山的路。
↳ the only way possible = the only way which is possible

・**Is it currently the only offer available to the shareholders?**
那是股東們目前可得到的唯一報價嗎？
↳ 這類形容詞後面若跟介系詞片語（如：to the shareholders）時，也置於名詞後面。

以 -able, -ible 結尾的形容詞，被另一個**最高級形容詞**或 **only** 等字修飾時，則可前置，也可後置，意義不變。

the only way possible = the only possible way 唯一可能的方法
the only offer available = the only available offer 唯一可得到的報價

・Of those people who applied for this position, Sue is the only person suitable. → 後置
= Of those people who applied for this position, Sue is the only suitable person. → 前置
在這個職務的應徵者當中，蘇是唯一的合適人選。

3 形容詞片語一般需要後置，相當於形容詞子句。

- a house twice as big as mine
  = a house that is twice as big as mine 一棟是我的房子兩倍大的房子

- Will this movie appeal to people interested in space exploration?
  = Will this movie appeal to people who are interested in space exploration? 這部影片會吸引對太空探索感興趣的人嗎？

8 可以置於名詞前，也可以緊跟在名詞之後的形容詞

一些形容詞置於名詞前和緊跟在名詞後面時，意思有所不同，例如：

名詞 + 形容詞	形容詞 + 名詞
the students concerned 參與（相關）的學生	a concerned look 擔憂的神情
all those people involved 所有參與的人	an involved reply 複雜的回答
all the people present 所有在場的人	the present principal 現任的校長
the person responsible 應（對某事）負責的人	a responsible teacher 有責任心的老師

英式 Claire was one of the people concerned in that corrupt affair.

美式 Claire was one of the people involved in that corrupt affair.

克萊兒是與那件貪污案有關的人員之一。

↑ concerned 置於名詞後，意思是「相關的、參與的」；美式英語常用 involved 來表示此意思。

concerned 置於名詞前或連綴動詞後，表示「擔心的、不安的、關心的、感興趣的」，如：

- He stared at me with a concerned look.
  他用擔憂的表情注視著我。
- She was concerned about your safety. 她很擔心你的安危。

形容詞的構成

1 形容詞常見的字尾

大多數形容詞的詞性可以由字尾判斷出來。下表列舉了最常見的形容詞字尾：

1 -able

- an acceptable answer 令人滿意的回答
- a believable story 可信的故事
- a comfortable climate 舒適的氣候
- a desirable profession 值得嚮往的職業
- an enjoyable job 有樂趣的工作
- a readable book 可讀性強的書
- a reliable friend 可信賴的朋友
- a remarkable novelist 傑出的小說家
- a suitable husband 速配的丈夫
- an unreasonable man 不講理的男人
- a valuable experience 寶貴的經歷
- variable weather 多變的天氣
- a washable dress 耐洗的洋裝

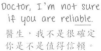

Doctor, I'm not sure if you are reliable.
醫生，我不是很確定你是不是值得信賴。

2 -al

- a biological miracle 生物學奇蹟
- cultural life 文化生活
- a digital clock 數字顯示式時鐘
- an environmental disaster 環境大災難
- a formal gown 禮服

- a global village 地球村
- a historical play 歷史劇
- industrial pollution 工業污染
- a national holiday 全國性假日
- an official stamp 官方印章
- a professional woman 職業女性
- a typical mistake 典型的錯誤

3 -ary

- an elementary student 小學生
- an extraordinary idea 離奇的想法
- a military truck 軍用卡車
- a necessary result 必然結果
- ordinary people 普通人
- a primary cause 主要原因
- a revolutionary idea 完全創新的構想
- a secondary school 中等學校
- a temporary inconvenience 一時的不方便
- an unnecessary war 沒必要的戰爭

military service
當兵

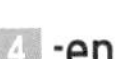

4 -en

- a broken leg 斷腿
- a drunken/drunk driver 酒駕者
- a frozen pond 結冰的池塘
- a golden opportunity 絕佳的機會
- the hidden treasure 藏起來的金銀財寶
- a rotten pear 腐爛的梨
- spoken English 英語口語
- a stolen purse 被偷的錢包
- a swollen face 浮腫的臉
- a wooden house 木頭房子
- a woolen sweater 羊毛衣
- a written assignment 書面作業

the hidden treasure
藏寶

a wooden house
木屋

5 -ful

許多字尾是 -ful 的形容詞，其意思是「充滿……的」（full of, filled with, having a lot of）。例如：joyful 的意思是「充滿了歡樂」（full of joy）。

- an awful earthquake 可怕的地震
- beautiful sunflowers 美麗的向日葵
- a colorful dress 鮮豔的洋裝
- a faithful dog 忠誠的狗
- a forgetful husband 健忘的丈夫
- a graceful skater 動作優美的溜冰者
- a harmful hobby 有害的嗜好
- a meaningful wink 意味深長的眼色
- a playful puppy 愛玩耍的小狗
- a useful grammar book 有用的文法書
- a wonderful journey 美好的旅程
- a youthful attitude 富於青春活力的態度

6 -ible

- a horrible sight 可怕的景象
- an impossible mission 不可能完成的任務
- a possible result 可能發生的結果
- a terrible mess 一片混亂
- visible nervousness 明顯的緊張

7 -ic

- an atomic bomb 原子彈
- an automatic door 自動門
- a basic grammar rule 基本文法規則
- an electronic dictionary 電子詞典
- a heroic act 英勇的行為
- a magic carpet 魔毯
- a public bathroom 公共廁所
- a romantic island 富有浪漫色彩的小島
- a scientific analysis 科學分析

a heroic act
英勇的行為

8 -ish

- a boyish game 男孩玩的遊戲
- a British novel 英國小說
- childish behavior 幼稚的行為
- a Danish singer 丹麥歌手
- a foolish habit 愚蠢的習慣
- a girlish game 女孩玩的遊戲
- Polish Air Force 波蘭空軍
- a selfish girl 自私的女孩
- a Spanish dancer 西班牙舞者
- a stylish hat 時髦的帽子

如果想表達某個東西帶有一點粉紅色、綠色、紅色、黃色等，可以在表示這些顏色的形容詞後面加 -ish，例如：

- greenish coat 淡綠色的大衣
- pinkish cheeks 帶桃紅色的面頰
- reddish berries 淡紅色的漿果
- yellowish paper 淡黃色的紙

9 -ive

- an expensive meal 昂貴的一餐
- festive costumes 節日服裝
- an imaginative teacher 有想像力的老師
- a native speaker 說母語的人
- a negative attitude 消極的態度
- an objective opinion 客觀的見解（objective 與 subjective 是反義詞）
- a passive outlook 消極的看法（passive 是 active 的反義詞）
- a positive attitude 積極的態度（positive 與 negative 是反義詞）
- a talkative man 健談的男人

festive costumes
節慶服裝

10 -less

以 -less 結尾的形容詞，意思通常是 without（沒有、無），例如：powerless 表示「無權力的，無力量的」。

- a careless motion 粗心的動作
- a clueless detective 毫無線索的偵探
- a cloudless sky 晴朗的天空
- an endless debate 無休止的辯論
- a fearless woman 大膽的女子

a clueless detective
毫無線索的偵探

- a harmless kitten 不會傷人的小貓
- a helpless baby 無依無靠的嬰兒
- a homeless woman 無家可歸的婦女
- a hopeless drunk 不可救藥的醉鬼
- a joyless marriage 沒有歡樂的婚姻
- a meaningless life 毫無意義的生活
- a merciless dictator 殘酷的獨裁者
- a spotless shirt 極其清潔的襯衫
- a useless computer 無用的電腦
- a worthless contract 毫無價值的契約

a merciless attack
無情的攻擊

11 -ly（很多副詞也是以 -ly 結尾。參見 257 頁〈Unit 6 副詞〉。）

- bodily harm 肉體上的傷害
- a costly diamond 貴重的鑽石
- a cowardly act 懦弱的行為
- a daily newspaper 日報
- a deadly blow 致命的一擊
- an early warning 預警；先兆
- an elderly barber 上了年紀的理髮師
- a friendly dog 友善的狗
- a holy book 宗教書
- an hourly broadcast 每小時的廣播節目
- a kindly smile 和藹的微笑
- a likely story 說得像真的一樣（實際上不可信）
- a lively discussion 熱烈的討論
- a lonely mountain village 偏僻的山村
- a lovely view 宜人的景色
- a monthly magazine 月刊
- a silly story 無聊的故事
- an ugly building 難看的建築物
- an unlikely solution 不太可行的解決方法
- a weekly meeting 週會

a lively discussion
熱烈的討論

12 -ous

- an adventurous woman 愛冒險的女子
- a courageous pilot 勇敢的飛行員
- dangerous behavior 危險的行為
- a furious boss 狂怒的老闆
- a generous heart 寬宏大量的心胸
- a humorous remark 幽默的話
- a marvelous experience 奇特的經歷
- a mountainous path 山路
- a nervous bridegroom 緊張不安的新郎
- a poisonous snake 毒蛇
- a precious gift 珍貴的禮物
- a serious mistake 嚴重的錯誤
- a victorious shout 勝利的呼喊

a marvelous experience
奇特的經歷

13 -some

- an adventuresome young woman 有冒險精神的年輕女子
- an awesome waterfall 令人敬畏的瀑布
- a bothersome noise 令人討厭的嘈雜聲
- a burdensome responsibility 沉重的責任
- a fearsome explosion 可怕的爆炸
- a handsome man 英俊的男子
- a lonesome path 人跡罕至的小路
- tiresome work 令人疲勞的工作
- a troublesome child 令人煩惱的孩子
- a wearisome class 無聊的課
- a wholesome laugh 有益健康的笑

tiresome work
令人疲勞的工作

14 -y

- a cloudy sky 多雲的天空，陰天
- a dirty street 骯髒的街道
- an easy question 簡單的問題
- a foggy morning 霧濛濛的清晨

- a funny guy 滑稽可笑的人
- a gloomy face 陰沉的面孔
- a hairy monster 多毛的怪物
- a happy marriage 美滿的婚姻
- healthy teeth 健康的牙齒
- a juicy peach 多汁的桃子
- a messy man 邋遢的男人
- a muddy path 泥濘小徑
- a noisy machine 噪音大的機器
- a rainy day 雨天
- a rusty nail 生銹的釘子
- a sleepy bear 昏昏欲睡的熊
- a stormy evening 暴風雨的夜晚
- a sunny room 陽光充足的房間
- tasty soup 美味湯
- a windy city 多風的城市

a happy marriage
美滿的婚姻

a rainy day
雨天

✗ Her snappy puppy is unhappily.

✓ Her snappy puppy is unhappy. 她那隻脾氣暴躁的小狗很不快樂。

↳ 連綴動詞 be 後面要用形容詞 unhappy。

15 -ed

- an aged airplane 破舊的飛機
- an amused expression 被逗樂的表情
- a blessed event 喜事
- a crowded highway 擁擠的公路
- a detailed explanation 詳細的解釋
- a disabled man 殘障人士
- a frightened child 受驚嚇的孩子
- an interested party 當事人
- a learned mother 博學的母親
- a married man 已婚男人
- a one-legged woman 獨腳的婦女

a disabled man
身障人士

- a ragged coat 破爛大衣
- a so-called genius 所謂的天才
- a tired teacher 疲勞的老師
- an unemployed artist 失業的藝術家
- a united country 統一的國家
- a worried politician 憂慮的政治家

16 -ing

- an aging grandmother 逐漸蒼老的奶奶
- an amazing story 驚人的故事
- an amusing performance 令人捧腹大笑的表演
- a frightening sight 令人驚恐的景象
- an interesting man 有趣的人
- a tiring trip 令人疲倦的旅途

an amusing performance
令人捧腹大笑的表演

Diving Deep Into English 35 not happy 與 unhappy 的差別

以下這兩句，在意義上有沒有區別呢？

Annie is not feeling happy.

Annie is feeling unhappy.

這句話可以有三種含意：

ⓐ 安妮不高興，但也不至於傷心。
ⓑ 安妮也許有點傷心。
ⓒ 安妮也許傷心。

這句話可以做出各種解釋，意思較為含糊。現代寫作通常力求句子清楚、簡潔，盡量避免語意不清、模棱兩可。

這句話的意思相當於「Annie is feeling sad.」，意思是「安妮感覺痛苦。」否定字首 un- 比 not 更靠近形容詞 happy，這就使 unhappy 的意思清楚明瞭。運用字首、字尾可以將語意表達得較清楚。如果要表達某人傷心或痛苦，用 unhappy 比 not happy 更確切、更恰當。

2 -ful 與 -less 字尾的形容詞比較

下列成對形容詞，是在同一個字後面分別加字尾 -ful 或 -less 而構成的。以 -less 結尾的形容詞在意義上與以 -ful 結尾的形容詞**相反**，比較以下例子：

以 -ful 結尾的形容詞

careful 小心的	careless 粗心的
cheerful 快樂的	cheerless 悶悶不樂的
colorful 彩色的	colorless 無色的
faithful 忠貞的	faithless 不忠的
fearful 害怕的	fearless 不怕的
harmful 有害的	harmless 無害的
hopeful 有希望的	hopeless 無望的
meaningful 有意義的	meaningless 無意義的
merciful 仁慈的	merciless 無情的
powerful 強大的	powerless 軟弱的
painful 痛的	painless 無痛的
useful 有用的	useless 無用的

3 -ed 與 -ing 字尾的形容詞比較

有些字可以加 -ed 結尾，成為形容詞，也可以加 -ing 結尾，成為意義不同的形容詞。以 -ed 結尾的形容詞用來**描述人的感覺**（某人覺得……）。以 -ing 結尾的形容詞用來描述**引起這些感覺的人或事物**（某事物令人感到……）。

以 -ed 結尾的形容詞			以 -ing 結尾的形容詞	
alarmed	受驚的	→	alarming	驚人的
amazed	吃驚的	→	amazing	令人吃驚的
bored	感到無聊的	→	boring	令人乏味的
excited	激動的	→	exciting	令人激動的
frightened	受驚的	→	frightening	令人驚恐的
interested	感興趣的	→	interesting	引起興趣的
pleased	滿意的	→	pleasing	令人滿意的
surprised	感到驚訝的	→	surprising	令人驚異的
tired	疲倦的	→	tiring	令人疲倦的
worried	擔心的	→	worrying	令人擔憂的

- She was interested in Jerry's speech. 她對傑瑞的演講有興趣。
- Bing said that Kim's speech was interesting.
  賓說，金姆的演講很有趣。
- Bob is often bored at work, because he's got a boring job.
  鮑勃工作時常感到厭倦，因為他的工作很無聊。
- Bing only talks about himself. He's really boring.
  賓只談論他自己，他真無聊。
  ↳ 賓讓別人覺得他無聊（Bing makes other people bored.）
  » 參見 214 頁〈Part 5 分詞形容詞〉。

4 「the + 形容詞」的用法

1 **泛指某一類人的複數用法**：某些形容詞可以與定冠詞 the 連用，構成「the + 形容詞」的結構，當**複數名詞**使用，**泛指某一類人**，後面不需要再接名詞。例如「the rich」泛指所有的富人，相當於 all rich people 或 the rich people，而不是指 the rich person。

» 參見 155 頁〈8 類指的用法，要加 the〉。

the + 形容詞 = 複數名詞

- the blind 視障人士
- the brave 勇士
- the dead 死人
- the deaf 聽障人士
- the disabled 身障人士
- the elderly 長者
- the free 自由之人
- the jobless 失業者
- the old 老人
- the sick 病人
- the unemployed 失業者
- the young 年輕人

Remember, Robin, our sales competitors are the rich and we are the poor.
記得，羅賓漢，我們的銷售競爭對手是富人，而我們是窮人喔。

= the blind people

- Jeff often helps the blind and the deaf.
  傑夫常幫助視障和聽障人士。 = the deaf people
  ↑ 這類「the + 形容詞」結構指具特定身體狀況或特定社會條件的人。

- At the beginning of the year, I was greatly annoyed when I joined the unemployed. 年初我加入了失業者的行列，感到很氣惱。
  = the unemployed people

  = the injured people

- After the train accident, the injured were carried on stretchers to a safe place.
  火車事故發生後，傷患者被放在擔架上，
  抬到了安全的地方。
  ↑ 這類「the + 形容詞」結構用作主詞時，述語動詞要用複數形。

stretcher 擔架

2 作單數使用的固定用法：在某些固定片語中，「the + 形容詞」代表**單數意義**，例如：

- the accused 被告
- the former 前者
- the latter 後者

- The accused was released on bail yesterday. 被告昨天被保釋了。
  ↑ 這類「the + 形容詞」的固定片語用作主詞時，
  述語動詞要使用單數形。

3 代表抽象觀念的用法：「the + 形容詞」有時可指一種籠統的抽象觀念，如：

- the beautiful 美人
- the unreal 非真實
- the supernatural 超自然現象；鬼神
- the impossible 不可能的事
- the unthinkable 難以想像的事

the supernatural
超自然現象

- Do you believe in the supernatural?
  你相信鬼神嗎？

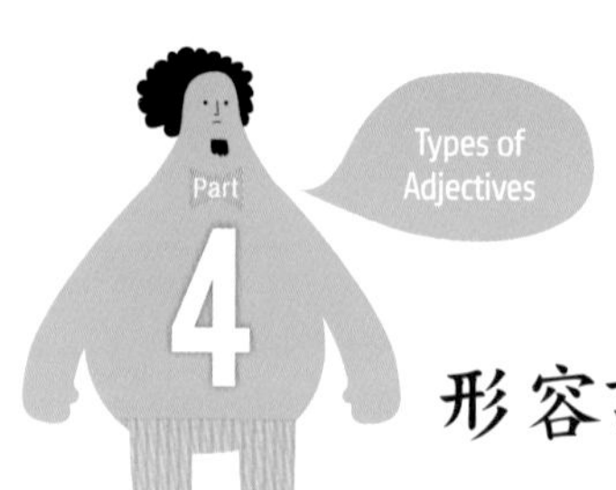

形容詞的種類

1 描述性形容詞（Descriptive Adjectives）

「描述性形容詞」，用來描述所修飾的名詞或代名詞的性質或狀態。

- **That handsome man with the blue hat is my brother Mat.**
  那位戴著藍帽子、相貌英俊的男子是我的弟弟麥特。
  ↳ handsome 和 blue 都是描述性形容詞，分別描繪名詞 man 和 hat。

- **The movie Ivy showed us yesterday was quite funny.**
  艾薇昨天放給我們看的電影很有趣。
  ↳ funny 是描述性形容詞。

2 專有形容詞（Proper Adjectives）

如果一個形容詞是從一個專有名詞衍生出來的，就稱為「專有形容詞」，要以**大寫字母**開頭。

- **Coco has decided to cook Chinese food tomorrow.** 可可決定明天做中國菜。
  ↳ Chinese 是從 China 衍生出來的專有形容詞，說明是哪一種食品。

- **Those Singaporean tourists enjoyed walking with their guide Paul on the top of the Great Wall.**
  那些新加坡遊客喜歡跟他們的導遊保羅一起在長城頂上漫步。
  ↳ Singaporean 是從 Singapore 衍生出來的專有形容詞，說明是哪一類的觀光客。

3 所有格形容詞／所有格限定詞（Possessive Adjectives/Possessive Determiners）

1 當所有格代名詞放在名詞前面修飾名詞時，就具有形容詞的作用，這樣的所有格代名詞即為**所有格形容詞**，包括 my、his、her、its、our、their、your、whose。這些所有格形容詞屬限定詞，亦稱為**所有格限定詞**。

- **My Aunt Kay visited her cousin in London in May.**
  我姑姑凱五月去倫敦探望了她的堂妹。
  ↥ My 和 her 都是所有格形容詞，分別修飾專有名詞 Aunt Kay 和一般名詞 cousin。
- **The two sailors put on their life jackets and jumped into the sea to rescue the captain's wife.**
  那兩名水手穿上他們的救生衣，跳進大海去救船長夫人。
  ↥ their 是所有格形容詞，修飾複合名詞 life jackets。
  » 參見 84 頁〈1 所有格限定詞〉。

2 還有一種表示「所有」或「擁有」的方法，那就是在名字或名詞後面，加上所有格符號（'）和字母 s，即「's」。

» 參見 50 頁〈Part 5 名詞的所有格〉。

cowboy hat 牛仔帽

- **Jane's kitten took a nap in Sam's cowboy hat.**
  珍的小貓在山姆的牛仔帽裡睡了個午覺。
- **Our dog's new collar is blue.** 我們狗狗的新項圈是藍色的。

4 指示形容詞／指示限定詞（Demonstrative Adjectives/Demonstrative Determiners）

指示形容詞包括 this、that、these、those，這些字用在名詞前，有形容詞的作用，因此被稱作指示形容詞。指示形容詞用來表示所指的是哪一個（哪一些）東西或人，因而也被稱為**指示限定詞**。

» 參見 67 頁〈Part 2 指示代名詞〉。

描述近物			描述遠物		
	this	→ 單數		that	→ 單數
	these	→ 複數		those	→ 複數

- My Uncle Ray gave me this robot as a gift on my eleventh birthday.
  這個機器人是我叔叔雷在我 11 歲生日時送我的生日禮物。
- That opening over there by Kent is the entrance to the circus tent. 肯特旁邊的那個開口是馬戲團帳篷的入口。
- These ballet dancers are the best in Norway.
  這些芭蕾舞者是挪威的頂尖舞蹈家。
- My four sons gave me those antique guns.
  那些古董槍是我的四個兒子給我的。

circus tent
馬戲團帳篷

5 作形容詞用的名詞（構成複合名詞）

1 有時候**名詞**也可以用來修飾其他名詞，當作**形容詞**用，與其所修飾的名詞構成複合名詞（名詞 + 名詞），如下列的套色字：

- a beauty shop 美容院
- a computer salesperson 電腦售貨員
- a garden chair 花園的椅子
- a gold ring 金戒指
- a horse race 賽馬
- a log cabin 木屋
- an English teacher 英文老師
- a race track 跑道
- a silk dress 絲質洋裝
- a sports shoe shop 運動鞋店
- a stone road 石頭路
- a telephone operator 電話接線員
- a war movie 戰爭片
- a woman general 女將軍

- This war movie is too scary for Mary. 這部戰爭片對瑪麗來說太恐怖了。
- Bess loves her silk dress. 貝絲喜歡她的絲質洋裝。

» 參見 27 頁〈5 複合名詞〉和 916 頁〈附錄 4 複合名詞表〉。

2 雖然有些名詞原本就另有形容詞的形式，但用其形容詞來修飾其他名詞，和直接用這個名詞來修飾其他名詞，意義卻不一樣。比較下列 a beautiful shop 和 a beauty shop 的不同。

- Pop sells clothes at a beautiful shop, and Mom works at a beauty shop. 爸爸在一家漂亮的商店賣衣服，媽媽在一家美容院工作。
  ↳ a beautiful shop 是指「一家漂亮的商店」（a very nice-looking shop）；a beauty shop 是指「美容院」（a shop for women to beautify themselves）。

3 「名詞 + 名詞」的結構中，即使後一個名詞用了複數形式，第一個名詞也必須用**單數**。此外，第一個名詞不能用所有格形式。這是因為第一個名詞作**形容詞**用，而形容詞並沒有單複數形式的變化，也沒有所有格形式。

- a foreign language teacher 一個外語教師
- two foreign language teachers 兩個外語教師
- a business student 一個讀商的學生
- two business students 兩個讀商的學生
- a telephone number 一個電話號碼
- two telephone numbers 兩個電話號碼
- a shoe store 一家鞋店
- two shoe stores 兩家鞋店

a shoe store
一家鞋店

- **He wrote his telephone number on a piece of lumber.** 他把他的電話號碼寫在一塊木料上面。
  ↳ 第一個名詞不能用所有格 telephone's，也不能用複數 telephones。
- **She went to a sale at the shoe store.** 她去了鞋店的大拍賣。
  ↳ 第一個名詞不能用複數 shoes，也不能用所有格形式 shoe's。

NOTE

1 上述規則也有例外。如果 woman 或 man 是複合名詞的一部分，而修飾的另一個名詞是複數，則可用複數 women 或 men，例如：

- women doctors 女醫師
- women teachers 女教師

2 不過，doctor、teacher、lawyer、nurse 這類名詞，指男性亦指女性，因此最好不要與 woman、man 等字用在一起構成複合名詞，除非是有特別原因需要區別性別。

3 涉及一種以上項目或行為的複合名詞，複合名詞中的第一個名詞通常用複數。

- the building materials industry 建築材料工業
- Ann Pool is going to encourage reading when she starts her new foreign languages school.
  等安・普爾創立了她新的外語學校後，她就要鼓勵閱讀。
  ↳ 「一所外語學校」要說 a foreign languages school，因為外語學校涉及多門語言。（不過英式也有用單數 a foreign language school。）

6 複合形容詞／片語形容詞（Compound Adjectives/Phrasal Adjectives）

1 由一個以上的詞所構成的形容詞，稱作**複合形容詞**或**片語形容詞**，用在名詞前時，複合形容詞的字與字之間有**連字號**（-）。

- a long-distance call 長途電話
- a well-dressed teacher 穿著體面的老師
- a well-known writer 著名作家
- an old-fashioned dress 舊式洋裝
- a three-year-old boy 三歲男孩
- user-friendly software 易使用的軟體

・**Tess loved her old-fashioned dress.** 黛絲喜歡她那件舊式的洋裝。

・**The well-dressed teacher, Mr. Brown, reminded me of a fancy preacher.** 那位穿著體面的老師，布朗先生，使我想起了一位花俏的傳教士。

2 複合形容詞中的**名詞**，不可以用複數形式。

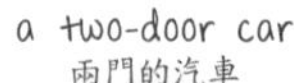

- a forty-five-minute walk 四十五分鐘的散步
- an ten-dollar bill 十美元的鈔票
- a two-door car 兩門的汽車
- an eight-hour day 八小時的一天
- a 50-year-old car 一輛五十年車齡的車

・**My niece has to write a two-thousand-word paper about Greece.**
我姪女要寫一篇關於希臘的兩千字報告。

Ⅰ 即使複合形容詞中數量詞（forty-five, ten, two 等）表示的含意是複數，複合形容詞中的名詞 minute、dollar、door、year、hour、word 等，不能用複數形式。

3 當修飾複數名詞時，構成複合形容詞的名詞也不用複數。

- three two-door cars 三輛雙門汽車
- two ten-dollar bills 兩張十美元的鈔票

4 複合形容詞作定語置於名詞之前時，通常要有連字號，而同樣的修飾詞如果不作定語，就不要連字號。

- **The Lord prefers common-looking people. That is why he makes so many of them.** (President Abraham Lincoln)
  上帝喜歡相貌平凡的人，所以既不美、也不醜的人，隨處可見。
  ↑ common-looking 是分詞構成的複合形容詞。

- **Last Saturday night, that third-rate ballet company gave a performance that was first rate.**
  上星期六晚上，那個三流的芭蕾舞團演出了一場一流的表演。
  ↑ 複合形容詞 third-rate 要有連字號，修飾複合名詞 ballet company。而當複合形容詞放在名詞（performance）和連綴動詞（was）後面時，就不要連字號。

an old-car saleswoman 和 an old car saleswoman，在意義上有何區別？

- Is Ruth an old-car saleswoman or an old car saleswoman?
  露絲究竟是一個賣舊車的女業務員，還是一個上了年紀的女汽車業務員？
  → an old-car saleswoman 是一個賣舊車的女推銷員（a saleswoman who sells old cars），形容詞 old 只修飾第一個名詞 car，用連字號把形容詞 old 和所修飾的第一個名詞 car 連接起來，構成複合形容詞，而整個**複合形容詞** old-car 修飾名詞 saleswoman。
  → an old car saleswoman 是指一個上了年紀的、賣汽車的女推銷員（an old saleswoman who sells cars），名詞 car 修飾 saleswoman，構成複合名詞，而形容詞 old 修飾整個**複合名詞** car saleswoman。

7 疑問形容詞／疑問限定詞（Interrogative Adjectives/Interrogative Determiners）

疑問形容詞包含 whose、what、which 三個字，這些字用在名詞前修飾名詞時，就是疑問形容詞，也是限定詞的一種，因此亦稱為**疑問限定詞**。

- **Whose computer did Jake break?**
  傑克把誰的電腦弄壞了？

- **What color should Claire dye her hair?**
  克萊兒應該把她的頭髮染成什麼顏色？

- **Which way leads to the new zoo?**
  哪一條路通往新的動物園？

Diving Deep Into English 36 which 和 what 的用法區別

❶ 許多情況下，which 和 what 都可以互換，意義上區別不大。

- **What college are you going to attend next year?**
  Which college are you going to attend next year?
  明年你要去哪一所大學讀書？

❷ 但如果談論的只有兩個東西或兩個人，或者供選擇的**數目有限**，就要用 which。通常 which 涉及的東西比 what 更具體。

- **Which android did she want, the new one on the floor or the old one on the shelf?**
  她要的是哪個機器人：地板上那台新的，還是架子上那台舊的？
  ↳ 可以選擇的機器人是已知的。
- **Which size do you want—small, medium, or large?**
  你想要哪個尺寸的——小的、中的，還是大的？
  ↳ 可以選擇的尺寸是已知的。 
- **Which way should we go to get to our hut?**
  去我們的小屋應該走哪一條路？
  ↳ 用 Which way，比 What way 更自然，因為指的是我們面前具體的幾條路。

❸ 沒有特別限定的數量時，就可以用 what。換句話說，當可供選擇的數量未知時，傾向於用 what。

- **What language do I need to know if I go to Togo?**
  如果我要去多哥，我需要懂哪一種語言？
  ↳ 這是泛指用法，可供選擇的語言數量未知，因為世界上有很多種語言。這裡用 What language 比 Which language 更自然。
- **What color is the ribbon that Claire likes to wear in her hair?**
  克萊兒喜歡戴在頭上的那條緞帶是什麼顏色？
  ↳ 這是泛指的用法，因為顏色的數量有很多。

» 參見 92 頁〈4 what 和 which〉。

8 數量形容詞（基數詞與序數詞）

一些文法學家把數量詞也看成是一種形容詞，叫做**數量形容詞**，數量形容詞包括**基數詞**和**序數詞**兩類。

1 **基數詞**：表明人、物、動物等的數量。

- one fluffy kitten 一隻毛茸茸的小貓
- five ugly ducklings 五隻醜小鴨
- twelve months 十二個月
- eight witches 八個女巫
- seven days 七天
- two polar bears 兩隻北極熊

・**In next week's parade, there will be ten movie stars and over two hundred valuable antique cars.**
有十位電影明星和兩百多輛昂貴的古董車將參加下週的遊行。
↳ ten 和 two hundred 是數字作形容詞，表數量；valuable 是描述性形容詞，表評價；antique 是描述性形容詞，表新舊。

2 如果數量詞指代的名詞很明確，就可以省略名詞。

・**"How many students does your school have?" "About two hundred."**
「你們學校有多少學生？」「大約兩百。」
↳ two hundred 顯然是指 two hundred students。

3 **序數詞**：如 first、second、third 等，這也是數量詞，表明人或東西一個接一個的順序。

- first 第一
- second 第二
- third 第三
- fourth 第四
- fifth 第五
- sixth 第六
- seventh 第七
- eighth 第八
- ninth 第九
- tenth 第十
- eleventh 第 11
- twelfth 第 12
- thirteenth 第 13
- fourteenth 第 14
- fifteenth 第 15
- sixteenth 第 16

・**The first week in January I'll go to see Mary, and the second week in February I'll go to visit Jerry.**
一月的第一個星期我要去探望瑪麗，二月的第二個星期我要去拜訪傑瑞。

表示**不定數量**的代名詞 some, any, many, much, a few, a little 等也可作形容詞，修飾名詞。

・I need some help from Eli. 我需要伊萊給我一些幫助。

Part
5
Adjectives
That Are
Participles

分詞形容詞

1 -ed 形式的形容詞，與 -ing 形式的形容詞之比較

1 分詞形容詞指動詞的 -ing 和 -ed 形式，在使用中比較容易出錯。

- **Are you a frightened child or are you a frightening child?**
  你是一個感到害怕的孩子，還是一個令人害怕的孩子？
  ↑ 假如某人或某物使你害怕，你就會 frightened（感到害怕的），用 -ed 形式；如果你使別人害怕，你對別人而言就很 frightening（可怕的），用 -ing 形式。

- **Are you confused or are you confusing after listening to Professor Glass in English class?**
  聽完格拉斯教授的英文課，你是感到困惑呢，還是你令人困惑呢？
  ↑ 如果你聽不懂格拉斯教授的課，那麼你就會 confused（感到困惑），用 -ed 形式，也就是格拉斯教授的教學使你困惑（Professor Glass's teaching confuses you.），而你被格拉斯教授的教學搞糊塗了（You are confused by Professor Glass's teaching.）。
  ↑ 如果格拉斯教授和其他學生聽不懂你的話，不能理解你在說什麼，那麼就是你令他們困惑（You are confusing to them.），用 -ing 形式。

- **The book you wrote about the king is interesting.**
  你寫的那本關於國王的書很有趣。

- **Bing is interested in your book about the king.**
  賓對你那本關於國王的書很感興趣。

Pam was surprised
by the result of
her English exam.

- **Pam was surprised by the result of her English exam.** 潘姆對英文考試的結果感到很意外。

- **The result of Pam's English exam was surprising to her.**
  潘姆的英文考試結果出乎她的意料之外。

2 一般說來，描述某人的感覺、表情，要用 -ed 形式，描述引起這種感覺的人、物、環境、事件，要用 -ing 形式。

» 參見 203 頁〈3 -ed 與 -ing 字尾的形容詞比較〉。

-ing 形式的形容詞	-ed 形式的形容詞
· My job is very satisfying. 我的工作很令人滿意。	· I am very satisfied with my job. 我對我的工作很滿意。
· She thinks politics is interesting. 她認為政治很有趣。	· She is interested in politics. 她對政治感興趣。
· That was shocking news. 那真是令人震撼的消息。	· I was shocked when I heard the news. 我聽到那則消息後，感到震驚。
· Bob says his job is boring. 鮑勃說他的工作很乏味。	· Bob is bored with his job. 鮑勃對他的工作感到厭煩。
· The magic tricks of the short robot were very amusing. 那台小個子機器人所變的魔術把戲很有趣。	· We were amused by how Ann juggled tennis balls with Dan. 安和丹用網球玩雜耍的方式把我們逗樂了。
· Fighting a water balloon battle was tiring. 打一場水球戰很累人。	· She was very tired from the trip to Tibet. 她從西藏之旅回來後，感到很疲憊。

2 -ed 形式的形容詞，搭配特定介系詞

以 -ed 結尾的形容詞常與特定的介系詞（at、by、in、from 等）並用。

1. I was amazed at how all around us the circus lights blazed.
   馬戲團的燈光在我們周圍閃耀，使我驚嘆不已。
2. I was amused by the clowns and the bicycles they used.
   小丑們和他們用的自行車把我逗樂了。
3. I was annoyed by the elephant near me because he suddenly began to pee. 我身旁的這頭大象很讓我生氣，因為牠突然小便了起來。
4. I was bored by the slow bumper car ride that I had tried.
   我試著坐了碰碰車，可是它慢得讓我覺得很無聊。

5. I was concerned about Mom riding a big elephant called Tom.
我不放心媽媽乘坐一頭叫湯姆的大象。

6. I was confused by the House of Mirrors and Ms. Sly.
鏡子屋和斯萊女士把我搞糊塗了。

7. I was disappointed by Mom not allowing me to be an explorer of the House of Horror. 媽媽不准我進鬼屋探險，這讓我很失望。

8. I was embarrassed by my baby brother, Ted, when he vomited on my mother. 我的小弟弟泰德在媽媽身上吐了，這讓我很尷尬。

9. I was exhausted from the roller coaster rides and the wild water slides. 乘坐雲霄飛車和玩瘋狂滑水道使我筋疲力盡。

10. I was excited about the blue cannon and the two human cannonball women.
那台藍色的大砲和那兩個當作砲彈的女子，讓我激動不已。

cannon
大砲

11. I was frightened by the blue cannon's boom, and I needed to go to the bathroom.
那台藍色砲發出的轟隆聲把我嚇壞了，我得上洗手間。

12. I was interested in how Claire milked the giant cow.
我對克萊兒給那頭巨大母牛擠奶的方式感興趣。

13. I was so irritated by the heat from Jake the Dragon that I drank a milkshake poured by Coco.
傑克龍身上散發出來的熱氣讓我很煩心，於是我喝了一杯可可倒給我的奶昔。

14. I was strongly opposed to going home, but Mom said, "It is late, and Ted is supposed to be in bed." 我強烈反對回家，可是媽媽說：「天色晚了，泰德應該上床睡覺了。」

15. I was satisfied with the red cotton candy sold by Ms. Sky. 我對斯蓋女士銷售的紅棉花糖感到很滿意。

16. I was shocked by the bang as a tire on our van went flat because of a piece of barbed wire. 一片帶刺的鐵絲網把我們的廂型車戳破了一個輪胎，破裂時發出的砰砰聲把我嚇了一跳。

17. I was surprised at how quickly Mom and I changed the tire that night in the moonlight and how happy Mom seemed to be as we arrived at our cottage near the sea.
那天晚上在月光下，媽媽和我換輪胎的速度之快，讓我感到很驚訝；當我們回到濱海別墅時，媽媽似乎非常高興，也讓我感到很驚訝。

18. After a while, I was tired from all the circus lights, sights, and delights. 過了一會兒，馬戲團的各種燈光、景象和歡樂使我疲倦了。

19. Late at night, because I was worried about all the animals in the dark, I said a prayer as Mom turned off my light. 深夜，因為我為所有在黑暗中的動物擔心，所以媽媽關掉我的燈時，我禱告了一下。

3 分詞形容詞的位置

1 分詞形容詞在句中的位置與其他形容詞相同，可以在名詞前做定語，也可以在連綴動詞後做主詞補語。

・Listen carefully to every complaint from disappointed customers.
細心聆聽失望的消費者的每一個投訴。 → 名詞前

・Sam was disappointed at his final exam results.
山姆對自己的期末考成績感到很失望。 → 連綴動詞後

2 一些分詞形容詞只能用於名詞之後，相當於形容詞子句。

- the land area taken up by urban development
= the land area that was/has been taken up by urban development 那塊農地區域已經被劃入都市發展
- the damage caused by the atomic bomb
= the damage that was caused by the atomic bomb
這是由原子彈所造成的損害
- Items Lost and Found 失物招領物品（慣用語）

・The mayor questioned in a bribery case in Norway applied for an American visa yesterday. 挪威那位疑似涉嫌賄賂的市長，昨天申請美國簽證。
↳ 分詞形容詞 questioned 只能放在所修飾的名詞之後。

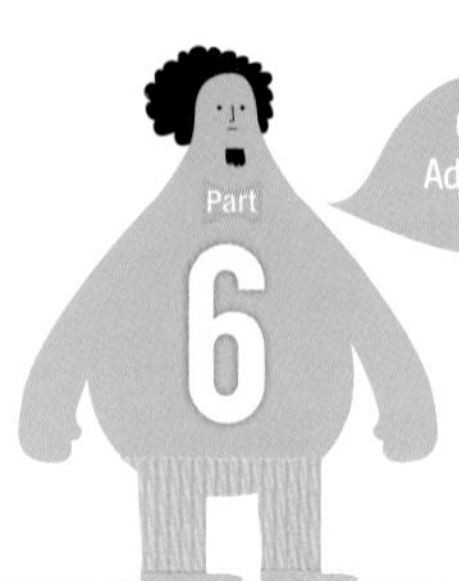

形容詞的排列順序

1 形容詞放在作形容詞用的名詞前面

當一個名詞同時由一個形容詞和名詞來修飾時，形容詞應該放在最前面。

- Mom and Pop work in a busy coffee shop.
  媽媽和爸爸在一家熱鬧的咖啡店工作。
- She works in a new robot store.
  她在一家新開張的機器人商店工作。
- Mr. Olive is an objective crime detective.
  奧利弗先生是一個公正無私的犯罪調查私家偵探。
- He is an excellent Spanish translator.
  他是個傑出的西班牙文翻譯。
- Paul climbed over the old stone wall.
  保羅翻過了那面古老的石牆。

a crime detective
犯罪調查私家偵探

2 用在名詞前的一系列形容詞的排列順序

形容詞的排列順序是英語文法中的一個難點。下頁表格總結了形容詞的排序規則，務必記牢。但要注意，在這個規則之外還有不少例外情況，不能任何時候都一味地按規則去套，應根據具體情況而變通。

用在名詞前的一系列形容詞的排列順序

	限定詞	品質／評價	外型描述					分詞	來源	材質	類型	用途 / 名詞作形容詞	名詞
			大小	長、高度	形狀	年齡	顏色						
1	an	exciting										bus	tour
2	an	expensive								diamond			ring
3	some	delicious							Italian				food
4	eight	beautiful					red						roses
5	those		huge			young			Chinese			basketball	players
6	her	attractive		long			black						hair
7	that	lovely	little				brown					hunting	cabin
8	our			tall		young			Japanese				teacher
9	a	beautiful	large							wooden			table
10	a		big		round			broken					plate
11	an								international		financial		center

1 一趟刺激的巴士之旅
2 一枚昂貴的鑽戒
3 一些美味的義大利食品
4 八朵美麗的紅玫瑰
5 這些高大年輕的中國籃球選手
6 她那動人的黑色長髮
7 那間可愛的棕色狩獵小屋
8 我們又高又年輕的日本老師
9 一張漂亮的大圓木桌
10 一個破碎的大盤子
11 國際金融中心

1 **限定詞**（determiner）：包含冠詞和其他限定詞（參見 138 頁〈Part 1 冠詞和限定詞〉），例如：

- a 一個
- an 一個
- all 全部
- few 少的
- five 五個
- her 她的
- many 許多的
- my 我的
- our 我們的
- several 幾個
- some 一些
- that 那個
- the 那
- these 那些
- this 這個
- those 那些
- three 三個
- two 兩個
- what 什麼
- which 哪個

2 **品質／評價**（observation）：表示主觀判斷的形容詞，例如：

- a beautiful lady 一位美麗的女士
- an expensive magic broom 一把昂貴的魔法掃把
- an interesting king 一個有趣的國王
- a perfect idea 一個完美的主意
- a real idiot 一個十足的傻子
- an ugly duckling 一隻醜小鴨

3 **大小／長度／高度／形狀**（size and shape）：表客觀基準的形容詞。例如：

- large 大的
- short 矮的
- round 圓的
- square 方的
- a small round table 一張小圓桌
- a long narrow street 一條又長又窄的街道
- a tall thin boy 一個又高又瘦的男孩

⤶ 表大小、長度、高度的形容詞（big, small, long, tall, short），一般放在表形狀和寬度的形容詞（round, fat, thin, slim, wide）之前。

4 **年齡**（age）：表示年齡的形容詞，例如：

- ancient 古代的
- new 新的
- old 老的
- young 年輕的
- a tall young woman 一個高高的年輕女子 → 高度 + 年齡

5 **顏色**（color）：表示顏色的形容詞，例如：

- black 黑色
- pale 灰白色
- red 紅色
- green 綠色
- pink 粉紅色
- white 白色
- a hard red ball 一個堅硬的紅球 → 品質 + 顏色
- big blue eyes 大藍眼睛 → 大小 + 顏色

6 **分詞形容詞**（participle adjectives），例如：

- broken 破碎的 ● retired 退休的 ● recently-built 剛修建的
- a small old broken plate 一個又舊又破的小盤子
  ↥ 大小 + 年齡 + 分詞形容詞

7 **來源**（origin）：表示所修飾名詞的來源的專有形容詞，例如：

- American 美國的 ● French 法國的 ● Japanese 日本的
- Chinese 中國的 ● Greek 希臘的 ● Nigerian 奈及利亞的
- an old French song 一首古老的法國歌曲 → 年齡 + 來源

8 **材料**（material）：表示材料的名詞或形容詞，例如：

- leather 皮革製的 ● gold 黃金製的 ● wooden 木製的
- plastic 塑膠製的 ● steel 鋼製的 ● woolen 羊毛製的
- a big black plastic bag 一個黑色的大塑膠包 → 大小 + 顏色 + 材料
- an new purple cotton shirt 一件紫色的新棉質襯衫 → 年齡 + 顏色 + 材料

9 **類型**（type），例如：

- digital alarm clock 數字顯示鬧鐘 → 類型（digital）+ 用途（alarm）

10 **用途**（purpose）/ **修飾詞**（qualifier）：常被看成是複合名詞的一部分，或者是作形容詞用的名詞，例如：

- book cover 書的封面 ● rocking chair 搖椅
- hunting cabin 打獵用的小屋 ● washing machine 洗衣機

· **Yesterday Mabel bought a round glass table.**
美博昨天買了一張圓玻璃桌。
↥ 順序：形狀（round）+ 材質（名詞 glass 作形容詞）

· **His wife often wears a colorful, modern silk blouse.**
他的妻子常穿色彩鮮豔、時髦的絲綢上衣。
↥ 順序：評價（colorful）+ 年齡（modern ）+ 材質（名詞 silk 作形容詞）

· **Our neighborhood has a tall, ancient redwood tree.**
我們這附近有一棵高大、古老的紅杉樹。
↥ 順序：高度（tall）+ 年齡（ancient）+ 材質（名詞 redwood 作形容詞用）

· Ted has a little blue house trailer and a red Japanese sports car.
泰德有一輛藍色的小型拖車屋和一輛紅色的日本跑車。

↳ 順序：a（限定詞）+ little（大小）+ blue（顏色）+ house（名詞作形容詞，表用途）。

↳ 順序：a（限定詞）+ red（顏色）+ Japanese（專有形容詞，表來源）+ sports（名詞作形容詞，表用途）。

· That cute, young Japanese woman ate a lot of fruit.
那位可愛、年輕的日本女子吃了很多水果。

↳ 順序：That（限定詞）+ cute（評價）+ young（年齡）+ Japanese（專有形容詞，表來源）

· There are many valuable old airplanes. 有很多有價值的舊飛機。

↳ 順序：many（限定詞）+ valuable（評價）+ old（年齡）

· I am looking at the clear blue sky. 我正望著萬里無雲的藍天。

↳ 順序：the（限定詞）+ clear（品質／評價）+ blue（顏色）

· I bought a Chinese glass flower vase.
我買了一個中國的玻璃花瓶。

↳ 順序：a（限定詞）+ Chinese（來源）+ glass（材質）+ flower（名詞作形容詞，表用途）

· She has a pair of red Mexican leather riding boots.
她有一雙紅色的墨西哥皮馬靴。

↳ 順序：red（顏色）+ Mexican（來源）+ leather（材料）+ riding（用途）

如果一系列的形容詞屬於同一種類（都是表示顏色或都是表示主觀判斷），那就不用特別排順序。

· She has a beautiful and valuable ring.
= She has a valuable and beautiful ring.
她有一枚美麗而貴重的戒指。

↳ valuable 和 beautiful 都是表示品質的形容詞（主觀判斷的基準），無論哪一個放在前面都無所謂。

· He is wearing a red and green shirt.
= He is wearing a green and red shirt. 他穿著一件紅配綠的襯衫。

↳ red 和 green 都是表示顏色的形容詞，無論哪一個放在前面都無所謂。

3 數量詞的次序

1 數量詞和形容詞的次序

a 數量詞 + 形容詞

數量詞（包含基數詞與序數詞）是限定詞，通常放在形容詞的前面。

b 序數詞 + 基數詞

序數詞和基數詞連用時，序數詞 first、next、last 等常放在基數詞 one、two、three 等前面，這一點與中文的語法順序一樣，很容易記住。

- five fat hippos 五匹胖河馬
- the first two applicants 最初的兩個申請人
- his last three jobs 他最後的三份工作
- the next four days 接下來的四天
- six big men 六個高大男子

- **Amy and Anna are two smart girls with pretty curls.**
  艾咪和安娜是兩個有著漂亮捲髮的聰明女孩。

- **Kay's dad said that the moonlight would be very bright for the next four nights.** 凱的爸爸說，接下來的四個晚上，月光會很亮。

2 數量詞修飾單數可數名詞的用法

a the + 序數詞 + 單數可數名詞

當序數詞（first、second、third 等）用來限定一個單數可數名詞時，前面要加定冠詞 the。

- the first chapter 第一章
- the third person 第三人稱；第三者

- **Labor Day in the USA is celebrated on the first Monday in September.**
  美國的勞動節是在九月的第一個星期一慶祝。

b 單數可數名詞 + 基數詞

基數詞（如 one、two、three、four 等）可用在單數可數名詞後面，代表排列順序。這時不用定冠詞 the，名詞和基數詞的首字母都需**大寫**。

- Last night Sue left before the beginning of Act Two.
  = Last night Sue left before the beginning of the second act.
  昨晚蘇在第二幕開始之前就離開了。

- Is there any glamor in Unit Six of *Comprehensive Grammar*?
  = Is there any glamor in the sixth unit of *Comprehensive Grammar*?
  在《文法大全》的第六單元裡有沒有什麼魅力？

- I'm reading Volume Two of *Poems for the New Millennium*.
  = I'm reading the second volume of *Poems for the New Millennium*.
  我在讀《新時代詩歌》第二冊裡的詩歌。

4 兩個以上的形容詞並列與 and

當兩個以上的形容詞並列在一起，有時在**最後一個形容詞**前面用 and 或 but，有時又不用 and 或者 but，請看下列說明。

1 連綴動詞後的一系列形容詞（用 and）

連綴動詞（be、seem、look 等）後面若接一系列的形容詞，要用逗號分開，通常在最後一個形容詞前面用 and 或 but、or 連接。美式英語中，在 and 的前面常常需要有一個逗號。連綴動詞後面的一系列的形容詞的順序，常把長的形容詞（音節多的形容詞）放在後面。

- The silk blouses Ted gave me on my birthday were blue, yellow, orange, or red. 我生日那天，泰德給我的絲質上衣有藍的、黃的、橙的或紅的。

- Ms. Annie Olive is short, dark, and attractive.
  安妮·奧利夫女士個子小、皮膚黑，又嫵媚動人。

- For Emma, a day with Grandma Wool is usually short, exciting, and blissful.
  對愛瑪來說，與伍爾奶奶共度的一天通常都短暫、令人興奮且充滿歡樂。

- Sensible Emma is sometimes exotic, mysterious, and incomprehensible. 明智的愛瑪有時很奇特、神祕，而且不可思議。
  ↑ 音節最多的形容詞（incomprehensible）放在最後。

2 名詞前的一系列同類形容詞（常省略 and）

如果**系列同類形容詞**出現在名詞前面，常省略 and 或 but，在這一系列形容詞之間用逗號即可，但也可以省略逗號，直接列出所有形容詞。

- a colorful stylish cotton shirt
  = a stylish colorful cotton shirt
  = a colorful, stylish cotton shirt
  = a stylish, colorful cotton shirt
  = a colorful and stylish cotton shirt
  = a stylish and colorful cotton shirt 一件色彩鮮豔、有型的棉質襯衫
  - cotton shirt 是複合名詞，與形容詞 stylish 之間不能用逗號分開，也不能用 and 連接，因為 colorful 和 stylish 修飾整個複合名詞 cotton shirt。
  - colorful 和 stylish 都是表示評價的形容詞（同類形容詞），兩者之間可用、也可不用逗號或 and 連接。凡是能夠用 and 連接的地方，就可以用逗號取代 and。
  - 同類形容詞如果都是多音節詞或都是單音節詞，沒有特定的順序，可以把 colorful 置於 stylish 前面，也可以把 stylish 置於 colorful 前面。

- **Pearl is a beautiful (and) smart girl.**
  = **Pearl is a beautiful, smart girl.** 珀兒是個美麗、聰明的女孩。
- **Dan is a cruel (and) vicious man.**
  = **Dan is a cruel, vicious man.** 丹是一個殘忍、邪惡的男人。
- **Those are tired but happy cheerleaders.**
  = **Those are tired, happy cheerleaders.** 那些是疲勞但快樂的啦啦隊長。
  - 參見 790 頁〈2 修飾同一個名詞的形容詞〉。

NOTE

兩個表示顏色的形容詞之間，要加 and（不能省略 and）。

- a yellow and blue flag 黃藍旗幟
- a red and white shirt 紅白襯衫

3 名詞前的一系列不同類形容詞

a **不同類的形容詞**之間是否要用逗號分開，取決於這些字之間是否可以用 and。

✗ the dear and little and old lady
✗ the dear, little, old lady
✓ the dear little old lady 可愛的小個子老太太
↑ dear 修飾整個片語 little old lady。

✗ the established and British political system
✗ the established, British political system
✓ the established British political system 現有的英國政治體系
↑ established 修飾整個片語 British political system。

- that polite, tall Russian man 一個彬彬有禮的高大俄羅斯男子
  = that polite and tall Russian man = that polite tall Russian man
  ↑ polite 和 tall 之間可以用 and 連接，也可以用逗號來替代 and。
  ↑ Russian man 視為一個整體，tall 和 Russian 之間就不能用 and，也不能插入逗號。polite 和 tall 都修飾 Russian man。

b 複合名詞與修飾複合名詞的形容詞之間，不用 and 或逗號連接。

- **Joan jumped off that old stone wall and broke her right thigh bone.**
  瓊安從舊石牆上跳下來，造成右腳的大腿骨折了。
  ↑ stone wall 是複合名詞，與形容詞 old 之間不用 and 或逗號連接。

- **Marilyn lives in that lovely white hunting cabin.**
  瑪麗蓮住在那間可愛的白色獵屋裡。
  ↑ 順序：限定詞（that）+ 評價（lovely）+ 顏色（white）+ 用途（hunting）
  ↑ 這一系列不同類的形容詞不能用 and 連接，也就不能插入逗號，第一個形容詞 lovely 修飾「第二個形容詞 white + 複合名詞 hunting cabin」（white hunting cabin 被看成是一個整體）。

» 參見 790 頁〈2 修飾同一個名詞的形容詞〉。

系列形容詞置於名詞前，最後一個形容詞與名詞之間，不能用逗號。

✗ Kay put in a long, hard, demanding, day on Friday.
✓ Kay put in a long, hard, demanding day on Friday.
凱在星期五時度過了一個漫長、辛苦又吃力的一天。

形容詞的比較級和最高級

1 形容詞「級」的作用與類別

1 形容詞的「級」（degree）：形容詞可用級的變化來表達要修飾的等級，如：

- **Lily is a rich woman, Sally is richer than Lily, and Ms. Sherry Brown is the richest woman in town.** 莉莉是一位富有的女子，莎莉比莉莉更富有，而雪麗．布朗女士卻是城裡最富有的女子。

  ↑ rich → richer → richest 富有→更富有→ 最富有

2 形容詞有三種級：原級、比較級和最高級。

a **原級**（positive degree）：被形容的人或物並未與另一個人或物進行比較，那麼就應該用形容詞的原級，原級的形容詞沒有形的變化。

b **比較級**（comparative degree）：比較兩個人或兩個物時，表達其中一個比另一個「更……」，要用形容詞的比較級。

c **最高級**（superlative degree）：比較三個或三個以上的人或物時，該用形容詞的最高級，表示哪一個「最……」。

fat 胖　fatter 較胖　fattest 最胖

- **Her new hat is sillier than her skirt made out of fur.**
  她的新帽子比她那件毛皮裙還可笑。

  ↑ sillier 是比較級，兩個東西 hat 和 skirt 之間進行比較。

- **Yesterday was the longest day of the year in the Northern Hemisphere.** 昨天是北半球一年中最長的一天。
  ↥ longest 是最高級，比較的是兩天以上（最長）。
- **Lily has a more positive attitude than Sally (does).**
  莉莉的態度比莎莉來得更積極向上。
  ↥ more positive 是比較級，在兩個人（Lily 和 Sally）之間進行比較；形容詞 positive 前加 more。
- **Mary Brown is the most cheerful woman in Cape Town.**
  瑪麗·布朗是開普敦市最快樂的女子。
  ↥ most cheerful 是最高級，比較三個或三個以上的人；在形容詞 cheerful 前面加 most。

2 形容詞「級」的規則變化

1 單音節形容詞

a 比較級：單音節形容詞 + -er → 單音節的形容詞，通常在原級後面加 -er，就變成比較級。

最高級：單音節形容詞 + -est → 在原級後面加上 -est，就變成最高級。大部分形容詞皆依此規則變化。

原級			比較級		最高級
bright	明亮的	→	brighter	→	brightest
broad	寬闊的	→	broader	→	broadest
cheap	便宜的	→	cheaper	→	cheapest
cold	寒冷的	→	colder	→	coldest
cool	涼爽的	→	cooler	→	coolest
fast	快速的	→	faster	→	fastest
great	優秀的	→	greater	→	greatest
high	高的	→	higher	→	highest
kind	親切的	→	kinder	→	kindest
light	明亮的	→	lighter	→	lightest
long	長的	→	longer	→	longest
loud	大聲的	→	louder	→	loudest

• low	低的	→ lower	→ lowest
• near	近的	→ nearer	→ nearest
• old	老的	→ older	→ oldest
• proud	驕傲的	→ prouder	→ proudest
• rich	有錢的	→ richer	→ richest
• short	短的	→ shorter	→ shortest
• slow	慢的	→ slower	→ slowest
• strong	強壯的	→ stronger	→ strongest
• tall	高的	→ taller	→ tallest
• young	年輕的	→ younger	→ youngest

ℓ 上表中有一些詞也可以作副詞。

NOTE

1 子音字母加 -y 結尾的單音節形容詞，去 y 加 -ier 或 -iest，形成比較級或最高級：• dry 乾的 → drier 比較乾的 → driest 最乾的

2 形容詞 like（相似的）的比較級和最高級，一定要用 more 和 most。

- Tom is more like his dad than his mom.
  湯姆長得比較像他父親，不像母親。

3 -ed 結尾的單音節形容詞，比較級和最高級要用 more/less、most/least。

• tired 疲倦的 → more/less tired 較疲倦的（較不疲倦的）
→ most/least tired 最疲倦的（最不疲倦的）

Diving Deep Into English 37 何謂音節？

❶ **音節**是發音的單位，一個音節由**一個母音**加上一個或一個以上的子音構成。或者說，音節是構成一個字（或字的一個部分）的一個音。

❷ 有的單字只有一個音節，有的則多達數個音節。有幾個音節，唸起來就有幾個音，例如：一個音節的字，唸起來就只有一個音，而兩個音節的字，唸起來就有兩個音。

• bright → bright /braɪt/（一個音節）
• common → com-mon /ˈkɑmən/（兩個音節）

b **比較級**：「單母音 + 單子音」重複字尾子音 + -er
最高級：「單母音 + 單子音」重複字尾子音 + -est

以「單母音 + 單子音」結尾的單音節形容詞的比較級和最高級，先重複字尾子音後，再加 -er 或 -est。

原級			比較級		最高級
big	大的	→	bigger	→	biggest
dim	暗淡的	→	dimmer	→	dimmest
fat	肥胖的	→	fatter	→	fattest
hot	熱的	→	hotter	→	hottest
mad	發狂的	→	madder	→	maddest
sad	悲傷的	→	sadder	→	saddest
slim	苗條的	→	slimmer	→	slimmest
thin	薄的、瘦的	→	thinner	→	thinnest

唯獨子音字母 w 不適用此規則，不可重複字尾：
- low 低的 → lower 較低的 → lowest 最低的

c **比較級**：字尾是 -e 的單音節 + -r
最高級：字尾是 -e 的單音節 + -st

以 -e 結尾的單音節形容詞，加 -r 構成比較級，加 -st 構成最高級。

原級			比較級		最高級
close	近的	→	closer	→	closest
large	大的	→	larger	→	largest
late	遲的	→	later	→	latest
nice	好的	→	nicer	→	nicest
rude	粗魯的	→	ruder	→	rudest
safe	安全的	→	safer	→	safest
wide	寬的	→	wider	→	widest

2 雙音節形容詞

a 比較級：字尾是 -y 的雙音節形容詞， 去 y + -ier
最高級：字尾是 -y 的雙音節形容詞，去 y + -est

以 -y 結尾的雙音節形容詞在構成比較級和最高級時，要先把 y 變成 i，再加 -er（比較級）或 -est（最高級）。

原級			比較級		最高級
busy	忙碌的	→	busier	→	busiest
chilly	冷颼颼的	→	chillier	→	chilliest
dirty	髒的	→	dirtier	→	dirtiest
early	早的	→	earlier	→	earliest
easy	容易的	→	easier	→	easiest
funny	有趣的	→	funnier	→	funniest
happy	快樂的	→	happier	→	happiest
heavy	重的	→	heavier	→	heaviest
hilly	多山丘的、陡的	→	hillier	→	hilliest
juicy	多汁的	→	juicier	→	juiciest
jumpy	跳動的	→	jumpier	→	jumpiest
lively	活潑的	→	livelier	→	liveliest
lovely	可愛的	→	lovelier	→	loveliest
nasty	惡劣的	→	nastier	→	nastiest
noisy	嘈雜的	→	noisier	→	noisiest
pretty	漂亮的	→	prettier	→	prettiest
silly	愚蠢的	→	sillier	→	silliest
smelly	臭的	→	smellier	→	smelliest
tidy	整潔的	→	tidier	→	tidiest

b 比較級：more/less + 非 -y 字尾的雙音節形容詞
最高級：most/least + 非 -y 字尾的雙音節形容詞

大多數不以 -y 結尾的雙音節形容詞，要用 more/less 來構成比較級，用 most/least 來構成最高級（more 和 most 具有肯定意義，而 less 和 least 具有否定意義）。

原級		比較級	最高級
active	活躍的	→ more/less active	→ most/least active
brutal	殘忍的	→ more/less brutal	→ most/least brutal
careless	粗心的	→ more/less careless	→ most/least careless
charming	迷人的	→ more/less charming	→ most/least charming
cheerful	快樂的	→ more/less cheerful	→ most/least cheerful
famous	有名的	→ more/less famous	→ most/least famous
foolish	愚笨的	→ more/less foolish	→ most/least foolish
harmful	有害的	→ more/less harmful	→ most/least harmful
hopeful	有望的	→ more/less hopeful	→ most/least hopeful
polite	客氣的	→ more/less polite	→ most/least polite
worried	擔心的	→ more/less worried	→ most/least worried

Diving Deep Into English 38 少數非以 -y 結尾的雙音節形容詞，可以用兩種方式構成比較級和最高級

在上述規則之外，少數非以 -y 結尾的雙音節形容詞，可加 -er/-est 或 -r/-st（字尾是 -e）構成比較級和最高級，也可加 more/less 和 most/least，來構成比較級或最高級，如下面表格所示。不過有些文法學家認為，下面這些形容詞只能用 -er 和 -est 的形式來構成比較級和最高級，用 more/less 和 most/least 反而是錯誤的。在考試中如果出現這種情況，最好還是用 -er 和 -est 的形式，因為這種形式是最正規的，不會出錯。

原級	比較級	最高級
clever 聰明的	→ cleverer more/less clever	→ cleverest most/least clever
common 普通的	→ commoner more/less common	→ commonest most/least common
handsome 英俊的	→ handsomer more/less handsome	→ handsomest most/least handsome
mature 成熟的	→ maturer more/less mature	→ maturest most/least mature
narrow 狹窄的	→ narrower more/less narrow	→ narrowest most/least narrow

原級		比較級		最高級
obscure 晦澀的	→	obscurer more/less obscure	→	obscurest most/least obscure
quiet 安靜的	→	quieter more/less quiet	→	quietest most/least quiet
shallow 淺的	→	shallower more/less shallow	→	shallowest most/least shallow
simple 簡單的	→	simpler more/less simple	→	simplest most/least simple
stupid 愚蠢的	→	stupider more/less stupid	→	stupidest most/least stupid
subtle 微妙的	→	subtler more/less subtle	→	subtlest most/least subtle

3 多音節形容詞

比較級：more/less + 多音節形容詞
最高級：most/least + 多音節形容詞

具有三個或三個以上音節的形容詞，稱為**多音節形容詞**。多音節形容詞在原級前面加 more 或 less 構成比較級，加 most 或 least 構成最高級。

三個音節	beautiful 漂亮的	→ beau-ti-ful	/ˋbjutəfəl/
	expensive 昂貴的	→ ex-pen-sive	/ɪkˋspɛnsɪv/
三個以上的音節	comfortable 舒服的	→ com-for-ta-ble	/ˋkʌmfətəbl̩/
	reasonable 合理的	→ rea-son-a-ble	/ˋriznəbl̩/

原級			比較級		最高級
acceptable	可接受的	→	more/less acceptable	→	most/least acceptable
capable	能幹的	→	more/less capable	→	most/least capable

- confident 自信的 → more/less confident → most/least confident
- delicious 美味的 → more/less delicious → most/least delicious
- difficult 困難的 → more/less difficult → most/least difficult
- expensive 昂貴的 → more/less expensive → most/least expensive
- generous 慷慨的 → more/less generous → most/least generous
- important 重要的 → more/less important → most/least important
- interesting 有趣的 more/less interesting most/least interesting
- powerful 強大的 more/less powerful most/least powerful
- practical 實際的 more/less practical most/least practical
- reasonable 合理的 more/less reasonable most/least reasonable
- valuable 有價值的 more/less valuable most/least valuable

Diving Deep Into English 39 以「子音 + -y」結尾的多音節形容詞

❶ 以 -y 結尾的雙音節形容詞，加上字首 un- 之後的反義詞雖然是多音節，但其比較級和最高級仍然要去字尾 y 加 -ier 和 -iest，例如：

- unhappy 不快樂的 → unhappier → unhappiest
- untidy 不整潔的 → untidier → untidiest

❷ 你可以掌握另一種記憶原則，亦即以「子音 + -y」結尾的形容詞，一律去字尾 y，加 -ier/-iest 構成比較級或最高級。

3 形容詞（與副詞）「級」的不規則變化

1 不規則變化的形容詞

有些形容詞和副詞的比較級和最高級，不是加 -er 或 -est，也不是加 more/less 或 most/least，而是不規則變化。這類的形容詞只能靠你努力去記住！

原級			比較級		最高級
bad	壞的	→	worse	→	worst
good	好的	→	better	→	best
well	好的；健康的	→	better	→	best
ill	生病的	→	worse	→	worst
far（指距離）	遠的	→	farther	→	farthest
far（指程度、距離）	遠的	→	further	→	furthest
few（修飾可數名詞）	少數的	→	fewer	→	fewest
little（修飾不可數名詞）	少量的		less		least
many（修飾可數名詞）	許多的		more		most
much（修飾不可數名詞）	許多的		more		most
old	年老的；舊的		older		oldest
old（指年齡）	年老的		older, elder		oldest, eldest

↥ 上表中的一些詞也可以作副詞（如：far 遙遠地、well 很好地）。

↥ 上表中的 fewer/fewest、older/oldest 屬於規則形容詞的變化，放在上表中與 less/least、elder/eldest 比較。

- **Kay, please put in more sugar than you did yesterday.**
  凱，請多放一點糖，比你昨天放的還要多。
  ↥ much（許多的）的比較級形式是 more（更多的）。

- **Walking is the best possible exercise. Habituate yourself to walk very far.**
  (President Thomas Jefferson)
  步行是最佳的可行運動，要養成長距離步行的習慣。
  ↥ good 的最高級是 best。

2 far 的兩種比較級和最高級

far

farther / farthest

→ 指**距離**（英式英語也常用 further 和 furthest 來指距離）

- **The farthest car in the parking lot is mine.**
  停車場裡最遠的那輛車是我的。
  ↥ 指距離遙遠，英式英語也可以用 furthest（the furthest car in the parking lot）。

- **It's a long way from here to the airport—farther than I thought.** 從這裡去機場好遠啊，比我想像的還遠。

further / furthest

→ 指「更進一步的；另外的；（空間或時間）更遙遠的／最遙遠的」。

● further news 進一步報導

- **Sam will give you further instructions later.**
  之後山姆會給你進一步的指示。
  ↥ further 指程度，表示「進一步的」。

- **Robin Hood thought further back into his childhood.**
  羅賓漢回想起更遙遠的童年時代。
  ↥ further 在這個句子中是副詞，修飾動詞 thought。
  ↥ further 指時間上更久遠，可以指過去，也可以指未來。

3 old 的兩種比較級和最高級

a old 的比較級和最高級，通常用 older 和 oldest 表示。older 和 oldest 可以和 than 連用。如：

- the oldest house in our village 我們村子裡最古老的房子
- my oldest son 我的長子
- his older sister 他的姐姐

- **Ann is six years older than her husband Dan.** 安比她的先生丹大六歲。

b 英式英語也用 elder 和 eldest 來比較人的年齡，尤其是指同一個家庭裡的成員。elder 和 eldest **只能用在名詞前面**，不能和 than 連用。如：

- his elder sister 他的姐姐
- my eldest son 我的長子

C 美式英語則用 older 和 oldest 來比較人的年齡，無論是同一家庭成員，還是非家庭成員都可以用。

| 美式 | **Lily is the oldest child in her family.**
| 英式 | **Lily is the eldest child in her family.** 莉莉是家中的長女。
| 美式 | **My older brother Henry is married to my old friend Mary.**
| 英式 | **My elder brother Henry is married to my old friend Mary.**
我的哥哥亨利娶了我的老朋友瑪麗。

4 less 與 fewer 的差異

less 與 fewer 都指「較少的」，差別如下：

little/less/least + 單數名詞（通常是不可數名詞）	few/fewer/fewest + 複數名詞
• less bad weather 較少的壞天氣	• fewer snowstorms 較少暴風雪
• less energy 較少的精力	• fewer chores 較少家事
• less knowledge 較少的知識	• fewer facts 較少事實
• less air traffic 較少的飛機流動量	• fewer airplanes and helicopters 較少飛機和直升機
• less interest 較不感興趣	• fewer interested participants 較少感興趣的參與者

- **Dan has less knowledge than Ann.** 丹不如安有學問。
- **Daniel knows far fewer girls than Mark.**
  丹尼爾認識的女孩比馬克認識的少得多。
  ↳ far 是副詞，修飾形容詞比較級 fewer，表示程度。

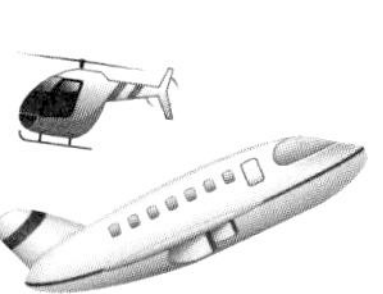

- **There's less air traffic near the airport tonight than last night.** 今晚機場附近的飛機流動量比昨晚少。
- **There are fewer airplanes and helicopters near the airport tonight than last night.** 今晚機場附近的飛機和直升機比昨晚少。

» 參見 132 頁〈14 few、a few、little、a little：限定詞或代名詞〉。

4 錯誤的比較級和最高級形式

1 含「絕對」意義的形容詞，無比較級和最高級

有些形容詞沒有比較級或最高級形式，如：correct、ideal、perfect、unique 等。以 correct 這個詞來說，某事要嘛正確，要嘛就不正確，沒有「更正確的」（more correct）或「最正確的」（most correct），因此 correct 的比較級就無意義。有些作者會用這些形容詞的比較級和最高級，例如 more perfect、fuller、straighter 等，但最好避免這種累贅的用法。這類形容詞在意義上表示「絕對的，無與倫比的」，由它們轉換成的副詞（如：absolutely, entirely）也沒有比較級和最高級。例如：

- absolute 絕對的
- alone 孤獨的
- basic 基本的
- blind 瞎的
- certain 無疑的
- complete 完整的
- correct 正確的
- dead 死的
- deadly 致命的
- empty 空的
- entire 全部的
- essential 必要的
- final 最後的
- full 滿的
- excellent 優等的
- ideal 理想的
- harmless 無害的
- meaningless 無意義的
- obvious 明顯的
- perfect 完美的
- round 圓的
- single 單一的
- square 正方形的
- superior 上等的
- straight 筆直的
- total 全體的
- unique 獨一無二的
- universal 全球的
- wrong 錯誤的

- **Bob is an ideal candidate for this job.** 鮑勃是做這份工作的理想人選。
- **At every crisis in one's life, it is absolute salvation to have some sympathetic friend to whom you can think aloud without restraint or misgiving.** (President Thomas Woodrow Wilson)
  在人生的每個危機時刻，有個富有同情心的朋友，你可以與之推心置腹，傾訴衷腸，這絕對是一種拯救之路。

2 避免雙重比較

不能在一個以 -er 構成的比較級形容詞前面又加上 more，或是在一個以 -est 構成的最高級形容詞前面又加上 most，造成雙重比較。

✗ I wish my interpreter were more quieter.
✓ I wish my interpreter were quieter. 但願我的翻譯少說點話。

✗ Is the climate in Singapore more warmer than that of Labrador?
✓ Is the climate in Singapore warmer than that of Labrador?
新加坡的氣候比拉布拉多半島的氣候溫暖嗎？

3 描述 how much 和 how many 的形容詞

a 描述 how much 和 how many 的形容詞常被錯誤使用。如果是**可以一個個數的東西**，就要用 fewer 或 many。如果談論的是「**量**」（quantity），無法一個個數，就要用 less、much。

不可數
- less money 較少的錢
- less knowledge 較少的知識

可數
- fewer days 較少天數
- fewer rockets 較少火箭

- **Kate paused to poach a few French fries off my plate.**
凱特停下來，然後從我的盤子裡偷了一些薯條。
↳ French fries 是一條條可以數的。要用 a few 修飾，不用 a little 修飾。

- **Sue eats less mashed potatoes than you do.** 蘇吃的馬鈴薯泥比你少。
↳ potato 雖然是可數名詞（one potato, two potatoes），但馬鈴薯泥無法數。這裡指的是 a smaller quantity of mashed potatoes。

b 在一些與統計和數字相關的片語中，要用「less than + 數量詞 + 複數可數名詞」。

- less than twenty miles to Chicago 去芝加哥的路程不到 20 英里
- less than five feet tall 高度不到五英尺
- spend less than two hundred dollars on the trip 旅費不到 200 塊美元
- less than five weeks 少於五星期

↳ 這裡的 twenty miles、five feet、two hundred dollars、five weeks 被看成是整體的「量」（quantity），而不是一個個數的個體。

- **Less than 20 people attended Sue's Christmas party.** 蘇舉辦的聖誕聚會，參加人數不到 20 人。
↳ 這句也可以用 fewer than，但用 less than 更符合慣用法，把 20 people 看成是一個整體，而不是一個個數的個體。

比較級的用法

1 表示「相等」（equality）的句型

1 as + 形容詞原級 + as（達到與……相同的程度）

要表達人、東西等在某方面是相等的，可用「as + 形容詞原級 + as」的結構。

- Weep Lake is as deep as Leap Lake.
  威浦湖跟利浦湖一樣深。

- Lilly's job is as difficult as Sally's.
  莉莉的工作跟莎莉的工作一樣難。

- Your hands are as cold as ice.
  Do you want a cup of hot chocolate?
  你的手像冰一樣冷。你想喝一杯熱巧克力嗎？

- Is she as busy as before?
  她像從前那樣忙碌嗎？

- Those identical twin girls are nearly as tall as their mother.
  那對同卵雙胞胎女孩幾乎跟她們的母親一樣高了。
  ↑ 可以在「as + 形容詞原級 + as」前面加上 just、nearly、not quite 等副詞修飾。

2 not so/as + 形容詞原級 + as（沒有達到與……相同的程度）

在否定句中，可以用「not so/as + 形容詞原級 + as」結構。

Paul is not so tall as his brother Saul.
= Paul is not as tall as his brother Saul.
保羅沒有他的兄弟所羅高。

- Is Sue not so slim as Lulu?
  = Is Sue not as slim as Lulu? 蘇沒有露露那麼苗條嗎？

- My eyes are not so good as yours.
  = My eyes are not as good as yours. 我的視力沒有你好。

1 在傳統文法中，so . . . as 結構可以用於否定句、疑問句和一些以 if 引導的子句中。但 so . . . as 結構在美式英語中越來越罕見，而 as . . . as 結構現在可用於所有的句型結構中：肯定句、否定句、疑問句、 if 引導的子句。

- Tom is not so tall as Mom. 湯姆沒有媽媽高。（否定句）
- Is Ted so bad as you said? 泰德真的有你說的那麼壞嗎？（疑問句）
- If it is so bad as you say, you ought to leave right away.（if 子句）
  如果情況如你所說的那麼糟糕，你應當立即離開。
  ⤴ 上面三個例句現在都可以用 as . . . as 結構來替代。

2 如果只是表示「沒有那麼」，並不表示「沒有達到與……相同的程度（not as/so . . . as）」，在一些慣用語中要用 not so，而不用 not as，如：

- She's not so sure. 她沒有那麼肯定。
- The situation is not so bad. 形勢沒有那麼糟。
- Not so loud, please. 請不要那麼吵鬧。
- Her health is not so good. 她的健康沒有那麼好。

3 as + 形容詞原級 + a/an + 單數可數名詞 + as（肯定句）
not as + 形容詞原級 + a/an + 單數可數名詞 + as（否定句）
not such + 形容詞原級 + 複數名詞 + as（否定句）

如果形容詞和第二個 as 之間有一個單數可數名詞，需要在這個名詞前加 a 或 an，否定句在形容詞前用 not as。否定句中的複數名詞只能用 not such。

- They are not such good swimmers as I expected.
  他們游泳不像我預料的那樣出色。
  ⤴ not as 不能和複數名詞連用，複數名詞要用 not such。

- She is as hardworking a student as I have ever known.
  她是我認識的學生中最用功的。 → 單數可數名詞前要加 a/an。

- Dee is not as excellent a volleyball player now as she was last year.
  = Dee is not such an excellent volleyball player now as she was last year.
  蒂打排球沒有去年打得那麼好了。 → 注意上面兩個句子的語序不同。

4 as . . . as possible（盡可能……）
as . . . as + I/he/she + can/could（盡可能……）

- Sue needs to learn not to be gullible as soon as possible. 蘇得盡快學會不要輕易受騙。
- How can Mabel and I get to the hospital as fast as possible? 美博和我要如何才能盡快趕到醫院？
- I'm walking as fast as I can. 我正在盡快地走。
  ↑ 上面三個例句的 as . . . as 片語都是作副詞，修飾句中的動詞。

5 表示倍數的數詞 + as + much/many + as（表示倍數）

✗ This Fun in the Sun swimsuit is prettier, but it costs twice more than the other one. → 倍數詞（twice, three times）後面不能用 more than。

✗ This Fun in the Sun swimsuit is prettier, but it costs as much twice as the other one. →as much 和 as many 的後面，不要用倍數詞。

✗ This Fun in the Sun swimsuit is prettier, but it costs twice so much as the other one. → 在倍數詞後面應該用 as，不要用 so。

✓ This Fun in the Sun swimsuit is prettier, but it costs twice as much as the other one.
這件名叫「陽光下的歡樂」的泳衣更漂亮，不過，價錢是另外一件的一倍。

6 表示倍數的數詞 + as + 形容詞原級 + as
表示倍數的數詞 + 形容詞原級 + as（不常用）

three times
as big as

- Ann's dog is three times as big as Dan's.
  = Ann's dog is three times big as Dan's. 安的狗是丹的狗的三倍大。
  ↑ 可以省略第一個 as（如上面第 2 句），但不常用這種句型。
- Mary is twice as lively as her brother Jerry. 瑪麗比她哥哥傑瑞活潑一倍。

7 **the same as**（和……相同）
the same + 名詞 + as

- Your salary is the same as mine.
  = You get the same salary as me. 你的薪水和我的薪水是一樣的。
- Dee is the same age as me. 蒂的年齡和我一樣。

2 表示「不均等」（inequality）的句型

1 **比較級 + than**（比較……）

要表達**兩個**人、物、地方等在某方面不均等，用「形容詞比較級 + than」。

- Dan Bold is 12 years old, and Ann Bold is 14 years old. Ann is older than Dan. 丹．伯爾德 12 歲，安．伯爾德 14 歲，安的年紀比丹大。
- My English is better than my Polish. 我英語比我的波蘭語好。
  ↑ 比較級要用 than，不要用 as。
- Jean is happier now than she was when she first came aboard this submarine. 琴現在比她初登潛水艇時快活。→ happy 的比較級是 happier。
- Our town is less crowded today than five years ago.
  = Our town isn't as crowded today as five years ago.
  我們的城鎮現在沒有五年前那麼擁擠了。→less . . . than 與 not as . . . as 的意義相似。

2 **taller than I am 與 taller than me 的比較**（主格和受格之分）

當用 than 進行比較時，後面應該接主格形式（I、he、we），還是受格形式（me、him、us）？應該是 taller than I am，還是 taller than me 呢？

正式文體 用主格形式（I/she）+ 動詞
口語體 用受格形式（me/her）

Formal Amy, Pam, and Mary are older than I am.
Informal Amy, Pam, and Mary are older than me.
艾咪、潘姆和瑪麗的年紀比我大。
↑ 用主格（I、he、she、we、they）時，
後面最好要接動詞（than I am, than she is）。

1 在使用「I like him better than she/her.」這類句子時，應注意句意的差別。比較下列句子：

- I like him better than she. → better在這裡用作副詞well的比較級。
  ↳ 使用主格，意思可能是：我喜歡這位男子，勝過她喜歡這位男子。
- I like him better than her.
  ↳ 使用受格，意思可能是：我喜歡這位男子，勝過我喜歡這位女子。

2 為了避免歧義，上面的句子應當改寫成：

- I like him better than she does. 我喜歡他，勝過她喜歡他。
- I like him better than I like her. 我喜歡他，勝過我喜歡她。

3 在這類含有 like、love 等的句子中，即使在 than 後面用名詞，語意也不一定清楚。

- I like Dan better than Joe.
  ↳ 這句話的意思可能是「我喜歡丹，勝過喜歡喬。」
  也可能是「我喜歡丹，勝過喬喜歡丹。」

4 為了避免歧義，最好明確寫明：

- I like Dan better than I like Joe. 我喜歡丹，勝過喜歡喬。
- I like Dan better than Joe does.
  = I like Dan better than Joe likes Dan. 我喜歡丹，勝過喬喜歡丹。

3 倍數詞（數字 + times）+ 比較級 + than

可以用「數字 + times + 比較級 + than」這個結構來代替「數字 + times + as + 原級 + as」的結構。

- She said running a marathon was three times more difficult than swimming across the Amazon.
  = She said running a marathon was three times as difficult as swimming across the Amazon.
  她說，馬拉松賽跑比游泳橫越亞馬遜河艱苦兩倍。

- His house is three times bigger than mine.
  = His house is three times as big as mine.
  他的房子比我的房子大兩倍。

NOTE

twice 和 half 雖然也是倍數詞，卻不能用在「倍數詞 + 比較級 + than」的結構中，twice 和 half 只能用在「twice/half + as + 原級 + as」的結構中。

✗ Nan is twice livelier than her older sister Ann.
✓ Nan is twice as lively as her older sister Ann.
南比她姐姐安活潑一倍。

✗ Nan's English is half better than Ann's.
✓ Nan's English is half as good as Ann's.
南的英語只有安的英語一半好。

✗ Nan is half taller than Ann.
✓ Nan is half as tall as Ann. 南只有安的一半高。

4 much 和 far 等修飾比較級

比較級不能用 very 修飾，而是用以下的詞來修飾：

- a bit 有點〔口語〕
- a little 少許的
- a lot ……得多〔口語〕
- any 少許；稍微
- even 甚至
- far …… 得多
- no 一點也不
- rather 相當
- much ……得多
- very much 非常多

- I'm much/far older than Pam.
  我的年齡比潘姆大得多。

Pam
I'm much older than Pam.

- Larry's cooking is even better than Jerry's.
  賴瑞的廚藝甚至比傑瑞還好。
- Is Kay feeling a little better today?
  凱今天是不是感覺好一點了？
- Sue looks no older than her daughter Lulu.
  蘇看起來一點也不比她女兒露露歲數大。
- Joy is a bit more sensible than her boyfriend Roy.
  喬伊比她的男朋友羅伊明智一點。

- Joe is a lot/much happier today than ten years ago.
  喬比十年前幸福得多。 → a lot 是口語用法。

- Jerry is a head taller than Larry.
  傑瑞比賴瑞高一個頭。
  ↳ 也可用 a head、two years 等來修飾比較級，
  如：a head taller、two years older。

a head taller than

5 成雙的比較級表達「越來越……」

1 more and more + 原級 → 這種成雙的比較級可用來表達某事正在發生變化。
2 -er and -er

- Kay is walking more and more slowly every day.
  凱走路走得一天比一天慢。 → slowly 在這個句子中用作副詞。

- My sister Wendy is growing taller and taller. 我妹妹溫蒂長得越來越高。

- Is it possible she is getting more and more susceptible to the virus?
  她有可能對那種病毒越來越容易感染嗎？

- It's getting harder and harder to find a job.
  = It's getting more and more difficult to find a job. 找工作越來越難了。

- We're getting closer and closer to sending tourists to the Moon.
  我們離把旅客送上月球的那一天，愈來愈近了。

the . . . the . . . → the + 比較級（附帶名詞）+ 主詞 + 動詞
↳ 前後兩個子句都用同樣的次序。

此結構表示兩個事物同時發生變化，或將兩個可變的數量依因果關係互相聯繫。在這種句型中，第一個比較級表「原因」，第二個表「結果」。

- The older Liz gets, the happier she looks.
  隨著年齡的增長，莉茲看上去也越來越幸福。
  ↳ The + 比較級（older）+ 主詞（Liz）+ 動詞（gets），
  the + 比較級（happier）+ 主詞（she）+ 動詞（looks）。

- The less Max's stocks earn him, the less he will pay in income taxes.
  馬克斯的股票賺的錢越少，他要繳的所得稅也就越少。
  ↥ little 的比較級形式是 less，不是 lesser。

- The faster Coco runs, the sooner she will see Joe.
  可可跑得越快，就能越快見到喬。
  ↥ 在這個句子中，faster 和 sooner 分別是副詞 fast 和 soon 的比較級形式。

- The more we read, the more we will learn.
  我們讀得越多，就能學得越多。

- The more money Tom made from his 3D computer game, the more confused he became.
  湯姆從立體電腦遊戲中賺的錢越多，就變得越糊塗。

- The more she thought about the plan, the less she liked it.
  她越考慮這個計畫，就越不喜歡它。
  ↥ more 和 less 分別是副詞 much 和 little 的比較級，修飾動詞 thought 和 liked。

句型三 the + 比較級 + the better → 這是比較級「the . . . the . . .」結構的簡短句型，通常以 the better 結尾。

- "How do you like your coffee?" asked Sue.
  Tom replied, "The stronger the better."
  蘇問：「你的咖啡要濃一點還是淡一點？」湯姆回答：「越濃越好。」

- Trish asked, "When do you want to start to learn Spanish?"
  I replied, "The sooner the better."
  翠西問：「你什麼時候想開始學西班牙語？」我回答：「越快越好。」

6 比較級 + than any other + 單數名詞

- Mark is more stubborn than any other student in his class.
  馬克比他班上任何其他學生都固執。
  ↥ 「比較級 + than any other」後面不能用複數名詞。

- This ring Jane is going to buy is more expensive than any other ring in this store.
  珍要買的這枚戒指，比這家商店裡任何其他一枚戒指都貴。
- Mary is more helpful to me than any other politician in Washington, D.C. 瑪麗比任何其他一位在華盛頓特區的政客，對我的幫助都更多。

3 合理的比較

1 類似的事物才能比較

要比較的東西在邏輯上要具有可比性，例如 John's English 和 Jane 不能比較（一個是語言，一個是人），John's English 只能和 Jane's English 比較。為了使兩樣東西之間的比較合乎邏輯，並避免重複，常用 that 和 those 來取代名詞，有時也用省略了名詞的**所有格形式**（比如：Jane's），這時千萬不要漏掉了 that、those 或所有格符號（'s）。

✗ This year's output is higher than last year.
 ↑ 把 this year's output（今年的產量）與 last year（去年）拿來比較，不合邏輯。

✓ This year's output is higher than last year's. 今年的產量比去年高。
 ↑ last year's 後面省略了名詞 output，今年的產量和去年的產量就可以比較。

✗ Dr. Brown's class about Mark Twain was less interesting than Dr. Harbor.
 ↑ Dr. Brown's class（課程）和 Dr. Harbor（人物）沒有可比性，只有同類的東西才能比較。

✓ Dr. Brown's class about Mark Twain was less interesting than Dr. Harbor's. 布朗博士開的馬克·吐溫的課不如哈伯博士的課有趣。
 ↑ 句尾的所有格形式 Dr. Harbor's 後面省略名詞 class，相當於 Dr. Harbor's class。

✗ The prices in this store are higher than in that store called Rice's Devices. → 不要漏掉 those。

✓ The prices in this store are higher than those in that store called Rice's Devices.
 ↑ 這裡的 those 相當於 the prices。
這家商店的價格比那家名叫「萊斯裝置」商店的價格高。

✗ The CD interest rate at the Rank Credit Union is higher than the Miami Bank. → 不要省略 that at。

✓ The CD interest rate at the Rank Credit Union is higher than that at the Miami Bank.
阮克儲蓄互助社的定期存款利率比邁阿密銀行的定存利率高。

2 than anything 與 than anything else 的區別

✗ I enjoy mountain climbing more than anything.

✓ I enjoy mountain climbing more than anything else.
我喜歡爬山勝過其他任何運動。

↳ 如果少了 else，就是把 mountain climbing 也包括在 anything 裡面，第一句的意思暗示了「喜歡爬山勝過爬山」，意思不通，所以要加 else，表示「喜歡爬山勝過其他任何運動。」

4 兩個相關屬性的比較（與其說是……，倒不如說……）

對比兩個相關的屬性時，要用 more，不用 -er。這裡的 more . . . than 意思不是「比……更」，而是「與其說是……，倒不如說……」。這種涵意也可以用 not so/as much . . . as 或 rather than 來表達。

✗ Mary is sadder than angry.
↳ sad 和 angry 是兩個相關的屬性，都指情感。對比的成分結構上不是平行結構，一個是比較級（sadder），一個是原級（angry）。

✓ Mary is more sad than angry.
= Mary is sad rather than angry.
= Mary is not so much angry as (she is) sad.
與其說瑪麗生氣，倒不如說她是傷心。

- Sue says my eyes are more green than blue.
  = Sue says my eyes are green rather than blue.
  = Sue says my eyes are not so much blue as green.
  蘇說，我的眼睛與其說是藍色的，倒不如說是綠色的。
  ↳ green 和 blue 是兩個相關的屬性，都指顏色，要用 more，不用 -er。
  ↳ 也可以用 not so/as much . . . as 或 rather than 來表達。

5 than 和 as 後面省略的詞彙

在比較級的子句中，有時 than 和 as 就如同關係代名詞，常代替主格代名詞或受格代名詞，這些被替代的詞在 than 或 as 之後被省略。這種用法主要用於正式文體。

✕ Collecting more taxes than it is absolutely necessary is legalized robbery.

✓ Collecting more taxes than is absolutely necessary is legalized robbery.

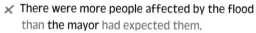

(President John Calvin Coolidge)

徵收比實際需要更多的稅收，是合法化的搶劫。

↳ than 代替主格代名詞 it。

✕ There were more people affected by the flood than the mayor had expected them.

✓ There were more people affected by the flood than the mayor had expected.

遭受洪水之害的人數比市長預料的還要多。

↳ than 代替受格代名詞 them。

✕ Jim sleeps more than it is good for him.

✕ Jim sleeps more than what is good for him.

✓ Jim sleeps more than is good for him.

吉姆睡的比適合他的睡眠時間還多。

↳ than 代替主格代名詞 it 或關係代名詞 what。

✕ Mary and Jerry's marriage isn't as happy as it was expected.

✓ Mary and Jerry's marriage isn't as happy as was expected.

瑪麗和傑瑞的婚姻沒有原來預料的那麼幸福。

↳ as 代替主格代名詞 it。

形容詞最高級的用法

1 使用最高級的原則

1 什麼情況下用形容詞的最高級？如果是某人、某地、某物與**其所屬的整個團體**（**兩個以上**的人、東西、地方等）進行比較，就要用最高級。

»（最高級的拼寫規則，參見 228 頁〈2 形容詞「級」的規則變化〉。）

- **Of all the candidates, Ted has never lied to us and is probably the most qualified.**
  在所有的候選人中，泰德從不對我們說謊，而且可能是最符合要求的。
  ↳ 當被比較的人或物數量在三個或三個以上時，要用最高級 the most（不用 the more）。此句是 Ted 與其所屬的整個團體進行比較（Ted 是所有的候選人之一）。

- **All these pictures are very good, but the one drawn by Susan is the best.** 這些畫都很好，但是蘇珊畫的那張是最好的。
  ↳ 當被比較的人或物數量在三個或三個以上時，要用最高級 the best（不用 the better）。

- **Bob is the tallest of all my classmates.** 鮑勃是我所有的同學裡最高的。
  ↳ 當被比較的人或物數量在三個或三個以上時，要用最高級 -est 的形式（不用 -er 形式）。

- **The worst movie in the history of Norway was released yesterday.**
  昨天上映了一部挪威史上最糟糕的影片。
  ↳ 不規則形容詞的最高級形式應牢記：good → best、bad → worst、little → least、many → most、far → farthest，不要誤用規則的形式（-est/most）。

- **Whose karate kicks are the best, Amy's or Jane's or Sue's?**
  誰空手道的踢腿踢得最好，艾咪、珍還是蘇？ → 三人之間進行比較，用最高級。

- **Amy Glass is the prettiest of all the girls in our class.**
  = Amy Glass is the prettiest girl in our class.

艾咪．葛拉斯是我們班上最漂亮的女孩。

↑ 注意上面兩種句型：the + 最高級 + of + 複數名詞／the + 最高級 + 單數可數名詞

- Tom is the strongest of our school's soccer players.
  = Tom is the strongest of all the soccer players in our school.
  = Tom is the strongest soccer player in our school.
  湯姆是我們學校最強壯的足球隊員。

2 整個團體只有兩名成員時，用比較級。

當整個團隊只有**兩名**成員時，要用**比較級**，不用最高級。有些人認為，在這種情況下可以用比較級，也可以用最高級，但大多數文法學家認為用最高級是錯誤的。在考試時要用比較級，這樣可以確保不會被扣分。

- I like both Sue and Lulu, but I think Lulu is the nicer of the two.
  蘇和露露我都喜歡，但我認為在這兩個人當中露露更友善。
  ↑ 團隊只有兩個人（Sue 和 Lulu），要用比較級。注意這種比較級句型需要定冠詞 the。
  ↑ 比較級用 the，是因為 nicer 後面有介系詞片語（of the two）限定。
- Sue is 21 years old, and Lulu is 22 years old. Lulu is the older of the two. 蘇 21 歲，露露 22 歲，露露是兩人之中年紀比較大的。

3 兩組人或物進行比較時，仍用比較級。

三個或三個以上的人或物進行比較時，並非一定都用最高級。如果被比較的人或物是當作**兩組人或物進行比較**時（一組是單一的項目，另一組是一系列的項目），就要用**比較級**而不是最高級。

- Amy was earlier than Wendy, Susan, and me. 艾咪比溫蒂、蘇珊和我都早。
  ↑ Amy 不包含在另一組的比較對象之中（Wendy, Susan, and me）。
- Ann's robotic toys are better than those of the three boys.
  安的玩具機器人比那三個男孩的玩具機器人好。
  ↑ 兩組進行比較，用比較級。

- Mary is shorter than her three sisters, Sue, Claire, and Lulu.
  瑪麗比她的三個姐妹——蘇、克萊兒、露露都矮。
  ↑ Mary 與其他三個姐妹比較，兩組進行比較，用比較級。
- Of the four girls, Mary is the shortest. 在四個女孩中，瑪麗的個子最矮小。
  ↑ Mary 是四個女孩中之一，用最高級。

- **Tom is taller than all the other basketball players on the team.**
  湯姆比籃球隊裡所有其他的隊員都高。 → 兩組進行比較，用比較級。

- **Tom is the tallest basketball player on the team.**
  湯姆是籃球隊裡最高的隊員。 →Tom 是籃球隊的成員之一，用最高級。

- **This hotel is more expensive than all the others in town.**
  這家旅館比城裡其他的所有旅館都貴。 → 兩組進行比較，用比較級。

- **This hotel is the most expensive in town.** 這家旅館是城裡最貴的旅館。
  ↑ 這家旅館是城裡所有旅館之一，與所屬的團體裡的成員進行比較，用最高級。

2 最高級常與 the 連用

1 名詞被形容詞最高級修飾時，要用定冠詞 the。

- **Kay Brown is the richest woman in our town.**
  凱·布朗是我們鎮上最富有的女子。

- **Ted said it was the best book he had ever read.**
  泰德說那是他至今讀過的最好的一本書。

2 接在 be 動詞後面的最高級形容詞也常加 the，但口語中有時會省略 the。

- **Which of the men is (the) strongest?** 這些男人之中哪一個最強壯？

- **Kate thinks her electronic dictionary is (the) best.**
  凱特認為她的電子詞典是最好的。

- **Liz Mist thinks that she is (the) greatest. With her nose up in the air, she often tries to interfere with a teacher's teaching and a cook's cooking.** 莉茲·密斯特覺得自己最棒，她傲氣十足，老師上課和廚師做菜時，她老想插手。

3 be 動詞後的最高級與限定性片語（形容詞子句或介系詞片語）連用時，就不能省略定冠詞 the。

- **This dictionary for the blind is the best (that) I could find.**
  這本盲人用的詞典是找能找到的最好的一本。
  ↑ 最高級（best）後面有形容詞子句，不能省略 the。

・**Mary thinks she is the smartest of all the staff.**
瑪麗認為自己是所有員工中最聰明的。
↑ 最高級（smartest）後面有介系詞片語（of all the staff），不能省略 the。

3 最高級後面的介系詞

1 指一個地方或一個團體的**單數名詞**，位於最高級後面時要用 in；在 team、farm、island 等字的前面，則用 on。

- the longest river in the world 世界上最長的河流
- the nicest room in the hotel 旅館裡最好的房間
- the best student in the class 班上最好的學生
- the oldest person on the island 島上最老的人

・**He is the happiest husband in France.** 他是法國最幸福的丈夫。
↑ in + 地點名詞（France）

・**Is Dwight the oldest violin player in the orchestra tonight?**
杜威特是今晚管弦樂隊裡年紀最大的小提琴演奏者嗎？
↑ in + 指一群人的單數名詞（orchestra）

・**She is the fastest basketball player on our team.**
她是我們籃球隊裡動作最快的運動員。 → 要用 on 和 team 搭配。

・**Do you know why Sirius is the brightest star in the sky?**
你知道為什麼天狼星是天上最明亮的星星嗎？

2 但是在**複數名詞**或**代名詞**，以及 year（年）、life（一生）、lot（一批人）、bunch（一幫人）等**單數量詞**前面，要用 of，不要用 in。

・**Saul is the fastest runner of them all.**
所羅是他們所有人中跑得最快的。
↑ of + 複數代名詞（them）

・**This Arrive 2025 computer is the most expensive of the five.**
這台「成功 2025」電腦是這五台電腦裡最貴的。
↑ the five 在這裡等於 the five computers，為了避免重複，省略名詞 computers。
↑ of + 複數名詞（computers）

- **Kim is the best shooter** of the four women.
  金姆是這四個女子中最好的射擊手。
  ⤷ of + 複數名詞（women）

- **Is today the shortest day** of the year?
  今天是一年中最短的一天嗎？

- **What was the saddest day** of your life?
  在你一生中，最悲傷的一天是哪一天？
  ⤷ of 可以用於表示一段時間的詞，如：year、life。

- **Scot is the best** of the lot. 史考特是那些人中最好的。

- **Liz thinks that Nick is the worst** of the bunch.
  莉茲認為尼克是那幫人中最壞的。

4 oldest 與 eldest 比較

1 old 的最高級形式是 oldest。

- **That church is** the oldest **building in this town.**
  那座教堂是鎮上最老的建築物。

2 談論家人時，英式常用 eldest，而美式用 oldest。

| 美式 | **My** oldest **child is 10 years old.**
| 英式 | **My** eldest **child is 10 years old.** 我最大的孩子十歲了。

5 much 等程度副詞修飾最高級／比較級

最高級或比較級可以由**程度副詞**修飾，例如：

- almost 幾乎
- by far 顯然；無疑
- easily 無疑；確實
- a little 一點點
- a lot . . . 很多……
- nearly 幾乎
- much 非常；很
- so much 非常；很
- practically 實際上
- quite 相當；很

- Ms. Jean Pool is nearly/almost the tallest student in our school.
  琴·普爾小姐差不多是我們學校裡個子最高的學生。
- He is practically the silliest man I've ever met.
  實際上，他算是我認識的男人中最傻的。
- I'm going to be a little more careful this time. 這次我會更小心一點。
- Ms. Mist is walking by far the fastest. 密斯特小姐無疑是走得最快的。
- Slowly picking herself up from the slime, Lily began to move a lot more carefully as she stared at the bully.
  莉莉從爛泥巴裡慢慢爬起來，瞪著那惡霸，動作也小心得多了。
  ↑ 上面最後兩句，by far 和 a lot 修飾副詞最高級（fastest, more carefully）。

6 very 強調最高級

可以用 very 來強調最高級以及 first、next、last 等字，這時需要在 very 前面加一個限定詞，如：the、my、her 等。

- Tess put on her very best dress. 黛絲穿上了她最好的洋裙。
- This may be your very last chance to dance with Kay.
  這也許是你最後一次與凱共舞的機會了。
- Amy Smith is the very first woman he has fallen in love with.
  艾咪·史密斯是他愛上的第一個女子。

7 one of the + 最高級 + 複數名詞

- Seattle is one of the safest cities I've ever visited.
  西雅圖是我去過的最安全的城市之一。
- This movie called *Fears* is one of the best movies I've seen.
  這部名叫《恐懼》的電影是我看過最好的片子之一。
- Reading interesting stories in English is one of the most important things Sue likes to do. 閱讀有趣的英語故事書，是蘇最喜歡做的事情之一。

UNIT

06 副詞

Adverbs

副詞的定義、用法與形式

1 副詞的定義與用法

副詞 修飾 → 動詞、形容詞、另一個副詞、整個句子

副詞是用來修飾動詞、形容詞、另一個副詞或整個句子的詞。副詞說明某件事是在什麼時候、什麼地方、以什麼方式、什麼程度、在何種條件下發生的，換句話說，副詞表明事情發生的時間、地方、方式、結果、程度、手段、情況等。副詞包括以下幾大類：

時間 Time	頻率 Frequency	地點 Place	方式 Manner	程度 Degree
now 現在	always 總是	here 這裡	brightly 明亮地	too 太
last night 昨晚	frequently 頻繁地	there 那裡	quietly 安靜地	quite 很
today 今天	often 常常	everywhere 到處	loudly 吵鬧地	very 非常
this year 今年	seldom 很少	nowhere 任何地方都不	madly 瘋狂地	really 確實；十分
last year 去年	sometimes 有時	abroad 在國外	quickly 迅速地	completely 完整地
soon 很快	usually 通常	home 回家／在家	slowly 緩慢地	rather 相當

1 動詞 + 副詞（副詞修飾動詞）

- **Dwight snored loudly last night.** 杜威特昨晚鼾聲大作。
  - ↳ loudly 是方式副詞，修飾動詞 snored，說明杜威特打鼾的狀況（How did Dwight snore?）。
- **She is leaving soon.** 她就快要離開了。
  - ↳ soon 是時間副詞，修飾動詞 is leaving，說明何時離開（When is she leaving?）。
- **After school, he went home.** 放學後，他就回家去了。
  - ↳ home 是地方副詞，修飾動詞 went，說明去了哪裡（Where did he go?）。
  - ↳ 在 go home、get home、be home 這些片語中，home 是副詞，因此不要說成 went to home.

2 副詞 + 形容詞（副詞修飾形容詞）

- **Margo is often tired when she flies to Chicago.**
  瑪歌飛往芝加哥時，常常感到疲倦。
  - ↳ often 是頻率副詞，修飾形容詞 tired，說明疲倦的頻率（How frequently is Margo tired?）。
- **Billy is very naughty.** 比利很頑皮。
  - ↳ very 是程度副詞，修飾形容詞 naughty，說明比利有多頑皮（How naughty is Billy?）。

3 副詞 + 副詞（副詞修飾副詞）

- **Mr. Wright snored very loudly last night.**
  賴特先生昨晚鼾聲如雷。
  - ↳ very 是程度副詞，修飾另一個副詞 loudly，說明賴特先生的鼾聲有多大（How loudly did Mr. Wright snore?）。

4 副詞 + 片語／數詞（副詞修飾片語或數詞）

有些副詞，如 quite、roughly、about、approximately 等，也可修飾其後面的名詞片語、介系詞片語和數詞。

- **She sobbed, "My life is rather/quite a mess right now."**
  她嗚咽道：「我現在的生活真是一團糟。」
  - ↳ 副詞 rather 或 quite 修飾名詞片語 a mess（不定冠詞 + 名詞），作定語，說明混亂的程度。

- In the evening, **she is** usually at home **reading news on the Internet.**
  晚上，她通常在家上網讀新聞。
  ↳ 「副詞 + 介系詞片語」結構：頻率副詞 usually 修飾介系詞片語 at home，說明她在家的頻率（How often is she at home?）。
  ↳ In the evening 和 at home 是介系詞片語，用來說明什麼時候（晚上）和在哪裡（在家）。In the evening 在這裡是作副詞，at home 在這裡作主詞補語。當介系詞片語起副詞作用時，有些文法學家也將之稱為副詞片語。

- **At Ocean View College,** roughly 95 **percent of the students have cellphones with an Internet connection.**
  在海觀學院，大概有 **95%** 的學生擁有上網手機。
  ↳ 副詞 roughly 修飾數詞 95。

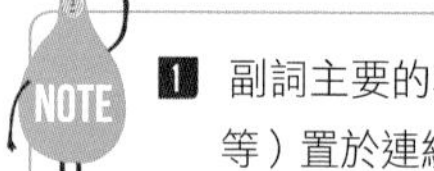

1 副詞主要的功能是作**狀語**，只有少數的副詞（如：on, off, here, there 等）置於連綴動詞後，作**主詞補語**，表示主詞的方位、方向或狀態。

- "Where is my wallet?" "It's there, right in front of you."
  「我的皮夾在哪裡？」「在那裡，就在你前面。」
- The lights in the gym are all on. 體育館的燈都打開了。

2 個別副詞可以置於受詞後面作**受詞補語**。

- I've got a whole month off. 我有一整個月的假。
- Don't keep the TV on all night. 不要整晚都開著電視。

3 個別副詞也可以置於名詞片語（a/an + 名詞）前或名詞片語（如：the + 名詞、my way 等）後作定語。

- quite a surprise 非常吃驚
- rather a mess 一團糟
- on my way home 在我回家的路上
- the man over there 那邊的那個男人

2 副詞的形式

1 不由其他字衍生而成的副詞或副詞片語

a 副詞（包括與形容詞同形的副詞）

- almost 幾乎
- already 已經
- close 接近
- dead 突然地；完全的
- fast 迅速地
- fine 精巧地；很好地
- long 長遠地
- low 低聲地；低地
- pretty 非常
- quite 頗
- short 簡略地；突然地
- soon 不久
- still 仍然
- straight 筆直地
- then 然後
- well 很好地
- wide 張得很大地
- yesterday 昨天

・**How soon will Sue learn how to milk her cow?**
蘇多快能學會幫她的牛擠牛奶？

b 副詞片語

- at last 最後
- at night 晚上
- by the way 順便一提
- in the end 最後
- in the morning 早上
- kind of 有一點兒
- of course 當然
- out of the blue 意外地

・**I have lived in Yellowknife all my life.**
我這一生都住在黃刀鎮。

out of the blue
意外地

2 由其他詞構成的副詞

a 形容詞 + -ly，構成副詞

① 大多數副詞是在形容詞後面加上 -ly 構成。

» 參見 266 頁〈2 以 -ly 結尾的副詞〉

・**After becoming economically successful, he finally went to visit his old grandparents.** 他事業有成之後，終於去見了年邁的祖父母。
↳ economical → economically 在經濟上
↳ 副詞也可以描述所評價事物的某一特別方面。

② 以 -le 結尾的形容詞，去 e+-y。

・**Rick felt terribly sick.** 瑞克覺得身體非常不適。
↳ terrible → terribly

feel terribly sick

③ 以 -y 結尾的形容詞，去 y+-ily。

・**The newlyweds Olive and Roy both enjoy novels, sports, and laughter, and they hope to live happily ever after.** 奧麗芙和羅伊這對新人都喜歡小說、運動和歡笑，他們希望從此可以開開心心地生活。
↳ happy → happily

在美語口語中，以下的字常用作副詞：

- bad 壞 → 代替 badly
- cheap 便宜 → 代替 cheaply
- loud 大聲 → 代替 loudly
- quick 快 → 代替 quickly
- real 真正 → 代替 really
- sure 確定 → 代替 surely
- tight 緊 → 代替 tightly
- wrong 錯 → 代替 wrongly

b 複合詞形式的副詞

- some + times → sometimes 有時
- some + where → somewhere 某處
- out + doors → outdoors 戶外
- out + side → outside 在外面

outdoors 戶外
outside 在外面

- **Finish writing your book report before you go outside to play.** 先把你的閱讀報告寫完，再出去玩。
- **Claire asked, "Have you seen my purse anywhere?"**
克蕾兒問：「你有在哪裡看到我的錢包嗎？」
- **The human body has two ends on it: one to create with and one to sit on. Sometimes people get their ends reversed.** (President Theodore Roosevelt) 人體的身軀有兩端，一端是用來創造的，另一端是用來坐的，而人們有時會反過來使用。

c 名詞／介系詞 + -ward/-wise，構成副詞

- after → afterward 之後
- home → homeward 朝向家地
- health → healthwise 在健康上
- money → moneywise 在金錢上

- **We could go to a movie and afterward have a pizza.**
我們可以去看電影，之後再去吃披薩。

3 勿混淆形容詞與副詞

不要把形容詞當作副詞使用。副詞用來修飾動詞、形容詞或另外的副詞，而形容詞用來修飾名詞。

Informal She is eating healthier than before.

Informal She is eating more healthy than before.

Formal She is eating more healthily than before. 她的飲食比以前健康。

↑ 動詞（is eating）+ 副詞（healthily）

↑ 口語用法雖然很普遍，不過在正式用語或考試中還是要遵循文法規則。

- He is eating more healthy foods than before.
  他比以前吃更多的健康食品了。
  ↑ 形容詞（healthy）+ 名詞（foods）；形容詞（more）+ 名詞片語（healthy foods）
- He is eating healthier foods than before. 他現在吃的東西比以前健康。
  ↑ 形容詞（healthier）+ 名詞（foods）
  ↑ healthy（原級）→ healthier（比較級）→ healthiest（最高級）

- She sang beautifully last night at the party.
  她在昨晚的晚會上唱得很優美。
  ↑ 動詞（sang）+ 副詞（beautifully）
- She looked beautiful last night at the party.
  在昨晚的晚會上，她看上去很美。
  ↑ 連綴動詞（looked）+ 形容詞（beautiful）

- Ted read the directions carefully before putting the computer helmet on his head. 泰德在把電腦安全帽戴到頭上之前，仔細看了使用說明。
  ↑ 動詞（read）+ 副詞（carefully）
- I don't remember Del very well. 我不太記得戴爾了。
  ↑ 動詞（remember）+ 副詞（well）；副詞（very）+ 副詞（well）
- He is running unusually fast. 他跑得快得不得了。
  ↑ 動詞（is running）+ 副詞（fast）；副詞（unusually）+ 副詞（fast）
- Sam is a little sick. 山姆的身體有點不適。
  ↑ 副詞片語（a little）+ 形容詞（sick）
- Kim was madly in love with Jim. 金姆瘋狂地愛上了吉姆。
  ↑ 副詞（madly）+ 介系詞片語（in love with Jim）
- I looked and noticed the steak was well cooked.
  我看了一下，發現牛排已經煮好了。 → 副詞（well）+ 過去分詞（cooked）

副詞和形容詞

1 同形的副詞和形容詞

一般來說，副詞是由形容詞變化而來的。有一些副詞與其形容詞同形，例如 clear、early、easy、fast、hard、late、loud、near、straight 等。那麼，怎麼辨別一個詞是副詞還是形容詞呢？方法很簡單，如果這些字修飾**名詞**，就是**形容詞**；如果這些字修飾**動詞**、**形容詞**或其他**副詞**，就是**副詞**。

	形容詞	副詞
bright	明亮的	明亮地
cowardly	膽小的	膽小地
daily	每天的	每天地
dear	親愛的	疼愛地
deep	深的	深深地
easy	容易的	輕鬆地
early	早的	早地
fast	快的	快地
fresh	新鮮的	剛剛地
hard	困難的	努力地
hourly	每小時的	每小時地
kindly	親切的	親切地
late	遲的	遲地
less	較小的	較小地
little	少的	少地
lively	活潑的	活潑地
long	長的	長久地
loud	大聲的	大聲地
low	低的	低地
monthly	每月的	每月地
near	近的	近地；接近
only	唯一的	只；僅僅
straight	直的	直地
timely	及時的	及時地
true	真實的	真實地
weekly	每週的	每週地

1 **For three days Sue's boyfriend was in the daily news.**
蘇的男朋友出現在每日新聞裡三天了。 → 形容詞（daily）+ 名詞（news）

She happily decided to go dancing daily.
她興高采烈地決定每天都要去跳舞。 → 動詞（go）+ 副詞（daily）

❷ An early bird catches a worm and avoids every germ.
早起的鳥兒有蟲吃，還可以避開各種病菌。 → 形容詞（early）+ 名詞（bird）

Lily often gets up early. 莉莉經常早起。 → 片語動詞（gets up）+ 副詞（early）

❸ Her train was late. 她的火車誤點了。 → 連綴動詞（was）+ 形容詞（late）

He got up late this morning. 他今早起床晚了。
↑ 片語動詞（got up）+ 副詞（late）

❹ Now that the pig has escaped from the barn, she is a free sow.
既然那頭豬從圈裡逃了出去，她就是一頭自由的母豬了。
↑ 形容詞（free）+ 名詞（sow）

Children under three can travel free.
三歲以下的小孩可以免費旅遊。
↑ 動詞（travel）+ 副詞（free）

❺ His daughter leads a hard life. 他的女兒生活艱難。
↑ 形容詞（hard）+ 名詞（life）

He worked hard after joining the Coast Guard.
他加入了海上防衛隊後工作很努力。 → 動詞（worked）+ 副詞（hard）

❻ Dad bought a fast car. 爸爸買了一輛速度很快的車。
↑ 形容詞（fast）+ 名詞（car）

Dad drives fast. 爸爸開車開得很快。 → 動詞（drives）+ 副詞（fast）

❼ Bob has an easy job. 鮑勃的工作很輕鬆。 → 形容詞（easy）+ 名詞（job）

Go easy down the Zambezi! 輕鬆划下贊比西河吧！
↑ 動詞（go）+ 副詞（easy）

❽ She is a pretty girl. 她是一個漂亮的女孩。 → 形容詞（pretty）+ 名詞（girl）

I'm pretty busy. 我很忙。 → 副詞（pretty = rather）+ 形容詞（busy）

❾ The Neptune Band played a lively tune. 海神樂隊演奏了一首活潑的歌曲。
↑ 形容詞（lively）+ 名詞（tune）

Amy is singing now, so step lively, all you guys and gals!
艾咪在唱歌了，那麼，輕快地踏起步來吧，你們所有的小夥子和姑娘們！
↑ 動詞（step）+ 副詞（lively）

⑩ **Liz had an F on her weekly English quiz.**
莉茲在每週一次的英語測驗中得了 F（不及格）。
↑ 形容詞（weekly）+ 名詞（quiz）

Liz meekly agreed to read an English storybook weekly.
莉茲順從地同意每週讀一本英語故事書。
↑ 動詞（read）+ 副詞（weekly）

⑪ **"Well, Sue, how are you?"**
"I'm very well, thanks, and how are you doing, Del?"
「嘿，蘇，你好嗎？」「很好啊，謝謝。戴爾，你好嗎？」
↑ well 在這裡是形容詞，是形容詞 ill 的反義詞（I'm well. = I'm healthy.）。

Del and his team are playing well. 戴爾和他的球隊打得很好。
↑ well 在這裡是副詞，是副詞 badly 的反義詞。

2 以 -ly 結尾的副詞

1 形容詞 + -ly → 副詞：大多數副詞都是以 -ly 結尾的，這些副詞是在形容詞後面加上 -ly 構成的，例如把形容詞 quiet 加上 -ly，就變成副詞 quietly。

形容詞			副詞		
able	有能力的	→	ably	能幹地	→ 去 e 加 -y
absent	缺席的	→	absently	心不在焉地	
bad	壞的	→	badly	壞地	
			↑ 在美式口語中，bad 可以用作副詞，代替 badly。		
beautiful	美麗的	→	beautifully	美麗地	
careful	小心的	→	carefully	小心地	
clever	聰明的	→	cleverly	聰明地	
correct	正確的	→	correctly	正確地	
dangerous	危險的	→	dangerously	危險地	
dear	親愛的	→	dearly	充滿深情地	

● excited	興奮的	→	excitedly	興奮地
● expensive	昂貴的	→	expensively	高價地
● final	最後的	→	finally	最後地
● fond	深情的	→	fondly	深情地
● general	一般的	→	generally	一般地
● mad	瘋狂的	→	madly	瘋狂地
● magnificent	壯麗的	→	magnificently	壯麗地
● manual	手工的	→	manually	手工地
● mechanical	機械的	→	mechanically	機械地
● nervous	緊張的	→	nervously	焦急地
● normal	正常的	→	normally	正常地
● popular	大眾化的	→	popularly	大眾化地
● professional	專業的	→	professionally	專業地
● quick	快的	→	quickly	快速地
● strange	奇怪的	→	strangely	怪異地
● sure	確信的	→	surely	確信地
			↳ 在美語口語中，sure 常用作副詞，代替 surely。	
● slow	緩慢的	→	slowly	緩慢地
● terrible	可怕的	→	terribly	可怕地 → 去 e 加 -y
● thoughtful	深思的	→	thoughtfully	深思地
● truthful	誠實的	→	truthfully	信任地
● usual	通常的	→	usually	通常地
● wise	聰明的	→	wisely	聰明地
● wonderful	精彩的	→	wonderfully	精彩地

- **She is a careful driver.**
  她是一個非常小心的駕駛員。
- **She always drives carefully.**
  她開車總是小心翼翼。
- **This is your final chance.** 這是你最後的機會了。
- **He finally realized he had made a bad mistake.**
  他終於意識到自己犯了一個大錯誤。

2 **字尾是 -y 的形容詞，去 y + -ily → 副詞**：如果形容詞是以 -y 結尾的，把字母 y 變成 i，然後再加 -ly 構成副詞，例如形容詞 angry 的副詞為 angrily。

形容詞			副詞	
angry	生氣的	→	angrily	生氣地
crazy	瘋狂的	→	crazily	瘋狂地
easy	容易的	→	easily	容易地
greedy	貪婪的	→	greedily	貪婪地
happy	快樂的	→	happily	快樂地
heavy	沉重的	→	heavily	沉重地
messy	混亂的	→	messily	亂糟糟地
merry	愉快的	→	merrily	愉快地
noisy	嘈雜的	→	noisily	嘈雜地
gloomy	陰暗的	→	gloomily	陰暗地
ready	樂意的	→	readily	樂意地
sleepy	瞌睡的	→	sleepily	瞌睡地
tidy	整齊的	→	tidily	整齊地

- **I didn't go climbing yesterday because of the heavy rain.**
  昨天因下大雨，我沒有去爬山。
- **I didn't go climbing yesterday because it rained heavily.**
  昨天因雨下得很大，我沒有去爬山。

3 以 -ly 結尾的形容詞

1 並非所有以 -ly 結尾的詞都是副詞，有些以 -ly 結尾的詞可以是形容詞，例如：

- a costly diamond 昂貴的鑽石
- a cowardly act 懦弱的行為
- a deadly poison 致命的毒藥
- elderly parents 年邁的父母
- a friendly gesture 友好的姿態
- homely furniture 樸實無華的傢俱
- a lively performance 輕快活潑的表演
- a lonely widow 孤獨的寡婦
- a lovely dress 漂亮的洋裝
- be manly 有男子氣概的
- be womanly 女子氣的
- a silly story 無聊的故事
- an ugly duckling 醜小鴨
- seem unlikely 看上去不太可能的

NOTE

deadly 既可作形容詞，也可作副詞。

- 作形容詞：指「致死的」或「不共戴天的」
  - deadly combat 殊死的戰鬥
  - deadly enemies 不共戴天的敵人
- 作副詞：指「非常」或「死了一般地」
  - deadly cold 極度寒冷
  - deadly pale 死一般地蒼白

✗ Paul walked lonely through the huge banquet hall.

✓ Paul was lonely while walking through the huge banquet hall.
保羅穿過寬大的宴會大廳時，感到很孤獨。

↑ lonely 是形容詞，用在連綴動詞 was 後面作主詞補語，不能修飾動詞（walked）。

- Joyce might become a famous singer, because she's got a lovely voice. 喬伊絲可能會成為一個著名歌手，因為她有優美動人的歌喉。
- Joyce told me a silly story about how she once made a bad choice.
喬伊絲跟我講了一個無聊的故事，是關於她曾經如何做了一個錯誤的選擇。

2 這類形容詞不能作副詞，但有時可以使用帶有 fashion、manner 或 way 的介系詞片語使其具有副詞意義。

✗ Kay smiled friendly.

✓ Kay smiled in a friendly way. 凱友善地微笑。

✓ Kay gave me a friendly smile. 凱對我友善地微笑了一下。

↑ friendly 是形容詞，修飾名詞（way, smile），不能修飾動詞（smiled），但介系詞片語 in a friendly way 作副詞，修飾動詞 smiled。

4 兼作副詞和形容詞的 -ly 結尾字

有一些以 -ly 結尾的字既可以當形容詞，也可以當副詞。

- early 早（的）
- likely 可能（的）
- weekly 每週（的）
- daily 每天（的）
- monthly 每月（的）
- yearly 每年（的）

- Sue's newspaper always reviews the weekly news. → 形容詞
蘇的報紙總是對每週新聞進行評論。

- With her sleekly brushed dark hair, Claire reports the fashion news weekly. 烏黑秀髮梳得柔滑光亮的克萊兒，每週報導一次時尚資訊。 → 副詞

- Kay had an early lunch today. 凱今天午餐吃得很早。 → 形容詞
- Sue got up early to go sailing. 蘇起了個大早，去航海。 → 副詞

- Kate is likely to be late. 凱特有可能會遲到。
  ↑ 形容詞 likely 用在連綴動詞（is）後面，作主詞的補語。
- This summer Ann will quite likely go to Japan. 今年夏天安很可能會去日本。
  ↑ 副詞 likely（= probably）用在動詞（go）前面；通常在 likely 前面要有程度副詞 most、quite、very。

5 字尾有 -ly 與非 -ly 兩種形式的副詞

1 有兩種形式的副詞：有些副詞同時具有兩種形式，一種以 -ly 結尾，另一種不以 -ly 結尾，例如：

非 -ly 結尾	-ly 結尾	
bright	brightly	明亮地
close	closely	接近地
dear	dearly	深情地；昂貴地
deep	deeply	深地；深刻地
direct	directly	直接地
fair	fairly	公平地
fine	finely	很好地
loud	loudly	大聲地
quick	quickly	快地
right	rightly	正確地
slow	slowly	慢地
wide	widely	充分地；廣泛地

2 -ly 與非 -ly 結尾意義不同的副詞

a dead 確實地，全然地，完全地（= exactly; completely; very）
deadly 死了一般的；非常，極度（= in a way suggestive of death; extremely）

- dead drunk 酩酊大醉
- dead slow 出奇地慢
- sit deadly still 一動不動地坐著
- dead right 完全正確
- dead tired 筋疲力盡
- deadly serious 非常嚴肅

- **He often drives when he's dead drunk.**
  他常常醉醺醺的還開車。

- **Officer Louise Lee was deadly serious when she yelled, "Police! Freeze!"** 露易絲·李長官大喊「員警！不許動！」時是非常認真的。

b **deep 深入地；深遠地**（= in a deep way; to a deep extent）
deeply 強烈地；深刻地（= strongly; profoundly）

- **Let's dig deep into the research about lunar resources.** 讓我們深入去發掘關於月球資源的研究吧。

- **She's deeply in love with the idea of working and living on the moon.** 她非常喜歡去月球工作和居住的構想。

c **fine 很好地**（= well）
finely 優雅地；漂亮地；精巧地（= nicely; delicately）

- **Astronaut Mike Devine said, "Our new lunar colony is doing fine."**
  太空人邁克·迪瓦恩說：「我們在月球上新開闢的僑居地情況不錯。」

- **Ms. Bold wore a fishnet dress that was made out of finely crafted platinum and gold.**
  伯爾德小姐穿了一件用鉑和金經過精細加工製成的漁網洋裝。

d **free 免費地**（= for free）
freely 自由地；無拘束地（= in whatever way you like; without controls or limits）

- **Today everyone can eat free at my restaurant.**
  今天大家都可以在我的餐廳裡免費用餐。
  ↳ free 指「不付錢」(without payment)。

- **Can we speak freely about those sensitive political issues?**
  我們可以自由地談論那些敏感的政治問題嗎？
  ↳ freely 指「不受限制」(without restriction)。

e **hard 努力地**（= with a lot of effort）
hardly 幾乎不；很少（= almost not）

- **Mark thought hard about how to succeed.**
  馬克認真地思考如何才能成功。
- **Mark is a professional basketball guard, and he works very hard.**
  馬克是一個職業籃球後衛，他打起球來很拚。
- **It's so dark that I can hardly see Mark.**
  天太黑，我幾乎看不見馬克。
- **Anna hardly knows Mark.** 安娜不太認識馬克。

f **high 表示高度很高**（= in, at, to, or toward a high degree, level, place, position, etc.）
highly 表示程度很高或評價高（= greatly; with high approval or esteem）

- **I love to fly my rocket plane high in the sky.**
  我喜歡把我的火箭飛機高高地飛在天空中。 → 指高度
- **Brooke is highly critical of Coco's gobbledygook.**
  布魯克對可可的官樣文章表示極端不滿。 → 指程度

- **Mary speaks highly of her brother Jerry.**
  瑪麗對她的哥哥傑瑞贊許有加。 → 指評價高

g **late 遲到**（= after the usual, proper, or expected time）
lately 最近；不久前（= recently; a short while ago）

- **Kate read a book of proverbs, came to school late, and missed the grammar lesson about the use of adverbs.**
  凱特讀了一本諺語書，上學遲到了，結果錯過了關於副詞用法的那堂文法課。
- **Lately, Lily seems to be a little lazy.** 最近莉莉似乎有點懶惰。

h **pretty 很；非常；相當**（= rather）
prettily 漂亮地；優美地；可愛地（= in a pretty way; beautifully）

- **Kim is pretty annoyed with Jim.** 金姆很生吉姆的氣。
  ↳ pretty 相當於 rather，意為「很、非常、相當」。
- **Isn't Sally dressed prettily tonight!** 莎莉今晚穿得好漂亮啊！

i **right 向右方**（= opposite to left）
rightly 理所當然地（= with reason; justifiably）

- **Turn right at the third traffic light.** 在第三個紅綠燈右轉。
- **Jenny is rightly proud of the contributions she has made to the company.** 珍妮理所當然會為自己對公司所作的貢獻感到驕傲。

j **short 突然**（= suddenly）
shortly 不久；馬上（= in a short time; soon）

- **Seeing the accident, I hit my brakes hard, and my car stopped short.**

看見事故，我用力地踩煞車，車一下子就停住了。
- **Shortly after Sally became a judge, she became courtly.**
莎莉當了法官後不久，就變得有威嚴了。

3 -ly 與非 -ly 結尾意義相同的副詞

a 正式／非正式用法

有的副詞有兩種形式，字尾可以加 -ly，也可以不加 -ly，意思相同，應根據語體決定選用哪一種形式：加 -ly 結尾的副詞較正式，不加 -ly 結尾的副詞通常用在非正式的情境中。

Informal	cheap	loud	quick	real（美式）
	sure（美式）	tight	wrong	clear
Formal	cheaply	loudly	quickly	really
	surely	tightly	wrongly	clearly

Informal Dee vowed to speak loud.
Formal Dee vowed to speak loudly.
蒂鄭重宣布要大聲講話。

Informal Is Lee going to sell his jeep cheap?
Formal Is Lee going to sell his jeep cheaply?
李打算把他的吉普車便宜賣掉嗎？

Informal Sue, think quick; otherwise, our boss will fire you.

Formal Sue, think quickly; otherwise, our boss will fire you.

蘇，快想想辦法，不然我們老闆就要炒你魷魚了。

b 習慣用法

在一些情境裡，究竟是要用 -ly 結尾還是非 -ly 結尾的副詞，應根據**語言習慣**去判斷。一些動詞習慣與以 -ly 結尾的副詞連用，一些動詞則習慣與非以 -ly 結尾的副詞連用。

- Louise, go slow, please. 露易絲，請慢慢走。
- Paul proceeded slowly down the hall.
  保羅沿著大廳慢慢地走。
  ↥ slow 作副詞時，主要用在祈使句中，與表示動作的短動詞連用，例如 drive slow、go slow、run slow。

- Please come close. 請走近一點。
- Watch Dan closely if you can.
  可以的話，就請你嚴密監視丹。
  ↥ 一些動詞（如：watch）習慣和副詞 closely 連用。又如：closely related、be closely guarded。

- Claire asked us to play fair.
  克萊兒要我們公平行事。
- Dee doesn't treat others squarely and yet is quick to complain when she isn't treated fairly.
  蒂對別人不公正，可是當她自己受到不平等對待時，又急著抱怨。
  ↥ fair 和 fairly 都可作副詞。但動詞 play 常和 fair 連用（play fair 公平行事，公平地比賽）。

- Please open your mouth wide. 請把嘴巴張大。
- Lily has traveled widely. 莉莉遍遊了各地。
  ↥ wide 可作形容詞，比如：a wide river。也可以作副詞，常和動詞 open 連用，指「（張得）很大地」（如：open the door wide）。指「廣泛地」時，通常用 widely，不過副詞 wide 也可指「廣泛地」，但只用於片語 far and wide（到處）。

6 連綴動詞 + 形容詞；行為動詞 + 副詞

1 **連綴動詞**通常接**形容詞**。感官動詞也可以作連綴動詞，有些一般動詞也可以作連綴動詞，這時要接形容詞。

感官動詞	連綴動詞	一般動詞
feel 覺得	appear 似乎	get 變得；成為
look 看起來	be 是	grow 成長；變得
smell 聞起來	become 變成	keep 保持
sound 聽起來	seem 似乎	prove 證明是
taste 嚐起來		remain 保持
		turn 變得；成為

- He seemed pretty happy to see me. 他似乎很高興見到我。
- Please keep calm while I defuse this A-bomb.
  我拆這顆原子彈的時候，請保持鎮靜。
- She became famous. 她出名了。
- His voice sounded strange to Joyce. 他的聲音在喬伊絲聽來有點怪怪的。
- I got lucky after I met Scot. 我認識史考特後，運氣也好了起來。
- Scot knew the weather would turn hot. 史考特知道天氣會變熱。
- Building the dam proved difficult without Sam.
  結果證明，沒有山姆，很難修建這座水壩。
- Saul has grown big and tall. 所羅長得又高又大。

2 上表中有些動詞可以作連綴動詞，也可以作行為動詞。作**行為動詞**時，要用**副詞**修飾。

- Why did that big pig look mean and sly?
  為什麼那隻大豬看起來卑鄙又狡猾？
  ↑ 連綴動詞（look）+ 形容詞（mean, sly）
- Sally and Lily looked suspiciously at the boar standing by the door.
  莎莉和莉莉疑心地看著站在門口的公豬。
  ↑ 行為動詞（looked）+ 副詞（suspiciously）

- Sally felt sad that the boar was snorting and clearly mad.
那頭公豬在哼鼻子，顯然是瘋了，莎莉感到挺傷心的。
↳ 連綴動詞（felt）+ 形容詞（sad）
- Lily felt carefully for the trigger of her gun as the boar began to charge. 那頭公豬展開攻擊，這時莉莉小心翼翼地觸摸著手槍的扳機。
↳ 行為動詞（felt）+ 副詞（carefully）

7 易誤用的形容詞和副詞

1 good 與 well

a well 是副詞，修飾動詞。
good 是形容詞，修飾名詞。

plays the piano well

- Del plays the piano well. 戴爾的鋼琴彈得很好。
↳ well 是副詞，修飾動詞 plays。
- Did you and Del eat well while on your canoe trip? 你和戴爾在獨木舟之旅中吃得還好嗎？
↳ well 是副詞，修飾動詞 eat。

canoe trip

- Roy is a good boy. 羅伊是一個好男孩。
↳ good 是形容詞，修飾名詞 boy。
- Tom had a good time on the island of Guam. 湯姆在關島過得很快活。
↳ good 是形容詞，修飾名詞 time。

b 在**連綴動詞**（be、appear 等）或用作連綴動詞的**感官動詞**（look、sound 等）後面，要用形容詞 good，不用副詞 well。
» 參見 275 頁〈6　連綴動詞 + 形容詞；行為動詞 + 副詞〉。

- The fish smells good. 魚聞起來好香。
- Sorry, but this neighborhood doesn't look good.
對不起，不過這附近的環境看起來不太好。

c 在連綴動詞後面可以用 well 表示**健康狀況**，這時 well 是形容詞，不是副詞。
- "How are you, Sue?" "I'm very well, and how about you, Dr. Mime?"
「你好嗎，蘇？」「我很好，你呢，邁姆醫生？」 → I'm well. = I'm healthy.

✕ Dan is a well man.

✓ Dan looks well. = Dan looks healthy. 丹看起來很健康。

= Dan is a healthy man. 丹是個健康的男子。

↳ well 表示「健康的、安好的」，放在連綴動詞（be、look 等）之後，不放在名詞前。

- look good = look attractive/well-dressed/fine 看起來嫵媚動人／穿得好／健康
- look well = look healthy 看起來很健康
- feel good = feel contented/happy/satisfied 感覺很滿足／高興／滿意
- feel well = feel healthy 感覺很健康

2 bad 與 badly

a **bad 是形容詞，修飾名詞。**

badly 是副詞，修飾動詞、形容詞或其他副詞。

- **I am sorry, but I have some bad news for you.**
  很遺憾，我有些壞消息要告訴你。 → bad 是形容詞，修飾名詞 news。
- **Fortunately, she wasn't badly injured in the accident.**
  幸運的是，她在事故中傷得不重。 → badly 是副詞，修飾動詞 wasn't injured。

b 在**連綴動詞**和表示人的**感情**的動詞後面，要用形容詞 bad。

✕ Yesterday Dad vomited and felt badly.

✓ Yesterday Dad vomited and felt bad. 昨天爸爸吐了，覺得不舒服。

↳ 除非你沒有手指或手指受傷，觸摸物體時感覺不靈敏，才有可能 feel badly。

- **I felt bad about leaving without saying goodbye.**
  我對於不告而別感到很愧疚。 → 有人會用 feel badly，但在正式用語中要用 bad。
- **I asked Dad if the weather was getting really bad.**
  我問爸爸天氣是否會變得很壞。 → was getting 在這裡是連綴動詞，意思是「變成」。

c go bad 和 go badly 之間的區別：

- go bad 不再新鮮
- go badly 不順利；不成功

・The meat will soon go bad if you leave it out here in the noon heat.
如果你把這塊肉放在外面這裡，暴露在中午的熱氣之中，它很快就會壞掉。
↑ go 在這裡是連綴動詞，意思是「變為」。

・If her trip through time goes badly, a dinosaur could eat Lily.
如果莉莉的時空之旅進展得不順利，她可能會被恐龍吃掉。
↑ go 在這裡是行為動詞，意思是「進行、進展」。

d 在美語口語中，bad 可以用作副詞。但在正式用語或在考試中，不應把 bad 用作副詞。

Informal Trish did bad on the quiz because she did not know that "bad" is not acceptable as an adverb in formal English.

Formal Trish did badly on the quiz because she did not know that "bad" is not acceptable as an adverb in formal English.
翠西的測驗成績不理想，因為她不知道在英語的正式用語中，bad 不能作副詞用。

3 everyday 與 every day

everyday : 形容詞，意思是「每天的、日常的、常有的、平常的」。
every day : 副詞，意思是「每天」。

- everyday food 便飯
- everyday story 司空見慣的事
- everyday English 日常英語
- jog every day 每天慢跑
- laugh every day 每天笑
- study English every day 每天學英語

・"I feel most comfortable in my everyday clothes," said Kay.
「我穿便服感覺最舒服了。」凱說。

・Kay says "Hello" to her teachers every day.
凱每天都要對她的老師說「您好」。

4 such 與 so

such 是形容詞：	such a/an（ + 形容詞）+ 單數可數名詞 such（ + 形容詞）+ 複數名詞／不可數名詞
so 是副詞：	so + 形容詞 so + 副詞

- such a long way 這麼遠的路程
- such a silly story 多麼無聊的故事
- such nice people 多麼友好的人
- such lovely weather 多麼好的天氣

- so far 這麼遠
- so silly 多麼無聊
- so nice 多麼友好
- so lovely 多麼美好；多麼可愛

・We haven't seen each other for such a long time.
= We haven't seen each other for so long. 我們已經好久沒有見面了。

5 altogether 與 all together

副詞 altogether 意思是「完全；全部、合計；總的說來」。
副詞片語 all together 意思是「一道、一起；每一件東西都……」。

・If we don't do something now, the glaciers in North America may disappear altogether.
如果我們現在不採取行動，北美的冰河就有可能完全消失。

・Kay noticed that there were altogether only twenty-two people watching the play. 凱注意到來看戲的人總共才 22 個人。

・Because the room was very small, Heather and her sisters were squeezed all together.
= Because the room was very small, Heather and her sisters were squeezed together. 房間很小，所以希瑟和姊妹們緊緊擠在一起。

6 healthful 與 healthy

healthful 意思是「有益健康的」，不能指「健康的 」。
healthy 的主要意思是「健康的、沒有病的、運轉良好的」。
healthy 的反義詞是 unhealthy、sick、diseased。

- a healthful climate 有益健康的氣候
- healthful country air 有益健康的鄉村空氣
- a healthy body 健康的身體
- a healthy mind 健康的頭腦

・Dee is wealthy, but her teeth aren't very healthy. 蒂很有錢，但她的牙齒不是很健康。

不應使用副詞的情況

不要用意思與動詞一樣的副詞來修飾該動詞（參見 864 頁〈Part 2 如何避免重疊詞和累贅修飾語〉），比如：return（返回），已經包含了 back（回來）的意思，所以就不要再用副詞 back 去重複動詞 return 的意思。

× assemble together	✓ assemble 集合	× merge together	✓ merge 合併
× first begin	✓ begin 開始	× mingle together	✓ mingle 混合
× cancel out	✓ cancel 取消	× mix together	✓ mix 混合
× continue on	✓ continue 繼續	× raise up	✓ raise 舉起
× finish up/finish off	✓ finish 完成 1	× repeat again	✓ repeat 重複
× follow up	✓ follow 跟隨 2	× retreat back	✓ retreat 撤退
× join together	✓ join 參加	× return back	✓ return 返回
× leave from	✓ leave 離開	× share in common	✓ share 共享
× lower down	✓ lower 放低	× share together	✓ share 分享

1 如果指「完成」，只需要用 finish。
片語動詞「finish up」、「finish off」指「用完；吃完」。 finish off 還指「毀滅」。

- finish up/off everything in the fridge
  把冰箱裡的所有東西都吃光光了

2 表示「跟隨」，不能說 follow up。follow up 是片語動詞，意思不是跟隨，而是「在做過某事之後，採取進一步行動以確保達到目的」。比如：

- Follow up your interview with a thank-you letter.
  面試之後，要寫封感謝信致意。

1. **Ben cancelled his meeting with Amy again.**
班又取消了與艾咪的約會。
↑ 不能說 cancelled out 。

2. **She said that we needed to cooperate in order to fight HIV.**
她說，我們必須攜手戰勝愛滋病病毒。
↑ 不能說 cooperate together 。

3. **Louise, please refer to Chapter Two.** 露易絲，參見第二章。
↑ 不能說 refer back。

4. **We decided to advance.** 我們決定要前進。
↑ 不能說 advance forward。

5. **When did you begin to get thin?**
你是什麼時候開始變瘦的？
↑ first begin 在口語中可以接受，但不符合文法規則，在正式用語和考試中不要使用。

6. **Did you continue?** 你繼續下去了沒有？
↑ 不能說 continue on。

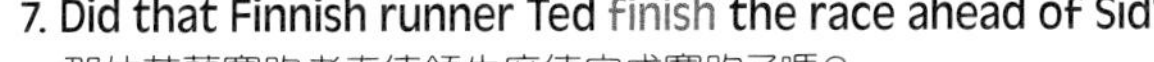

7. **Did that Finnish runner Ted finish the race ahead of Sid?**
那位芬蘭賽跑者泰德領先席德完成賽跑了嗎？
↑ 不能說 finish up。

8. **Kay wants to raise her English grade.** 凱想提高她的英語成績。
↑ 不能說 raise up。

9. **Paul likes to repeat everything said by his grandfather.**
保羅喜歡重複他爺爺說的每一句話。
↑ 不能說 repeat again。

10. **I'll return to school and begin to learn.**
= I'll go back to school and begin to learn. 我要回到學校重新開始學習。
↑ 不能說 return again 或 return back。

11. **They will follow the trail.** 他們將沿著這個蹤跡前進。
↑ 不能說 follow up。

副詞的種類

1 時間副詞或片語（Adverbs/Adverbial Phrases of Time）

時間副詞或片語：用來表示某事發生的時間（when）。

- already 已經
- early 早
- finally 最後；終於
- first 最初；第一個
- immediately 立刻
- last night 昨晚
- last week 上星期
- long ago 很早以前
- next year 明年
- now 現在
- recently 最近
- second 居第二位；其次
- soon 很快
- still 還；依舊
- then 那時；然後
- this morning 今天早上
- this year 今年
- today 今天
- tomorrow 明天
- yesterday 昨天

- **Ms. Mary Pool finally arrived at our school.**

  瑪麗·普爾女士終於抵達我們的學校了。

  ↳ finally 是時間副詞，回答 when 的問題，修飾動詞 arrived。

- **Kay left early today.** 凱今天很早就離開了。

  ↳ early、today 是時間副詞，回答 when 的問題，修飾動詞 left。

- **Mike finished his job first.**

  邁克是第一個完成工作的人。

  ↳ first 是時間副詞，回答 when 的問題，修飾動詞 finished。

- **My pink pants were too large last year, they fit me this year, but they will be too small next year.**

  我的粉紅褲子去年穿太大，今年穿剛好，明年穿就會太小了。

  ↳ last year、this year、next year 都是時間副詞片語，回答 when 的問題。

2 頻率副詞或片語（Adverbs/Adverbial Phrases of Frequency）

頻率副詞或片語：用來表示某件事或某動作發生的頻率或次數（how often）。

- always 總是
- annually/yearly/once a year 一年一次
- daily/every day 每天
- ever 從來
- frequently 頻繁地
- hourly/every hour 每小時
- monthly/every month 每月
- never 從不
- often 常常
- once 一次
- seldom 很少
- sometimes 有時
- three times 三次
- twice 兩次
- usually 通常
- every week 每星期
- weekly/once a week 一星期一次

- **The bus is always late by the time it gets to my school gate.**
  每當公車到達學校大門口時，都已經遲到了。
  ↑ always 是頻率副詞，修飾形容詞 late，回答 how often 的問題。
- **Kay takes the subway to work every workday.** 凱每個工作日都坐地鐵上班。
  ↑ every workday 是頻率副詞片語，修飾動詞片語 takes the subway，回答 how often。
- **She usually rides to school in her father's car.**
  她通常坐她父親的汽車去上學。
- **We go camping monthly near the Black Sea.**
  我們每個月去黑海附近露營一次。

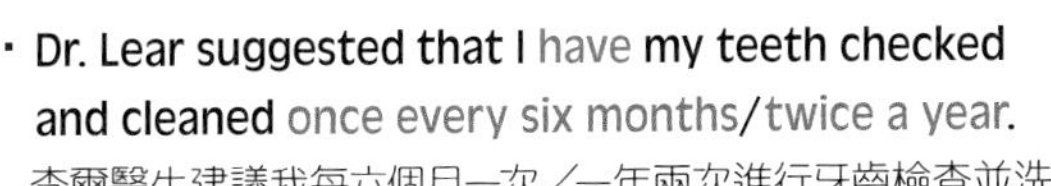

- **Dr. Lear suggested that I have my teeth checked and cleaned once every six months/twice a year.**
  李爾醫生建議我每六個月一次／一年兩次進行牙齒檢查並洗牙。

3 持續性時間副詞或片語（Adverbs/Adverbial Phrases of Duration）

持續性時間副詞或片語：表明某事持續多長時間（how long）。

- a long time 很長一段時間
- all day 整天
- all night 整晚
- briefly 短暫地
- for a while 一會兒
- for ages 很久
- forever 永遠
- long 長時間

- We haven't seen each other for ages. 我們已經很久沒見面了。
  ↳ for ages 是持續性時間副詞，修飾動詞 haven't seen，回答 how long 的問題。
- Excuse me, I'll be back in a minute or two.
  抱歉，我離開一會兒，馬上就回來。
- She talked on the phone for an hour.
  她講了一個小時的電話。
- I stayed awake all night. 我徹夜未眠。

talk on the phone
for an hour
講了一個小時的電話

以介系詞開始的副詞片語，例如 for ages、for a while，也稱作介系詞片語。

4 地點副詞或片語（Adverbs/Adverbial Phrases of Place）

1 地點副詞或片語：說明事情發生的地點，或是某人某物要去哪裡（where）。

- down 在下面；向下
- up 在上面；向上
- near 附近
- far 很遠
- in 在裡面；在家
- out 在外面；不在家
- inside 在／往裡面
- outside 在／往外面
- downstairs 在／往樓下
- upstairs 在／往樓上
- indoors 在／往室內
- outdoors 在／往戶外
- everywhere 到處
- nowhere 任何地方都不
- somewhere 在／到某處
- anywhere 任何地方
- here 這裡
- there 那裡
- abroad 在／往國外
- at home 在家
- away 離開；外出
- at hand 在手邊

- Amy has lived in Yellowknife all her life. 艾咪一生都居住在黃刀鎮。
  ↳ in Yellowknife 是地點副詞片語，修飾動詞 has lived，回答 where 的問題（住在何處）；in Yellowknife 可看作是介系詞片語，作地點狀語。
- Amy once made a vow never to leave Yellowknife, and she still lives there now. 艾咪曾發誓永遠不離開黃刀鎮，她現在仍然居住在那裡。
  ↳ there 是地點副詞，修飾動詞 lives，回答 where 的問題。

- The purse was nowhere near Claire. 手提包根本不在克萊兒身旁。
- Claire asked everyone, "Have you seen my purse anywhere?
  克萊兒問大家:「你們有沒有在哪兒看到我的手提包?」

2 當 up、down、upstairs、downstairs、inside、outside、far 和 near 等後面沒有接名詞時，就是副詞。

- an upstairs room 一個樓上的房間 → 形容詞修飾名詞
- live upstairs 住在樓上 → 副詞修飾動詞
- an outside toilet 戶外的廁所 → 形容詞修飾名詞
- wait outside 在外面等 → 副詞修飾動詞

- After Amy sipped her cup of coffee, she looked up.
  艾咪喝了一小口咖啡,然後把頭抬了起來。
  ↳ up 是地點副詞,修飾動詞 looked,回答 where 的問題(朝何處看)。
- Mom was looking for Claire's purse upstairs and downstairs.
  媽媽樓上樓下地幫克萊兒找手提包。

5 方式副詞(Adverbs of Manner)

方式副詞(又稱**情狀副詞**):說明某事的進行方式，回答 how 的問題，這類副詞通常以 -ly 結尾。

- brightly 明亮地
- carefully 仔細地
- carelessly 粗心地
- cheaply 便宜地
- cheerfully 愉快地
- clearly 清楚地
- closely 緊密地;嚴密地
- correctly 正確地
- cunningly 狡猾地
- differently 不同地
- freely 自由地;坦率地
- loudly 大聲地;吵鬧地
- peacefully 平靜地
- playfully 愛玩地;開玩笑地
- quickly 迅速地;馬上
- safely 安全地
- skillfully 巧妙地;精巧地
- slowly 緩慢地
- suddenly 突然;意外地
- well 很好地;成功地
- wildly 粗暴地;瘋狂地

- Nancy sat quietly during the entire presentation.
  南西在整個報告期間都坐著沉默不語。
  ↳ quietly 是方式副詞，回答 how 的問題，修飾動詞 sat。
- My wife carefully explained the importance of maintaining a positive attitude toward life. 我妻子仔細地解釋了保持人生積極態度的重要性。
  ↳ carefully 是方式副詞，回答 how 的問題，修飾動詞 explained。
- When the witch began to zoom around on her broom, we moved slowly out of the huge classroom.
  當女巫開始騎著她的掃把環繞飛行時，我們緩緩地走出了大教室。
  ↳ slowly 是方式副詞，回答 how 的問題，修飾動詞 moved。
- My dog playfully jumped over the log. 我的狗愉快地跳過了圓木頭。
- Bob and Joy decided to enjoy their laughter and live happily ever after. 鮑勃和喬伊決定享受他們的歡笑，從此要過幸福快樂的生活。
- The moon began to shine brightly when the thief was about to steal the truck loaded with wine.
  當小偷剛想偷走一輛裝滿葡萄酒的卡車時，月亮開始明亮地照耀起來。

6 程度副詞／強調性副詞（Adverbs of Degree/Emphasizing Adverbs）

程度副詞：表示「到某種程度」（to what extent），又稱**強調性副詞**，常用在形容詞或其他副詞前。

- absolutely 絕對地
- almost 幾乎
- completely 完全地
- entirely 徹底地
- exceedingly 極度地
- extremely 極端地；非常
- fairly 簡直；完全地
- just 實在；非常
- pretty 相當
- quite 完全；相當；很
- rather 有點；相當
- really 實在；其實；的確
- simply 純粹地；完全地
- too 非常；太
- truly 非常；真正地
- utterly 十足地
- very 很

- I felt quite uncomfortable, sitting in the very noisy and smelly bar.
  我坐在又吵又臭的酒吧裡，渾身不自在。
  ↳ quite 和 very 都是程度副詞，回答 to what extent 的問題，分別用來修飾、強調形容詞 uncomfortable 和 noisy、smelly。

- "The new space elevator is simply unbelievable!" exclaimed Sue.
  「那座新的太空電梯簡直不可思議！」蘇驚呼道。

- Are you absolutely sure that Jake can swim across the lake?
  你百分之百確定傑克能夠游過這個湖嗎？

- Bobby declared, "This is an extremely exciting hobby." 鮑伯宣稱：「這是一項刺激透頂的嗜好。」
  ↳ 程度副詞 extremely，修飾分詞形容詞 exciting。

- She is quite a good dancer.

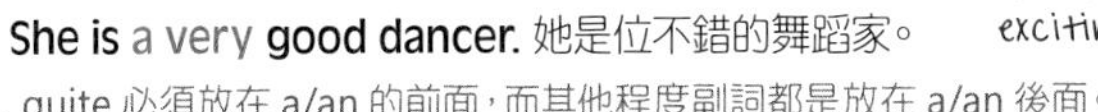

  = She is a very good dancer. 她是位不錯的舞蹈家。
  ↳ quite 必須放在 a/an 的前面，而其他程度副詞都是放在 a/an 後面。

7 目的副詞或片語（Adverbs/Adverbial Phrases of Purpose）

目的副詞或片語：用來回答「為什麼」（why）。不定式片語常作目的副詞，這時我們也可以說不定式片語在句中作目的狀語。

- Gus ran as fast as he could to catch the school bus.
  ↳ 目的副詞片語
  加斯為了趕上校車拼命地跑。
  ↳ 目的副詞片語在句子中作狀語，回答 why 的問題，修飾動詞 ran。

- That FBI agent's plan for the summer is to go to Hanoi to meet his girlfriend's parents.
  ↳ 目的副詞片語
  那位聯邦調查局的特務人員今年夏天計畫去河內見他女朋友的父母。
  ↳ 目的副詞片語在句子中作狀語，回答 why 的問題，修飾動詞 go。

8 疑問副詞（Interrogative Adverbs）

疑問副詞引導疑問句，是用來發問、提出問題的副詞，常見的疑問副詞有：

- when 何時
- where 哪裡
- why 為何
- how 怎麼

↳ when、where、why 也可以作關係副詞。

» 參見 320 頁〈Part 4 關係副詞與形容詞子句〉。

- When did Trish start to learn Spanish and English?
  翠西是何時開始學習西班牙語和英語的？
  ↑ When 是疑問副詞，用來引出疑問句，指時間，修飾動詞 (did) start。

- How could Louise and I learn to speak and write excellent Chinese?
  露易絲和我怎樣才能說出並寫出漂亮的中文呢？
  ↑ How 是疑問副詞，用來引出疑問句，指方式（怎麼、怎樣），修飾動詞 (could) learn。

- How deep can Jake scuba dive in that lake?
  傑克能在那個湖裡水肺潛水多深？
  ↑ How 是疑問副詞，用來引出疑問句，指程度，修飾形容詞 deep。

- Where is that cute and funny bunny that stole my money?
  偷走我金錢的那隻可愛又可笑的小兔子在哪裡？ → 指地點。

- Why do you waste your time crying over a friend who is always lying? 為什麼要浪費你的時間為一個老愛撒謊的朋友哭泣？ → 指原因。

比較 That's the reason why Kay came to Taipei. 那就是凱來臺北的原因。
↑ 關係副詞 why 引導一個形容詞子句，修飾先行詞 reason。

9 句副詞／分離副詞（Sentence Adverbs/Disjunct Adverbs）

1 一些副詞或副詞片語用來表示說話者對某種行為的態度。這類副詞被視為是**句副詞**或**分離副詞**，常置於句首，用來修飾後面的整個句子，並用逗號與句子的其他部分分開。比如：

- astonishingly 令人驚訝地
- clearly 顯然地
- frankly/to be frank 坦率地說
- generally 大體而言
- honestly/to be honest 老實說
- hopefully 但願
- interestingly (enough) 有趣地
- luckily 幸運地
- naturally 自然地；當然
- obviously 顯然地
- oddly enough 說也奇怪
- personally 就本人而言
- surprisingly 出人意外地
- to my disappointment 令我失望地
- unbelievably 難以置信地
- understandably 可理解地
- unfortunately 可惜；遺憾地

- **To be honest, I don't care whether or not he comes to my party.**
  實話說，我不在乎他是否來參加我的聚會。
  ↳ 不定式片語 To be honest 作句副詞。

- **Frankly, I don't care about what she thinks of me.**
  坦白說，我才不管她怎麼看我呢。
  ↳ Frankly 是句副詞，置於句首，用逗號分開，意思是「坦白說」，修飾後面整個句子。
  ↳ 句副詞也可以放在句尾，也要用逗號分開。（= I don't care about what she thinks of me, frankly.）

2 在這些分離副詞中，有些可以用來表示**態度**，也可以用來表示**方式**。

- **Clearly, the desert is growing and our land is becoming covered by sand.** 顯然地，沙漠區逐漸擴大，我們的陸地開始被沙石所覆蓋。
  ↳ 分離副詞 clearly = obviously, decidedly（顯然地）

- **It is difficult for me to explain this clearly.**
  要我把這一點解釋清楚，很難啊。
  ↳ 方式副詞 clearly = in a clear manner（清楚地）

10 其他副詞

一些副詞或副詞片語用來表示**說話者是從哪個角度來談論事情**的，比如：

- biologically 生物學上地
- chemically 化學上地
- environmentally 有關環境方面地
- financially 財政上
- ideologically 意識形態上
- logically 邏輯上
- morally 道德上
- outwardly 表面上
- physically 身體上
- politically 政治上
- technically 技術上
- visually 外表上；視覺上
- from a technical point of view 從技術的角度看
- as far as the environment is concerned 從生態環境考慮

- **My identical twin girls are alike physically, but they have very different personalities.**
  我的同卵雙胞胎女孩外表看上去很像，但她們的性格很不一樣。

作副詞用的子句和片語

1 副詞子句（Adverbial Clauses）

如果一組詞裡包含一個主詞和一個動詞，並在句子裡擔任副詞的角色，修飾句子裡的述語或主要動詞，這組詞就叫做**副詞子句**（或稱狀語子句）。

- As soon as Steve gets to Honolulu, **he will marry Sue.**
  史蒂夫一到達檀香山就會娶蘇。
  ↑「As soon as . . .」引導一個副詞子句，其中有主詞 Steve 和動詞 gets，子句在句中起副詞作用，指出主句述語動詞「will marry」的時間。
- After I learn these adverbs, **I'm going to use them** when I write some proverbs. 學了這些副詞之後，我會在寫諺語的時候去使用。

2 用作副詞的片語（Phrases Used as Adverbs）

1 **介系詞片語**是一組不包含主詞和動詞的詞，可作副詞來修飾動詞，故又稱作**副詞片語**。

go to the movies

- **Is Dwight going** to the movies **tonight?**
  今晚杜威特要去看電影嗎？
  ↑ to the movies 是介系詞片語，作地點狀語。
- **Kay's boyfriend works even** on Sundays. 凱的男朋友連星期天也要工作。
  ↑ on Sundays 是介系詞片語，作時間狀語。

2 **不定式片語**（**to + 動詞原形**），常作副詞使用，通常用來回答 why 的問題。

- **Santa Claus arrived on Christmas Eve** to deliver a present **to little Dawn Wu.** 聖誕老公公在聖誕夜到來，為小朵安．吳送來了禮物。
  ↑ to deliver a present 是目的副詞片語，修飾動詞 arrived，回答 why 的問題。
  » 參見 287 頁〈7 目的副詞或片語〉和 741 頁〈2 不定式的用法〉。

副詞的位置和語序

1 副詞在句中的位置

1 副詞置於所修飾的形容詞、其他副詞和名詞片語之前，比如：

- pretty good 非常好 → 副詞 pretty 修飾形容詞 good
- very well 很好 → 副詞 very 修飾副詞 well
- quite a shock 很震驚 → 副詞 quite 修飾名詞片語 a shock（不定冠詞 + 名詞）

2 修飾動詞或表示方式、時間和地點的副詞，在句中有多個不同位置。

1 方式副詞可置於句中不同位置

a 方式副詞的位置比較靈活，可置於句首、動詞前，或「動詞 + 受詞」後。

・Slowly, he opened the car door. → 句首（主詞前面）
= He slowly opened the car door. → 句中（主詞和述語動詞之間）
= He opened the car door slowly. → 句尾（述語動詞和受詞之後）
他慢慢地開了車門。

・Quickly, Mr. Ox opened the two locks on the box and found three rocks.
= Mr. Ox quickly opened the two locks on the box and found three rocks.
= Mr. Ox opened the two locks on the box quickly and found three rocks.
歐克斯先生很快打開盒子上的兩個鎖，找到了三塊石頭。

・Yesterday Mr. Qing, the schoolmaster, asked me not to talk publicly about the new policy before the annual meeting.
= Yesterday Mr. Qing, the schoolmaster, asked me not to talk about the new policy publicly before the annual meeting.
昨天，卿校長要我在年會之前，不要公開討論新政策。

↳ 雖然方式副詞的位置比較靈活，可以放在動詞前（publicly talk），但因這裡是不定式 to talk，不要把 publicly 置於不定式前，否則就成了分裂不定式（× not to publicly talk about）。

b 方式副詞 well、badly、hard 等要置於句尾。

- **Margo Bell plays the piano well.** 瑪歌．貝爾的鋼琴彈得很好。
  ↳ 動詞 + 受詞 + well
- **Ms. Card is a conscientious professional administrator, and she works very hard.** 卡德小姐是一個盡職盡責的專業管理人，她工作很勤奮。
  ↳ 動詞 + hard

c 方式副詞通常要靠近所修飾的動詞。

✗ **My dog ran to catch the thief very fast.**
✓ **My dog ran very fast to catch the thief.**
我的小狗飛快地跑去抓小偷。
↳ 方式副詞片語 very fast 要緊靠所修飾的動詞 ran。

2 不確定頻率副詞、程度副詞常置於句中

下列副詞常置於句中：

- almost 差不多
- already 已經
- always 總是
- certainly 無疑地
- completely 完全地
- definitely 明確地
- even 甚至
- finally 徹底
- hardly 幾乎不
- just 正好；僅僅
- nearly 幾乎
- never 從未
- now 現在
- only 只有
- probably 大概
- quite 頗
- rarely 很少
- really 真地；實在
- still 仍然
- suddenly 突然地

a 副詞 + 述語動詞

- **I never get up before nine on Sundays.** 我星期天不曾在九點之前起床過。
- **Jerry often visits his Aunt Mary.** 傑瑞經常拜訪瑪麗姨媽。
- **Jane really hates traveling by airplane.** 珍實在不喜歡乘飛機旅行。

b 連綴動詞 + 副詞

- **She is always late for her date.** 她約會向來都會遲到。
  ↳ 頻率副詞 always, often 等置於連綴動詞之後（is always）。

c 助動詞 + 副詞 + 主要動詞

- Sue has never been to Honolulu.
  = Never has Sue been to Honolulu. 蘇沒有去過檀香山。
  ↑ 表示否定意義的詞位於句首，句子要倒裝。
- Dan has rarely visited his Aunt Ann. 丹很少拜訪安姑姑。
- I have completely forgotten how to solve that math problem.
  我完全忘記了要怎麼算那道數學題目。

為了強調，這類副詞可移到助動詞和 be 動詞之前。
（在口語中，需要把重音放在副詞上面表示強調。）

- Lee Glass certainly is the best student in his class.
  李．葛拉斯無疑是班上最優秀的學生。
  ↑ 副詞 certainly 位於 be 動詞之前作強調。
- I pray Grace never has been and never will go to such a dangerous place. 我祈禱葛麗絲從來沒有、也永遠都不要涉足那樣一個危險的地方。
  ↑ 副詞 never 位於助動詞之前作強調。

still、sometimes、certainly、definitely、probably 等置於否定助動詞之前，而不是之後。也可以置於句首，表示強調。

- Bob probably won't accept your offer of a carpentry job.
  ↑ 否定助動詞之前
  = Probably Bob won't accept your offer of a carpentry job.
  ↑ 句首（強調）
  鮑勃大概不會接受你提供的這個木工工作。

3 置於句尾的副詞

a 確定頻率副詞：daily、weekly、monthly、annually 等置於句尾。

- The astronomy club's meeting is held monthly.
  = The astronomy club's meeting is held once a month.
  天文俱樂部的會議每個月舉辦一次。

b **頻率副詞片語**：every day、every year 等，通常置於句尾或句首。

✗ Kay every day jogs home.

✓ Kay jogs home every day.

= Every day Kay jogs home. 凱每天都慢跑回家。

↑ 頻率副詞片語（every day、every month 等），通常不置於主詞（Kay）和述語動詞（jogs）之間，而是置於句首或句尾。

c 副詞 yet、a lot、any more、any longer、too、as well 常置於句尾。

- I can't trust Lenore any more. 我再也不相信蕾諾兒了。

  ↑ any more、any longer、as well 等置於句末（受詞之後）。

2 各種副詞的排列順序

1 當句中有多個副詞時，這些副詞須依照基本的順序規則排列：

主詞	動詞	方式副詞	地點副詞	頻率副詞	時間副詞	目的副詞
She	swims	enthusiastically	in the pool	every morning	before dawn	to keep fit.
Jan	naps		on her classroom floor	every afternoon	before dinner.	
Sue Brown	walks	fast	to town	every morning	after trimming the lawn.	

2 由於副詞的位置非常靈活，上述表格內例句中的部分副詞修飾語（頻率和時間副詞），也可以移動到句子的最前面。例如：

- Every morning before dawn, she swims enthusiastically in the pool to keep fit. 她每天早上天亮之前都要在游泳池裡興致勃勃地游泳，以保持健康。
- Every afternoon before dinner, Jan naps on her classroom floor. 簡每天下午晚飯之前，都要在教室的地板上打個盹兒。
- Every morning after trimming the lawn, Sue Brown walks fast to town. 蘇‧布朗每天早上修剪了草坪後，就快步走路到城裡。

3 副詞排列的一般原則

1 較短的副詞片語放在較長的副詞片語之前：無論是哪一種副詞片語，**較短**的副詞片語應該位於較長的副詞片語之前。

- His wife swam in a pool before dawn almost every day of her life.
  他的妻子一生中幾乎每天天亮之前都在游泳池裡游泳。
  ↑ 頻率副詞片語 every day of her life 位於時間副詞片語 before dawn 之後，因為 every day of her life 比 before dawn 長。

2 較具體的副詞片語在前：在同類的副詞片語中，語意較為**具體**、**細微**的副詞片語放在前面。

- Aunt Sally was born in a tiny hut in a Tibetan valley.
  莎莉姨媽出生在一個西藏山谷的小屋裡。
  ↑ in a tiny hut 和 in a Tibetan valley 都是地點副詞片語，in a tiny hut 比 in a Tibetan valley 更具體，因此放在前面。

- Kay's sisters rarely get up before nine on Saturdays.
  凱的姊妹們星期六很少會在九點以前起床。
  ↑ 時間副詞片語 before nine 比時間副詞片語 on Saturdays 更為具體、細微，應該放在前面。

3 有些副詞放在句首，起強調作用：有時為了強調某個副詞，可將之置於句首，尤其是方式副詞。

- Slowly and carefully, she opened the door.
  她小心翼翼地慢慢把門打開。
  ↑ slowly、carefully 是方式副詞。

- Grace sometimes stays up late at night, reading articles on the Internet about space.
  = Sometimes Grace stays up late at night, reading articles on the Internet about space.
  葛麗絲有時會熬夜上網看天文網站。
  ↑ sometimes 是頻率副詞。

副詞的比較級和最高級

1 副詞「級」的類別

1 副詞和形容詞一樣，也有原級、比較級和最高級形式：**原級**不與另一個人或物進行比較；**比較級**用於兩者之間的比較；**最高級**用於三者之間的比較。

原級　**Claire sang beautifully in the clean, clear mountain air.**
克萊兒的歌聲在未受污染的、潔淨的高山空氣中十分動聽。

比較級　**Claire sang more beautifully than Sally.**
克萊兒唱得比莎莉還要動聽。

最高級　**Claire sang the most beautifully of all the singers that were there.**
在場的所有歌手中，克萊兒唱得最動聽。

2 副詞比較級與最高級的形式

1 比較級（Comparative）

單音節副詞 + -er + than
more/less + 雙音節／多音節副詞 + than

- **Mike finished the English quiz faster than Trish.**
  邁克比翠西先寫完英語測驗。 → fast 一個音節
- **Mike wrote his English quiz essay more rapidly than Liz.**
  邁克的英語測驗論文比莉茲寫得快。 → rapidly 三個音節

- **Mike wrote his English quiz essay less rapidly than Bess.**
  邁克的英語測驗論文比貝絲寫得慢。 → rapidly 三個音節

2 最高級（Superlative）

the + 單音節副詞 + -est
the most/least + 雙音節／多音節副詞

- **Paul wrote his English quiz essay the most rapidly of all.** → rapidly 三個音節
  = Paul wrote his English quiz essay the fastest of all. → fast 一個音節
  保羅在所有人中最快地寫完了英語測驗論文。

- **Saul wrote his English quiz essay the least rapidly of all.** → rapidly 三個音節
  所羅是所有人中最慢寫完英語測驗論文的人。

1 副詞的比較級和最高級不能只用原級的形式。
2 雙音節和多音節的副詞，其比較級不能用 -er，要加 more 或 less。
3 單音節的副詞，其比較級不能用 more 或 less，要用 -er。

- She always arrives at work later than me.
  她總是比我晚到辦公室。
  ↳ late 是單音節詞，比較級要用 -er，不能用原級。
- Dee wants to see you more frequently. 蒂希望更常見到你。
  ↳ frequently 是多音節詞，比較級要用 more。
- Sally can shout louder than Lily.
  莎莉喊的聲音可以比莉莉更大。
  ↳ loud 是單音節詞，比較級要用 -er，不用 more。

有些以 -y 結尾的雙音節副詞，如 early、lively 等，也可以作形容詞用，這些副詞的比較級和最高級不要用 more/less 或 most/least，而要把字尾 -y 改成 i，再加 -er 或 -est。

✗ Today Amy arrived at school half an hour more early than me.
✓ Today Amy arrived at school half an hour earlier than me.
艾咪今天比我早半個鐘頭到學校。

3 副詞的比較用法

1 副詞的比較句型

a 原級：主詞 A + 動詞 + as + 副詞（原級）+ as + 主詞 B

- Ann plays jazz as lively as Nan.
  安演奏起爵士樂跟南一樣輕快活潑。
- Did little Sid run as fast as his big sister Liz?
  小席德跑得跟他姐姐莉茲一樣快嗎？
- Mary does not get up as early as Larry.
  瑪麗沒有賴瑞起得早。
- Mary does not drive as carefully as Larry.
  瑪麗開車沒有賴瑞那麼小心。

b 比較級：主詞 A + 動詞 + 副詞（比較級）+ than + 主詞 B

- Ann gets up earlier than her husband Dan.
  安比她丈夫丹早起床。
- Ann gets up later than her sister Nan.
  安比她姐姐南晚起床。
- Larry drives more carefully than Mary.
  賴瑞開車比瑪麗謹慎。
- Larry drives less carefully than Jerry.
  賴瑞開車沒有傑瑞謹慎。
- Jan's husband talks more than she does, but she thinks more (than he does).
  簡的丈夫比簡愛說話，不過簡比較愛思考。

c 比較級：主詞 + 動詞 + 副詞（比較級）

- Can't you please walk a little bit faster, Louise?
  露易絲，你可以走快一點嗎？

- Can you eat your cheese more quietly, please?
  可以請你吃起司的聲音小聲一點嗎？

- After the accident, Bess evidently acted less confidently.
  事故發生後，貝絲顯然沒有過去那麼自信了。

- I sing badly out of tune, but Jill sings worse and sounds like a dog howling at the moon.
  我歌唱得很糟糕，完全走調，不過潔兒唱得更糟糕，聽起來就像一隻對著月亮咆哮的狗。

d 最高級：主詞 + 動詞 + (the) 副詞（最高級）+ of (in、on)

- Claire screams the loudest of all the cheerleaders.
  在所有的啦啦隊長中，克萊兒的尖叫聲最大。
  ↑ of + 複數名詞（cheerleaders）

- Who runs the fastest in your class?
  你們班上誰跑得最快呢？
  ↑ in + 指團體的單數名詞（class）

- She runs the fastest of all the kids in my class.
  在我班上所有的孩子中，她跑得最快。

- Sam has flown that rocket plane the highest of all our pilots.
  在我們所有的飛行員中，山姆駕駛的那架火箭飛機飛得最高。

- She dances the most beautifully of all my ballet students.
  在我所有的芭蕾舞蹈學生中，她的舞跳得最優美。

2 沒有比較級和最高級形式的副詞

某些副詞具有「絕對」、「到達極限」的意思，是不能比較的，完美就是完美，完全就是完全，沒有「更完美、更完全」或「最完美、最完全」的説法，因此沒有比較級和最高級，比如下面的這些副詞：

- almost 幾乎
- again 再一次
- back 向後
- before 以前；較早
- by 在旁邊
- exactly 確切地；完全地
- ever 在任何時候
- here 這裡
- never 從未
- no 沒有
- not 不
- now 現在
- perfectly 完美地
- then 那時
- there 在那裡
- thus 如此
- too 太
- very 非常
- yes 是的

✕ Short Amy stood straighter and asked shy tall Paul, "Will you marry me?"

✓ Short Amy stood straight and asked shy tall Paul, "Will you marry me?"

個子嬌小的艾咪筆直地站著，對害羞的高個子的保羅問道：「你會娶我嗎？」

✕ Lulu looked more exactly like Sue.

✓ Lulu looked exactly like Sue.

露露和蘇完全像是一個模子刻出來的。

✕ Lily Lee dives most perfectly.

✓ Lily Lee dives perfectly.

莉莉‧李跳水跳得很完美。

UNIT

07 關係詞與形容詞子句和名詞子句

Relatives in Adjective Clauses and Noun Clauses

關係代名詞和形容詞子句

1 關係詞的定義

關係詞分為關係代名詞、關係形容詞和關係副詞。主要的關係詞有：

- who
- whoever
- whom
- whomever
- whose
- that
- which
- whichever
- what
- whatever
- as
- than
- where
- when
- why

2 關係代名詞引導形容詞子句

1 引導一個從屬子句，並與句子裡的一個名詞或代名詞有關聯的代名詞，稱作**關係代名詞**。

2 關係代名詞指代的名詞或代名詞，稱作**先行詞**。這類從屬子句在文法上稱為**形容詞子句**、關係子句或定語子句。關係代名詞一般包括：

- who
- whom
- that
- which
- as
- than

- **The woman is an American. She won the prize.**
  那個女子是美國人，她贏得了獎品。 → 由兩個簡單句組成。

- **The woman who won the prize is an American.**
  贏得獎品的那個女子是美國人。
  ↑ woman 為先行詞，who 為關係代名詞，用來引導形容詞子句 who won the prize，在子句中作動詞 won 的主詞，並與先行詞 woman 相關聯。

- **Did you find the honey (that) you were looking for?** 你找到你要的蜂蜜了嗎？
  ↑ (that) you were looking for 是一個形容詞子句，修飾名詞 honey；關係代名詞 that 是形容詞子句動詞片語 were looking for 的受詞，作受詞時，that 可省略。

・The guy (whom/that) Nancy married is my old friend Sam.
娶南西的那個男人是我的老朋友山姆。

⤷ (whom/that) Nancy married 是一個形容詞子句，修飾名詞 guy；關係代名詞 whom/that 是形容詞子句動詞 married 的受詞，作受詞時，whom/that 可省略。

3 關係代名詞的用法（who, whom, which, that, as, than）

1 常用關係代名詞的使用規則

who	① 只能指人，不能指物。 ② 可以作主詞，在口語中也可以作受詞。
whom	① 只能指人，不能指物。 ② 只能作動詞或介系詞的受詞。 ＊介系詞後面只能用 whom 和 which，不能用 who 和 that。
which	① 作關係代名詞用時，只能指動物或東西，不能指人。 ② 比較：作疑問代名詞用時，which 可以指人，這時後面跟 of 片語（比如：which of us, which of the ladies）。
that	① 可以指人、動物、東西。 ② 不能用在非限定性形容詞子句中。 ③ 關於非限定性形容詞子句。 » 參見 324 頁〈2 非限定性形容詞子句〉。
as	① 與 such、the same、as 等連用。 ② 在形容詞子句中作主詞或受詞。
than	① 與「形容詞比較級 + 名詞」結構連用。 ② 在形容詞子句中作主詞或受詞。

✗ In our class, Lily is the only one which can speak Spanish fluently.

⤷ which 作疑問代名詞時可以指人，如 which of you（參見 89 頁〈Part 5 疑問代名詞〉）。which 作關係代名詞時，則只能指物，不能指人。

✓ In our class, Lily is the only one who can speak Spanish fluently.
莉莉是我們班上唯一能流利地用西班牙語進行會話的人。

⤷ 指人時要用關係代名詞 who 作主詞。

· Here's the money that you were looking for. 你找的錢在這裡。

↳ 關係代名詞 that 可以指人，也可以指物。that 在這裡指代先行詞 money（物）。

2 who（指「人」；作主詞）

✗ This is Andrew, that works with Sue.

↳ 這是非限定性形容詞子句，不能用 that。

✗ This is Andrew, whom works with Sue. →whom 不能用作主詞。

✓ This is Andrew, who works with Sue.

這位是安德魯，他和蘇一起工作。

↳ who 指的是 Andrew（人），作形容詞子句（who works with Sue）的主詞。

· Is that the waitress who served us yesterday?

那位就是昨天為我們服務的服務生嗎？

↳ 關係代名詞 who 是形容詞子句動詞 served 的主詞，與前面主句裡的名詞 waitress（人）有關聯。

3 whom（指「人」；作受詞）

✗ This is Ms. Sue Powers, with that I am working on an e-car project.

✗ This is Ms. Sue Powers, with who I am working on an e-car project.

↳ that 和 who 都不能用在介系詞後面

✗ This is Ms. Sue Powers, that I am working with on an e-car project.

↳ 先行詞是特定的人，要用非限定性形容詞子句，而在非限定性子句中，不能用 that。

✓ This is Ms. Sue Powers, with whom I am working on an e-car project.

✓ This is Ms. Sue Powers, whom I am working with on an e-car project.

這位是蘇·鮑爾斯女士，我和她一起在進行一項電動車專案的工作。

↳ whom 指的是 Ms. Sue Powers，作形容詞子句裡的介系詞 with 的受詞。

↳ 介系詞 with 可以放在關係代名詞之前（with whom），也可以放在動詞之後（whom I am working with）。

· Roy Smith, whom I hope you hire, can drive large trucks.

羅伊·史密斯能夠駕駛大卡車，我希望你雇用他。

↳ 主句的主詞是 Roy Smith。whom 指的是 Roy Smith，作子句裡動詞 hire 的受詞。

4 who 與 whom 的正式和非正式用法

關係代名詞 who 和疑問代名詞一樣，who 作主詞，口語中也可以作受詞；而 whom 只能作受詞，比 who 作受詞更正式。

Informal Mike is married to someone who I really like.
Formal Mike is married to someone whom I really like.
邁克娶了一個我很喜歡的人。

Informal The man who I marry will be both honest and persistent.
Formal The man whom I marry will be both honest and persistent.
我要嫁的男人既要忠誠老實，又要持之以恆。

5 that/who（指「人」；作主詞）

a 在**限定性形容詞子句**中，先行詞不是具體人名（如：the couple、the doctors），美式英語常用 that 指人，也可以用 who 指人，who/that 作子句的主詞。

- **Have you ever spoken to the couple that/who lives next door?**
  你跟住在隔壁的那對夫妻說過話嗎？ ↑ 形容詞子句
  ↑ that/who 作子句（that/who lives next door）的主詞。

b 如果先行詞是具體的人名（如：Mr. Brown、Mike），要用**非限定性形容詞子句**，子句只能用 who 指人。that 不能用於非限定性形容詞子句。

- **Have you ever spoken to Sue Bore, who lives next door?**
  你跟住在隔壁的蘇·波爾說過話嗎？
  ↑ 先行詞是一個具體的人名（Sue Bore），只能用非限定性形容詞子句。

c 先行詞為 one、ones、the only one、anyone 或 those 時，用 who。

- **Those who have not yet registered should do so as soon as possible.** 還未登記的人，請盡速辦理登記。

- **I enjoy singing songs written by those song writers who are my friends.** 我喜歡唱我朋友們所寫的歌。
  ↑ 先行詞 song writers 有 those 修飾。

- **Anyone who doesn't take truth seriously in small matters cannot be trusted in large ones either.** (Albert Einstein, 1879–1955)
  小處不用心的人，難以託付大任。

6 that/which（指「物、動物、地點」，用於限定性形容詞子句）

- Daniel gave me the keys that/which opened both his door and the safe hidden in his floor. ↥ 形容詞子句
  丹尼爾把可以打開房門和藏在地板下保險箱的鑰匙給了我。
  ↥ 傳統文法規定，在限定性子句中，用來指「物」的關係代名詞只能用 that，不用 which，但現代英語可以用 which。
  ↥ that 或 which 指 keys（東西），作形容詞子句的主詞。

- Is Jake acting like a mole that/which lives in a black hole? 傑克表現得就像一隻住在黑洞裡的鼴鼠嗎？
  ↥ 關係代名詞 that/which 是形容詞子句動詞 lives 的主詞，並且與前面主句裡的動物 mole 有關聯。限定性子句更常用 that。

✗ This is the hospital in that I was born.

✓ This is the hospital in which I was born.
  ↥ 介系詞後面要用 which，不用 that。

✓ This is the hospital (which/that) I was born in.
  我就是在這家醫院出生的。
  ↥ 介系詞 in 移動到動詞後面，作介系詞受詞的 that/which 可以省略。
  ↥ that/which 在這裡指地點（hospital）。
  » 參見 310 頁〈4 關係代名詞的省略用法〉。

7 which（指「物、動物、地點」，用於非限定性形容詞子句）

- The cat, which is a popular pet, is one of the smartest domestic animals. 貓這種受大眾喜愛的寵物，是家畜動物中最聰明的動物之一。
  ↥ which 指 cat（動物），作形容詞子句（加底線的部分）的主詞，這裡的子句是一個非限定性形容詞子句，僅提供補充說明，不能用 that 來引導非限定性子句。

- Alice got a job as a well-paid model in Paris, which really surprised her friends from the Scottish island of Lewis and Harris.
  艾麗絲在巴黎獲得了一個待遇優渥的模特兒工作，這的確使來自蘇格蘭路易斯哈里斯島的朋友們大吃一驚。
  ↥ 一些非限定性形容詞子句不是修飾主句裡的名詞或代名詞，而是修飾整個主句，表示「這個事實」（the thing or fact that），與其他非限定性子句一樣，關係代名詞要用 which，而不能用 that。

Diving Deep Into English 40 which 與 that 的比較

❶ **非限定性子句**（which）：which 可以引導**附加說明**的子句（這種子句從主句中刪除後，不會改變句子的基本意思），此即非限定性子句，通常會用一個或兩個逗號與主句分開。注意 非限定詞形容詞子句不能用 that。

- **I lent Anna my brand-new GMC truck, which she soon drove into a big oak tree.**

  我把我的新 GMC 卡車借給了安娜，不久後，她就開著它撞上了一棵大橡樹。

  ⤴ which 引導的是非限定性形容詞子句，用逗號與主句分開，起附加說明的作用，如果把這個子句刪除，句子的基本意思不變。

  ⤴ GMC = General Motors Corporation 通用汽車公司

  » 關於限定性子句和非限定性子句，參見 323 頁〈Part 5 關係詞在限定和非限定性子句中的用法〉。

❷ **限定性形容詞子句**（that 或 which）：that 常用來引導限定性的子句，該子句通常與主句不可分離，如果刪除了 that 子句，句子的意思就不完整，因此，that 引導的子句不要用逗號分開（即，關係代名詞 that 不可能出現在逗號後面）。現在有很多人既用 that、也用 which 來引導限制性子句，但更常用 that。

- **The ballet shoes that I just bought last week were stolen today.**

  = The ballet shoes which I just bought last week were stolen today.

  我上星期剛買的那雙芭蕾舞鞋今天被人偷了。

  ⤴ 如果刪除了 that 子句，句子的意思就不完整。

  ⤴ which 和 that 都可以指「物」，不過限定性定語子句裡更常用 that。

❸ **限定性形容詞子句**（which）：但在下列情況中更常用 which，而非 that。

1 句子裡有兩個或更多個平行的限制性子句時，關係代名詞要用 which。

- **I am taking acting classes which will improve my stage performances and which may also lead to some work as a TV actress.** 我在上表演課，這些課有助於我改進舞臺表演，也許還能使我獲得做電視演員的工作。

2 如果句中已經使用過 that，關係代名詞要用 which。

- **That is a movie which you should not miss.** 那是一部你不應該錯過的電影。

③ 當先行詞前面有 that/this/these/those 修飾時，關係代名詞要用 which，比如 this . . . which、that . . . which、these . . . which 或 those . . . which。

- **I was explaining to Sam those words which I had already taught Pam.**
  我當時正在對山姆解釋我已經教過潘姆的那些字。

④ 介系詞後面必須用 which。介系詞用在關係代名詞前面（介系詞 + 關係代名詞 + 主詞 + 動詞），這時關係代名詞必須用 which，而且關係代名詞不能省略，用於非常正式的文體中。

- **Bounty always receives part of its value from the manner in which it is bestowed.** (Samuel Johnson, 1709–1784)
  慷慨總是從慷慨的方式中獲得其部分價值。

❹ 限定性形容詞子句（that）：在下列情況中，要用 that，不用 which。

① 在 something、anything、few、all 等不定代名詞以及在最高級形容詞之後，要用 that 作受詞（或省略關係代名詞）或主詞，不用 which。

- **She is one of the most interesting women (that) I have ever met.**
  她是我見過最有趣的女子了。 ↑ 受詞

- **Is there anything (that) I can do for you?** 我能為你做些什麼？（that：受詞）

- **Is this all that is left?** 就剩這些嗎？（that：主詞）

② 當先行詞被 the only、the last、the very、the first（序數詞）等修飾時，用 that。

- **Paris is the very place that I would like to visit next summer.**
  巴黎正是我明年夏天想去的地方。

- **The only thing that matters is to stay healthy.**
  唯一要緊的事，就是保持健康。

8 as 作關係代名詞的用法

a 引導**限定性**形容詞子句：要與 such、the same、as 等連用，表示「與……相同的事物或人」。

- **I have the same health problem as my mom does.**
  我的健康問題和我媽一樣。
  ↳ as 引導形容詞子句，修飾先行詞 problem；as 在子句中作動詞 does 的受詞。

- **Sue is no longer the same honest person as I once knew.**
  蘇不再是我以前所認識那個誠實的人了。
  ↳ as 的先行詞是 person；as 作形容詞子句動詞 knew 的受詞。

- **The world sometimes witnesses extreme nationalism such as occurred just before World War Two.**
  世人有時候會見證到極端的民族主義，例如在二次世界大戰爆發的前夕之際。
  ↳ as 引導限定性形容詞子句，修飾先行詞 nationalism；as 在子句中作動詞 occurred 的主詞。

b 引導**非限定性**形容詞子句：意味「正如，像」，在句中的位置很靈活，可置於句首、句中或句尾。

- **As is reported on the Internet, talks between those two countries have ended in failure.**
  根據網路報導，那兩個國家的談判以失敗告終。
  ↳ as 引導非限定性形容詞子句，修飾後面的整個主句；as 在子句中作主詞。

- **As is noted above, HPV is a sexually transmitted virus that can cause many kinds of cancer.**
  如前所述，人類乳突病毒透過性行為所傳染，能導致多種癌症。

9 than 作關係代名詞的用法

than 作關係代名詞必須具備以下條件：① than 前面必須是「形容詞比較級 + 名詞」結構；② 比較級所修飾的名詞即為 than 的先行詞。

- **I don't want to borrow more money than is needed.**
  我需要多少錢就借多少錢，不想多借。
  ↳ than 前面是比較級 more + money。
  ↳ than 引導一個形容詞子句，修飾先行詞 money。在子句中 than 是主詞。

- Collecting more taxes than is absolutely necessary is legalized robbery. (President John Calvin Coolidge)
  徵收比實際需要更多的稅收是合法化的搶劫。

4 關係代名詞的省略用法

1 在**限定性**形容詞子句裡，常省略受格關係代名詞，尤其在口語中。

Very formal I feel sorry for the man whom Mary is going to marry.
Informal/Common I feel sorry for the man Mary is going to marry.
我對要娶瑪麗的那個男人深表同情。
↳ 這是限定性形容詞子句，受格關係代名詞 whom 是動詞 marry 的受詞，可省略。

- Here is the honey that you were looking for to do your cooking.
  = Here is the honey you were looking for to do your cooking.
  你剛才在找、要用來做飯的蜂蜜就在這裡。
  ↳ 這是限定性形容詞子句，關係代名詞 that 是動詞片語 were looking for 的受詞，可省略。

2 在**非限定性**形容詞子句中，不能省略受格關係代名詞。

✗ Last year at a conference in New York City, Jane met my brother Daniel, she later married.
✓ Last year at a conference in New York City, Jane met my brother Daniel, whom she later married.
去年在紐約召開的一個會議上，珍認識了我哥哥丹尼爾，後來還嫁給了他。
↳ whom 是動詞 married 的受詞；非限定性形容詞子句不能省略受格關係代名詞。

3 關係代名詞作**主詞**時，也不能省略關係代名詞。

- Mom has bought a new car that goes over 60 miles on a gallon of gasoline. 媽媽買了一輛一加侖汽油可跑六十多英里的新車。
  ↳ that 是動詞 goes 的主詞；關係代名詞作主詞時，不能省略。

✗ The government, was designed for the people, has got into the hands of the bosses and their employers, the special interests.
✓ The government, which was designed for the people, has got into the hands of the bosses and their employers, the special interests.
(President Thomas Woodrow Wilson)

政府本來是為人民而設計的，卻落入了特定利益集團老闆或雇主之手中。

↑ 關係代名詞 which 是形容詞子句的主詞，不可省略。這句為非限定性形容詞子句，所以關係代名詞無論是作主詞還是受詞，都不可省略。

5 介系詞在形容詞子句中的位置

1 介系詞 + 關係代名詞 whom 或 which（不可省略）

在非常正式的文體中，介系詞可以用在關係代名詞前面，這時關係代名詞要用 whom 或 which，不能用 who 和 that，同時關係代名詞不能省略。

● in which ● with whom ● for whom ● to whom

・**Nancy is respected by everyone with whom she works.**

凡是與南西一起工作的人都很尊敬她。

↑ 介系詞 with 用在受格關係代名詞 whom 前面，後面不能接代名詞 who 或 that。

・**This is the cottage in which Liz and Mitch Thorn were born.**

莉茲·索恩和米奇·索恩就是在這棟別墅裡出生的。

↑ 介系詞 in 用在關係代名詞 which 之前，which 不可省略。

2 關係代名詞（可省略）+ 動詞 + 介系詞

口語中，介系詞也可放在動詞或形容詞子句後面，當介系詞位於動詞後面（介系詞與關係代名詞不連用）時，who、whom、which 和 that 可省略。

Informal/Common **The woman who always has a grin owns the apartment (that/which) Mat left his hat in.**

↑ 介系詞 in 用在形容詞子句的末尾，that/which 可以省略。

Very formal **The woman who always has a grin owns the apartment in which Mat left his hat.**

麥特的帽子留在那個總是露出牙齒咯咯笑的女子的公寓裡。

↑ 介系詞 in 用在關係代名詞 which 之前，which 不可省略。

Informal/Common **The young Japanese woman (whom/that/who) I was looking at smiled sweetly and said, "I'm Louise."**

↑ 介系詞 at 位於動詞 was looking 之後，whom/that/who 可省略。

Very formal The young Japanese woman at whom I was looking smiled sweetly and said, "I'm Louise."
我在凝視的那位年輕日本女子甜甜地微笑說：「我是露易絲。」
↑ 介系詞 at 放在關係代名詞 whom 之前，whom 不可以省略。

3 關係代名詞（可省略）+ 片語動詞

如果形容詞子句裡的動詞是片語動詞（例如：come across, fill in, look after, put up with），不要把介系詞放在關係代名詞前面。

✗ Sue is one of the few women to whom I look up.
↑ 片語動詞 look up to 不能分開。

✓ Sue is one of the few women (that/who) I look up to.
蘇是我所尊敬的少數幾個女子之一。

- Here is the form (that/which) you need to fill in. 這是你需要填寫的表格。
↑ 片語動詞 fill in 不能分開。

6 人稱代名詞及關係代名詞不能並用

不要用人稱代名詞重複表達關係代名詞的意思。在形容詞子句中，用 who、which 等來代替 he、him、she、it 等就好，不要兩者同時使用。

✗ The person who she/he leaves last should always turn off our bright blue searchlight.
↑ who 是關係代名詞；she/he 是人稱代名詞，關係代名詞和人稱代名詞不能並用。

✓ The person who leaves last should always turn off our bright blue searchlight. 最後離開的人應該關掉明亮的藍色探照燈。

✗ Here's the haunted house (which/that) Mat wanted it.
↑ which/that 是關係代名詞，作子句動詞 wanted 的受詞；it 是人稱代名詞，不要用人稱代名詞重複關係代名詞的意思。

✓ Here's the haunted house (which/that) Mat wanted. 麥特想要的鬼屋就在這裡。

不定關係代名詞和名詞子句

1 不定關係代名詞 what 的用法

1 what 可以代替 the thing(s) which/that 或 anything that。what 引導一個**名詞子句**，整個子句用作名詞，在句中可以作主詞、受詞或主詞補語。

✗ The food what you were cooking made me sneeze.

↳ what 前面不能有名詞（即不能有先行詞），what 不引導形容詞子句，that 才引導形容詞子句，修飾先行詞 food。

✓ What you were cooking made me sneeze.

= The food that you were cooking made me sneeze.

= The thing(s) that you were cooking made me sneeze.

你煮的食物使我打了個噴嚏。

↳ what 引導的整個名詞子句在句中作主詞；what 指「物」，在子句中作動詞 were cooking 的受詞。

- I'm sorry about what happened to you yesterday.
  = I'm sorry about the thing that/which happened to you yesterday.
  我對你昨天的遭遇深表同情。
  ↳ what 引導的名詞子句在句中作介系詞 about 的受詞。what 在子句中作主詞。

- Steve gave me a talking doll, and that's just what I wanted on Christmas Eve.
  = Steve gave me a talking doll, and that's just the thing that/which I wanted on Christmas Eve.
  史蒂夫給了我一個會講話的洋娃娃，那正是我想要的聖誕夜禮物。
  ↳ what 引導的名詞子句放在動詞 be 後面，作主詞補語。
  ↳ what 是子句中動詞 wanted 的受詞。

2 在 anything、something、nothing、everything、all 和 the only thing 等詞後面，關係代名詞要用 that，不能用 what，即 what 不引導形容詞子句。

- Mat can take anything (that) he wants from the hut. → 形容詞子句
  = Mat can take what/whatever he wants from the hut. → 名詞子句
  麥特可以從小屋裡拿走任何他想要的東西。

- All (that) Mat could do was to say his prayers with his eyes shut.
  = What Mat could do was to say his prayers with his eyes shut.
  麥特所能做到的事，就是閉上眼睛祈禱。

- Money and power are the only things that matter to her.
  = Money and power are what matter to her.
  對她來說，金錢和權力是唯一重要的東西。

- I can't give you everything (that) you ask for.
  = I can't give you what/whatever you ask for.
  我無法給你想要的一切。

2 不定關係代名詞 whoever, whomever, whichever, whatever 的用法

1 whoever, whomever, whatever, whichever（引導名詞子句）

a 除了 what，不定關係代名詞還包括：

- whoever = any person that
- whomever（為 whoever 的受格）
- whatever = everything that
- whichever = any one of the two or more

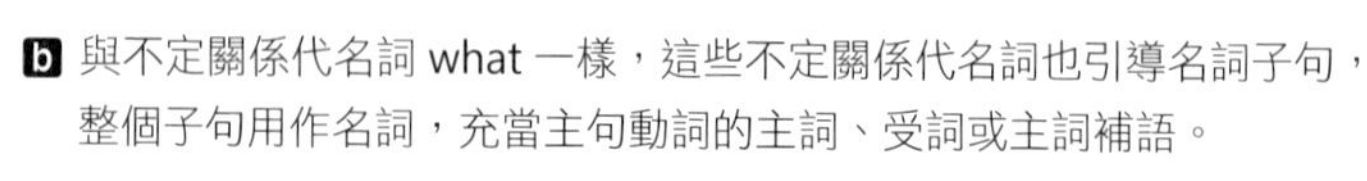

b 與不定關係代名詞 what 一樣，這些不定關係代名詞也引導名詞子句，整個子句用作名詞，充當主句動詞的主詞、受詞或主詞補語。

- **Give a map of our city to whoever asks for one.**
  = Give a map of our city to anyone who asks for one.
  無論誰想要，就給他一張我們城市的地圖。
  ↥ whoever 引導的整個名詞子句，當作主句的介系詞 to 的受詞。
  ↥ whoever 在名詞子句中充當主詞。

- **You should not give Lulu whatever she wants.**
  = You should not give Lulu everything (that) she wants.
  你不應該給露露她想要的一切。
  ↥ whatever 引導的整個名詞子句，當作主句的動詞 give 的直接受詞。
  whatever 在名詞子句中是動詞 wants 的受詞。

- **Whichever you like will be yours.**
  = Whichever one you like will be yours. 你喜歡哪一個，你就拿去吧。
  ↥ 上面第一句的 whichever 引導的整個名詞子句作句子的主詞。
  ↥ whichever 在名詞子句中是動詞 like 的受詞。
  ↥ 第二句的 whichever 是關係形容詞，修飾代名詞 one。
  » 參見 317 頁〈Part 3 關係形容詞與形容詞子句、名詞子句〉。

- **Will the manager of our store be whoever marries Jill?**
  無論誰和潔兒結婚，就會成為我們的商店經理嗎？
  ↥ whoever 引導的名詞子句在連綴動詞 be 後面作主句的主詞補語。
  ↥ whoever 在名詞子句中是主詞。

2 who, whoever, whom, whomever 用主格還是受格？

當整個名詞子句作動詞或介系詞的受詞時，學生們常傾向於使用受格形式的 whom 或 whomever，但這樣選擇有時會出錯。究竟應該用主格（who/whoever）還是受格（whom/whomever），應該取決於這個關係代名詞在**名詞子句**中是主詞還是受詞。

- **Do you know who received the most beauty pageant votes and became Ms. Hawaii?** 你知道誰以最高的得票數獲選為夏威夷小姐嗎？
  ↥ 整個名詞子句（who received . . .）作述語動詞 know 的受詞。
  ↥ 儘管整個子句是主句述語動詞 know 的受詞，但 who 卻是受詞子句裡動詞 received 的主詞，因此應該用主格 who，而不是用 whom。

- **The Prom King will be selected by whomever you have elected as Queen.** 班級舞會的國王將由你們選出的皇后來挑選。
  - ⮤ 整個名詞子句 (whomever you have elected . . .) 是介系詞 by 的受詞。
  - ⮤ whomever 在受詞子句中作動詞 have elected 的受詞，因此要用受格 whomever，不能用主格 whoever。

- **A free trip to Honolulu will be given to whoever wins "The Best-Dressed" in the Chicago Fashion Contest.**
  無論誰贏得芝加哥時裝比賽的「最佳穿著獎」，都能免費去檀香山旅行。
  - ⮤ 整個名詞子句（whoever wins . . .）作介系詞 to 的受詞。
  - ⮤ 但 whoever 在受詞子句中作動詞 wins 的主詞，因此應該用主格 whoever。

- **The manager of the After-School Reading Program will hire whomever she likes.** 「課外閱讀課程」的主任想雇用誰就雇用誰。
  - ⮤ 整個名詞子句（whomever she likes）是主句動詞 hire 的受詞。
  - ⮤ whomever 在受詞子句中作動詞 likes 的受詞，因此應該用受格 whomever。

- **Whoever gets the job of being the Prom King will ride in my convertible.** 誰當選了班級舞會的國王，誰就可以乘坐我的敞篷車。
  - ⮤ 整個名詞子句（Whoever gets the job . . .）是句子的主詞。
  - ⮤ Whoever 是子句中動詞 gets 的主詞，因此應該用主格 Whoever。

關係形容詞與形容詞子句、名詞子句

關係形容詞包括 whose, what, whatever, which, whichever，這些字的後面要接名詞，例如 whose mother、whatever books，故稱為關係形容詞。whose 引導**形容詞子句**，而 what、whatever、which、whichever 則引導**名詞子句**。

1 whose（限定詞，指「人、動物、物、地點」；引導形容詞子句）

whose ① whose 須用在名詞前面，不能單獨使用，表示所屬關係。

② whose 可以指人、動物、東西或地點（of whom, of which）。

③「whose + 名詞」結構在形容詞子句中作主詞或受詞。

④ 不要把關係形容詞和疑問代名詞 whose 弄混淆。疑問代名詞 whose 只用來指人，意思是 belong to whom。

- **I have a cute dog, whose name is Scot.**

  我有一隻可愛的狗狗，牠叫作史考特。

  ⤷ whose 引導的形容詞子句修飾先行詞 dog（動物）；whose 用在名詞 name 前；「whose + name」在形容詞子句中作連綴動詞 is 的主詞。

- **My friend Lily lives in a house whose roof is covered with a lovely garden.**

  我朋友莉莉的房子屋頂上覆蓋了一片美麗的花園。

  ⤷ whose roof = the roof of the house; whose 表所屬關係，指 house（地點）。

  ⤷ 「whose + roof」在形容詞子句中作主詞。

• Last month our small town was struck by a flood, from whose effects we are still suffering.

我們的小鎮上個月遭受一場洪水的襲擊，

我們至今還受到災後的影響。

↳ whose effects = the effects of the flood:
whose 表所屬關係，指物（flood）。

↳ 「whose + effects」在形容詞子句中作介系詞 from 的受詞。
這是一個非限定性形容詞子句。

2 what/whatever（指「物」；引導名詞子句）

what/whatever ① 可作關係形容詞，意思為「任何的，無論怎樣的」。

② 「what/whatever + 可數／不可數名詞」引導名詞子句。

③ whatever 比 what 語氣更強。

• I will share with you what/whatever information I learn about that new rocket engine.

= I will share with you all the information (that) I learn about that new rocket engine. → that 引導形容詞子句。

只要我有那個新火箭發電機的新資訊，我都會分享給你。

↳ what/whatever 引導名詞子句，整個子句作主句動詞 share 的受詞。

↳ 在這個子句中，「what/whatever + 名詞（information）」是動詞 learn 的受詞。

• His wife spent whatever money he had saved, and then she left him.

= His wife spent all the money (that) he had saved, and then she left him. 他妻子把他存的錢全部花光後就離開了他。

關係形容詞 what/whatever 也可引導讓步副詞子句。

» 參見 345 頁〈Part 5 從屬連接詞與副詞子句〉。

3 which/whichever（指「物、地點」；引導名詞子句）

which/whichever ① 可作關係形容詞，意思為「無論哪個／哪些」。
② 「which/whichever + 可數名詞」引導名詞子句。
③ whichever 比 which 語氣更強。

- **You may choose which/whichever books on this shelf you are interested in.** 你可以選擇書架上任何一本你感興趣的書。
  - ↑ which/whichever 引導名詞子句，整個子句作主句動詞 choose 的受詞。
  - ↑ 「which/whichever + 名詞（books）」是動詞片語 are interested in 的受詞。

4 whichever 和 whatever 的區別

1 whichever 和 whatever 接**可數名詞**時，有時可以互換，有時不能互換；兩者的區別與 what 和 which 之間的區別一樣，通常 whichever 涉及的東西比 whatever 更具體。

- **You may take whatever/whichever measures you think are necessary.** 你認為有必要採取什麼樣的措施，就可以採取什麼樣的措施。
  - ↑ 這句 whatever 和 whichever 可以互換。

- **Whichever debate team wins on Saturday will go on to the national competition.** 無論哪一個辯論組在星期六贏了，就會去參加全國性的競賽。
  - ↑ 比賽是在具體的、已知的隊伍之間進行，因此，這句要用 whichever。

2 **不可數名詞**要用 whatever 修飾，不用 whichever。

- **Ann's lazy boyfriend foolishly spends whatever money she earns.** 無論安掙多少錢，她懶惰的男朋友都要胡亂地花光。
  - ↑ money 為不可數名詞，要用 whatever。

關係副詞與形容詞子句

1 where（指「地點」；引導形容詞子句）

1 where 是關係副詞，也可以像關係代名詞一樣，用來引導一個形容詞子句（關係子句），修飾主句裡表示地點的名詞。where 在子句中充當地點副詞（at that place）修飾動詞，其先行詞通常是**表示地點的名詞**（如 house、place、town 等）或**含有地點意義的名詞**（如 case、point、situation 等）。

- This is the church where my grandpa used to be the minister.
  我爺爺就是在這座教堂裡當過牧師。
  ↳ where 引導的形容詞子句修飾先行詞 church，在形容詞子句中 where 作副詞。

- Some writers insist that the word "that" cannot be used to refer to people, but in situations where the people are not specifically named, it is acceptable.
  有些作者堅持 that 這個字不能用來指「人」，不過當先行詞是非特別指定的人的情況下，則可以用 that 來指「人」。
  ↳ where 引導一個形容詞子句，修飾含有地點意義的先行詞 situations。
  ↳ 在形容詞子句中，where 作副詞，修飾動詞 are not named。

比較

- The point in history at which we stand is full of promise and danger.
  (President Franklin Delano Roosevelt)
  我們所處的這個歷史時刻，充滿了希望與危險。
  ↳ 先行詞雖是 point，但這裡因為有介系詞 at，不能用 where（at which = where）。

2 並非所有表示地點的先行詞，都要求用 where 來引導形容詞子句。判斷的關鍵，端視關係詞在子句裡所擔任的角色。關係代名詞 which 或 that 在形容詞子句裡作主詞或受詞。關係副詞 where 在形容詞子句中作狀語，不能作主詞或受詞。

✕ Nancy has never been to Paris, but it is the city where she most wants to see.

↑ 這句的形容詞子句動詞 see 需要接受詞，但這裡的 where 不能作 see 的受詞。

✕ Nancy has never been to Paris, but it is the city that she most wants to see it.

↑ 此句在句尾多了一個代名詞 it，受詞重複了。

✔ Nancy has never been to Paris, but it is the city she most wants to see.

南西沒去過巴黎，不過那是她最想去看一看的城市。

↑ 此句省略了作受詞的關係代名詞 that 或 which。

2 when（指「時間」；引導形容詞子句）

when 是關係副詞，引導形容詞子句，在子句中充當時間副詞（at that time）修飾動詞，其先行詞必須是**表示時間的名詞**（如 day、time、year 等）。在限定性子句中可以用 that 來代替 when, 但可以省略 when/that。

- We are living in a fantastic age, when the whole world has become a small village.

  我們生活在一個奇異的時代，在這個時代裡世界成了一個小村莊。

  ↑ when 引導非限定性形容詞子句，修飾先行詞 age；在形容詞子句中 when 作副詞，修飾動詞 has become；非限定性形容詞子句中的 when 不能省略。

- I will never forget the day when I first met you in Honolulu.
  = I will never forget the day that I first met you in Honolulu.
  I will never forget the day I first met you in Honolulu.
  我永遠也不會忘記我在檀香山初次見到你的那一天。
  ↥ when 引導限定性形容詞子句，修飾先行詞 day；這裡是限定性子句，可以用 that 代替 when, 但 that 和 when 都可以省略。

- Does Amy still remember the occasion when she fell in love with Del?
  艾咪還記得她愛上戴爾的那個場合嗎？
  ↥ when 引導的限定性子句，修飾主句裡表時間的先行詞（occasion），在子句裡充當時間副詞（at that time）。

3 why（指「原因」；引導形容詞子句）

why 引導形容詞子句，在子句中作原因副詞，其先行詞是名詞 **reason**（the reason why = the reason for which）。也可以用 that 代替 why，還可以省略 why 或 that。

- Did Sam understand the reason why/that he failed yesterday's English exam?
  = Did Sam understand the reason he failed yesterday's English exam?
  = Did Sam understand why he failed yesterday's English exam?
  山姆知道他昨天英文考試不及格的原因嗎？
  ↥ 第一句 why 是關係副詞，可用 that 取代 why，引導形容詞子句，修飾先行詞 reason。
  ↥ 第二句 why/that 被省略。
  ↥ 第三句刪除了先行詞 reason，由疑問連接詞 why 引導一個名詞子句，整個子句作動詞 understand 的受詞。why 指 the reason for which。

» 參見 359 頁〈Part 6 從屬連接詞或關係代名詞引導名詞子句〉。

關係詞在限定和非限定性子句中的用法

1 限定性形容詞子句（Restrictive/Essential Adjective Clauses）

1 限定性形容詞子句（由 that, which, who, whom 所引導）在句子中是不可缺少的成分，用以提供句子的重要訊息，與主句之間不用逗號分開；如果把它從句子裡刪除，主句的意思就會變得不清楚。

2 限定性子句的先行詞通常是**非特定**的人、物、地點等（如：the lady, the book, a house 等）。

✗ **Where is the lady, that rings the bell and gives the weather forecast?**
↑ 這是一個限定性形容詞子句，不能用逗號與主句分開。

✓ **Where is the lady that/who rings the bell and gives the weather forecast?** 那位搖鈴鐺、做氣象報告的女士在哪裡？
↑ that 和 who 都可以用來指 lady（人），在子句中作主詞，如果把子句刪除，句子的意思（Where is the lady）就會變得不清楚或不完整。

- **That's the police officer who helped us find Sue.**
  就是那位警官協助我們找到蘇的。
  ↑ 如果刪除 who 所引導的子句，主句（那是那位警察）的句意就不完整。因此這個形容詞子句是限定性的，不能刪除。主句的主詞是 that，為了避免重複，關係代名詞要用 who，不用 that。

- **The book (that) Dee's mom bought yesterday came with six valuable DVDs.** 蒂的媽媽昨天買的那本書附贈六張珍貴的 DVD。
  ↑ that 所引導的限定性形容詞子句（關係子句）不可少，如果刪除，那麼主句「The book came with six valuable DVDs.」（那本書附贈六張貴重的 DVD。）的意思就不清楚了，聽者或讀者可能會不知道在談論的是哪一本書。

- **Yesterday I met a young woman whose beauty took my breath away.**
  我昨天碰到了一個美得令我屏息的年輕女子。
  ⮡ whose 引導的形容詞子句修飾先行詞 woman（人）。
  ⮡ 「whose + beauty」在限定性形容詞子句中作動詞 took 的主詞。如果刪除了這個形容詞子句，主句（昨天我碰到了一個年輕女子）的意思就不完整。

- **You know, once in a while I get to the point, with everybody staring at me, where I want to go back indoors and pull down the curtains.**
  (President Dwight David Eisenhower)
  有時候呢，當每個人都目不轉睛地看著我時，我就想走回屋子裡，然後把窗簾拉下。
  ⮡ 關係副詞 where 指代先行詞 point，引導限制性形容詞子句。
  ⮡ 句中雖有逗號把 where 子句與先行詞 point 分開，但這並非意味就是非限定性子句。where 前面加上逗號，是因為先行詞和子句中間插入 with 引導的介系詞片語。

2 非限定性形容詞子句（Nonrestrictive Adjective Clauses）

1 非限定性形容詞子句（由 which, who, whom 所引導）不是句子不可缺少的成分，只是附加的成分，提供額外的訊息，如果刪除，也不會改變句子的基本意思。非限定性形容詞子句常會以一個逗號或一對逗號（位於句子中間時），來和句子的其他部分分開。

2 非限定性子句的先行詞通常是一個**特定的**人（Ann Smith）、物 (my new car, a book called *The Old Man and the Sea*) 或地點（Paris）。

- **My friend Trish Pool, who now teaches English at the National University of Singapore, never liked English in high school.**
  我的朋友翠西·普爾，她當年讀高中時根本就不喜歡英語，現在卻在新加坡國立大學教英語。
  ⮡ 關係代名詞 who 的先行詞是特定的人（Trish Pool）。who 所引導的是非限制性形容詞子句（關係子句），可刪除，不會改變主句的意思。
  ⮡ 子句置於句中時，要用一對逗號與句子其他成分分開。

- My friend Trish Pool never liked English in high school.

  我的朋友翠西·普爾當年讀高中時根本就不喜歡英語。

  ⤷ 這是上一句複合句的基本意思。上一句由 who 所引導的非限定性形容詞子句（關係子句）刪除後，主句的基本意思絲毫沒有改變。

- Her latest book, which deals with backpackers, has sold very well.

  她的新書賣得很好，那是一本談論徒步旅行者的書。

  ⤷ 關係代名詞 which 的先行詞是特定的物（her latest book）。which 所引導的非限制性形容詞子句（關係子句），在句中並非不可少，可以刪除，而不會改變主句的基本意思。這個子句放在句子中間，前後要用逗號隔開。

- Her latest book has sold very well. 她的新書賣得很好。

  ⤷ 這一句是上一句複合句的基本意思。which 所引導的非限定性形容詞子句（關係子句）刪除後，主句的基本意思絲毫沒有改變。

✗ I lent her a book called *Standard American English*, that is easy and fun to read.

✓ I lent her a book called *Standard American English*, which is easy and fun to read.

我借給她一本叫做《標準美式英語》的書，這本書讀起來輕鬆有趣。

⤷ which 引導的是非限定性形容詞子句，用逗號與主句分開，這個子句對特定的物（Standard American English）只起附加說明的作用。

⤷ 如果把這個子句刪除，句子的基本意思不會改變，意思依然清楚、完整（知道說話人所指的是哪一本書）。

⤷ 非限定性形容詞子句不能用關係代名詞 that。

✗ This is Ann Smith, that teaches EFL in Japan.

✓ This is Ann Smith, who teaches EFL in Japan.

這是安·史密斯，她在日本教 EFL。

⤷ EFL = English as a foreign language 以英語為外語（教學或研究）

⤷ 先行詞是特定的人物（Ann Smith），要用非限定性子句修飾。雖然 that 可以指人，但不能用在非限定性形容詞子句中。

- Sometimes the angel Sue flies high with the fairy Lulu, whose home is in Honolulu.

  有時小天使蘇會與小妖精露露一起在天空高飛；露露的家在檀香山。

  ↥ 關係代名詞 whose 指特定的人（Lulu），whose 與所修飾的名詞一起（whose home）作動詞（is）的主詞。這是一個非限定性形容詞子句。

- Last summer I returned to Long Ridge Village, where I had spent my childhood with Midge.

  去年夏天，我回到了長山脈村莊，我的童年就是和米姬一起在那裡度過的。

  ↥ where 引導一個非限定性子句，修飾主句裡特定的地點（Long Ridge Village），在子句裡充當地點副詞（at that place）。

- We picked up three boat-loads of refugees, some of whom had been at sea for weeks.

  = We picked up three boat-loads of refugees, of whom some had been at sea for weeks.

  我們救起了三船的難民，他們當中有些人已經在海上漂流數週之久了。

  ↥ 在非限定性子句中，some, any, none, all, both, several, many 等可以與 of whom, of which, of whose 連用。

UNIT

08 連接詞與並列句和從屬子句

Conjunctions, Compound Sentences, and Dependent Clauses (Adverbial Clauses and Noun Clauses)

連接詞的定義與類型

連接詞是用來連接單詞、片語、簡單句和從屬子句與主句的詞。最常見的連接詞有下列三種：

對等連接詞	成對連接詞	從屬連接詞
• and 和 • but 但是 • or 或 • nor 也不 • so 因此 • for 由於 • yet 可是	• both . . . and . . . 既……又…… • as well as 不但……而且…… • either . . . or . . . 不是……就是…… • neither . . . nor . . . 既不……也不…… • not . . . but 不是……而是 • not only . . . but also . . . 不僅……而且…… • whether . . . or 是……抑或	• as 如同；因為 • because 因為 • if 如果 • when 當……時 • though/although 雖然 • so that 以便 • unless 除非 • that 引導名詞子句（也可作關係代名詞，引導形容詞子句，參見 301 頁 Unit 7）

- Mom and Dad are mad at my brother Tom.
  媽媽和爸爸對我的弟弟湯姆大發脾氣。
  ⮤ 對等連接詞 and 連接兩個對等的名詞 Mom 和 Dad。
- Joe is making great progress, but he still has a long way to go.
  喬有很大的進步，不過仍然有很大的進步空間。
  ⮤ 對等連接詞 but 連接兩個獨立子句，即兩個簡單句，構成一個並列句。
- Daisy Heart is neither a writer nor a fighter.
  黛絲·哈特既不是作家，也不是戰士。
  ⮤ 成對連接詞：neither + 名詞；nor + 名詞
- Sam was depressed because he did not know how to solve the problem. 山姆很沮喪，因為他不知道如何解決這個問題。
  ⮤ 從屬連接詞 because 引導一個表示原因的從屬子句。

對等連接詞（兼論並列句）

1 對等連接詞的作用

1 **對等連接詞**又稱**並列連接詞**，用以把文法上各自獨立的兩個或多個字、片語和獨立子句連接起來。用對等連接詞連接獨立子句（又稱簡單句），就構成並列句（參見 721 頁〈Part 2 並列句和複合句〉）。對等連接詞包括下列詞彙：

- and 和
- but 但是
- or 或
- nor 也不
- for 由於
- so 因此
- yet 可是

有些文法學家把 for、so 和 yet 看作從屬連接詞。

2 對等連接詞連接的字或片語須具相同的文法作用，即連接「**並列詞類**」，例如：「名詞 + 名詞」、「動詞 + 動詞」、「片語 + 片語」、「獨立子句 + 獨立子句」。被連接的句子（即簡單句或獨立子句）在文法形式和結構上也要一致，具相同的重要性，沒有主次之分。

2 對等連接詞的用法

1 and 和；又；並且

a and 表示附加和補充；用 and 連接的句子成分須對等。

✗ Sighting the whale was interesting and excitement.

✓ Sighting the whale was interesting and exciting.
看見鯨魚是一件有趣又興奮的事。

↳ and 連接兩個對等的形容詞 interesting 和 exciting。
↳ 所謂對等成分，在文法形式和結構上須相同。

- **In the advancing crowd, everyone was singing and dancing.**
  在行進的人群中，每個人都在唱歌跳舞。
  ↳ and 連接兩個對等的動詞 was singing 和 (was) dancing。

- **Sam is expected to work hard and to succeed on the exam.** 山姆應該用功念書，通過考試。
  ↳ and 連接兩個對等的不定式片語 to work hard 和 to succeed on the exam。

- **Please open the window and air out the bathroom.**
  請打開窗戶，讓洗手間通通風吧。
  ↳ and 連接對等的祈使句 open the window 和 air out the bathroom。

- **Sally and Lily both love chocolate candy.**
  莎莉和莉莉都喜歡吃巧克力糖。
  ↳ and 連接兩個對等的名詞 Sally 和 Lily，作複合主詞，述語動詞要用複數（love）。

- **Bob failed his driving test and had to leave his job.**
  鮑勃沒考上駕照，不得不辭掉工作。
  ↳ and 連接前後的兩個動詞片語，表示一個動作是另一個動作的結果。

- **Mr. Flower came home early and took a quick shower.**
  弗勞爾先生早早回到家裡，很快地沖了個澡。
  ↳ and 連接動詞片語 came home 和 took a quick shower，表時間順序。

b 對等連接詞若連接兩個獨立子句（構成並列句），則 and 前面通常要加逗號。

- **Alvin is playing his violin. His wife Margo is playing her piano.**
  ↳ 兩個獨立子句／兩個簡單句

- **Alvin is playing his violin, and his wife Margo is playing her piano.** 艾爾文在拉小提琴，他的妻子瑪歌在彈鋼琴。
  ↳ and 把兩個獨立子句連接起來，成為一個句子（即並列句），在 and 前面要加逗號。

c 用 and 連接三個以上的詞彙時，要用逗號分開被連接的成分，並在最後兩個成分之間用 and 連接。

・Louise speaks Italian, Spanish, English, Japanese, and Chinese.
露易絲會講義大利文、西班牙文、英文、日文和中文。
↳ and 連接並列五種語言，美式英語在 and 前要加逗號，英式英語則可不加逗號。

・She is beautiful, intelligent, and hardworking.
她美麗、聰明，又勤奮。
↳ and 連接三個並列的形容詞 beautiful、intelligent、hardworking。

d 當句子中有三個字並列出現時，可以在每兩個字之間都加上連接詞 and，不用逗號，表強調。

・I love milk and coffee and tea.
MILK, COFFEE, and TEA
= I love milk, coffee, and tea. 我喜歡喝牛奶、咖啡和茶。
↳ 也可用逗號分開被連接的成分，並於最後兩個成分之間加上連接詞。

e 請看下列兩個例句的結構分析：

・Jane found out that she was in the wrong line and in the wrong building and that she was obviously wasting her time.
珍發現她排錯了隊，又走錯了大樓，根本是在浪費時間。
↳ 第一個 and 連接兩個介系詞片語，第二個 and 連接兩個 that 引導的受詞子句。

・Kay was tired and irritable, and she had lost her way.
凱又累又煩躁，而且還迷路了。
↳ 第一個 and 連接兩個形容詞；第二個 and 連接兩個獨立子句。

使用並列結構時，注意不要遺漏介系詞。

✗ She is interested and skillful at playing pingpong.
✓ She is interested in and skillful at playing pingpong.
她對乒乓球很感興趣，而且球技不錯。

用 and 時，通常不再重複多餘的詞。

Redundant Coco can sing and Coco can play the piano.
Better Coco can sing and play the piano. 可可會唱歌和彈鋼琴。

f and 也用來構成下面的複合結構，這些結構當作一個整體看待，在句中作主詞時，述語動詞須用**單數**形式。例如：

- horse and carriage 馬車
- curry and rice 咖哩飯
- law and order 法律與秩序
- time and tide 歲月
- bread and butter 抹了奶油的麵包；生計；謀生之道
- strawberries and cream 抹了奶油的草莓

curry and rice
咖哩飯

- Curry and rice always tastes good to Sue.
  蘇總是喜歡咖哩飯的味道。
  ⮤ curry and rice 是複合單位，看作一個整體，在本句中作主詞；當這種當作整體的複合成分在句中作主詞時，通常接單數述語動詞，所以要使用單數動詞 tastes。
- Time and tide waits for no one, not even the king's bride.
  歲月不待人，就算是國王的新娘也不例外。
- Is bread and butter good for Ted?
  抹了奶油的麵包對泰德有好處嗎？

bread and butter
奶油抹麵包

- Which is Ted's main bread and butter, his writing or his teaching?
  泰德主要靠什麼謀生，寫作還是教學？

2 but 但是

a and 表示補充和附加；but 則表示轉折，引入一個不同的概念，強調句子的兩個成分之間的對立。

- Today the weather is sunny and warm.
  今天的天氣陽光燦爛，溫暖宜人。
  ⮤ sunny and warm：表示意義的疊加。
- Today the weather is sunny but cold.
  今天出太陽了，但卻很冷。
  ⮤ sunny but cold：表示意義的對比。

- Mountain climbing is difficult but interesting. 爬山雖然艱難，但很有趣。

b 用 but 連接的句子成分必須對等。

- I had the impression that his resignation wasn't a bad thing but a happy release from stress and depression.

我覺得他的辭職並不是一件壞事，而是從壓力和沮喪下幸福地解脫出來了。

↑ but 是對等連接詞，連接兩個名詞片語。

- She is making lots of money but can't find happiness and peace.
  她賺了很多錢，卻找不到幸福和安詳。 → but 連接兩個動詞片語。

c 用 but 連接兩個獨立子句時，but 前面要加逗號。

- Grandma Corning is 84 years old. She still goes swimming every morning. → 兩個獨立子句／兩個簡單句
  = Grandma Corning is 84 years old, but she still goes swimming every morning. 科寧奶奶已經 84 歲了，但每天早晨還是會去游泳。
  ↑ but 把兩個獨立子句連接起來，成為一個句子（即並列句），在 but 前面要加逗號。

- I'm not the smartest fellow in the world, but I can sure pick smart colleagues. (President Franklin Delano Roosevelt)
  我不是世界上最聰明的傢伙，但我有能力選出聰明的同事。
  ↑ but 連接兩個獨立子句，構成一個並列句。

3 or 或；否則

a or 用來連接可供選擇的人或物，表示選擇（alternative）。

b 在句子裡，or 通常只放在最後一個可供選擇的選項前面，其餘選項之間用逗號分開；如果列舉的項目不多，也可以用 or 連接所有的選項。

c 用 or 連接的句子成分須對等。

- Is Gus going to school on foot, by car, or by bus?
  = Is Gus going to school on foot or by car or by bus?
  加斯打算走路、開車，還是坐公車去學校？
  ↑ or 連接三個介系詞片語 on foot、by car 和 by bus。

- Which color does Sue want—red, green, yellow, purple, pink, or blue?
  蘇想要哪一個顏色——紅色、綠色、黃色、紫色、粉紅色，還是藍色？
  ↑ or 連接六個名詞，or 只用在最後一個選項前面。

- **Paul and his friends will go to the beach on Sunday to surf or to play volleyball.** 保羅和他的朋友們星期日要去海灘衝浪或打排球。
  - ⮤ or 連接兩個不定式片語 to surf 以及 to play volleyball。
  - ⮤ 第二個不定式可以省略 to（如：to surf or play volleyball）。

d or 連接兩個字，構成複合主詞，要用**單數**動詞。
and 連接兩個字，構成複合主詞，要用**複數**動詞。

- **Ann or Dan is coming to pick you up at 10 a.m.**
安或丹上午十點會來接你。
  - ⮤ Ann or Dan 是複合主詞，要用單數動詞（is coming）。
- **Ann and Dan are coming to pick you up at 10 a.m.**
安和丹上午十點會來接你。
  - ⮤ Ann and Dan 是複合主詞，要用複數動詞（are coming）。

e **否定句**中，or 用來包含另一個人或另一件事，表示「也不」（and not）。

- **My wife never skis or skates.** 我的太太從不滑雪，也不溜冰。
- **After the skunk's stink reached Amy, she didn't cry or blink.**
艾咪聞到臭鼬的臭味後，沒有哭也沒有眨眼。

f 連接詞 or 也用來表示：如果某人不去做某事，將產生什麼樣的後果。表達警告、威脅、建議的語氣，譯為「否則、要不然」，連接一個祈使句和一個獨立子句。

- **Hurry up, Jane. You'll miss today's last train to Maine.** → 兩個簡單句
- **Hurry up, Jane, or you'll miss today's last train to Maine.**
快一點，珍，否則你會錯過今天開往緬因州的末班火車。
  - ⮤ or 連接兩個簡單句（一個祈使句和一個獨立子句），需要用逗號分開。
  - ⮤ 意即：If you don't hurry up, you'll miss today's last train to Maine.

- **Get out of my house at once, or I'll shoot.**
  - ⮤ 意即：If you don't leave my house at once, I'll shoot.

= Get out of my house at once before I shoot.
馬上離開我的房子，不然我開槍了。
  - ⮤ before 也可以表示「否則；要不然」，這時，before 引導的副詞子句通常置於主句後面，且不加逗號，before 子句中的述語動詞要用簡單現在式來表示未來式。

4 nor 也不

a 在否定陳述的後面，如果要加另一個否定陳述，可以用 nor（也可以用 or）。nor 的意思是 and not、or not 或 not either，不過 nor 不常用在 not . . . nor 結構中。

Less Common He could not read nor write.

Common He could not read or write.

Common He could neither read nor write. 他不識字，也不會寫字。

↳ or 常用在 not . . . or 結構中（如上面第二句）；nor 常用於成對連接詞 neither . . . nor 中（如上面第三句）。

» 參見 337 頁〈Part 3 成對連接詞（兼論並列句）〉。

b nor 如果放在獨立子句前面，需要倒裝，如下面例句將助動詞 does、could 放在主詞前面。

- **Claire doesn't brag, nor does she swear.** 克萊兒不會吹牛，也不會罵髒話。
- **Ted could not speak English, nor could he understand anything we said.** 泰德不會講英文，也聽不懂我們說的話。

  ↳ 與其他對等連接詞一樣，如果 nor 連接兩個獨立子句，其前面要加逗號。

5 for 因為；既然；由於

a for 作連接詞時，**只能用在兩個獨立子句之間**，需用逗號把兩個子句分開。for 引導的獨立子句對前面子句的內容加以解釋，說明原因，故不放句首。

b for 比 because 更正式，用來為前面的陳述提供證據或解釋。

- **Please comfort Dan, for he looks sad about his divorce from Ann.** 請安慰丹，因為他跟安離了婚，看起來很傷心。
- **Mack began to grow nervous, for his wife had not come back.** 麥克開始緊張起來，因為他妻子還沒有回來。

  ↳ for 連接兩個獨立子句，構成一個並列句。

6 so 所以；於是

a 連接詞 so 和 for 一樣，**只用於連接兩個獨立子句**，構成並列句，需要逗號把兩個子句分開。so 引導的獨立子句表示結果，因此不放在句首。

- That night Jenny had no money, so she had to sleep at the airport.
  那晚珍妮身上沒有錢，只好睡在機場。 → so 表示「因此、所以」。

- The old road was blocked by a rockslide, so Mack had to turn around and go back.
  那條老路被落石堵住，麥克只好調頭往回走。 → so 表示「於是」。

- Ann's mom has always been nervous in large gatherings, so she tries to avoid crowds. → 表結果
  人聚集很多時，安的媽媽總是很緊張，所以她都盡量避開人群。
  = Ann's mom tries to avoid crowds, for she has always been nervous in large gatherings. → 表原因
  安的媽媽儘量避開人群，因為人聚集很多時，她總是會很緊張。

b 區別副詞 so 的用法：

- I like singing, and so does my girlfriend.
  = I like singing; so does my girlfriend.
  我喜歡唱歌，我女友也喜歡唱歌。
  ↳ and 連接兩個並列子句，so 是副詞，表示「也一樣」，後用倒裝結構。
  ↳ 也可以不用連接詞 and，用分號分開兩個並列子句。

- So, Claire is glad that she has broken up with Brad.
  這麼說，克萊兒很高興她已經和布萊德分手了。
  ↳ 這句的 so 不是連接詞，而是副詞。
  ↳ 在非正式用語中，副詞 so 可以放在句首，起總結或過渡的作用。在這種情況下，so 後面常加逗號，與句子的其他部分分開。

7 yet 可是；然而

a 連接詞 yet 的意思相當於 but，但比 but 更為正式。

b yet 常**連接兩個獨立子句**，構成並列句，需要逗號把兩個子句分開。

- Kate had promised me that she would be on time for our date at the ballet, yet/but she arrived an hour late.
  凱特答應我會按時赴約會去看芭蕾舞，但她卻晚到了一個小時。

成對連接詞（兼論並列句）

1 成對連接詞的定義

成對連接詞不能單獨使用，必須成對使用，又稱作**關聯連接詞**，被當作一個整體看待。這類成對連接詞可以看作是成對的**對等連接詞**，連接兩個在文法上平行的結構，如：兩個名詞、兩個形容詞、兩個獨立子句、兩個動詞、兩個副詞。

» 參見 845 頁〈Unit 19 平行結構〉。

- as well as 不但……而且
- both . . . and 既……又
- not . . . but 不是……而是
- either . . . or 不是……就是
- not only . . . but also 不僅……而且
- neither . . . nor 既不……也不
- whether . . . or 是……抑或

2 成對連接詞的用法

1 not . . . but 不是……而是

a not . . . but 是成對連接詞，須**成對使用**，用來排除 not 後面的成分，如：名詞、形容詞、動詞、副詞等，而涵蓋 but 後面的成分。

b not . . . but 不可誤用成 not . . . only 或 not . . . but only。

c not 和 but 後面的成分須平行。

✗ It was not they offered him good money but the job itself that attracted Bob.

↳ 這句 not 後面接的是獨立子句，而 but 後面接的卻是名詞，二者不平行。

✓ It was not the money but the job itself that attracted Bob. 吸引鮑勃的不是錢，而是工作本身。

↳ 平行結構：not + 名詞（money）；but + 名詞（job）

- Lee could have made himself understood if he had spoken not louder but more slowly.
如果當時李講話不是放大聲音，而是放慢速度，聽眾就聽得懂他的話了。
↑ 成對連接詞 not 和 but 連接兩個副詞比較級 louder 和 more slowly。

- Ruth did not tell a fairy tale but spoke the bitter truth.
露絲講的不是天方夜譚，而是殘酷的現實。
↑ 成對連接詞 not 和 but 連接兩個動詞 tell 和 spoke。

- We must always remember that America is a great nation today not because of what government did for people but because of what people did for themselves and for one another.
(President Richard M. Nixon)
我們必須時刻牢記：今天美國之所以成為一個偉大的國家，不是因為政府為人民做了什麼，而是因為人民為他們自己、為他們彼此做了什麼。
↑ 平行結構：not + because of . . .；but + because of . . .

2 both . . . and/as well as 也；都

a both 必須與 and 搭配，不能與 as well as 搭配。both . . . and 只用以連接**兩個平行結構**。

b as well as 必須按先後次序，連接**兩個**或**三個**平行結構。

c both . . . and 只用來連接兩個平行結構，若要連接三個或三個以上的平行結構，要用 as well as。

✗ Jane and John speak both English as well as Chinese at home.
↑ both 和 as well as 不可連用。

✓ Jane and John speak both English and Chinese at home.
↑ 平行結構：both + 名詞 (English) + and + 名詞 (Chinese)

✓ Jane and John speak English as well as Chinese at home.
珍和約翰在家中既講英文，也講中文。
↑ 平行結構：名詞 (English) + as well as + 名詞 (Chinese)

- I have a hunch that Amy can both kick and punch.
  = I have a hunch that Amy can kick as well as punch.
  我有一種預感，艾咪既會打拳，也會踢腿。
  ↳ both . . . and 是成對連接詞，連接兩個動詞 kick 和 punch；as well as 也是成對連接詞，連接兩個動詞 kick 和 punch。

d 「(both) A and B」只能連接兩個平行結構；如果是三個平行結構，就要用「A and B as well as C」或「both A and B as well as C」。

✗ She is both attractive, intelligent, and considerate.
✓ She is attractive and intelligent as well as considerate.
✓ She is both attractive and intelligent as well as considerate.
她迷人、聰明又體貼。
↳ (both +) 形容詞 (attractive) + and + 形容詞 (intelligent) + as well as + 形容詞 (considerate)

- To be successful, our team must plan and work as well as dream.
  = To be successful, our team must both plan and work as well as dream. 要想成功，我們的隊伍就必須要有計劃，要努力，還要有夢想。
  ↳ 動詞 (plan) + and + 動詞 (work) + as well as + 動詞 (dream)
  ↳ both + 動詞 (plan) + and + 動詞 (work) + as well as + 動詞 (dream)

1 下面四對成對連接詞連接複合主詞時，動詞的單複數要與第二個連接詞（but also, or, nor）後面的主詞一致。

- not only . . . but also
- neither . . . nor
- either . . . or
- whether . . . or

2 這四對成對連接詞連接兩個獨立子句時，不要用逗號把子句分開。

3 not only . . . but also 不僅……而且

a not only 不能只用 not，but also 不能只用 but。

b not only 和 but also 後面的結構必須平行。

✗ My wife is not only beautiful but wise. → 錯誤的成對連接詞。

✗ My wife is not beautiful but also wise. → 錯誤的成對連接詞。

✗ My wife not only is beautiful but also wise. → 非平行結構。

✓ My wife is not only beautiful but also wise.
我妻子不僅美麗而且聰明。
↑ 平行結構為：not only + 形容詞（beautiful），but also + 形容詞（wise）

✗ He not only is a great runner but also an excellent rugby kicker.

✓ He is not only a great runner but also an excellent rugby kicker.
他不僅是一名優秀的賽跑選手，而且還是一名傑出的橄欖球射手。
↑ not only 後面接名詞（runner），but also 後面也接名詞 (kicker)，是平行結構。

4 either . . . or 不是……就是；或者

either 和 or 後面的結構必須平行。

- Either Annie or Jenny will get the programming job at my company.
不是安妮就是珍妮會得到我公司電腦程式設計的工作。
↑ 成對連接詞 either 和 or 連接兩個並列主詞 Annie 和 Jenny，構成複合主詞。

- Mary can take the oath either at the county courtroom or at the city library. 瑪麗可以在縣法庭上宣誓，也可以在市立圖書館宣誓。
↑ 成對連接詞 either 和 or 連接兩個介系詞片語 at the county courtroom 和 at the city library。

- Either Ted is telling the truth or he has already dropped out of high school. 要嘛泰德說的是實話，要嘛他已經從高中綴學了。
↑ either + 獨立子句；or + 獨立子句；不用逗號分開兩個獨立子句。
↑ 兩個獨立子句由成對連接詞連接起來，就構成一個並列句。

5 neither . . . nor 既不……也不

neither 和 nor 後面的結構必須平行。

- He neither smokes nor drinks.
他既不抽菸，也不喝酒。
↑ 成對連接詞 neither 和 nor 連接兩個動詞 smokes 和 drinks。

- **Trish speaks neither English nor Spanish.**
  翠西既不會講英語，也不會講西班牙語。
  ↳ 成對連接詞 neither 和 nor 連接兩個專有名詞 English 和 Spanish。

- **Neither Claire nor I want to go there.** 克萊兒和我都不想去那裡。
  ↳ 成對連接詞 neither 和 nor 連接兩個並列主詞（Claire, I），構成複合主詞。
  ↳ 動詞 want 與 nor 後面的主詞 I 一致，不能用單數動詞 wants。

6 whether . . . or 是……抑或

whether . . . or 也是成對連接詞，表示兩種可能性不管哪一種成立，結果都是相同的。

- **Jenny has a lovely handwriting, whether she writes with a colored pencil or with a pen.**
  珍妮不論是用彩色鉛筆還是原子筆，寫的字都很漂亮。
  ↳ 成對連接詞 whether 和 or 連接兩個獨立子句：she writes with a colored pencil 和 (she writes) with a pen。
  ↳ 為避免重複，可以將第二個子句中的主詞 she 和動詞 writes 省略。
  ↳ 注意 這種省略必須是兩個獨立子句的主詞和動詞是相同的。

- **Jill passed the test, whether by skill or (by) luck.**
  無論是因為有實力，還是因為運氣，總之，潔兒通過了考試。
  ↳ 成對連接詞 whether 和 or 連接兩個介系詞片語：by skill 和 by luck。

- **Whether you like it or (whether) you don't, Sue is in love with Andrew.**
  = Whether you like it or not, Sue is in love with Andrew.
  = Whether or not you like it, Sue is in love with Andrew.
  不論你是否喜歡，蘇愛上安德魯已經是事實了。
  ↳ 成對連接詞 whether 和 or 連接兩個獨立子句：you like it 和 you don't (like it)。
  ↳ 當 or 後面的部分是否定式時，可以有幾種不同的表達方式，如這例的三個句子。

從屬連接詞與從屬子句

1 從屬連接詞的定義與作用

1 除了對等連接詞和成對連接詞外，還有一類連接詞稱作**從屬連接詞**，如 because、if、when、where、that、which、why 等。

2 從屬連接詞用來引導**從屬子句**，包括副詞子句和名詞子句，並連接從屬子句和主要句子，構成複合句。下表的連接詞，除了引導名詞子句的 that 和 whether，其他都屬於從屬子句的一部分，在子句中充當副詞、主詞或受詞。

- after 在……之後
- although 雖然
- as if 猶如
- as long as 只要
- as though 好像
- as 依照；隨著；因為
- because 因為
- before 在……以前
- even if 即使
- even though 即使
- ever since 自從
- except 要不是
- how 如何（用於間接疑問句）
- if only 只要；但願
- if 假如
- in order that 為了
- now that 既然
- once 一旦
- provided 假如
- rather than 而不是
- since 自從
- so that 以至於
- than 比
- that 引導名詞子句（也可作關係代名詞，引導形容詞子句，參見 301 頁 Unit 7）
- though 雖然
- till 直到
- unless 除非
- until 直到
- whenever 每當
- when 當……的時候
- where 在……處
- whereas 反之
- wherever 無論何地
- whether 是否（用於間接疑問句）
- while 當……的時候
- why 為何（用於間接疑問句）

ℓ why, how, whether 引導名詞子句用於間接疑問句中。
ℓ when, where 可以引導副詞子句，也可以引導名詞子句用於間接疑問句中。
ℓ than 和 as 也可作關係代名詞，引導形容詞子句。參見 Unit 7。

3 上表列舉的從屬連接詞中，有的也可以用作介系詞，如：as、after、before、except、since、unless、until 等。如果後面接名詞或代名詞便是介系詞，如果接從屬子句就是連接詞。如：

介系詞 after dinner 飯後（after + 名詞）

連接詞 after he got married to Jan 他跟簡結婚後（after + 從屬子句）

2 子句與片語的區別

1 **片語**（phrase）：是一組相關的詞，但其中不包含「主詞－動詞」的關係，如：

- in the morning 早上
- in her office 在她的辦公室
- having grown used to this cold weather 越來越習慣這種冷天氣
- running down the beach 沿著海灘跑

2 **子句**（clause）：由一群相關的詞構成，包含一個主詞和一個動詞，子句可分為兩種：

a **獨立子句**：即主要句子（簡稱主句），表達一個完整的概念，可以不需要任何附加成分，單獨成為一個句子。兩個獨立子句由對等連接詞連接，就構成**並列句**；一個獨立子句和一個從屬子句，如果由從屬連接詞或關係代名詞連接，就構成**複合句**。

b **從屬子句**：即附屬子句，不能獨立存在，若不附屬在主句裡，本身就沒有完整的意義。

- **Jim felt tired.** 吉姆感到疲倦。
  ↑ 獨立子句：可以獨立存在。
- **. . . until the cheerleader Amy began to dance.**
  ……直到啦啦隊長艾咪開始跳舞時。
  ↑ 從屬子句：不能獨立存在，必須附屬在主句裡，否則意義不完整。
- **Jim felt tired until the cheerleader Amy began to dance.**
  啦啦隊長艾咪開始跳起舞時，吉姆的倦意就消失了。
  ↑ 從屬連接詞 until 連接主句和從屬子句，構成一複合句。

3 獨立子句作為簡單句

當獨立子句單獨作為一個句子時，就稱作簡單句。一個簡單句只包括一個子句。（參見 715 頁〈Unit 15 句子的結構〉。）

- **I started to shout and jump.** 我開始又喊又跳。
- **Baby Daisy was beginning to smell bad.** 小嬰兒黛絲開始有臭味了。
- **Coco will fly from Chicago to Tokyo.** 可可要從芝加哥飛往東京。

4 從屬子句的定義

1 有一些子句雖然包含一個主詞和一個動詞，但子句本身無法提供完整的意義，這類子句就叫做從屬子句或附屬子句。

2 從屬子句在句子裡可以擔任副詞、形容詞、名詞等各種成分，為主句提供更多的資訊。從屬子句不能獨立存在，必須依賴獨立子句／主句才能表達完整的概念或意義。請記住，從屬子句含有主詞和動詞，但不能單獨存在。

✗ **Amy will be a teaching assistant. When she goes to Michigan State University.**

✓ **Amy will be a teaching assistant when she goes to Michigan State University.** 艾咪去密西根州立大學讀書時會兼任助教。

↳ 第一句是破句，結構不完整，從屬子句不能獨立成一個句子，必須依賴主句（Amy will be a teaching assistant）意義才完整。從屬連接詞 when 引導的從屬子句扮演副詞的角色，指出時間，是時間副詞子句。

主句 / 獨立子句　　條件副詞子句

- **Kay can borrow this DVD as long as she brings it back on Monday.**
  只要凱能在星期一歸還這張 **DVD**，她就可以把它借回家。

  ↳ as long as 引導的從屬子句扮演副詞的角色，指出條件，是條件副詞子句。從屬子句不能單獨存在，必須依賴主句（Kay can borrow this DVD）意義才完整。

3 從屬子句通常由從屬連接詞或關係詞引導，構成複合句。參見 301 頁〈Unit 7 關係詞與形容詞子句和名詞子句〉；關於複合句的說明，請參見 715 頁〈Unit 15 句子的結構〉。

4 根據在句中的作用，從屬子句可分為三種：**副詞子句**、**形容詞子句**、**名詞子句**。其中副詞子句又稱狀語子句，形容詞子句又稱定語子句。

從屬連接詞與副詞子句

當從屬連接詞引導的從屬子句用來修飾整個主句時，這個子句就稱為**副詞子句**（或狀語子句）。副詞子句在整個句子中扮演副詞（即狀語）的角色，為主句（即獨立子句）提供更多的資訊：在哪裡、什麼時候、為什麼、如何、到什麼程度、在什麼條件下，即表明條件、地方、時間、原因、結果、目的、方式、讓步、比較。

1 條件副詞子句（Adverbial Clauses of Condition）

1 **條件副詞子句**常由下列表**條件**的從屬連接詞引導，表達事件發生的條件或環境。條件句指可能的未來事件時，要用簡單現在式表示未來的含義。

- if 如果
- so long as 只要
- on (the) condition that 只要
- supposing (that) 假如
- as long as 只要
- only if 只要
- unless 除非
- provided 假如

- **Bob Card will** not **pass the exams** unless he starts to work hard.
  除非鮑勃·卡德開始用功，否則他考試不會及格的。
  ⮡ unless 引導的從屬子句扮演副詞的角色，指出條件，是條件副詞子句。主句用 will not 表示未來，但 unless 引導的子句用簡單現在式（starts）表示未來的含義。

- Unless the strike is cancelled, **there will be** no **buses and taxies tomorrow.** 除非罷工取消，否則明天將沒有公車和計程車。
  ⮡ unless 所引導的從屬子句，可以放在主句前面，也可以放在主句後面。

- **Your expenses will be paid by the company** on the condition that/as long as/providing that/only if you submit all of your receipts.

= Your expenses will not be paid by the company unless you submit all of your receipts. 你只要呈上所有的收據，公司就會支付你的開銷。

↳ on the condition that、as long as、providing that、only if 等引導的從屬子句扮演副詞的角色，指出條件，是條件副詞子句。

↳ 條件句中用簡單現在式（submit）表示未來。

- If tomorrow there is a hurricane in Jakarta, Sue will not be able to fly to Honolulu. 如果明天雅加達刮颶風，蘇就不能飛往檀香山了。

↳ If 引導的從屬子句扮演副詞的角色，指出條件，是條件副詞子句。

↳ 這裡的條件句指可能的將來事件，主句是未來式（will not be able），條件句用現在式（there is）。

1 當 if 具有與 whether（是否）大致相同的意思時，if 之後可以跟 will。

- Sue will let me know soon if/whether she will be able to come to the US. 蘇是否可以來美國，她會很快通知我的。

2 表示「意願」時，if 引導的句子可以用未來式。

- You won't be able to get into college if you do not work hard.
  如果你不用功念書，就進不了大學。
  = You won't be able to get into college if you won't work hard.
  如果你不願意用功念書，就進不了大學。
  ↳ 第二句 If you won't work hard 不是表示單純的將來，而是強調「意願」。

2 如果條件子句表達的不是事實，而是想像的條件，則必須用假設語氣。關於 if 的假設語氣用法，參見 695 頁〈Part 6 假設語氣〉。

- Susan would look much younger if she got more rest.
  假如蘇珊多休息一點，她看起來可能就會年輕得多。

↳ 不過，蘇珊沒有足夠的休息，所以她看起來不年輕。

↳ 從屬子句 if she got more rest 具有副詞的作用，指條件（非真實條件），所以這是一個假設語氣的條件副詞子句。

- If I were you, I would feel satisfied with the test results.
  如果我是你，就會對考試結果感到滿意。

↳ 這句是假設語氣，與現在事實相反（Fact: I am not you），if 條件子句用 were；主句用「would + 動詞原形」。

2 地方副詞子句（Adverbial Clauses of Place）

地方副詞子句由表**地點**的從屬連接詞 where 或 wherever 引導，回答「Where?」的問題。

Kay, stay.
凱，待著。
Where? 待在哪裡？
Where you can play.
你能玩耍的地方。
主句+副詞子句
Kay, stay where you can play. 凱，待在你可以玩耍的地方。

從屬子句

- **Her boyfriend will eat pistachio nuts** wherever he goes.
  她的男友無論走到哪裡都要吃開心果。
  ↳ wherever 引導的從屬子句具有副詞作用，指地點，所以是地方副詞子句。

- **I advised Liz to live** where the climate is warm and dry.
  我建議莉茲應該住在氣候溫暖乾燥的地方。
  ↳ where 引導的從屬子句具有副詞作用，指地點，所以是地方副詞子句。

- Where there is a will, **there is a way.**
  有志者，事竟成。
  ↳ 表示抽象含義時，where 引導的子句要放在主句之前。

NOTE

比較從屬連接詞 where 和關係副詞 where：

- My advice to you is to live where the weather is warm all year round. 我給你的忠告，是去一個氣候終年溫暖的地方居住。
  ↳ 從屬連接詞 where 引導的地方副詞子句，用來修飾前面主句的動詞 live。

- She found a good job in Hawaii where the weather is warm all year round. 她在氣候終年溫暖的夏威夷找到了一份好工作。
  ↳ 這句的 where 是關係副詞，引導一個形容詞子句，修飾先行詞 Hawaii。

» 參見 320 頁〈Part 4 關係副詞與形容詞子句〉。

3 時間副詞子句（Adverbial Clauses of Time）

時間副詞子句通常以下列表**時間**的從屬連接詞引導，回答「When?」的問題。

- when 當……之時
- while 當……之時
- till 直到
- until 直到
- since 從……開始
- as soon as 一……就……
- after 之後
- before 之前
- as 當……之時

He blew a kiss to Jane. 他給了珍一個飛吻。

When? 何時給的飛吻？→ As he climbed onto the train. 在上火車時。

主句＋副詞子句 → He blew a kiss to Jane as he climbed onto the train. 他在上火車時給了珍一個飛吻。

從屬子句

- **Please email me** as soon as you arrive. 請你一到達就寄電子郵件給我。
  - ↑ 這句從屬子句指時間，所以是時間副詞子句。

- **The phone rang** while/when Mabel was setting the table.
  當美博正在擺碗筷時，電話響了起來。
  - ↑ 從屬子句是 while/when Mabel was setting the table，具有副詞的作用，指時間，所以是時間副詞子句。

- **The wedding ceremony was already over** before Bob arrived in his old Land Rover.
  = Before Bob arrived in his old Land Rover, **the wedding ceremony was already over.**
  在鮑勃駕駛著他那輛用舊了的荒原路華越野車到達之前，婚禮就已經結束了。
  - ↑ before 引導的從屬子句，具有副詞的作用，指時間，所以是時間副詞子句。
  - ↑ before 引導的時間副詞子句可置於主句前或主句後。

- **Sam Sun should look at many sports cars** before he buys one.
  山姆·孫應該多看幾輛跑車再買。
  - ↑ 在 before 引導的時間從屬子句中，要用簡單現在式（buys）表示未來。

- Dan moved to Chicago after he got married to Jan.
  = After he got married to Jan, Dan moved to Chicago.
  丹跟簡結婚後就搬到了芝加哥。
  ↳ after 引導的時間副詞子句可置於主句前或主句後。

- Jim has not heard from Kim since she left him.
  自從金姆離開吉姆後，吉姆就沒有她的消息了。
  ↳ 本句中的 since 從屬子句是限定性的，since 前面不用逗號。
  這裡的 since 表示「自……以來」。
  ↳ since 引導的時間副詞子句，動詞要用簡單過去式（left），
  主句的動詞要用完成式（has not heard）。

  比較 I'll do what she asks me to do, since she is my wife.
  她要我做什麼我就要做，因為她是我老婆。
  ↳ 本句中的 since 從屬子句是非限定性的，since 前面須加逗號。
  這裡的 since 表示「既然、因為」。

- I am going to stay in school until/till I get my PhD in chemistry.
  我要一直留在學校讀書，直到我拿到化學博士學位。
  ↳ until/till 用於肯定句中，表示主句的動作一直持續到子句的動作發生為止，
  主句的述語動詞是延續性動詞或狀態（stay）。

- Ann did not go to bed until her husband came home from the conference. 安一直等到她丈夫開會回家，才上床睡覺。
  ↳ not . . . until 意思是「直到……才」。主句述語動詞是非延續性動詞（go to bed）。
  = Not until her husband came home from the conference did Ann go to bed.
  ↳ 可以將 Not until 置於句首，後面的主句須用倒裝結構（did Ann go to bed）。
  = It was not until her husband came home from the conference that Ann went to bed.
  ↳ 這句也可以用強調句型 it is/was not until . . . that。

1. until 和 till 常可以互換，但 until 引導的子句可以置於句首，而 till 不可以。
2. 在「not . . . until」和「it was not until . . . that」的句型中，不可以用 till 來替換 until。

Diving Deep Into English 41 表示時間的從屬連接詞 while 和 when

❶ **延續性動詞**（如：was talking, was walking）用於附屬連接詞 while 引導的副詞子句中，while 表示某一時間段（during that time）；附屬連接詞 when 也可以用於延續動詞，表示時間段，但通常用於過去進行式。

- **The cellphone vibrated while/when I was talking to Andrew.**
= While/When I was talking to Andrew, the cellphone vibrated.
我在跟安德魯用手機通話時，手機震動了起來。
↥ while/when 引導的時間副詞子句可以置主句前或主句後。

❷ **非延續性動詞**（短暫動作，如：vibrated, came home）只能用於 when 引導的副詞子句中，when 表示某個時間點（at that time）。

- **I was talking to Andrew when the cellphone vibrated.**
- **When Glen came home, he found that monstrous mouse in his house again.** 格蘭回到家時，發現那隻可怕的大老鼠又在他的房裡了。
↥ 短暫性動詞片語 vibrated、came home 與 when 連用，不與 while 連用。
↥ 參見 584 頁〈5 過去進行式和簡單過去式的比較〉。

4 原因副詞子句（Adverbial Clauses of Reason）

原因副詞子句通常以表**原因**的從屬連接詞 because（因為）、as（因為）、since（既然）、now that（既然）或 in case（以防）引導，回答「Why?」的問題。

Insure your wife Dee's life and your own life. 替你太太蒂和你自己的生命買份保險。

Why? 為何要買保險？因為 →

In case your family has a tragedy you couldn't foresee. 以防你的家人發生你無法預料的悲劇。

Insure your wife Dee's life and your own life, in case your family has a tragedy you couldn't foresee.
替你太太蒂和你自己的生命買保險吧，以防天有不測風雲。

・Because he was sick, **Bing could not come to our wedding.**
賓生病了，因此不能來參加我們的婚禮。
↑ Because 引導的從屬子句具有副詞的作用，指原因，所以是原因副詞子句。

・As Daisy was a bit crazy and lazy, **she was fired.**
因為黛絲有點古怪又有點懶惰，所以被解雇了。
↑ As 引導的從屬子句具有副詞的作用，指原因，所以是原因副詞子句。
↑ as 引導的原因子句常置於句首。

・Since you insist, **I will travel to Japan with Ann.**
= Now that you insist, **I will travel to Japan with Ann.**
既然你堅持，那麼我將跟安一起去日本旅遊。
↑ Since 引導的從屬子句具有副詞的作用，指原因，所以是原因副詞子句。
↑ since 和 now that 引導的原因子句常置於句首。

Diving Deep Into English 42 because 和 so

❶ 中文可以說「因為……所以」，但英語只能在 because（從屬連接詞）和 so（對等連接詞）之間擇一使用，不能兩個同時使用。

✗ Because **Sue blew a big bubble during class,** so **she got into trouble.**
✔ Because **Sue blew a big bubble during class, she got into trouble.**
↑ because 表示原因。
✔ **Sue blew a big bubble during class,** so **she got into trouble.**
因為蘇在課堂上吹破了一個大泡泡，所以惹上麻煩。→ so 表示結果。

❷ because 引導的從屬子句，可以放在句首，也可以放在主句後面。一般說來，當 because 引導的子句放在句首時，後面通常要用逗號與主句分開；當子句放在主句後面時，如果僅僅是對主句作補充說明，則需要用逗號與主句隔開；但如果子句對主句具有限制作用，就不用逗號。

・Because **Ted was drowsy, he went to bed.** → 句首
= **Ted went to bed** because he was drowsy. → 主句後（對主句有限制作用）
= **Ted was drowsy,** so **he went to bed.** 因為泰德睏了，所以上床睡覺了。
↑ so 引導的獨立子句前面需要用一個逗號與前面的獨立子句分開。

・I need to have three copies of our financial report for this month by 6:30 p.m., because I am leaving for New York City on a flight at 10 tonight. 我在今天下午六點半之前要拿到三份的當月財政報告，因為我晚上十點要飛往紐約。

↑ 主句意思是完整的，because 引導的子句作補充說明用，需要用逗號與主句隔開。

Diving Deep Into English 43 because 和 because of 的差別

兩者都表示「因為」，但 because 是連接詞，後面接從屬子句；because of 是複合介系詞，後面接名詞或名詞片語。

・Mary stayed at home the whole day, because it was snowing.
= Mary stayed at home the whole day because of the snow.
因為下雪，瑪麗整天都待在家裡。

・Ann can swim fast, because her coach trained her well.
= Ann can swim fast because of the excellent training she received from her coach. 安游泳之所以游得快，是因為她的教練教得好。

5 結果副詞子句（Adverbial Clauses of Result）

結果副詞子句是以「so . . . that」和「 such . . . that」引導，意思是「如此……以至於」，用於強調某事實，連接詞 that 後面的從屬子句表示結果。

a so + 形容詞 / 副詞 + that 子句（表結果）

・Coco was so tired that she fell asleep at the car show.
可可精疲力竭，結果在車展上睡著了。 ↑ 從屬子句

↑ 這句 that 引導的從屬子句具有副詞的作用，指結果，所以是結果副詞子句。

・The monkey is so heavy that I cannot lift it.
= The monkey is too heavy for me to lift it.
那隻猴子太重了，我抬不起來。

↑ that 引導的結果副詞子句是否定式時，也可以用「too + 形容詞 / 副詞 + to 不定式」的句型替代，談論「如此……以至於不能」。

b such + 名詞 + that 子句（表結果）

- Kay is such a funny teacher that she makes her students laugh a lot every day. 凱是一個非常滑稽的老師，她讓她的學生每天都笑個不停。
  - ⤷ 這句 that 引導的從屬子句具有副詞的作用，指結果，所以是結果副詞子句。

- Politics is such a torment that I advise everyone I love not to mix with it. (President Thomas Jefferson)
  政治是一種折磨，所以我奉勸每一個我愛的人不要捲入其中。

6 讓步副詞子句（Adverbial Clauses of Concession）

讓步副詞子句以下列表示**讓步**的從屬連接詞引導：

- although 雖然
- (even) though 雖然
- whereas 而
- while 儘管
- as 雖然
- even if 即使
- whether 無論
- whenever 無論何時

- Although/Though Bill, the maitre d', is pleasant and hardworking, his daughter Daisy is cranky and lazy.
  雖然餐廳的侍者總管比爾和藹可親又勤快，但他女兒黛絲的脾氣暴躁又懶惰。
  - ⤷ Although 引導的從屬子句具有副詞作用，指讓步，所以是讓步副詞子句。
  - ⤷ although 與 though 兩者意思相同，一般可以互換。

- Whether I win or lose, I will fight.
  = I will fight whether I win or lose. 無論輸贏，我都要奮戰。
  - ⤷ whether 引導的從屬子句具有副詞作用，指讓步，所以是讓步副詞子句，可以置於主句前或主句後。

- We enjoy living in Michigan, even though it is sometimes very cold.
  = Even though it is sometimes very cold, we enjoy living in Michigan.
  我們喜歡住密西根，雖然有時候會很冷。
  - ⤷ even though 引導的從屬子句具有副詞作用，指讓步，所以是讓步副詞子句。
  - ⤷ 從屬連接詞 although、though、even though、even if 等引導的讓步副詞子句可以出現在主句前或後。

- Whenever you do a thing, act as if all the world were watching. (President Thomas Jefferson) 無論何時做事，都要像全世界的人都在看著你一樣。
  - ⤷ whenever (= no matter when) 是從屬連接詞，引導一個讓步副詞子句。
  - ⤷ as if 後面的子句是假設語氣（all the world were watching）。

whatever、whichever、whoever、whenever、wherever、however 可以引導讓步副詞子句，其中 whatever、whichever、whoever 是關係詞，其餘是連接詞。

- Whatever you are, be a good one. (President Abraham Lincoln)
  = No matter what you are, be a good one.
  無論你做什麼，都要潔身自好。
  ↑ 關係代名詞 whatever 是子句的主詞補語，引導一個讓步副詞子句。
- Whenever Eve is ready, then we'll leave.
  = No matter when Eve is ready, then we'll leave.
  等伊芙一準備好，我們就可以動身了。
  ↑ 從屬連接詞 whenever 在子句中作副詞，引導一個讓步副詞子句。

- As highly respected as he is, Dr. Limb made a small mistake last week and it almost caused my death.
  = Highly respected as he is, Dr. Limb made a small mistake last week and it almost caused my death.
  雖然萊姆醫生德高望重，但他上星期犯了一個小小的錯誤，差點就要了我的命。
  ↑ 這兩句都是 as 引導倒裝讓步副詞子句，as 意為「雖然」，句型為：
  過去分詞片語（Highly respected） + as + 主詞（he） + 述語動詞（is）。

比較

- My ex-wife is not living a happy life, though/although she is quite rich. → 從屬連接詞
  = My ex-wife is quite rich, but she is not living a happy life. → 對等連接詞
  = Rich as she is, my ex-wife is not living a happy life.
  = As rich as she is, my ex-wife is not living a happy life.
  我的前妻雖然很有錢，但生活過得並不快樂。
  ↑ 最後兩句的從屬連接詞 as 引導倒裝讓步副詞子句，
  即主詞補語（rich）置於句首，放在「as + 主詞 + 動詞」之前。

- Although/Though he had little experience, Bob did a good job.
  鮑伯雖然只有一點點經驗，但是他做得很好。 → 從屬連接詞
  = Bob had little experience, but he did a good job. → 並列連接詞
  = Little experience as he had, Bob did a good job.

= As little experience as he had, Bob did a good job.
鮑伯雖然沒有什麼經驗，但這項工作他做得很好。

↳ 後兩句的從屬連接詞 as 引導倒裝讓步副詞子句，即受詞（little experience）置於句首。

Diving Deep Into English 44 although 和 but

中文常說「雖然……但是」、「因為……所以」，但在英語中 although 和 but、because 和 so 不能同時使用。

✗ Although Pam was sick. She passed the exam.
↳ 句子結構不完整，從屬子句不能獨立成一個句子。

✗ Although Pam was sick, but she passed the exam.
↳ 在 although 和 but 之間只能擇一使用，不能同時使用兩個連接詞。

✔ Although Pam was sick, she passed the exam.
= Pam passed the exam, although she was sick. →although 是從屬連接詞。
↳ although 引導的從屬子句，可以放在句首（如上面第一句），也可以放在主句後面（如上面第二句），無論置於句首還是主句後面，都要用逗號與主句分開。
= Pam was sick, but she passed the exam. → but 是對等連接詞。
雖然潘姆生病了，但她還是通過了考試。
↳ but 引導的獨立子句前面常用一個逗號與前面的獨立子句分開。

Diving Deep Into English 45 連接詞 although 和複合介系詞 in spite of 的差別

❶ 介系詞通常出現在名詞或代名詞之前，表示該名詞或代名詞與其他詞彙的關係。如：under the chair（在椅子下）、on the bed（在床上）。

❷ although 和 in spite of 都表示「雖然」，但 although 是連接詞，後面接從屬子句；而 in spite of 是複合介系詞，後面接名詞或名詞片語。

- Although it was raining hail, Dan ran out of the cabin to help Sue.
  = Dan ran out of the cabin to help Sue in spite of the hailstorm.
  儘管外面在下冰雹，丹還是從小屋跑出去幫助蘇。

- Although I was interested in Professor Lee's lecture on using glass in architecture, I fell asleep in class. 雖然我對李教授關於在建築上使用玻璃的演講很感興趣，但我還是在課堂上睡著了。
- I fell asleep in class in spite of Professor Lee's interesting lecture on using glass in architecture.
儘管李教授關於在建築上使用玻璃的演講很有趣，我還是在課堂上睡著了。

7 目的副詞子句（Adverbial Clauses of Purpose）

1 目的副詞子句通常以 so that（為了）、in order that（為了）或 so（因而；以便）引導，回答「What for?」或「For what purpose?」（目的是什麼）的問題。

Midge Flower quickly put the milk in the fridge. 米姬．弗勞爾很快把牛奶放進了冰箱。

What for? 為何要放進冰箱？因為 ➔

So it wouldn't go sour. 為了不讓牛奶酸掉。

主句＋副詞子句

Midge Flower quickly put the milk in the fridge so it wouldn't go sour. 米姬．弗勞爾趕快把牛奶放進冰箱，這樣牛奶就不會酸掉。

2 口語中常用 so，但在書面語和正式語中，so that 較為常用。

3 so that、in order that 或 so 通常與 can、will 或 may 等情態動詞連用。

4 表示目的的副詞子句要置於主句後，不用逗號與主句分開。

正式 Sue, I am telling you about that big snake so that you can decide what to do.

正式 Sue, I am telling you about that big snake in order that you can decide what to do.

口語 Sue, I am telling you about that big snake so you can decide what to do.

蘇，我要告訴你那隻大蛇的事，你好決定該怎麼辦。

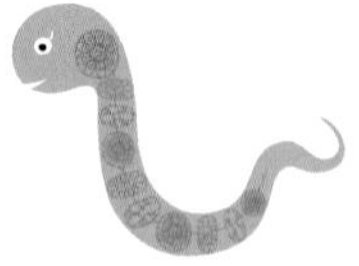

↑ so that 引導的從屬子句具有副詞的作用，指目的，所以是目的副詞子句。

↑ 也可以用 in order that 和 so 引導目的副詞子句。

- Listen to Jake carefully so that you understand everything about that snake.
  = Listen to Jake carefully so as to/in order to understand everything about that snake.
  仔細聽傑克的話，這樣你便可以對那隻蛇瞭若指掌。
  ↳ 也可以用 so as to/in order to 後面接不定式的句型，來談論某人做某事的目的。

Diving Deep Into English 46 「so (that) 指目的」和「so 指結果」的用法比較

- **We work hard so (that) our team may win.**
  我們努力工作，這樣我們隊就可以贏。
  ↳ 目的（= in order that）；so (that) 是從屬連接詞，所連接的從屬子句與前面的主句不用逗號分開。
- **We worked hard, so our group won.**
  我們努力工作，因此我們小組贏了。
  ↳ 結果（= therefore）；對等連接詞 so 連接兩個獨立子句，要用逗號分開。

8 方式副詞子句（Adverbial Clauses of Manner）

方式副詞子句以下列詞彙引導，回答 how 的問題。

- as 依照
- exactly as 完全就像
- just as 就像是
- as if 好像
- as though 好像
- in the way/manner 以……的方式
- just like 就像
- the way 以……的方式

I want to get my hair cut. 我想剪頭髮。

How? 剪成什麼樣？剪成 →

In the (same) way Ann has hers. 就像安的頭髮樣式。

主句＋副詞子句

I want to get my hair cut in the (same) way Ann has hers.
我想剪頭髮，就照著安的頭髮樣式剪。

· **Daniel dreamed of marrying Jenny,** as though having her as his wife <u>were</u> his only ambition in life.

丹尼爾渴望娶到珍妮，好像娶她為妻是他這一生中唯一的抱負。

↳ as though 是從屬連接詞，連接方式副詞子句（having her as his wife were . . .）與前面的主句（Daniel dreamed of marrying Jenny）。

↳ 從屬子句（as though having her . . .）用動詞 were，而不是動詞 was，因為這是假設語氣。

» 參見 707 頁〈6 as if 和 as though（就好像）〉。

· **Just do** as you are told, **and don't be so bold.**

照要求去做吧，不要這麼冒失。

↳ 從屬子句 as you are told 具有副詞作用，指方式，所以是方式副詞子句。

· **Treat others** the way you want to be treated.

你希望別人怎麼對待你，你就要怎麼對待別人。

↳ 從屬子句（the way you . . .）具有副詞作用，指方式，所以是方式副詞子句。

9 比較副詞子句（Adverbial Clauses of Comparison）

比較副詞子句以 than（比）、as . . . as（像……一樣）等引導。

· **Anna turned out to be smarter** than I thought.

結果安娜比我想像得還要聰明。

↳ 從屬子句 than I thought 具有副詞作用，指比較，所以是比較副詞子句。

· **Amy is not** as **bossy** as you said.

艾咪不像你說的那樣愛指使別人。

↳ 從屬子句 as you said 具有副詞作用，指比較，所以是比較副詞子句。

» 參見 227 頁〈Part 7 形容詞的比較級和最高級〉。

從屬連接詞或關係代名詞引導名詞子句

1 名詞子句的定義

1 當從屬連接詞、疑問連接詞或關係代名詞引導的子句，在句中作受詞（包括介系詞的受詞）、主詞、主詞補語或同位語時，這個子句就是**名詞子句**。名詞子句作名詞用，凡是名詞所具有的功能，名詞子句也有。名詞子句主要分為**受詞子句**、**主詞子句**、**主補子句**、**同位語子句**。

從屬連接詞	句子類型	在名詞子句裡充當的成分
that	陳述句	ㄨ
whether, if	間接一般疑問句	ㄨ
when, where, why, how	間接特殊疑問句	副詞

關係代名詞／關係形容詞	句子類型	在名詞子句裡充當的成分
who, whom, what/whatever	間接特殊疑問句	主詞、受詞
which, whose, what	間接特殊疑問句	形容詞

2 疑問詞 whether, if, when, where, why, how, who, what, whose 等引導的名詞子句是間接疑問句，但詞序要用陳述句的詞序，不用疑問句詞序，即，不用助動詞 do、does 或 did，be 動詞或情態動詞 can、may 等不能放在名詞子句的主詞前面。

» 關係代名詞和關係形容詞引導名詞子句，參見 313 頁〈Part 2 不定關係代名詞和名詞子句〉、第 317 頁〈Part 3 關係形容詞與形容詞子句、名詞子句〉。

2 受詞子句（Object Clauses）

從屬連接詞或關係代名詞引導的名詞子句若在句中作受詞，則稱為受詞子句。

1 主詞 + 動詞 + 連接詞 that 引導的受詞子句

從屬連接詞 that 只起連接作用，在受詞子句中不扮演主詞或受詞的角色。

- **Mike told Dee a lie.** 邁克對蒂撒了一個謊。
- **Mike told Dee that he loved me.** 邁克告訴蒂說他愛我。
  ↥ that 引導的受詞子句的作用，和第一句的名詞 a lie 類似，是主句動詞 told 的受詞。

- **He knew (that) I was about to cry.** 他知道我快要哭了。
  ↥ that 引導的是名詞子句，是主句裡動詞 knew 的受詞。
- **Trish suggested that Coco go to the University of Chicago to get her Ph.D. in English.** 翠西建議可可去芝加哥大學拿英語博士學位。
  ↥ that 引導的是名詞子句，是主句裡動詞 suggested 的受詞。
  ↥ 如果主句的動詞是 suggest, demand 等，受詞子句要用假設語氣：動詞要用動詞原形（go），或用「should + 動詞原形」。

  » 參見 695 頁〈Part 6 假設語氣〉。
- **Do you believe (that) Steve wants to marry Eve?**
  你相信史蒂夫想娶伊芙嗎？
  ↥ Steve wants to marry Eve 是名詞子句，是主句裡動詞 believe 的受詞。
- **I don't believe (that) swimming across the Amazon River is much more difficult than running a marathon.**
  我相信游泳橫越亞馬遜河，並不會比跑馬拉松難到哪裡去。
  ↥ 主句主詞是第一人稱而且為簡單現在式，主句的述語動詞是 think, believe, imagine, suppose, expect, consider 等時，通常要把否定詞轉移到主句述語上（don't believe），受詞子句述語動詞用肯定形式（is）。

Diving Deep Into English 47 何時可以省略連接受詞子句的從屬連接詞 that？

❶ 連接詞 that 引導受詞子句時常可以省略。

- **Mike said (that) he loved me.** 邁克說他愛我。

❷ 如果受詞子句前有插入語時，通常不省略 that。

- **Mike said many times that he loved me.** 邁克說了很多次他愛我。

❸ 受詞子句置於間接受詞（me, him, her 等）之後時，通常不省略連接詞 that。

- Kate told me that love lasts much longer than hate.
  凱特跟我說，愛比恨長存許多。

❹ 當 it 作形式受詞，後接 that 引導的受詞子句時，不要省略 that。

- I don't think it proper that you try to interfere with this legal case. 你想介入這個法律案件，我認為不妥。

❺ 當 that 引導的受詞子句中有副詞子句，而副詞子句位於主句前面時，不要省略 that。

- I promised God that if I survived my lung cancer, I would help poor students to have access to a good education.
  我向上帝承諾說，我要是能戰勝肺癌，我就要幫助貧困學生接受良好的教育。

2 主詞 + 動詞 + whether 引導的受詞子句

連接詞 whether/if 意味「是否」，只起連接主句和受詞子句的作用，在子句中不扮演任何成分。

- Please ask Sally whether she can go with us to the movies tonight.
  = Please ask Sally if she can go with us to the movies tonight.
  請問一下莎莉，看她今天晚上能不能跟我們一起去看電影。
- She asked me whether/if I liked milk tea. 她問我是否喜歡喝奶茶。

比較

- Please ask Sally whether or not she can go with us to the movies tonight. → 與 or not 連用，只能用 whether，不用 if。
- There is no doubt about whether Sally can go with us to the movies tonight. 毫無疑問，莎莉今晚能跟我們一起去看電影。
  ↑ 子句作介系詞受詞時，只能用 whether，不用 if。
- I haven't decided yet whether to take a vacation in Hawaii or California. 我還沒有決定好是要去夏威夷還是加州度假。
  ↑ 在不定式前只能用 whether，不用 if；與 or 連用時，也只能用 whether。

Diving Deep Into English 48 doubt 後面用 that 還是 whether 引導的受詞子句？

❶ 在**否定句**中，doubt 後面要接 that 引導的受詞子句，表示「肯定」（sure, certain）。即，當受詞子句的內容是肯定的，通常 doubt 後面要接 that，不用 whether。

- I never doubted for a minute that hardworking Ted would move ahead.
  = I was always certain that hardworking Ted would move ahead.
  勤奮的泰德會向前發展，對此我從未懷疑過。

❷ 在**肯定句**中，doubt 後面接 whether 還是 that，要看意思而定。當暗示主詞「不信、懷疑」（disbelief）時，後面接 that；當表示主詞「不確定」（uncertainty）時，後面通常接 whether（非正式用語中也可以用 if）。

- I doubt that Mary wants to marry Jerry.
  = I don't think that Mary wants to marry Jerry.
  我懷疑瑪麗會想嫁給傑瑞。 → 表示不相信，用 that。
- I doubt whether/if Kay can go fishing with us on Sunday.
  = I am not sure whether/if Kay can go fishing with us on Sunday.
  我認為凱不太可能星期天跟我們一起去釣魚。
  ↑ 表示「不肯定」，用 whether 或 if。

3 主詞 + 動詞 + 疑問詞引導的受詞子句

a 疑問連接詞 where, why, when, how 在受詞子句中起副詞作用。受詞子句雖有疑問詞，但要用陳述句句型。

✗ Can you tell Liz where is the police station?
✓ Can you tell Liz where the police station is?
你能告訴莉茲警察局在哪裡嗎？
↑ 在受詞子句中，be 動詞（is）不能放在子句的主詞前面。
↑ 疑問連接詞 where 在受詞子句中起副詞作用。

✗ Does Robert Frost's mom know how much does it cost?
✓ Does Robert Frost's mom know how much it costs?
羅伯特·弗羅思特的媽媽知道它的價錢嗎？

↳ 在受詞子句中，不用助動詞 do、does 或 did 構成疑問句，要用陳述句的詞序。
↳ 疑問連接詞 how much 在受詞子句中起副詞作用。

- I cannot understand why men should be so eager after money.
  (President Abraham Lincoln) 我無法理解人為什麼這麼汲汲於金錢。
  ↳ 疑問連接詞 why 引導的名詞子句作主句動詞 understand 的受詞。
  ↳ why 在受詞子句中起副詞作用。

b **疑問關係代名詞** what, whatever, who, whom 雖是疑問詞，但引導的受詞子句要用陳述句句型。關係代名詞在受詞子句中主要作主詞、受詞或主詞補語。

» 關係代名詞引導名詞子句，參見 313 頁〈Part 2 不定關係代名詞和名詞子句〉。

✗ Ted didn't understand what did she say.
✓ Ted didn't understand what she said. 泰德沒聽懂她說的話。
↳ 在受詞子句中，疑問代名詞（what）後面不要用助動詞 did 構成疑問句的語序。
↳ 關係代名詞 what 作受詞子句中動詞 said 的受詞。

✗ Could you please tell me what time does the movie start?
✓ Could you please tell me what time the movie starts?
請你告訴我電影什麼時候開始，好嗎？
↳ 在受詞子句中，疑問詞後面不要用助動詞 does 構成疑問句的語序。
↳ what 是關係形容詞，修飾名詞 time。

» 關係形容詞，參見 317 頁〈Part 3 關係形容詞與形容詞子句、名詞子句〉。

- Liz doesn't know what it is. 莉茲不知道那是什麼。
  ↳ what 是關係代名詞，在受詞子句中，作主詞補語。
- I read several news articles about what Mr. Sun had done. 我看了幾篇講述孫先生事蹟的文章。
  ↳ what 引導的名詞子句作介系詞 about 的受詞；
  what 在受詞子句中，作動詞 had done 的受詞。
- Do whatever you want to do, as long as it is legal.
  你想做什麼就做什麼吧，只要合法就好。
  ↳ 關係代名詞 whatever 在受詞子句中作不定式動詞 to do 的受詞。
- Ann Rice is trying to sell her house to whoever meets her low market price. 安·賴斯試圖把她的房子賣給任何支付她所出的底價的人。
  ↳ whoever 引導的是名詞子句，是主句裡介系詞 to 的受詞。whoever 在子句中作主詞。

3 主詞子句（Subject Clauses）

1 連接詞或關係代名詞引導的子句若在句中作主詞用，稱為主詞子句。句型為：

名詞子句（主詞）＋動詞

- Why he married Amy puzzles me.
  他為何娶了艾咪，令我百思不解。
  ↥ 主詞（Why he married Amy）＋ 述語動詞 puzzles。
  ↥ Why 是疑問連接詞，在主詞子句中起副詞的作用，表「原因」。

- Whatever Ann wants is no concern of mine.
  無論安想要什麼，都與我無關。
  ↥ 主詞（Whatever Ann wants）＋ 連綴動詞 is。
  ↥ Whatever 是疑問關係代名詞，在主詞子句中作動詞 wants 的受詞。

2 在主詞子句中即使有疑問詞，也不要用疑問句的語序，而要用陳述句的語序。也就是說，不需要用助動詞 do、does 或 did，動詞 be 不能放在主詞子句的主詞前面。疑問連接詞（when, where, why, how）在子句中作副詞，因此也稱為「連接副詞」。

✗ How did Anna die is still a mystery.
✓ How Anna died is still a mystery.
安娜的死至今仍然是一個謎。
↥ 在主詞子句中，疑問連接詞（How）後面不要用助動詞 did 構成疑問句的語序。How 在子句中起副詞作用。

✗ Where is Ms. Bliss going is not my business.
✓ Where Ms. Bliss is going is not my business.
布利斯女士要去哪裡，不關我的事。
↥ 在主詞子句中，助動詞 be 不能放在子句的主詞前面。
↥ 疑問連接詞 Where 在子句中起副詞作用。

3 連接詞 whether 在主詞子句中不扮演任何成分。

- Whether Sally is coming to the party is not known.
  還不確定莎莉是否要來參加聚會。
  ↥ Whether 引導的主詞子句置於句首，不能用 If 替代。

= It is not known whether/if Sally is coming to the party.

↑ 也可以把 whether 引導的主詞子句置於句尾，用 it 作形式主詞置於句首，這時就可以用 if 替換 whether。

= It is not known whether or not Sally is coming to the party.

↑ 與 or not 連用時，只能用 whether，不用 if。。

4 連接詞 that 在主詞子句中不充當任何句子成分。

- **That Paul is not honest is obvious to us all.**

  保羅不誠實，這一點我們大家都很清楚。

  ↑ That 引導主詞子句置於句首時，that 不能省略。

  = It is obvious to us all that Paul is not honest.

  ↑ 常見句型是用 it 作形式主詞，把 that 引導的主詞子句置於後面。

4 主補子句（Subject Complement Clauses）

1 連接詞或關係代名詞引導的子句若用在**連綴動詞**後面，在句中作主詞補語，則稱為主補子句。

2 從屬連接詞 that 連接主句和從屬子句（主補子句），在從屬子句中不充當任何成分。

miss the plane

- **It may have been that Jane missed the plane.**

  珍有可能錯過了班機。

  ↑ that 引導的是名詞子句，用在連綴動詞 may have been 後面作主詞補語。

play chess against sb.

- **The trouble was that Harry had never played chess against Jerry.**

  麻煩的是，哈利沒跟傑瑞下過棋。

  ↑ that 引導的是名詞子句，用在連綴動詞 was 後面作主詞補語。

- **It is not that Mr. Wise isn't friendly but that he often tells lies.**

  並不是因為懷斯先生不夠友善，而是因為他常說謊。

  ↑ 這裡的兩個 that 子句都用在連綴動詞 is 後面作主詞補語。「not that . . . but that」意思是「並非……而是」。在這個結構裡 that 不可省略。

3 在主補子句中連接詞 whether 不充當任何成分，不能用 if 替換。

- **The test of our progress is not whether we add more to the abundance of those who have much；it is whether we provide enough for those who have little.**
  (President Franklin Delano Roosevelt)
  對我們進步的檢驗，不在於我們是否給富人錦上添花，而在於我們是否給窮人解決衣食之憂。
  ↳ 主句是 The test of our progress is not 以及 it is。
  ↳ 兩個 whether 引導名詞子句置於連綴動詞 is 後面，為主補子句。
  ↳ 兩個 who 引導的子句都是修飾其前面的先行詞 those，所以 who 是關係代名詞，引導形容詞子句，who 在子句裡作主詞。

5 同位語子句（Appositive Clauses）

從屬連接詞 that 引導的子句若對其前面的名詞之內容作補充説明，這種名詞子句就是同位語子句。 that 在同位語子句中不扮演任何成分，作同位語的 that 不可省略。

- **This morning Skip received the great news that Northern Michigan University has offered him a $20,000 scholarship.**
  今天上午，史奇普接獲大好消息，北密西根大學已經提供給他兩萬塊的獎學金了。
  ↳ 從屬連接詞 that 只起連接作用，引導的同位語子句補充說明 news 的內容。

比較 從屬連接詞 that 和關係代名詞 that

- **The fact that smokers are much more likely to get lung cancer is well known.** 吸菸者比較容易罹患肺癌，這個事實眾所皆知。
  ↳ 這句的 that 不充當子句中的成分，因此，that 是連接詞，引導同位語子句，補充說明 fact 的內容。

- **The fact (that) he had been hiding from the police appeared in the Internet news story.**
  他一直不想讓員警知道的真相，結果被披露在網路的新聞報導中。
  ↳ 這句的 that 作子句動詞 had been hiding 的受詞（that 作受詞時可以省略），因此，that 是關係代名詞，引導形容詞子句，修飾先行詞 fact。

UNIT

09 介系詞

Prepositions

介系詞的定義與用法

1 介系詞的定義與作用

1 介系詞通常出現在名詞或代名詞之前，表示這個名詞或代名詞與句中其他成分之間的關係。例如：

- about us 關於我們
- between you and Jerry 在你和傑瑞之間

2 換句話說，介系詞把其後的名詞或代名詞與句中的另一成分，如動詞、名詞、形容詞等連接起來。例如：

- go to the store 去商店 → 連接名詞和動詞
- the sound of loud music 嘈雜的音樂聲 → 連接名詞和名詞
- bad for you 對你不好 → 連接代名詞和形容詞

· **That little baby with a sweet smile is my brother Pete.**
那個面帶甜蜜微笑的小嬰兒是我弟弟彼特。
↳ with 是介系詞，表示 baby 和 smile 之間的關係。

3 介系詞所表示的意義是多種多樣的，主要表示以下幾種關係：
地點（place）、方向（movement）、時間（time）。

地點
- on 在……上
- in 在……裡面
- near 在……附近
- under 在……下面
- behind 在……的後面
- in front of 在……的前面
- at 在……地方

時間
- on (Sunday) 在星期天
- in (the summer) 在夏天
- in (the morning) 在早上
- at (noon) 在中午
- at (7 a.m.)（早上七點）時
- before (7 a.m.)（早上七點）之前
- after (7 a.m.)（早上七點）之後

方向
- up 上
- down 下
- to 至
- toward 朝向

- **When will they start making that romance movie on the International Space Station?** → 表地點
  他們什麼時候要開始在國際太空站上製作那部浪漫影片？
- **The play *React* was so boring that we left the theater after the first act.** 《反應》這齣戲真乏味，第一幕結束後，我們就離開了劇院。→ 表時間
- **He moved slowly toward the edge of the cliff.** → 表方向
  他慢慢地朝懸崖邊移動。

2 常見介系詞

1 簡單介系詞：只有一個詞的介系詞，稱作簡單介系詞。

- aboard 上（船、飛機）
- about 大約；關於
- above 在……上面
- across 橫越
- after 在……以後
- against 反對
- alongside 在……旁邊
- along 沿著
- amid 在……之間
- among 在……之中
- around 圍繞
- as 作為；如同
- at 在……
- before 在……以前
- behind 在……後面 / 之後
- below 在……下面
- beneath 在……之下
- beside 在……旁邊
- between 在……之間
- beyond 在……的那一邊
- but 除……以外
- by 被；靠
- considering 就……而論
- despite 不管
- down 在……下方
- during 在……期間
- except 除……之外
- for 為
- from 從
- in 在……裡
- including 包括
- inside 在……裡面
- into 到……裡
- like 像
- minus 減去
- near 靠近；附近
- of 屬於……的
- off 離開……
- on 在……上
- onto 到……之上
- out 通過……而出
- outside 在……外
- over 在……之上
- past 通過
- per 經
- plus 加
- regarding 關於
- since 從……至今
- through 穿過
- throughout 遍及
- till 直到……為止
- to 向
- toward 向
- under 在……下面
- unlike 不像
- until 直到……為止
- up 向……上
- upon 在……之上
- via 經由
- with 與……一起
- within 在……內部
- without 沒有

↳ 上表的 considering、including 和 regarding 是分詞介系詞。

- Saul and I walked through the woods toward(s) the beautiful waterfall. 所羅和我穿過樹林，走向美麗的瀑布。

- I flew to Chicago via Shanghai. 我經由上海飛往芝加哥。

- She is resting in the shade. 她在蔭涼處休息。

2 **複合介系詞**：由兩個以上的字組成的介系詞，稱作複合介系詞（也稱片語介系詞）。

- according to 根據
- across from 在……的對面
- along side of 沿著……邊緣
- along with 與……在一起
- because of 因為
- by way of 經由
- due to 由於
- from under 從……下面出來
- in addition to 除……之外
- in case of 萬一
- in front of 在……的前面
- in spite of 不管
- instead of 代替
- out of 自……離開

- That mean dog leaped at me from under the table.
  那隻惡犬從桌子下面跳出來向我撲過來。

- Coco ran toward the scared child in spite of the approaching tornado.
  = Coco ran toward the scared child despite the approaching tornado.
  可可不顧即將來臨的龍捲風，跑向那位受驚的小孩。
  ↑ 複合介系詞 in spite of 等於簡單介系詞 despite。

3 介系詞與其受詞

1 介系詞後面要接名詞、名詞片語、代名詞、動名詞或what引導的名詞子句，來作為受詞。

- Is Coco wearing diamond rings on her toes? → on 後面接名詞片語。
  可可在腳趾上戴著鑽戒嗎？

- Is Ms. Bold talking about the price of gold?
  伯爾德女士在談論金子的價格嗎？
  ↳ about 後面接名詞片語。

- Sue isn't joking when she says she is strongly against smoking.
  當蘇聲稱她強烈反對抽菸時，她是認真的。
  ↳ 介系詞 against 後面接動名詞 smoking。
  ↳ 以 -ing 結尾的動名詞具有名詞的性質，但也保留了動詞的句法特徵。
  » 詳細說明參見 731 頁〈Unit 16 分詞、不定式與動名詞〉。

- Do not trouble other people for what you can do for yourself.
  自己能做的事，就不要去麻煩別人。
  ↳ 介系詞 for 後面接 what 子句。

2 代名詞位於介系詞後面時要用受格形式，如 me、him、her、us、them。

✗ Is Nancy trying to get between you and I?
✓ Is Nancy trying to get between you and me?
南西企圖挑撥你我之間的關係嗎？
↳ me 是受格代名詞，作介系詞 between 的受詞。

- Did Dwight go out with her last night?
  杜威特昨晚跟她出去了嗎？
  ↳ her 是受格代名詞，作介系詞 with 的受詞。

3 在一些固定片語裡，介系詞可以接形容詞或副詞作受詞。

- She gave me these clothes for free. 她免費送我這些衣服。
  ↳ 介系詞 for 後面接形容詞 free。

- Someone dropped a glove on my head from far above.
  有人從高處把一隻手套丟到我頭上。
  ↳ 介系詞 from 後面接兩個副詞 far、above。

- In a quick motion, Joe tackled her from behind just before the explosion occurred outside the window.
  就在窗外的爆炸發生之前，喬迅速地從後面抱住她，撲倒在地。
  ↳ 介系詞 from 後面接副詞 behind。

4 介系詞片語

1 介系詞片語 = 介系詞 + 修飾詞 + 受詞

2 介系詞不能單獨使用，須與別的詞連用，構成介系詞片語。介系詞片語包括介系詞、由名詞或代名詞充當的介系詞受詞，以及該受詞的其他修飾語，這些修飾語出現在介系詞與其受詞之間。介系詞片語依照功能可分為兩種：

① 起**形容詞**作用：修飾名詞或代名詞，作定語和補語。
有些文法學家把這類介系詞片語稱作「形容詞片語」。

② 起**副詞**作用：修飾動詞、形容詞或副詞，作狀語。
有些文法學家把這類介系詞片語稱作「副詞片語」。

3 起形容詞作用的介系詞片語（作定語和補語）

- **Jake and I just bought a** cottage near Deer Lake.
傑克和我剛在鹿湖旁邊買了一棟別墅。
↳ near Deer Lake 起形容詞作用，修飾名詞 cottage。

- **Is that** man with a long beard and a funny hat **your husband Dan?**
那位留著長鬍子、戴著滑稽帽子的男人，就是你的先生丹嗎？
↳ with a long beard and a funny hat 起形容詞作用，修飾名詞 man，作定語。

- **The story** is about a boy who lives in a cupboard.
這個故事是在講一位住在櫥櫃裡的男孩。
↳ 「about . . . cupboard」起形容詞作用，置於連綴動詞 is 後面，作主詞的補語。

4 起副詞作用的介系詞片語（作狀語）

- **Why** is **Jim** walking **around** in the gym?
吉姆為什麼在體育館裡踱來踱去？
↳ in the gym 起副詞作用，修飾動詞 (is) walking。

- The fog was so thick in the early morning **that it seemed crazy for Sue to** drive on Highway 2.
大清早的霧很濃，蘇要在二號高速公路開車，似乎有點瘋狂。
↳ in the early morning 起副詞作用，修飾主句 The fog was so thick。
↳ on Highway 2 起副詞作用，修飾動詞 drive。

5 介系詞片語在句中的位置（避免垂懸結構）

介系詞片語要緊靠其修飾的詞，如果放錯位置，就會造成誤會，還可能鬧出笑話。

✕ Were all the tall men born in July in my office in Mumbai?

↳ 介系詞片語 in my office in Mumbai 像是在修飾動詞 born，這就引起了誤會。天下所有高大男人都是在我孟買的辦事處出生的嗎？哎喲！這不可能啊！

✔ Were all the tall men in my office in Mumbai born in July?
在我孟買的辦事處，所有高大的男人都是七月出生的嗎？

↳ 介系詞片語緊靠其修飾的名詞 men，整個片語為修飾名詞（men）的定語，而不是修飾動詞（born）的狀語。

» 詳細說明參見 851 頁〈Unit 20 分詞片語和垂懸結構〉。

5 多餘的介系詞

下列句型不需要加介系詞：

✕ Sam asked, "Where's Pam at?"

✔ Sam asked, "Where's Pam?"
山姆問：「潘姆在哪裡？」

✕ Where are you going to?

✔ Where are you going? 你要去哪裡？

↳ where 是副詞，不應該用介系詞。

✕ Mr. Glass shouted at us, "Stay off of the grass."

✔ Mr. Glass shouted at us, "Stay off the grass."
格拉斯先生對我們喊著：「不要踩草坪。」

↳ 用了 off，就沒必要再用 of。

↳ 這是一個常見的錯誤，甚至英美人士也常犯這個錯誤。

Stay off the grass.

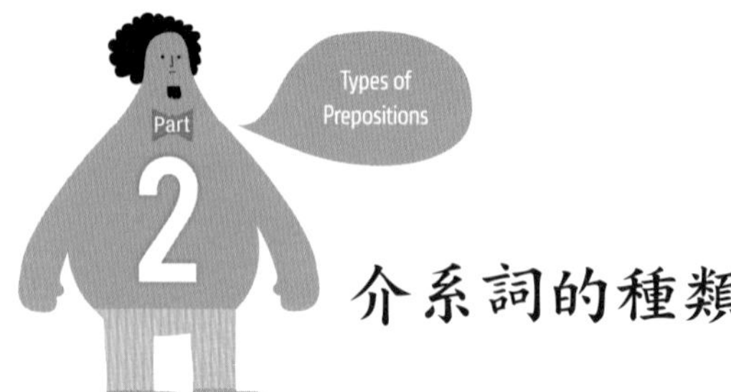

介系詞的種類

1 表示時間的介系詞 (1)：at, in, on

1 指時間時，介系詞 in、on 和 at 意思相似，但用法有別。一般規則是：

at + 具體的鐘點 → at 6 a.m.
on + 較短的時間單位 → on Sunday
in + 較長的時間單位 → in November 2002

- **Sue was born at 6 a.m. on the last Sunday in November 2002.**
  蘇出生於 2002 年 11 月最後一個星期天的早上六點。

2 **at + 時間**：指具體時間（時間點、時間段、較短的假期）。

- at noon 在中午
- at lunchtime 在午餐時間
- at night 在夜晚
- at midnight 在半夜
- at dawn 在黎明
- at midday 在正午
- at sunrise 在日出時
- at sunset 在日落時
- at present 目前
- at the moment 此刻
- at 9:00 在九點

- at Easter 在復活節
- at Christmas/Christmastime
  在聖誕節期間
- at the end of something
  在某事結束時
- at the beginning/start of something
  某事一開始

- Our bus to Bethlehem will leave at 10:15 a.m.
  我們要去伯利恆的公車將在上午 10 點 15 分出發。
- Sometimes at night the sky on Mars is full of bright stars.
  火星的夜空有時星光燦爛。
- Ann will be in Alaska at Christmastime. 安在聖誕節期間會在阿拉斯加。
- Steve was alone at the beginning of New Year's Eve.
  史蒂夫在除夕剛開始時是獨自一人。

  What do your Greek friends enjoy doing at the end of the week? → 美式
  = What do your Greek friends enjoy doing on the weekend? → 美式
  = What do your Greek friends enjoy doing at the weekend? → 英式
  你的希臘朋友們通常喜歡在週末做什麼？
  ↥ 美式英語用 on the weekend 或 at the end of the week。
  ↥ 英式英語用 at the weekend。

3 **on + 日期／星期**：on 指具體的某一天，以及諸如 Monday morning 和 Friday afternoon 這類表示特定時段的片語。

- on Monday 在星期一
- on Monday morning 在星期一的早上
- on New Year's Day 在元旦那天
- on May 12, 2008 在 2008 年五月 12 日
- on a rainy night 在一個下雨的夜晚
- on the night of May 25 在五月 25 日的晚上

- Kay is coming home with her new baby boy on the 25th of May.
  凱五月 25 日要帶著她剛出生的男嬰回家。
- Dwight is going to have a welcome home party for Kay on Friday night. 杜威特要在星期五晚上為凱舉行一個接風的聚會。
- Kay's family usually sleeps late on Sundays.
  凱一家人星期天通常都睡得很晚。
- Kay always prepares a special feast on New Year's Day.
  元旦那天，凱通常會準備一頓特別的宴席。

4 **in** 用來指一天、一個月、一個季節或者一年中非特定的一段時間。in 也可用來指「某事在一個時間段內發生」。in 還可以表示「花了多長時間完成某事」或「某事在未來的一段時間後結束」。

a **in + 年／月／季節／世紀**

- in March 在三月
- in April 2012 在 2012 年四月
- in the fall 在秋天
- in the 1990s 在 20 世紀 90 年代
- in (the) winter 在冬天
- in the 21st century 在 21 世紀
- in 2015 在 2015 年

- **Sue immigrated to Australia** in 2002. 蘇在 2002 年移民到澳洲。
- **It's too cold** in (the) winter **for Mona to jog outside.**
  冬天太冷了，夢娜不能到外面慢跑。
- In September **Ann is going to marry Dan.** 安將在九月嫁給丹。
- **His documentary was about the terrible wars** in the 20th century.
  他的紀錄片是關於發生在 20 世紀的可怕戰爭。

b **in + 一天中的一段時間**

- in the morning 在早上
- in the evening 在傍晚
- in the afternoon 在下午

✗ **Last year Dwight had a job** in the night.
✓ **Last year Dwight had a job** at night.
去年杜威特有一份上夜班的工作。
↑ 通常不用片語 in the night，在正式英語中要用 at night、in the middle of the night、during the night 等。

- **Our class about the moon starts at four** in the afternoon.
  我們研究月球的課在下午四點開始。
- **Anna King was born at 6:30** in the evening. 安娜·金在傍晚六點半出生。
- **I like to jog** in the morning. 我喜歡在早上慢跑。

c **in + 一段時間**：表示「某事在一個時間段內發生」，指「**在……期間**」。

- in the week 在那個星期
- in the past year 在過去的一年
- in the last two minutes 在最後兩分鐘

· **Ann and Dan are going to Malaysia** in the second week **of June.**
安和丹要在六月的第二個星期去馬來西亞。

· **Emma Clear finally got her divorce** in the middle of the year.
愛瑪·克利爾終於在年中時離婚了。

d **in + 一段時間**：表示「**花了多長時間完成某事**」或「某事在未來的一段時間後結束」，意思是「**在……以後**」。

- in five weeks 五個星期後／用了五週的時間
- in a minute 一分鐘後／用了一分鐘

· **She carved this statue** in a week. 她用一個星期雕刻了這座雕像。

· **Our dinner will be ready** in/within half an hour.
我們的晚餐再過半個小時就好了。 → 用 within 更正式。

· **"When will Brook have the checkbook?"** "In/Within three days, **if there aren't any delays."**「布魯克什麼時候能夠拿到支票簿？」「如果沒有任何耽擱，三天後就可以拿到支票簿。」

Diving Deep Into English 49 不與介系詞 in、at、on 連用的字

❶ 帶有下列詞彙的片語前面不加介系詞：

- this
- that
- next
- last
- every
- each
- all
- any
- today
- tomorrow

不要 in/at/on
- all morning
- next Saturday
- this weekend

要 in/at/on
- in the morning
- on Saturday
- on/at the weekend

· **Where were you** last Friday afternoon?
上個星期五的下午，你到哪兒去了？

· **She visits her relatives in Greece** every summer.
她每年夏天都要去希臘拜訪她的親戚。

· **"When did you meet Sue?" "I met Sue** last year **when she did surgery on my ear."**
「你是什麼時候認識蘇的？」「我是去年蘇幫我動耳朵手術時認識她的。」

❷ 介系詞 about、around 表示「大約」，指不確定的時間，不與時間介系詞 in、at、on 連用。

✕ **Sue was born at about 8 a.m. on September 1, 2012.**
✔ **Sue was born at 8 a.m. on September 1, 2012.**
蘇 2012 年 9 月 1 號上午八點出生。
✔ **Sue was born around 8 a.m. on September 1, 2012.**
蘇 2012 年 9 月 1 號上午大約八點出生。

2 表示時間的介系詞 (2)：for 和 since

1 **for + 一段時間**：for 表示時間的持續（for a period of time），用來指時間的長短（seconds、minutes、hours、days、months、years、decades、centuries）。因此，for 後面要接一段時間，而不接一個具體的時間。

- for three years 三年
- for a week 一星期

- **His parents have lived in Singapore for two decades.**
  他的父母在新加坡住了 20 年了。
- **Kyle held his breath for a little while.** 凱爾屏息了一會兒。
- **I've been waiting at the bus stop for half an hour.**
  我在公車站已經等了半個小時。

hold her breath
屏息

2 **since + 一個特定時間**：since 用來描述一個具體的時間或日期（since a point of time），雖然也表示一段時間的持續，但還意味著從何時開始（beginning when），表示某個事件從某時間點開始，一直持續到現在，意指「自從……至今……」。要注意與 for 的用法相區別。

- since New Year's Day in 2012 從 2012 年的元旦起

✕ **My parents have lived in New York City for 2009.**
✔ **My parents have lived in New York City since 2009.**
從 2009 年起，我的父母就住在紐約。

t. for 後面要接一段時間（如：for two hours, for three weeks）；
since 後面接一個具體的時間（如：since 2009, since 2:30 a.m.）。

- **Kate has been waiting for the bus since eight.**
  凱特從八點開始就一直在等公車。

- **Sue has lived in this tiny room since January 2012.**
  蘇從 2012 年一月就一直住在這間小房間裡。

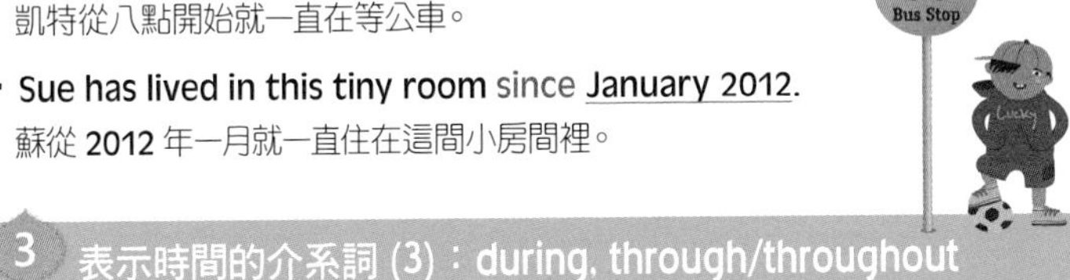

3 表示時間的介系詞 (3)：during, through/throughout

1 during + 一段時間：during 表示某事在某段時間內持續的時間，意思是「在……整個期間」，或「在……期間的某一時候」（when）。

- during the summer 在夏季
- during the day 在白天
- during the night 在夜晚

- **She slept for twenty minutes during the class.** 她在課堂上睡了20 分鐘。
- **Dee Wright is a great pilot, but she crashed three helicopters during her training in Tennessee.** 蒂·賴特是一名優秀的飛行員，但在田納西州進行訓練期間，她撞毀了三架直升機。

NOTE

1 某事在某段時間內持續了部分或全部時間（all through），可以用 during，也可以用 over，指「在……整個期間」。

- during/over the past few days 在過去幾天期間
- During/Over the Christmas vacation, I stayed with my Aunt Ann.
  在聖誕節假期期間，我同安姨媽住在一起。

2 某事發生在某段時間內的某時間點上（at some point in the course of），不用 over，要用 during，指「在 . . . 期間的某一時候」。

- during the performance 在表演期間
- During the play *Romeo and Juliet*, my sister began to cry.
  在戲劇《羅密歐與茱麗葉》表演期間，我妹妹開始哭起來。

1 during 和 in 都可以表示某事發生在某一個特定的時期內。

- during/in the last decade 在過去的十年裡
- during/in her four years in college 在她大學的四年裡

2 表示某事與另一件事同時發生，而不是強調這件事在某個特定時期內發生時，要用 during，不用 in。

- The President made a speech during a visit to Northern Michigan University. 總統在訪問北密西根大學期間做了一次講演。

2 **through/throughout + 一段時間**：through 表示「從開始至結束；在……整個期間」；throughout 強調「從頭到尾；貫穿整個時段」。

Kay said that the drug dealers liked to move around at night and sleep through (= during) the day. 凱說，那些毒販喜歡晚上行動，白天睡覺。

- **Dee Wright flew her airplane on patrol all through the night.** 蒂·賴特徹夜駕駛飛機巡邏。 →all through = throughout = all the way through
- **Mark was Dee's copilot throughout the last war.** 上一場戰爭整個期間，馬克都擔任蒂的副駕駛。

4 表示時間的介系詞 (4)：until/till, from . . . to, by

1 **until/till** 表示某個行動或狀況的「結束時間」。

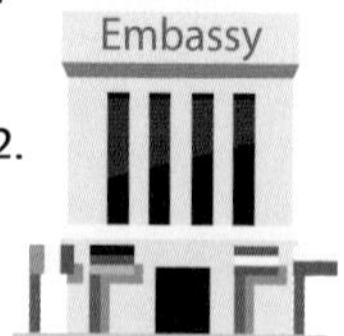

- **Kay and I played computer games until/till 11 p.m.** 凱和我玩電腦遊戲，一直玩到晚上 11 點。
- **Sue worked at our embassy in Tokyo until/till 2012.** 蘇在我們東京的大使館一直工作到 2012 年。
  ↑ 肯定句中的動詞用延續性動作（如：played, worked）。
- **Kate did not start to study English until the age of eight.** 凱特直到八歲才開始學英語。
  ↑ until 用與否定句中（not . . . until）表示「直到……才」。
  ↑ 否定句中的動詞要用短暫性動作（如：start）。

2 from . . . to, from . . . until/till, from . . . through，表某行為或狀況的「開始和結束」。

・Kate usually sleeps from midnight until/till eight.
= Kate usually sleeps from midnight to eight.
凱特通常從半夜一直睡到早上 8 點鐘。 → from . . . until/till 可以代替 from . . . to。

美式 Kay said the Coffee Castle was open from Monday through Saturday.

英式 Kay said the Coffee Castle was open from Monday to Saturday.
凱說，咖啡城堡從星期一到星期六都有營業。 → 包括星期六在內。

3 by (= not later than) 表示某事發生在某一特定時刻，或此特定時刻之前。

- by March 6 在三月六日（或更早）
- before March 6 在三月六日之前（即在五日或更早）

・Kay will return the DVD by 6 p.m. on Monday.
凱在星期一下午六點以前，要歸還那塊 DVD。 → 表示不能晚於星期一晚上六點。

・Mary will move to Amherst by January 1.
瑪麗將在一月一日之前搬到（美國麻州）艾默斯特市。

5 表示地點的介系詞：at, on, in

1 當指地點時，in、on、at 意思類似，但與不同的地點連用。一般規則為：

at + 小型地點／位址號碼
on + 中型地點
in + 大型地點（有時也用於很小的地點）

2 at 表示「某個點」的地理概念，而不是某個地區，與具體的位址連用。

a at + 小地點

- at home 在家
- at school 在學校
- at a factory 在工廠
- at the gas station 在加油站
- at the bus stop 在公車站
- at Harvard University 在哈佛大學

・He works at the graveyard. 他在墓地工作。

b at + 門牌號碼

- at 29 Washington Street 在華盛頓街 29 號
- at 25 Adam Road 在亞當路 25 號

・Do you live at 75 Fourth Street? 你住在第四街 75 號嗎？

3 on 與街道、河川、海岸名稱等連用。

a on + 街道／河川／海岸名稱

- on Tenth Street 在第十街
- on Park Avenue 在公園路
- on the Yellow River 在黃河
- on the East Coast 在東岸

・Sue lives on Park Avenue. 蘇住在公園路。

↥ 對比：Sue lives at 25 Park Avenue. 蘇住在公園路 25 號。

・They often deliver goods to the barges floating on the Colorado River. 他們常把貨物運到行駛在科羅拉多河的駁船上面。

1 用街道名稱來指稱某條街上的某個機構時，要用 at 取代 on。

・They are going to meet at Downing Street tomorrow.
他們明天要在唐寧街會面。 → 指英國政府內閣

2 但是，在代表金融機構的 Wall Street 之前要用 on。

・What is the latest news about the New York City mass demonstration against financial greed on Wall Street?
紐約市抗議華爾街金融貪婪的大示威，有什麼最新消息？

b 慣用語

- on Mars 在火星上
- on a ship 在船上
- on a plane 在飛機上
- on Earth 在地球上
- on a train 在火車上
- on a farm 在農場裡

・She dreamed of a baboon eating breakfast at a restaurant on the moon. 她夢見一隻狒狒在月球上的一家餐廳吃早餐。

・Jane wants to travel across Canada on a train. 珍想搭火車橫越加拿大。

- She works on her farm and makes a lot of money.
  她在自己的農場工作，賺了很多錢。

比較 She works in a car parts factory. 她在一家製造汽車零件的工廠工作。

4 in 與大陸、國家、州、縣、城鎮的名稱等連用。

a in + 大陸／國家／州／省／縣／城鎮名稱（大地點）

- in Asia 在亞洲
- in Russia 在俄國
- in Michigan 在密西根州
- in Alberta 在亞伯達（加拿大西部一省）
- in Marquette County 在馬凱特郡
- in Rome 在羅馬

- **Margo will meet her boyfriend's family in Chicago.**
  瑪歌將在芝加哥和她男朋友的家人碰面。

- **I live in Miami, which is in the southeastern part of the United States of America.** 我住在美國東南部的邁阿密。

b 慣用語：in + 小地點

- in a corner 在街角
- in a building 在建築物裡
- in a department 在系裡；在部裡
- in a car 在汽車裡
- in a room 在房間裡
- in a park 在公園裡
- in a boat 在小船上

- **They will cross the river in a boat.** 他們將乘一艘小船過河。
  ↳ 比較：on a ship 和 in a boat。

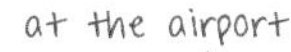

1 一般而言，at 用在小地方，例如：
- at Saint Leo University 在聖利奧大學
- at the airport 在機場

2 in 則用在大地方，例如：
- in New York City 在紐約市
- in Tokyo 在東京
- in Calcutta 在加爾各答市
- in Britain 在英國

3 但有時 in 也用在很小的地點前面，例如：
- in the math department at Northern Michigan University
  在北密西根大學數學系

5 in、on、at 的用法比較

- **Kay's mom is going to stay in New York City for a few days.** 凱的媽媽要在紐約待幾天。
- **Sue lives on Fifth Avenue.** 蘇住在第五大道。
- **The mime master arrived at Tampa International Airport on time.** 默劇大師準時抵達坦帕國際機場。
- **Steve was born in South Africa on Christmas Eve.**
  史蒂夫在聖誕節前夕出生於南非。
- **I learned a wide diversity of writing styles while studying in the English department at Saint Leo University.**
  我在聖利奧大學英語系讀書時，學到多種寫作風格。
  ↳ in + department; at + university

Diving Deep Into English 50 in the street 和 on the street 的差別

❶「在街上」用 in the street 或 on the street。

- **"Tom, don't run in/on the street," warned Mom.**
  媽媽告誡說：「湯姆，不要在街上跑。」

❷ 當談到具體的哪一條街時，美式英語則要用 on，英式英語常用 in。

美式	英式
• on Third Street	• in Third Street
• on Oakwood Street	• in Oakwood Street
Do you live on Washington Street? 你住在華盛頓街嗎？	**Do you work in Washington Street?** 你在華盛頓街工作嗎？

6 in、at、on 的一些固定搭配（兼論無介系詞）

a 當 downtown、uptown、downstairs、upstairs、home、inside 和 outside 作副詞時，前面不需要與任何介系詞連用。

b 以下有 * 符號的地點或場所的詞，可以與不同的介系詞連用（比如：in the hospital/at the hospital）。

at 在……地點	on 在……上	in 在……裡	無介系詞（作副詞用）
at the library* 在圖書館	on the bed* 在床上	in (the) bed* 在被窩裡	downtown 在（往）城市的商業區
at home 在家	on the floor 在地板上	in the house 在屋裡	upstairs 在（往）樓上
at school* 在學校	on the bus 在公車上	in school* 在學校	downstairs 在（往）樓下
at work 在工作	on the train 在火車上	in the car 在車裡	inside 在裡面
at the desk* 在桌前	on the horse 在馬上	in the hospital* 在醫院	outside 在外面

- **Mat is at work now.** 麥特現在正在工作。

✗ **She lives in downtown.**
✓ **She lives downtown.** 她住在商業區。 → 無介系詞

Diving Deep Into English 51 at school 與 in school

❶ 指具體的地理位置（physical location），表示講話的此刻正在學校上課，at school 和 in school 可以互換使用。

- **"Where is Claire?" "She is at/in School."**「克萊兒在哪兒？」「她在學校。」
  - ↑ at school：指具體的地理位置，表示講話的此刻正在學校上課。
  - ↑ in school：①也可以指具體的地理位置，表示講話的此刻正在學校上課；②還可以表示在校接受教育。

- **"Today there will be an earthquake drill at/in school," explained Kay.**「今天學校有地震演習。」凱說明道。 → 具體地理位置

❷ 表示在學校接受教育（participation in education），要用 in school。

- **Last year Jenny worked for a computer company, but now she is in school full time.** 去年珍妮在一家電腦公司工作，不過現在是專職的學生。
  - ↑ 在校接受教育

Diving Deep Into English 52 in 和 at 接場所名稱時的差別

❶ 許多句型中，用 in 或 at 都可以，但意義稍有不同。

❷ 談論某人在某處做的「活動」時，常用 at。

❸ 談論做某活動的「場所」時，常用 in。

- **Kay and I had lunch together at the Play Cafe.**
  凱和我在遊戲咖啡店共進午餐。 → 活動

- **It was too hot for us to stay in the Play Cafe.**
  遊戲咖啡店熱得我們無法待在那裡。 → 場所本身

- **They were popular at Cannes.** 他們在坎城影展上很受歡迎。
  ↑ 這裡指 Cannes Film Festival（事件）。

- **They were popular in Cannes.** 他們在坎城很受歡迎。
  ↑ 用 in 表示在這個城市裡（場所）。

❹ at 意思是「在……地點」，而 in 強調「在……裡」（= inside）。

- **Does Mark want to meet us at Central Park?**
  馬克要在中央公園跟我們碰面嗎？ → inside or outside Central Park

- **Does Mark want to meet us in Central Park?**
  馬克要在中央公園裡面跟我們碰面嗎？ → inside Central Park

6 表示「移動」的介系詞（兼論無介系詞）

1 **to**、**into** 和 **out of**：to 表示朝著一個地方移動；into 表示「進入……中」；out of 表示「自……離開」。

- **Does this highway lead to Taipei?** → lead to 是固定搭配。
  這條公路通往臺北嗎？

- **Yesterday afternoon I went to the dentist's**
  昨天下午我去了牙科診所。
  ↑ the dentist's = the dentist's office

✗ They went to inside the tent.

✓ They went inside the tent.

= They went into the tent. 他們走進帳篷裡。

⤴ 這裡的 inside 是介系詞，相當於 into；介系詞片語 inside the tent 作副詞用，修飾動詞 went，不需要與表示方向的介系詞 to 連用。

- **Fire! Get out of the house!** 起火了！撤出房子！

  ⤴ out of（從……離開）是 into（到……裡）的反義詞。

2 **toward** 和 **towards**：也是表達朝著某方向移動的介系詞。美國人喜歡用 toward，英國人喜歡用 towards。

- **Face the fact that we humans have taken a big step toward exploring outer space.** 面對這個事實吧，我們人類已經朝外太空探索邁出了一大步。
- **Floyd's family wants to move outward toward/towards the asteroids.** 福羅伊德一家想移民到小行星去。

3 **at** 和 **to**：接在某些動詞（如：shout、throw）之後，可以用 to（受動者主觀願意接受動作），也可用 at（受動者不願接受動作）。

- **I quickly threw the baseball to Lulu.** 我迅速把棒球傳給露露。
- **Don't ever throw stones at my puppy.** 不要對我的小狗丟石頭。

4 **up** (to) 和 **down** (to)：表示北上或南下的移動。up 指「北」；down 指「南」。up 和 down 也表示「沿著」，常與河流和道路連用。

- go up north 往北走
- go down south 往南走
- come up to Michigan from Florida 從佛羅里達州往北前往密西根州
- come down to Florida from Michigan 從密西根州往南前往佛羅里達州
- drive up the street 開車沿著街道而上
- drive down the street 開車沿著街道而下
- swim up the river 沿河往上游去
- swim down the river 沿河往下游去

5 **across**、**through** 和 **over**：across 和 through 的意思都是「穿過」。across，指從一邊移動到另一邊；through 指穿越物體內部的移動。over 指「越過」，也可以表示「先上後下、越過障礙物的移動」。

- walk across the square 走過廣場 → 地面是平的
- pass through a tunnel 通過隧道 → 穿過物體內部
- leap over the fence 跳過籬笆 → 先上後下越過

6 介系詞通常只與名詞或代名詞連用，不與副詞連用。下列的字作**副詞**用時，不加表示移動的介系詞 to 或 toward：

- home 回（到）家
- downtown 在（往）市中心
- inside（在）往裡面
- outside（在）往外面
- downstairs 下樓
- upstairs 上樓

・**He went outside with his cellphone and began to walk and talk.**
他帶著手機出門，開始一邊走路一邊說話。

・**After taking a quick shower, Dan went upstairs quietly so as not to wake up Ann.** 丹迅速地沖了個澡，輕輕地走上樓，以免吵醒安。

・**She came home from work at 3 a.m.** 她凌晨三點才下班回到家。
↑ 這裡的 home 是副詞，前面不要用表示移動的介系詞 to。
↑ 固定片語：go home、come home（回家）。

比較 Is Jerry at home? 傑瑞在家嗎？
↑ 這裡的 home 是名詞，at 是表示地點的介系詞。
↑ 固定片語：be (is, am, are, was, etc.) at home（在家）。

7 一些表示移動的慣用語：

- get into a car 上車
- get out of a car 下車
- get to a place 到達某地
- get on a bus/train/plane/ship 上公車、火車、飛機、船
- get off a bus/train/plane/ship 下公車、火車、飛機、船

・**I'll get off the bus at the next stop.** 我要在下一站下公車。

Diving Deep Into English 53 get to a place、arrive in a place 與 arrive at a place 的用法

表示到達某地可用 get to a place 或動詞 arrive（arrive 後面不接 to），例如：

arrive at + 小地方
arrive in + 大地方

- **It took four hours for Sue King's airplane to get to Colorado Springs.**
  蘇·金的飛機花了四個小時才到科羅拉多州斯普林斯市。
- **Kate arrived in Tokyo before eight.** 凱特八點前抵達了東京。
- **I was dead tired when I arrived at the Hilton Hotel.**
  我到達希爾頓飯店時已經精疲力竭了。

7 表示位置的介系詞 (1)：above, over, on, below, under

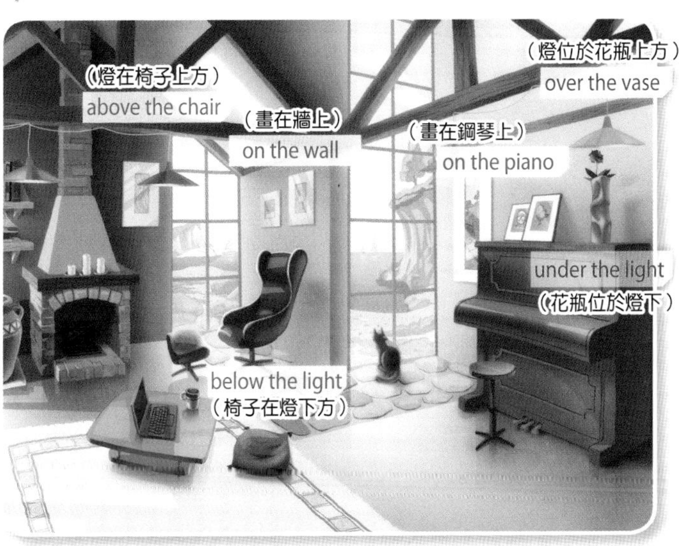

1 on（緊鄰在……之上；在……旁邊）

sit on my shoulders

a on 表示在一個平面之上並與這個平面有接觸。

- on the desk 在書桌上
- on my shoulders 在我肩上
- on the ceiling 在天花板上
- a kiss on the cheek 面頰上一個親吻

- **She fell asleep on a cave floor.** 她在一個洞穴的地板上睡著了。
- **Mabel is dancing on a big oak table.** 美博在一張大橡木桌上跳舞。
- **After swimming in a creek, they went home to their cabin on a mountain peak.** 他們在小河裡游完泳後，回到山頂的小屋裡。
- **Keep your eyes on the stars, and your feet on the ground.** (President Theodore Roosevelt) 抬頭仰望滿天繁星，雙腳站穩人間大地。

b on 也表示某物掛在另一物上面，以其為支撐。

- **What is Paul going to hang on the wall?** 保羅要在牆上掛些什麼？

c on 表示某物靠近另一物，在另一物旁邊（= near, by）。

- **Mabel was sitting on my right, and Paul was sitting on my left.**
  美博坐在我的右邊，保羅坐在我的左邊。
  ↥ sit on my left/on my right 是固定搭配，只能用 on。

2 above（在某物上方）和 below（在某物的下方）

a above 通常表示某物在另一物的上方，但非正上方；有時候也指一物在另一物的正上方。

b above 的反義詞 below。below 通常用來説明某物位置比另一物低，指非正下方或正下方。

- below sea level 低於海平面
- above sea level 高於海平面
- below the horizon 地平線下
- above the horizon 地平線上

- **The bees are flying above the trees.** 蜜蜂在樹的上方飛翔。
- **Devil Cave extends about 200 feet below sea level.**
  魔鬼洞穴低於海平面大約 200 英尺。

- **Mike lives in the apartment below/above mine.**
  邁克就住在我樓下（／樓上）的公寓房間裡。

- **Dee's new skirt ends just above/below her knees.**
  蒂的新裙子剛好在膝蓋上方（／下方）。
  ⤴ 裙子比較長，剛好在膝蓋下方，用 below；反之，就用 above。

above 和 below 還可以表示「水準」或「級別」。

- Is a captain above or below a lieutenant?
  上尉比中尉的軍銜高還是低？

above 也可以表示「優於；勝過；比……更重要」。

- A people that values its privileges above its principles soon loses both. (President Dwight David Eisenhower)
  將特權淩駕於原則之上的民族，要不了多久就會兩者皆失。
  ⤴ 這裡的 above 意指「rather than; in preference to」。比如：favor one child above the other（愛一個孩子勝過愛另一個）。
  ⤴ 介系詞 over 也可以表達此意，比如：chosen over another applicant。

3 over（在某物正上方；越過 ） 和 under（在某物正下方）

a over 表示某物在另一物的正上方。

b 表示「正上方」時，可以用 over 或 above；不在正上方時，只能用 above。

- over the door = above the door 在門的正上方

- **She became excited when her plane was flying over/above Madrid, Spain.** 她的飛機在西班牙馬德里市上空飛翔時，她興奮了起來。

- **I began to shiver as I stood in the rain on the old bridge over the Cold River.** 我在雨中站在冷河上方那座舊橋上，開始發起抖來。
  ⤴ 習慣用 over the river。

c 表示一物覆蓋在另一物之上並與之有接觸，用 over，不用 above。

- spread a new carpet over the floor 在地板上鋪新地毯

・**Jan was drunk last night and began to smell really bad after she ran her bicycle over a skunk.** 簡昨晚喝醉了，她的自行車從一隻臭鼬身上碾過去後，她身上開始散發一股非常難聞的氣味。

d over 的反義詞為 under（在……正下方）。under 也指「被另一物覆蓋」。

・**We were sitting and talking under the big oak tree when we heard some thunder.** 我們坐在大橡樹下聊天，這時聽見了雷聲。

・**I hid the money under my pillow.** 我把錢藏在了我的枕頭下面。
↑ money 被 pillow 覆蓋了。

over 和 under 也能表示「水準」或「級別」，用法等同 above 和 below。

・In the Army, is a major over/above a captain?
在陸軍裡，少校的軍階高於上尉嗎？

・In the Army, is a captain under/below a major?
在陸軍裡，上尉的軍階低於少校嗎？

8 表示位置的介系詞 (2)：beneath 和 underneath

1 **beneath** 的意思相當於 below（地位等「低於」）和 under（在……之下）。

- beneath (= below) a major 位階低於少校
- beneath (= under) the same roof 在同一個屋簷下
  ↑ 更常用 under the same roof

2 **underneath**

a 表示某物在另一物的下面，尤其是被另一物覆蓋，與 under 同義。

b 也可以表示「在……的喬裝下」，用來談論某人的真正性格和感情。

c 還可表示地位等「低於」（under the control of; in a lower position）。

- wear a swimming suit underneath your clothes
  在你的衣服下穿一件泳衣 → 在……下面（被另一物覆蓋）

- underneath a mask of friendliness 在友善的面具下 → 在……的喬裝下
- underneath the department heads 在部門主管的位階之下 → 地位低於

· **Ted hid the teddy bear** underneath **the bed.** 泰德把泰迪熊藏在床底下。

· **Matt left the key** underneath **the mat.** 麥特把鑰匙藏在腳踏墊下。

Diving Deep Into English 54 表示「地位低於……」的用法

❶ after 也可以表示「地位低於」。

· **"As you move lower in the ranks, does a captain** come after **a major?" "Yes, a captain is** below/under **a major."**「軍階從上到下來看，少校下來是上尉嗎？」「是的，上尉在少校的下面。」

ℒ 上面第一句不能用 below/under。雖然 below/under 也可表示「級別」高低（上尉軍階低於少校。），但上面第一句的 come after（緊跟）是固定的片語。after 指在一個表格裡或排列順序裡，某人或某物的位置緊跟在另一個人或物的後面；after 常和動詞 come 連用。比如：

· C comes after B in the alphabet.
在英語字母表裡，字母 B 的後面接著的是 C。

· A captain's rank is after a major's. 上尉的軍階在少校的下面。

❷ 可以用其他不同的詞表示相同的意思：

· **A captain is** beneath/lower than/inferior to/subordinate to/subservient to **a major.** 上尉的軍階在少校的下面。

9 表示位置的介系詞 (3)：by, beside, near, against

1 by = beside （在……旁邊；靠近）

・Dee is going to sit by/beside me. 蒂要坐在我旁邊。

・We camped by/beside Snake Lake. 我們在蛇湖邊露營。

2 near = next to = close to （在……的附近）

● a cottage near Deer Lake
= a cottage close to/next to Deer Lake
= a cottage by Deer Lake 鹿湖附近的一間小屋

・Jake said there was a beautiful beach near his campsite on Clear Lake. 傑克說，在他清水湖畔的營地附近，有一片美麗的海灘。

・She asked me if Jake was near Clear Lake.
她問我傑克在不在清水湖附近。

英式英文常用 on 表示「在……旁」（= near, by）。

● a wooden house on the highway（主要為英式用法）
= a wooden house near/by the highway 公路旁的一間木屋

● a hotel on the sea（英式用法）
= a hotel by the sea 一家靠海的旅館

Diving Deep Into English 55 介系詞 besides 和 beside

beside 指「在旁邊」(= by the side of, next to, by)。
besides 指「除……之外（其他的也）」。

・Audrey Ride knelt down beside her bed and prayed for the sick and hungry. 奧德莉・賴德跪在床邊，為病人和饑餓的人祈禱。
ℓ beside = next to, by

・A free man obtains knowledge from many sources besides books. (President Thomas Jefferson)
除書本之外，一個不受約束的人還可以從許多別的來源獲取知識。

3 against （ 靠；對著 ）

- Did Coco leave my motor scooter leaning against the shop window?
  可可把我的小型摩托車靠在商店窗戶上了嗎？
- Nicole rubbed her back too hard against the tent pole.
  妮可靠著帳篷柱子用力摩擦背部。

10 表示位置的介系詞 (4)：behind, in front of, in the front of, before, opposite, across

1 behind （ 在……後面 ）：反義字為 in front of。

- Ann sat behind Dan. 安坐在丹後面。
  = Dan sat in front of Ann. 丹坐在安的前面。
- Behind us, Dwight's car automatically beeped and flashed its headlights. 杜威特的車在我們身後自動響起汽笛，閃起頭燈。
- I saw Dee hiding behind the tree. 我看見蒂正躲在那棵樹後面。

2 in front of （ 在……前面 ）

- Gus stared at the road in front of his bus.
  加斯盯著公車前面的道路。
- It seemed impossible to all of us, but there was a horrible huge rat in front of the bus.
  也許在我們大家看來不太可能，不過那輛公車前面的確有一隻恐怖的巨鼠。
- The mean rat was hungrily eating a dead skunk in front of us when Gus rammed it hard with the bus.
  那隻凶惡的老鼠正在我們面前狼吞虎嚥地吃一隻死臭鼬，突然，加斯開著那輛公車狠狠地向牠撞去。

3 in the front of （ 在……的最前部 ）

in the front of 表示「在……的前部」，指在某物的內部，其反義詞是 at the back of；in front of 指在某物外部的前面。

- In the front of the bus sat the driver Gus, staring at the dead rat in front of us. 司機加斯坐在公車的最前面，盯著我們前方的死老鼠。
- In the front of the bus was the strong bumper with which Gus had killed the rat in front of us.
  加斯就是用公車前面的保險桿，撞死我們前方那隻老鼠的。
- While in second grade, I always sat at the back of the classroom.
  我讀小學二年級時，都是坐在教室的最後一排。

4 before 在……之前；在……前面

a before 為「在……之前，先於」，通常指時間。

- Will Mark get home from the park before dark?
  馬克會在天黑之前從公園回家嗎？

b 在非常正式的英語，如古英語或文學用語中，before 可以表示位置，意思相當於 in front of。

- Anna Wing knelt before the king. 安娜．溫在國王面前跪下。
- Before the old temple gate stands a statue of Buddha.
  古寺門前豎立著一尊佛像。
  ↑ 表示位置的介系詞片語（before）位於句首，句子用倒裝形式（動詞 stands 置於主詞 a statue of Buddha 前面）。
  » 參見 726 頁〈3 用倒裝句來作強調〉。

5 opposite 和 across 在……對面

opposite 和 across：兩者具有「對面」的意思。美式用 across，英式用 opposite。

|主要為英式| sit opposite each other 坐在彼此的對面

|主要為美式| sit across from each other

↑「sit across from」是美式固定搭配的片語。

|主要為英式| Please put the radio on the table opposite the piano.

請把收音機放在鋼琴對面的桌子上。

|主要為美式| Pete is standing over there across the street.

彼特站在對街那一邊。

介系詞 opposite 也可以指「與……聯合主演」，用於片語「play opposite somebody」中。

- Sadie's brother has played opposite many leading ladies.

  莎蒂的兄弟和許多一線女演員領銜演出。

  ↑ = in a complementary dramatic role to

11 表示「原因」：from 和 for

1 from + 名詞 / 動名詞（-ing）：from 意為「由於；出於；因為」

- is trembling from fear 因害怕發抖
- faint from hunger 因飢餓暈倒

- **Kay got sunburned from staying out on her sailboat all day.**

  凱由於整天都待在帆船上，皮膚被曬傷了。 → from + 動名詞

- **Tess has been suffering from too much stress.** 黛絲飽受壓力沉重之苦。

  ↑ from + 名詞；suffer from 是固定搭配，指「因……而痛；受……之苦」。

2 for 也可以表示「因為；由於」。

- a city famous for its beauty 一座以美景著稱的城市
- jump for joy 高興得跳起來

- **Amy felt sorry for what she had done to me.**

  艾咪為她對我所做的事感到抱歉。

  ↑ 雖然 for 和 from 都可以表示「原因」，但兩者並不能互換，要根據習慣用語而選擇。

Diving Deep Into English 56 表原因的複合介系詞

❶ 表原因的複合介系詞有：

- owing to
- because of
- as a result of
- on account of
- due to

❷ owing to, because of, as a result of, on account of 在句中的位置比較靈活，可以置於句首或動詞後面。

- Owing to/As a result of/Because of **the mistakes made by the new accountant, some of us received incorrect checks.**
  由於新來的會計犯的錯誤，我們一些人收到了錯誤的支票。
- **I was told that our school would be closed** owing to/as a result of/because of **the dust storm.** 我被告知，我們學校因沙塵暴要停課。

❸ 在正式用語中，due to 要放在連綴動詞 be 或 seem 等後面，作主詞補語，意思是 caused by, resulting from。

- **Kirk knows that success in life** is due to **hard work.**
  柯克明白，人生的成功應歸功於辛勤工作。 →resulting from 起因於
- **Paul knows the difference in his behavior** is due to **alcohol.**
  保羅明白，他的舉止改變都是因為酒精而造成的。 →caused by 由 . . . 而造成

❹ 在非正式用語中，due to 可以放在句尾（但不放句首），等同於 owing to/because of/as a result of/on account of。。

- **Our business is in deep financial trouble** due to **global warming.**
  因為全球暖化的緣故，我們的企業深陷財務困境。

Diving Deep Into English 57 from 的其他用法

- from 8 am. to 8 p.m. 從早上八點到晚上八點（從……起）
- twenty miles from the airport 從機場有 20 英里路（離）
- relieve you from your responsibility 免去你的職責（免去）
- know right from wrong 能夠辨別是非（區別）

- **She's from India.** 她是印度人。／她來自印度。
  ↑ 意思是「出自；從……來」。
- **Wine is made** from **grapes.** 葡萄酒是由葡萄釀成的。
  ↑ 表示原料，意思是「由」。

12 表示「目的」：for

a 名詞 + for + 名詞：for 用在名詞前，表示某行動的目的或物體的用途。
b 名詞 + for + 動名詞（動詞 -ing 形式）：用於提及一個儀器的特定使用方式。
c 名詞 + 不定式：for 不能與不定式和動詞原形連用。

- **I use this balcony for my telescope.** 我用這個陽臺來放我的望遠鏡。
  ↑ 名詞（balcony）+ for + 名詞（telescope）：指明陽臺的用途。
- **I use the computer and joystick for controlling the telescope.**
  = I use the computer and joystick to control the telescope.
  我用電腦和搖桿來控制我的望遠鏡。
  ↑ 名詞 + for + 動名詞：指明儀器（電腦和搖杆）的特定作用。
  ↑ 名詞 + 不定式：表達目的最常用的是不定式（如：to control the telescope）。
- **Dwight, please use the red button for turning on the light.**
  = Dwight, please use the red button to turn on the light.
  杜威特，請按那個紅色按鈕來開燈。
  ↑ 「名詞 + for + 動名詞」表示紅色按鈕的作用。
- **Joe's mom built a new closet for storing her winter clothes.**
  = Joe's mom built a new closet to store her winter clothes.
  喬的母親修建了一個新廚櫃，用來放她的冬裝。

Diving Deep Into English 58 for 的其他用法

- leave for Singapore 出發去新加波（往）
- for the idea or against it 贊成或反對這個觀點（支持）
- sell the house for only $10,000 只以一萬美元把房子賣了（以……交換）

- **Sue usually has some time and a smile for Andrew.**
  蘇通常都會留點時間和微笑給安德魯。 → 為了
- **Tom bought a new sports car for his mom.**
  湯姆買了一輛新跑車送給他媽媽。 → 為了
- **Mary said this grammar book was too easy for me.**
  瑪麗說，這本文法書對我來說太簡單了。 → 就……而言

個別介系詞的固定搭配

1 at

・"Is Dwight at home with Liz?" "No, Dwight is at work, and he will be home at midnight."
「杜威特和莉茲一起在家嗎?」「沒有啊,杜威特在工作,他要半夜才回家。」
↳ at home(在家)、at work(在工作)、at midnight(半夜)是固定片語。

1 at 意為「從事於;忙於」,表示某人正在某處做某事,或正在參加某項活動。

- at a party 在聚會上
- at a concert 在音樂會上
- at a meeting 在開會
- at the theater 在戲院看戲
- at a football game 在觀看美式足球賽
- at a conference 在開會

2 at 表示某人在某個教育機構學習。

- at school 在學校
- at college 在大學

3 at 表示某人正在用餐(主要用於英式英語)。

- at breakfast 在吃早餐
- at brunch 在吃早午餐
- at lunch 在吃午餐
- at dinner 在吃正餐
- at supper 在吃晚餐
- at mealtime 在進餐時間
- at snack time 在點心時間
- at teatime 在喝茶時間

4 at 表示某人或某事所處的狀態。

- at rest 休息中
- at peace 和平狀態
- at war 戰爭中

・If civilization is to survive, we must cultivate the science of human

relationships—the ability of all peoples, of all kinds, to live together, in the same world at peace. (President Franklin D. Roosevelt)
要讓文明萬載長存，我們就必須修好人際關係這門學問——不同民族、不同種族生活在一起，在同一個世界和平共處的能力。

5 at 表示某個特定時刻或時期。

- at Christmas 在聖誕節期間
- at Easter 在復活節
- at New Year 在元旦期間
- at night (during any night) 在晚上（泛指任何一晚）
- at midnight 午夜時分
- at noon 在正午時分
- at the age of three 在 3 歲時
- at sixteen 在 16 歲時
- at present 目前
- at the moment 此時此刻
- at the time 在那時

1 the middle of . . . 要與 in 連用：
- in the middle of the night 在半夜
- in the middle of July 在七月中旬

2 比較：at the moment（= now）和
in a moment（= in a short period of time）

- She's at a meeting at the moment. 此刻，她正在開會。
- I'll be back in a moment. 我馬上就回來。

6 at 表示某人或某物所在的地點。

- at a restaurant 在餐廳
- at the gas station 在加油站
- at the bus stop 在公車站
- at the corner 在角落裡
- at the main entrance 在正門口
- at home 在家
- at the supermarket 在超市
- at the office 在辦公室
- at work 在工作場所；在工作
- at the doctor's 在看醫生
- at the dentist's 在看牙醫
- at the hairdresser's 在美容院
- at the bank 在銀行

↳ 對比：in the bank、in the supermarket、in a restaurant 等，強調在建築物裡面。

7 at 表示在某人家中。

- at Daniel's 在丹尼爾家
- at the Fosters' 在福斯特公館
- at Sally's 在莎莉家
- at the Smiths' 在史密斯宅

↑ 複數形式的姓氏前面要加 the，表示一家人。

8 at 與 the beginning、the end、the bottom、the top 連用。

- at the beginning of the 21st century 二十一世紀初
- at the end of this year 今年年底
- at the bottom of the mountain 在山腳下
- at the top of the stairs 在樓梯頂
- at the end of the week/at the weekend 在週末

↑ 美式用 on the weekend 和 at the end of the week。

9 at 表示價格、溫度、速度等。

- at $15 a piece 15 美元一個
- at 40 km per hour 時速 40 公里
- at high temperatures 高溫
- at high speeds 高速

2 in

1 in 表示在一個地點、地區、城市、國家範圍內。

- in America 在美國
- in Hong Kong 在香港
- in the park 在公園裡
- in the world 在世界上

・**Kay and Mark had a picnic in the park last Saturday.**
凱和馬克上星期六在公園野餐。

2 in 表示特定的一段時期（年、月、季節、世紀），或一天內的一部分。

- in 2012 在 2012 年
- in June 在 6 月
- in the fall 在秋天
- in (the) winter 在冬天
- in the morning 在早上
- in the afternoon 在下午
- in the 1990s 在 20 世紀 90 年代
- in the twentieth century 在 20 世紀

・**The football season began in the fall.** 美式足球賽季是在秋天開始的。

・**Kay is going to study judo in May.** 凱打算五月去學柔道。

↑ 月份和季節（summer、winter、April、March 等）要與 in 連用，不與 on 連用。

3 in 表示穿著。

- in a hat 戴帽子
- in a suit 穿西裝
- in a shirt 穿襯衫
- in a skirt 穿裙子

・**Did Bess look fantastic in that red dress?** 貝絲穿那件紅色洋裝好看嗎？

・**Did that red dress look fantastic on Bess?** 那件紅洋裝穿在貝絲身上好看嗎？

↑ 人穿戴服飾要用「人 + in + 服飾」；服飾穿戴在人身上則用「服飾 + on + 人」。

4 in 表示使用某種語言。

- in Russian 用俄文
- in Spanish 用西班牙文
- in French 用法文
- in Chinese 用中文

・**Can Professor Blish explain this Spanish grammar rule in English?**
布利西教授能夠用英文來解釋這一條西班牙語文法規則嗎？

5 in 表示書寫或作畫的工具，後面接複數，不可數名詞，以及單數可數名詞（不要冠詞）。

- in pen 用筆
- in pencil 用鉛筆
- in ink 用墨水
- in oils 用油墨
- in watercolors 用水彩
- in chalk 用粉筆

・**She drew a picture in chalk on the sidewalk.**
她用粉筆在人行道上畫了幅畫。

也可以用介系詞 with 來表示相同的意思（書寫和作畫的工具），但 with 後面需接**可數名詞**，單數要用不定冠詞 a/an，比如：

✔ with a pen	✘ with pen
✔ in chalk	✘ with chalk
✔ in ink	✘ with ink

✘ Did he fill in the forms with ink or with pencil?
✔ Did he fill in the forms in ink or in pencil?
✔ Did he fill in the forms with a pen or with a pencil?
他是用鋼筆還是鉛筆填表的？

↑ 這裡如果用 in ink or with a pencil 文法好像正確，但不是平行結構。
↑ 要用 in ink or (in) pencil 或 with a pen or (with) a pencil 保持結構平行。

6 in 指天氣。

- in the rain 在雨中
- in the snow 在雪中
- in the hurricane 在暴風雨中
- in the breeze 在微風中

・ **Coco and I hate driving in the snow.** 可可和我討厭在雪中開車。

7 in 指自然界。

- in the air 在空氣中
- in space 在太空中
- in the sky 在天空中

・ **There isn't a cloud in the sky, but that thunder was really loud.**
天空沒有一絲雲,可是雷聲卻很響。

8 in 指在圖文中。

- in a picture 在圖中
- in a book 在書裡
- in a story 在故事裡
- in a photo 在照片裡
- in the newspaper 在報紙上

・ **Sue looked much younger in this picture taken last year.**
在去年拍的這張照片裡,蘇看起來比她本人年輕多了。

・ **Reading about nature is fine, but if a person walks in the woods and listens carefully, he can learn more than what is in books, for they speak with the voice of God.** (President George Washington)
閱讀有關自然的書固然很好,但如果你走在樹林裡仔細聆聽,就能學到比書本上更多的東西,因為透過樹林可以聽見上帝的聲音。
↑ in the woods(在樹林裡);in books 在書中

9 用 in 指聲音、看法。

- in a . . . voice 用……聲音
- in one's opinion 依……的看法(不用 according to 或 after)

・ **Joyce always speaks in a soft voice.** 喬伊絲總是輕聲細語。

・ **In Bob's opinion, Amy is a silly girl.** 依鮑勃之見,艾咪是一個傻女孩。

10 in a car/taxi 在汽車、計程車裡

・ **They arrived in a rainbow-colored taxi.**
他們坐著一輛塗著彩虹顏色的計程車抵達。

除了 car 和 taxi 用 in 之外，其他交通工具則要用 on。

- on a bus/train/plane/ship 在公車、火車、飛機、船上
- Gus is leaving on the 4:30 bus. 加斯要搭四點半的公車離開。
- Jane loves to travel around Spain on the train.
  珍喜歡搭火車周遊西班牙。
- I'll put on my hat and go home on foot.
  我要戴上帽子，然後走路回家。
  ⮤ on foot 是固定短語，沒有冠詞。
- I was going to school on my bicycle when I was nearly hit by a falling icicle.
  我騎自行車去學校的路上，突然有塊冰柱掉落，差點打到我。

11 慣用語

- in the direction of 朝……方向
- in progress 進行中
- in cash 用現金
- in business 經營；做生意
- in the end 終於；最終

- In the end, Lisa got a U.S. visa.
  麗莎終於拿到了美國簽證。

in the end 意為「終於」，而 at the end 則表示事物的「盡頭；末端；最後部分」。

- She thinks my book is a bit weak at the end.
  她認為我的書在結尾處寫得有點牽強。
- It behooves every man to remember that the work of the critic is of altogether secondary importance, and that, in the end, progress is accomplished by the man who does things. (President Theodore Roosevelt)
  每一個人都應該記住，評論家的工作完全是次要的，要有所進步最終還是要靠做事的人。

3 on

1 on 說明某事發生的日子。

- on Saturday 在星期六
- on the 27th of November 在 11 月 27 號
- on a rainy day 在下雨天
- on a cold night 在寒冷的夜晚
- on Christmas Day 在聖誕節
- on New Year's Eve 在除夕夜

· **Dee graduated from college on June 15, 2003.**
蒂於 2003 年六月 15 日大學畢業。

2 on 表示頁數，這種情況下不能用 in 或 at。

· **My story about Sue is on page 2.** 我關於蘇的報導在第二頁。

· **I found a mistake on the first page.** 我在第一頁發現了一個錯誤。

3 on 表示「關於」（concerning）或「就……而言」，與 about 的意思一樣。

a 在下面動詞和名詞之後用 on 或 about 都可以：

動詞
- advise 勸告
- lecture 演講
- talk 談論；演講
- agree 意見一致
- speak 談論
- write 寫
- disagree 爭論
- speculate 推測

名詞
- advice 勸告
- consultation 磋商
- lecture 演講
- agreement 一致
- decision 決定
- opinion 意見
- article/book/paper 文章／書／論文
- idea 見解
- question 問題
- information 資訊

· **She speculated about/on my motives.** 她推測我的動機。

· **I need your advice about/on which university I should attend.**
我需要你的建議，我應該上哪一所大學。

b 在下面動詞之後用 on，不用 about：

- comment 評論
- focus 集中
- reflect (= think) 深思；反省
- concentrate 集中
- insist 堅持

· **I will concentrate on studying English this summer.**
今年夏天我會專心學英語。

c 在下面動詞和名詞之後用 about，不用 on：

動詞

- argue 爭論
- ask 詢問
- care 關心
- complain 抱怨
- enquire/inquire 查詢
- find out 查明
- hear 聽說
- joke 開玩笑
- know 知道
- laugh 笑
- learn 學
- protest 抗議
- quarrel 爭吵
- read 讀到
- teach (someone) 教導
- tell (someone) 告訴
- think 思索
- wonder 想知道
- worry 擔心

名詞

- argument 爭論
- chat 聊天
- fuss 小題大做
- joke 玩笑
- misunderstanding 誤解
- quarrel 爭吵

- **Do you know any jokes about politicians?** 你知道任何關於政客的玩笑嗎？
- **Eventually, you will be able to laugh about some of your foolish mistakes.** 最終，你將會對你犯過的一些愚蠢的錯誤感到好笑。

4 表示位置（在……上；靠近」）

- stand on my left 站在我的左邊
- a scar on her face 她臉上的一個疤

- **Can you stand on your hands?** 你會倒立嗎？

stand on your hands

5 是……的成員；屬於

- on the basketball team 籃球隊隊員

6 慣用語

a 度假

- on vacation 在度假
- go on (a) vacation 去度假

go on vacation

- **Will Coco soon go on vacation to San Francisco?**
可可快要去舊金山度假了嗎？ → 美式英語中也說 go on a vacation。

b 電子媒介

- on the radio 在收音機上
- on TV 在電視上
- on the phone 在電話上
- on the computer 在電腦上
- on the Internet 在網路上
- on the blog 在部落格上

- **Dirk likes to listen to the news** on the radio **while he's driving to work.** 德克喜歡在開車上班時聽新聞廣播。
- **She is** on her cellphone. 她在講手機。

- **He is always** on the Internet. 他總是在上網。

c 著火

- on fire 著火

- **The kitchen is** on fire. 廚房著火了。

d on time 準時

- **Is Liz ever** on time? 莉茲有沒有準時過？

on time 是「準時」，按照計畫的時間，不早不遲。
in time 則是「及時」，表示在最後時刻之前還有足夠的時間做某事。

- I got to Titusville just in time to see the launch of the space shuttle. 我抵達泰特斯維爾時，剛好趕上看太空梭發射。

4 by

1 by 表示**寫書**、**作曲**、**作畫**的人。

- a book (written) by Brooke 布魯克寫的書
- a concerto (composed) by Mozart 莫札特創作的協奏曲
- a sketch by Leonardo de Vinci 李奧納多・達文西畫的素描
- a movie (directed) by Clint Eastwood 克林・伊斯威特導演的電影

2 by 表示某事完成的方式或手段，意為「**靠；用；通過**」。

- by mail/by post 用郵寄
- by email 用電子郵件
- by phone 用電話
- by fax 用傳真
- by hand 用手
- by force 用武力
- by credit card 用信用卡
- by heart 熟背下來

・**Del made a reservation by emailing the hotel.** 戴爾用電子郵件向飯店訂房。
  ↳ 介系詞 by 表示手段，回答 how 的問題：How did Del make a reservation?（戴爾是怎麼訂房的？）

by, with, through（以……手段／材料／行為）

1 by + 動名詞：by 表示透過**某種行為**做某事（through the activity or effort of）。

2 by + 單數可數名詞（不帶冠詞）：by表示透過**某種方式**做某事（through the means of）。

3 with + 可數名詞（複數和單數）：with 表示用**某種物品**來做某事（by means of; using）。

- by calling 911 給 911 打電話
- by phone 用電話
- to eat with chopsticks 用筷子吃飯
- to play tennis with a new racket 用新球拍打網球

・Scot learned English by reading a lot.
史考特用大量閱讀的方式來學習英語。
  ↳ 介系詞 by 後面要用動名詞（-ing 形式），不能用不定式。

・Please send your recording by email. 請用電子郵件把你的錄音寄來。

・Open the bottle with a bottle opener. 用開瓶器打開那個瓶子。

・I cut it with the scissors. 我用剪刀剪它。

4 through 指透過仲介、工具來做某事；也表示「**因為**」。

- through outside aid 透過外援
- through my brother 透過我的兄弟
- yield through fear 因為恐懼而屈服
- wounded through carelessness 因不小心而受傷

3 by 表示**交通工具**或**交通方式**。

- by car 開車
- by road 經公路
- by train 坐火車
- by boat 乘船
- by air 經空運
- by sea 經海路
- by airplane 坐飛機
- by bike 騎自行車
- by land 經陸路
- by bus 搭公車

- **Jane went to Spain by train.** 珍坐火車去了西班牙。

  ↑ 對比：She's on the bus/on the airplane/on the train/in the taxi. 她在公車上／飛機上／火車上／計程車裡。

4 by 表示**某事發生的原因或肇事者**，有「被；由」的意思，常用於被動式。

- destroyed by fire 被火所燒毀

- **The mess was made by John, not Bess.**
  這一團混亂是約翰造成的，不是貝絲造成的。

- **The math problem that had confused Jenny was solved by Danny.**
  困擾珍妮的那道數學題被丹尼解出來了。

5 by 表示在某個特定時間或日期之前（before 或 until），意為「**不遲於；在……之前**」。

- by the time . . . 到……的時候

- **Jenny said the astronomy meeting would be over by 11 p.m.**
  珍妮說，天文學會議晚上 11 點之前結束。

比較 by **與** until

1 **by**：表示某件事在某個特定的時間之前或在最近的某個時間發生。

- We have to be at the gym by 3:30 p.m.
  我們要在下午三點半之前到體育館。 → 比賽在三點半開始。

2 **until**：表示某件事一直持續到某個特定的時間。

- We have to be at the gym until 3:30 p.m.
  我們要留在體育館直到下午三點半。 → 在三點半之前不能離開。

比較 at 和 by

✗ At the time Kay was twelve, she had already learned to speak four languages and was reading over 25,000 English words every day.

✓ By the time Kay was twelve, she had already learned to speak four languages and was reading over 25,000 English words every day.
凱滿十二歲時，就已經學會講四國語言，而且每天都讀超過二萬五千字的英語閱讀量。

- by 表示在某個特定時間或日期之前（before 或 until），意為「到⋯⋯的時候；到⋯⋯之前；不遲於」。
- 句子是過去完成式（had already learned），指「已經學會」，只能用介系詞 by 引導的時間片語，不用介系詞 at the time/at the age of twelve。

・At the age of three, Kay started to read simple storybooks in English every day. 凱在三歲時，開始每天讀簡單的英語故事書。
- 述語動詞是簡單過去式（started），用介系詞 at，指「在三歲時⋯⋯」。

6 by 表示靠近某人或某物，意為「**在⋯⋯旁邊；靠近；在⋯⋯手邊**」。

- by = beside = near = close to = next to

・**Put the plastic dinosaur by the door.**
把那個塑膠恐龍放在門邊。

・**Dee stayed in a hotel by the sea.**
蒂住在一家靠海的旅館。

表示在城市或鄉鎮的附近，用 near 不用 by。

✗ They live in a big house by Miami.

✓ They live in a big house near Miami.
他們住在邁阿密附近的一幢大房子裡。

7 by 表示「**以⋯⋯計算；按**」：

・**Speeches that are measured by the hour will die with the hour.**
(President Thomas Jefferson)
以時間長短來衡量的講演，會隨著時間的流逝而被遺忘。

8 慣用語

a 逐一地

- day by day 逐日地
- item by item 逐條地
- little by little 逐漸地
- one by one 一個一個地
- step by step 逐步地
- week by week 一個星期又一個星期

・Kay said her mom's health was improving little by little/step by step/day by day. 凱説她媽媽的健康在逐漸／逐步／逐日改善。

b 靠自己；獨自地

- (all) by yourself 靠你自己
- (all) by itself 靠它自己
- (all) by himself 靠他自己
- (all) by myself 靠我自己

・I went to talk to the doctor all by myself.
我獨自去跟醫生談話。 → alone

・Henry has learned Chinese all by himself.
亨利全靠自修學會了中文。 → independently

c 靠運氣；失誤

- by mistake 錯誤地
- by luck 出於好運

・By a stroke of luck, she was elected president. 她選上總裁全憑運氣。

・Sorry, Jake, I put salt into your tea by mistake.
對不起，傑克，我錯把鹽倒進你的茶裡了。

d by the way 順便一提

・By the way, his English is getting better day by day.
對了，他的英語一天比一天進步了呢。

e 依照、根據（某種標準，某種規定）

- by modern standards 依照現代標準
- by any standards 依照任何標準
- by somebody's standards 依照某人的標準
- act by the rules 按規定行事

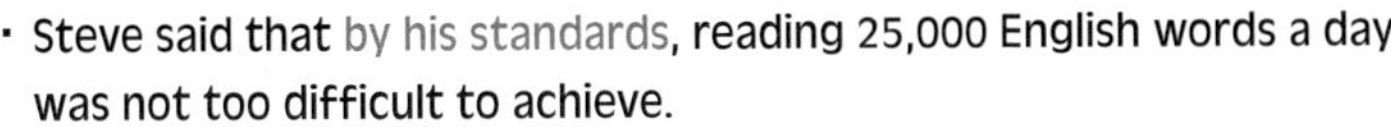

- **Steve said that by his standards, reading 25,000 English words a day was not too difficult to achieve.**
  史蒂夫說，按照他的標準，一天閱讀 25,000 個英文字並不難。

- **I ask you to judge me by the enemies I have made.**
  (President Franklin Delano Roosevelt) 請你以我所樹立的敵人來評價我。

5 between, among

1 剛好兩個實體，只用 between：當具體指定了兩個人或物供選擇時，只能用 between，不能用 among。

- the choice between good and evil 善惡之間的抉擇
- between right and wrong 對錯之間
- the difference between night and day 黑夜和白天的區別

- **"I sat between my parents at the party," said Pat.**
  派特說：「聚會上我坐在父母中間。」
  ↑ 父母是兩個人（兩個具體的實體），因此用 between。

- **The long friendship between Great Britain and the United States is valuable.** 英美之間長久的友誼很珍貴。
  ↑ between 與兩個國家（Great Britain 和 the United States）連用。

- **Just between you and me, I like Lulu better than I like Sue.**
  不要告訴別人喔，我喜歡露露勝過喜歡蘇。 → between 與代名詞 you 和 me 連用。

- **Jenny and Danny sat side by side between the two huge rocks.**
  珍妮和丹尼肩並肩地坐在那兩塊巨石中間。

2 三個及三個以上實體（用 among 或 between）

a among 指**某個人或物在特定的一整群人或物之中**的狀態。把人或物看作是某個組織或整體的一部分（one of/some of），也要用 among。

- **Jenny and Danny sat among the huge rocks.**
珍妮和丹尼坐在巨石中間。
↳ among 指某人或某物在一群東西中間。

- **My little girl crawled among a football, doll, toy robot, and pinecone.**
我的小女孩在一個足球、一個洋娃娃、一個玩具機器人和一個松果中間爬行。
↳ among 表示在一個地方移動，而周圍被人或東西包圍著。

- **Emma is among the best of the young actresses in Africa.**
愛瑪是非洲最優秀的一位年輕演員。
↳ among 指某人或某物是某個整體的一部分（= one of）。

- **"Divide the candy among you," instructed Sue.**
蘇指示說：「你們自己把糖果分一分。」
↳ among 指每人分一份。

- **Among other things, I enjoy reading and writing.**
除了別的愛好，我還喜歡閱讀和寫作。
↳ among other things 是固定片語，指「除了別的以外」。

b between 也可以用來指「在三者或三者以上」，這時將這些實體看作**獨立的個體**，而不是總體，強調每個個體之間的關係，指「每兩者之間」。當提及的各個實體是用來確定一個範圍界限，那麼表示在這個範圍內時，也要用 between。

- a treaty between four powers 四大強國之間的條約
↳ 獨立的個體

- **They searched the area between the river, the university, and the lake.** 他們搜尋了河流、大學、湖泊之間的區域。

- **It was reported that the truck driver who caused the accident had been drinking beer between stops.**
據報導，那位肇事的卡車司機在每次停車休息之間都不斷地喝啤酒。
↳ 表示特定的範圍：他停車的公路上。

- **She takes the flight between Iran, Pakistan, and Afghanistan.**
  她乘坐的航班來往於伊朗、巴基斯坦和阿富汗之間。

c between 也可以指一個（人或物）與一組（人或物）之間。

- **There is no disagreement between Mary and her three brothers.**
  瑪麗和她的三個兄弟之間並未意見相左。
  ↑ 一個人和一組人，用 between。

d 表示比較和相互關係時，要用 between，不用 among。

- a difference between . . . ……之間的區別
- a connection between . . . ……之間的聯繫
- a friendship between . . . ……之間的友誼
- a link between . . . ……之間的關係

- **Do you know the differences between soccer, rugby, and American football?** 你知道英式足球、橄欖球和美式足球之間的區別嗎？

Diving Deep Into English 59 用 between 還是 among?

❶ 許多文法書說，between 只用於兩者之間，不能用於兩者以上，這是錯誤的說法。涉及兩個以上、數目不明確的實體（人或物）時，要根據作者或講話人的意圖來決定究竟要用 between 還是 among。

❷ 當這些實體被看作相互獨立的個體或單位（distinct individuals or units）時，無論是兩個還是兩個以上的人或物，都要用 between。

❸ 當這些實體被看作一個整體／群體（group or mass）時，用 among。在正式英語中，among 只與兩個以上的人或物相關。某人／物在一群人或物之中，用 among。

❹ 若指定具體兩個實體（人或物），就只能用 between，如 between her brother and mother（在她哥哥和母親之間）、to choose between tea and coffee（在茶和咖啡之間選擇）。

Diving Deep Into English 60 between . . . and . . ./ from . . . to . . . 在 . . . 之間

❶ between 和 and 連用，from 和 to 連用。

- **Was it sometime between midnight and 12:15 a.m. that you heard an owl hoot and a wolf howl?**
  = Was it sometime from midnight to 12:15 a.m. that you heard an owl hoot and a wolf howl?
  你是在午夜至淩晨 12 點 15 分之間聽見貓頭鷹和狼叫的嗎？

❷ 當「between . . . and . . .」後面接同一個單數名詞（比如：floor）時，between 後面的名詞（floor）可以被省略，這時 and 後面的名詞就要用複數（floors、streets）。

❸ 當「from . . . to . . .」後面接同一個單數名詞（比如：floor）時，from 後面的名詞（floor）可以被省略，這時 to 後面的名詞仍然用單數（floor）。

- between the 1st floor and the 3rd floor
  = between the 1st and the 3rd floors 在一樓到三樓之間
- from the 1st floor to the 3rd floor
  = from the 1st to the 3rd floor 從一樓到三樓

6 besides, except (for), but

1 besides 和 except (for)

a besides 表示「包括、加之」；如同 with、as well as 或 plus (+)。

b except 表示「不包括、例外」；如同 without、with the exception of、other than 或 minus (-)。

- **Besides Mark, Sue and Lulu went to the park.**
  除了馬克，蘇和露露也去了公園。 → 馬克去了公園。

- **We all decided not to drink any alcohol except (for) Paul.**
  = Except for Paul, we all decided not to drink any alcohol.
  除了保羅外，我們大家決定一點酒都不喝。 → 保羅決定喝酒。

2 except 和 except for

a except = except for：except 和 except for 都表示「不包括在內」；都可用在以下表概括性的詞之後：

- all
- anything
- everybody
- no
- whole
- anybody
- every
- everything
- nowhere

・Nobody listened to me except for Amy.
= Nobody listened to me except Amy. 除了艾咪以外，沒有人聽了我的話。
↑ nobody 後面既可用 except，又可用 except for。

b except ≠ except for：但如果 all、every、nobody、anybody 這類詞在句子的後面，那麼，句首就要用 except for，不能用 except。

・Except for Ms. Tool, nobody dove into the swimming pool.
除了圖爾女士外，沒有人跳進游泳池。
↑ nobody 在句子的後面，句首要用 except for 而不用 except。

c except ≠ except for：如果句中沒有 all、every、nobody、anybody 這類詞，要用 except for，不用 except。

・Paul cleaned the fifth floor except for the meeting hall.
除了會議廳，保羅把五樓的其他地方都打掃了。

d except ≠ except for：在介系詞片語、不定式動詞或子句前用 except（這種用法的 except 是連接詞）。except for 後面只能接名詞或代名詞。

・Yesterday Lily did not laugh except when she saw the giraffe.
昨天莉莉看見長頸鹿時才笑了笑，其餘時間都沒有笑過。
↑ 在子句前用連接詞 except，而不用複合介系詞 except for。

・The representative of the shipping line had nothing to tell us except that the ship had been delayed. → 在子句前用連接詞 except。
航運公司的代表除了告訴我們船延誤了，就什麼也沒有告訴我們。

・Jane did nothing except complain all the time on our train trip to Spain. 在我們乘火車去西班牙的路途中，珍除了抱怨，就什麼也沒有做。
↑ 在不定式動詞前要用連接詞 except，而不用 except for；在連接詞 except 前如果有 nothing，anything 等字，就要用「except + 動詞原形」（如：did nothing except complain）。

- While picking grapes off a vine, Jane did not open her mouth except to complain about the hot sunshine.
  珍在摘採葡萄藤架上的葡萄時，沒有開口講話，除了抱怨陽光太熱之外。
  ⮤ 在 except 前如果沒有 nothing、anything 這類字，except 後面接帶 to 的不定式。

e **except ≠ except for**：表示「要不是由於」（= if it were not for; but for），要用「except for + 名詞」，不用「except + 名詞」。口語中也可用連接詞「except + that 子句」，表示「要不是、但是」。

- I would travel around the world except for a lack of money.
  要不是因為缺錢，我會去環遊世界。
  ⮤ except for = but for = if it were not for

- He is a good husband except for his inability to save money.
  他是個好丈夫，只是他缺乏存錢的能力。

- I would have watched the weight lifting competition, except that I had to work late.
  〔口語〕要不是因為得加班，我就會看那場舉重比賽。
  ⮤ 介系詞後面不可以接 that 子句。這裡的 except 是連接詞。
  「except + that 子句」，常用於口語中，指「若不是因為」。

- I could have played in that volleyball game, except that I overslept.
  〔口語〕我本來可以參加那場排球賽，但是我睡過了頭。
  ⮤ except 在這裡是連接詞。

3 except 和 but

but 也可以作介系詞，意思等同於 except (for)（除了……之外），尤其用在 nothing、nobody、all 等字的後面。

- No one in our class knows how to ski but you and me.
  = No one in our class knows how to ski except (for) you and me.
  Everyone but/except him wants tea. 除了他以外，大家都想喝茶。
  » 參見 81 頁〈10 except 和 but 後面，要用受格代名詞〉。

同形的副詞和介系詞

1 behind、down、in、up，是介系詞還是副詞？

有些副詞也可以作介系詞用，例如 behind、down、in、over、under、up 等，那麼，如何辨別一個詞到底是副詞，還是介系詞呢？其實很簡單！如果這些字後面接了**受詞**，就是作**介系詞**用；如果沒有接受詞，就是作**副詞**用。

- Andrew is like a stubborn mule and doesn't like to fall behind schedule. 安德魯就像一頭固執的騾子，不喜歡進度落後。 → 介系詞
- Those that lack education lag behind. 缺乏教育的人會落後。 → 副詞

- I followed him down the mountain. 我跟在他後面，朝山下走。 → 介系詞
- Please ask that clown with the tall hat to sit down.
請叫那位戴著高帽子的小丑坐下來。 → 副詞

- Paul is in the mall. 保羅在購物中心。 → 介系詞
- Please ask Kim to come in. 請金姆進來。 → 副詞

- She is climbing up the giant statue's leg. 她在爬那座大雕像的腿。 → 介系詞
- It's 7 a.m., and I bet Mike is not up yet.
現在是早上七點，我打賭邁克還沒有起床。 → 副詞

2 分辨副詞與介系詞

1 「介系詞 + 名詞」的介系詞片語：下列片語中的 behind、down、in、up 都接有受詞，所以是介系詞，這些片語稱為介系詞片語，又因為在句中起到副詞的作用，故也稱為副詞片語。

- behind schedule 進度落後
- in the mall 在購物中心裡
- down the mountain 下山
- up the giant statue's leg 在巨大雕像的腿上

2 **不及物的片語動詞**：下列片語動詞中，behind、down、in、up 後面沒有受詞，因此為副詞，而非介系詞。

- to lag behind 落後
- to come in 進來
- to sit down 坐下
- be (is) up 起床

3 **及物的片語動詞**：下列及物片語動詞中的 up、in、on、off 是副詞，不是介系詞。

- to look up the definition 查詢定義
- to put on a puppet show 表演木偶戲
- to trade in RVs 從事房車買賣
- to write off our losses 勾消我們的虧損

4 鑑別方法：觀察**片語動詞**（如：put on a show）或**動詞片語**（如：dance on the stage）後面的名詞，是否可以移到介系詞或副詞前面，如果可以，就是副詞；如果不可以，就是介系詞（因為介系詞後須接名詞）。

- to write off <u>your losses</u> on your taxes = to write <u>your losses</u> off on your taxes 在賦稅時購銷你的虧損
  ↳ off 是副詞。
- to turn on <u>the TV</u> = turn <u>the TV</u> on 打開電視
  ↳ on 是副詞。
- to keep off the grass 不踩草地
  ↳ off 是介系詞。
  ↳ 注意：to keep the grass off 是錯誤用法。
- to dance on the stage 舞臺上跳舞
  ↳ on 是介系詞。
  ↳ 注意：to dance the stage on 是錯誤用法。

・**She put on <u>her jacket</u> and went outside.**
= She put <u>her jacket</u> on and went outside. 她穿上夾克，走到戶外。
↳ 名詞 jacket 可以移到 on 前面，變成 put her jacket on，所以 on 是副詞。

・**Are you going to take part in <u>next month's beauty contest</u> in Taipei?**
你要參加下月在臺北舉辦的選美會嗎？
↳ 名詞 beauty contest 不能移到 in 前面，所以這個片語動詞中的 in 是介系詞。

和特定介系詞搭配的名詞、動詞和形容詞

在慣用語中，許多名詞、動詞和形容詞都搭配特定的介系詞，不能光靠猜測去選用介系詞，須熟記與特定介系詞搭配的片語。常用的介系詞片語列舉如下：

1. afraid of 害怕（不用 by）

- Are your aunts afraid of cockroaches and ants? 你的阿姨們怕不怕蟑螂螞蟻？
- Peg didn't jump off the tree, because she was afraid of breaking her leg. 佩格沒有從樹上跳下去，因為她怕把腿摔斷。

2. angry with a person for doing something 因為某事生某人的氣

- I am still angry with Amy for lying to me. 艾咪對我撒謊，我還在生她的氣。

3. angry at or about something 為某事生氣

- Eve got so angry about it that she began to shout. 伊芙對那件事氣得大吼大叫了起來。

4. apologize to somebody for (doing) something 為某事向某人道歉

- You should apologize to her for acting so rude and crude. 你應該為自己如此粗魯的行為向她道歉。

5. apply for a position 應聘職位

- Is Eve going to apply for a new job, or is she going to leave and marry Bob? 伊芙打算找個新工作，還是打算離開，然後與鮑勃結婚？

6. argue about something 為某事爭吵

- You and Kay argued about silly things every hour of the day. 你和凱無時不為愚蠢的小事爭吵。

7. **arrive at/in** 到達（不用 to）

- What time did you arrive at Newark Liberty International Airport?
  你是什麼時候到達紐阿克自由國際機場的？
- When did Jane arrive in Spain? 珍何時到達西班牙的？

8. **ask about/inquire about** 詢問某人或某物的資訊

- Don't ask about/inquire about his private life. 不要打聽他的私人生活。
- I am calling to ask about/inquire about my mother, Susan Smith. How is she doing now?
  = I am calling to ask after/inquire after my mother, Susan Smith. How is she doing now?
  我正在打電話要問候我母親蘇珊·史密斯。她現在怎樣呢？
  ⮤ 英式用 ask after/inquire after 詢問某人狀況，尤其是健康狀況，美式用 ask about/inquire about。

9. **ask for** 要求；請求見到

- I asked for a cup of coffee, not tea. 我要了一杯咖啡，沒要茶。
- She asked for the manager. 她要求見經理。
  ⮤ ask for 是片語動詞。
  » 參見 451 頁〈Part 5 片語動詞〉。

10. **bad at** 不擅長（不用 in）

- Jake is bad at teaching his son how to add. 傑克不擅長教他兒子加法。

11. **because of** 因為

- Ms. Rice bought the car because of its low price.
  賴斯小姐因為便宜而買下那輛車。

12. **care about** 關懷

- She doesn't care about anyone except herself.
  除了她自己，她不關心任何人。 → feel concern or interest

13. **care for** 喜歡；照料；想要

- Do you really care for her? 你真的喜歡她嗎？ → feel love or a liking

- Please care for my baby while I am away.
= Please take care of/look after my baby while I am away. 我不在時，請照顧好我的寶貝。
- Would you care for a cup of milk tea? 你想喝杯奶茶嗎？ →want/wish for
  ↑ take care of、look after, care for 是片語動詞。

14. compare to 比作（兩個不同事物，不能用 with。）
- Mr. Lee often compares life to a river. 李先生常常把生命比作成河流。
  ↑ life 與 river 是完全不同的東西，儘管兩者之間有相似之處。

15. compare with/to 比較（兩個類似事物）
- Please compare the London of today with the London of the late 1940s. 請把今日的倫敦與 20 世紀 40 年代末的倫敦進行比較。
  ↑ 兩個類似之物進行比較：the London of today 和 the London of the late 1940s.
  ↑ 比較兩個類似事物，傳統用法只用 with，現代用法也可以用 to，但更常用 with。
- Compared with/to me, Paul looks pretty tall.
和我比起來，保羅看上去就很高啊。
  ↑ 人與人進行對比。在過去分詞 compared 後面，無論是比較同類型的或不同類型的事物，to 和 with 都可以用。

16. congratulate/congratulations on 祝賀
- Kay's dad congratulated her on getting a pay raise.
凱的爸爸恭喜她加薪。
- Congratulations on your marriage and recent purchase of a baby carriage! 恭喜你結婚了，也恭喜你剛買了嬰兒車！

17. convenient for 合適；方便
- What time will be most convenient for you? 你什麼時候最方便？

18. convenient to 近而方便（得到）
- The beautiful island of St. Vincent has a location convenient to anyone in Miami who wants a lovely weekend vacation.
美麗的聖文森特島地理位置優越，對任何想度過一個愉快週末的邁阿密人來說，都非常方便。

19. depend/dependent on 依靠；取決於（不用 from 或 of）

- She said the beach party would depend on the weather.
  她說海灘聚會的舉辦要視天氣而定。
- His theory is that modern youth should work hard, make their own choices, and not always be dependent on their parents.
  他的理論是，現代青年應該努力工作，自己作主，不要總是依靠父母。

比較 independent of 不必依賴

- With a car, you can be independent of public transportation and travel around the whole nation.
  有了車子，你就不用搭大眾交通工具來全國走透透了。
  ↳ independent 後面則要用 of。

20. different from/than 不同

- The effects of the disease were different from what the doctor had told Louise. 這種疾病的影響，和醫生對露易絲講的不一樣。
  ↳ different from 較為常用，不過在美式口語中也可以用 different than。不過，在下面的例句中用 than 則較為自然。
- He views love in a different way than his wife does. → 較自然
  他對愛情的看法與他妻子相左。
- He views love in a different way from the way in which his wife does. → 不太自然

21. disappointed with somebody 對某人感到失望

- Don't be disappointed with me. I'll do better next time. 不要對我失望啦，我下次會做好一些。

22. disappointed with/at/about something 對某事感到失望

- Pam's parents are pretty disappointed with/at/about the results of her final exams. 潘姆的父母對她的期末考結果非常失望。

23. discuss something 討論某事（不加介系詞）

- Will Ann discuss her divorce? 安會討論她離婚的事嗎？

24. discussion about something 討論某事

- I had a long discussion with Louise about love and divorce. 我跟露易絲長談過愛情和離婚的事。

discussion about love and divorce

25. divide into 分成（不用 in）

- Art's computer classroom is divided into four parts. 亞特的電腦教室被分成四部分。

26. dream of 夢想；渴望

- As a little kid, I often looked at the stars and dreamed of someday exploring Mars. 我小時候常望著天上的星星，夢想有一天上火星探險。

dream of

27. dream about/of 夢見（睡眠中）

- Why does Jane often dream about/dream of flying to the moon? 為什麼珍常夢見飛向月球？

dream about

28. dressed in 穿著（不用 with）

- Is that pretty Kay dressed in a pink miniskirt today? 那個俏麗的凱今天穿了一件粉紅色的迷你裙嗎？

29. drive into 撞上（不用 against）

- I begged her not to flunk me on my driving test simply because I drove into a big skunk. 我懇求她不要因為我撞上一隻大臭鼬，就不發駕照給我。

drive into

30. enter a place 進入某處（不加介系詞）

- Danny entered my office and told me he was going to start up a new company. 丹尼走進我的辦公室告訴我，他要著手成立一家新公司。

31. enter into an agreement/a dialog/a discussion 進入談判、會談、討論

- Danny and Jenny have entered into discussions with the Stars & Mars Company. 丹尼和珍妮已經開始和「恆星與火星」公司談判了。

↑ enter into 是片語動詞。

32. example of 範例（不用 for）

- That textbook shows examples of compositions with errors in using prepositions. 那本課本列舉了誤用介系詞的作文範例。

33. explain something to somebody 對某人解釋某事
（不是 explain somebody something）

- Could you please explain to Louise how to put the cheese on the peas? 請你向露易絲解釋如何把起司撒在豌豆上，好嗎？
- Mr. Lee, could you please explain this grammar rule to me?
李老師，可以請您跟我說一下這個文法規則嗎？

34. get in/into (or get out of) a car/taxi/boat 上（下）汽車 / 計程車 / 小船

- As soon as Pete got into his van, he saw a huge snake coiled up on the back seat. 彼特一進入他的廂型車，就看見一隻大蛇盤繞在車子的後座上。
- Pete got out of his van and ran as fast as he could to find Ann.
彼特從箱型車裡出來，以最快的速度跑去找安。

35. get on/onto (or get off) a train/plane/bus/ship/bike/horse
上（下）火車 / 飛機 / 公車 / 船 / 自行車 / 馬

- Gus decided to get on the bus. 加斯決定上公車。
- President Powers will be getting off the plane in two hours.
還有兩個小時，鮑爾斯總統就要下飛機了。

be good at telling lies

36. good at 擅長（不用 in）

- Isn't Tom good at telling a pack of lies to his mom! 湯姆真會對他媽媽撒謊！

37. hear about/hear of 聽說；得知

- I heard about/of your promotion from Sam. 我從山姆那裡得知你晉級。

38. hear from 收到……的信／來電（等）

- I haven't heard from Sherry since she moved to the Philippines.
自從雪麗搬去菲律賓之後，我就沒有她的消息了。 → hear from 是片語動詞。

39. **impressed with/by** 對……印象深刻

- Are you impressed with/ by her artwork?
  你對她的藝術品印象深刻嗎？

40. **increase in activity, output, etc.** 活動或產量的增加（不用 of）

- Leading language experts know that fluency requires you to make a huge increase in reading.
  知名的語言專家知道，語言要流利，就得大幅地增加閱讀量。

41. **independent/independence from** 獨立；自主

- Did India become independent from Britain in 1947?
  = Did India gain independence from Britain in 1947?
  印度是 1947 年脫離英國獨立的嗎？

42. **independent of** 不受……支配；不依賴……的

- Does Jenny want to be independent of her family's money?
  珍妮不想依賴家裡的錢嗎？

43. **insist on** 堅持認為；強烈要求（不用 to）

- Coco insisted on getting a job three year ago.
  三年前，可可堅持要找工作。 → insist on 是片語動詞。

44. **instead of** 代替（接名詞、副詞或形容詞）

- I decided to immigrate to Australia instead of America.
  我決定移民到澳洲，而不是到美國。 → 名詞 + instead of + 名詞（America）

- Dirk stayed at home all day instead of going to work.
  德克整天待在家裡，沒有去上班。 → 動詞 + instead of + 動名詞（going）

- "Treat the cat gently instead of roughly," suggested Pat.
  「不要對那隻貓粗暴，要溫柔。」派特建議。 → 副詞 + instead of + 副詞（roughly）

- You should be tough instead of soft when dealing with a person like Andrew. 你對付安德魯這種人應該要強硬，而不是軟弱。
  ↳ 形容詞 + instead of + 形容詞（soft）

1 instead of 是複合介系詞。和其他介系詞一樣，instead of 用在名詞或動名詞的前面，但和其他介系詞不同的是，instead of 後面也可以跟形容詞或副詞。

1 instead 單獨用時被看作是**副詞**，用在句子的末尾。不可以在名詞前用副詞 instead。

比較 **instead（副詞）反而；卻；替代**

- I decided to immigrate to Australia instead.
  我卻決定移居澳洲。（而沒有移居其他地方）
- Dirk stayed at home all day instead.
  結果，德克一整天都待在家裡。（而沒有外出）
- "Treat the cat gently instead," suggested Pat.
  派特建議說：「應該對這隻貓溫柔一點。」（而不要粗暴）
- You should be tough instead. 你反而應該潑辣一點。（而不要軟弱）

45. interest/interested in 對⋯⋯感興趣（不用 for）

- When did she first show an interest in Mars?
  她是什麼時候開始表現出對火星感興趣的？
- Are you really interested in English grammar?
  你真的對英文文法感興趣？

46. kind to 善待（不用 with）

- Please be kind to your little sister Louise. 請善待你的小妹妹露易絲。

47. lack of (n.) 缺少

- My bitterness comes from your total lack of respect for females.
  你對女性毫不尊重，給我帶來很大的痛苦。

48. lack (v.) 缺乏（不加介系詞）

- Although the lunar colonies lacked laser cannons, they attacked the deadly UFO. 雖然月球殖民地缺乏鐳射炮，他們還是擊敗了致命的不明飛行物。

49. be lacking in 缺乏

- She is lacking in grace. 她不夠優雅。

50. laugh at 嘲笑

- Don't laugh at Jim just because of his heavy accent.
  不要因為吉姆口音重就嘲笑他。 → laugh at（嘲笑）是片語動詞。

51. laugh about/at 因……而笑

- Someday Jill will laugh about her first kiss.
  總有一天，潔兒將對她的初吻感到好笑。
  ↑ 因想起以前某些有趣的事、人或情形而發笑，用 laugh about。
- I didn't laugh at his crude jokes. 對他粗野的玩笑，我沒有笑。
  ↑ 因某些有趣的事、人或情形而發笑，而這些事情就發生在眼前時，用 laugh at。

52. listen to 聽，聽從

- My brother always tries to listen to our mother.
  我哥總是盡量聽媽媽的話。 → listen to 是片語動詞。

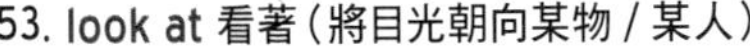

53. look at 看著（將目光朝向某物／某人）

- Why is Mat looking at my dress like that?
  麥特為什麼用那種眼神看我的洋裝？

54. look after (= take care of) 照顧，照看

- Are you going to look after your baby sister tonight? 今晚你要照顧你的小妹嗎？

55. look for (= try to find) 尋找（努力要找到）

- The Mount Hood police are looking for the robber in our neighborhood. 胡德山的警方正在鄰近地區尋找那個強盜。
  ↑ look at、look after、look for 都是片語動詞。

56. marriage to; get/be married to 結婚（不用 with）

- Is Eve really going to get married to Steve? 伊芙真要跟史蒂夫結婚嗎？
- Eve's marriage to Steve will be a happy match made in heaven.
  伊芙與史蒂夫的婚姻將是上天安排的美滿婚姻。

57. nice to 善待（不用 with）

- My brother said we should be nice to each other. 我哥說我們要善待彼此。

58. operate on a patient 為病人動手術

- Kate came back home late, because she had operated on a little girl. 凱特很晚回家，因為她為一個小女孩動了手術。

59. pleased with somebody 對某人感到滿意

- My boyfriend Jim is very polite, and I am really pleased with him. 我男朋友吉姆很有禮貌，我對他十分滿意。

60. pleased with/about something 對某事／某物感到滿意

- Bob is pleased with/about his new job. 鮑勃對他的新工作很滿意。

61. point at/to/toward 指向

- "Your dog is over there," said Claire, pointing at/to/toward the garden. 克萊兒指著花園說：「你的狗在那邊。」

62. point something at 把……指向；把……對準（挑釁性）

- Don't point your finger at me. 不要把你的手指指向我。

63. polite to 對……有禮貌（不用 with）

- Mom told my sister, my brother, and me to be polite to one another. 媽媽要我妹妹、我弟弟和我對彼此有禮貌。

64. prevent . . . from + -ing 阻止（不用不定式）

- Last night the loud beeping noise from the house next door prevented me from sleeping.
昨晚從隔壁房子傳來很大的嗶嗶聲，害我睡不著覺。

65. proof of 證據（不用 for）

- She provided clear proof of my innocence.
她提供了明顯的證據，證明我是清白的。

66. **reason for 理由（不用 of）**

- What was the reason for Mary canceling her date with Jerry? 瑪麗為什麼取消與傑瑞的約會？

remind me of my home

67. **remind someone of 使某人回想起**

- The beautiful view reminded me of my home in Tibet. 這片美麗的風景使我想起了我的家鄉西藏。

68. **remind someone about 提醒**

- Kay, please remind me about my appointment with the president next Monday. 凱，請提醒我下星期一與總裁有約。

69. **responsible for (doing) something 對某事負責**

- Was the truck driver responsible for the accident? 那位卡車司機是否該為這次事故負責？
- Does Dirk understand he is responsible for doing his chores and homework?
= Does Dirk understand that he has (the) responsibility for doing his chores and homework? 德克知道他有責任做他的家務事和家庭作業嗎？

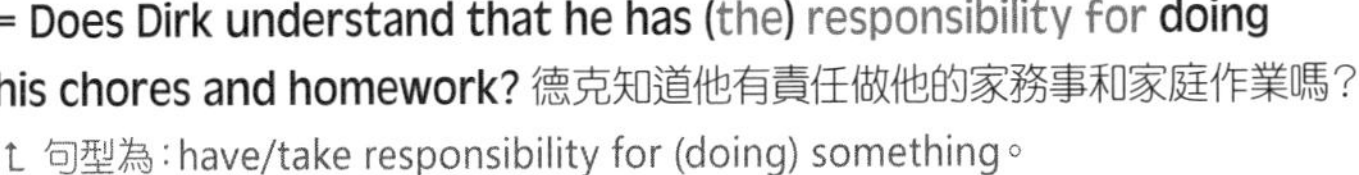
Who is responsible for the accident?

↳ 句型為：have/take responsibility for (doing) something。

70. **responsible to somebody 對某人負責（有責任的）**

- The American President is responsible to the American people. 美國總統要對美國人民負責。

71. **rude to 對某人無禮（不用 with）**

- Your slurs are rude to all females. 你的毀謗冒犯了所有女性。

72. **search (= look through; look everywhere in/on) 搜查（不加介系詞）**

- Today at customs, the officers searched everybody's luggage.
海關工作人員今天搜查了每個人的行李。

73. **search for (= look for) 搜尋；尋找**

- The police were searching for weapons and drugs at the airport.
警方在機場搜尋武器和毒品。　→ search for 是片語動詞。

74. shocked at/by 對某事感到震驚

- Eve was shocked at/by the news of the terrorist bombing in Tel Aviv. 恐怖分子在特拉維夫市的轟炸，讓伊芙震驚萬分。

75. shout at 對……吼叫（挑釁性）

- Mat shouldn't shout at you like that. 麥特不應該對你那樣吼叫。

76. shout to (= call to) 對……喊叫（沒有敵意）

- Gus shouted to us to come into the garage and see his new bus. 加斯對我們喊叫，要我們進車庫看他新買的公車。

77. smile at 對某人微笑

- Whenever Kyle smiles at Amy, she has trouble with math for a while. 每當凱爾對艾咪微笑，她就會一時做不出數學題。

78. sorry about something that has happened 對某事的發生感到遺憾

- I am sorry about Bob not getting that job. 鮑勃沒得到那份工作，我感到遺憾。

79. sorry about/for something that one has done 為做出某事感到抱歉

- I'm really sorry about/for losing your cellphone. 我弄丟你的手機，我很抱歉。

80. sorry for somebody 對某人感到同情

- Jim is really poor, and I feel sorry for him. 吉姆真的很窮，我對他深表同情。

81. speak to/with somebody 與某人談話

- I spoke to/with Ms. Jan Tower for about an hour. 我與簡·陶爾女士談了一個鐘頭左右。

speak to somebody

82. suffer from 受……之苦

- Grandpa Jones is suffering from six broken bones. 鐘斯爺爺飽受了折斷六根骨頭的痛苦。

83. surprised at/by 對某事物感到驚訝

- Joe wasn't surprised at/by the breaking news that a big UFO had landed in Tokyo.
  一個巨大不明飛行物在東京登陸，但這則驚人的新聞並沒有使喬感到驚訝。

84. take part in 參加（不用 at）

- Is Margo going to take part in next month's beauty contest in Chicago? 瑪歌要參加下個月在芝加哥舉行的選美比賽嗎？
  ⤷ take part in 是片語動詞。

85. think about 思索（考慮了較長時間）

- I haven't thought about my divorce for a long time. 我很久沒有去想我的離婚了。

86. be thinking about 想（此刻腦海正浮現的事）

- "What's Mary thinking about right now?" "She is probably thinking about her hometown again."「瑪麗在想什麼呢？」「她可能又在想家了。」

87. think of 突然想到；想起來；認為（用來徵求意見）

- I suddenly thought of Bob. Perhaps he could do the job. 我突然想到了鮑勃。也許他可以做這項工作。
- What do you think of my new cellphone?
  你覺得我的新手機如何？

88. be thinking of 考慮（考慮一個計畫，但沒有最終確定）

- Are you thinking of applying for a job with NASA?
  你在考慮去美國國家太空總署應聘工作嗎？
  ⤷ think of 和 think about 是片語動詞。

89. the thought of 念頭（不用 to）

- The very thought of facing Mark at school makes me feel sick. 一想到在學校要面對馬克，我就想吐。

90. throw . . . at somebody 扔向某人（挑釁性）

・ I remember throwing a shoe at Mark and then vomiting in his canoe.
我記得我曾經把一隻鞋朝馬克扔去，然後又在他的獨木舟裡嘔吐。

91. throw . . . to somebody 扔給某人（沒有敵意，例如在球賽中）

・ Jim is teaching his dog how to catch the ball and throw it to him.
吉姆在教他的狗如何接住球，再把球扔給他。

92. translate into 翻譯（不用 in）

・ Trish has translated twenty-two books from Japanese into English.
翠西已經把 22 本日文書翻譯成了英語。

93. typical of 有代表性的；典型的；特有的（不用 for）

・ Your aggressive attitude is typical of men who are rude toward females. 只有對婦女粗魯的男人才會具有你那種挑釁的態度。

94. wait for somebody/something 等待

・ Gus was attacked from behind while he was waiting for a bus.
加斯在等公車時，有人從背後攻擊他。 → wait for 是片語動詞。

95. wait on somebody 侍候；服務

・ Don't wait on him or he will become lazy. 不要侍候他，否則他會變懶惰。

96. wonder about (= to think curiously about) 納悶；想知道

・ Do you wonder about the origin of all the ice on the Moon? 你想知道月球上所有的冰的起源嗎？

wonder about
想知道

97. wonder at (= to be surprised at) 覺得驚奇

・ I wondered at Sally's ability to deal with such a crisis.
我對莎莉應付此類危機的能力感到驚訝。

98. wrong with 問題（不用 about）

・ What's wrong with Lilly, and why is she so cranky toward Sally?
莉莉怎麼了？她幹嘛對莎莉這麼暴躁？

UNIT

10 動詞

Verbs

動詞的定義與類型

動詞是句子的重點，用來描述行為動作、感覺或心理過程。不同的動詞，接不同種類的詞和文法結構。

動詞種類	說明	舉例
主要動詞／述語動詞	每一個完整的句子都包括一個主要動詞，即述語動詞。	包括行為動詞、連綴動詞、使役動詞、及物和不及物動詞。
助動詞	與主要動詞連用，構成疑問句、否定句、進行式、完成式或被動語態。	do, have, be
情態動詞／情態助動詞	與主要動詞連用，表達「必然性」、「可能性」或「許可」等。	can, may, must
行為動詞	表示「活動或動作」。	play, read, run
連綴動詞	表示「狀態或特性」（包括感官動詞和狀態動詞）。	be
	感官動詞：表達人的器官感覺。	look, smell, feel, taste, sound
	狀態動詞：表示「過程」（從一種狀態變成另一種狀態）。	appear, become, get, grow
使役動詞	表示一個行為引發另一個行為的發生，或某人讓另一人做某事。	make, have, let
擁有動詞	表示「擁有」。	have, has
there is/are 動詞結構	表示某處存在某物／某人。	there is . . ., there are . . .
及物動詞	要接受詞。	arrest, love, memorize
不及物動詞	不接受詞。	come, go, sleep
規則動詞	動詞詞態作規則變化。（過去式和過去完成式）	call → called → called
不規則動詞	動詞詞態作不規則變化。（過去式和過去完成式）	break → broke → broken
單一動詞	由一個字組成。	play, leave, talk
片語動詞	由一個字以上組成。	belong to, run into, get along with

be 動詞

1 be 動詞的現在式 am, is, are 的使用規則

am

I am . . . → Hi, I am Sam. 嗨，我是山姆。

is

he is . . .
she is . . .
it is . . . → She is Emma, my best friend. 她叫愛瑪，我最好的朋友。

單數名詞 + is . . . → Claire is an excellent swimmer. 克萊兒游泳游得很好。

are

we are . . .
your are . . .
they are . . . → We are from Seoul. 我們是從首爾來的。

複數名詞 + are . . . → The trees are tall, the walls are high, and eagles can fly above them all. 樹高牆也高，老鷹可以在它們上方飛翔。

由 and 連接兩個或兩個以上的名詞或代名詞，與 are 連用。 → Bart and his sweetheart are both smart. 巴特和他的情人都很聰明。

2 be 動詞現在式的各種形式

	肯定	肯定縮寫	否定	否定縮寫	疑問
單數	I am	I'm	I am not	I'm not	am I?
	you are	you're	you are not	you're not = you aren't	are you?
	he is	he's	he is not	he's not = he isn't	is he?
	she is	she's	she is not	she's not = she isn't	is she?
	it is	it's	it is not	it's not = it isn't	is it?
複數	we are	we're	we are not	we're not = we aren't	are we?
	you are	you're	you are not	you're not = you aren't	are you?
	they are	they're	they are not	they're not = they aren't	are they?

1 縮寫用法：在口語和非正式用語中常用縮寫。

- She's a friend of Mary's. 她是瑪麗的朋友。
- You're my best friend. 你是我最好的朋友。

2 疑問句：**am, are, is + 主詞**

用 be 動詞提問時，am, are, is 要放在主詞前面。

- "Is this your baggage?" "Yes, it is."
  「這是你的行李嗎？」「是的。」
  ↳ 簡短肯定回答不要用縮寫形式。

- Is the taxi here? 計程車到了嗎？

3 否定句：**主詞 + am, are, is + not**

be 動詞用於否定句時，not 要放在 am, are, is 或 'm, 're, 's 的後面，或用否定的縮寫形式「n't」。

✗ I amn't going out with you or Scot.
✓ I'm not going out with you or Scot. 我不會跟你或史考特約會。

- Kay and Ann are not belly dancers, but they are studying ballet.
  凱和安不是肚皮舞孃，不過她們在學跳芭蕾舞。

- They aren't happy with Sue and her brother Andrew. 他們對蘇和她哥哥安德魯不滿。
- He isn't handsome or smart, but he sure is good at driving a go-cart.
  他長得不帥，也不聰明，但他的確很會開卡丁車。
  ↑ sure（非正式）= surely

go-cart racing

Diving Deep Into English 61 疑問詞與 is 的縮寫形式

疑問詞		加 is 的縮寫	
who 誰	where 何地	who's	where's
what 什麼	why 為何	what's	why's
when 何時	how 如何	when's	how's

↑ when's 是非正式用語

- Pat, who's that? 派特，那是誰？
- What's this? 這是什麼？
- Why's everybody picking on Dee and me? 為什麼人人都在找蒂和我的碴？
- How's your friend Larry? 你的朋友賴瑞還好嗎？
- Sue, when's your baby due? 蘇，你的預產期是什麼時候？ → when's：非正式
- Where's my money? 我的錢在哪裡？

3 be 動詞的過去式 was, were 的使用規則

be 動詞過去式	說明	用法
was	is 和 am 的簡單過去式	I was . . . he was . . . she was . . . it was . . . 單數名詞 + was . . .
were	are 的簡單過去式	you were . . . they were . . . we were . . . 複數名詞 + were . . .

- Where were you last night, Claire? 克萊兒，你昨晚在哪裡？
  ⤴ 指「昨晚」，用過去式（were you . . .?）。
- I was with Jim last night, and we were at the gym.
  昨晚我和吉姆一起在體育館裡。 → 指「昨晚」，用過去式 I was, we were。
- Where was Dwight last night? 昨晚杜威特在哪裡？
  ⤴ 單數名詞要用 was。疑問句要把 were 或 was 放在主詞前面。
- Dwight and I were at home last night. 昨晚杜威特和我一起在家。
  ⤴ 複合主詞要用 were。
- They were not at the art museum yesterday afternoon.
  昨天下午他們不在藝術博物館裡。 → 否定詞 not 位於 were 之後。

4 be 動詞過去式的各種形式

	肯定句	否定句	否定縮寫	疑問句
單數	I was	I was not	I wasn't	was I?
	you were	you were not	you weren't	were you?
	he/she/it was	he/she/it was not	he/she/it wasn't	was he/she/it?
複數	we were	we were not	we weren't	were we?
	you were	you were not	you weren't	were you?
	they were	they were not	they weren't	were they?

- Where were you and Jake during yesterday's earthquake? 昨天地震的時候，你和傑克在哪裡？

- Were you at Kay and Pam's party last Saturday? 你上星期六參加了凱和潘姆的聚會嗎？
  → Yes, I was. 是的，我參加了。
  → No, I wasn't. 沒有啊，我沒有參加。
- Was Kay in the Banana Milkshake Shop yesterday?
  凱昨天在香蕉奶昔商店嗎？
  → Yes, she was. 是的，她在。
  → No, she wasn't. 沒有，她不在。

5 be 動詞的未來式（will be）

	肯定句	肯定縮寫	否定句	否定縮寫	疑問句
單數	I will be	I'll be	I will not be	I won't be	will I be?
	you will be	you'll be	you will not be	you won't be	will you be?
	he/she/it will be	he'll/she'll/it'll be	he/she/it will not be	he/she/it won't be	will he/she/it be?
複數	we will be	we'll be	we will not be	we won't be	will we be?
	you will be	you'll be	you will not be	you won't be	will you be?
	they will be	they'll be	they will not be	they won't be	will they be?

- Jenny says it will be an excellent Christmas party. 珍妮說那將是一次完美的聖誕聚會。
- Lisa thinks we will be able to dance under a full moon during the party.
  麗莎覺得，派對時，我們可以在滿月下跳舞。
- I won't be late to pick up Kate. 我會準時接凱特的。
- Jill thinks everybody will be here on time.
  潔兒認為大家都會準時到達。

- Will your van be full if Jill and her chum come?
  如果潔兒和她的好友一起來，你的廂型車會擠滿人嗎？
  » 關於 will 的詳細說明，參見 553 頁〈2 簡單未來式 will〉。

6 be 動詞的完成式（have/has been, had been）

1 has/have been 是 be 動詞的**現在完成式**。代名詞單數第三人稱（he, she, it）和單數名詞（Amy, my son）用 has been，其餘的用 have been。

- My friend Mary has been to Cairo many times, but I have never been there. 我的朋友瑪麗去過開羅好幾次，但我還沒去過。

2 had been 是 be 動詞的**過去完成式**，不分單複數，用於所有人稱。

- She asked me whether I had been to Israel. 她問我有沒有去過以色列。
  » 參見 589 頁〈Part 9 簡單現在完成式〉，和第 615 頁〈Part 12 簡單過去完成式〉。

連綴動詞

1 連綴動詞的定義與類別

1 大多數動詞用來表達行為或動作，但有些動詞則用來描述或確認句中主詞的**狀態**，這種動詞稱為**連綴動詞**（又稱**連繫動詞**）。連綴動詞連接主詞和主詞補語（主詞補語簡稱為「主補」，又稱「表語」）。

2 **be 動詞**是最常見的連綴動詞，還有其他一些動詞可以用作連綴動詞。

» be 動詞的用法，參見 437 頁〈Part 2 be 動詞〉。

be 動詞（最常見的連綴動詞）	• be • am • is • are • was • were • have/has been • had been • will be • shall be
感官動詞（作連綴動詞用）	• taste 嚐起來 • sound 聽起來 • look 看起來 • smell 聞起來 • feel 覺得
表示**狀態或狀態變化**的詞	• seem 似乎 • grow 漸漸變得 • come 變成 • appear 看起來好像 • turn 變得 • keep 保持某一狀態 • prove 證明是 • remain 保持 • stay 保持某一狀態 • run 變得 • go 變成 • lie 呈 . . . 狀態 • get 成為 • become 開始變得；成為 • turn out 證明是

Diving Deep Into English 62 連綴動詞 be 和助動詞 be

- **Jan is cute in her pink swimsuit.** 簡穿上粉紅色的泳衣很可愛。
  ↳ is 是連綴動詞，接形容詞 cute 作主詞補語，描述主詞的狀態。
- **Joe is leaving Chicago tomorrow.** 喬明天要離開芝加哥。
  ↳ is 是助動詞，協助主要動詞 leaving 構成進行式。

2 連綴動詞的用法

1 主詞 + 連綴動詞 + 主詞補語（名詞 / 代名詞 / 形容詞）

連綴動詞連接句子的主詞（名詞或代名詞）和主詞補語。主詞補語可以是名詞、代名詞或是形容詞，用來修飾句中的主詞，因此在連綴動詞後面作主詞補語的代名詞應該用**主格**。

- **Scot is thirsty and hot.** 史考特又渴又熱。
  ↥ 這個句子不是說明史考特做什麼事（what Scot does），而是描述史考特的狀態（what he is）；「連綴動詞（is）+ 主詞補語（thirsty、hot）」描述主詞的狀態或特性。
- **Those young people are all college students, and they are trying to increase their knowledge.** 那些年輕人都是大學生，他們在努力增長知識。
  ↥ are 是連綴動詞；名詞 students 作主詞補語，說明主詞 Those young people 的身分。
- **Pam felt nervous even though she was well prepared for the exam.** 潘姆為這次考試作了充分的準備，但還是很緊張。
  ↥ felt（feel 的過去式）是連綴動詞；形容詞 nervous 作主詞補語，說明主詞 Pam 的狀態。
- **The hungry child ran wild.** 那個饑餓的孩子開始撒野。
- **The little girl first got mad and then later became sad.** 那個小女孩先是發怒，後來又傷心起來。
- **Sally's face turned red, and she said, "I won't marry Ted."** 莎莉紅著臉說：「我不要嫁給泰德。」
  ↥ become、grow、turn、get、go、come、run 等表「狀態變化」，意思是「變得」。

✗ His room smells badly.

✓ His room smells bad. 他房間的氣味很難聞。

↥ smells 是感官動詞作連綴動詞；形容詞 bad 作主詞補語，修飾主詞 room。與一般行為動詞不同，連綴動詞後面通常不能接副詞，只能接名詞、代名詞或形容詞。

↥ 「連綴動詞 + 形容詞」；「行為動詞 + 副詞」。

✗ It was me who called your niece and the police.

✓ It was I who called your niece and the police.
是我給你的侄女和員警打電話的。

↥ be 動詞（屬於連綴動詞）後面的代名詞要用主格（they, I），不用受格（them, me）。

» 參見 80 頁〈8 動詞「to be」的後面，要用主格代名詞〉。

2 作主詞補語的形容詞或名詞前，有時要用 to be。

a 在 appear 和 seem 後面常接 to be（也可以不要 to be），再接形容詞。

- **She seems (to be) very excited.** 她好像很激動。

b 但在 alive、alone、asleep、awake 等形容詞前面，一定要用 appear to be 或 seem to be。

- **I think you can go in now. He appears to be awake.** 我想你可以進去了。他好像醒了。

c 在「動詞 -ing」前面要用 appear to be 或 seem to be。

- **My cold seems to be growing worse.**
  我的感冒好像更嚴重了。

d 美式英語在名詞前面通常要用 appear to be 或 seem to be。

- **He seems to be a responsible and hardworking employee.** 他好像是一位有責任感而且工作認真的員工。

3 become、get、come、go、grow、turn (into)，都可以用來描述某個變化過程。

a 如果連綴動詞後面的名詞描述某種工作上的變化，要用 become。

- **He became America's ambassador to France.**
  他成了美國的駐法大使。

- **She is on her way to becoming the best surgeon in our city.**
  她就要成為我們城市最優秀的外科醫生了。

b 祈使句和下列片語要用 get。

- get married 結婚
- get lost 走失
- get dressed 穿好衣服
- get broken 破產
- get killed 被殺；死了
- get caught in the rain 被雨淋了

- **Don't get upset about it.** 不要為此感到苦惱。
- **Don't get mad at me.** 不要生我的氣。 → 祈使句用 get。

c go 用來表示某種令人不愉快的變化，例如，某人變聾、啞、瞎、禿頭等。（不用 turn 或 get）。

- go bad 變壞了
- go blind 變瞎
- go deaf 變聾
- go wrong 發生故障
- go missing 失蹤
- go bald 變禿頭

・**Why do people go deaf?** 人為什麼要變聾？

d turn 用來表示某人到了某個年齡；turn into 表示某物質或東西變成另一種。

・**I will turn eighteen next week.** 下星期我就滿十八歲了。

・**The water in the basin has turned into ice.** 盆子裡的水已經變成了冰。

e go 或 turn 用來表示顏色變化（不用 get）。

・**Her face went/turned red with embarrassment.**
她因難堪而臉紅了。

turn red

f 在 come、get、grow 後面可以用帶 to 的不定式。
become 後面不能用帶 to 的不定式。

・**She eventually came/grew to appreciate my work and personality.**
她終於開始賞識我的工作和品格。

・**You get to meet lots of interesting people when you travel around the world.** 你環遊世界時，會認識許多有趣的人。

4 有些詞既可以作連綴動詞，又可以作一般動詞，該如何區分呢？

- 可以用 be 動詞取代，這些動詞就是**連綴動詞**。
- 不能用 be 動詞取代，這些動詞就是**一般動詞**（即行為動詞）。

look	**Dee looked angry with me.** 蒂看起來在生我的氣。	**≈ Dee was angry with me.** ← 用 was 取代 looked 後，語句通順，語意不變，則 looked 是感官動詞作連綴動詞，描述外觀、狀態。。
	He looked at the sky. 他望著天空。	**≠ He was at the sky.** ← 用 was 取代 looked 後，語意改變，語句不合邏輯，所以 looked 是感官動詞作一般行為動詞，描述感官動作。

feel	This red blanket feels soft under my head. 我頭下枕著的這條紅色毛毯感覺很柔軟。	≈ This red blanket is soft under my head. ← 連綴動詞（意思是「給人某種感覺」）
	Art felt a great pain in his heart. 亞特感到心臟劇烈疼痛。	≠ Art was a great pain in his heart. ← 一般動詞（意思是「感覺；感知」）
	Mitch felt along the wall for the light switch. 米奇摸著牆壁，尋找電燈開關。	≠ Mitch was along the wall for the light switch. ← 一般動詞（意思是「摸索著尋找」）
remain	Despite the troubles that came their way, they remained friends anyway. 儘管他們之間有點糾紛，他們還是朋友。	≈ Despite the troubles that came their way, they were friends anyway. ← 連綴動詞（意思是「保持；仍是」）
	Bob said his financial problems remained even after he found a good job. 鮑勃說，找到好的工作後，他的經濟問題還是沒解決。	≠ Bob said his financial problems were even after he found a good job. ← 一般動詞（意思是「繼續存在」）
smell	This meat smells good, and so does this beet. 這塊肉和這顆甜菜聞起來都很香。	≈ This meat is good, and so is this beet. ← 連綴動詞（意思是「聞起來有某種氣味」）
	Come and smell these roses with your curious noses. 過來用你們好奇的鼻子聞聞這些玫瑰花。	≠ Come and be these roses with your curious noses. ← 一般動詞（意思是「聞」）
taste	The wine tasted fine. 這葡萄酒味道不錯。	= The wine was fine. ← 連綴動詞（意思是「嚐起來」）
	We tasted the fine wine. 我們品嚐了那美味的葡萄酒。	≠ We were the fine wine. ← 一般動詞（意思是「品嚐」）

及物動詞與不及物動詞

1 及物動詞

行為動詞可分為及物動詞和不及物動詞。及物動詞把行為施加在一個人或物（受詞）身上，所以不能單獨使用，須搭配一個名詞或代名詞作受詞。

1 及物動詞 + 直接受詞

直接受詞：是直接受動詞的動作所影響的人或物。及物動詞後面一般都與直接受詞連用。

- **Jim loves Kim.** 吉姆愛金姆。
  - ㄴ loves whom?（愛誰？）動詞 love 後面要加受詞（Mom、Dad、books、movies 等）。
  - ㄴ 及物動詞（loves）+ 直接受詞（Kim）
- **Kay's brother wants a pay raise.** 凱的哥哥想要加薪。
  - ㄴ wants what?（想要什麼？）動詞 want 後面要加受詞（a robotic toy、a hundred dollars 等）。
  - ㄴ 及物動詞（wants）+ 直接受詞（a pay raise）
- **Scot, please help me untie this knot.** 史考特，請幫我解開這個結。
  - ㄴ untie what?（解開什麼？）動詞 untie 後面要加受詞（the shoelace、the knot 等）。
  - ㄴ 及物動詞（untie）+ 直接受詞（this knot）
- **Kay and her friends help one another every day.**
  凱和她的朋友們每天都互相幫助。
  - ㄴ 及物動詞（help）+ 直接受詞（one another）
- **She gave $50,000 to the church.** 她捐給教會 50,000 美金。
  - ㄴ 及物動詞（gave）+ 直接受詞（$50,000）

• He loves coffee, she loves tea, and they both love to swim in the sea. 他愛喝咖啡，她愛喝茶，他們兩個都愛在大海裡游泳。

↳ loves 和 love 是及物動詞；coffee、tea 和 to swim 是受詞。

2 及物動詞 + 間接受詞（人）+ 直接受詞（物）

a 有些及物動詞可以接兩個受詞：直接受詞和間接受詞。當你「給某人某物」或「為某人做某事」時，你給某人的**東西**或你為某人做的**事**，叫做直接受詞；接受該物品的**人**，叫做間接受詞。間接受詞通常放在直接受詞前面。

b 可以接雙受詞的常見動詞有：

- bring 帶來
- buy 買
- cost 花費
- do 給予
- get 拿
- give 給
- hand 遞交
- leave 留給
- lend 借
- make 做；製造
- offer 提供；給予
- owe 欠；應給予
- pass 傳遞
- pay 付款
- play 演奏
- promise 答應
- read 朗讀
- refuse 不准
- send 寄
- show 出示
- sing 為……唱歌
- teach 訓練；教
- tell 告訴
- wish 祝福
- write 寫信

• Please give me the money! 請把錢給我！

= Please give the money to me!

↳ give me what?（給我什麼？）動詞 give 後面要加一個直接受詞（the money）和一個間接受詞（me）。

↳ 及物動詞（give）+ 間接受詞（me）+ 直接受詞（the money）

↳ 及物動詞（give）+ 直接受詞（the money）+ 介系詞（to）+ 間接受詞（me）

↳ 通常把間接受詞（me）放在直接受詞（the money）前面。

• She has left me some food in the fridge.
她在冰箱裡留了一些食物給我。

↳ fridge（非正式）= refrigerator

• I bought Kay some roses for her birthday.
我買了一些玫瑰給凱當作生日禮物。

- **Please sing us a song, Louise.** 露易絲，請為我們唱一首歌。
- **Mom is reading a funny story to my little brother, Tom.** 媽媽在為我小弟弟湯姆唸一個有趣的故事。
  - ↳ 如果間接受詞比較長（如：my little brother, Tom），要把間接受詞放在直接受詞後面，並用介系詞 to。

2 不及物動詞

不及物動詞可以單獨使用，不用接受詞。如：come（來）、go（去）、fall（跌倒；落下）、smile（微笑）等，都是不及物動詞。

- **Standing alone on the island, I could only shout to avoid my fears and tears.**
  我孤獨地站在小島上，只能靠喊叫來忘記恐懼，不讓自己哭出來。
  - ↳ 不及物動詞 shout 單獨使用，不接受詞。
  - ↳ 不定式片語 to avoid my fears and tears，相當於 in order to avoid my fears and tears，用作目的狀語，而不是動詞 shout 的受詞。

- **Does Kay jog every day?** 凱每天都慢跑嗎？
- **Those joggers who wanted to get thinner went out for a light dinner.** 那些想瘦身的慢跑者出去吃清淡的晚餐。
- **A giant bee is hiding behind that big oak tree.**
  一隻巨大的蜜蜂躲在那棵大橡樹後面。

3 可作及物動詞，也可作不及物動詞的動詞

一些動詞既可以當及物動詞，也可以當不及物動詞。

不及物動詞	及物動詞
• **Kay sings every day.** 凱每天都要唱歌。 ↳ 不及物動詞 sings 單獨使用，不接受詞。	• **Kay sings spirituals every day.** 凱每天都要唱聖歌。 ↳ 及物動詞 sings 接受詞（spirituals）。

不及物動詞	及物動詞
・Soon after the insurance policy lapsed, the building collapsed. 保單剛失效，那棟大樓就倒塌了。 ↑ 不及物動詞 collapsed 單獨使用，不接受詞。	・The huge elephant collapsed the small house by pushing against it. 那頭巨象推撞那間小房子，結果把房子弄垮了。 ↑ 及物動詞 collapsed 接受詞（the small house）。
・“That will do,” said Andrew. 安德魯說：「那可以。」 ↑ 不及物動詞 do 單獨使用，表示「適合」，不接受詞。	・I do the crossword puzzle every day with my Aunt Sue. 我每天都跟蘇姨媽一起玩填字謎遊戲。 ↑ 及物動詞 do 接受詞（the crossword puzzle）。
・The huge kite is flying high in the sky. 那個巨大的風箏正在天空中高高地飛翔。	・Joe is flying a kite. 喬在放風箏。
・She is walking happily along the beach. 她正快樂地沿著海灘溜達。	・She is walking her dog along the beach. 她正沿著海灘遛狗。
・Ann runs faster than her husband Dan. 安跑得比她先生丹快。	・Anna runs a publishing house in Arizona. 安娜在亞利桑那州經營一家出版社。
・Henry took part in the ballet competition but lost. 亨利參加了芭蕾舞比賽，但是輸了。	・Henry wore his lucky black leotard but still lost the ballet competition to Jerry. 亨利穿上他的幸運黑色緊身連身褲，但是在芭蕾舞比賽中還是輸給了傑瑞。
・Mark and Mike are playing in the park. 馬克和邁克在公園玩。	・Paul and Saul are playing basketball. 保羅和所羅在打籃球。

片語動詞

片語動詞由一個**動詞**接一個**介系詞**或**副詞**組成，片語動詞可能是不及物動詞，也可能是及物動詞。

- **Bing was lounging around, doing nothing.** 賓在混日子，什麼事也不做。
  ↑ 這個片語是不及物動詞。
- **Mr. Peach called off the meeting.** 皮奇先生取消了會議。
  ↑ 這個片語是及物動詞。

★以下例句中，6、23、25、26、28 是不及物動詞，其餘是及物動詞。

1. **Jake and Jeff can't agree with each other about which path to take.**
   對於到底該走哪一條路，傑克和傑夫意見不一。
2. **Midge said the terrorists shot a woman and then tried to blow up the bridge.** 米姬說，恐怖分子槍殺了一名女子，然後企圖炸毀大橋。
3. **The clown suit belongs to the richest man in town.**
   那件小丑衣是城裡最富有的男人的。
4. **It isn't easy to bring up children nowadays.** 這年頭養小孩真不容易啊。
5. **Joe, the referee, called off the game because of the cold and snow.**
   由於又冷又下雪，裁判喬取消了比賽。
6. 不及 **Bess dressed up as a princess.** 貝絲裝扮得像一個公主。
7. **Fill out/Fill in this application form, and give it to Jill.** 填寫這張申請表，然後交給潔兒。

8. **Dee found out being a cheerleader meant that she had to shout.** 蒂發現，要當一名啦啦隊隊長，就得大聲喊叫。
9. **Kim Straw gets along well with her mother in law.**
   金姆·斯特勞和她婆婆相處融洽。

ℓ 片語動詞也可以由三個字組成，如：drop out of（退出）、hang on to（緊急抓住）、run out of（用完）、set out for（出發去某處）、sign up for（報名）、watch out for（注意）等。

10. Jean and Andrew handed in their term papers and then left for Honolulu. 琴和安德魯交了學期論文後，就動身前往檀香山。

11. She hung up the phone. 她掛斷了電話。

hang up the phone

12. A pretty lass asked us to keep off the grass. 一位美麗的少女要我們不要踩草坪。

13. Kate's hard work helps her to keep up with her classmates. 由於凱特很用功，所以跟得上同班同學。

14. What are you looking for? 你在找什麼？

15. If you don't understand this phrasal verb, you can look it up in a dictionary. 你如果不懂這個片語動詞的意思，可以查詞典。

在「及物動詞 + 副詞」的結構中，代名詞作受詞時，要放在動詞後、副詞前（如：look it up）；當名詞作受詞時，常放在副詞後，但也可放在副詞前。例如：

- Please look up this phrasal verb in a dictionary.
  = Please look this phrasal verb up in a dictionary.

16. Mary doesn't listen to anyone, and she's made up her mind to marry Jerry. 瑪麗誰的話都不聽，下定決心要嫁給傑瑞。

17. Dad is always mixing up the twins. 爸爸老是分不清這對雙胞胎。

18. He tries to put away money for his retirement. 他設法存點錢，退休要用。

19. Has Kate put on a lot of weight? 凱特胖了很多嗎？

20. The firefighters have put out the fire. 消防隊員已經把火撲滅了.

21. Kim ran across her ex-boyfriend at the high school gym. 金姆在高中體育館裡遇到了她的前任男友。

22. Kay ran into her English professor in the hallway.
凱在走廊上碰到她的英文老師。
 run into = run across = meet by chance 偶遇

不及 23. Is it rude to say "Shut up!" 說「閉嘴」，這樣會很粗魯嗎？

24. Dee took off her wet boots and went into her RV.
蒂脫下濕靴子，然後走進房車。

不及 25. Kay turned away and said in a whisper, "I can't give my daughter any milk today." 凱轉過身低聲說：「我今天不能給我女兒餵奶。」

不及 26. Jane unexpectedly turned up at the party. 珍出人意料地出現在聚會上。

27. Sometimes, when it gets really busy, Ms. Able, the owner, has to wait on the long table. 有時很忙的時候，老闆娘艾博也得替那張長桌服務。
 wait on somebody/wait on a table
= serve people in a store or restaurant 服侍

不及 28. Watch out, or you'll get wet. 小心，不然你會弄濕自己的。

還有一種片語動詞的形式是「**動詞 + 名詞 + 介系詞**」。

- find fault with 挑剔
- get hold of/lose hold of 抓住／沒有抓住
- give rise to 引起
- keep an eye on 注意；照看
- lay foundation for 為……打基礎
- lose sight of 看不見
- make a fool of 嘲弄
- make friends with 交朋友
- make fun of 取笑
- make peace with 與……講和
- make preparations for 為……做準備
- make room for 讓出地方給
- make sense of 理解
- make use of 利用
- make way for 讓路給
- pay attention to 注意；關心
- put an end to 結束
- say goodbye to 告別
- set foot in 進入
- shake hands with 和……握手
- show interest in 對……表現出興趣
- take account of 考慮到
- take advantage of 利用；佔……便宜
- take care of 照顧
- take charge of 負責
- take notice of 注意到
- take part in 參加
- take pride in 以……而自豪
- take the place of 代替

• It's not polite to make fun of her pronunciation. 嘲笑她的發音是很不禮貌的。

使役動詞

用來引發另一個行為的動詞，叫做使役動詞，通常表示某人不直接做某個動作，而使另一個人做這個動作。常見的使役動詞有：

- make
- have
- let
- get
- help

1 make

1 make + 人／物 + 原形動詞（使某人或某物做某事）

make 當使役動詞用時，後面所接的動詞要用原形動詞，不能使用帶 to 的不定式或動詞 -ing 形式。

- Mom made Dirk do his homework.
  媽媽讓德克做家庭作業。
- Dirk can't make his cleaning robot do any work. 德克叫不動他的清潔機器人做任何工作。

make 用在被動式（is/was made）的句子裡時，要用帶 to 的不定式。

- The captain makes everyone on the big houseboat do his or her share of the work.
  = Everyone on the big houseboat was made to do his or her share of the work (by the captain).
  船長令大船屋上的每個人各盡職責。

» 參見 631 頁〈Unit 12 主動語態和被動語態〉。

2 make + 人／物 + 過去分詞（含有被動意義）

- Did Ted make himself understood?
  = Did everybody understand what Ted said?
  = Did Ted express himself clearly?
  泰德把自己的意思表達清楚了嗎？
  ↑ 這裡用過去分詞 understood，表示被動意義。

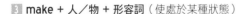

make himself understood

- I will make it known that we are hiring carpenters.
  我會讓公眾知道，我們要招聘木工。

3 make + 人／物 + 形容詞（使處於某種狀態）

- My plan of driving across America made her excited, and she wanted to go with me. 我開車周遊美國的計畫讓她很興奮，她想跟我一起去。
  ↑ 過去分詞 excited 作形容詞。
- We have some guests coming. Please make the bathroom clean and tidy. 我們有一些客人要來，請把洗手間弄乾淨整潔。

make 除了用作使役動詞，也可以用作一般動詞，表示「製造」。

- Dwight made a plastic kite. 杜威特做了個塑膠風箏。
  ↑ 這裡的 made 相當於 built（建造）。

2 let

let + 人／物 + 原形動詞（允許某人做某事；允許某事發生；給出指示或命令）

let 是使役動詞，要用原形動詞，不能用帶 to 的不定式或動詞 -ing 形式。

- Dr. Pam Smith let us write a paper instead of taking the final exam.
  潘姆．史密斯博士讓我們寫一篇論文來代替期末考試。 → 允許某人做某事
- I will let my car get cool before I drive it to school.
  我要先讓我的汽車冷卻下來，再開車去學校。 → 允許某事發生
- Don't let Andrew and his foolish talk bother you.
  不要讓安德魯和他的蠢話來煩你。 → 否定式用「don't let + 人／事 + 原形動詞」

3 have

1 have + 人 + 原形動詞（給出指示或命令；安排某人做某事）

have 可以作使役動詞，語氣沒有 make 和 get 強烈，意指用勸說或強制的方式使某人做某事。當 have 後面的受詞是人時，其後的動詞用原形，不用帶 to 的不定式。

- **Mr. Mill had his lawyer change his will.**
  米爾先生讓他的律師更改了他的遺囑。
  ↳ have + someone + 原形動詞：發命令、給指示。
- **Professor Ann Creek has her EFL students read seven short novels every week.** 安．克里克教授要她的 EFL 學生每星期閱讀七本短篇小說。
  ↳ EFL = English as a Foreign Language 以英語為外國語
- **Claire had her boyfriend do her hair.** 克萊兒讓她男友幫她設計髮型。

2 have + 物 + 過去分詞

當 have 後面的受詞是物時，其後的動詞用過去分詞，表示被動意義，不用原形、帶 to 的不定式或動詞 -ing 形式。

a have + something + done：指「安排他人做某事」（含被動意義）。

- **Has Kay had her temperature taken today?** 凱今天量體溫了沒有？
- **I like the way you had your hair cut.** 我喜歡你剪的髮型。
- **I want to have this book renewed, please.** 我要續借這本書。

b have + something + done：也可以指「發生了意外」。

- **Kay had two of her fingers badly cut yesterday when she ran into a car with her bike.** 昨天凱騎自行車撞到汽車時，把兩根手指嚴重割傷了。

3 have + 人 + 過去分詞（讓某人經歷了某種感覺）

- **Amy had me worried for the whole night.**
  艾咪讓我擔心了一整晚。

4 have 後面可以接**動詞 -ing** 形式，**強調「正在進行」**，意思不是「用勸說或強制的方式使某人做某事」。

a have + 人 + 動詞 -ing（讓某人經歷了某種狀態〔experience/undergo〕；使某人按照某種方式做某事〔make someone do something in a particular way〕）

- **Sue had us laughing all through the dinner.**
  蘇整個晚餐期間讓我們笑個不停。
- **Last night I had so many guests at my house that I had some of the guests sleeping on the floor.**
  昨晚我家來了很多客人，我不得不讓一些客人睡在地板上。

b have + 物 + 動詞 -ing（使某物按照某種方式做某事）

- **Mayor Anna Bud had her car going nowhere owing to the storm and the mud.** 暴風雨和泥坑讓安娜．巴德市長的汽車寸步難行。
- **I had my car moving in neutral.** 我的汽車以空檔在移動。

have 除了作使役動詞，也可以作行為動詞。

- Tom asked, "When are we going to have dinner, Mom?"
  湯姆問：「媽，什麼時候吃晚飯？」→ have = eat（吃）
- Adam said that his voice always seemed hoarse and (that) he had a difficult time after his divorce. 亞當說，他的聲音好像總是很沙啞，還說他離婚後的日子很不好過。→ 經歷

» 參見 460 頁〈Part 7 have, has, there is, there are 的用法〉。

4 get

1 get + 人 + 不定式（帶 to）（勸說某人做某事；讓某人做某事）

get 可以用作使役動詞，但語氣沒有 make 強烈，表示「說服、使得」。當 get 的受詞是人時，其後的動詞要用帶 to 的不定式，不用原形動詞或動詞 -ing 形式。

・Can you get Jane to give us a ride to Maine?
你可以叫珍載我們去緬因州嗎？→ get + somebody + to do（帶 to 的不定式）

・Kay, please get someone to fix the RV right away.
凱，請馬上找人來修房車。

2 若 get 的受詞是物（a thing），則其後的動詞用過去分詞，表示被動意義，不用原形動詞、帶 to 的不定式或 -ing 形式。

a get + 物 + 過去分詞（使某事得以完成；安排他人或由自己完成某事，含被動意義〔get something done = find a way to ensure this happens, one way or the other〕）

・I need to get my motorcycle fixed before I go to see Jane in Spain.
在去西班牙拜訪珍之前，我得先修好我的摩托車。
↳ get + something + done（過去分詞）

・Coco is planning to get her house painted and roof fixed before it snows. 可可正打算在下雪前找人把房子粉刷好，並把屋頂修好。

b 「get + 物 + 過去分詞」：與 have 的用法一樣，「get something done」也可以指「發生了意外」(something bad has happened to people or their possessions)，意為「讓……經歷某事（experience/undergo）」，而不是「讓某人／某物做某事」。

・I had/got my wallet stolen yesterday in New York. 我昨天在紐約時皮夾被扒走了。
↳ 讓某人經歷了某事。

BEWARE PICKPOCKET

・My poor dog had/got his leg caught in the door a few days ago. 我可憐的狗狗前幾天時腿被門夾到了。
↳ 「get + something + 過去分詞」可以描述異常、意外的行為動作。

3 **get + 人或物 + 形容詞**（使處於某種狀態）

・Arguing about politics got all of us tired.
爭論政治使我們都累了。

・He got his jacket all wet. 他的上衣全濕了。

4 get + 人或物 + 動詞 -ing（使某人按照某種方式做某事；使某物運行）

get 後面可以接動詞 -ing 形式，強調「正在進行」。

- You'd better get the soldiers moving faster, or they will be late for supper. 你最好讓那些士兵行軍快一些，否則他們晚飯會遲到的。
- Ben finally got my computer working again. 班終於讓我的電腦又可以正常運作了。

get 除了作使役動詞，也可以作行為動詞。

- Please get some novels from Ann and then mail them to Dan. 請跟安拿一些小說，然後寄給丹。
  ↑ get 也可以用作一般動詞，在這裡指「得到、取」。
- Jim declared, "We got him!" 吉姆宣布：「我們抓到他了！」
  ↑ get = catch 抓到

5 help

help + 人 + 原形動詞／帶 to 的不定式（幫助某人做某事）

help 可以作使役動詞，用來表示某人幫助另一個人做事；在「a person + help + another person」的後面，要用原形動詞或是帶 to 的不定式，不能用動詞 -ing 形式。

- Lee is helping Dee carry the monkey.
  = Lee is helping Dee to carry the monkey.
  李正在幫蒂抱這隻猴子。
  ↑ help somebody (to) do（help 可接帶 to 的不定式或原形動詞）。
- Did your Uncle Bob help you get this wonderful job?
  = Did your Uncle Bob help you to get this wonderful job?
  是你的鮑勃叔叔幫你得到這份好工作的嗎？

have, has, there is, there are 的用法

1 have, has（擁有）

	肯定句		否定句		疑問句		
現在式	I	have	I	do not have	do	I	have?
	you		you			you	
	we		we			we	
	they		they			they	
	he	has	he	does not have	does	he	have?
	she		she			she	
	it		it			it	

	肯定句		否定句		疑問句		
過去式	I	had	I	did not have	did	I	have?
	you		you			you	
	we		we			we	
	they		they			they	
	he		he			he	
	she		she			she	
	it		it			it	
未來式	I	will have	I	will not have	will	I	have?
	you		you			you	
	he		he			he	
	she		she			she	
	it		it			it	
	we		we			we	
	they		they			they	

縮寫形式
- do not have = don't have
- does not have = doesn't have
- did not have = didn't have
- will not have = won't have

→ I'll, you'll, etc., have

✗ Does Claire has long hair?

✓ Does Claire have long hair? 克萊兒是長頭髮嗎？

- Will Jenny ever have lots of money? 珍妮將來會不會很有錢？
- He won't have a dog or a hog. 他不會養狗，也不會養豬。
- Did his movie only have two actors? 他的電影裡只有兩個演員嗎？

Diving Deep Into English 63 have（擁有）的美式與英式用法

❶ have 表示「擁有」時，大多數美國人喜歡在否定句和疑問句中用助動詞 do（does, did）與動詞 have 搭配使用，英國人則有時將 have 單獨使用，不用助動詞 do (does, did) 與動詞 have 搭配。

英式 Mary and I haven't any children.
↑ 這種形式不太自然，不常用了。
美式／英式 Mary and I haven't got any children.
美式 Mary and I don't have any children.
瑪麗和我沒有孩子。

❷ 在英式英語中，當 have 表示「擁有」時，「代名詞 + have」可以縮寫為 we've、you've、they've。

- They've a big indoor swimming pool in their school.
他們的學校有一個很大的室內游泳池。
↑ 不過最好避免這種用法，當 have 用作助動詞時，才用這種縮寫式。

1 have/has 可以當作及物動詞，表示「擁有」（持有、佔有，具有某種特徵或屬性，處於某種關係等）。

- Jake's electric scooter does not have good brakes. 傑克的電動小摩托車的煞車不好。
- Believe it or not, my classmate Claire Harbor has green hair. 信不信由你，我同學克萊兒·哈伯的頭髮是綠色的。
- Midge has four sisters, and besides being cute, they all have a great deal of courage. 米姬有四個姐妹，她們不但可愛，還個個都很勇敢。
- My dog won't have any fear of that mean hog.
我的狗一點兒也不會怕那隻脾氣暴躁的豬。

- Did you have time to read any of Mary's stories?
  你有時間讀瑪麗的故事了嗎？

2 have/has 作「擁有」解釋時，不能用在進行式或被動語態中。

✗ Coco is not having any common sense.
✓ Coco doesn't have any common sense.
✓ Coco has got no common sense. → has got 是非正式用法。
✓ Coco has no common sense. 可可一點兒常識也沒有。

2 have got, has got（擁有，只用於現在式）

肯定句	肯定縮寫	否定句	否定縮寫
I have got = I have	I've got = I have	I have not got = I do not have	I haven't got = I don't have
you have got = you have	you've got = you have	you have not got = you do not have	you haven't got = you don't have
he/she/it has got = he/she/it has	he's/she's/it's got = he/she/it has	he/she/it has not got = he/she/it does not have	he/she/it hasn't got = he/she/it doesn't have
we have got = we have	we've got = we have	we have not got = we do not have	we haven't got = we don't have
they have got = they have	they've got = they have	they have not got = they do not have	they haven't got = they don't have

疑問句	簡短回答
Have I got . . .? = Do I have . . .?	Yes, you have. No, you haven't. = No, you don't have.
Have you got . . .? = Do you have . . .?	Yes, I have. No, I haven't. = No, I don't have.
Has he/she/it got . . .? = Does he/she/it have . . .?	Yes, he/she/it has. No, he/she/it hasn't. = No, he/she/it doesn't have.

Have we got . . .? = Do we have . . .?	Yes, we have. No, we haven't. = No, we don't have.
Have they got . . .? = Do they have . . .?	Yes, they have. No, they haven't. = No, they don't have.

注意 簡短回答中不能用 have/has got。

- **We've got a swimming pool in our school.** → 肯定句
  = We have a swimming pool in our school. 我們學校有一個游泳池。
- **My mom hasn't got/has not got a brother called Tom.** → 否定句
  = My mom doesn't have/does not have a brother called Tom.
  我媽媽沒有一個名叫湯姆的弟弟。
- **Have you and Kay got an appointment today?** → 疑問句
  = Do you and Kay have an appointment today? 你和凱今天有約會嗎？

1 在**非正式語**中，可以用 I have got、we have got 這樣的結構，來代替 I have、we have 等，用以表達「擁有；佔有；具有」之意。美式更常用 have/has，而英式更常用 have/has got。但 have/has got 只能用在簡單現在式中。這裡的 got 並不是 get 的過去式，也不是動詞 get 的過去分詞。

- **Claire has got dark curly hair.** → 非正式
  = Claire has dark curly hair. 克萊兒有一頭黑色的捲髮。 → 正式
- **My cat has got a long tail, beautiful fur, and a lovely purr.** → 非正式
  = My cat has a long tail, beautiful fur, and a lovely purr. → 正式
  我的小貓有一條長尾巴和一身漂亮的毛髮，叫聲也很可愛。

2 構成否定句和疑問句時，have/has got 不能與助動詞 do/does 連用，have/has 才可以與助動詞 do/does 連用。

- **Jim and Jenny haven't got any children.**
  = Jim and Jenny don't have any children.
  吉姆和珍妮沒有孩子。
- **Has Sue got a new sailboat?**
  = Does Sue have a new sailboat? 蘇有一艘新帆船嗎？

3 have/has got（擁有）只能用於簡單現在式，在過去式中要用 had。不要用「I/you/we/they/she/he/it had got」表示擁有。

- Sally Eagle had a collie and a beagle. → 過去式
  莎莉·伊果有過一隻蘇格蘭柯利牧羊犬和一隻畢哥小獵犬。
- Sally Eagle has got a collie and a beagle. → 現在式（非正式）
- Sally Eagle has a collie and a beagle. → 現在式（正式）
  莎莉·伊果有一隻蘇格蘭柯利牧羊犬和一隻畢哥小獵犬。
- I had a sports car for two years when I was in college.
  大學期間，有兩年的時間我擁有一輛跑車。

4 在未來式中，要用 will have 的形式，不能用 will have got 表示「擁有」；have/has got（擁有）只能用於現在式。

- Sue and you will have a problem or two. 蘇和你將會有一、兩個難題。
- I won't have this old cellphone for much longer. I'm getting a new one next week. 這支舊手機我用不久了，我下星期就會買一支新手機。

5 在帶 to 的不定式和情態動詞後面以及 have 的 -ing 形式，用 have 表示「擁有」（如：to have, having, may have），不用 have got 的形式。

- She finds having no cellphone very inconvenient.
  她發現沒有手機很不方便。 → 不用 having got。
- Do you want to have a big house someday?
  你希望將來有一天擁有一棟大房子嗎？

Diving Deep Into English 64 美式英語：have/has got（擁有）／have/has gotten（獲得；得到）

- Sue has got a new sailboat. 蘇有一艘新帆船。
  - has got = has (possess; own)
  - 句子用了現在式。動詞 has got 與 has 的意思完全相同，表示「擁有」，是 have 的單數第三人稱簡單現在式的形式，而非 get 的現在完成式形式。
- Sue has gotten a new sailboat. 蘇得到了一艘新帆船。
  - has gotten = has acquired（行為動作）
  - 句子用了現在完成式。在美式英語中，get 的過去分詞是 gotten。

Diving Deep Into English 65 英式英語中 have/has got 有兩種意思

- **My mother has got three sisters and a brother.**
  我媽媽有三個姐妹和一個兄弟。
  ↳ has got = has (possess; own)
- **She could have got more money for her house if she'd sold it to me.** 如果她把房子賣給了我，她就會得到更多錢了。
  ↳ have got = have obtained（行為動作）
  ↳ 句子用了完成式。在英式英語中，get 的過去分詞是 got，可用於帶 to 的不定式、-ing 形式和情態動詞之後。這句是假設語氣，表示實際上她沒有把房子賣給我。

» 假設語氣參見 695 頁〈Part 6 假設語氣〉。

3 表達其他行為的 have 片語

1 have 在很多常見片語中用來表達行為動作。談論這些行為動作時，不能用 have got 結構。

吃；喝
- have breakfast/lunch/dinner 吃早餐／午餐／晚餐
- have tea/coffee 喝茶／咖啡
- have something to eat/drink 吃／喝點什麼
- have fish for lunch 午餐吃魚

經歷
- have a good time 玩得愉快
- have fun 玩得愉快
- have a bad day 度過了糟糕的一天
- have a nice evening 度過一個愉快的夜晚
- have a good trip/journey/flight 旅途愉快

執行；從事
- have a talk/have a conversation 談話
- have an argument 爭論，辯論
- have a shower/have a bath 沖淋浴／泡個澡
- have a meeting 開會
- have a wild party 舉辦狂歡會

感染疾病；受疾病折磨
- have a headache 頭痛
- have a fever 發燒

生育	● have a baby 生孩子
獲取；得到	● have news of someone 得到某人的消息 ● have a look at it 看看某物
表達感覺	● have pity on somebody 憐憫某人
容忍（否定句）	● won't have this nonsense 絕對不容忍這種胡言亂語

✗ I usually have got breakfast at 8 a.m.

✓ I usually have breakfast at 8 a.m. 我早上通常八點吃早餐。 → 吃；喝

- I won't have a mouse in my house. 我不能容忍房子裡有老鼠。 → 容忍
- Yesterday the young couple next door had a fight that lasted almost all night. 隔壁的那對年輕夫婦，昨晚吵了幾乎一整晚。 → 經歷
- When Anna comes back from Italy, we will have a welcome home party. 等安娜從義大利回來，我們要舉行一個歡迎會。 → 執行
- I had an email from my boyfriend Dan.
  我收到了男友丹寫給我的電子郵件。 → 收到
- Maybe Sue is going to have a really big baby.
  也許蘇真的會生下一個胖寶寶。 → 生孩子

be going to have a baby

- I have my doubts that learning English is best done with shouts.
  有人說學英語最好的方法是大聲喊出來，我對此持懷疑態度。 → 心中懷有、持有

2 這些慣用 have 的片語中，現在式、過去式和未來式的疑問句和否定句，要用助動詞 do/does、did 及 will。

- The bathroom of her hotel room was so filthy that Sue didn't have a bath. 旅館房間的浴室太髒啦，所以蘇沒有洗澡。
- Ted does not have coffee or tea before going to bed. 泰德睡前不喝咖啡，也不喝茶。
- Will Sue have fun teaching her boyfriend how to swim and float? 蘇會開心地教她的男友游泳和漂浮嗎？

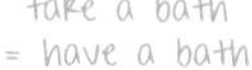

- I won't have lies and nonsense from you. 我不能容忍你撒謊和胡說八道。

4 there is, there are（現在式）

	肯定句	否定句	疑問句
單數	there is = there's	there is not = there isn't	is there?
複數	there are	there are not = there aren't	are there?

1 意義：there is/are (not) 表示某物存在於某處，或某物不存在，表示看得見或聽得到某物的存在，其後面常接 a/an、some、any、many 等。

- There is a big green frog on your mean hog.
  = A big green frog is on your mean hog.
  你那隻凶惡的豬身上有一隻綠色的大青蛙。
  ↑ 表示某物存在於某處，用 there is 句型較為自然，因此上面第一句比第二句自然。

- Mark says there are many gorillas in this park.
  馬克說，這座公園裡有很多大猩猩。
- Are there any apples left in the fridge? 冰箱裡還有蘋果嗎？
- How much gold is there in that treasure chest?
  那個藏寶箱裡有多少金子？

- I asked in a whisper, "How many thieves are there in our backyard?" 我低聲問：「有多少小偷在我們家的後院？」

2 在 there is、there are、there seems to be 等結構中，句首的 there 用來引導句子，並不是句子的主詞，真正的主詞在動詞（is/are）的後面，動詞（is/are）的單複數要與動詞後面的主詞一致。

- There is a snake under the table behind Jake. 傑克身後的桌子下面有隻蛇。
  ↑ 單數動詞（is）+ 單數主詞（a snake）
- There are a lot of big alligators in this river. 這條河裡有很多隻大鱷魚。
  ↑ 複數動詞（are）+ 複數主詞（alligators）
- Is there anything wrong with Jane practicing her violin at midnight?
  珍半夜練小提琴有什麼不妥嗎？ → 單數動詞（Is）+ 單數主詞（anything）

3 當 there be 句型中含有複合主詞時，述語動詞的形式要與最靠近的名詞一致。儘管整個主詞是複數概念，但如果最靠近述語動詞的是單數名詞，通常習慣用單數動詞 there is。

Idiomatic There is **a kangaroo jumping around outside** and **a rabbit hopping around inside.**

Unnatural There are **a kangaroo jumping around outside** and **a rabbit hopping around inside.**

有一隻袋鼠在外面跳來跳去，有一隻兔子在裡面跳來跳去。

↑ 第一句實際上是省略了第二個主詞前面的 there is。

↑ 第一句比第二句更符合語言習慣。第二句雖然符合文法規則，但不自然。

» 參見 873 頁〈Part 3 There be 句型的主詞與動詞〉。

Diving Deep Into English 66 It is 與 There is

it is 指已經提過的或人們已知的事物，there is 則單純表達某物的存在。

✗ **"How's your new job, Sue?"** "There's **the pits."**

✓ **"How's your new job, Sue?"** "It's **the pits."**

「蘇，你的新工作如何啊？」「糟透了。」

↑ the pits（口語）: 指一件很糟糕的事。這裡的 it 是指前面提及的 new job。

✗ It's **a neat park and a public swimming pool on Clark Street.**

✓ There is **a neat park and a public swimming pool on Clark Street.** 克拉克大街上有一座很棒的公園和一個公共游泳池。

5 there was, there were（過去式）

	肯定句	否定句	疑問句
單數	there was	there was not = there wasn't	was there?
複數	there were	there were not = there weren't	were there?

- Last year there were lots of sweet grapes here that attracted many apes.
  去年這裡大量的甜葡萄吸引了很多無尾猿。

an ape

- Once upon a time, there was a beautiful blue lady who lived in a giant shoe.
  從前，有一個美麗的藍色女子住在一個巨大的鞋子裡。

- “There weren’t any accurate world maps in the 15th century,” stated Jenny.
  珍妮說：「15 世紀時還沒有精確的世界地圖。」

an old map

- How many people were there at the party last night? 昨晚的聚會上有多少人？

6 there will be（未來式）

	肯定句	否定句	疑問句
單複數	there will be	there will not be = there won’t be	will there be?

- I think there will be lots of health spas on the moon in 2110.
  我認為，到了 2110 年，月球上面會有許多健身水療俱樂部。
- According to Andrew, there won’t be any poor people in 2222.
  根據安德魯的看法，2222 年就不會再有任何窮人了。
- In 2100, will there be cars and trains and buses on Mars?
  2100 年時，火星上會有汽車、火車和公車嗎？

7 there have been, there has been（完成式）

	肯定句	否定句	疑問句
單數	there has been	there has not been = there hasn’t been	has there been?
複數	there have been	there have not been = there haven’t been	have there been?

- There have been three bank robberies in our city in the last two weeks. 過去兩星期，在我們市裡就發生了三次銀行搶劫案。
- There has been a lot of snow this week.
  這星期下了很多雪。

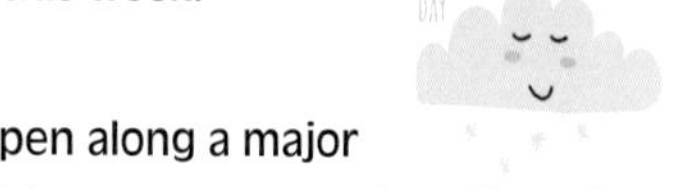
Snowy
DAY

- An earthquake is likely to happen along a major fault line where there haven't been many recent earthquakes.
  在近期地震並不多的主要斷層帶，很可能會發生地震。

8 have (has) 與 there is (are) 的比較

1 當 have 表示「擁有」時，是一般動詞，不與 there 連用，不會出現「there have ＋名詞」這樣的句型。

✕ There have a traffic jam on Sam Road, because a truck has spilled ten thousand jars of jam.

✓ There is a traffic jam on Sam Road, because a truck has spilled ten thousand jars of jam.
一輛卡車撒落了一萬罐的果醬，導致山姆公路堵車。
↳ there 不與表示「擁有」的 have 連用。

2 have 作「擁有」解釋時，要注意主詞的合理性，有些東西可以「擁有」另一樣東西，有些卻不行。

✕ "My home has three cars," said sweet little Dee.
✓ "We have three cars," said sweet little Dee.
✓ "My family has three cars," said sweet little Dee.
「我家有三輛汽車。」可愛的小蒂說。

My family has three cars.

↳ have 表示「擁有」時，要用「人」作主詞。
如果要用動詞 have，就要把 my home 改成 we 或 my family，因為只有 people（人）、family（家人）才能擁有汽車，home（家／住家）卻不能。

✕ "My home in Rome has a swimming pool and a whirlpool," said Jerry.

✔ Jerry says there is a swimming pool and a whirlpool in his house in Rome. → there is 表示某物存在於某處。

✔ Jerry says his house in Rome has a swimming pool and a whirlpool.
傑瑞說，他在羅馬的房子有一個游泳池和一個按摩溫水浴池。
↑ have 表示「擁有；佔有」。房子（house）可以擁有某些設備（所屬關係）。

✔ Jerry has a swimming pool and a whirlpool in his house in Rome.
傑瑞在羅馬的房子有一個游泳池和一個按摩溫水浴池。
↑ 人可以擁有某些設備（所屬關係）。
↑ 人或房子（house）可以擁有某些設備，但 home 不能。可以說「My house has a balcony.」(我的房子有個陽臺。)，但不能說「My home has a balcony.」。

3 have 也可以用作**助動詞**。

a have 作助動詞時，與**過去分詞**連用構成完成式，表達動作的完成，如「I have done, I had done, I will have done, I would have done」等。

b 當 have 作助動詞，而非表示「**擁有**」的行為動詞時，就可以和 there 連用，構成 there have/has been 結構（這是 there are/is 的簡單現在完成式）。

- **There have been many friends dropping by all day.**
  整天都有很多朋友順道來訪。
  ↑ 句中 have 作助動詞，不是表示「擁有」的行為動詞。

再複習一次 have/has 與 there is/are 的用法：

1 動詞 have 可表示所屬關係，意為「擁有，佔有」，作「擁有」講時，不要與 there 同時使用。

2 there is/are (not) 的結構，表示某處存在（或不存在）某物。

3 動詞 have 也常用於其他表示行為動作的片語裡，例如：
- have a look 看一下
- have dinner 吃晚餐

4 have 也可以作助動詞，與過去分詞連用構成完成式（have/has studied, there have/has been）。

助動詞 do, have, be, will

助動詞又稱為**協助動詞**，與行為動詞連用，表示動詞的時態，或構成疑問句、否定句、被動式或簡略回答。常見的助動詞有四類：

1 **do** → 用來構成否定句、疑問句，做簡略回答，或代替主要動詞，或在肯定句中置於原形動詞之前以加強語氣。

- do
- does
- did

- She does not know anything about it. → 否定句（簡單現在式）
  她對此一無所知。
- Where did you hide my bunny bank filled with money? → 疑問句（過去式）
  你把我裝滿錢的兔子撲滿藏去哪裡了？
- Sue runs faster than I do. → 代替主要動詞（run）。
  蘇跑得比我快。

Sue runs faster than I do.

- I do care for you. 我是真的喜歡你。
  ↑ 用在動詞原形 care 前，加強語氣。（簡單現在式）

Dan Do you and Kay go swimming every day? → 疑問句（簡單現在式）
Ann Yes, we do. → 簡略回答
Dan 你和凱每天都要去游泳嗎？
Ann 是的。

do、does、did 除了當助動詞用，也可以作行為動詞，談論行為動作。

- Usually Mom does the shopping, Dirk does the cooking, and I do my homework. 通常是媽媽負責採購，德克做飯，而我做功課。

2 **have** → 與過去分詞一起構成各種完成式。
- have ● has ● had

- **Have you ever seen such a horrible scene!** → 現在完成式
- 你目睹過這麼恐怖的場面嗎！

- **Sue Flowers has been jogging for over two hours.** → 現在完成進行式
  蘇·弗勞爾斯已經慢跑兩個多小時了。

- **Kay's brother Lee and his girlfriend Dee had been canoeing down the river for three days.** → 過去完成進行式
  凱的哥哥李和他的女友蒂已經沿著河划了三天的獨木舟。

- **Having worked all day, I was too tired to argue and I simply walked away from Kay.** → 分詞完成式
  工作了一整天，我累得沒有力氣爭吵，只是從凱身邊走開。

3 **be** → 與現在分詞一起構成各種進行式，或與過去分詞一起構成被動式。
- am/is/are ● was/were ● being ● been

- **Our cooking contest winner is making dinner.**
  我們的烹飪賽冠軍正在做晚餐。
  ↳ 助動詞 is 與動詞現在分詞 making 一起構成現在進行式。

- **Last night two people were injured in a car accident.** 昨晚的車禍中有兩人受傷。
  ↳ 助動詞 were 和動詞過去分詞 injured 一起構成被動式（過去式）。

4 **will** → 與動詞原形一起構成未來式。
- will ● would

- **Don't worry, because Jill and Gus will win the game for us.**
  不要擔心，潔兒和加斯會為我們贏得這場比賽的。
  ↳ will 可以作助動詞，與另一個動詞構成簡單未來式。

- **Mike said he would retire in two years, and then he would move to Shanghai.** 麥克說，他兩年內會退休，然後搬去上海住。
  ↳ would 和動詞原形 retire, move 一起構成過去未來式。

情態動詞／情態助動詞

1 情態動詞的定義和形式

1 **情態動詞**與另一個動詞連用，表示能力、可能性、許可、必要、意圖等。情態動詞包括：

- can
- may
- must
- shall
- will
- dare
- could
- might
- ought to
- should
- would
- need

2 情態動詞是一種特殊的助動詞，又稱為**情態助動詞**。有些文法學家則把助動詞和情態動詞統稱為「助動詞」，不過，情態動詞不只輔助動詞，本身還帶有一定的含意，而助動詞本身是沒有含意的。情態動詞和助動詞一樣，不能單獨使用，只能與其他動詞（亦即主要動詞）連用。

- She may arrive tonight. 她今晚可能會抵達。
  ⇡ 情態動詞 may 意思是「也許」，不能單獨使用，要和主要動詞（arrive）連用。

情態動詞一覽表

情態動詞	否定式	簡略否定式	註
can	cannot	can't	cannot 是一個字，不是兩個字。否定式 can not 是不標準的。
could	could not	couldn't	
may	may not	mayn't	英式英語有時用縮寫形式 mayn't，但不常見；在美式英語中，mayn't 是錯誤的拼寫。
might	might not	mightn't	不常用縮寫式 mightn't。
will	will not	won't	
would	would not	wouldn't	

shall	shall not	shan't	縮寫形式 shan't 只用於英式英語，而且不常見。
should	should not	shouldn't	
must	must not	mustn't	
ought to	ought not to	oughtn't	縮寫式 oughtn't 不常用。
need	need not	needn't	need 可作一般動詞，即實義動詞。
dare	dare not	daren't	* 縮寫形式 daren't 不常用。 * dare 可作一般動詞。
had better	had better not		
have to has to had to will have to	do not have to does not have to did not have to will not have to	don't have to doesn't have to didn't have to won't have to	* 英式口語的肯定句中可用 have got to。 * have to 不是情態動詞，只是意義和情態動詞 must 相同。

2 情態動詞的特徵（區別於一般動詞）

1 情態動詞沒有變化形式，因此第三人稱單數不以 -s 結尾。

- **Bess may know his address.** 貝絲也許知道他的地址。
- **Bess knows his address.** 貝絲知道他的地址。

 ↳ 簡單現在式，第三人稱單數（如：he, she, it, Mary 等）的動詞要以 -s 結尾。

 » 參見 528 頁〈2 第三人稱單數的動詞變化形式〉。

- **Ann can belly dance.** 安會跳肚皮舞。

2 情態動詞沒有不定式、現在分詞和過去分詞的形式，必要時可以用其他同義句型。

● can → be able to

- **Jane would like to be able to fly an airplane.** 珍希望能夠駕駛飛機。

3 情態動詞的疑問句、否定句和簡略回答，不用助動詞 do/does。

◆ 疑問句：將情態動詞移至主詞之前。

◆ 否定句：在情態動詞後面加否定詞 not。

- **Can she water-ski? = Does she water-ski?** 她會滑水嗎？

✗ Mike doesn't should be shouting at Pat like that.
✓ Mike shouldn't be shouting at Pat like that.
邁克不應該那樣對派特大吼大叫。

- May I help you, Kay? 凱，我可以幫你嗎？
  ↑ 含情態動詞的疑問句，將情態動詞移至句首。
- Do you need my help, Sue? 蘇，你需要我的幫忙嗎？
  ↑ 含實義動詞的疑問句，在句首加助動詞（do 或 does）。

- Brook cannot cook. 布魯克不會做飯。
  ↑ 含情態動詞的否定句，情態動詞後面加 not。
- Del doesn't cook very well. 戴爾的烹調技術不好。
  ↑ 含實義動詞的否定句，加助動詞與否定詞 not
  （do no/don't 或 does not/doesn't）。

4 情態動詞後面只能用原形動詞，不能接帶 to 的不定式、動名詞或分詞（ought to 例外）。

✗ must to speak ✗ must spoken ✗ must speaks
✗ must speaking ✗ must spoke

- Wow! Kim really can dive and swim! →can + 原形動詞（dive, swim）
  哇！金姆真的會跳水和游泳呀！
- He might stop to visit me on his way to France. →might + 原形動詞（stop）
  他在去法國的路上也許會順道來看我。
- Sue may stay with us for a week or two. →may + 原形動詞（stay）
  蘇也許會跟我們一起住一、兩星期。

比較 You can use my cellphone to call Sue. 你可以用我的手機打電話給蘇。
↑ 情態動詞（can）後面只能接原形動詞。
Joan wants to use my xylophone. 喬恩想要用我的木琴。
↑ 在許多一般動詞後面則要用不定式。

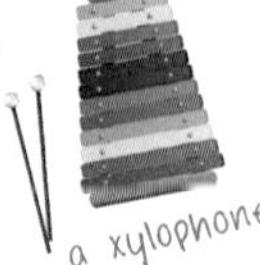
a xylophone

5 情態動詞沒有未來式。

- Kay may go to Britain for further study next May.
  明年五月凱可能要去英國進修。
  ↑ 談論未來的事情，但情態動詞（may）不變形，沒有未來式，不能寫成 will may。

- **If Trish works hard, she'll learn English.** 如果翠西努力學習，就能學好英文。
  ↑ 談論未來的事情，一般動詞（learn）與助動詞 will 構成未來式。

6 一般而言，情態動詞沒有過去式，然而，could、might、would（原本是用來表示「可能性、請求」的情態動詞）有時被看作 can、may、shall、will 的過去式；must、ought to、should 的過去式則要改用其他句型。

現在式、未來式	過去式、過去未來式
● can go	● could go 許可、能力
● may go	● might go 可能（用於間接引語）
● shall go〔主英式〕	● would go（表示單純的未來）將
● will go	● would go（表示單純的未來）將
● must go	● had to go
● ought to go	● ought to have gone
● should go	● should have gone
● ought to + 動詞原形	● ought to have + 過去分詞
● should + 動詞原形	● should have + 過去分詞

- **Can you swim more than a mile?** 你能游超過一英里嗎？ → 現在式
- **Could you swim more than a mile when you were young?**
  你年輕時能游超過一英里嗎？ → 過去式

- **If she wants to do international business, Trish must work hard at her English.** 如果翠西想從事國際貿易，就得努力學習英語。 → 現在／將來
- **Kay is really tired now, because she had to work hard for 14 hours yesterday to get the project done.**
  凱現在真的很累，她昨天為了完成這個案子，不得不努力工作了 14 個小時。 → 過去

- **You ought to be more polite to Andrew.**
  你應該對安德魯更禮貌一點。 → 現在／將來
- **You ought to have been more polite to Andrew.**
  = You should have been more polite to Andrew.
  你本應該對安德魯更禮貌一點的。 → 過去

can, could 的用法

1 can 的句型

肯定句	I/You/He/She/It/We/They can go.
疑問句	Can I/you/he/she/it/we/they go?
否定句	I/You/He/She/It/We/They cannot go.

縮寫：cannot = can't

- **If I can do it, you can do it, too.** 如果我能做這件事，你也能夠做。 → 肯定句
- **I can't hear you!** 我聽不到你的聲音！ → 否定句
- **Can she beguile Dan with her smile?** 她能夠用她的微笑吸引丹嗎？ → 疑問句

1 can 沒有未來的形式。can 本身可以表示現在，也可以表示未來。

2 若要強調某人**未來才有能力**（future ability）做某事，或某事在**未來**發生的可能性（尤其是要經過一段較長的時間），則要改用 will be able to。

- **Trish can speak Chinese, Spanish, and English.**
  翠西會講中文、西班牙文和英文。 → 指現在的能力。

- **When can you pay Jan and Nan?** 你何時能付薪水給簡和南？
  ↑ 計畫即將要做的事。

- **Will Coco be able to speak Russian fluently before she goes to Moscow?** 可可能夠在去莫斯科之前就講得一口流利的俄文嗎？
  ↑ 強調某人未來才有能力做某事。

- **Sixty years from now, tourists will be able to visit Neptune's moons.**
  六十年後，觀光客就能夠拜訪海王星的衛星。
  ↑ 未來發生的可能性（經過很長一段時間）。

3 can 沒有不定式或 -ing 形式，也沒有完成式，在這種情況下，要用 be able to 來表示「**有能力或有辦法做某事**」。

- **She wants to be able to water-ski and scuba dive.** → 不定式形式
  她想要能夠會滑水和做水肺潛水。
- **I enjoy being able to speak five languages.** → -ing 形式
  我很能享受於自己能夠講五種語言。
- **Meg hasn't been able to go bowling since last month when she injured her leg.** → 完成式
  梅格上個月傷到腳之後就無法去打保齡球了。

4 can 的否定式是 cannot，在口語或非正式用語中，常縮寫為 can't。

- **My little sister Kay cannot dance, but she can smile.**
  我的小妹妹凱不會跳舞，但會微笑。
- **No, Dee and I can't surf or scuba dive, but we can ride bikes and go on hikes.**
  不會，蒂和我不會衝浪和水肺潛水，但我們會騎自行車和健行。

Diving Deep Into English 67 can not 和 cannot 的用法

1 can 的否定形式是 cannot，口語中常用縮寫式 can't。
can not 不是標準的英語，最好避免使用。

Not standard　I can not dance.
Common　I cannot dance. = I can't dance. 我不會跳舞。

2 注意 片語 can not only 中，not 應該與 only 視為一個整體（not only），而不是跟 can 搭配的，與上述不標準的否定縮寫形式 can not 不可混為一談。

- **Trish can not only speak in English, but she can also speak and write in Polish.** 翠西不僅會講英文，還會說、會寫波蘭文。
  t. 在「not only . . . but also」這個結構中，not 不是 can 的否定形式。

2 could 的句型

肯定句	I/You/He/She/It/We/They could go.
疑問句	Could I/you/he/she/it/we/they go?
否定句	I/You/He/She/It/We/They could not go.

縮寫：could not = couldn't

- **Dan couldn't find his way out of the maze, because he was in a romantic daze.**
  丹走不出迷宮，因為他已經被浪漫沖昏了頭。

3 can 和 could 的意義

1 can 和 could 表示**能力**（ability, skill），通常指有能力或有辦法做某事，可指身體、心理或精神上的各種能力。

現在式 / 未來式 can　　過去式 could

- **Anna can scuba dive, fix engines, read Greek, and make me laugh.**
  安娜會水肺潛水，會修理引擎，看得懂希臘文，而且還會逗我笑。 → 現在式
- **Anna could scuba dive when she was five.**
  安娜五歲時就會水肺潛水了。 → 過去式

- **I think I can finish writing the magazine article about Hawaii by 6 p.m. tomorrow.**
  我想我在明天下午六點以前，能夠寫完那篇夏威夷的雜誌專文。
  ↑ 未來
- **She asked me whether I could visit her on the weekend.**
  她問我週末可不可以去找她。
  ↑ 表示過去有能力或有辦法做某事，要用 can 的過去式 could。
  ↑ could 用於間接引語中。主句是過去式動詞 asked，子句用 could。

Diving Deep Into English 68 比較 could 和 was/were able to（過去式）

❶ could 是 can 的過去式，**泛指在一般情況下**，過去有能力或有辦法做某事（也可以用 was/were able to），但不說明實際上是否有做某事；was/were able to 指**在特定情況下**，透過努力成功做成某事的能力。

- **New York City used to be a place where anyone could start a business.**
  = New York City used to be a place where anyone was able to start a business.
  紐約市以前是一個人人都可以在那裡創業的地方。
  ↑ 泛指在一般情況下，過去有能力或辦法做某事。(general ability)

start a business

✗ **After I climbed on the table, I could open that window.**
✓ **After I climbed on the table, I was able to open that window.**
我爬上桌子之後，就可以打開窗子了。
↑ 指在特定情況下，透過努力而做成某事（= managed to open/succeeded in opening）。(particular occasion)

❷ 在以下情況下，可以用 could 表示在**特定的情況**下，有能力或有辦法做成或沒做成某事：

a 與 see, hear, taste, feel, smell, understand, remember, follow, remember, guess 連用時：

- **She could smell something burning.**
  = She smelled something burning. 她能聞到有東西在燒的味道。
- **I couldn't understand what she was talking about.**
  = I didn't understand what she was talking about.
  我聽不懂她在講什麼。
- **From the top of the hill, Joe could see the village below.**
  喬從山頂上可以看到下面的村落。

b 在子句中：

- **I'm glad that you could come.** 我很高興你可以來。

c 在否定句中：

- I was able to find the street, but I couldn't find her house.
  我找得到街道，但找不到她的房子。

d 與 hardly、only 連用時：

- I could hardly believe my ears. 我真不敢相信我的耳朵。
- She could only buy two eggs. 她只能買兩顆蛋。

2 can、could、may 都可表達「**請求許可**」，指現在或未來。表達此意時，could 並不是 can 的過去式。

現在式 / 未來式 can, could, may

- can/could/may I/we (please) . . . ? 請求許可做某事
- can/could/may I/we (please) have . . . ? 請求許可得到某物

- Mom, can/may/could I please go to the prom with Tom tonight?
  媽媽，今晚我可以跟湯姆一起去參加班級舞會嗎？ → 未來（請求許可做某事）
- Bess, can/may/could I have your email address?
  貝絲，可以告訴我你的電子郵寄地址嗎？ → 現在（請求許可得到某物）

3 can 和 could 表示**准許與否**（permission），用於肯定句和否定句。

現在式 / 未來式 can 過去式 could

a 表示准許與否，只能用 can 或 can't 指現在或未來；could 和 couldn't 用於過去式。

- I told Jake, "You can take a nap while Kay is practicing ballet."
  = I told Jake that he could take a nap while Kay was practicing ballet.
  我跟傑可說：「趁凱在練芭蕾之際，你可以小睡一下。」
  ↳ 第一句是直接引語，第二句是間接引語。在直接引語中，用 can 表示「許可」，指現在或未來；在間接引語中，用 could 表示「許可」，指過去。

✗ Sorry, Mary, but you couldn't make a lot of noise in this library.
✗ Sorry, Mary, but you are not able to make a lot of noise in this library.
✓ Sorry, Mary, but you can't make a lot of noise in this library.

= Sorry, Mary, but you must not make a lot of noise in this library.
= Sorry, Mary, but you are not allowed to make a lot of noise in this library. 很抱歉，瑪麗，本圖書館內不能製造這麼多噪音喔。

↳ 表示「不准許」，要用 can't（也可用 must not），指現在和將來，不能用 couldn't。
↳ be able to 表示「能夠」，不表示「許可」或「不許可」。

- You can eat now, or you can wait for Pete.
  你可以現在吃飯，也可以等彼特一起吃。
  ↳ 表示「准許」，要用 can，指現在和將來，不能用 could。

- "Could/Can I bother you for a minute?" "Yes, you can."
  「可以耽誤你一分鐘嗎？」「可以啊。」
  ↳ 疑問句（現在式）：請求許可做某事，可以用 can，也可以用 Could。
  ↳ 回答表示「准許」只能用 can，不用 could。

b 比較 can 和 could 表示「**准許與否**」

- Sue's mom said to Tom, "You can't take my daughter to the prom."
  蘇的媽媽對湯姆說：「你不能帶我女兒去舞會。」 → 現在式（不允許）

- Sue's mom told Tom that he couldn't take her daughter to the prom. 蘇的媽媽告訴湯姆，他不能帶她女兒去舞會。 → 過去式（不允許）
  ↳ 這是間接引語句子。主句用過去式 told，子句也用過去式 couldn't。

- Even today, women still can't vote in some countries.
  = Even today, women are still not allowed to vote in some countries.
  甚至在今天，一些國家的婦女仍然沒有選舉權。
  ↳ can't 或 are/is not allowed to，用來表示現在普遍不被允許做的事。

- Two hundred years ago, women couldn't vote.
  = Two hundred years ago, women were not allowed to vote.
  兩百年前，婦女沒有選舉權。
  ↳ couldn't 或 were/was not allowed to，用來表示過去普遍不被允許做的事。

4 can 和 could 可用來表示**請求**和**邀請**（request or invitation），表達此意時，could 並不是 can 的過去式。

現在式／未來式　can, could

正式 could you . . . ? → 跟陌生人、長輩、老師、上司談話時用，較為客氣。
非正式 can you . . . ?

- **Mom, could you pass me the butter, please?** → 現在
  媽媽，可以請你把奶油遞給我嗎？
  ↑ 表「請求」可以用 can 或 could；用 could 更客氣。

- **Can/Could you go out for dinner with me tonight?** → 將來
  今晚跟我一起出去吃晚飯，好嗎？
  ↑ 表「邀請」可以用 can 或 could；用 could 更委婉。

5 can 和 could 也可用來提出**建議**（suggestions or advice），意為「可以」或**主動提議做某事**（offers），could 不是過去式，而是指現在或未來，口氣比 can 委婉。

現在式 / 未來式 can, could

- **You can/could lend her your car if hers isn't fixed by Sunday.**
  如果她的車子到星期天還沒有修好，你可以把你的車借給她。 → 建議（將來）

- **Can/Could I help you with the dinner?**
  = Should/Shall I help you with the dinner? 我幫你做晚餐，好嗎？
  ↑ 提議做某事（現在）

- **Can/Could I offer you and Pete something to eat?**
  我拿點吃的給你和彼特好嗎？ → 提供物品（現在）

6 can 和 could 可以用來表示做某事的**機會**或**選擇**（opportunities, choices），could 在此不是 can 的過去式。could 這種用法類似 might，表示可能性較小。

現在式 / 未來式 can, could, might

- **If the weather is good tomorrow, we can/could/might go camping with Joe.** 如果明天天氣好，我們就可以和喬一起去露營。 → 選擇

- **You can/could/might still win—the game is not over yet.**
  你仍然有可能贏的，比賽還沒有結束。 → 機會

7 can 和 could 可用來表示**邏輯推論**。

a 在疑問句和否定句中，can 表對**現在**的邏輯推論（present logical possibility），詢問現在的某事是否是真的，或表示現在的某事不可能是真的。

現在式 can → 用於疑問句或否定句中

- There's the doorbell. Who can that be? 門鈴在響。會是誰呢？
- Look at Mitch and his old clothes, and you'll know he can't be rich.
看看米奇和他那一身舊衣服，你就知道他不可能是有錢人。

b 在肯定句中，要用 could（= may, might）表示對**現在**的邏輯推論，意思是「**或許**」（perhaps, maybe）。表達此意時，不用 can，而是用 could。could 在此用法中並非是 can 的過去式。

現在式 could → 用於肯定句中

- There could be life on Mars or on planets that orbit distant stars.
= There may/might be life on Mars or on planets that orbit distant stars.
= Perhaps there is life on Mars or on planets that orbit distant stars.
在火星上，或是在遠遠繞著恆星運行的行星上，有可能有生命的存在。

c 在肯定句中，can 和 only 或 hardly 連用時，可以表示對**現在**的邏輯推論。表示偶然發生的**可能性**可以用 can，意為「有時會⋯⋯」。

現在式 can → 用於肯定句（與 only、hardly 連用）

- "Who's that at the door?" "It can only be your sister." → 與 only 連用
「在門邊的那個人是誰？」「一定是你妹妹，不會是別人。」
- Sometimes it can be extremely busy at the Play Day Café. → 偶然發生
遊日咖啡廳有時會忙翻了。

d 在肯定句中，不用 can，而要用 could（= may, might）推測**未來**要發生的事。

未來式 could

- War between those two nations could break out soon.
= War between those two nations may/might break out soon.
這兩國之間隨時可能爆發戰爭。

8 「could have + 過去分詞」表對過去的邏輯推論。

在**疑問句**和**否定句**中，「could have + 過去分詞」可以表達對**過去**的邏輯推論，詢問過去的某事是否是真的（疑問句），或表示過去的某事可能不是真的（否定句）。

- Jake, could that strange noise have been our ape killing a snake?
  傑克，剛才那奇怪的聲音會不會是我們的無尾猿把蛇殺死的聲音？
  ↳ 疑問句：過去某事可能是真的（無尾猿剛才可能殺死了一隻蛇）。

- Bart couldn't have fixed my car, because the motor still won't start.
  巴特應該還沒修我的車，因為馬達還是發不動。
  ↳ Perhaps Bart did not fix my car.
  ↳ 意指「Bart 不可能修好了我的車」。對過去情況的否定推測，美式用「couldn't have + 過去分詞」，英式有時也用「can't have + 過去分詞」。

9 「could have + 過去分詞」也可以表示假設語氣。

「could have + 過去分詞」也可以表示**過去**可能發生，但實際上未發生的事，是一種假設語氣。

- Joyce could have been married to Mark Wood if she had made a different choice. 假如喬伊絲當初作了不同的選擇，她可能就嫁給了馬克·伍德。
  ↳ 事實上喬伊絲沒有嫁給馬克·伍德。

- Mike was lucky—he could have been killed when the grizzly bear tore up his tent. 邁克很幸運——當那隻凶悍的灰棕熊撕破他的帳篷時，他可能就沒命了。 → 事實上他沒有被黑熊殺死。

比較

- Annie, can that scary noise be from a howler monkey?
  安妮，那個可怕的聲音會不會是吼猴的聲音呢？
  ↳ 指現在：Perhaps/Maybe that scary noise is from a howler monkey.

- Annie, could that scary noise have been from a howler monkey?
  ↳ 指過去：Perhaps/Maybe that scary noise was from a howler monkey.

- Lily and Millie could do that, because they're both so kind and friendly.
  莉莉和米莉有可能會做那件事，因為她們兩個都很好心、很友善。
  ↳ could do 指現在或未來特定的可能性，憑經驗或證據進行推測，意思為 might, may。

- Lily and Millie couldn't have done that, because they're both so kind and friendly.
  那件事不可能是莉莉和米莉做的，因為她們兩個都很好心、很友善。
  ↳ 「couldn't have + 過去分詞」表示過去某事可能不是真的（他們不可能做過那件事）；「couldn't have + 過去分詞」常用來表示驚訝或懷疑。

may 和 might 的用法

1 may 和 might 的意義與句型

may 和 might 是表示**可能性**或**許可**的情態動詞。may 用於現在式；might 用於過去式，也可以用在現在式或未來式，使語氣較為委婉（同 could）。may 和 might 的句型如下：

肯定句	I/You/He/She/It/We/They may/might go.
疑問句	May/Might I/you/he/she/it/we/they go?
否定句	I/You/He/She/It/We/They may/might not go.

↥ 英式英語有時將 may not 縮寫為 mayn't（不規範），但在美式英語中這種拼寫是錯誤的。

- I might see Bing again someday—who knows what the future might bring? 也許有一天我還會見到賓，誰知道未來會怎樣？
  ↥ might 或 may 後面要接原形動詞。
- May I offer you a cup of coffee or tea? 我可以幫你倒杯咖啡或茶嗎？
  ↥ 疑問句中，might 或 may 要放在句首，即放在主詞前面。
- Ann said that she might not call Dan. 安說，她可能不會打電話給丹。
  ↥ 否定句中，might 或 may 後面接 not。

2 may 和 might 表「可能性」（用於肯定句和否定句，不用於疑問句）

1 may 和 might 指**事情發生的可能性**，此時 might 被視為 may 的過去式，用於間接引語中；may 則用於現在式或未來式。

現在式／未來式 may　　過去式 might

- **We may stop to see Disney World on the way to Miami.**
  去往邁阿密的路上，我們可能會順道停下來參觀迪士尼樂園。 → 未來的可能性

- **Nicole told me that she might stop to see me on her way to Seoul.**
  妮可跟我說，她可能會在前往首爾的路上順道來看我。
  ↳ 主句的動詞用了過去式（told），因此間接引語的子句中動詞也應該用過去式（might），指過去的可能性，不能用現在式／未來式（may）。

- **Sally was afraid that she might be in trouble for blowing her huge green bubble.**
  莎莉擔心她會因為吹綠色大泡泡而惹禍上身。 → 過去式

NOTE 比較直接引語和間接引語中 may 和 might 的用法：

- Susan said, "I may go to Martinique next week." → 直接引語
  蘇珊說：「我下星期也許會去馬提尼克島。」
- Susan said that she might go to Martinique next week. → 間接引語
  蘇珊說她下星期也許會去馬提尼克島。
  ↳ 間接引語由過去式動詞（said）轉述，要用 might（may 的過去式）。

» 參見 649 頁〈Unit 13 直接引語與間接引語〉。

2 might 也可以用於現在式或未來式，表示**微弱的可能性**。此時的 might 和 may 之間不是時態的差異，而是可能性程度的分別，may 表示可能性較大（大約 50% 的可能性），might 表示可能性較小（大約 30% 的可能性），相當於 could。

現在式 **may, might**　未來式 **may, might** → may 的可能性比 might 大

- **It may snow tomorrow.**
- **It might snow tomorrow.**
  = It could snow tomorrow. 明天可能會下雪。
  ↳ might 表示未來的可能性，可能性小於 may。

- **Mike and Mark may need your help pretty soon.**
  邁克和馬克也許很快就會需要你的幫忙了。

- I don't think Dwight needs any help, but he might.
  我想杜威特不需要任何幫忙，但也有可能需要。
  ↑ 可能性小，用 might（指現在或未來）。

- I'd better write her birthday on my calendar, or I may/might/could forget it. 我最好把她的生日寫在日曆上，否則我可能會忘記。

- Kay isn't in her office. She may/might/could be working at home today. 凱不在她的辦公室。她今天也許在家工作。
  ↑ 「may/might/could + be + V-ing」可以表示「現在可能正在發生的事」。

- She might/could be a billionaire one day—but who knows when?
  她有一天也許會成為億萬富翁，不過誰知道是什麼時候？ → 可能性小

3 may 表「可能性」時，不用於疑問句；might 也很少用於疑問句。
疑問句要用 could 或片語 be likely 等。

Not common	Might it rain?
Common	Could it rain? 會下雨嗎？

- Do you think it may/might snow tonight?
  你想今晚會下雪嗎？
  ↑ 在疑問句的受詞子句中，可以用 may/might 表示「可能性」。

- Jane said, "It may/might not rain." 珍說：「可能不會下雨。」
  ↑ 用於否定句。

- Joe said, "It might/may snow." 喬說：「可能會下雪。」 → 用於肯定句。

Diving Deep Into English 69 may not be 與 can't be

may not be 是**也許不會**（= perhaps not）
can't be 是**一定不會**（= certainly not）

- Jerry may not be in his cabin; please call him to find out.
  傑瑞可能不在他的小屋，請打電話跟他確認一下。 → 也許不在

- It's very late, so Kate can't be in her office.
  天色已經很晚了，凱特不可能在她的辦公室。 → 一定不在

3 may 和 might 表「請求許可」

與 can 和 could 一樣， may 和 might 都可以用來**請求許可**，用於正式場合。

現在式 / 未來式 may, might

- May I hold your hand? 我可以握著你的手嗎？
- May Mitch and I ask you how to get rich?
  米奇和我可以向你請教致富之道嗎？

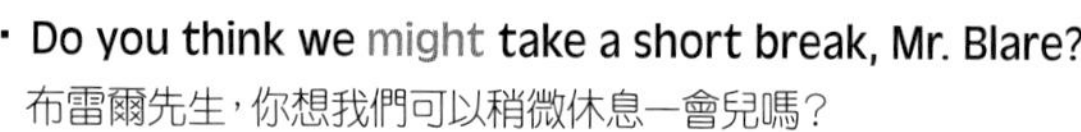

- Do you think we might take a short break, Mr. Blare?
  布雷爾先生，你想我們可以稍微休息一會兒嗎？
  ↳ 更客氣的用法（might 常用於疑問句的受詞子句中）。

» may 表示請求許可，參見 482 頁〈2 can、could 和 may 都可表達「請求許可」〉。

NOTE

can、could、may 都可以表示請求許可，但語氣不同，可以依照具體的場合使用不同的詞。

Casual	Can I/we . . . ?	→ 一般朋友間使用
More Formal	Could I/we . . . ?	→ 跟陌生人、長輩、老師、上司談話時用
Very Formal	May I/we . . . ?	→ 非常正式的場合使用（美式用 may，英式也可以用 might）

- Can I use your robotic dinosaur for a day, Dan?
  丹，我可以借你的機器恐龍用一天嗎？ → 非正式的場合（跟朋友說話）
- Mr. Smith, could Kay and I leave a little early today?
  史密斯先生，凱和我今天可不可以早點走？
  ↳ 正式的場合（跟老師或上司說話）
- Mrs. Otter, may I please have your permission to marry your daughter? 奧特太太，請同意讓我娶您的女兒，好嗎？
  ↳ 非常正式的場合
- Can't/Couldn't I stay at the party a little bit longer? Please?
  請讓我在聚會上再多待一會，好嗎？
  ↳ 擔心提出的請求可能會被拒絕，因此特別希望某人能給肯定的回答，可以用「can't/couldn't I/we . . .?」。

4 may 表「准許與否」（非常正式的場合）

you may 或 you may not 用於非常正式的場合，表示准許與否。在非正式的場合，更常用 can/cannot。

- You may kiss my granddaughter Sue only after you two get married. 在你們兩人結婚後，你才可以親吻我的孫女蘇。
- You may not leave until the principal has finished her speech. 要等到校長的演講結束，你才可以離開。

5 may 和 might 表「客氣的請求或提議」

may 和 might 都可以用於**客氣的請求或提議**（只與 I 和 we 連用）。美式更常用 may。

現在式 / 未來式 may, might

- "May I see your ID, please?" asked Sheriff Ray Lee.
  「我可以看你的身分證嗎？」雷·李警長問。 → 客氣的請求或要求

crackers and cheese

- May I offer you some crackers and cheese?
  要我給你拿些餅乾和起司來嗎？ → 客氣的提供食品
- Jake, might I make a suggestion to you about that huge snake?
  傑克，關於那隻大蛇，我可以給你個建議嗎？ → 客氣的提議

6 may 表「願望」

may 也可以表示**願望**或**祝福**，句型為「may + 主詞 + 動詞原形」。

- Sue, may happiness always be with you! 蘇，願你永遠幸福！
- May you live long and happy, Ray. 雷，祝你幸福長壽。
- May all your Christmases be white! 祝你每年都有個白色的聖誕節！
- May you succeed in your new business, Kay!
  凱，祝你新的事業成功！

7 may/might have + 過去分詞

1 「**may/might have + done（過去分詞）**」表示**對過去可能性的猜測**，用來談論過去可能發生的事，但不確定到底有沒有發生，與 could have done 的用法一樣。

- something may/might have happened
  = perhaps something happened
  指過去可能發生過的事

- **All of the deaths may/might have been caused by the jeep driver falling asleep.**
  = All of the deaths could have been caused by the jeep driver falling asleep.
  = Perhaps all of the deaths were caused by the jeep driver falling asleep.
  所有的死亡都可能是由於吉普車司機睡著所造成的。
  ↑ might/may + have been caused（過去分詞）

- **Jill may/might have changed her mind and decided not to go to Brazil.**
  = Jill could have changed her mind and decided not to go to Brazil.
  = Perhaps Jill changed her mind and decided not to go to Brazil.
  潔兒可能已經改變心意，決定不去巴西了。
  ↑ might/may + have changed（過去分詞）

2 「**might have + done（過去分詞）**」也用來表示**與過去事實相反的假設**，談論過去可能發生、實際上卻未發生的事，是一種假設語氣，與 could have done 的用法一樣。表示假設語氣，不用 may 和 can。

- something might have happened
  某事在過去可能發生，但事實上並沒有發生

- **Lisa said, "You might have been killed in that stupid war."**
  = Lisa said, "You could have been killed in that stupid war."
  麗莎說：「你本來可能會在那場愚蠢的戰爭中喪生的。」
  ↑ might + have been killed（過去分詞）

比較：「may have + 過去分詞」與「might have + 過去分詞」

1 表示特定的過去可能性，但不確定到底有沒有發生，可以用「may have + 過去分詞」，也可以用「might have + 過去分詞」。

- The pilot Jane Wu may/might have been killed in the helicopter crash in Spain.
  飛行員吳珍可能已經在這次西班牙的直昇機墜機中喪生。
  ↳ 還未收集到具體的資訊，新聞廣播最初報導一次事故（還不確定飛行員是否遇難）。

2 表示過去實際上未發生的事（假設語氣），只能用「might have + 過去分詞」，不用「may have + 過去分詞」。

- Without a timely rescue, the pilot Jane Wu might have been killed in the helicopter crash in Spain.
  假如沒有及時救援，飛行員吳珍就有可能在這次西班牙的直昇機墜機中喪生。
  ↳ 收集到具體的資訊後，新聞廣播再次報導墜機事故。事實：飛行員吳珍沒有死。

3 「**may/might**（不用 can）**have + done（過去分詞）**」也用來表示未來某個時候，某件事可能已經發生了。

- something may/might have happened
  某事在未來可能已經發生

- **By next Saturday, they may/might have installed the solar panels.**

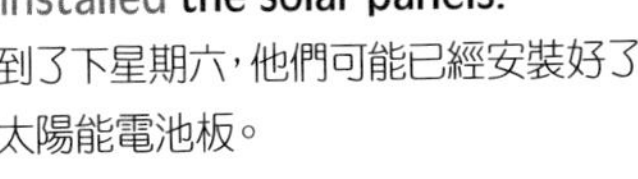

到了下星期六，他們可能已經安裝好了太陽能電池板。

shall, will, should, would 的用法

1 shall 和 will 為助動詞（簡單未來式）

1 過去的文法教學，不論是美式英語或英式英語，第一人稱簡單未來式都用 I shall、we shall，不用 I will、we will。然而英語在不斷演變，隨著時間流逝，shall 逐漸被 will 取代，用於簡單未來式。現代英語中，美式英語已經完全摒棄了 I shall、we shall 這種簡單未來式的用法，而用 I will、we will；英式英語雖然仍用 I shall、we shall，但也越來越少見。

第一人稱簡單未來式

傳統用法	現代用法	
	英式〔少用〕	美式／英式〔常用〕
• I shall • we shall	• I shall • we shall	• I will • we will

- I shall be very busy tomorrow. → 英式英語
- I will be very busy tomorrow. 我明天會很忙。 → 現代英語

- We shall visit Jill again soon. → 英式英語
- We will visit Jill again soon. 我們很快就會再去探望潔兒。 → 現代英語

- He will tell you the result tomorrow, but not today.
  他明天會把結果告訴你，但今天不會。 → 單數第三人稱（he），用 will，不用 shall。
- School will start next week for Jill and Bill. 潔兒和比爾下星期要開學了。
  ↑ 單數名詞（school），用 will，不用 shall。

- "Who do you think will win on Sunday?" asked Lynne.
  琳恩問:「你覺得星期天誰會贏?」
  ↑ 疑問代名詞(Who),用 will,不用 shall。
  » 參見 553 頁〈2 簡單未來式 will〉。

2 shall 和 will 作助動詞，表示未來式時，其**過去式**應該是 would（過去的未來），而不是 should（英國人有時用 should 作 shall 的過去式，但很少見）。

- I told Joe that I would leave tomorrow.
  我告訴過喬我明天要離開。
  ↑ 過去未來式
- We told Linda that we would visit her again soon.
  我們跟琳達說過，我們很快就會去探望她的。 → 過去未來式
  » 參見 587 頁〈3 過去未來式〉。

3 在傳統用語中，shall 也可以與第三人稱或第二人稱連用，常用在正式的場合中（法律檔、規章、條約、會議記錄等），表示「義務，規定，責任」，意思是「應該；必須」；但現代語可以用 will 或 should 取代 shall。

Traditional She finished her speech by noting "Horse thieves shall be punished."
↑ shall 用於傳統用語或非常正式的場合。

Modern She finished her speech by noting "Horse thieves will/should be punished."
她以指明「盜馬賊應該受到懲戒」來結束演講。

2 shall 作情態動詞：表「提供；提議；請求建議」

疑問句中，shall 仍可和 I/we 連用，用來徵求對方意見，表示**提供**（make an offer）、**提議**（make a proposal）或**請求建議**（ask for advice）。此時，shall 作情態動詞用，而不是表示簡單未來式的助動詞。

- The waiter asked, "Shall I take your coat, Ms. Moat?"
  服務生問:「莫特女士，我幫您拿大衣好嗎?」 → 提議

- Shall I make a pot of coffee for you and Scot?
  我幫你和史考特煮一壺咖啡好嗎？ → 提供

- What shall we do now? 我們現在該怎麼辦？ → 請求建議
  ↑ 表示「請求建議」，美式英語更常用 should I/we（如：What should we do now?），而英式常用 shall I/we。

3 will 作情態動詞：表「提議；命令；意願」

1 will 作情態動詞時，用來表示可能性、客氣的提議、客氣的請求、命令、規則、必然性，以及（現在）習慣性的行為。

- Will your habit of leaving garbage everywhere make people think you're messy?
  你亂扔垃圾的習慣，會不會讓人們認為你是一個邋遢的人？
  ↑ 可能性

- Won't you stay here a little bit longer?
  再多待一會兒好嗎？
  ↑ 客氣的提議、請求

- Will you please be quiet? 請你們安靜一點兒好嗎？
  ↑ 客氣的請求（也可以用 would/could/can 表示「請求」）

- Dirk, you will not go out until you finish your homework.
  德克，你作業沒寫完就不准出去。 → 命令

- At the meeting, the manager emphasized the requirement, "All the staff members will punch in by 8 a.m."
  會議中，經理強調了那條規定：「所有的工作人員都要在早上八點準時打卡。」
  ↑ 強烈的責任或要求／規定

- Wendy, you will regret this.
  溫蒂，你會為此後悔的。 → 必然性

- Whenever Jill tells a joke, she will wiggle and giggle.
  潔兒一講笑話就會咯咯笑著扭動身子。 → （現在）習慣性的行為

» 表過去習慣性的行為，參見 500 頁〈6 would 可以作助動詞（用於過去式）〉。

2 will not 或 won't 可以表示不願意做某事，也可以表示某物不能正常運作。

- **If you won't tell Jill the truth, I will.** → 不願意
  如果你不願意告訴潔兒事實，我會告訴她。
- **Something is wrong with my car. It won't start.** → 不能正常工作
  我的車子有問題，發動不起來。

3 'll 的用法

a 'll 是 will 的縮寫，常與下列代名詞連用：

- I'll
- we'll
- he'll
- you'll
- she'll
- they'll
- it'll
- who'll

b 正式英語中，'ll 通常不與名詞和上述之外的代名詞連用，that'll、this'll、when'll、there'll 等都不是標準英語，口語中尚能接受，正式用語必須避免。're、've、'd 的縮寫與代名詞的搭配也是同樣用法。

Informal **"When'll that be?" asked Jill.**
Formal **"When will that be?" asked Jill.** 潔兒問：「那將是什麼時候呢？」
Informal **Where're my green jeans?**
Formal **Where are my green jeans?** 我的綠色牛仔褲在哪裡？
Informal **"That'd be good," said Pat Wood.**
Formal **"That would be good," said Pat Wood.** 派特·伍德說：「那樣可以。」

4 should 為情態動詞（現在式或未來式）

肯定句	I/You/He/She/It/We/They should leave.
疑問句	Should I/you/he/she/it/we/they leave?
否定句	I/You/He/She/It/We/They should not leave.

* 縮寫：shouldn't = should not

1 should 表示「做某事的合理性」（應該；必須）時，是情態動詞，不是助動詞 shall 的過去式。should 用於現在式和未來式中，表示某事是恰當的、合理的、正確的、義不容辭的（義務，責任，建議，命令，決定）。

- Amy wrote an interesting book—you should read it.
  艾咪寫了一本很有趣的書。你應該讀一讀。
- There should be a law against smoking near schools.
  應該要有一條法律禁止在學校附近抽菸。
- Gus, you shouldn't smoke on the bus. 加斯，你不該在公車上吸菸。
- Wayne, you shouldn't drive fast in the rain.
  韋恩，你不應該在下雨天開快車。

2 should 還用於**請求給予確認或建議**的疑問句中。

- Should skinny Kim swim in cold Lake Minnie?
  瘦巴巴的金姆該不該在寒冷的米妮湖游泳？
- Who should/shall I talk to about getting the job?
  要得到那份工作，我該跟誰談談？
- Should/Shall I wear a tie? 我應該打領帶嗎？
  ↑ 表示「請求建議」，美式常用 should I/we，英式常用 shall I/we。

3 should 也可表**強烈的可能性**，確信某事會發生或期待某事發生。

- Sue will show a scary video at her Halloween party, so it should be fun. 蘇要在她辦的萬聖節派對上放映恐怖錄影片，所以派對應該會很好玩。
- Henry is a hardworking student, and he should graduate with honors. 亨利是一個用功的學生，他應該會以優異的成績畢業。

4 should 表達**語氣較強的假設**（萬一；如果），可用在 if 子句中或取代 if 來描述某事發生的可能性。

- Tom muttered, "If anything should happen to me, please contact my mom." 湯姆低聲喃喃道：「萬一我出了什麼事，請跟我媽媽聯絡。」
  ↑ should 用在 if 後面。
- Should we have a bad snowstorm, our school will be closed.
  ↑ should 用來取代 if，置於句首。
  = If we have a bad snowstorm, our school will be closed.
  萬一下暴風雪，我們學校就會停課。 → if 引導的條件句要用現在式表示未來。

5 should have + 過去分詞

1 should have + 過去分詞：表示過去應做而未做的事，是一種假設語氣。當某人沒做該做的事（好事或重要的事），我們就說 he/she/you should have done it。

2 shouldn't have + 過去分詞：表示過去做了不該做的事，是一種假設語氣。當某人做了錯事，我們可以說 he/she/you, etc., shouldn't have done it。

- **You should have taken my advice and should not have married Joyce.** 你早就該聽我的話，不應該跟喬伊絲結婚。
  - ⮤ should have + taken（過去分詞）：表示過去該發生而未發生的事（你沒聽我的建議；你沒做該做的事。）
  - ⮤ should not have + married（過去分詞）：表示不該發生而已經發生的事（你已經跟喬伊絲結婚了；你做錯了。）

- **I acknowledge that I should have studied harder during my last year in college.**
  我承認，我本應該在大學的最後一年更用功一點。

- **Ray is really sick, and he should have gone to the doctor yesterday.**
  雷病得很重，他昨天就應該去看醫生的。

- **I'm sorry, I shouldn't have yelled at you last night.**
  對不起，昨晚我不應該對你大聲叫喊。

- **She shouldn't have eaten so much junk food.**
  她不應該吃那麼多垃圾食物。

3 should have done 也可指一個很可能已經發生的事情或活動。

- **Your prize-winning cow should have arrived in Macao by now.**
  你那頭得獎的乳牛現在應該已經抵達澳門了。
  - ⮤ should have + arrived（過去分詞）：表示很可能已經發生的行為。

6 would 可以作助動詞（用於過去式）

1 would 作助動詞時，是 will 的過去式，表示過去的習慣，或用在過去未來式中表示過去將發生的事。

直接引語 Dee said, "I'll never forgive you."

間接引語 Dee said that she would never forgive me.
蒂說她永遠也不原諒我。
↑ would 用在間接引語中，表示過去將發生的事。

- **While vacationing in Michigan, Larry met Kay, whom he would marry one day.**
  賴瑞在密西根度假的時候認識了他未來的新娘凱。
  ↑ 過去未來式

- **Whenever we went to Aunt Amy's farm, we would play hide-and-seek.** 每當我們去艾咪姨媽的農場，我們都要玩捉迷藏的遊戲。
  ↑ 用 would 表示過去的習慣時，需要有某個含有重複性的時間或場合（如：whenever, on warm summer nights）。

- **On warm summer nights with clear skies, we would gaze through our telescopes until sunrise.**
  在溫暖夏夜的晴空下，我們常用望遠鏡凝望，直到第二天日出。
  ↑ 過去的習慣（重複性）

- **Last night we gazed through our telescopes until sunrise.**
  昨天夜晚，我們用望遠鏡凝望，直到第二天日出。 → 過去某個特定的事件

2 比較 used to 和 would

a used to 後接原形動詞，沒有人稱和數的變化。used to 表示「過去常常」，但過去習慣性的動作或狀態現在已結束，有「今昔對比」的含義。

- **Lee used to smile all the time, but now he often looks unhappy.**
  李以前總是笑臉常開，但現在常常看起來不開心。

b would 表示過去經常發生的習慣性動作，但沒有「今昔對比」的含義。

- **While in college, I would visit Grandma every summer at her farm.**
  在大學時，我每年暑假都會去奶奶的農場拜訪她。

7 would 可作情態動詞，表「意願、可能、客氣的提議或請求」

would 也是情態動詞（作情態動詞用時，不是過去式），表示意願、可能性、請求或客氣的提議等。would 跟 will 的意思一樣，但語氣更委婉，可能性較小。

現在式 would　未來式 would

- Ann, I would/will be glad to answer any of your questions about becoming a vet. 安，我很樂意回答你任何有關當獸醫的問題。 → 意願
- I think she would/will come to your birthday party.
  我想她可能會參加你的生日聚會。 → 可能性
- I will give Sue some money. Would/Will $500 be enough for Sue to buy milk for her hungry baby?
  我會給蘇一些錢。不知道五百塊美金夠不夠蘇給她飢餓的小寶貝買牛奶？ → 可能性

- Would/Will you please wait outside? 請你在外面等好嗎？ → 請求
- Would/Will it be all right if I use your cellphone to call Joan?
  我可以用你的手機給喬恩打電話嗎？ → 請求許可

8 would like 的用法

1 would like something：would 常用於 I'd like (= I would like) 片語中。I'd like something 表示希望得到某樣東西，語氣比 I want something 客氣。

- I'd like a window seat, please. 我想要一個靠窗的座位。

2 would like/love/prefer to do something：表示想做某事。

- I'd like to buy a good telescope to look at Mars and the stars.
  我想買一個好的望遠鏡，可以用來看火星和星星。
- "I would love to have twin sisters," declared little Mike.
  小邁克表示：「我想要一對雙胞胎妹妹。」

- I think she would prefer to talk to you alone.
  = I think she would rather talk to you alone. 我認為她更希望單獨跟你談話。
  ↳ would prefer to do = would rather do

- I wouldn't like to be taller, but it would be nice if my waist were a bit smaller. 我不想再長高了，但是我的腰能細一點就好了。

3 **would you like to . . . ?**：用來提出邀請。

- Dee, would you like to go to the movies with me?
  蒂，想不想跟我去看電影？ → 邀請

Chicago
Miami

Ann Would you like to enjoy New Year's Eve in Miami with Joy and Steve? → 邀請

Dan I'd love to, but I can't, because I have already told my mom I will go to Chicago and see my brother Tom.

Ann 你想不想跟喬伊和史蒂夫一起去邁阿密歡度除夕？

Dan 我想啊，可是不行，因為我已經告訴媽媽我要去芝加哥看我的弟弟湯姆了。

4 **would you like . . . ?/would you like to have . . .?**：用來提供物品。

- Dee, would you like a cup of hot chocolate milk or coffee?
  蒂，你要來杯熱巧克力牛奶或咖啡嗎？
  ↳「would you like . . .」表禮貌提供物品，不用「will you like . . .」。

- Would you like to have a brownie? 你想不想要來個巧克力布朗尼？
  ↳ 提供物品

Diving Deep Into English 70 would like 與 like 的用法區別

- would like = want 想要
- like = enjoy 喜歡

- I'd like some green tea, please.
  = I'd like to have some green tea, please. 請給我來點兒綠茶。
  ↳ I'd like 等於 I want（我想要），這句不能用 I like（喜歡）。

- I like green tea, but I don't like coffee. → like = enjoy
  我喜歡綠茶，但不喜歡咖啡。

- Would you like to go for a walk tonight?
今晚你想去散步嗎？
⤴ 這裡的「Would you like . . . ?」等於「Do you want . . . ?」，不能用 Do you like（喜歡）。

- Do you like to walk at night? 你喜歡晚上散步嗎？
⤴ 這裡的 like 等於 enjoy。

9 「would have + 過去分詞」（假設語氣）

在帶有 if 條件句的假設語氣中，主句用「would have + 過去分詞」，表示**與過去事實相反的假設**。

- Mike would have brought flowers for me if he had known I was here.
如果邁克知道我在這裡，他就會帶花給我。
⤴ would have + brought（過去分詞）：表示過去沒有發生的事（邁克不知道我在這裡，所以他沒有帶花來）。

» 參見 699 頁〈3 If（與事實相反的假設）〉。

10 will 與 would 的比較

1 will 用來表達**可能實現的期待**（不用 would）。

主詞	+	hope（希望） believe（相信） expect（預料）	+	someone something	+	will . . .

- Jill hopes that the big Swede will succeed.
潔兒希望那個高大的瑞典人成功。

- Mr. Peer believes that China's stock market will rise next year.
皮爾先生相信中國的股市明年會上漲。

2 would 用來表達**感激**（不能用 will be grateful）。

主詞 + would be grateful + if you could/would . . .

- I would be grateful **if you** could **help me baby-sit Lulu.**
  如果你能幫我照顧一下露露，我會很感激的。

- I would be grateful **if you** would **help me phone Dan in Iran.**
  如果你願意幫我打電話給伊朗的丹，我會很感激的。

英式英語中，若主詞為第一人稱 I/we，有時可用 should 代替 would 來表達感激之情（should be grateful）。

- I should be grateful if you would send me more information about Hollywood.
  如果你告訴我更多好萊塢的消息，我會很感激。

3 would 與 wish 連用，表示**希望**某事發生或某種情況產生變化，是一種假設語氣。would 不能換成 will。

主詞 + wish（希望）+ someone / something + would . . .

✗ I wish **it** will **stop snowing and blowing.**
✓ I wish **it** would **stop snowing and blowing.**
要是風雪能停就好了。

- I wish **Jerry** would **marry my sister Mary.**

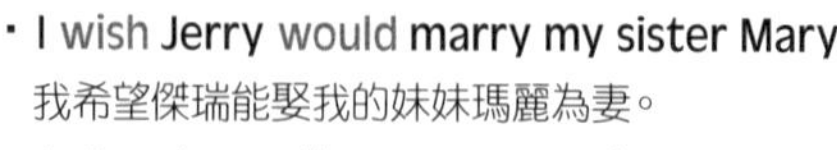

我希望傑瑞能娶我的妹妹瑪麗為妻。
↳ Fact: Jerry will not marry my sister Mary.

must 的用法

1 must 表「義務、必要」

肯定句	I/You/He/She/It/We/They must leave.
疑問句	Must I/you/he/she/it/we/they leave?

1 在肯定句和疑問句中，must 用來表示「義務；責任；必要性」，談論某件我們**不得不做的事情**。

2 must 用於否定句的用法，參見 508 頁〈5 mustn't 與 needn't 的區別〉。

- **You must pay your taxes.**
  你必須繳稅。 → 職責

- **I must defend my right to say no, because I'm tired of eating dust.**
  我必須捍衛我說「不」的權利，因為我再也受不了含垢忍辱了。 → 必要性

- **Tom, you must get your hair cut before you go home to see your mom.**
  湯姆，你必須先剪頭髮再回去見你媽媽。 → 好主意

get your hair cut

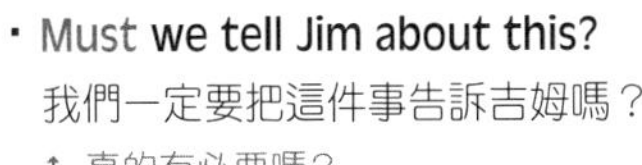

- **Must we tell Jim about this?**
  我們一定要把這件事告訴吉姆嗎？
  ↑ 真的有必要嗎？

2 must 與 should 的差別

should 表示**應該**做的事；must 表示**必須**做的事。

- **My wife says I should eat lots of vegetables and fruit if I want to live a long life.**
  我妻子說，如果我想長壽，就應該吃大量的蔬菜和水果。
- **Should I tell Sue the truth about Ruth?**
  我該把露絲的事對蘇實話實說嗎？
- **You shouldn't depend on the wisdom of John, your fair-weather friend.** 你不應該信賴約翰的看法，他不是個能夠共患難的朋友。
  ↥ shouldn't 表示「不應該」。
- **"Sue, you must be home by 10 p.m.," demanded Dad.**
  爸爸命令說：「蘇，你必須在晚上十點以前回到家。」

- **Gus said to all of us, "You mustn't smoke on a bus."**
  加斯對我們大家說：「公車上禁止吸菸。」
  ↥ mustn't 表示「禁止」。

3 must 表「對現在的合理推論」（用於肯定句）

1 在**肯定句**中，must 也可用來表示合乎邏輯的推論、合理的結局，意思是「一定是、八成是」。

- **He must be very tired after his long trip.** 長途旅行後，他一定很累了。
  ↥ 對現狀的邏輯推論（我斷定他很累了）。
- **Look at Jan's body and jewelry; she must be very healthy and wealthy.** 瞧瞧簡的身材和首飾，她一定很健康也很有錢。
  ↥ 對現狀的邏輯推論（我斷定她健康富有）。
- **The line is busy, and someone—Mom, Dad, or my sister Joan—must be using the phone.**
  電話佔線中，一定是媽媽、爸爸或我妹喬恩在打電話。
  ↥ 對現狀的邏輯推論（我斷定其中一人在打電話）。

2 表示推論的句型也有「現在進行式」。「must be + V-ing」表示「**想必正在發生的事**」，「can't be + V-ing」表示「**想必沒有在發生的事**」。

- **Margo must be sleeping right now. You'd better call her tomorrow.**
  瑪歌想必現在正在睡覺，你最好明天再打電話給她。
- **She can't be out dancing with Joe because she has an English exam early tomorrow morning.**
  她現在不可能在跟喬跳舞，因為她明天一大早就有一場英文考試。

Diving Deep Into English 71 否定句和疑問句用 can 表達對現狀的邏輯推論

只有在肯定句中才用 must 表達必然性，在表示**疑問**和**否定**的句子中則要用 can 來表示對現狀的邏輯推論，來談論必然性。

- **You must be Ann Otter's daughter—you look just like her.**
  你一定是安．奧特的女兒，你長得好像她。
  ↳ 肯定句：我斷定你是安．奧特的女兒。
- **Glen just had a big lunch, and he can't be hungry again.**
  葛倫剛剛才吃了一頓豐盛的午餐，不可能又餓了。
  ↳ 否定句：我肯定葛倫還不餓。
- **Somebody is riding my motorcycle down the street, and I wonder who that can be.**
  有人騎著我的摩托車，沿著街上行駛，我在想那會是誰呢？
  ↳ 這句雖然不是疑問句，但子句（who that can be . . .）表示疑問，要用 can 來表達對現狀的邏輯推論。
- **It can't be Kim at the door; it's only 4 p.m., and she is supposed to get here at 7 p.m.**
  在門口的不可能是金姆，現在才四點，她應該七點才會到。

4 「must have + 過去分詞」表「對過去的推論」（用於肯定句）

something must have happened 的句型，表示確定過去某事已經發生，用於肯定句中，對過去發生之事的邏輯推論。

- Amy says that her car is not in the garage and her husband must have taken it.
  = Amy is sure that her husband took her car. 艾咪說她的車子不在車庫裡，一定是她先生把車開走了。

- Jim can't find his wallet and thinks he must have left it at home.
  = Jim is sure he left his wallet at home.
  吉姆找不到他的皮夾，他猜想一定是忘在家裡了。

Dan Last summer Sue and I visited India. 去年夏天，蘇和我去了印度旅遊。

Ann It must have been wonderful to see India with Sue.
= I am sure it was wonderful for you to see India with Sue.
跟蘇一起去印度旅遊一定很棒。

Diving Deep Into English 72 疑問句和否定句用「could have + 過去分詞」表達對過去的推論

只有在肯定句中才用「must have + 過去分詞」表達對過去的推論，在**疑問句**和**否定句**中要用「could have + 過去分詞」。

- Where could Kay have put my jar of Sunny Honey?
  She couldn't have given it to Dee.
  凱把我那罐陽光牌蜂蜜放到哪裡去了？她不會拿給蒂了吧。

5 mustn't 與 needn't 的區別

1 mustn't 表示「不可以」，即「不要做這件事」（It is forbidden.）。英式英語常用 mustn't，而美式英語常用 don't 引導的祈使句。

2 needn't 表示「不需要」，即「沒有這個必要」（It is not necessary.）。
needn't 相當於 don't/doesn't need to 或 don't/doesn't have to。

- **Nick, you mustn't smoke in the house, because smoke will make our baby sick.**
  = Nick, don't smoke in the house, because smoke will make our baby sick. 尼克，不准在房裡抽菸，香菸會讓我們的寶寶生病。

- **You mustn't waste your time with computer games if you want to go to college.**
  = Don't waste your time with computer games if you want to go to college. 如果你想上大學，就不可以浪費時間玩電腦遊戲。

- **You mustn't eat chocolate before dinner or you will spoil your appetite.**
  = Don't eat chocolate before dinner or you will spoil your appetite. 飯前不要吃巧克力，否則你會沒有食欲。

- **You needn't pay me now, because I won't need the money until May.**
  = It is not necessary for you to pay me now, because I won't need the money until May.
  = You don't have to/You don't need to pay me now, because I won't need the money until May.
  你不需要現在就付錢給我，因為我到五月份才需要那筆錢。

- **Lulu needn't be in such a hurry, because she has lots of time to catch her train to Paris.**
  = It is not necessary for Lulu to be in such a hurry, because she has lots of time to catch her train to Paris.
  = Lulu doesn't have to be in such a hurry, because she has lots of time to catch her train to Paris.
  = Lulu doesn't need to be in such a hurry, because she has lots of time to catch her train to Paris.
  露露不用這麼匆忙吧，她還有很多時間可以趕上開往巴黎的火車。

have to, must, need 的用法

1 have to, had to, will have to（必須）

had to 是 have to 的過去式；will have to 是 must 和 have to 的未來式。注意，have to、had to、will have to 都不是情態動詞，但其含意和用法與情態動詞 must 或 need 是相似的。

have to（現在式）

	第一人稱／第二人稱／複數第三人稱	單數第三人稱
肯定句	I/You/We/They have to leave.	He/She/It has to leave.
疑問句	Do I/you/we/they have to leave?	Does he/she/it have to leave?
否定句	I/You/We/They do not have to leave.	He/She/It does not have to leave.

* 縮寫：• do not have to = don't have to • does not have to = doesn't have to

had to（過去式）

肯定句	I/You/He/She/It/We/They had to leave.
疑問句	Did I/you/he/she/it/we/they have to leave?
否定句	I/You/He/She/It/We/They did not have to leave.

* 縮寫：did not have to = didn't have to

will have to（未來式）

肯定句	I/You/He/She/It/We/They will have to leave.
疑問句	Will I/you/he/she/it/we/they have to leave?
否定句	I/You/He/She/It/We/They will not have to leave.

* 縮寫：will not have to = won't have to

- "Does your wife Kay have to work every Saturday?"
  "Yes, she has to work every Saturday."
  "No, she doesn't have to work every Saturday." → 現在式
  「你太太凱每週六都要工作嗎?」
  「是,她每週六都要工作。」
  「不,她不必每週六都工作。」

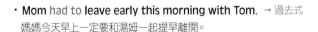

- Mom had to leave early this morning with Tom. → 過去式
  媽媽今天早上一定要和湯姆一起提早離開。

- Did you have to tell Jim about what had happened to Kim in the gym? 你真有必要把金姆在體育館裡所發生的事告訴吉姆嗎?
  ↑ 過去式 had to 的疑問形式

- Nick didn't have to pay for the meal after he began to feel sick.
  尼克開始覺得想吐以後,就不需要付這頓飯錢了。 → 過去式 had to 的否定形式

- If Sam Bard wants to be a doctor, he will have to study hard.
  如果山姆·巴德想當一名醫生,就得努力讀書。 → 單純表示未來(肯定句)

- Will your daughter Coco have to go to Miami soon?
  你女兒可可一定要盡早去邁阿密嗎? → 單純表示未來(疑問句)

- Ann won't have to go to that economics conference in Japan.
  安沒有必要去日本參加經濟學會議。 → 單純表示未來(否定句)

2 have to, must 表「義務與必要性」

1 談論**必要性**和**職責**(necessity and obligation),have to 並不是情態動詞,只是意義和情態動詞 must 相同。

美式 | Do I have to clean up this huge room by noon?
英式 | Must I clean up this huge room by noon?
我要在中午之前把這間大房子打掃乾淨嗎?
↑ 表示「必要」或「責任」時,疑問句中,美式英語常用 have to;英式英語常用 must。

· Today I have to work from one to ten.
今天我得從一點工作到十點。
↑ 這句用 have to work 比 must work 自然。

NOTE 比較這幾個句子，注意不要遺漏主詞。

英式 "Must I do it?" asked Sue. 蘇問：「我必須做這件事嗎？」
美式 "Do I have to do it?" asked Sue. 蘇問：「我必須做這件事嗎？」
美式／英式 "Do I need to do it?" asked Sue. 蘇問：「我需要做這件事嗎？」

2 表示「推論」，要用 must，不用 have to。

✗ This party is crowded. There have to be over 100 people here.
✓ This party is crowded. There must be over 100 people here.
這個聚會真擁擠，這裡一定有一百多人。

3 will have to, must, have to (has to), need 表「未來職責」

1 表示某人未來必須做某事，用 will have to、must、have to/has to 或 need。

2 have to 用於現在式（第三人稱用 has to）；在談論未來，如果要表示職責現在就存在，也可以用 have to。have to 還有常用的英式口語形式：have got to。

· Amy will have to find a job after she graduates from Michigan State University. → 單純表示未來。
= Amy must find a job after she graduates from Michigan State University. → 表「必須」（美式不常用 must）。
= Amy has (got) to find a job after she graduates from Michigan State University. → 表未來，但職責現在就存在。
= Amy needs to find a job after she graduates from Michigan State University. → 表「需要」。
艾咪從密西根州立大學畢業後就得找工作。
↑ 上面幾個句子，needs to 最常用。這裡的 need 是一般動詞。

- You'll have to tell Sue that she was not selected, even though it may make her feel dejected.
  = You must tell Sue that she was not selected, even though it may make her feel dejected.
  = You have (got) to tell Sue that she was not selected, even though it may make her feel dejected.
  = You need to tell Sue that she was not selected, even though it may make her feel dejected.
  你有必要告訴蘇她落選了，就算她知道後會很沮喪。
  ↑ 最後一句的 need 是一般動詞。

4 had to 和 must have done

had to 表「過去的職責」
must have done 表「確信過去發生了某事」

had to 是 have to 的過去式，用來表示**過去的職責**（past obligation）；must have done 用來表示對過去某件事有把握的**推論**（certainty or strong deduction about the past），而不是表示過去的職責（must have done ≠ had to）。

» 參見 508 頁〈4「must have + 過去分詞」表「對過去的推論」〉。

- Jim is not working in his office now; something urgent happened, and he had to go home.
  吉姆現在不在辦公室，發生了緊急的事情，他不得不回家。
  ↑ 過去的義務

- Jim is not working in his office now—he must have gone home.
  吉姆現在不在辦公室，他一定是回家了。
  ↑ 對過去的肯定推論

5 needn't, don't (doesn't) have to, mustn't（否定形式）的用法

1 have to 不是情態動詞，否定形式為 don't have to、doesn't have to，意義與用法同情態動詞 needn't，用來表達「沒有必要；沒有義務」。情態動詞 need 的用法參見 518 頁〈2 need 需要；必要〉。

2 must not、mustn't 表示「禁止；不准」（不可以用 mustn't 表達「不需要」）。

✗ You mustn't call Annie about the meeting, because she already knows about it.
✓ You needn't call Annie about the meeting, because she already knows about it.
✓ You don't have to call Annie about the meeting, because she already knows about it.
你不用打電話告訴安妮開會的事，因為她已經知道了。 → 沒必要

- You mustn't tell Dee about it, because this is just between you and me.
= Don't tell Dee about it, because this is just between you and me.
這件事你不准告訴蒂，因為這是你我之間的祕密。 → 禁止

- Passengers must not smoke in the bathroom.
乘客不准在洗手間抽菸。 → 禁止

- She does not have to get any thinner to be a winner.
= She needn't get any thinner to be a winner.
她不需要為了獲勝而變得更瘦。 → 沒必要

ought to 的用法

1 ought to 表「義務；建議；可能性」

1 ought to 表示「義務；責任」，語氣沒有 must 強烈，和 should 的意義非常接近。

- **Scot ought to pay his debts before he buys any new pets.**
  = Scot should pay his debts before he buys any new pets.
  史考特應該先還債，然後再買新寵物。

- **Sweet little Ruth ought to learn how to wash her smelly feet.**
  = Sweet little Ruth should learn how to wash her smelly feet.
  可愛的小露絲應該學會洗她的臭腳丫。

2 以 I 作主詞提出建議的時候，美式用 would，英式可以用 should，但不用 ought to。

- **I should/would keep a distance from Sue, if I were you.**
  如果我是你，我就會與蘇保持一定的距離（我就會疏遠蘇）。
  ↑ 提出建議（這句是假設語氣），不用 ought to。

- **I ought to/should visit my grandparents more often.** 我應該更常去看我的爺爺奶奶才是。
  ↑ 義務；責任

3 ought to (= should) 也可以表示「強烈的可能性」，但只限於指未來，不指現在。

- **It's a game that I ought to win.**
  = It's a game that I should win. 那是一場我應該要贏的比賽。

2 ought to have + 過去分詞

1 「**ought to have + 過去分詞**」等於「should have + 過去分詞」，表過去本來該做而未做的事（通常帶有指責或遺憾的語氣），這是一種假設語氣。

- **Little Jane Rice** ought to have listened **to my advice about her lice.**
  = Little Jane Rice should have listened **to my advice about her lice.**
  如果小珍·賴斯早點聽了我的建議來對付她身上的蝨子就好了。
  ↳ 一件本該發生但沒有發生的事（很遺憾她沒有聽我的建議）。

2 「**ought to have + 過去分詞**」等於「should have + 過去分詞」，也可以表示某件可能已經發生的事。

- **The farmers' meeting on cow diseases** ought to have finished **by now.**
  = The farmers' meeting on cow diseases should have finished **by now.**
  那些農夫關於如何解決乳牛疾病的會議到現在應該結束了吧。
  ↳ 一件很可能已經發生的事。

dare 和 need 的用法

dare 和 need 這兩個動詞可以當作**情態動詞**，也可以當作**一般動詞**，意義相同。dare 和 need 作情態動詞用時，主要用於**疑問句**和**否定句**。

1 dare（敢……）

	情態動詞	一般動詞
肯定句	✕	主詞 + dare/dares + 不定式（帶 **to**）
否定句	主詞 + dare not + 原形動詞	主詞 + do/does not + dare + 不定式（帶 **to**）
疑問句	Dare + 主詞 + 原形動詞？	Do/Does + 主詞 + dare + 不定式（帶 **to**）？

✗ She dare not to lie.

✓ She dare not lie.

↳ dare 是情態動詞（接原形動詞），直接加 not 構成否定句。

✓ She doesn't dare to lie. 她不敢撒謊。

↳ dare 是一般動詞（接不定式），加助動詞 does 及否定詞 not 來構成否定句。

- Dare Ruth tell her mom the truth?
  = Does Ruth dare to tell her mom the truth? 露絲敢跟媽媽說實話嗎？
  ↳ 第一個疑問句中的 Dare 是情態動詞；第二個疑問句中的 dare 是一般動詞。

✗ Beautiful Jenny White dare go out of the house alone at night.

✓ Beautiful Jenny White dares to go out of the house alone at night.
美麗的珍妮．懷特夜晚敢獨自出門。

↳ 作情態動詞用的 dare 和 need，只能用於疑問句和否定句。

↳ 肯定句只能用一般動詞。

2 need（需要；必要）

1 need 作**情態動詞**時，多用於**否定句**中，有時也用於疑問句。

	情態動詞	一般動詞
肯定句	×	主詞 + need/needs + 不定式（帶 to）
否定句	主詞 + need not + 原形動詞	主詞 + do/does not + need+ 不定式（帶 to）
疑問句	Need + 主詞 + 原形動詞？	Do/Does + 主詞 + need + 不定式（帶 to）？

✗ You need not to worry about Mary. She's very tough.
✓ You need not worry about Mary. She's very tough.
✓ You don't need to worry about Mary. She's very tough.
你不需要替瑪麗擔心。她很堅強。
↳ need (not) 是情態動詞，後面接原形動詞（worry）；
(don't) need 是一般動詞，否定句要加助動詞 don't，
後面接不定式片語（to worry）。

• Need I pay now for this lovely cow?
= Do I need to pay now for this lovely cow?
= Do I have to pay now for this lovely cow?
我現在就得付錢買這頭可愛的乳牛嗎？

↳ 第一個疑問句中的 Need 是情態動詞；
第二個疑問句中的 need 是一般動詞。
不過，「Do I have to . . .」是最常用的句型。

2 過去式 didn't need to 也是表示「沒有必要做某事」，但這種用法並沒有明確指出「事情是否已經做了」，除非句子裡有另外說明。

• I didn't need to buy four new tires, but I bought them anyway.
我沒必要買四個新輪胎，可是我還是買了。
↳ 沒必要買，但後面的句子說明了「事情已經做了」。

• I didn't need to buy a new car, so I didn't.
我沒必要買一輛新車，所以我沒買。
↳ 沒必要買，而後面的句子說明了「事情還沒做」。

had better 和 should 的用法

肯定句	I/You/He/She/We/They had better leave.
否定句	I/You/He/She/We/They had better not leave.

* 縮寫：I'd better, you'd better; I'd better not, you'd better not, etc.

1 在口語中，表示某件事是明智的或可取的，常用 had better 代替 should。had better 形式雖像過去式，但要用於**現在式**，不能用於過去式。

2 had better 的否定形式為 had better not（not 放在 had better 之後）。

- **You'd better leave now. It's getting dark outside.**
  = You should leave now. It's getting dark outside.
  你該走了，外面天色已經黑了。

- **You'd better not make a fuss about your breakfast, or you will be late for the school bus.**
  = You should not make a fuss about your breakfast, or you will be late for the school bus.
  你最好不要再為早餐發牢騷了，否則你就趕不上校車了。

3 指「現在最好 / 應該做某事」（指**具體**某件事）時，可以用 had better，也可以用 should。若指「**一般**說來做某事是應該的、恰當的」，只能用 should，不用 had better。

- **You should always drive with care.**
  你開車永遠都要小心。
  ↑ 這句有副詞 always 修飾動詞 drive，表示「總是應該」，要用 should，不用 had better。

・Slow down, and you'd better (= should) drive with care.
開慢點，最好小心一點兒。
↳ 此刻應該做某事。

・I don't think parents should beat their children when they don't behave.
我不認為，孩子表現不好時父母就應該打他們。
↳ 做一般評價，不用 had better。

・If you have a fever, you'd better to stay at home.
= If you have a fever, you should stay at home.
如果你在發燒，最好（就應該）待在家裡。
↳ 做這件事是明智的；現在最好做這件事。

4 you'd better 帶有命令口氣，不可用來「禮貌地請求別人做某事」。

✗ Lily, you'd better pass me the salt.
↳ 這句的意思是「莉莉，你最好把鹽遞給我。」
you'd better 帶有命令口氣，顯得不禮貌。

✓ Lily, could you please pass me the salt?
莉莉，請把鹽遞給我好嗎？

・You'd better come and pick me up.
= I need you to come and pick me up.
你最好來接我。
↳ 意指「我需要你來接我」。

pick someone up

・Would/Could you please come and pick me up?
麻煩你來接我好嗎？
↳ 禮貌的請求。

UNIT

11 時態

Tenses

各種時態句型總結

1 時態的類別

1 動詞有不同的形式，這些形式被稱為「時態」。時態是動詞的特徵，用來表達行為動作發生的時間或動詞描述的狀態。英語共有 16 個時態。

2 動詞時態可根據**動作進行的狀態**，分為：**簡單式**、**進行式**、**完成式**、**完成進行式**。

3 動詞時態也可根據**動作進行的時間**，分為：**現在式**、**過去式**、**未來式**、**過去未來式**。現在式表示現在時間，過去式表示過去時間，未來式用來表示未來時間，而過去未來式則表示過去的未來時間。

4 除了簡單現在式和簡單過去式外，英語的時態是由「**助動詞 + 分詞**」（如：have talked、are walking, would have worked），或是「**助動詞 + 原形動詞**」（will run, would study）構成的。但在肯定句中，簡單現在式單數第三人稱動詞要加 -s 或 -es（比如：talks、walks、runs），簡單過去式要用動詞過去式（如：talked、walked、ran）。

時間	簡單式	進行式	完成式	完成進行式
現在	I work/she works	I am working	I have worked	I have been working
過去	I worked	I was working	I had worked	I had been working
未來	I will work	I will be working	I will have worked	I will have been working
過去未來	I would work	I would be working	I would have worked	I would have been working

2 簡單式（Simple Tenses）

1 **簡單現在式** 主詞 + 動詞現在式（第三人稱原形動詞 /-s/-es）

- Coco flies a kite every night. 可可每天晚上都要放風箏。
  ↑ 肯定句中，單數第三人稱動詞要加 -s 或 -es，或變 y 為 -ies（fly → flies）。

2 **簡單過去式** 主詞 + 動詞過去式

- Coco flew the hot air balloon designed by Scot.
  可可駕駛了史考特設計的熱氣球。
  ↑ 肯定句中，要用動詞的過去式（fly → flew）。

3 **簡單未來式** 主詞 + will/shall + 原形動詞

- Tomorrow Coco will fly to Chicago.
  可可明天將飛往芝加哥。

4 **過去未來式** 主詞 + would + 動詞原形

- Lee said many times that he would never forgive Dee.
  李說了好幾次，說他永遠都不會原諒蒂。

3 進行式（Progressive Tenses）

1 **現在進行式** 主詞 + am/is/are + 現在分詞

- I am diving with Sam. 我正在和山姆一起潛水。

2 **過去進行式** 主詞 + was/were + 現在分詞

- I was diving with Ray at noon yesterday.
  昨天正中午的時候，我正在和雷一起潛水。

3 未來進行式 主詞 + shall/will + be + 現在分詞

- I will be diving at 7:30 a.m. tomorrow with Jill.
  明天早上七點半時，我將正和潔兒一起潛水。

4 過去未來進行式 主詞 + would + be + 現在分詞

- I asked Mary whether she would be attending the NASA conference at 9 a.m. the next day.
  我問了瑪麗，是否會參加第二天早上九點的太空總署會議。

4 完成式（Perfect Tenses）

1 現在完成式 主詞 + have/has + 過去分詞

- Scot has finished designing a robotic rabbit toy for Roy.
  史考特已經為羅伊設計好了一個機器玩具兔子。

2 過去完成式 主詞 + had + 過去分詞

- By the time I arrived, Scot had finished designing a new dress for Bess.
  我到達時，史考特已經為貝絲設計好了一件新洋裝。

3 未來完成式 主詞 + shall/will + have + 過去分詞

- By the end of the week, Scot will have finished designing a robotic astronaut. 在這個週末之前，史考特將設計好一個機器太空人。

4 過去未來完成式 主詞 + would + have + 過去分詞

- She thought that she would have finished writing her romance story by the time Vance came back from his trip to France.
  她以為，等萬斯從法國旅遊回來，她就可以寫完她的羅曼史故事了。

5 完成進行式（Perfect Progressive Tenses）

1 現在完成進行式 主詞 + have/has + been + 現在分詞

- She has been looking around the bookstore for a book about the American Civil War.
  她一直在這家書店尋找一本關於美國內戰的書。

2 過去完成進行式 主詞 + had + been + 現在分詞

- Finally I found the diamond ring I had been looking for.
  我終於找到了一直在尋找的鑽石戒指。

3 未來完成進行式 主詞 + shall/will + have + been + 現在分詞

- By 8:30 a.m. tomorrow, Ms. Powers will have been looking for her dog for twenty-four hours.
  到明天早上八點半時，鮑爾斯小姐找她的狗就已經找了 24 小時了。

4 過去未來完成進行式 主詞 + would + have + been + 現在分詞

- Mark told us that by noontime he would have been jogging for four hours.
  馬克跟我們說，到中午時，他就慢跑了四個小時了。

Part 2 Simple Present Tense

簡單現在式

1 簡單現在式的動詞變化和句型

1 簡單現在式用來描述永久的、重複性的事件或動作，可以表示**事實**、**慣例**或**習慣**等。

2 在**肯定句**中，簡單現在式有自己的動詞形式，不需要使用助動詞。一般情況下用原形動詞，當句子的主詞是單數第三人稱（如 he, she, it, Kay 等）時，應在原形動詞後面加 -s，如：eats, comes; 或加 -es，如：goes、does。

3 在**疑問句**和**否定句**中，單數第三人稱的述語動詞，要和助動詞 does 一起使用，其餘情況下用述語動詞和助動詞 do。在疑問句和否定句中使用了 do 或 does，述語動詞就要用原形，不能加 -s/-es/-ies。

	人稱	單數	複數
肯定句	一	I jog every day.	We jog every day.
	二	You jog every day.	You jog every day.
	三	He/She/It jogs every day.	They jog every day.
疑問句	一	Do I jog every day?	Do we jog every day?
	二	Do you jog every day?	Do you jog every day?
	三	Does he/she/it jog every day?	Do they jog every day?
否定句	一	I do not jog every day.	We do not jog every day.
	二	You do not jog every day.	You do not jog every day.
	三	He/She/It does not jog every day.	They do not jog every day.

* 縮寫 • do not = don't • does not = doesn't

Do you **drink coffee every day?** 你每天都喝咖啡嗎？
Yes, I do. 是的，我每天都喝咖啡。
No. I don't. I drink **tea.** 不，我不喝咖啡，我喝茶。

Do Kay and Dee **drink tea every day?** 凱和蒂每天都喝茶嗎？
Yes, they do. 是的，他們每天都喝茶。
No, they don't. They don't **like tea.** 不，他們不喜歡喝茶。

Does Kay **play ball every day?** 凱每天都要打棒球嗎？
Yes, she does. 是的，她每天都要打棒球。
No, she doesn't. She swims **every day.** 不，她沒有每天打棒球，她是每天游泳。

肯定句 **Dwight** likes **to fly his kite.** 杜威特喜歡放風箏。
疑問句 Does **Dwight** like **to fly his kite?** 杜威特喜歡放風箏嗎？
否定句 **Dwight** does not like **to fly his kite.** 杜威特不喜歡放風箏。

用助動詞 does 來構成第三人稱單數的疑問句和否定句時，述語動詞不加 -s/-es/-ies，而要用原形動詞。

✗ "Does Paul plays volleyball?" "No, Paul doesn't plays volleyball."
✓ Does Paul play volleyball? 保羅打排球嗎？
No, Paul doesn't play volleyball. 不，保羅不打排球。

Diving Deep Into English 73 一個句子只能使用一個否定詞

✗ Nobody doesn't **trusts Tom, because his temper is like a ticking time bomb.**
✓ Nobody **trusts Tom, because his temper is like a ticking time bomb.** 沒有人信任湯姆，因為他的脾氣就像一顆滴答作響的定時炸彈。

✗ **Dee** doesn't never **talk to me.**
✓ **Dee** never **talks to me.**
✓ **Dee** doesn't **talk to me.** 蒂從不跟我說話。

2 第三人稱單數的動詞變化形式

1 原形動詞 → + -s

第一、二人稱及複數人稱的動詞，簡單現在式都用原形動詞；第三人稱單數則要變化動詞形式，大多數動詞在原形後面加 -s。

- eat → eats 吃
- drink → drinks 喝
- sell → sells 賣
- sit → sits 坐
- win → wins 贏
- work → works 工作

・**My Uncle Ray takes a long walk every day.** 我叔叔雷每天都走很遠的路。
↑ 簡單現在式第三人稱單數（Uncle Ray）作主詞，述語動詞後面要加 -s（takes）。

2 字尾為 -s、-sh、-ch、-o、-x、-z → + -es

以 -s、-sh、-ch、-o、-x、-z 結尾的動詞，用於第三人稱單數時，要在原形動詞後面加 -es。

- dress → dresses 穿著打扮
- pass → passes 傳遞
- wish → wishes 許願
- finish → finishes 完成
- teach → teaches 教導
- switch → switches 切換
- do → does 做
- go → goes 去
- fix → fixes 修理；固定
- fax → faxes 傳真
- mix → mixes 混合
- buzz → buzzes 嗡嗡叫

・**Anna misses her former dance teacher.** 安娜懷念上一個舞蹈老師。
↑ 以 -s 結尾的動詞，要在原形動詞後面加 -es (misses)。

3 子音字母 + y 字尾 → y 變 i， + -es

以「子音字母 + y字尾」(-dy、-fy、-ly、-py、-ry 等) 的動詞，要把y變成 i，然後再加 -es。

- apply → applies 應用；申請
- copy → copies 複製
- cry → cries 哭泣
- fly → flies 飛行
- hurry → hurries 趕緊
- marry → marries 結婚
- reply → replies 回覆
- satisfy → satisfies 滿足
- study → studies 學習
- terrify → terrifies 驚嚇
- worry → worries 擔心

- In order to practice her acting skills, Jill cries every Friday morning.
  為了練習演戲技巧，潔兒每星期五早上都要哭。
  ↑ 以一個子音 + y 結尾的動詞，要把 y 變成 i，然後再加 -es (cries)。

4 母音字母 + y 結尾 → + -s

以「母音字母 + -y」結尾的動詞，在原形動詞後面加 -s。即y 前面有母音 a、e、o、u（字尾為 -ay、-ey、-oy、-uy）時，保留 y，只需在 y 後面加 -s。

- annoy → annoys 惹惱
- buy → buys 購買
- enjoy → enjoys 享受
- obey → obeys 遵守
- pay → pays 支付
- play → plays 玩耍
- pray → prays 祈禱
- prey → preys 獵食
- say → says 說
- stay → stays 留下

- Kay plays her violin every night. 凱每晚都要拉小提琴。
  ↑ 以一個母音 + y 結尾的動詞，只需在原形動詞後面加 -s (plays)。

5 字尾為 -i → + -s

- taxi → taxis 乘計程車；用計程車運送
- ski → skis 滑雪

- During the winter, Kay skis every day. 冬天時，凱每天都會滑雪。

6 動詞 have → has

動詞 have 的第三人稱單數要用 has。動詞 have 的用法。
» 參見 460 頁〈Part 7 have, has, there is, there are 的用法〉。

單數 →	I have	he/she/it has	you have
複數 →	we have	they have	you have

7 連綴動詞 be 的簡單現在式為：

- I am
- he/she/it is
- we/you/they are ← 第二人稱 you 無論單數和複數都用 are。

3 簡單現在式用於永久成立的事實、習慣或反覆發生的事

動詞有不同的形式，叫做時態。動詞的時態說明動作是什麼時候發生的。簡單現在式用來來談論永久性的情況，或經常性、多次或不斷發生的事，或時而發生的事，或從未發生過的事情。

1 永久成立的事實（或現在存在的狀態或特徵，據我們所知會長期存在下去）

- My sister hates lice, cockroaches, and mice. → 現在的特徵
  我妹妹討厭蝨子、蟑螂和老鼠。
- Do penguins live in Antarctica? 企鵝生活在南極洲嗎？ → 永久的事實
- Does the sun appear to rise in the east and set in the west only because the earth turns toward the east? → 永久的事實
  太陽東升西落，只因為地球向東旋轉嗎？
- He is evil and would sell his mom down the river. → 現在存在的狀態
  他非常邪惡，會為錢出賣自己的媽媽。

2 習慣及反覆發生的事（或從未發生過的事情）

- We usually go to the movies on Saturday night with Aunt Dee.
  我們星期六晚上通常都會跟蒂姑姑一起去看電影。
- Every summer I go to Japan to see Uncle Dan.
  我每年夏天都要去日本探望丹姑父。
- She always washes her hands before each meal. 她吃飯前都要洗手。
- Amy is deaf and can't hear any sound, so she never crosses the street without looking around.
  艾咪是聽障人士，什麼也聽不到，所以每次過街時都要環顧一下四周。

3 常用簡單現在式的詞彙和片語

- all the time 一直
- always 總是
- every day 每天
- every morning 每天早上
- every Sunday 每個星期天
- every weekend 每個週末
- every year 每年
- never 從不
- often 常常
- once a day 一天一次
- sometimes 有時
- twice a year 一年兩次
- usually 通常

- I never smoke and usually love a good joke. 我從不抽菸，通常喜歡有趣的玩笑。
- Ms. Peach sometimes plays volleyball at the beach.
  皮奇小姐有時候在海灘打排球。
- Does Ray watch cartoons once a day? 雷每天都要看一次卡通嗎？

- Kim says her baby, Jim, does not get sick very often, because she breastfeeds him. 金姆說她的小寶貝吉姆不常生病，因為她用母乳餵他。

簡單現在式不能用來表達某事持續的時間（如 ：for ten years）。

- I have known my husband Jerry for twenty years, and we've been married for about a decade.
  我跟我先生傑瑞認識 20 年，結婚大概 10 年了。
  ↑ 表達某事持續時間，要用完成式，不用簡單現在式（know, are married）。

  » 詳細說 3 明參見 589 頁〈1 簡單現在完成式的句型〉。

4 簡單現在式用於請求和提供指示

問路、請求指示，或指路、給出指示時，常用簡單現在式。

- How do I get to the airport? 去機場怎麼走？ → 詢問方向
- You go straight to the first set of traffic lights, and then you turn left. 向前直走，第一個紅綠燈左轉。 → 告知方向

5 簡單現在式用於表示「確定的計畫和安排」

簡單現在式可以用來表示**時刻表**或**計畫表**上已經確定好的計畫和安排，常用於動詞 be, go, arrive, leave, start, stay, begin 等動詞。

- Flight 89 to London departs at 8:10 p.m.
  開往倫敦的 89 號班機於晚上八點 10 分起飛。 → 時刻表
- Next week my daughters go to our church's summer camp.
  下星期我女兒要參加我們教會的夏令營。 → 行程計畫

» 詳細說明參見 566 頁〈8 簡單現在式表示未來的用法〉。

6 從屬子句中的現在式用法

當主句為未來式時，由下列詞彙引導的從屬子句，要用現在式來表示未來含意（不能用簡單未來式 will）。

- where 哪裡
- wherever 無論到哪裡
- when 當……時
- whenever 無論何時
- until 直到……時
- before 在……以前
- after 在……之後
- as soon as 一……就
- as long as 只要
- unless 除非
- once 一旦
- provided that 只要
- if 如果
- whether 是否
- on condition that 只要

✗ If there will be a hurricane in Spain tomorrow, I will not get on the airplane in Maine.

✓ If there is a hurricane in Spain tomorrow, I will not get on the airplane in Maine.
明天西班牙如果有颶風，我就不在緬因州上飛機了。
↑ 主句用簡單未來式 will，if 子句用簡單現在式 there is。

- After I pass my driving test, I'll ride my motor scooter and go to see Jill.
= After I have passed my driving test, I'll ride my motor scooter and go to see Jill. 考上駕照以後，我要騎著我的小輪摩托車去見潔兒。
↑ After 子句可用簡單現在式 After I pass，也可用簡單現在完成式 After I have passed。

- I'll lend you the *The Giver* DVD as long as you promise to return it before Friday afternoon.
= I'll lend you the *The Giver* DVD if you promise to return it before Friday afternoon.
只要你允諾在週五下午之前歸還，我就把《記憶傳承人》的 DVD 借給你。

- Once Kitty Cork makes some friends in New York, she'll love that city.
一旦姬蒂．科克在紐約交了朋友，她就會愛上那座城市。

- I'll park my Land Rover under the bridge and wait until the hailstorm is over. 我要把我的荒原路華越野車停在大橋下，一直等到這場大冰雹過去。

- Sue will light two candles before Andrew arrives for dinner tonight.
蘇要在安德魯到達之前，為今晚的晚餐點上兩根蠟燭。

» 參見 553 頁〈2 簡單未來式 will〉、第 566 頁〈8 簡單現在式表示未來的用法〉。
» 從屬子句的用法，參見 345 頁〈Part 5 從屬連接詞與副詞子句〉。

現在進行式

1 現在進行式的構成方式和句型

現在進行式是動詞的進行式形式，由**助動詞 be** 和動詞的**現在分詞**構成，表示現在正在進行的動作或狀況。助動詞 be 包括 is、am、are。

主詞 + am / is / are + 現在分詞（即動詞 **-ing**）

原形動詞（簡單現在式）	現在分詞	現在進行式
learn 學習	→ learning	am/is/are learning 正在學習
sing 唱歌	→ singing	am/is/are singing 正在唱歌
jog 慢跑	→ jogging	am/is/are jogging 正在慢跑

現在進行式的句型

	人稱	肯定句	否定句	疑問句
單數	第一	I am crying. = I'm crying.	I am not crying. = I'm not crying.	Am I crying?
	第二	You are crying. = You're crying.	You are not crying. = You're not crying. = You aren't crying.	Are you crying?
	第三	He/She/It/Bing is crying. = He's/She's/It's/Bing's crying.	He/She/It/Bing is not crying. = He's/She's/It's/Bing's not crying. = He/She/It/Bing isn't crying.	Is he/she/it/Bing crying?

<table>
<tr><td rowspan="4">複數</td><td>第一</td><td>We are crying.
= We're crying.</td><td>We are not crying.
= We're not crying.
= We aren't crying.</td><td>Are we crying?</td></tr>
<tr><td>第二</td><td>You are crying.
= You're crying.</td><td>You are not crying.
= You're not crying.
= You aren't crying.</td><td>Are you crying?</td></tr>
<tr><td rowspan="2">第三</td><td>They are crying.
= They're crying.</td><td>They are not crying.
= They're not crying.
= They aren't crying.</td><td>Are they crying?</td></tr>
<tr><td>Bing and Amy are crying.</td><td>Bing and Amy are not crying.
= Bing and Amy aren't crying.</td><td>Are Bing and Amy crying?</td></tr>
<tr><td>特殊問句</td><td></td><td colspan="3">What's he reading? 他在讀什麼書？
Where's she reading? 她在哪裡讀書？
When is it + 動詞 -ing . . . 它什麼時候做……</td></tr>
</table>

Are you bouncing your basketball in the dining hall?
你在餐廳拍打籃球嗎？

→ **Yes, I am.** 是的，我在拍打。

→ **No, I'm not.** 没有，我没有拍打。

Is Paul throwing his bowling ball at the wall?
保羅在對著牆壁丟他的保齡球嗎？

→ **Yes, he is.** 是的，他在丟球。

→ **No, he isn't.** 不，他不在丟球。

Are you and Saul playing volleyball? 你和所羅在打排球嗎？

→ **Yes, we are.** 是的，我們在打排球。

→ **No, we're not.** 不，我們不在打排球。

Are Paul and Saul eating meatballs at an outdoor food stall?
保羅和所羅在戶外的小吃攤吃肉丸嗎？

→ **Yes, they are.** 是的，他們在吃。

→ **No, they're not.** 不，他們不在吃。

2 現在分詞的構成方式

1 大部分動詞 原形動詞→ + -ing

大部分動詞在原形後面加 -ing 構成現在分詞。

- cook → cooking 烹飪
- look → looking 看
- play → playing 玩耍
- sleep → sleeping 睡覺
- speak → speaking 講話
- study → studying 研讀
- throw → throwing 投擲
- walk → walking 行走

・Dad is sleeping. 爸爸在睡覺。

2 -e 結尾的動詞 字尾 -e → 去 e， + -ing

以 -e 結尾的動詞，先去掉 e，再加 -ing。

- arrive → arriving 抵達
- come → coming 來到
- drive → driving 駕駛
- hope → hoping 希望
- hustle → hustling 趕緊
- make → making 製作
- move → moving 移動
- rise → rising 上升
- shake → shaking 搖動
- smile → smiling 微笑
- take → taking 拿取
- write → writing 寫作

・Are you making a birthday cake for Sue? 你在為蘇做生日蛋糕嗎？

3 -ie 結尾的動詞 字尾 -ie → ie 變 y，+ -ing

以 -ie 結尾的動詞，先把 ie 變成 y，再加 -ing。

- lie → lying 說謊
- tie → tying 捆
- die → dying 死
- vie → vying 競爭

・I don't believe you. You are lying! 我不相信你。你在撒謊！

4 單母音 + 單子音結尾的動詞

a **單音節動詞**：以「一個母音 + 一個子音」結尾的動詞，要**重複最後一個子音**，再加 -ing。這些單音節的短音動詞，以 b、d、g、m、n、p、r、t 等子音字母結尾，而且在子音前只有一個母音字母（a、e、i、o、u）。

- cut → cutting 切割
- get → getting 獲得
- hit → hitting 打擊
- jog → jogging 慢跑
- rob → robbing 搶劫
- run → running 跑
- stop → stopping 停止
- sit → sitting 坐下

・Daisy is jogging along the beach. 黛絲正沿著海灘慢跑。

1 含兩個母音字母的單音節動詞，其現在分詞不重複字尾子音。

- sleep → sleeping 睡覺
- wait → waiting 等待

2 字尾為兩個子音的單音節動詞，其現在分詞不重複字尾子音。

- want → wanting 想要
- help → helping 幫助

b 重音在後的雙音節動詞：以「一個母音 + 一個子音」結尾的雙音節動詞，如果重音在最後一個音節，也要先**重複字尾的子音**，再加 -ing。

- begin → beginning 開始
- unplug → unplugging 拔去插頭
- control → controlling 控制
- patrol → patrolling 巡邏

・It's beginning to look like a white Christmas.
開始看上去像一個白色聖誕節了。

↳ begin /bɪˋgɪn/ 有兩個音節，並以「一個母音 + 一個子音」結尾，重音在最後一個音節上，因此要重複最後的子音 n。

c 重音在前的雙音節動詞：以「一個母音 + 一個子音」結尾的雙音節動詞，如果最後一個音節不是重音，則不要重複字尾的子音，只加 -ing。

- happen → happening 發生
- wonder → wondering 想弄明白

・Global warming is happening right now. 全球暖化此時此刻正在發生中。

↳ happen /ˋhæpən/ 也有兩個音節，也是以「一個母音 + 一個子音」結尾，但重音在第一個音節上，因此最後一個音節的子音 n 不重複。

- **program** /ˋprogræm/ → programming, programing

  ↳ program（給……編寫程式）動詞的重音在第一個音節，第二個音節是非重音。但比較特殊，可以重複字尾字音（重複更常見），也可以不重複。

- **travel** → travelling（英式要重複 l）
  → traveling（美式只需要加 -ing）

3 現在進行式的用法

1 談論「此刻」

現在進行式用來談論此刻（講話的時刻）正在進行的（或不在進行的）暫時動作或狀況。

- **Hurry up, Sue—we are all waiting for you!**
  蘇，快點，我們都在等你！
- **Dirk can't go bowling with you now because he is doing his homework.** 德克現在不能跟你去打保齡球，因為他正在做家庭作業。
- **Why are you crying, Sue? Is something wrong?**
  蘇，你怎麼在哭啊？怎麼回事呢？

2 談論「目前這段時間在發生的事」

現在進行式也可以用來談論目前這段時間正在發生的事（things in progress lately），不一定是說話時刻正在進行的動作。

- **Adam is working very hard at his English these days.**
  最近這些日子，亞當正非常努力地學習英語。
- **Right now Joe is looking for a job in Tokyo.**
  目前喬正在東京找工作。

3 表示「正在變化的情形」

現在進行式也可以用來談論正在**發展**、正在**變化**的情形。

- **May says the baby in her belly is getting bigger every day.**
  = May says the baby in her belly gets bigger every day.
  梅說她肚子裡的胎兒一天比一天大了。
- **Kay thinks my English is getting better and better every day.**
  = Kay thinks my English gets better and better every day.
  凱認為我的英語一天比一天進步。

Diving Deep Into English 74 get warmer（變暖和）的用法

- The climate of the Earth is getting warmer. 地球的氣候正在變暖。
  The climate of the Earth gets warmer every decade.（簡單現在式）
  = The climate of the Earth is getting warmer every decade.（現在進行式）全球氣候正以十年為期愈益變暖。
  ↳ 含 every decade 這一類時間副詞的句子，可以用現在進行式或簡單現在式，來表示「正在變化的情形」；如果沒有這類的時間提示語，則只能用現在進行式。
- Does it get warmer when it snows? 下雪時，天氣會變暖和嗎？
  ↳ 有副詞子句（when it snows）修飾，主句要用現在式（get warmer）。
- As the weather gets warmer, gas prices get lower.
  隨著天氣變暖，汽油價格也下跌了。
  ↳ 在副詞子句裡用現在式（gets warmer）。

4 談論「未來」

現在進行式有時可用來談論未來將要發生的事，通常是**已經計畫好**、**決定好**，或是**正開始發生**的事情。

- What are you and Dwight doing tonight? 你和杜威特今晚做什麼？
- Dwight and I are having a party tonight. 今晚我和杜威特要辦一個晚會。
- Who's bringing the pizza for the party? 誰會為派對帶披薩來？
- She's moving to Los Angeles this summer. 今年夏天她要搬往洛杉磯。

» 參見 558 頁〈3 現在進行式表示未來的用法〉。

5 現在進行式和簡單現在式常用的時間字彙和片語

a 常用**現在進行式**的詞彙和片語：

- now 現在
- right now 此刻；目前
- today 今天
- these days 這幾天
- recently 最近
- this morning 今天早上

- I'm driving right now. I can't talk on the cellphone.
  我正在開車，不能打手機。

b 常用**簡單現在式**的詞彙和片語：

- always 總是
- often 經常
- on Sundays 在每個星期天
- when it snows 當下雪時
- when I'm tired 當我疲倦時

・I don't drive when it snows. 下雪時我不開車。

c every day（每天）用於簡單現在式，但在特定情況下也可以用於現在進行式。下列兩句使用相同的時間副詞 every day，用簡單現在式和現在進行式的意義不同。

・**Kay plays ping-pong every day.** 凱每天都要打乒乓球。
　↳「打乒乓球」是一個反覆發生的行為。

・**Kay is now playing ping-pong every day.** 凱現在每天都要打乒乓球。
　↳ 這句用了 every day，但同時也用了 now，意味著「凱從前並未每天打乒乓球，現在則每天都打」，在這種情況下可以用現在進行式。

d always（總是）、continually（一直）、constantly（不斷地）、forever（老是、不斷地）等字也可以用於**進行式**，表達預料之外持續發生或重複發生的事。這種用法帶有強烈的感情色彩，通常表達對某件事感到不愉快。

・**When my niece Emma comes to see me, I always meet her at the airport.** 每當我侄女愛瑪來看我時，我都會去機場接她。
　↳ 固定的、有計畫的安排。

・**These days I'm always meeting Paul in the school dining hall.**
最近我常在學校的餐廳見到保羅。
　↳ 意外的、無計畫的見面。（注意 always 在進行式中，不與 not 連用。）

・**Nobody lives forever.** 沒有人會永生。　→ 永久的事實。

・**She is forever talking about her cats and dogs.**
她老是在談論她的貓和狗。　→ 暗示對她的行為感到不滿。

 4 不能用現在進行式的情況

1「持續時間過長」或「永久的情形」不用進行式

表達持續時間較長的或永久的情形，不能用現在進行式，而要用簡單現在式。

» 參見 526 頁〈Part 2 簡單現在式〉。

✕ Our old school is standing on a hill outside the town.

✓ Our old school stands on a hill outside the town.

我們古老的學校坐落在城外的一座小山丘上。 → 長期固定的情形

2 重複的行為和事件不用進行式

表示與講話時刻無密切聯繫的重複行為動作和事件，不能用現在進行式，而要用簡單現在式。

- Kay goes to Taipei to visit her relatives every May.
  凱每年五月都要去臺北拜訪親戚。 → 與講話時刻無關聯的重複事件
- Why is Ted jumping up and down on the bed?
  泰德為什麼在床上跳上跳下？
  ↥ 描述此刻正在進行的重複性的動作，可用進行式。

Ted is jumping
up and down
on the bed.

3 持續的事件不用進行式

現在進行式不用來談論某件事持續了多久，這種情形要用完成式。

» 參見 589 頁〈Part 9 簡單現在完成式〉至〈Part 15 過去未來完成式和過去未來完成進行式〉。

✕ I'm waiting for you since 9 a.m.

✓ I've been waiting for you since 9 a.m. 我從早上九點開始就一直在等你。

↥ 「等待」開始於過去，一直持續到現在（現在完成進行式）。

5 非進行式動詞（Non-Progressive Verbs）

1 概述

有些動詞通常用於簡單式，即使是表達現在正在進行的動作或狀態，也不用於進行式，這類動詞稱作**非進行式動詞**。比如下面句子中的動詞 smell、like、understand 和 hope，都只用於**簡單式**，不用於進行式。

- This flower smells so good! 這朵花真好聞啊。
- I like this music. 我喜歡這首曲子。

- I don't understand her lecture. 我聽不懂她的講座。
- "Is Joyce enjoying her Rolls Royce?" "I hope so."
  「喬伊絲喜歡她的勞斯萊斯汽車嗎？」「但願她喜歡。」

2 常見的非進行式動詞

a 表心理狀態、感情、認知的動詞

- adore 崇拜
- believe 相信
- consider 認為
- desire 渴望
- dislike 不喜歡
- doubt 懷疑
- feel (= have an opinion) 覺得；認為
- forgive 原諒
- guess 猜測
- hate 討厭
- imagine 想像
- impress 使感動
- intend 打算
- know 知道
- like 喜歡
- love 熱愛
- perceive 意識到
- prefer 偏好；更喜歡
- realize 領悟
- recognize 認出
- regard 認為
- remember 記得
- see (= understand) 理解
- suppose 猜想
- think (= have an opinion) 認為
- understand 瞭解
- want 想要
- wish 希望

- I don't believe you. 我不相信你。 → 不能用進行式 am not believing。
- Lisa loves the color of her own black skin.
  Her husband Mack often says, "I love black!"
  麗莎喜歡自己的黑皮膚。她老公麥克常說：「我喜歡黑色！」
  ↑ 不能用進行式 is loving、am loving。

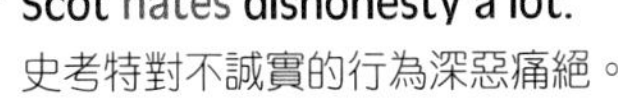

- Scot hates dishonesty a lot.
  史考特對不誠實的行為深惡痛絕。

- Do you know Joe? 你認識喬嗎？

- Do you understand that grammar rule? 你懂那條文法規則嗎？
- Do you see what I mean about how mean Dee can be?
  我說蒂有時候很刻薄，你明白我的意思嗎？
  ↑ see 作 understand 講時，不能用進行式 are you seeing。
- Dwight thinks highly of Lily. 杜威特認為莉莉很了不起。
  ↑ 當 think 指「認為；判斷」時，不能用進行式 is thinking。
  ↑ think highly of 指「尊重；崇拜」，不用於進行式。

b 感官動詞與連綴動詞

感官動詞

- hear（聽見）
- smell（聞起來）
- sound（聽起來）
- see（看見）
- taste（嚐起來）
- notice（注意到）

連綴動詞

- be（是）
- look（= seem）看起來
- appear（好像是）
- seem（似乎）

・**The milk tastes sour.** 這牛奶嚐起來酸掉了。
↑ 不能用進行式 is tasting。

MILK
The milk tastes sour.

・**He seems to be a good guy.** 他看上去好像是個好人。
↑ 不能用進行式 is seeming。

・**You sound depressed. What happened?** 你聽起來很沮喪，發生什麼事了？
↑ 不能用進行式 are sounding。

・**St John's Cathedral looks both solemn and majestic.**
聖約翰大教堂雄偉壯觀、莊嚴肅穆。 → 不能用進行式 is looking。

c 其他非進行式動詞

- agree 同意
- belong to 屬於
- consist of 由……構成
- contain 包含
- cost 花費
- deny 否認
- depend on 依靠
- deserve 應受
- disagree 不同意
- equal 等於
- exist 存在
- fit 合身；適合
- have 擁有
- include 包括
- involve 牽涉
- lack 缺少
- need 需要
- owe 欠
- own 擁有
- possess 持有
- promise 允諾
- recommend 推薦
- remain 保持
- require 要求
- satisfy 使滿意
- suggest 建議
- surprise 使吃驚
- weigh（= have weight）有……重量；稱起來

・**Kay needs some help today.** 凱今天需要一些幫忙。
↑ 不能用進行式 is needing。

・**Our astronomy club currently consists of ten people, but we hope to enroll more members soon.**
我們天文學俱樂部目前有 10 名成員，但我們希望可以很快招收更多的成員。
↑ 不能用進行 is consisting of。

・**Tom owes me $1,000.** 湯姆欠我一千塊美金。 → 不能用進行式 is owing。

NOTE

1 口語中，有些美國人也將上述這類的動詞用進行式，例如：

- I am liking this music. 我喜歡音樂。
- I'm hoping so. 希望如此。

2 不過，在正式場合，如商務英語、英文考試中，一定要遵守文法規則。

3 有一句流行廣告詞說：「I'm lovin' it!」，這句表達被當作慣用語而接受。不過，在正式英語中還應遵循文法規則，用 love 的現在式，即「I love it!」。

6 進行式與非進行式的用法

上面列舉的動詞中，有些可兼作一般行為動詞，這時就可以用進行式。比較以下這些動詞**非進行式**（表心理狀態和感情的動詞、感官動詞、連綴動詞等）和**進行式**（當作行為動詞）的用法。

1 feel

feel
行為動詞
可以用進行式
表「觸摸」。

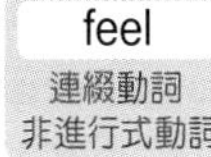
feel
連綴動詞
非進行式動詞
不可以用進行式
表「見解；覺得」或「（某物）給人某種感覺」。

- **Jerry is a blind boy, and he is feeling the elephant.**
  傑瑞是一個失明的男孩，他正在摸大象。
  ↳ 此處 feel 是行為動詞，意思是 touch（撫摸），後面接受詞（elephant）。

- **Jerry says he feels that the elephant is like a wall.**
  傑瑞說，他覺得大象就像一面牆。
  ↳ 此處 feel 是非進行式動詞，表「心裡狀態」，意思是 have an opinion（有一個見解），不能用進行式。

- **My bed is warm and my pillow feels soft. Oh, I don't want to get up on this cold, rainy day.**
  我的床暖暖的，枕頭很柔軟。啊，我真不想在這個寒冷的雨天起床。
  ↳ 此處 feel 是非進行式動詞，意思是「（某物）給人某種感覺」，不能用進行式。

Diving Deep Into English 75 涉及身體感覺的動詞（例如 feel），要用進行式還是簡單式？

❶ 下列涉及身體感覺（physical feelings/bodily sensation）的動詞可以用進行式，也可以用簡單式，意義相同。

- ache 疼痛
- feel 感覺
- hurt 疼痛
- itch 發癢

- **I'm** feeling **sick. = I** feel **sick.** 我覺得噁心。
  ⤴ feel sick、feel tired 這類片語可以用進行式，也可以用簡單式。
- **My nose** is itching**! = My nose** itches**!** 我的鼻子癢癢的！

❷ 片語 feel like 只能用簡單式，不能用進行式。

- **Mike** feels like **throwing up.** 邁克感覺想嘔吐。

2 look

look
行為動詞
✓ 可以用進行式
表「看……」或「尋找」。

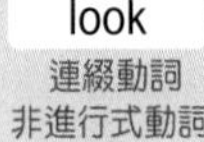

look
連綴動詞
非進行式動詞
✗ 不可以用進行式
表「看起來……」。

- **My cat** is looking at **my newborn baby.** 我的貓正看著我剛出生的寶寶。
  ⤴ is looking at 是行為片語動詞，指 turn eyes toward（看），後面接受詞（baby）。
- **Ann** looks **happy since she married Dan.** 安嫁給丹之後，看起來很幸福。
  ⤴ looks 作連綴動詞用的感官動詞（非進行式動詞），意思是「看起來」，相當於 seem 或 appear，後面接形容詞（happy），這時不能用進行式。

Diving Deep Into English 76 感官動詞 look、listen 與 see、hear 的不同

❶ look、listen 和 see、hear 都是感官動詞，都是「看，聽」的意思，但用法不同：

look
listen
感官動詞
✓「刻意進行的動作」，可以用進行式
意味著有意識地努力（conscious effort）去「看」或「聽」。

see
hear
感官動詞
✗「非刻意進行的動作」，不可以用進行式
沒有「努力」的含意，而是強調動作的完成（complete），表示「看見，聽見」，強調動作的結果。

✕ She is seeing the sky.

✔ She is looking at the sky. 她正望著天空。

↳ see（看見）不能用進行式；look at（看、瞧）是行為片語動詞，可用進行式。

- I'm listening to you. 我在聽你講話啊。

  ↳ hear（聽見）不能用進行式；而 listen 是行為動詞，可用進行式。

- Did you hear what Ted said? 你聽到泰德說的話沒有？

  ↳ hear（聽見）強調動作的結果，可用過去式。

❷ see、hear 常和 can/could 搭配。

- Where are you? I can't see you. 你在哪裡？我看不到你。
- Please speak a little louder. We can't hear you.
  請講大聲一點。我們聽不到你。

3 see

see	✔ 可以用進行式	see	✕ 不可以用進行式
行為動詞	表示「會見」。	心理狀態動詞 非進行式動詞	表示「明白、瞭解」。（see 表示「看見」時，也不可用進行式。）

- Are you seeing Joe tomorrow? 你明天要去見喬嗎？

  ↳ 此處 see 作行為動詞，意思是 meet（會見），後面接受詞（Joe）。

- I see what you mean when you say money is sweeter than honey.
  我知道你說金錢比蜂蜜還甜是什麼意思。

  ↳ 此處 see 意思是「明白、懂」（understand），表「心理狀態」，是非進行式動詞。

4 smell

smell
行為動詞
可以用進行式
表示「聞……」。
smell
連綴動詞
非進行式動詞
不可以用進行式
表示「聞起來……」。

- Why is she smelling the armpit of my shirt?
  為什麼她在聞我襯衫的腋窩處？

  ↳ 此處 smell 為行為動詞，意思是「聞」，可以用進行式，後面接受詞（the armpit）。

✗ Is our baby smelling bad?

✓ Does our baby smell bad? 我們的寶寶身上很難聞嗎？

↳ 此處 smell 是作連綴動詞用的感官動詞，為非進行式動詞，表示「聞起來……」，後接形容詞（bad）。

5 taste

taste	✓ 可以用進行式	taste	✗ 不可以用進行式
行為動詞	表示「品嚐」。	連綴動詞 非進行式動詞	表示「嚐起來……」。

- **Jim is tasting the soup to see whether it is done.**
  吉姆正在試湯的味道，看是不是已經煮好了。
  ↳ is tasting 是行為動詞，意思是「品嚐」，後面接受詞（soup）。

- **Kate exclaimed, "The fish tastes great!"**
  凱特喊道：「這魚味道真好！」
  ↳ tastes 意思是「嚐起來」，是當連綴動詞用的感官動詞，為非進行式動詞，後面接形容詞（great），不能用進行式。

6 think

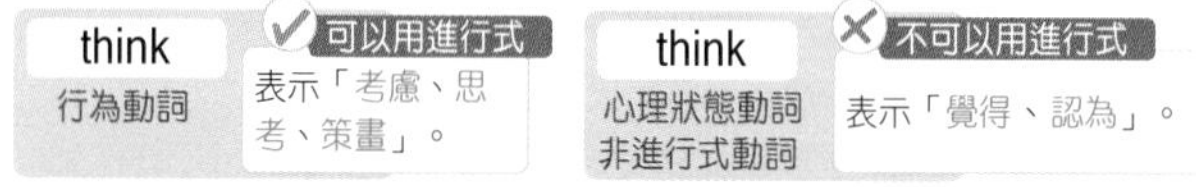

think	✓ 可以用進行式	think	✗ 不可以用進行式
行為動詞	表示「考慮、思考、策畫」。	心理狀態動詞 非進行式動詞	表示「覺得、認為」。

- **What are you thinking about right now?** 你現在正在想什麼？
  ↳ are thinking about 是行為片語動詞，意思是「細想；考慮」（consider），其受詞是 What。

- **I'm thinking of a way to solve the problem.**
  我正在努力想出解決問題的辦法。
  ↳ am thinking of 是行為片語動詞，意思是「考慮；思考；策畫」（plot, consider），接受詞（way）。

✗ What is Mom thinking of my new boyfriend Tom?

✓ What does Mom think of my new boyfriend Tom?
媽媽覺得我的新男友湯姆如何？

↳ think (about/of something/somebody) 意為「認為」（have an opinion），表「心理狀態」，是非進行式動詞。

7 weigh

- Claire is standing on the scales and weighing herself.
  克萊兒正站在體重計上量體重。
  ↳ is weighing 是行為動詞，意思是「稱……的重量」，接受詞（herself）。

✗ Claire is weighing 82 pounds when she's only wearing her underwear.
✓ Claire weighs 82 pounds when she's only wearing her underwear.
當克萊兒只穿內衣褲時，她的體重是 82 磅。
↳ weighs 的意思是「稱起來有……重」，是非進行式動詞。

8 appear

- Kay and Andrew are appearing in a new play. 凱和安德魯要演一齣新戲。
  ↳ are appearing 是行為動詞，意思是「演出；露面」。

✗ Tess is appearing to be very confident of success.
✓ Tess appears to be very confident of success.
黛絲看起來很有信心能夠成功。
↳ appears 是連綴動詞，為非進行式動詞，
意指「似乎；看起來」（seem, look），後面常接不定式片語。

She appears to be confident.

9 have

- They are having a wonderful time at the party.
  他們在派對上玩得很盡興。
  ↳ are having 是行為動詞，意思是「經歷、體驗」。

- **Annie** has **a big house and a lot of money, but she isn't happy.**
  安妮有一間大房子，還有很多錢，但她並不幸福。
  ⤴ has 意指「擁有」，為非進行式動詞，不能用進行式。

10 consider

- **She**'s considering **moving to Australia.** 她在考慮搬去澳洲。
- **I** consider **Mona to be a genius.** 我認為夢娜是一個天才。

7 be 動詞的進行式與非進行式的用法

1 be 動詞（is、am、are 等）強調「**一時的行為或表現**」時，可以用進行式（am/is/are being），後面也接形容詞；be 動詞表「**個性、狀態**」，作連綴動詞時，是非進行式動詞。

- **Kay** is being **haughty today.**
  = Kay is acting arrogant today.
  = Today Kay's behavior is haughty. 凱今天表現得很傲慢。
  ⤴ is being haughty 強調凱暫時的行為，而不是凱的個性。
- **Amy** is **very naughty.** 艾咪很頑皮。
  ⤴ is 是連綴動詞，表示艾咪的「個性頑皮」。

Kay is being haughty today.

- **Stop talking foolishly. You**'re being rude **to our parents.**
  不要再講傻話了。你對父母粗魯無禮。
  ⤴ 強調暫時的行為

・Mary is sometimes rude to her parents.
瑪麗有時候對她父母粗魯無禮。
↑ 有時發生的事

2 並非所有形容詞都適合接在 be being 的後面。

a 可用 be being 句型的形容詞：表示**動態**（dynamic）的形容詞

- careful 小心的
- careless 粗心的
- foolish 傻的
- funny 有趣的
- generous 大方的
- impatient 沒有耐心的
- impolite 沒禮貌的
- kind 親切的
- lazy 懶惰的
- naughty 頑皮的
- nice 好心的
- noisy 吵的
- pleasant 討人喜歡的
- polite 客氣的
- quiet 安靜的
- rude 粗魯的
- serious 嚴肅的
- unreasonable 不講理的

b 不用 be being 句型的形容詞：表示**狀態**（stative）的形容詞

- beautiful 美的
- handsome 帥的
- happy 快樂的
- healthy 健康的
- hungry 餓的
- old 老的
- short 矮的
- sick 生病的
- tall 高的
- thirsty 渴的
- well 安好的
- young 年輕的

✗ Paul is being tall.
✓ Paul is tall. 保羅個子高。
↑ 形容詞 tall 不能用進行式 is being 來表示（Paul has no choice about being tall.）。

✗ My mom is being sick.
✓ My mom is sick. 我媽媽生病了。
↑ 形容詞 sick 不能用進行式 is being 來表示（My mom has no choice about being sick.）。

・Look at her. She is being silly.
瞧瞧她。她表現得好傻啊。
↑ 形容詞 silly 可以用進行式 is being 來表示（She has chosen to be silly.）

8 簡單現在式和現在進行式的比較

兩種現在式：**簡單現在式**描述不變的經常性事件，而**現在進行式**描述此刻正在（不在）進行的事件。

簡單現在式	現在進行式
✓ 永恆的真理或永久成立的事實 ✓ 現在存在的狀態或特徵 ✓ 有時發生、從未發生過的事 ✓ 一直、反覆、經常發生的事 ✓ 長時間內的重複行為 ✓ 長期固定的行為或情境	✓ 此時此刻正在發生的事 ✓ 現在正要發生、即將發生的事 ✓ 目前正在發生的事或目前暫時發生的情況 ✓ 強調「重複頻率太高」 ✓ 短時間內重複發生的行為 ✓ 暫時行為；會有變化的情境
Does the sun rise in the east? 太陽是從東邊升起的嗎？ ↑ 永恆的真理	The sun is hiding behind a cloud. 太陽正藏在一朵雲的後面。 ↑ 此刻正在發生的事
Ray plays basketball every day. 雷每天都要打籃球。 ↑ 長時間內的重複行為	Ray is playing basketball now in Macao. 雷現在正在澳門打籃球。 ↑ 目前正在發生的事
We have fish once a week. 我們一星期吃一次魚肉。 ↑ 反覆的行為	What are you having for dinner, Sue? 蘇，你晚餐準備吃什麼？ ↑ 未來的安排和計畫（即將發生的事）
Margo teaches geography at a university in Chicago. 瑪歌在芝加哥的一所大學教地理。 ↑ 長久的狀況	Ann is teaching English in Japan this year. 安今年在日本教英語。 ↑ 暗示這可能是暫時的狀況
He never smokes or tells stupid jokes. 他從來不抽菸，也不講無聊的笑話。 ↑ 從未發生過的事	Is he smoking in the backyard? 他正在後院抽菸嗎？ ↑ 此刻正在發生的事

Water boils at 100˚ Centigrade. 水在攝氏 100 度就會沸騰。 ↑ 永久成立的事實	Isn't the water boiling yet? 水還沒滾嗎？ ↑ 此刻正在發生的事
Dwight often reads magazines at night. 杜威特晚上時常會讀雜誌。 ↑ 經常發生的事	Right now, Dwight is reading a story about how to milk a cow. 此刻杜威特正在讀一則如何幫牛擠奶的報導。 ↑ 此刻正在發生的事
Once a week Jake makes a chocolate cake. 傑克每星期做一次巧克力蛋糕。 ↑ 反覆的行為	It's 10 a.m., and Jake is making a chocolate cake. 現在是上午 10 點，傑克正在做一個巧克力蛋糕。 ↑ 此刻正在發生的事
Every day my robot Ted jumps up and down on the bed. 我的機器人泰德每天都要在床上跳上跳下。 ↑ 長時間內的重複行為	Ted is now jumping up and down on the bed. 泰德現在正在床上跳上跳下。 ↑ 短時間內重複發生的行為
I usually enjoy an art show, and so does Coco. 我通常都覺得藝術展很不錯，可可也是。 ↑ 經常發生的事	I'm not enjoying this art show, and neither is Coco. 我覺得這場藝術展不怎麼好看，可可也這樣覺得。 ↑ 此刻正在發生的事
She easily loses her temper. 她動輒就發脾氣。 ↑ 現在的特徵	I am always losing my cellphone. 我老是丟手機。 ↑ 強調「重複頻率太高」
On top of the hill stands an old temple. 一座古剎坐落在山頂上。 ↑ 長期固定的情境（表「位於」）	A police officer is standing outside our door. 我們門前站著一名警官。 ↑ 暫時行為（正在發生，但會有變化的情境）

簡單未來式

1 四種形式表示未來將要發生的事

有四種常見的方式可以用來表達未來將要發生的事：

1 用助動詞 will（簡單未來式）

- Tomorrow Pam and I will be at the beach from dawn till 9 a.m.
  明天潘姆和我從黎明時分到上午九點都會待在海灘上。

2 用 be going to 結構

- Is Kay really going to stop smoking on Friday?
  凱真的打算要在星期五戒菸嗎？

3 用現在進行式結構

- Are you visiting the Wright Aerospace Museum tonight?
  你今晚要參觀賴特航太博物館嗎？

4 用簡單現在式結構

- I'm sure my plane leaves here at 10 a.m. and arrives in Chicago at noon local time.
  我確定我的飛機會在上午十點離開這裡，於當地時間正午抵達芝加哥。
- I will call you as soon as Jill arrives home.
  潔兒一到家，我就會打電話給你。

2 簡單未來式 will

1 will 表示對未來事件的單純預測（簡單未來式）
2 will 表示「說話當時所做的決定」（簡單未來式）
3 will 表示「習慣」（不表示未來要發生的事）
4 will 表達意圖和說話態度
5 won't 的用法（表拒絕）
6 will 和 shall 的用法

肯定句	I/You/He/She/It/We/They will go.
疑問句	Will I/you/he/she/it/we/they go?
否定句	I/You/He/She/We/They will not go.

* 縮寫：I'll, you'll, he'll, she'll, it'll, we'll, they'll, won't (= will not)

在第一人稱 I 和 we 後面，有些人用 shall 來代替 will，意思相同，但現代英語較常用 will。

» 參見 494 頁〈1 shall 和 will 為助動詞（簡單未來式）〉。

1 will 表示對未來事件的單純預測

a **簡單未來式**（will + 原形動詞）：若是單純提供未來的資訊，或預料未來要發生的事件（prediction），用助動詞 will。

- **All their friends and relatives will be there for the wedding of Louise and Paul.** 所有的親戚朋友都會來參加露易絲和保羅的婚禮。
  ↑ 單純提供未來的資訊。
- **It will snow tomorrow.** 明天會下雪。
  ↑ 預料未來要發生的事件。

b will 構成的簡單未來式可表示在一定條件下將發生的事，即用於帶有附加條件的句子（比如 when 和 if 引導的子句）。

- **Claire will be relieved when the wedding is over and the bride and groom are on their honeymoon in Delaware.**
  婚禮結束後，新娘和新郎去德拉威州度蜜月，克萊兒就會如釋重負。
  ↑ 從屬子句用簡單現在式（is, are），主句用簡單未來式（will be relieved）。

» 參見 531 頁〈6 從屬子句中的現在式用法〉。

C will 用來預測未來時，常與下列詞語連用，描述我們主觀意識中所知道、認為、推測將要發生的事情：

- think 認為
- suppose 猜測
- perhaps 或許
- expect 期待
- hope 希望
- most likely 很可能
- wonder 納悶
- probably 可能
- sure 肯定

- Tonight Kate will probably come home late. 凱特今晚可能很晚回家。
- "Who do you think will win on Sunday?" "I think Lisa will win." 「你認為星期天誰會贏？」「我認為麗莎會贏。」
- She is a fast runner, and I'm sure she will win. 她跑得很快。我確定她會贏。

Diving Deep Into English 77 think、believe、suppose、imagine 的否定用法

❶ 否定詞 not 通常置於 think 等字的前面，與中文語序不同。

✗ I think/believe/suppose/imagine . . . won't
✓ I don't think/believe/suppose/imagine . . . will
我認為……不

- I don't think Mary will marry Gary. 我認為瑪麗不會嫁給蓋瑞。
  ↑ 這一句比「I think Mary won't marry Jerry.」更自然，更符合習慣。
- I don't believe she will buy that house. 我相信她不會買那棟房子。

❷ 若將否定詞置於 I thought（過去式）後面，則帶有「驚訝、意料之外」的意味。

- "Would you like to come to my birthday party this Saturday night?" "Yes! I thought you'd never invite me."「這星期六晚上來參加我的生日聚會好嗎？」「好啊，我還以為你永遠都不會邀請我呢。」

2 will 表示「說話當時所做的決定」

will（助動詞）可用來表達**說話當時所做的決定**（spontaneous decision），而這些未來事件並沒有預先計畫好（no plan），也不是明顯快要發生了。

- Please hold on. I'll get a pen and a piece of paper.
  請不要掛斷電話。我去拿筆和紙來。
  ↳ 在講話之前並沒有事先計畫好，而是講話時做出的決定。

Please hold on.

- "I guess we are lost," said Tess.
  "I'll go to ask someone the way," said Ray.
  黛絲說：「我想我們迷路了。」雷說：「我去問路。」
  ↳ 當場做出的決定，而不是事先打算要做的事。

如果是 be 動詞，即使我們談論的是事先計畫好的或事先決定的事，也可以用簡單未來式 will。

- Will Joe be at home tomorrow? 明天喬在家嗎？
- I'll be in Singapore next week. 我下星期會在新加坡。

3 will 表示「習慣」

will（情態助動詞）還可以用來表示「習慣」（此時，will 不表示未來）。

- Sue will bite her lip when she's nervous about something.
  蘇只要一緊張，就會咬嘴唇。
- She will often sit in the Happy Coffee House for hours, doing almost nothing. 她常在快樂咖啡廳一坐就是幾個小時，幾乎什麼事都不做。

4 will 表達意圖和說話態度

will（情態助動詞）也用來表示意圖以及對待他人的態度，當提供物品或幫助、提議、請求、威脅、許諾、意願、命令、職責等時，常常用 will。

» 參見 494 頁〈1 shall 和 will 為助動詞（簡單未來式）〉。

✗ I promise I send you lots of email.
✓ I promise I'll send you lots of email. → 許諾
我答應會寄很多電子信件給你。

- Ben cried loudly, "I won't do that again!" → 許諾
  班大聲叫道：「我不會再幹那種事了！」

- Will Sunday night be fine with you? → 可能
  你星期天晚上方便嗎?

- You will not go home without my permission. → 命令
  沒有我的許可,你們就不准回家。

- Joyce asked me with her sweetest voice, "Will you have a cup of coffee or tea?" → 提供物品
  喬伊絲用最甜的聲音問我:「你要來杯咖啡還是茶嗎?」

- I will have to report you and Coco to the principal tomorrow. → 職責
  明天我要向校長報告你和可可的行為。

- Will you please be quiet? 請你安靜一點好嗎? → 請求

5 won't 的用法(表拒絕)

will not 或 won't 可以用來表達「拒絕」。當某人不願意或某物不照要求去做,可用 will not 或 won't。

- She won't see Ben again. → 不願意
  她不願意再見到班。

- My baby is sick and won't eat his food. → 不願意
  我的寶寶生病了,不肯吃東西。

- It's too cold, and my car won't start. → 不能正常工作
  天氣太冷,我的車子發動不起來。

- He has tried many times, but the door won't open. → 不能正常工作
  他試了很多次,但門就是打不開。

- If you won't marry Jill, Gary will. 如果你不願意娶潔兒,蓋瑞就會娶潔兒。
  ↳ 表達「意願」時,情態動詞 will 和 won't 可用在 if 子句中。

6 will 和 shall 的用法

a 一般來說,**簡單未來式**的第一人稱(I、we)、第二人稱(you)、第三人稱(he、she、it、they)都用 will,而不用 shall。但在**非常正式的文件**(如「條約、規章、法令、會議記錄」)或講演中,shall 可以用**簡單未來式**,這時可以與第一人稱,甚至第二人稱或第三人稱搭配。

- **We shall never give up on the idea of exploring space.**
  我們將永不放棄探索太空的計畫。 → 表示職責(obligation)
- **Convicted killers shall spend years in prison.**
  被判有罪的殺人犯將被長期關監。 → 表示法令(mandatory action)

b 疑問句中，請求別人提供指示或建議，或向他人提供物品、提出建議時，要用 shall 與第一人稱（I、we）搭配。

» 參見 494 頁〈1 shall 和 will 為助動詞(簡單未來式)〉。

- **Shall we go now to make a video of your purple cow?** → 提議
  我們現在可以去替你的紫色乳牛拍影片嗎？
- **Shall I help you with your luggage?** → 提供幫助
  我幫你拿行李好嗎？
- **What shall I do if Jean refuses to go with me to Berlin?** → 請求建議
  如果琴拒絕和我一起去柏林，我該怎麼辦？

Diving Deep Into English 78 will 的用法小整理

❶ 表示純粹的預測（prediction）。

- **She will regret her decision to marry Gary.**
  她決定嫁給蓋瑞，她將為此決定而後悔。
- **It'll be spring soon, and then flowers will blossom everywhere.**
  春天就快到了，到時花兒將四處開放。

❷ 與 I think、expect、wonder、suppose、hope 等或 probably、perhaps 等字連用。

- **It's late. I wonder if she'll come.** 天色已晚。我不知道她是否會來。
- **I expect that Coco will not go to the party unless you say you will go.** 我預料可可不會參加聚會，除非你說你要去。

❸ 臨時的決定（spontaneous decision）。

- **It's windy. I'll close the window.** 風很大，我去關窗戶。

- Del said, "There's the doorbell." "I'll get it!" yelled Amy.
  戴爾說:「門鈴響了。」「我去開門!」艾咪叫道。

❹ 表示承諾（promise）。

- I will come back home before 10 p.m. 我會在晚上十點以前回來。
- Promise you will always love me. 向我保證，你要永遠愛我。

❺ 附帶某種情況。參見 531 頁〈6 從屬子句中的現在式用法〉。

- If Joe asks me to marry him, I will say no.
  如果喬要我嫁給他，我會拒絕。
- Will Lily be surprised when she sees me?
  莉莉見到我時會感到吃驚嗎?

❻ 表示意願（肯定句）或拒絕（否定句）。

- Ray will go, no matter what I say. 不管我說什麼，雷就是要去。
- Kay won't go, no matter what I say. 不管我說什麼，凱就是不去。

❼（不涉及未來）表示習慣（habit）。

- My sister will always make noise when I am trying to sleep.
  = My sister always makes noise when I am trying to sleep.
  每當我想讓自己睡著時，我妹就會製造噪音。

3 現在進行式表示未來的用法

現在進行式可用於描述未來的計畫和安排，主要是**個人的安排和確定的計畫**，其時間和地點大多已經確定下來，通常句中有明確的時間提示語。此時現在進行式並沒有「正在進行」的意義。

- "We're playing ping-pong and volleyball at the Smiths tonight," announced Paul. 保羅宣布:「今晚我們要在史密斯家打乒乓球和排球。」
  ↳ 史密斯家邀請了我們。

- **Liz Peak** is having **her kitchen redecorated next week.**
  下個星期莉茲·皮克要重新裝潢廚房。
  ↳ 莉茲·皮克下星期和室內設計師有約。

- I'm seeing **Kay this Sunday.** 這星期天我要去見凱。
  ↳ 這星期天我和凱有約。

4 be going to 表示未來的用法

	人稱	肯定句	否定句	疑問句
單數	一	I am going to dive	I am not going to dive	am I going to dive?
單數	二	you are going to dive	you are not going to dive	are you going to dive?
單數	三	he/she is going to dive	he/she is not going to dive	is he/she going to dive?
複數	一 二 三	we/you/they are going to dive	we/you/they are not going to dive	are we/you/they going to dive?

Coco and Sue are going to **dive tomorrow.**
可可和蘇明天要去潛水。

Coco and Sue are not going to **dive tomorrow.**
可可和蘇明天不去潛水。

Are **Coco and Sue** going to **dive tomorrow?** 可可和蘇明天要去潛水嗎？

1 be going to 用來表示「**意圖**」或「**先前的決定**」

be going to 用於未來式。在做出明確計畫或任何具體安排之前，可以用 be going to 來談論你的意圖，這種用法在口語中尤其常見。

- Are **you** going to **the prom with Tom?**
  你要和湯姆作伴去參加班級舞會嗎？

- **Del says he**'s going to visit **Eve in jail.** 戴爾說他要去監獄探望伊芙。

- **Bob, when** are **you** going to get a **job?**
  鮑勃，你打算什麼時候要去找工作？

- Claire is going to be an astronaut when she grows up. 克萊兒長大後要當一名太空人。
  ↑ 意圖或已做出的決定
  » 參見 563 頁〈6 表示未來的「現在進行式」與 be going to 的區別〉。

1 be going to 不能用來談論**突然產生的意圖**，或突然做出的決定。突然的情況要用 will。參見 561 頁〈5 be going to 與 will 的區別〉。

- Bess asked Sue, "Do you have Tess Brown's phone number and email address?" Sue answered, "I do, and I'll get it for you."
  貝絲問蘇：「你有黛絲・布朗的電話號碼和電子郵件地址嗎？」
  蘇回答說：「有啊，我找給你。」

2 避免使用累贅的「be going to go」結構，而要用 go 的現在進行式。

- My daughter Amy is going to high school next year.
  我女兒艾咪明年要上高中了

2 be going to 用來表示即將發生的事

be going to 還有另一個用法：根據**當前的跡象**或**我們對情勢的瞭解**，來預測未來，或者是表示未來即將發生或正開始發生的行為動作或事件。

» 參見 561 頁〈5 be going to 與 will 的區別〉。

- Next month she's going to have a baby girl.
  她下個月就要生一個女娃兒了。
  ↑ 一個快要發生的未來事件（我們對情勢的瞭解）。
- Sue's mom is going to be disappointed when she hears the news about Tom. 蘇的媽媽要是得知了湯姆的這個消息，會失望的。
  ↑ 根據我們對情勢的瞭解，預測未來要發生的事。
- Look at the sky—it's going to snow. 你看天空，要下雪了。
  ↑ 一個即刻就要發生的未來事件：看見了天空中的烏雲（根據當前的跡象）。
- Gus shouted, "That airplane is going to crash near us!"
  加斯大叫道：「那架飛機要在我們附近墜毀了！”
  ↑ 一個正在開始的未來事件：已經看見的眼前危險（根據當前的跡象）。

5 be going to 與 will 的區別

be going to
- ✓ 預先就有的意圖或決定
- ✓ 根據當前的跡象預測「快要發生的事」

will
- ✓ 突然的意圖或決定
- ✓ 根據自己的主觀意見或過去的經驗，而對未來提供預測的訊息

1 「事先決定」與「突然決定」的區別

a **be going to** 表「**計畫、預先的意圖**」：用來指在說話之前就已經存在的念頭，或是預先考慮過的想法。be going to 不能用來表示突如其來的意圖或決定。

» 參見 559 頁〈4 be going to 表示未來的用法〉。

b **will** 表「**突然的決定**」：will 構成的簡單未來式表示當下做出的決定，即突然的意圖和決定。當你一邊做決定、一邊告知他人時，就用 will。

» 參見 554 頁〈2 表示「說話當時所做的決定」〉。

- **Max declared, "You can have it for $250 plus tax." Kay quickly said with a big smile, "OK, I'll buy it."**
  馬克斯宣稱：「你出 250 美元再加稅，就可以買到它。」
  凱立刻面帶微笑地說：「好，我買了。」
  ↑ 宣布一個突然的決定或意圖，不能用 be going to。

- **Max declared, "You can have it for $250 plus tax." Kay was thinking to herself, "It's a lot of money, but I think I'm going to buy it."**
  馬克斯宣稱：「你出 250 美元再加稅，就可以買到它。」
  凱心想：「那可要花一大筆錢啊，不過我想我還是要買。」
  ↑ 表意圖，並沒有當場宣布一個突然的決定，就可以用 be going to。

2 「強調即將發生」與「單純預測未來」的區別

a **be going to** 表示「**快要發生的事**」：根據當前的跡象或瞭解到的情況預測未來，表示未來即將發生或正開始發生的行為動作或事件。

✗ Hold on, Paul! We will crash into the wall!

✓ Hold on, Paul! We're going to crash into the wall!

保羅，抓緊！我們要撞到牆了。

↑ 根據當前的跡象預測未來。

b will 表示「**單純提供未來的訊息**」：只是提供未來的訊息或預測未來的事件，並不表示已經決定了的或明顯快要發生的事情，而是根據自己的**主觀意見**或過去的經驗，表示我們認為或相信某事未來要發生。

- **Don't lend Lisa that video camera—she'll definitely break it.**
  不要把攝影機借給麗莎，她會把它弄壞的。 → 我相信她會把它弄壞。

- **Kay began to sob, "It will rain tomorrow on my wedding day!"**
  凱開始哭泣：「明天是我的婚禮，竟然要下雨啊！」
  ↑ 單純提供未來的訊息（預測明天要下雨）。

  比較 **Look at the sky—it's going to rain cats and dogs!**
  瞧瞧天空，快下大雨了！ → 明顯看得出馬上就要發生的事件。

will 也可以表達當前的徵兆，但通常與副詞（probably、definitely 等）連用。與這些副詞連用時，仍然表達的是「我們**主觀意識**中所認為、推測將要發生的事情」。

- Look at the sky—it will probably/definitely rain cats and dogs! 看看天空，大概快下大雨了！

3 be going to 和 will 有時區別不大，常可以互換。

- **I will be as rich and famous as Kay one day.** → 單純指對未來的預測
- **I am going to be as rich and famous as Kay one day.** → 強調意圖
  將來有一天，我要像凱一樣名利雙收。
  ↑ 兩句意義區別不大，可以互換。

- **You won't believe this.** → 對未來事件的預測
- **You are not going to believe this.** → 根據現實情況預測將發生的事
  你不會相信這一點的。
  ↑ 兩者意義區別不大，可以互換。

- **Next month things** will be **difficult for Jill.** → 單純指對未來的預測
- **Next month things** are going to **be difficult for Jill.** → 根據現實情況，預測未來要發生的事

潔兒下個月會很不好過。

↑ 兩句意義區別很小，可以互換。

6 表示未來的「現在進行式」與 be going to 的區別

1 兩者可以互換

許多情況下，現在進行式和 be going to 這兩個結構的意義相同，不過 be going to 強調「**意圖**」，而現在進行式則強調「**事先做好的安排**」。

- I'm taking <u>tomorrow</u> off to go fishing with Coco and Joe.

  ↑ 強調已經安排好的事。

  = I'm going to take <u>tomorrow</u> off to go fishing with Coco and Joe. 明天我休假，要跟可可和喬去釣魚。

  ↑ 強調意圖或先前的決定。當句中有具體的時間提示語（tomorrow）時，兩句意思幾乎一樣，完全可以互換。

- I'm sorry. I'd love to go bowling with you, but I'm taking Kay out <u>on Saturday</u>. → 強調已安排好的事。

  = I'm sorry. I'd love to go bowling with you, but I'm going to take Kay out <u>on Saturday</u>. → 強調意圖或先前的決定。

  不好意思，我是很想跟你去打保齡球，可是星期六我要帶凱出去。

  ↑ 句中有具體時間提示語（on Saturday），兩句完全可以互換。

2 「安排」與「意圖」之別

a **現在進行式**：強調「**確定的安排**」，有明確的時間和地點的安排或計畫。

b **be going to**：則強調「**意圖**」或「**先前的決定**」。當句中的時間指「**大概時間**」，而不是指「具體的時間」，通常要用 be going to 強調意圖。

✗ I'm taking a few days off <u>as soon as I can</u>.

✓ I'm going to take a few days off <u>as soon as I can</u>. 我想盡快休幾天假。

↑ 表意圖。由片語 as soon as I can 得知尚未安排休假的具體時間和地點，因此不用表示「已經安排妥當」的現在進行式，而是用表示 be going to 的句型。

- **Tomorrow I'm really going to tell Sue about your new girlfriend Lulu.** 明天我真的要跟蘇說說你新女友露露的事。
  ↥ 這句顯然是強調意圖，而不是強調「確定的計畫和安排」，應當用 be going to。
- **Ann is starting college on September 1.** 安九月一號要上大學了。
  ↥ 表示確定的安排（有明確的時間提示語），也可以用 be going to。
- **Kay's brother John is going to study Chinese in Beijing one of these days.** 有那麼一天，凱的哥哥約翰會在北京學中文。
  ↥ 表示意圖或先前的決定（沒有明確的時間提示語）。這句不能用現在進行式。

1 詢問**安排**：用**進行式**比用 be going to 自然，因為進行式強調安排，be going to 強調意圖，詢問他人的安排，比詢問他人的意圖更有禮貌。

- Are you and Joe doing anything special tomorrow?
  你和喬明天有什麼特別的事要做嗎？
  ↥ 比「Are you and Joe going to do anything special tomorrow?」更自然。

2 詢問**他人的先前決定**：**be going to** 比用進行式更禮貌。

- Are you going to do anything about that insurance claim letter from Mr. Andrew Lame?
  你打算對安德魯．蘭姆先生的保險索賠信做怎樣的處理嗎？
  ↥ 這比「Are you doing anything about that insurance claim letter from Mr. Andrew Lame?」更禮貌，後者聽起來帶有責備的含意。

7 現在進行式、will、be going to 三者的區別

1 三者的細微區別

a **現在進行式**：所陳述的未來與「現在」有關聯，強調「現在已經安排好」或「確定的」未來。

b **be going to**：也與「現在」有關，強調「現在的意圖」，含有人的意志；也可以用來表示「根據外在證據，來推斷將發生的事」。

c **will**：與現在沒有關聯，純粹表示對未來事件的預測，描述主觀意識中所知道、認為、猜測、推測將要發生的事情。

	與現在有關	已安排好	意圖	預測
現在進行式	✓	✓ 見例 4		
be going to	✓		✓ 見例 2	✓（根據當前證據，客觀預測）見例 1
will				✓（根據過去經驗，主觀預測）見例 3 見例 4

例 1 **Look out, Brook! You're going to fall and land on Paul.**
小心，布魯克！你快摔到保羅身上了。
↳ 有外在的、看得到的證據。

例 2 **If Mark comes to Paris, Bing is going to help me with the cooking.**
如果馬克來到巴黎，賓要幫我煮飯。
↳ 指事先想過的意圖或決定。

例 3 **I know Mary is a terrible driver, and if you lend her your car, she will destroy it.**
我知道瑪麗的開車技術很差，如果你把車借給她，她會把車撞壞的。
↳ 由說話者的知識所做出的預測；說話者相信要發生的事。

例 4 **I'm seeing Dee at eight tonight, but I wonder whether she'll recognize me.**
我今晚八點要跟蒂見面，不過我不知道她是不是認得我。
↳ I'm seeing 表示現在已經做好的安排；這裡用 I'm going to see Dee 也可以。
↳ she'll recognize 表示與現在沒有關聯，單純表達說話者推測將要發生的事。

因為進行式只用來表示「個人的**未來計畫**和**安排**」，所以不能用來描述人類無法控制的事件（如氣象）。這種情況要用 be going to 或 will。

✗ According to the weather forecast, it's raining tomorrow.
✓ According to the weather forecast, it's going to rain tomorrow.
= According to the weather forecast, it will rain tomorrow.
根據氣象報導，明天會下雨。

2 完全可以互換的情況

某些句子用現在進行式、be going to 還是簡單未來式（will），對語意的影響不大。我們再整理一下這三種用法之間的細微區別：

現在進行式 → 強調與現在有關且已確定的安排。

be going to → 與現在有關的意圖。

will → 單純預測或描述未來事件。

- **What are you and Ray doing during your vacation in May?**
  ↳ 強調已安排好的計畫。

- **What are you and Ray going to do during your vacation in May?**
  ↳ 強調主觀意圖。

- **What will you and Ray do during your vacation in May?**
  你和雷五月的假期時要做什麼?
  ↳ 單純提供未來的訊息。以上三句的區別不大,可互換。

8 簡單現在式表示未來的用法

簡單現在式通常不用於談論未來事件。但某些情況下也有例外,見下述說明。

1 時刻表上的行程

談論時刻表、計畫表上的計畫或安排時,可以用簡單現在式,這種情況下的簡單現在式常具有未來的含意。

» 參見 531 頁〈5 簡單現在式用於表示「確定的計畫和安排」〉。

- **June says her ship leaves at noon.**
  = June says her ship will leave at noon.
  茱恩說,她的船中午時分起航。
  ↳ 簡單現在式可以表示時刻表上已經確定的安排;這類句子還常用簡單未來式 will,意思相同。

- **This year the Fun With American English Summer Camp starts on July 1.** 今年的「美國英語快樂夏令營」於七月一日開營。

- **What time does your flight arrive in Miami?**
  你的班機何時抵達邁阿密?

- **Dwight says the movie starts at 9:30 and ends at midnight.**
  杜威特說,電影九點半開始,半夜結束。

1 談論**非正式的個人計畫**或對未來事件做出**預測**時，不用簡單現在式，要用 will、going to 或現在進行式。

✗ I'm tired and I stay in bed today.

✓ I'm tired and I'm going to stay in bed today.
我累了，我今天要待在床上。
↳ 非正式的個人安排，不可用簡單現在式。

- I expect Kay will come to visit me today.
我預料凱今天會來找我。 → 對未來預測，不用簡單現在式。

2 如果某個行為或事件是**正式安排**（如**時刻表**或**計畫表**），可用簡單現在式。

- When do you and Sue go to Paris?
你和蘇什麼時候去巴黎？ → 以你們的旅遊行程表為根據。
- Is Amy Bend on duty this weekend?
艾咪・班德這個週末要值班嗎？ → 以計畫表為根據。

2 在從屬子句中表未來

在表示**未來時間的從屬子句**中，簡單現在式常具有未來的含意。

- **Don't worry, Mary. As soon as Jake gets a job, he will pay you back.**
不要擔心，瑪麗。傑克一找到工作就會還你錢。
↳ 從屬子句用簡單現在式（gets）表示將來；主句用簡單未來式 will。
- **After I find out what has happened to Coco, I'll let you know.**
等我查明可可究竟發生了什麼事之後，我就會通知你。
↳ 從屬子句用簡單現在式（find）表示將來；主句用簡單未來式 will。

» 參見 531 頁〈6 從屬子句中的現在式用法〉。
» 從屬子句的用法，參見 345 頁〈Part 5 從屬連接詞與副詞子句〉。

3 請求指示或提供指示

簡單現在式可用來「**請求指示**」或「**提供指示**」，在這種用法中，簡單現在式具有未來含意。

- **How do I get from Bart's apartment to the Institute for Performing Arts?** 從巴特的公寓去藝術學院要怎麼走？
  ↑ 請求指示

- **After you go under the overpass, you turn to the left on Toad Road, walk straight for about 200 meters, and then catch a No. 2 bus on the right-hand side of the road.**
  你從高架橋下通過之後，左轉到蛤蟆路，再往前走兩百公尺，然後在馬路右邊搭乘二路公車。
  ↑ 提供指示

» 參見 531 頁〈4 簡單現在式用於請求和提供指示〉。

Diving Deep Into English 79 表「未來」的另外兩個句型

❶「be about to + 原形動詞」：表示「即將發生的事情」

表示未來即將發生的事，還可以用 be about to do。這個結構一般不與時間狀語連用。

- **Hurry up, Steve! Eve is about to leave.**
  史蒂夫，快點！伊芙要走了。
- **"This bridge is about to collapse!" shouted Sue.**
  蘇叫喊道：「這座橋要塌了！」
- **Art, the football game is about to start!**
  = Art, the football game is going to start! 亞特，美式足球賽要開始了！

❷「動詞 be + 不定式」：表示未來

「動詞 be +（帶 to）不定式」結構也可表示未來（可能性、職責、義務、意圖）。不過，這種結構只用於非常正式的文體中。

- **We should not look back unless it is to derive useful lessons from past errors, and for the purpose of profiting by dearly bought experience.** (President George Washington)
  我們不應該往後看，除非是為了從過去的錯誤中得到有益的教訓，為了從付出高昂代價得到的經驗中受益。

未來進行式

1 未來進行式的用法

1 未來某一時刻正在進行的事

will be + 現在分詞：未來進行式表示未來某一時刻正在進行的動作。在使用未來進行式的句子中，通常會提到未來某個時刻（例如 when you come back from class 或 this time next week）。

- **When you come back from class, I will be watching CNN, so please do not disturb me then.**
  你上完課回來時，我會正在看美國有線電視新聞網，因此那個時候請不要打擾我。
- **This time next week I'll be lying next to Coco on a sunny Florida beach, dreaming of Christmas snow.** 下星期的這個時候，我將躺在佛羅裡達一個豔陽高照的海灘上，躺在可可的身邊，夢想著聖誕的白雪。

2 已確定或決定的未來事件

a 未來進行式可以指「已經確定的未來事件」或「已經確定的安排」，並沒有正在進行的含意。

- **Good luck with your job hunting, Bob. I'll be praying for you.**
  鮑勃，祝你找工作好運！我會為你祈禱的。
  ↑ 已經決定的未來事件
- **Next week the coach will be training our basketball team hard to prepare for the championships.**
  下週，教練會對我們的籃球隊進行嚴格訓練，為錦標賽做準備。
  ↑ 已經確定的未來事件

- I'm sorry, Susan, but I won't be coming to your party, as I have an appointment with a client from Baghdad.
  對不起，蘇珊，我不能參加你的聚會，因為我和一個來自巴格達的客戶有約。
  ↥ 已經確定的安排（日程的一部分）

- I will be talking more about this topic in my next lecture.
  在我下一次的演講中，我會進一步談論這個題目。
  ↥ 已經確定的安排

b 在一些句子中，**未來進行式**和**現在進行式**都可以表示個人已經計畫或安排好的未來事件，可以互換。

- I'll be leaving/I'm leaving for Hong Kong at 9:30 tonight.
  我今晚九點半要起程去香港。

- He'll be making/He's making a speech at the conference next week. 他要在下週的會議上做演講。

3 按照事物的正常發展過程未來應該發生的事

未來進行式也可以表示「**猜測**」，指按照事物的正常發展過程應該會發生的未來事件，不表示事先的計畫、安排，在這種情況下，未來進行式並不包含個人意圖，也沒有正在進行的含意，純粹指「到時候會發生……」。

- Ms. Rover, I will be seeing you again, as soon as this war is over.
  羅維小姐，這場戰爭一結束，我就會再見到你。
  ↥ 按照事物的正常發展過程將要發生的事件，並沒有為此做什麼安排。

4 未來進行式的其他用法

a **禮貌的疑問句**：詢問某人的未來計畫和安排時，用**未來進行式**比用簡單未來式 will 聽起來更禮貌，表示你並不希望因你的詢問，而改變對方的計畫和安排。（用簡單未來式 will，會讓人感覺是在提出要求，語氣比較生硬。）

- Mike, will you be using your car this afternoon?
  邁克，今天下午你要用你的車嗎？
  ↥ 禮貌詢問對方已經做出的決定，只是想知道對方的計畫，並不想影響其意圖或決定。

- Claire, how long will you be staying there? 克萊兒，你會在那裡待多久呢？
  ↥ 禮貌詢問對方已經做出的決定，只是想知道對方的計畫，並不想影響其意圖或決定。

- Claire, how long will you stay there? 克萊兒，你要在那裡待多久？
  ↥ 在打聽別人的意圖、意願，語氣比較生硬。

b **委婉的否定句**：否定句中，用**簡單未來式**可能帶有**拒絕**的意味，若本意並非拒絕，最好用**未來進行式**。例如，要表達因外在環境因素而非個人主觀因素（例如有約在先），所以無法在未來時間做某事，最好用未來進行式。

- Steve won't be coming to my wedding. 史蒂夫不會來參加我的婚禮。
  ↥ 基於某種外在環境因素，史蒂夫不能來參加我的婚禮。
- Sue won't come to my wedding. 蘇不會來參加我的婚禮。
  ↥ 可能暗示蘇拒絕來參加我的婚禮。

- Dwight won't be cooking tonight, because he will be busy observing Jupiter until midnight. 杜威特今晚不能煮飯，因為他將忙著觀察木星直到深夜。
  ↥ 由於某種環境因素，杜威特今晚不能煮飯。
- Dwight won't cook tonight. 杜威特今晚不煮飯。
  ↥ 可能暗示杜威特拒絕今晚煮飯。

» 參見 556 頁〈5 won't 的用法（表拒絕）〉。

2 比較簡單未來式和未來進行式

簡單未在式（will）	未來進行式
✓ 對未來的預測 ✓ 允諾、邀請、願意 ✓ 疑問句：打聽對方的決定 ✓ 否定句：拒絕	✓ 未來某時刻正在進行的事 ✓ 已經安排好的未來事件 ✓ 疑問句：禮貌詢問對方的安排 ✓ 否定句：因客觀因素而未來不能做某事
It will snow tonight. 今晚要下雪。 ↥ 對未來的預測。	This time next week I'll be sitting on Waikiki Beach in Honolulu. 下星期這個時候，我將正坐在檀香山的懷基基海灘上。 ↥ 未來某時刻正在進行的事。
Amy will help me clean the sailboat. 艾咪會幫忙我清理帆船。 ↥ 願意幫助。	Amy will be helping me clean the sailboat. 艾咪要幫忙我清理帆船。 ↥ 已經確定的安排。

Will you please come to my birthday party? 可以請你來參加我的生日派對嗎？→ 發出邀請。	Will you be coming to my birthday party? 你能來參加我的生日派對嗎？ ↑ 禮貌地詢問你已經做出了什麼決定。
Will you eat with us tonight? 你今晚要跟我們一起吃嗎？ ↑ 打聽你的決定。	Will you be eating with us tonight? 你今晚會跟我們一起吃嗎？ ↑ 禮貌地詢問你的安排。
When will you finish this project? 這個方案你什麼時候會完成？ ↑ 直接詢問，如上司對下屬。	Will you be interviewing Kay Brown tomorrow morning? 你明天上午要面試凱·布朗嗎？ ↑ 禮貌詢問對方已做出的決定，如下屬對上司。
I won't see Ben again. 我不想再見到班了。 ↑ 不願意再見到班。	I am afraid I won't be seeing Ben again. 我恐怕再也見不到班了。 ↑ 由於某種環境因素，不能再見到班。

3 未來進行式、簡單未來式 will 與 be going to 的細微區別

在某些句子中，使用未來進行式、簡單未來式 will 或 be going to 都正確，意義上無太大區別，只是強調的重點不同而已。

- Dwight, will you be studying English tonight? → 禮貌地詢問
  杜威特，你今晚要學英語嗎？
- Dwight, will you please study English tonight? → 指示或命令
  杜威特，拜託你今晚學英語好不好？
- Dwight, are you going to study English tonight? → 催促對方做出決定
  杜威特，你今天晚上要不要學英語啊？

- Ray, will you be attending our party on Saturday? → 禮貌地詢問
  雷，星期六你會來參加我們的聚會嗎？
- Dwight, will you attend our party tonight? → 邀請
  杜威特，今晚來參加我們的聚會好嗎？
- Joe, are you going to attend our party tomorrow? → 催促對方做出決定
  喬，你明天要不要來參加我們的聚會啊？

簡單過去式

1 簡單過去式的句型

簡單過去式的**肯定句**中，要用動詞的過去式（如：called, danced, nodded, hurried, swam）；**疑問句**和**否定句**則由「助動詞 did + 原形動詞」構成，主要動詞一律不加 -ed 或 -d。

肯定句	I/he/she/it/we/you/they played
疑問句	did I/he/she/it/we/you/they play?
否定句	I/he/she/it/we/you/they did not play

* 縮寫 didn't = did not

- Last night I cooked for Dwight. 昨晚我為杜威特做了飯。
  ↑ 肯定句中用動詞 cook 的過去式 cooked。
- Last night I did not cook for Scot. 昨晚我沒有為史考特做飯。
  ↑ 否定句中用助動詞 did + not 和原形動詞 cook（沒有 -ed）。
- Did you cook last night for Brook? 昨晚你為布魯克做飯了嗎？
  ↑ 疑問句中用助動詞 did 和原形動詞 cook（沒有 -ed）。

2 規則動詞的過去式

a 大多數規則動詞→ + -ed

- accept → accepted 接受
- allow → allowed 允許
- bother → bothered 打擾
- call → called 致電
- consider → considered 考慮
- happen → happened 發生
- need → needed 需要
- rain → rained 下雨
- stay → stayed 留下
- visit → visited 拜訪
- wash → washed 清洗
- work → worked 工作

- I washed the dishes yesterday, so today it's your turn.
  昨天是我洗的碗，今天該輪到你洗碗了。

b 以 -e 結尾的動詞→ + -d

- believe → believed 相信
- blame → blamed 責備
- care → cared 關心
- confuse → confused 使困惑
- dance → danced 跳舞
- hate → hated 憎恨
- hope → hoped 希望
- include → included 包括
- inspire → inspired 鼓舞
- like → liked 喜歡
- phone → phoned 打電話
- realize → realized 實現

- Grandpa Shaw believed in working hard. 蕭爺爺堅信勤奮工作。

c 單音節動詞：「單母音 + 單子音」字尾 → 重複字尾子音字母 + -ed

以「一個母音字母＋一個子音字母（w 或 y 除外）」結尾的單音節動詞，要重複字尾的子音字母，再加 -ed。這類動詞有如下幾個特徵：

1 為短音動詞。

2 只有一個音節。

3 字尾只有 b、d、g、m、n、p、r、t 等一個子音字母。

4 字尾子音前只有一個母音字母（a、e、i、o、u）。

drum	+ m + ed	→ drummed 打鼓
grab	+ b + ed	→ grabbed 抓取
hop	+ p + ed	→ hopped 單腳跳
nod	+ d + ed	→ nodded 點頭
pat	+ t + ed	→ patted 輕拍
pet	+ t + ed	→ petted 寵愛；愛撫
plan	+ n + ed	→ planned 計畫
rob	+ b + ed	→ robbed 搶劫
skip	+ p + ed	→ skipped 跳過
slip	+ p + ed	→ slipped 滑行
step	+ p + ed	→ stepped 跨步；踩住
stop	+ p + ed	→ stopped 停止
whip	+ p + ed	→ whipped 鞭打

- Jim grabbed his towel and headed for the outdoor shower.
  吉姆抓起他的毛巾，朝戶外的淋浴間走去。

1 含有兩個**母音字母**的單音節動詞，其過去式不重複字尾子音字母。

- seem → seemed 似乎
- wait → waited 等待

2 字尾有兩個**子音字母**的單音節動詞，其過去式不重複字尾字母。

- want → wanted 想要
- help → helped 幫助

3 以 -w 或 -y 結尾的單音節動詞（「單母音 + 單子音」），其過去式不重複字尾子音字母。

- bow → bowed 低頭；鞠躬
- play → played 玩耍

d 雙音節動詞／多音節動詞：重音在後的「單母音＋單子音」字尾 → 重複字尾子音字母 + -ed

重音在後的雙音節或多音節動詞，且以「一個母音字母＋一個子音字母」結尾的動詞（字尾 w、x、y 除外），要重複字尾的子音字母，再加 -ed。

- prefer [prɪˋfɝ] → preferred 寧願
- refer [rɪˋfɝ] → referred 意指
- regret [rɪˋgrɛt] → regretted 後悔

・**It was a cold wet day, and Ted preferred to stay in bed.**
那是一個又冷又濕的一天，泰德寧願待在床上。

比較 betray → betrayed → betray 是雙音節動詞，而且是重音在後的「單母音＋單子音」，但因以 -y 結尾，不需要重複字尾的子音字母。

e 雙音節動詞／多音節動詞：重音在前的「單母音＋單子音」字尾 → + -ed

重音在前的雙音節或多音節動詞，則不需要重複字尾子音字母。

- wonder [ˋwʌndɚ] → wondered 納悶
- thunder [ˋθʌndɚ] → thundered 打雷

・**I wondered if I was the only one who realized that she was a big liar.**
我納悶，是否只有我才意識到她是一個大騙子。

- travel → travelled（英式要重複字母「l」）
  → traveled（美式只需要加 -ed）

f 以「子音字母 + -y」結尾的動詞 → y 變 i + -ed

字尾為子音加上 -y 的動詞，先把 y 變成 i，再加上 -ed。

- apply → applied 申請
- copy → copied 複印
- cry → cried 哭泣
- envy → envied 羡慕
- hurry → hurried 趕緊
- rely → relied 依靠
- reply → replied 回復
- study → studied 研讀
- try → tried 嘗試
- worry → worried 擔心

- I envied your good luck in marrying Sue. 我真羡慕你的好運，能娶到蘇。

  ↑ envy → envied

g 以「母音字母＋ -y」結尾的動詞 → 保留 y + -ed

- betray → betrayed 背叛
- delay → delayed 耽擱
- display → displayed 展示
- enjoy → enjoyed 享受
- obey → obeyed 遵守
- play → played 玩耍
- pray → prayed 祈禱
- stay → stayed 留下

- Uncle Dennis stayed with us in Washington, D.C. for a month.

  丹尼斯叔叔在華盛頓時在我們家裡住了一個月。

h 以 -i 結尾的動詞 → + -ed

- ski → skied 滑雪
- taxi → taxied 飛機緩慢滑行；乘計程車；用計程車運送

- Jill skied down the hill. 潔兒滑雪下山。
- The airplane taxied down the runway. 飛機在跑道上緩慢滑行。

3 不規則動詞的過去式

1 規則動詞的過去式和過去分詞只能逐一記憶，別無他法。

» 參見 904 頁〈附錄 1 不規則動詞表〉。

- come → came 來
- dive → dove 跳水
- hold → held 抓住；舉行

- Joy dove into the lake to save a drowning boy.

  喬伊跳進湖裡去救一個快淹死的男孩。

有些字同時具有規則和不規則變化，但意義不同，例如：

規則動詞 • hang → hanged → hanged 吊死；絞死（一個人）
不規則動詞 • hang → hung → hung 把……掛起（一幅畫）

- My little sister hung the ribbon from a branch of the big tree in front of our house. 我的小妹妹把絲帶掛在我家前面一棵大樹的樹枝上了。
- They hanged that vile dictator at noon, and soon after that everyone had a smile.
  他們在中午時分把那個邪惡的獨裁者絞死了，很快大家都有了笑容。

2 下列不規則動詞的**過去式與原形動詞同形**，這類動詞也屬於不規則動詞。

- beat → beat 打
- bet → bet 打賭
- broadcast → broadcast 廣播
- cost → cost 花費
- cut → cut 切割
- hit → hit 打
- hurt → hurt 傷害
- let → let 讓
- put → put 放置
- read [rid] → read [rɛd] 閱讀
- set → set 豎立
- shut → shut 關閉
- split → split 劈開
- spread → spread 伸展
- upset → upset 使心煩
- wet → wet 弄濕

- **Last night after dinner, Mary read me a funny story about a robotic bunny.** 昨天晚飯後，瑪麗給我讀了一個關於一隻機器兔子的滑稽可笑的故事。
- **Kent's mom bought me a pretty ring yesterday, and it cost only three dollars and ten cents.**
  昨天肯的媽媽給我買了一枚漂亮的戒指，她只花了三美元 10 美分。
- **Dee put some honey in my tea, and then we sat quietly and watched the waves dancing in the sea.** 蒂在我的茶裡加了一些蜂蜜，然後我們靜靜地坐著，觀看波浪在海上翩翩起舞。

4 簡單過去式的用法

1 表「過去事件」

a 簡單過去式用以表示過去曾經存在或發生過的事。

- **Clive began to dive at the age of five.** 克萊夫五歲就開始潛水。

b 這種用法還可以細分為以下三種情況：

短暫 Last week Meg had a bad fall while ice-skating and broke her leg. 梅格上星期溜冰時狠狠摔了一跤，把腿摔斷了。

持續較長 Pat spent much of her childhood at a boarding school in Texas. 派特在美國德州的一所寄宿學校度過了她大部分的童年。

重複發生 While in college, Ann fell in love four times before she married Dan. 安在大學時談了四次戀愛，後來嫁給了丹。

2 常用的時間提示語：簡單過去式常與表示**過去的時間副詞**連用。

- yesterday 昨天
- last night 昨晚
- a month ago 一個月前
- last week 上星期
- a week ago 一星期前
- in 2011 在 2011 年
- last year 去年
- a year ago 一年前

- **Where did you go with Andrew White last night?**
  昨晚你跟安德魯·懷特一起去哪兒了？
  ↳ 表示過去時間的 last night 要與簡單過去式連用。

- **Romeo and Juliet lived many years ago.**
  羅密歐和茱麗葉生活在很多年以前。
  ↳ ago 要與簡單過去式連用。

Romeo and Juliet

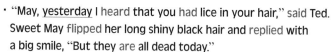

- **Mom asked sweetly, "Please wash the dishes, Tom." Tom replied, "No, I washed the dishes yesterday and the day before, and lazy Jane did nothing but complain!"**
  媽媽溫柔地請求：「湯姆，請把碗洗了。」
  湯姆回答說：「我不洗，昨天和前天都是我洗碗的，
  而懶惰的珍除了抱怨之外，什麼也沒做！」

- **"May, yesterday I heard that you had lice in your hair," said Ted. Sweet May flipped her long shiny black hair and replied with a big smile, "But they are all dead today."**
  「梅，我昨天聽說你頭上長了蝨子。」泰德說。
  可愛的梅輕輕甩了一下烏黑亮麗的長髮，面帶微笑答道：「牠們今天都死光啦。」
  ↳ yesterday 與過去式連用；today 與現在式連用。

3 **用於「故事」**：簡單過去式常用來敘述故事，或談論故事裡發生的事。

- **Sally noticed that her nose and toes grew longer every time she told a lie or stole a cherry pie.** 莎莉注意到，每次她撒了謊或偷了櫻桃派時，她的鼻子和腳趾就會變長。

5 簡單過去式的特殊用法

1 在**時間和條件副詞子句**中，用動詞過去式**代替過去未來式**。

- **Amy told me that she would be a teaching assistant when she went to Michigan State University.**
  安跟我說，她去了密西根州州立大學之後，就會當助教。
  ↑ 在 that 引導的受詞子句中，when 引導的時間副詞子句動詞要用過去式（went），表示過去的未來，而主句動詞則用過去未來式（would be）。

比較

- **Amy has already told me that she will be a teaching assistant when she goes to Michigan State University.**
  安已經跟我說過，等她去了密西根州州立大學，她就會當助教。
  ↑ 時態要一致。在 that 引導的受詞子句中，when 引導的時間副詞子句動詞用現在時（goes），表示未來，而主句動詞則用簡單未來式（will be）。

2 在**假設語氣**中，可以用動詞的過去式，表示**與現在事實或未來事實相反**的主觀設想或主觀願望。

» 參見 665 頁〈Unit 14 語氣〉。

- **Claire wishes her dad were a millionaire.** 克萊兒但願她爸爸是百萬富翁。
- **If only I could see my old parents more often, but I can't.**
  我要是能更常看到我年邁的父母親就好了，可是卻不行。

3 為了使請求更加**委婉客氣**，有些**情態動詞**用動詞過去式表示現在或未來的含義。

» 參見 474 頁〈Part 9 情態動詞／情態助動詞〉。

- **"Can/Could you wait?" "No, I'm pretty late."**
  「你能等等嗎？」「不行啦，我已經遲到很久了。」

過去進行式

1 過去進行式的句型

過去進行式的構成：was/were + 現在分詞

was/were 是 be 動詞的過去式，屬於助動詞，協助主要動詞構成過去進行式。was/were 加上動詞的現在分詞就構成了過去進行式。

» 參見 472 頁〈Part 8 助動詞 do, have, be, will〉。

	人稱	肯定句	疑問句	否定句
單數	第一	I was playing	was I playing?	I was not playing
	第二	you were playing	were you playing?	you were not playing
	第三	he/she/it was playing	was he/she/it playing?	he/she/it was not playing
複數	第一	we were playing	were we playing?	we were not playing
	第二	you were playing	were you playing?	you were not playing
	第三	they were playing	were they playing?	they were not playing

* 縮寫：wasn't → was not; weren't → were not

2 過去進行式的用法

1 過去進行式表示「過去某一時刻正在進行的事」。

✗ When I got up this morning, the birds chirped and the bells rang.

✓ When I got up this morning, the birds were chirping and the bells were ringing. 今天早上我起床時，小鳥兒在鳴叫，鈴鐺在叮噹響。

- "Jan, what was your boyfriend Clark doing at eight last night in the park?" "At eight last night, Clark was walking and talking in a warm and romantic fog with his heartthrob."
「簡，昨晚八點時，你的男朋友克拉克在公園做什麼？」
「昨晚八點時，克拉克正跟他心愛的人一起在溫馨、浪漫的霧靄中散步、聊天。」

- "What was your dog Mark doing when you got home yesterday evening?" asked Kay. Jan laughed and said, "When I got home, Mark was barking and jumping up and down in the living room and he insisted that he needed to do some walking in the park."
「昨天傍晚你回家時，你的狗馬克在做什麼？」凱問道。簡笑著說：「我回到家時，馬克正在客廳裡一邊吠叫，一邊跳上跳下，還堅持要去公園散步。」

2 過去進行式也用於「強調在過去某段時間中，某個行為動作無時無刻都在持續進行」。

- Kim said Paul and his classmates were quarreling all morning today at the gym. 金姆說，保羅和他的同學們今天整個上午都在體育館吵個不停。

3 過去進行式可以使「請求、建議或疑問」顯得更客氣、更具試探性。這種情況常用動詞 think、wonder 等。

- I was wondering whether I should invite my ex-girlfriend Sue Bedding to my wedding.
= I was thinking about whether I should invite my ex-girlfriend Sue Bedding to my wedding.
我在想，該不該邀請我的前任女友蘇‧貝丁來參加我的婚禮。

4 過去進行式常和簡單過去式搭配

a **過去進行式**：通常指「持續了較長時間」的行為動作或情境。

b **簡單過去式**：指「短暫的」行為動作或事件，該短暫動作或事件通常發生在持續較長時間的行為動作之中，或打斷了長時間的動作。

- As the young shepherdess was walking down the hill, she saw the murder. 當那年輕的牧羊女正在下山時，目睹了那場兇殺案。
↑ saw 是短暫動作，發生在持續較長時間的行為動作 was walking 的過程中。

・Grandpa Lindbergh died of a stroke while he was driving a sick friend to a hospital in St. Petersburg.
林德伯格爺爺在開車送一個生病的朋友前往聖彼德堡一家醫院的路上，突然中風去世了。
↑ died 是短暫動作，發生在持續較長時間的行為動作 was driving 的過程中。

・Wendy stopped by while I was enjoying a candlelight dinner with Ted. 我和泰德正在享受燭光晚餐的時候，溫蒂順道來訪。
↑ stopped by 是短暫動作，發生在持續較長時間的行為動作 was enjoying 的過程中。

C 過去進行式也常用來講故事，與簡單過去式搭配使用。此時，用「**過去進行式**」來說明「故事背景」，用「**簡單過去式**」來描述「事件」。

・Last Sunday I was happily bicycling on a path through a large forest. Suddenly a big wolf jumped onto the path and gave me a hungry look. We stared at each other. Pretending to be a furious tiger, I howled wildly at the animal. A few seconds later it turned around and ran away. After it disappeared into the forest, I found myself wet with sweat and trembling all over with fear.
上個星期天，我在一條小路上開心地騎著自行車，穿越一大片森林。突然，小路上跳進來了一隻大野狼，對我露出飢餓的樣子。我們目不轉睛地看著彼此。我假裝成一隻凶猛的老虎，對那隻動物發出狂野的怒吼。不一會兒，牠便調頭逃跑了。在牠逃進森林不見蹤影後，我發現自己被嚇出了一身汗，直打哆嗦。

3 不能用過去進行式的動詞

非進行式動詞不用於現在進行式，也不用於過去進行式，而只能用於簡單現在式或簡單過去式。
» 參見 540 頁〈5 非進行式動詞〉。

・Pam ate a piece of the cinnamon bread to see how it tasted before she added some jam.
塗果醬之前，潘姆先吃了一片肉桂麵包，想先嚐嚐滋味如何。
↑ 不能用進行式 was tasting。

- **Last night Dad drank a lot of beer and smelled bad.**
  昨晚老爸喝了很多啤酒，氣味難聞死了。
  ↑ 不能用進行式 was smelling。

- **Theodore heard a knock on the door.**
  希歐多爾聽見有人在敲門。
  ↑ 不能用進行式 was hearing。

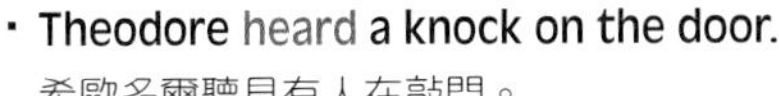

- **Mary believed your gory story about finding the Glory Galaxy UFO near an observatory.** 瑪麗相信你講的那個在天文臺附近發現葛洛瑞銀河系飛碟的令人毛骨悚然的故事。
  ↑ 不能用進行式 was believing。

4 when 和 while 要用於進行式還是簡單式？

a **while**：用於「延續較長時間」的動作或情境，不用於短暫的動作，常與**進行式**連用。

b **when**：可用於短暫的動作或持續性的動作，可與**進行式**或**簡單式**連用。

✗ **Ms. Lace claims that she was at a friend's house while the explosion took place.**

✓ **Ms. Lace claims that she was at a friend's house when the explosion took place.**
勒斯女士聲稱，爆炸發生時她正在一個朋友的家裡。
↑ 短暫的行為動作（took place）不能與 while 連用，只能與 when 連用。

- **The doorbell rang when/while Sue Fang was eating dinner with Steve Lang.**
  ↑ when 和 while 都可以用於持續較長時間的動作 was eating。
  = Sue Fang was eating dinner with Steve Lang when the doorbell rang. 就在蘇·方和史蒂夫·藍在共進晚餐時，門鈴響了。
  ↑ when 可以用於短暫動作 rang，但 while 不行，不能說 while the doorbell rang。

- **Paul sprained his ankle while/when he was playing basketball.**
  保羅打籃球時扭傷了腳踝。
  ↑ when 和 while 都可以用於持續較長時間的動作 was playing。

- Ann and Dan were enjoying their picnic near the lake when the hailstorm began.
  安和丹正在湖邊享受野餐時，突然下起了雹暴。
  ↳ when 與一個短暫的動作 began 連用。

- When Ann came home, Dan was cooking dinner for her, himself, and their son Stan.
  = Dan was cooking dinner for Ann, himself, and their son Stan when Ann came home.
  = Ann came home when/while Dan was cooking dinner for her, himself, and their son Stan.
  昨晚安回家時，丹正在為她、他自己以及兒子斯坦做飯。
  ↳ 上面第一句和第二句 when 與一個短暫動詞 came 連用。
  ↳ 上面第三句 when/while 都可以與較長時間的動作 was cooking 連用。

5 過去進行式和簡單過去式的比較

1 暫時行為與長期固定行為的區別

a **暫時行為**：**過去進行式**與現在進行式相同，用來指暫時的行為動作和情境，不能與表示時間跨度的片語連用（如：how long, for six years）。

b **長期固定行為**：若要談論長期的或固定的行為或情境，應該用**簡單過去式**。

✗ Roy was living in India for six years when he was an adventurous little boy.

✓ Roy lived in India for six years when he was an adventurous little boy.
當羅伊還是一個愛冒險的小男孩時，他在印度居住了六年。
↳ 過去進行式 was living 不能與表示時間跨度的片語 for six years 連用。

- Joy was looking for a job that she could truly enjoy.
  喬伊在尋找一個她可以真正喜歡的工作。
  ↳ 找工作是暫時的情況。

- When she was a child, Margo played the piano. 瑪歌小時候彈過鋼琴。
  ↑ When she was a child 是一個長期的情境，不能用 was playing。
- Lily was working/worked as a waitress during the summer of 2013. 莉莉在 2013 年夏天當過飯店服務員。
  ↑ 這句 was working 和 worked 都可以。

- Her father worked hard all his life.
  她的父親在生前辛勤工作了一輩子。
  ↑ 這句不能用 was working。

2 動作結束與否的區別

a **動作尚未結束**：表示過去正在進行、尚未完成的動作，要用**過去進行式**。

b **動作已經結束**：表示過去已經完成或結束的動作（無論是延續性動作還是短暫動作），要用**簡單過去式**。

- Yesterday my husband worked in his office from 8 a.m. to 11:30 p.m.
  昨天我丈夫從早上八點到晚上 11 點半都在辦公室工作。
  ↑ 已經結束
- When my husband came home last night, I was reading a book by the fireplace. 昨晚我丈夫回到家時，我正在壁爐旁看書。
  ↑ 尚未結束

3 **過去重複的行為或過去的習慣**，要用**簡單過去式**：涉及過去事件完成的次數（如：twice、three times、many times 等），不用過去進行式，而要用簡單過去式。

- Sue called you six times. 蘇打了六通電話給你。
  ↑ 重複動作要用簡單過去式，不用進行式 was calling。
- She jogged along the beach almost every day last year.
  她去年幾乎每天都會沿著海灘慢跑。
  ↑ 不能用進行式 was jogging。
- Midge fell in love twice when she was in college.
  米姬在大學時談了兩次戀愛。 → 不能用進行式 was falling in love。

4 詢問某件事「**發生的時間**」，只能用**簡單過去式**，不用過去進行式。

- **What time did you wake up this morning?**
  你今天早上幾點醒來的？

- **When did you start to wear make-up?**
  你什麼時候開始化妝了？

5 描述過去某個時間**先後發生**的兩個或多個行為或事件時，都用**簡單過去式**。

- **Screaming, she jumped out of the bed and ran to the kitchen.**
  她尖叫著跳下床，朝廚房跑去。

6 **always 與簡單過去式和過去進行式**

a always 與「**簡單過去式**」連用：表示過去某事不斷發生。

b always 與「**過去進行式**」連用：表示**對過去某事抱怨**。

- **Sue always called me when she was in trouble.**
  蘇遇上麻煩時總是給我打電話。

- **When we were in college, Dwight was always calling me late at night.**
  我們在讀高中時，杜威特老是在夜深時給我打電話。

7 **非進行式動詞**（hear、taste、sound、believe 等）不用於現在進行式，也不用於過去進行式，而只能用於簡單現在式或簡單過去式。

» 參見 540 頁〈5 非進行式動詞〉。

- **Midge and I couldn't have been more pleased when we heard that you had graduated from college.**
  聽到你大學畢業了，米姬和我是再高興不過了。
  ↳ 不能用進行式 was hearing。

- **Did Coco believe your story about seeing a UFO?**
  可可相信你說的看到了飛碟的事嗎？
  ↳ 不能用進行式 was believing。

過去未來式

1 過去未來式的構成

將簡單未來式的助動詞或 be 動詞改為過去式，即形成過去未來式。

簡單未來式		過去未來式
will	→	would
is/am/are going to	→	was/were going to
is/am/are doing	→	was/were doing
is/am/are about to	→	was/were about to

2 過去未來式的用法

a 談論**從過去觀點看將要發生的事情**，也就是在過去的某個時刻還沒有發生的事情，要用過去未來式。

- **In 2008 I arrived in Yellowknife, Canada, where I would spend the next four years of my life.**

  我於 2008 年來到加拿大的黃刀鎮，將在那裡度過我生命中的四年。

  ⤷ 過去未來式「would + 動詞原形」，常用於子句中，主句動詞通常是簡單過去式。

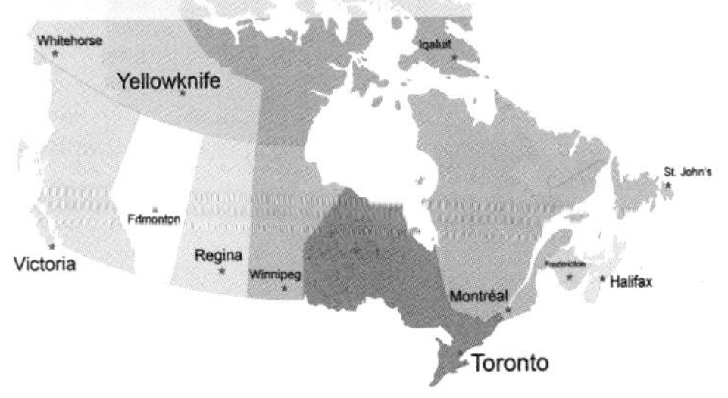

- I remember the last time I saw Bob he was going to start a new job.
記得我上次看見鮑勃時，他正要開始一份新的工作。
ℓ 從過去的視角描述未來的意圖。

- Yesterday I saw Jan Flower at the airport, but she didn't have much time to talk with me because she was leaving for Pakistan in an hour.
昨天我在機場看見簡·福勞爾，但她沒太多時間跟我聊天，因為她在一小時內就要動身前往巴基斯坦。
ℓ 過去進行式表示「從過去的視角描述已經安排好的未來事」。
ℓ 過去進行式在這裡沒有進行的含意，而表示按計劃將發生的事。

- Amy was about to be hanged when the governor's pardon came.
艾咪正要被絞死的時候，總督的赦免令到了。
ℓ was/were about to do 表示「過去某時刻剛要發生某事，突然另一事發生了」。

b 「was/were + going to」句型：也可以表示「該事件並未發生」。

- Danny was going to sell his house and move to the Philippines, but he changed his mind.
丹尼原本打算賣了房子，然後搬去菲律賓，但他最後改變了主意。

- I was going to visit Kay on Friday night, but I had to call her to cancel my visit because my husband got sick.
我本來打算星期五晚上去找凱，但因為我先生病了，我只好給她打電話取消我的拜訪計畫。

簡單現在完成式

完成式用來表達「在說話時已經完成的動作或狀況」。完成式分為八種：簡單現在完成式、現在完成進行式、簡單過去完成式、過去完成進行式、簡單未來完成式、未來完成進行式、過去未來完成式、過去未來完成進行式。

1 簡單現在完成式的句型

簡單現在完成式簡稱「現在完成式」，其結構是「**助動詞 have**（複數）/ **has**（單數）+ **動詞的過去分詞**（worked、seen、done 等）」。

	人稱	肯定句	疑問句	否定句
單數	第一	I have worked	have I worked?	I have not worked
	第二	you have worked	have you worked?	you have not worked
	第三	he has worked she has worked it has worked	has he worked? has she worked? has it worked?	he has not worked she has not worked it has not worked
複數	第一	we have worked	have we worked?	we have not worked
	第二	you have worked	have you worked?	you have not worked
	第三	they have worked	have they worked?	they have not worked

* 縮寫：• I've (not), you've (not), we've (not), they've (not)
• he's (not), she's (not), it's (not) • have not = haven't • has not = hasn't

Affirmative **Jerry and Mary have arrived in Canterbury.**
傑瑞和瑪麗已經到達坎特伯雷了。

Interrogative **Have Jerry and Mary arrived in Canterbury?**
傑瑞和瑪麗到達坎特伯雷了嗎？

Negative **Jerry and Mary haven't arrived in Canterbury.**
傑瑞和瑪麗還沒有到達坎特伯雷。

2 規則動詞的過去分詞

規則動詞的過去分詞跟其過去式一樣，以 -ed 結尾。

» 詳細說明參見 573 頁〈2 規則動詞的過去式〉。

1 原形動詞 → + -ed（大部分動詞在原形動詞後面加 -ed，即成過去分詞。）

原形動詞	過去式	過去分詞
• call	called	called 打電話
• help	helped	helped 幫助
• kiss	kissed	kissed 親吻
• rain	rained	rained 下雨

2 以 -e 結尾的動詞 → + -d（字尾為 -e 的動詞，後面只加 -d。）

原形動詞	過去式	過去分詞
• dance	danced	danced 跳舞
• believe	believed	believed 相信
• confuse	confused	confused 使困惑
• divide	divided	divided 分開

3 單音節動詞：「單母音 + 單子音」字尾 → 重複字尾子音字母 + -ed

a 以「一個母音字母 + 一個子音字母（w 和 y 除外）」結尾的單音節動詞，要重複字尾的子音字母，再加 -ed。

b 這類動詞是短音動詞，只有一個音節，字尾只有一個子音，為 b、d、g、m、n、p、r、t 等，同時在這些子音前面只有一個母音（a、e、i、o、u）。

原形動詞	過去式	過去分詞
• drum + m + ed	drummed	drummed 打鼓
• grab	grabbed	grabbed 抓取
• hop	hopped	hopped 單腳跳
• nod	nodded	nodded 點頭
• pat	patted	patted 拍打
• plan	planned	planned 計畫
• rob	robbed	robbed 搶劫
• skip	skipped	skipped 跳過

• slip	slipped	slipped 滑動
• step	stepped	stepped 踏；踩
• stop	stopped	stopped 停止

NOTE

1 若字尾子音前有兩個母音字母，則不要重複子音，直接加 -ed 構成過去分詞。

• seem → seemed → seemed 似乎
• wait → waited → waited 等待

2 若字尾為兩個子音，也不重複子音，直接加 -ed 構成過去分詞。

• want → wanted → wanted 想要
• help → helped → helped 幫助

3 以 -w 或 -y 結尾的單音節動詞（單母音 + 單子音），其過去式不重複字尾子音字母。

• mow → mowed → mowed 割（草等）
• stay → stayed → stayed 停留

4 雙音節動詞：重音在後的「單母音 + 單子音」字尾 → 重複字尾子音字母 + -ed

重音位於字尾的雙音節動詞，規則同字尾為「一個母音字母 + 一個子音字母」的單音節動詞，要重複字尾的子音字母，再加 -ed 構成過去分詞。

• prefer → preferred → preferred 寧願
• refer → referred → referred 意指

5 雙音節動詞：重音在前的「單母音 + 單子音」字尾 → + -ed

重音位於第一音節的雙音節動詞，其過去分詞則不需要重複字尾子音字母。

• wonder → wondered → wondered 納悶
• thunder → thundered → thundered 打雷

6 以 -i 結尾的動詞 → + -ed

• taxi → taxied → taxied 飛機緩慢滑行；乘計程車；用計程車運送
• ski → skied → skied 滑雪

7 以「子音字母 + y」結尾的動詞→ y 變 i + -ed

字尾為「子音字母 +y」的動詞，要先把 y 改成 i，再加 -ed。

原形動詞	過去式	過去分詞
• apply	applied	applied 申請
• copy	copied	copied 影印
• cry	cried	cried 哭泣
• envy	envied	envied 羨慕
• fry	fried	fried 煎煮
• hurry	hurried	hurried 趕緊
• study	studied	studied 研讀
• worry	worried	worried 擔心

8 以「母音字母 + y」結尾的動詞→ + -ed

字尾為「母音字母（a、e、o）+y」的動詞，只加 -ed。

原形動詞	過去式	過去分詞
• betray	betrayed	betrayed 背叛
• delay	delayed	delayed 耽擱
• enjoy	enjoyed	enjoyed 享受
• obey	obeyed	obeyed 遵守
• play	played	played 玩耍
• portray	portrayed	portrayed 畫肖像
• pray	prayed	prayed 祈禱
• stay	stayed	stayed 停留

3 不規則動詞的過去分詞

不規則動詞的過去分詞往往與過去式不同形，必須逐一記憶。

» 參見 904 頁〈附錄 1 不規則動詞表〉。

- drive → drove → driven 駕駛
- eat → ate → eaten 吃
- mean → meant → meant 意味著
- shake → shook → shaken 搖動

4 簡單現在完成式的用法

1 對現在有影響的過去行為動作

我們用簡單現在完成式來強調「與現在有關聯的、已經完成了的」行為動作或事件（the finished/completed actions or events），即，對現在有影響的過去發生的行為動作或事件。如果我們說「something has happened」，我們會同時想到**過去**和**現在**。

- **I've emailed Jan about her cow, so she knows what's happening now.**
  我已經發了電子郵件告訴簡她的乳牛的事，因此她知道現在的情況。
  ↳ have emailed 這一動作已經完成，且對現在產生了影響（亦即她知道現在的情況）。
- **Meg cannot attend your wedding, because she has broken her left leg.** 梅格不能參加你的婚禮，因為她摔斷了左腿。
  ↳ has broken 這一動作已經完成，且對現在產生了影響（她左腿斷了，無法來參加婚禮）。
- **Sue asked Mabel, "Have you read the Bible?"**
  蘇問美博：「你讀過聖經嗎？」
  ↳ 你現在對聖經熟不熟悉？
- **Jerry and Mary haven't arrived in the village of Cherry.**
  傑瑞和瑪麗尚未抵達切麗山莊。
  ↳ 他們現在不在切麗山莊。

比較
- **"An hour ago, Mom let my dog out," said Tom.**
  「一小時前，媽把我的狗放出去了。」湯姆說。
  ↳ let 在這裡只強調「媽媽把狗放出去」這個過去事件，而不強調對現在產生了什麼後果或影響。
- **"Mom has let my dog out," said Tom.**
  「媽已經把我的狗放出去了。」湯姆說。
  ↳ has let 強調過去的事件（放狗）對現在產生的效果或影響（狗此刻在外面）。
- **"Mom lets my dog out," said Tom.**
  「媽放我的狗出去。」湯姆說。
  ↳ 用簡單現在式，表示「媽媽放狗出去」是一個重複的行為。

2 動作或事件到目前為止的持續時間

a 描述「從過去某個時刻一直持續到現在」的某個過去事件，要用現在完成式。

b 現在完成式常用來表達或詢問某事「到目前為止持續了多長時間」。

c 表達行為或狀態持續的「時間跨度」時（如：how long, for ten years, since 2013），不能使用簡單現在式，要用現在完成式。

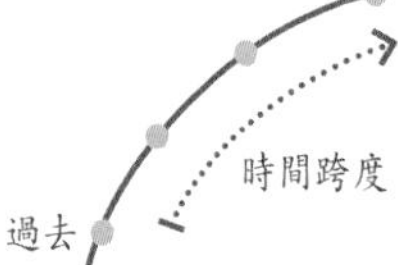

- Kay has been here since Monday. 凱從星期一就待在這裡。
  ↳ 從過去（Monday）到現在。

✗ How long is Mr. Howe a lawyer?
✓ How long has Mr. Howe been a lawyer?
豪先生當律師有多久了？

✗ My daughter Trish studies Spanish for seven years.
✓ My daughter Trish has studied Spanish for seven years.
我女兒翠西學西班牙文已經七年了。

✗ Kate knows Joe since 2008.
✓ Kate has known Joe since 2008. 凱特從 2008 年就認識喬。
↳ 不能用簡單現在式（is、studies、knows）談論目前的情形已經持續的時間長短。

還可以用**現在完成進行式**來表示「**從過去一直到現在的持續行為**」。

- Clive Sears has been living in Singapore for five years.
  = Clive Sears has lived in Singapore for five years.
  克萊夫．西爾斯在新加坡已經住了五年了。

» 參見 608 頁〈4 簡單現在完成式與現在完成進行式的比較〉。

3 **目前為止已發生的過去事件**：現在完成式描述「到目前為止已發生或未發生」的「過去事件」，事件發生的確切時間並不重要，只知道是在某段時間內發生，因此常與下列不特指某個時間點的時間副詞連用，暗示「到現在為止的任何或某個時刻」（at some/any time up to now），有時也可以將這些時間副詞省略。

- ever 曾經
- never 從未
- already 已經
- still 仍然
- just 剛剛
- yet 還沒
- before 之前

1 副詞 already、just、ever、never 要放在助動詞 have/has 後面。
- have/has already written 已經寫了……

2 在疑問句和否定句中，yet 通常出現在句尾。

3 在完成時態的否定句中，still 置於助動詞 have/has 之前。
- still have/has not paid 尚未支付

- **Dee, you've already done a lot for me.** 蒂，你已經為我做了很多了。
  ↑ 意味著「直到現在」。
- **Has Joe ever seen *Romeo and Juliet*?** 喬看過《羅密歐和茱麗葉》嗎？
- **Jenny has never yelled at me.** 珍妮不曾對我大聲叫喊過。
- **The train has just stopped, so we must be in Spain.**
- 火車剛停了下來，我們一定是在西班牙了。
- **Have you ever met Henry before?** 你以前見過亨利嗎？
- **Sue asked Jake, "Have you spoken to the boss yet?" "No, not yet," replied Jake.** 蘇問傑克：「你跟老闆談過了嗎？」傑克回答說：「還沒。」
- **"Has Annette made up her mind yet?" "No, she hasn't made up her mind yet about whether she wants to marry Joe."**
  = No, she still hasn't made up her mind about whether she wants to marry Joe.「安妮特做了決定了嗎？」「還沒，她還沒有決定是不是要嫁給喬。」
  ↑ still 常置於助動詞「have/has + not + 過去分詞」前面。
  ↑ yet 常置於疑問句和否定句句尾。

4 **至今已完成的事物分量（多少）**：現在完成式

可用來談論「到目前為止已經做了多少」。

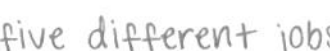

- **Joe has had five different jobs since Christmas.**
  喬從聖誕節起已經換過五個不同的工作了。
- **Kitty has lived in ten different houses since she graduated from Michigan State University.**
  姬蒂從密西根州立大學畢業後，已經住過十棟不同的房子了。

- I am saving $50 a month. I started a year ago, and up to now, I have saved $600. 一年前開始，我每個月存五十塊美金，到現在已經有六百塊美金了。

5 **事件至今發生的次數或頻率**：現在完成式可用來談論「到目前為止事件發生的次數」。

- I'm in love with the music of Paul Grimes, and I have been to his concerts four times.
  我非常鍾愛保羅・格萊姆斯的音樂，我去過他的音樂會四次。
- She has often wanted to go and visit Paris. 她常常想去巴黎觀光。
- I have seen Kay with Mark twice today.
  我今天已經兩次看到凱和馬克在一起了。
- How many times have you been out on a date with Midge since she graduated from college? 米姬大學畢業後，你和她約會過幾次？

6 **談論新聞事件**：現在完成式常用於談論新聞事件。

- The British Prime Minister Joan Blair has arrived in Washington, D.C. for talks with President Trent.
  英國首相喬恩·布雷爾已經抵達華盛頓，與總統崔恩特會談。
- Mort announced, "A plane has crashed at Kennedy International Airport. One person died and ninety-seven people survived."
  莫特宣布說:「一架飛機在甘迺迪國際機場墜毀了。一個人死亡，九十七個人倖存。」
  ↑ 新聞報導常用現在完成式（has crashed）引出某個事件，然後用簡單過去式（died, survived）詳述細節。

5 have been to、have gone to 和 went

1 **have been to 和 have gone to：都可以表示「去某地」**

a have been to：表示「去過」，意味著人現在已經回來，不在那個地方了。

b have gone to：表示「去了」，人已經出發，已到達某地或在返回途中，但還沒回來。

✗ Have you ever gone to Vietnam?

✓ Have you ever been to Vietnam? 你去過越南嗎？

↳ 用 gone 表示「去了某地」，人不在這裡。當對 you 提問時，you 這個人必定在現場，不在別處，因此不能說「have you gone to . . .」。

↳ 同樣道理，代名詞 I 也不能和「have gone to」連用。

- Sue has been to New York lots of times but has never been to Paris. 蘇去過紐約很多次，但沒有去過巴黎。
  ↳ 蘇現在不在紐約，也不在巴黎。
  ↳ 過去的動作對現在造成影響：蘇對紐約有了一定程度的瞭解。

- "Is June at home?" "She has gone to the bank, and she will be back soon." 「茱恩在家嗎？」「她去了銀行，很快就會回來。」
  ↳ 過去的動作對現在造成影響：茱恩去了銀行，現在還沒有回家。

2 用現在完成式 have been/gone 和簡單過去式 went 有什麼不同？

a **現在完成式** have been/gone：表示「對現在有影響的過去動作或事件」，暗示「人現在在何處」。

b **過去式** went：單純表達一個過去的動作，對現在的狀態沒有任何暗示。

- She has gone to the Daisy Computer Store. 她去了黛絲電腦商店。
  ↳ 她不在這裡，她現在在黛絲電腦商店，或是去往商店的路上，或是回來的途中。

- Kim Corning has been to Max's Gym this morning. 金姆·科寧今早去過邁克斯體育館。
  ↳ 金姆去過邁克斯體育館，但現在不在那裡（說話時依然是上午）。

- June went to Kumamoto this afternoon. 茱恩今天下午去了熊本市。
  ↳ 只強調「去」的過去行為動作。（熊本市為日本的一個地名。）

- Coco has gone to Tokyo. 可可去了東京。
  ↳ 可可不在此地，她現在在東京或在路途中，強調過去動作對現在的影響。

- Jenny has been to New Delhi many times. 珍妮去過新德里很多次。
  ↳ 珍妮現在不在新德里，不過因為去過幾次，所以對新德里有了一定的瞭解，強調過去動作對現在的影響。

- Dad went to Islamabad twice last year. 爸爸去年去過伊斯蘭馬巴德兩次。
  ↳ 只著重「去」的過去行為動作。

6 現在完成式與簡單過去式的比較

1 對現在有影響和對現在無影響的區別

a **對現在有影響**：談論過去的事件及其對現在產生的效果，就用**現在完成式**。

b **對現在無影響**：強調過去的行為動作或發生在過去的事因，而不強調對現在產生了什麼後果或影響，就用**簡單過去式**。

✗ How has Mr. Star gotten that facial scar?

✓ How did Mr. Star get his facial scar?
斯達先生臉上的疤是怎麼來的？
↳ 強調事因發生於過去，不能用現在完成式。

- Look what Dee has given me!
  瞧瞧蒂給我的東西！
  ↳ 強調的是禮物，而不是動作。

- Pat, who gave you that?
  派特，那個東西是誰給你的？
  ↳ 強調的是過去動作 gave，不能用現在完成式（has given）。

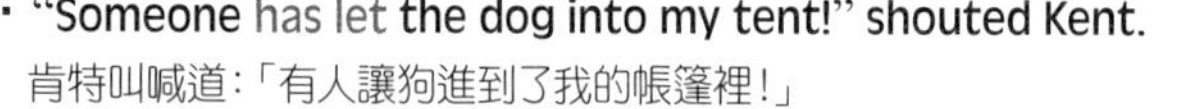

- "Someone has let the dog into my tent!" shouted Kent.
  肯特叫喊道：「有人讓狗進到了我的帳篷裡！」
  ↳ 強調現在的效果：此刻狗在我的帳篷裡，很可能正把我的帳篷搞得亂七八糟。

- Kent asked angrily, "Who let the dog into my tent?"
  肯特氣呼呼地問：「是誰讓狗進我的帳篷裡的？」
  ↳ 強調過去行為動作，這句不能用現在完成式（has let）。

- Would you like some of this chocolate cake I've made?
  想嚐嚐我做的巧克力蛋糕嗎？
  ↳ 強調對現在產生的效果：我現在正在提供蛋糕給你。

- I made a cake for my daughter Bess, but she didn't like it.
  我為女兒貝絲做了一個蛋糕，可是她不喜歡。
  ↳ 強調過去動作：我談論的不是現在，我想到的只是過去的事件或動作。

NOTE

美式和英式的區別

美式 I already saw the movie.

英式 I have already seen the movie. 我已經看過那部電影。

↑ 現在完成式（have seen）強調與現在有關聯（我現在知道電影的內容）。

↑ 簡單過去式（saw）只強調過去的動作。這種情況美式英語常用過去式，英式英語常用完成式。

美式 Would you like some of this chocolate cake I made?

英式 Would you like some of this chocolate cake I've made?

你要吃看看我做的這個巧克力蛋糕嗎？

2 與現在有關聯和與現在無關聯的區別

a **與現在有關聯**：用**現在完成式**表示某種狀態過去存在，現在仍然存在。

b **與現在無關聯**：用**簡單過去式**表示某種狀態現在已經不存在了。

- **I have belonged to the Tampa Space Club since I moved to Florida.**
  我搬到佛羅里達州之後，就是坦帕太空俱樂部的成員了。
  ↑ 「屬於」這種狀態過去存在，到現在仍然存在。

- **Linda belonged to the Tampa Space Club when she was living in Florida.** 琳達住在佛羅里達州時，是坦帕太空俱樂部的成員。
  ↑ 「屬於」這種狀態過去存在，到現在已經不存在了。

3 可能還會發生的重複性動作和不再發生的重複性動作

a **可能還會發生的重複性動作**：用**現在完成式**表示這個重複性動作或事件「有可能再次發生」。

b **不再發生的重複性動作**：用**簡單過去式**表示這個重複性動作或事件「已經結束，不再發生」。

- **Susan has written 32 books, and she plans to write 10 more before she retires.**
  蘇珊已經寫了 32 本書，她計畫在退休之前再寫 10 本。
  ↑ 「寫了 32 本書」這種重複性的行為到現在還沒有結束，還可能再次發生。

- Sam wrote 5 books before he was killed by a drunk driver.
  山姆被一個酒醉駕駛的司機害死之前，寫過五本書。
  ↳「寫過五本書」這種重複性的行為到現在已經結束，將不再發生。

4 起始時間與持續時間

a **起始時間**：談論某個現在的情況是什麼時候開始（when），而不是已經持續了多長時間（how long），用**簡單過去式**。

b **持續時間**：談論某行為或狀況到現在為止持續了多長時間，要用**現在完成式**。

簡單過去式 說明什麼時候開始	**現在完成式** 說明持續了多長時間
When did Sue arrive in Honolulu? 蘇是什麼時候到達的檀香山？	How long has Sue been in Honolulu? 蘇在檀香山有多長時間了？
Margo moved into this cottage a month ago. 一個月前瑪歌搬進了這棟別墅。	Margo has lived in this cottage for a month. 瑪歌在這棟別墅裡已經住了一個月了。

c 如果過去某個行為或事件「與現在無關聯」，也可以用**簡單過去式**表示該行為或事件持續了多長時間。

- How long did you save up for your first car?
  為了買你的第一輛車，你存錢存了多久？
- Last summer Aunt Amy stayed with me for two weeks.
  去年夏天，艾咪姨媽跟我在一起住了兩個星期。
  ↳ 她現在不跟我住在一起。

5 與現在完成式和簡單過去式連用的時間副詞

a **表示「尚未結束」的時間副詞**：與現在完成式連用的時間副詞，不會是描述已經結束的過去時間，必須是一個還沒有結束的時間，因為現在完成式表示的是「到現在為止已經完成或尚未完成的事」。

b **表示「已經結束」的時間副詞**：要與簡單過去式連用。

現在完成式 與「尚未結束」的時間副詞連用	**簡單過去式** 與「已經結束」的時間副詞連用
• today 今天	• yesterday 昨天
• this week 這星期	• last week 上星期
• this month 這個月	• last month 上個月
• this year 今年	• last year 去年
• this morning* 今天早上	• this morning* 今天早上
• this afternoon* 今天下午	• this afternoon* 今天下午
• this evening 今天傍晚	• last evening 昨天傍晚
• tonight 今晚	• last night 昨晚
• ever* 從來	• never* 從不
• just* 剛剛	• just* 剛才
• already* 已經	• already* 已經
• during the last/past three years 過去三年中	• when I saw him 當我看到他時
• before 之前	• two hours ago 兩個小時前
	• at 7 a.m. 早上七點
	• in 2013 在 2013 年

★ 以上標示「*」的字，可以指「已經結束」，也可以指「尚未結束」，根據說話當時的具體時間而定。

★ ever 主要用於疑問句，也可以用在否定句中，強調某件事情從沒有發生過，或永遠不應該發生。

- I don't believe she has ever called me. 我不相信她給我打過電話。

✗ What have Glen done then?

✓ What did Glen do then? 那時葛倫在做什麼？

↳ 過去時間副詞 then 只能用於簡單過去式。

- I saw Ray yesterday. 昨天我看見了雷。

  ↳ saw（簡單過去式）和已結束的時間副詞 yesterday 連用。

- I have seen Ray today. 今天我看見過雷。

  ↳ have seen（現在完成式）和尚未結束的時間副詞 today 連用。

- Joe, have you ever seen a UFO? 喬，你見過飛碟嗎？
  ↥ 詢問直到現在是否發生過的事。

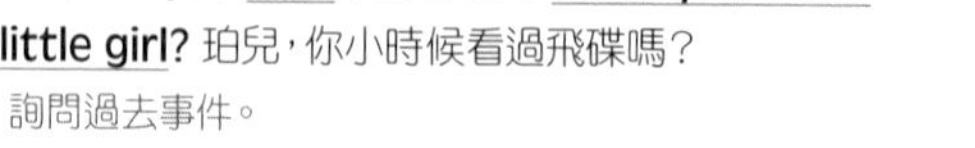

- Pearl, did you ever see a UFO when you were a little girl? 珀兒，你小時候看過飛碟嗎？
  ↥ 詢問過去事件。

- I'm sure we've met before, Pam. 潘姆，我確定我們見過面。
- Margo, I'm sure we met two weeks ago.
  瑪歌，我確定我們兩個星期前見過面。
  ↥ before 常用於現在完成式，ago 只用於簡單過去式。

- Lisa has never apologized for anything in her whole life.
  麗莎一生中從未對任何事情道過歉。
  ↥ never 用於現在完成式，表示到目前為止「還從來沒有」。
- When he was young, Tom never apologized for any mistakes he made. 湯姆年輕時從不對自己所犯的錯誤道歉。
  ↥ never 用於簡單過去式，表示過去已經結束的一段時間「從來沒有」。
- Nancy did not apologize for yelling at her little brother Dwight last night. 南西沒有為昨晚對小弟弟杜威特吼叫的事道歉。
  ↥ 表示過去的時間 last night，只能用於簡單過去式。

- How many times has Jenny Fife been in love in her life?
  珍妮·斐夫一生中戀愛過幾次了？
- How many times was Mike in love last year? 邁克去年戀愛過幾次？
- How many times was Mona Fife in love in her life?
  夢娜·斐夫生前戀愛過幾次？
  ↥ 這句用 was，表示 Mona Fife 已經死了。

- I've written two emails to Sue Corning this morning.
  我今天上午已經寫了兩封電子郵件給蘇·科寧。
  ↥ 表示現在還是早上，用現在完成式。
- I wrote two emails to Sue Corning this morning.
  今天上午我寫了兩封電子郵件給蘇·科寧。
  ↥ 表示現在已經是下午或晚上，相對而言，早上已經是過去時間。

- "Has Andrew come to work yet?"
  "Yes, he is in his office with Ms. Anna Coffee."
  「安德魯來上班沒有？」
  「來了，他在辦公室和安娜·卡菲女士在一起。」

- "Did Emma come this morning?" "Yes, she worked in her office for two hours, and then she left to meet with a client called Jenny Flowers."「愛瑪今天上午來過了嗎？」「來過了，她在辦公室工作了兩個小時，然後就出去見一個名叫珍妮·福勞爾斯的客戶。」

Diving Deep Into English 80 for、ago、since 的時態比較

❶ 重點提示

a **簡單現在式**：不能用來談論目前的情形已經持續了多長時間（how long）。

b **for**：可以用於現在完成式，也可以用於簡單過去式。

c **ago**：只能用於簡單過去式。

d 表示「從何時開始」：要用 **since**。

- since Monday 從星期一起

e 表示「時間持續了多久」：要用 **for**。

- for three years 三年來

f **since**（指時間）：無論引導的是從屬子句還是表示時間的詞，主句要用完成式。

主句（完成式）+ since 子句（過去式）
主句（完成式）+ since + 過去時間

- **Clive and Emma have been friends since they were five.**
  克萊夫和愛瑪從五歲起就一直是好朋友。
  ↳ 主句用完成式（have been），since 子句用過去式（were）。
  ↳ 過去是好朋友，現在仍然是，這時用現在完成式銜接過去和現在。

- Coco and Joe were friends two years ago.
  可可和喬兩年前是好朋友。
  ⤷ ago 只能用於簡單過去式。
  ⤷ 簡單過去式只著重於對過去事件或狀態的描述，現在情況則不明（很可能他們現在不是好朋友了）。

- How many years has it been since Denny met his first love, Jenny? 丹尼認識他的初戀情人珍妮幾年了？
- Did Margo first meet her husband Joe in Jericho ten years ago? 瑪歌是不是十年前在耶利哥與她丈夫喬初次見面的？

❷ 在含有 since 的句子中，主句一般用現在完成式（或過去完成式），表示現在的情形持續了多久，但有時也用簡單現在式（或簡單過去式），尤其是為了表示現在的情形與過去有所變化。

- Midge hasn't come to see us since her graduation from college. 米姬大學畢業後，就一直沒有來看過我們。
  ⤷ 現在完成式：表示情況一直持續到現在。
- Midge doesn't come to see us so much since her graduation from college.米姬大學畢業後就不常來看我們了。
  ⤷ 簡單現在式：表示現在的情形與過去有所變化。

- It's (been) a long time since I kissed Dee.
  我親吻蒂已經是很久以前的事囉。
  ⤷ 可以用現在式 it is，也可以用完成式 it has been。

❸ for 可以用於簡單現在完成式，也可以用於簡單過去式。

- Despite Amy Chow's fears about crime and earthquakes, she has lived in Los Angeles for five years.
  雖然艾咪·曹很怕犯罪活動和地震，但她在洛杉磯已經住了五年了。
  ⤷ 涉及過去和現在，艾咪·曹現在居住在洛杉磯。
- Coco lived in Chicago for four years. 可可曾在芝加哥住過四年。
  ⤷ 只著重於「住」的過去行為動作，可可現在住在哪裡，我們並不知道。

現在完成進行式

1 現在完成進行式的句型

現在完成進行式的構成方式：**have/has been + 現在分詞**。

	人稱	肯定句	疑問句	否定句
單數	一	I have been working	have I been working?	I have not been working
	二	you have been working	have you been working?	you have not been working
	三	he/she/it has been working	has he/she/it been working?	he/she/it has not been working
複數	一	we have been working	have we been working?	we have not been working
	二	you have been working	have you been working?	you have not been working
	三	they have been working	have they been working?	they have not been working

Affirmative I've been waiting for Fanny Flowers for over three hours.
我已經等芬妮·福勞爾斯等了三個小時。

Interrogative Have you been waiting long for Sue?
你已經等蘇很久了嗎？

Negative I haven't been waiting long for Linda.
我還沒有等琳達很久。

2 現在完成進行式的用法

1 表達事情至今的持續時間：現在完成進行式用來描述一個開始於過去，但現在還在進行的動作或狀態；或者剛結束並且對現在產生了影響的事件。

- **It** has been snowing **all day!** 已經下了一整天雪了！
  ↑ 很可能還在下雪。

- **Paul's wife** has been painting **the kitchen walls.**
  保羅的妻子一直在粉刷廚房的牆壁。
  ↑ 強調行為動作的連續，很可能還在粉刷。

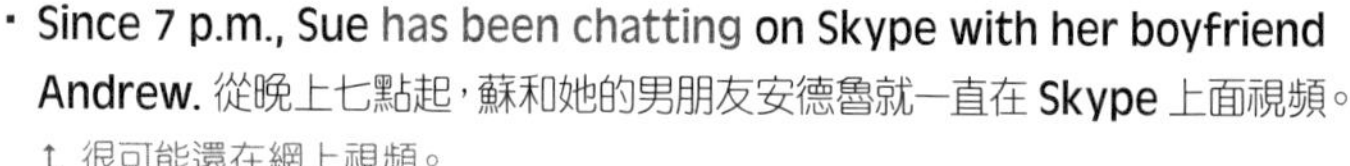

- **Since 7 p.m., Sue** has been chatting **on Skype with her boyfriend Andrew.** 從晚上七點起，蘇和她的男朋友安德魯就一直在 Skype 上面視頻。
  ↑ 很可能還在網上視頻。

- **I** have been living **here for ten years, and I think it's time I moved on.** 我在這裡已經住了十年了，我想我應該搬家了。
  ↑ 強調動作的連續，我還住在這裡。「it's time I moved on」中的動詞 moved 不是過去式動詞，而是假設語氣。
  » 參見 713 頁〈9 It is time that 和 would rather that〉。

move on

- **Her eyes are red and swollen.** Has **she** been crying?
  她的眼睛又紅又腫。她一直在哭嗎？
  ↑ 「哭」的動作剛結束，對現在產生的效果是「眼睛紅、腫」。

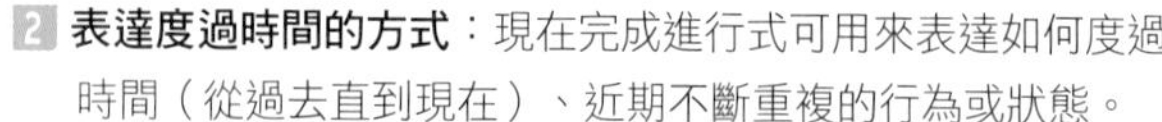

2 表達度過時間的方式：現在完成進行式可用來表達如何度過時間（從過去直到現在）、近期不斷重複的行為或狀態。

- **I'm sorry I haven't sent you any email—Dee and I** have been sailing **around the Mediterranean Sea.**
  對不起，我沒有寄電子郵件給你，因為蒂和我一直在繞著地中海航行。
  ↑ 如何度過時間

- **Ray's girlfriend** has been playing **a lot of basketball during the past few days.** 雷的女朋友最近幾天一直在打籃球。
  ↑ 近期不斷重複的行為

3 過去進行式、現在進行式、現在完成進行式的比較

1 表示**已經結束**的時間副詞或片語要與**過去式**連用，不能用現在完成進行式。

- until 3 p.m. 直到下午三點
- until yesterday 直到昨天
- at 3 p.m. 下午三點

✗ Joe said gently, "You look tired, Coco." "I have been working non-stop until 11 p.m." replied Coco with a yawn.

✓ Joe said gently, "You look tired, Coco." "I was working/worked non-stop until 11 p.m." replied Coco with a yawn.

喬溫柔地問：「可可，你看起來很疲倦啊。」
可可打了個哈欠回答說：「我一直不停地工作到了晚上 11 點。」

↳ 已經結束的時間副詞片語（until 11 p.m.），要與過去式連用。

2 **過去進行式**與過去時間搭配，描述過去某個時刻正在進行的事。

- Kim was watching TV at 4 p.m. 金姆下午四點時在看電視。

↳「at 4 p.m.」是一個過去時間點，要用過去進行式。

3 **現在進行式**與 now 連用，描述現在正在進行的事。

- Now Claire's brothers are watching TV and eating pears.
克萊兒的兄弟們現在正邊看電視邊吃梨。→ 描述此刻（now）正在進行的事。

4 **現在完成進行式**與 since、for、how long 連用，表狀態或行為動作的**持續**。

- Kay said with a concerned look, "It is already 10 p.m., and you look tired, Ray." "I have been working pretty hard since 6 a.m., so I guess it's time to quit for the day," sighed Ray.
凱用關心的神情說：「現在已經是晚上十點了。雷，你看起來很疲倦啊。」
雷嘆了口氣說：「我從早上六點開始就一直在拚命工作，我想今天該到此為止了。」
↳ 現在完成進行式表示「我現在正在工作」（動作開始於過去，現在還在進行）。

- Wade's mom has been studying English for three decades.
韋德的媽媽學英語已經三十年了。→ 很可能還在學習。

- How long have you been waiting for the bus?
你等公車等有多久了？→ 還在等車。

4 簡單現在完成式與現在完成進行式的比較

1 兩種現在完成式（簡單現在完成式和現在完成進行式）都可以用來談論對現在產生效果，及最近發生過的行為和情境。不過，兩者之間有「**動作完成與否**」的區別。

簡單現在完成式	現在完成進行式
通常表示動作已經結束（少數動詞例外）。	不說明動作是否結束（可能結束，也可能仍在進行），只強調動作或情形本身的持續性。
I've washed the car. 我洗車了。 ⮑ 強調動作的完成及所產生的效果：車現在很乾淨了。	I have been washing the car. 我一直在洗車。 ⮑ 強調動作的連續，是否已經洗完則不清楚。
My mom has read *The Maze Runner*. 我媽媽讀過《移動迷宮》。 ⮑ 強調動作的完成及效果：現在瞭解書了。	Trish has been reading *The Maze Runner*. 翠西一直在讀《移動迷宮》。 ⮑ 強調動作的連續，是否讀完則不清楚。
Clive has learned how to drive. 克萊夫學會開車了。 ⮑ 強調動作的完成及效果：現在會開車了，「學習」這個動作已經結束。	Kay has been learning how to be a pilot since May. 凱從五月起就一直在學開飛機。 ⮑ 強調動作的連續，「學開飛機」這個動作是否結束則不清楚，凱有可能還在學開飛機。
Gary has traveled to forty-two countries since he married Sherry. 蓋瑞與雪麗結婚後，已經去過 42 個國家旅遊。 ⮑ 強調動作的完成及效果：去過 42 個國家。	Sam and Jenny Plumber have been traveling across Africa all of this summer. 山姆和珍妮·普朗伯今年整個夏天都在非洲旅行。 ⮑ 強調動作的連續，旅行是否已經結束則不清楚。

My daughter has learned all of the common irregular verbs. 我女兒已經掌握了所有常見的不規則動詞。 ↳ 強調動作的完成及效果：知道了所有常見的不規則動詞。	Susan Corning has been learning irregular verbs all morning. 蘇珊‧科寧整個上午都在學習不規則動詞。 ↳ 強調動作的連續，是否已經學會則不清楚。（注意 時間仍然在上午。）

2 表示「持續很長時間、沒有變化的情境」，要用**簡單現在完成式**；表示「持續較短時間，且會有變化的情境」，可以用**現在完成進行式**，也可以用簡單現在完成式。比較下列兩句用法：

- **For eight centuries, this church has stood here on this hill.**
  這座教堂聳立在這座小山上已經有八個世紀了。
  ↳ 固定的情況（時間較長的、沒有變化的情境）。
- **Ann Flower has been standing/has stood there for an hour.**
  安‧勞爾站在那裡有一個小時了。
  ↳ 暫時的情況（比較短暫、有變化的情境）。

3 表示事情進行了多久（how long），可以用**簡單現在完成式**或**現在完成進行式**（但不能用簡單現在式和現在進行式），兩者區別不大。兩種完成式都可以與 for 或 since 連用。

✗ Kate lives here since 2008.
✗ Kate is living here since 2008.
✓ Kate has lived here since 2008.
✓ Kate has been living here since 2008.
凱特從 2008 年就住在這裡。

✗ I study astronomy for ten years.
✗ I'm studying astronomy for ten years.
✓ I've studied astronomy for ten years.
✓ I've been studying astronomy for ten years.
我學天文學已經有十年了。

4 表示「事件發生的頻率」，要用**簡單現在完成式**。

✗ Tom has been visiting Libya twice in the last three months.

✓ Tom has visited Libya twice in the last three months.
湯姆最近三個月去過利比亞兩次。

5 強調某種情況到目前為止的一段時期內，已經發生了變化並有可能**繼續變化**，用**現在完成進行式**。如果是談論在已結束的一段時期內發生的某個特定的變化，並強調這個變化的**結果**時，則用**簡單現在完成式**。

- **The problem of global warming has been getting worse during the last decade.**
  全球氣溫上升的問題在這十年內變得越來越嚴重了。
  ↑ 可能會繼續惡化。
- **Oil prices have increased by 7%.** 汽油價格已經上漲了 7%。
  ↑ 強調結果。

6 當句中使用 be 動詞、have（擁有）、know 和其他不能用於進行式的動詞時（非進行式的動詞），即使動作一直持續到現在還沒有結束，也要用**簡單現在完成式**，而不能用於現在完成進行式（也不用於現在進行式、過去進行式）。

» 詳細說明參見 540 頁〈5 非進行式動詞〉。

- **Annie has had this motor scooter since 2010, and now it is time to replace it.** 安妮從 2010 年就有了這輛小輪摩托車，現在也該換一輛了。
  ↑ 不能用現在完成進行式 has been having。
- **Sue has been in Nigeria since 2002.** 蘇從 2002 年起就一直在奈及利亞。
  ↑ 不能用現在完成進行式 has been being。
- **Anna and Wade have known each other for a decade.**
  安娜和韋德已經認識十年了。
  ↑ 不能用現在完成進行式 has been knowing。
  ↑ 簡單現在完成式通常表示動作或狀態已經結束，但少數動詞例外。非進行式動詞 be、have（擁有）、know（認識）和其他非進行式動詞，就可用簡單現在完成式來描述一直持續到現在，並且仍在進行的動作或狀態。因此，這句的意思是，十年之前他們就已經認識，「認識」這種狀態仍在進行。

簡單過去式、簡單現在完成式、現在完成進行式的總比較

簡單過去式、簡單現在完成式、現在完成進行式，這三個時態都與過去有關聯。

1 簡單過去式的使用

1 **已結束、完成的行為動作**，與現在沒有關聯，要用簡單過去式。

- **Adam flew back to New York City last night.** 亞當昨晚飛回紐約。
- **As Joan Chen exited her spaceship, she was glad to be back home on Mars again.** 當陳沖從太空船出來時，她很高興能再次回到在火星上的家。

2 簡單過去式與**表示已經結束的時間詞語**連用，例如下列時間副詞或片語：

- yesterday 昨天
- ago 在……以前
- last year 去年
- in 2011 在 2011 年
- then 當時
- when 什麼時候

- **When did Jane sell her airplane?** 珍是什麼時候賣了她的飛機？
- **I helped Grandpa Grey bale hay last Sunday.** 上星期天我幫格雷爺爺把乾草打成一捆一捆的。

3 講故事常用過去式。

> One sunny day while driving through a quiet intersection, I noticed the intersection camera light briefly turn on. My car was the only vehicle at that intersection. I was driving very slowly, way below the speed limit of 60 km, and the traffic light just turned green before I got to the intersection. Why did the camera take a

picture of my car? I felt puzzled. Curiously, I decided to find out whether something was wrong with the camera. I turned around and went through the intersection again to see what would happen. It turned on again. My curiosity and persistence prompted me to try again and again. I made my "scientific tests" three times.

Yesterday an envelope marked Police Department was in my mail box. In it there were 4 tickets, with a total fine of US$400. The reason for the tickets was "Our camera recorded a total of 4 times when you did not use your seat belt."

一個晴朗的日子裡，我在開車經過一個安靜的十字路口時，注意到紅燈照相機亮了一下。十字路口就只有我一輛車啊，我開得這麼慢，遠遠低於限速的60公里，而且在我開進十字路口之前，就變綠燈啦，怎麼我的車子會被照相呢？我覺得很奇怪。出於好奇，我決定去看一下照相機是否有問題。我把車子調頭，再度穿過十字路口，想看看結果會如何。結果，照相機又亮了一下。在好奇心和固執的作祟下，我又試了兩次。這個「科學實驗」我一共進行了三次。

昨天，我的信箱裡有一封信封上標有警局的來信，信封裡有四張罰單，罰款金額一共是四百美元。開罰單的原因是，「照相機記錄您行車未繫安全帶，共計四次。」

2 簡單現在完成式的使用

表示已經完成的過去行為動作，且與現在有關聯，用簡單現在完成式。

1 同時考慮到過去和現在的情況時

- **Mary has read your email, and I'm sure she'll want to publish your story about the dragon.**
  瑪麗已經看了你的電子郵件，我想她一定會發表你關於龍的故事。
  ↳ 「閱讀」動作已經結束，她現在知道了你的龍故事。

2 用於新聞報導

- President Gore has left for Singapore.
  戈爾總統已經動身前往新加坡了。

- "A UFO has just flown over Chicago," reported Margo.
  瑪歌報導說：「一架幽浮剛從芝加哥上空飛過。」

3 直到現在：用於呈現事件的次數

- I'm not joking when I say I have tried many times to quit drinking and smoking. 我說的是真話，我戒菸酒戒了很多次了。
- I have been to Prague twice. 我去過布拉格兩次。

4 直到現在（用於疑問句和否定句）：尚未發生的事（常用 ever 和 never）

- "My sister Susan has been a soldier for more than a decade."
  "Really? Has she ever fought in a war?"
  「我妹妹蘇珊當兵已經十年多了。」
  「真的嗎？她上過戰場打仗嗎？」

- Susan has never told me anything about her experiences during the last war. 蘇珊不曾跟我說過她在上一次戰事中的任何經歷。

5 直到現在：與 already 或 yet 搭配

- Haven't you made the pizza yet? 你還沒有做披薩？

- Has Jerome already gone home? 傑羅姆是不是已經回家了？

簡單現在完成式**不能與過去的時間**連用。

✕ I've seen Sherry last week. She has told me she was going to marry a man who has four sons.

✔ I saw Sherry last week. She told me she was going to marry a man who has four sons.

我上個禮拜看見過雪麗。她告訴我她就快要嫁給一個有四個兒子的男人了。

3 現在完成進行式的使用

現在完成進行式可以表示從過去某個時間開始，一直持續到現在，已結束或還沒有結束的動作（大多數的動詞）。

1 表示**時間持續的長度**（常與 since 和 for 連用）時，不能用簡單現在式或現在進行式，而是要用現在完成進行式。

✗ I'm driving/I drive for five hours and feel more dead than alive. Maybe it's time for you or Clive to drive.

✓ I've been driving for five hours and feel more dead than alive. Maybe it's time for you or Clive to drive.
我已經開了五個小時的車，累死我了，也許該換你或克萊夫來開了。

- "How long have you been waiting for your flight to Baghdad?"
  "I have been waiting since 8:30 a.m."
  「你等候飛往巴格達的班機等了多久了？」「我從早上八點半一直等到現在。」

2 現在完成進行式表示**到目前為止度過時間的方式**。

"You look a little tired," hinted Sue. "I've been working on this news story since four this morning," replied Joyce in a hoarse voice.
蘇暗示說：「你看起來有點累了。」
喬伊絲用沙啞的聲音回答說：「我從今天凌晨四點就一直在寫這篇新聞報導。」

1 現在完成進行式通常**不用來談論長久的、不變的情境**。

✗ This tree has been standing in Hidden Valley for over 400 years.

✓ This tree has stood in Hidden Valley for over 400 years.
這棵樹已經聳立在深隱山谷四百多年了。

2 現在完成進行式**不和非進行式的動詞連用**，非進行式動詞如 be 動詞、have（擁有）、know 等。

✗ I've been knowing Dee since Christmas, 2003.

✓ I've known Dee since Christmas, 2003.
我從 2003 年的聖誕節就認識蒂了。

簡單過去完成式

1 簡單過去完成式的句型

簡單過去完成式也稱「過去完成式」，由「had ＋ 過去分詞」構成，其中 had 不受人稱和數的影響。

» 過去分詞參見 904 頁〈附錄 1 不規則動詞表〉。

肯定句	I/he/she/it/we/you/they had seen Jean
否定句	I/he/she/it/we/you/they had not seen Jean
疑問句	had I/he/she/it/we/you/they seen Jean?

縮寫： * I'd, you'd, he'd, she'd, it'd, we'd, they'd　* had not = hadn't

例 I had seen = I'd seen

I had not seen = I'd not seen = I hadn't seen

肯定句 **Sam had worked as the Royal Translator for Princess Kim before she married him.**

山姆在娶公主金姆之前，是公主御用的翻譯員。

否定句 **Sam hadn't worked as the Royal Translator for Princess Kim before she married him.**

山姆在娶公主金姆之前，還不是公主御用的翻譯員。

疑問句 **Had Sam worked as the Royal Translator for Princess Kim before she married him?**

山姆在娶公主金姆之前，就是公主御用的翻譯員嗎？

2 簡單過去完成式的用法

1 過去的過去

簡單過去完成式（也稱過去完成式）的基本意義是「更早的過去」，或「過去的過去」，或「**過去某個特定時間之前**或**過去某個動作之前**已經完成的行為動作」。如果已經用過去式談論過去，可是還要再繼續回溯時，那就要用過去完成式，表示在談論的這個過去時間之前某事已經發生了。所以，過去完成式通常和簡單過去式搭配使用，表達相對的時間關係。

✗ Meg already broke her leg before I arrived with Peg.

✓ Meg had already broken her leg before I arrived with Peg.

在我和佩格到達之前，梅格已經摔斷了腿。

↳ 兩個過去發生的動作：先發生的動作用過去完成式（had broken），後發生的動作用過去式（arrived）。

- When Emma arrived at the party, Sue and Jerome had already gone home.

  當愛瑪到達聚會時，蘇和傑羅姆已經回家了。

  ↳ 行為動作 had gone home（過去完成式）在過去某個時刻已經完成，而且是在另一個過去行為動作 arrived 之前完成的。

  ↳ 不能用現在完成式 has already gone home 和過去式 went home。

- I didn't visit Jenny in Hong Kong, because she had gone on a business trip to Germany.

  在香港我沒有去看珍妮，因為她去德國出差了。

  ↳ 過去（didn't visit）；更早的過去（had gone）

- Annie realized that she had met Sam before.
  安妮發覺她曾經見過山姆。
  ↳ 過去(realized);過去的過去(had met)

- Andrew hadn't known Sue for very long before they got married and moved to Hollywood.
  安德魯認識蘇後不久,他們就結婚,並且搬到了好萊塢。
  ↳ 過去(got married, moved);更早的過去(hadn't known)

2 兩個接連發生的過去事件

a **簡單過去式**常用來表達兩個行為動作或事件**一個接一個地發生**。這種情況也可以用**過去完成式**,表達兩個過去動作的時間層次,強調一個動作在前(過去完成式),另一個動作在後(過去式)。

[美式/英式] As soon as Glen put the phone down, it rang again.
[英式] As soon as Glen had put the phone down, it rang again.
葛倫才剛把電話放下,電話就又響起來了。

↳ 兩個過去動作一個接一個地發生,可以都用簡單過去式,尤其是美式英語(如第一句)。
↳ 英式英語也可以用一個簡單過去式,一個過去完成式,強調動作的先後(如上面的第二句)。

[美式/英式] As soon as Jane came into the house, it started to rain.
[英式] As soon as Jane had come into the house, it started to rain.
珍一進到屋子裡,就下起雨了。

b 但強調第二件事是第一件事的結果,兩件事都要用**簡單過去式**。

- When Mr. Smith came into the classroom, all the students stopped talking.
  當史密斯先生走進教室,所有的學生都停止了說話。

3 already 和 just 與過去完成式：already 和 just 常用於過去完成式。

- I had just come into the house when the phone rang.
  我才進到屋子裡，電話就響了起來。

- Amy had already left by the time I arrived at the party.
  當我到達聚會時，艾咪已經離開了。

4 過去未實現的願望或未發生的事：過去完成式也可以用於假設語氣，表示過去未能實現的願望，或表示與過去事實相反的事。

» 參見 695 頁〈Part 6 假設語氣〉。

- My Uncle Jim had hoped that I would go into business with him.
  吉姆叔叔曾希望我跟他一起從商。
  ↥ 事實上，我沒有跟他從商。

- Dad had intended to make a birthday cake and write a rhyme for me, but he ran out of time.
  爸爸本來打算要為我做一個生日蛋糕，再寫一首詩，可是他沒有時間了。
  ↥ 事實上，爸爸沒有為我做生日蛋糕，也沒有寫詩。

- If I had gone on to attend a university, I would have studied history.
  假如我繼續讀了大學，我就會學歷史。
  ↥ 事實上，我沒有進大學繼續讀書。

- Mary wishes Jerry had married her instead of Sherry.
  瑪麗但願傑瑞娶的是她，而不是雪麗。
  ↥ 事實上，傑瑞沒有娶瑪麗。

過去完成進行式

1 過去完成進行式的句型

過去完成進行式由「had been + 現在分詞」構成，例如：

- had been snoring

肯定句	I/he/she/it/we/you/they had been fighting
否定句	I/he/she/it/we/you/they had not been fighting
疑問句	had I/he/she/it/we/you/they been fighting?

縮寫： * I'd (not), you'd (not), he'd (not), she'd (not), it'd (not), we'd (not), they'd (not)
* had not = hadn't 例 I had not = I'd not = I hadn't

2 過去完成進行式的用法

1 和簡單過去完成式一樣，過去完成進行式也是指「過去某一時刻之前或過去某個動作之前」發生的過去動作（**過去的過去**）；同時又和一般的進行式一樣，「**強調動作的持續**」。即，過去完成進行式表示「一直持續到過去某一時刻」的「比較長的行為動作」，常和簡單過去式搭配。

- **When Sam arrived at Daisy's house, he could see that she had been crying hard.** 山姆到達黛絲家時，他看得出來她傷心地哭過。
  - ↑ 過去動作（crying）一直持續到過去某個時刻（When Sam arrived at Daisy's house）。
  - ↑ had been crying 這一動作發生在 arrived 這一動作之前。

- Daisy's eyes were red and swollen, because she had been crying for a long time about what Ted had said.
黛絲的眼睛又紅又腫，因為她為泰德告訴她的事哭了很久。
  ↑ 過去完成進行式（一直在哭泣）解釋導致過去某個結果的原因，如處境或外貌表情（眼睛又紅又腫）的原因。had been crying 這一過去動作發生在 eyes were red and swollen 這一個過去狀況之前。

- Kate was exhausted because she had been working on her research project all day.
凱特累壞了，因為她整天都在做她的研究專案。
  ↑ 過去完成進行式（整天一直在工作）解釋導致過去某個結果（疲倦）的原因。

- Kay went to see the doctor last week. She hadn't been feeling well for two days.
凱上星期去看過醫生。她已經有兩天感覺不舒服了。
  ↑ 過去完成進行式（兩天感覺不舒服）解釋導致過去某個結果（去看醫生）的原因。

go to see the doctor

- The doctor asked what I had been eating recently. 醫生問我最近吃了什麼食物。
  ↑ 過去完成進行式可用在間接引語中，指「過去的過去」，並強調動作在過去持續進行。

- Her eager fans had been waiting with armloads of flowers for over two hours.
她熱情的粉絲們抱著大束的花，已經等她等了兩個多鐘頭了。
  ↑ 強調動作在過去持續進行。

2 **過去完成進行式**表示過去某事正在持續進行時（通常是持續時間比較長的動作或事件），另一件事發生了（通常是短暫動作，用簡單過去式）。

- We had been playing volleyball at the beach for about an hour when it started to rain heavily. 我們在海灘打了大約一個小時的排球後，天空開始下起了大雨。
  ↑ 過去某事正在持續進行時（had been playing）發生了另一件事（it started to rain）。

play beach volleyball

- Kim had been wondering whether to call her boyfriend Tom when he came to her door.

  金姆一直在納悶要不要打電話給她男友湯姆時，他就出現在她的門口了。

  ↑ 過去某事正在進行時（had been wondering）發生了另一件事（he came to her door）。

- I had been watching the movie on my cellphone for only ten minutes when Amy phoned and interrupted me.

  我用手機看影片才看了十分鐘，艾咪的電話就打進來打斷我了。

  ↑ 過去完成進行式（had been watching），強調動作的持續，後面接具有「突然」意義的 when 子句。

1 過去完成進行式（與其他進行式一樣）通常**不用來談論長久的、不變的情境**。

✗ Yesterday I visited the house where my grandparents had been living for about 80 years.

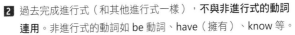

✓ Yesterday I visited the house where my grandparents had lived for about 80 years.

昨天我參觀了我祖父母曾經居住八十個年頭的房子。

2 過去完成進行式（和其他進行式一樣），**不與非進行式的動詞連用**。非進行式的動詞如 be 動詞、have（擁有）、know 等。

✗ I had been knowing Jim for ten years before we got married.

✓ I had known Jim for ten years before we got married.

我認識吉姆十年後我們才結婚。

3 比較過去完成進行式與簡單過去完成式

過去完成進行式	簡單過去完成式
➤ had been doing 強調行為動作	➤ had done 強調行為動作的結果
Larry had been working **hard, so he decided to take a week off.** 賴瑞一直很辛勤地工作，於是他決定休假一星期。 ↑ 強調行為動作（持續）	**Mary** had worked **hard, and her research project was finally finished.** 瑪麗一直努力地工作，她的研究專案終於完成了。 ↑ 強調行為動作產生的結果
➤ 強調動作持續	➤ 強調動作已經完成
I had been reading **a fantasy novel, and my mind was full of dragons and sword fights.** 我一直在看一本奇幻小說，我大腦裡充滿了龍和劍術的比武。 ↑ 過去動作在過去某個時間還在持續	**I** had read **all of today's important news on the Internet, and my brain was beginning to get tired.** 今天網路上重要的新聞我都看過啦，我的腦開始疲倦啦。 ↑ 過去某個時間（我的大腦疲倦的時候）已經完成的行為動作
➤ 持續的時間	➤ 發生的次數
I had been travelling **in India for a month before I got sick.** 我在印度旅行了一個月後生病了。	**Sam's parents** had let **him get away with his bad behavior so many times that he finally ended up in jail.** 山姆行為不良時，他的父母卻多次讓他逃避責罰，結果他最後被關進了牢房。
➤ 暫時的行為或情境	➤ 永久的情境
Grandma was tired because she had been standing **by her bedroom window for a long time.** 奶奶累了，因為她在她臥室的窗戶邊站了好久。 ↑ 暫時的行為（也可用簡單過去完成式 had stood）	**We lived in a stone house which** had stood **on Gold Mountain for over 100 years.** 我們曾住在一間已經在金山屹立超過百年的石屋裡。 ↑ 長久的情境

4 比較現在完成進行式與過去完成進行式

現在完成進行式	過去完成進行式
➤ have been + V-ing	➤ had been + V-ing
"Why are you out of breath?" **"I have been jogging for an hour."** 「你為什麼上氣不接下氣?」 「我慢跑了一個小時了。」 ↑ 簡單現在式與現在完成進行式搭配	**Sue was out of breath. She had been jogging for an hour.** 蘇上氣不接下氣。她已經慢跑了一個小時。 ↑ 簡單過去式與過去完成進行式搭配
I hope Sally will come soon. I've been waiting for her for half an hour. 我希望莎莉快來。我已經等她半小時了。 ↑ up to now(Sally 還沒有來)	**Finally Tom came. I'd been waiting for him for half an hour.** 湯姆終於來了。我已經等他半小時了。 ↑ before Tom came

5 比較過去進行式與過去完成進行式

a **過去進行式**(was/were + V-ing):指過去某個時刻正在進行的動作。

b **過去完成進行式**(had been + V-ing):表示一直持續到過去某一時刻的比較長的行為動作,該動作可能已經結束。

- **Emma was lying on the couch resting. She felt tired because she had been working very hard on her research project.**
  愛瑪正躺在沙發上休息。她感覺疲倦,因為她一直認真地在做她的研究專案。
  ↑ 「躺」這個動作正在進行;「工作」一直持續到「她感覺疲倦了」這個時刻。

- **It wasn't snowing when Coco got up and looked out of the window. The sun was shining. But it had been snowing, for the ground was covered with snow.** 可可起床後朝窗外望去,天空沒有在下雪,陽光燦爛。但是一直下過雪,因為地上覆蓋著白雪。
  ↑ 「had been snowing」表示這個持續的行為到可可起床時已經結束。

簡單未來完成式和未來完成進行式

1 簡單未來完成式的句型

簡單未來完成式也稱「未來完成式」，其構成是用「will have + 過去分詞」（done、finished、flown 等）。

肯定句	I/he/she/it/we/you/they will have finished
否定句	I/he/she/it/we/you/they will not have finished
疑問句	will I/he/she/it/we/you/they have finished?

2 未來完成式的用法

1 當一個「開始於過去」的行為動作，「現在還沒完成，將在未來的某個時刻完成」，就要用未來完成式。

2 未來完成式常和表示「直到未來某時刻」的時間副詞或片語連用。例如：

- by then 到那時
- by the end of the year 今年年底
- by that time 到那時
- on September 10 this year 今年九月十號
- by midnight 到半夜時
- before midnight 半夜之前
- when I get to the bottom of the mountain 當我到達山底時

- **By next New Year's Day, Roy will have been mayor of Adelaide for a decade.**
  到了明年元旦，羅伊擔任阿得雷德市的市長就滿十週年了。

- Ray will have finished writing the huge grammar book by May.
  到了五月，雷就會寫完那本大部頭的文法書了。

- How long will the robots have worked non-stop on building the new hotel by the end of this year?
  到今年年底，那些馬不停蹄地蓋新飯店的機器人就工作了多久了呢？

- June and I will have reached the top of the mountain before noon.
  在中午之前，茱恩和我就會到達山頂。

- On September 10 we will have been married for ten years.
  九月十號時，我們的婚姻就滿十週年了。

- When we get back to the bottom of the mountain, Jane and I will have been in the snowstorm for two days.
  當我們返回山腳下時，珍和我就在暴風雪裡度過了兩天了。
  ↑ 子句用簡單現在式指未來，主句用未來完成式指未來某時完成的狀態或動作。

Diving Deep Into English 81 比較三種簡單完成式

- Jane has written a book about Mark Twain.
  珍寫過一本關於馬克·吐溫的書。
  ↑ 簡單現在完成式（到目前為止）

- Jane had written a lot of books before I met her two years ago in Spain.
  我兩年前在西班牙認識珍之前，她就已經寫了很多書了。
  ↑ 簡單過去完成式（過去的過去）

- Jane will have written 20 pages of her new story by the time she gets off the airplane in Maine.
  珍在緬因州下飛機之前，會寫完二十頁的新故事。
  ↑ 簡單未來完成式（現在還未完成，未來才會完成）

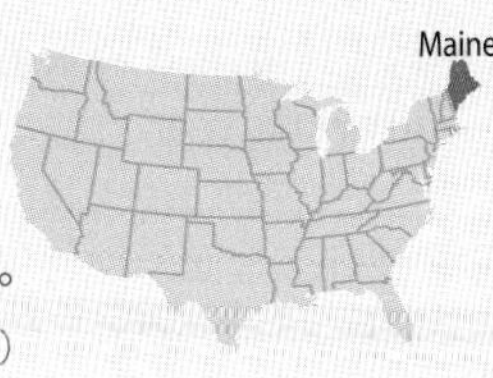

3 未來完成進行式的句型

未來完成進行式的構成方式：「will have been + 現在分詞」。

肯定句	I/he/she/it/we/you/they will have been eating
否定句	I/he/she/it/we/you/they will not have been eating
疑問句	will I/he/she/it/we/you/they have been eating?

4 未來完成進行式的用法

1 表示一個行為動作「在未來的某個特定時刻，已經發生並持續下去」，就用未來完成進行式。

2 這個時態常和 by 引導的表示「直到未來某時刻」的時間片語連用。

- Trish says that by the end of summer camp, she will have been eating fish for so many days that she will never want to see another fish.

  = Trish says that by the end of summer camp, she will have eaten fish for so many days that she will never want to see another fish.

  翠西說，等到夏令營結束時，她已經吃了好幾天魚了，膩得永遠都不想再看到魚。

  ↑ 第一句是未來完成進行式，這種時態比較少用，通常用簡單未來完成式（如第二句）就可以表達同樣的意思。

- I will have been teaching for 20 years by the end of this year.

  = I will have taught for 20 years by the end of this year.

  = I will have had 20 years of teaching by the end of this year.

  到今年年底時，我的教書生涯就滿二十年了。

  ↑ 兩種時態都描述動作開始於「過去」，「現在」還沒結束，將在「未來」的某個時刻完成。

5 未來完成進行式和簡單未來完成式的區別

1 **未來完成進行式**用來描述「尚未完成的、未打斷的行為」。如果要描述「重複的動作或事件」、「數量多少」、「將來某時刻已經完成的動作」，就要用**簡單未來完成式**。

- **When I reach fifty, I'll have been building boats for 25 years.**
  當我滿五十歲時，我就已經修建船 25 年了。
  ↳ 一個未完成的行為（one incomplete activity）。

- **When I reach fifty, I'll have built more than 25 boats.**
  當我滿五十歲時，我就已經修建了 25 艘船。
  ↳ 25 次重複的行為（more than 25 individual actions）。

- **By noon, Jill will have been cleaning her van for an hour.**
  到中午時，潔兒就已經清洗她的箱型車一個小時了。
  ↳ 一個未打斷的行為（one uninterrupted activity）。

- **By noon, Jill will have cleaned her van and changed the tires.**
  到中午時，潔兒就已經清洗完了她的箱型車，換好輪胎了。
  ↳ 兩個在未來某時刻將已經陸續完成的行為（two completed activities that will be done one after another）。

2 非進行式動詞不用於未來完成進行式，只能用於**簡單未來完成式**。

✗ **I'll have been knowing Kay for 10 years by May.**
✓ **I'll have known Kay for 10 years by May.**
到了五月，我就認識凱十年了。

過去未來完成式和過去未來完成進行式

1 過去未來完成式

1 過去未來完成式的構成方式 ：「would have + 過去分詞」。

2 過去未來完成式表示「某個過去開始的動作，將在過去未來的某個時刻完成」，常與表過去未來的時間副詞連用。（過去未來完成式，不是常用的時態。）

- Before she saw her publisher, Brooke would have finished writing five chapters in her new book.
  在和出版商見面之前，布魯克會寫完她的新書的五章內容。
  ↑ 子句（簡單過去式）+ 主句（過去未來完成式）
  ↑ 主句用過去未來完成式（would have finished），子句要用簡單過去式（saw）表示「過去將來」的含意。

比較

- Before she sees her publisher, Brooke will have finished writing five chapters in her new book.
  ↑ 子句（簡單現在式）+ 主句（未來完成式）
  ↑ 主句用未來完成式（will have finished），子句要用簡單現在式（sees）表「未來」。

2 過去未來完成進行式

1 過去未來完成進行式的構成方式：「would have been + 現在分詞」。

2 過去未來完成進行式表示「動作從過去某一時間開始，一直延續到過去未來某一時間」。動作是否繼續下去，要視具體情況而定。（過去未來完成進行式，不是常用的時態。）

- Wade told me that by the end of the month he would have been studying English for a decade.
魏德跟我說，到月底時，他學英語就已經長達十年了。

Diving Deep Into English 82 比較六種常用的完成式

❶ **簡單現在完成式**（主詞 + have/has + 過去分詞）

- **Kay has practiced on her piano for two hours today.**
凱今天花了兩小時練習鋼琴。

❷ **現在完成進行式**（主詞 + have/has + been + 現在分詞）

- **She has been practicing her speech every night all week, so she is ready for the English speech contest.**
她已經每晚練了一整個星期的演說，所以她已經為英語演講賽做好準備了。

❸ **簡單過去完成式**（主詞 + had + 過去分詞）

- **By the time I arrived, she had already debugged her computer's operating system.** 我到達時，她已經把她電腦作業系統的問題解決了。

❹ **過去完成進行式**（主詞 + had + been + 現在分詞）

- **Finally Lenore found her cellphone she had been looking for.**
蕾諾兒終於找到了一直在尋找的手機。

❺ **簡單未來完成式**（主詞 + will + have + 過去分詞）

- **Susan will have written more than ten pages by the time she gets off the train in Phnom Penh.**
等到蘇珊在金邊（柬埔寨首都）下火車時，她將寫完十幾頁的內容。

❻ **未來完成進行式**（主詞 + will + have + been + 現在分詞）

- **By 9 p.m. tomorrow, Ms. Powers will have been looking for her cat for twelve hours.**
截止到明天晚上九點，鮑爾斯小姐尋找她的貓將長達 12 小時了。

UNIT

12 主動語態與被動語態

The Active Voice and the Passive Voice

主動語態和被動語態的區別

1 主動語態和被動語態

1 英語有主動和被動兩種語態：

a **主動語態**：表明「主詞做某事」，主詞為動作的**執行者**。

b **被動語態**：表明「主詞被⋯⋯」，主詞為動作的**承受者**。

2 要用主動還是被動語態，視需要強調的重點而定：

a 要強調動作的**執行者**，就用**主動**語態。

b 強調動作的**承受者**，就用**被動**語態。

3 此外，也可以根據修飾的需要，選用適當的成分作主詞，以保持句子結構的平衡。

4 被動語態的構成：「**be 動詞 + 過去分詞**」。

» 詳細說明參見 638 頁〈Part 2 被動語態的動詞形式〉。

Active **Yesterday a terrible** hurricane hit **Spain.**
昨天有一場可怕的颶風侵襲了西班牙。
↳ 動詞的主詞是動作的執行者：主詞 hurricane 是 hit 這一動作的執行者。

Passive **Yesterday** Spain was hit **by a terrible hurricane.**
西班牙昨天遭受了一場可怕的颶風侵襲。
↳ 動詞的主詞是動作的承受者：主詞 Spain 是 hit 這一動作的承受者。

Active **Most** Canadians **speak** English.

Passive English **is spoken by most** Canadians. 大多數加拿大人都說英語。

Passive English **is spoken in Canada.** 在加拿大，人們說英語。

2 優先使用主動語態

相較而言，被動結構不如主動結構簡潔。可以用主動語態來代替被動語態表達時，最好使用主動語態。

Passive A teaching certificate was awarded to Jenny.
教師資格證頒給了珍妮。 → 句子共使用 7 個字。

Active Jenny received a teaching certificate.
珍妮得到了教師資格證。 → 句子共使用 5 個字。

Passive A big chunk of cheese was received by each of Lee's employees.
一大片起司被李的每一個職員都收到了。 → 句子共使用 12 個字。

Active Each of Lee's employees received a big chunk of cheese.
李的每一個職員都收到了一大片起司。 → 句子共使用 10 個字。

3 不自然的被動結構

有的被動結構在文法上來看雖然沒有錯誤，但實際中很少使用，要避免這類不自然的表達。

Unnatural A dessert was eaten by Kyle. 一份甜點被凱爾吃了。
↑ 雖然文法正確，但冗長、不自然，不是道地的英文。

Natural Kyle ate a dessert. 凱爾吃了一份甜點。
↑ 文法正確，而且簡潔、自然。

Unnatural Jerry is thought to be hairy and scary by Mary.
傑瑞被瑪麗認為是毛茸茸的，很可怕。

Natural Mary thinks Jerry is hairy and scary.
瑪麗覺得傑瑞毛茸茸的，很可怕。

4 適合用被動語態的情況

雖然主動語態更簡潔，但在下列情況下常用被動語態。

1 強調**動作的承受者**時，使用被動語態。

- **Ms. Flowers was robbed during the early morning hours.**
  福勞爾斯女士在淩晨的時候被搶劫了。
  ↑ 強調的是福勞爾斯女士被搶劫，而不是強調搶劫犯。

- **We believe that all men are created equal because they are created in the image of God.** (President Harry S. Truman)
  我們相信所有的人生而平等，因為人都是按照上帝的形象來創造的。
  ↑ 只強調動作的承受者（all men）。

2 動作的行為者是**泛指的一般人**或**顯而易見**時，使用被動語態。

- **That distant star can sometimes be observed at night if the moon isn't bright.** 晚上月光不是很亮時，有時候可以看見遠處的那顆星星。
  ↑ 動作的行為者是泛指的一般人。

- **Her dad is being treated at Miami General Hospital.**
  她的爸爸正在邁阿密總醫院接受治療。
  ↑ 動作的行為者是醫生，這是顯而易見的。

3 動作的行為者是**未知的**或是**不重要的**時，使用被動語態。當動作的行為者是未知的時，在口語中常用 people、they、we、you 或 somebody 作主詞；在正式用語**中或書面用語中，則常使用被動句。**

Active **They are going to finish the construction of a new highway from Mexico City to Houston next year.**

Passive **The construction of a new highway from Mexico City to Houston is going to be finished next year.**
明年就將修建好從墨西哥城到休斯頓的一條新高速公路。

Active **I hope they will accept me into Rice University.**
我希望他們招收我進入賴斯大學。

Passive **I hope to be accepted into Rice University.** 我希望被賴斯大學招收。

4 被動語態用於**轉述常言之語**。

a 被動語態的「it is said」（據說、聽說）、「it is believed」（一般認為），**相當於主動語態的「people say」或「people believe」，當說話者是未知的時候，就用這種被動式來表明**「據說、聽說」、「一般認為」。

Active People say that a tomcat has nine lives and no wives.

Passive It is said that a tomcat has nine lives and no wives.

Passive A tomcat is said to have nine lives and no wives.

據說公貓有九條命，但沒有老婆。

b 下列動詞可用於「it is + 過去分詞 + that 子句」的句型：

- acknowledge 承認
- agree 承認
- announce 聲稱、宣佈
- calculate 推測
- claim 聲稱
- consider 認為
- decide 決定
- declare 聲明
- discover 發現
- estimate 估計
- expect 預料
- know 知道
- propose 提議
- recommend 建議
- report 報導
- show 證明、表明
- suggest 建議
- suppose 認為
- think 認為
- understand 據聞

- It is reported that the mayor has resigned.
  = The mayor is reported to have resigned.
  據報導，市長已經辭職。
  ↳ 此句型可用「主詞 + 動詞被動式 + 帶 to 的不定式」來替代。

c 下列動詞可用於「it is + 過去分詞 + 帶 to 的不定式」的句型：

- agree 同意
- decide 決定
- forbid 禁止
- hope 希望
- plan 計畫
- propose 提議

- It has been proposed to use large supercapacitors as energy storage devices. 據提議，要把特大的超級電容器，當作能量儲存裝置。

5 為求措辭上的得體，避免把責任具體推給某人時，使用被動語態。

Active "You did not number the pages correctly," said Scot.
史考特說：「你把這幾頁的頁碼弄錯了。」
↳ 含有譴責的語氣，意指對方做錯了事。

Passive "The pages were not numbered correctly," said Scot.
史考特說：「這幾頁的頁碼弄錯了。」
↳ 強調動作承受者（pages）的狀況，不涉及誰需要承擔責任，顯得更得體。

Active You did not clean Room Twenty-two and set the tables in Dining Room Two.

你沒有打掃 22 號房，也沒有給 2 號餐室的桌子擺碗筷。

Passive Room Twenty-two needs to be cleaned, and the tables need to be set in Dining Room Two.

22 號房需要打掃，2 號餐室的桌子需要擺碗筷。

↳ 被動語態可以用來禮貌地提醒對方該做而未做的事，以此強調需要做的事情，而不強調誰該承擔責任。

6 **為保持句子結構的平衡**：有時可以用被動語態把含有較長修飾成分的主詞（動作的行為者）放在句尾，使整個句子看起來更自然，以保持句子結構的平衡。如果主詞是一個較長的片語或子句，句子通常改用被動語態。

Active My daughter's decisions to drop out of school, marry that lazy Dan, and move to Japan surprised me. → 不自然

↳ 主詞（My daughter's decisions）後面有三個不定式片語作修飾，使得主詞很長，而述語動詞和受詞很短，句子看上去不平衡、不自然。

Passive I was surprised by my daughter's decisions to drop out of school, marry that lazy Dan, and move to Japan. → 自然

我女兒要退學，嫁給那個懶惰的丹，然後搬去日本。她的決定讓我很吃驚。

Active While we were camping on the top of Citizen Hill last night, how the Earth's rotation slowly brought Mars above the horizon delighted Sue and me. → 不自然

Passive While we were camping on the top of Citizen Hill last night, Sue and I were delighted by how the Earth's rotation slowly brought Mars above the horizon.

昨晚在市民山的山頂露營時，看到地球的自轉，讓火星慢慢地浮出地平線之上，蘇和我真是開心。

↳ 通常如果主詞是一個較長的片語或子句，則句子常改用被動語態。這句如果使用主動語態，把 how 子句作為主詞，那麼主詞太長，不自然。

為求簡潔清楚，應盡量使用主動語態，但以下情況通常會使用**被動語態**：

1 為避免把責任具體推給某人。

2 要強調動作的承受者。

3 動作的執行者是未知的，或是泛指一般人，或是顯而易見的。

4 為求句子結構的平衡。

5 主動語態和被動語態不能混用

當兩個或更多的動作是由同一個行為者完成時，不要將主動語態和被動語態在同一個句子裡混合使用。

✗ Ann's dad approved the plan, and her schedule was revised by him so that it matched Dan's.
安的爸爸同意這項計畫，於是安的行程表被他修改了，以便和丹的行程表一致。

↳ approved 和 revised 這兩個動作由同一個執行者（Ann's dad）所完成，這時就不要在同一個句子裡混合使用主動語態和被動語態。

✓ Ann's dad approved the plan and revised her schedule so that it matched Dan's.
安的爸爸同意這項計畫，並修改了安的行程表，以便和丹的行程表一致。

↳ 一致使用了主動語態，保持了句子結構的平衡。

✗ On December 27, 2013, the Royal Cheese Company approved of a plan that included corporate social responsibilities, and then a set of measures to turn the financial crisis into profitable opportunities was adopted.

✓ On December 27, 2013, the Royal Cheese Company approved of a plan that included corporate social responsibilities and then adopted a set of measures to turn the financial crisis into profitable opportunities. 2013 年 12 月 27 日，皇家起司公司通過一項含企業社會責任的計畫，接著採取一系列措施，來將財務危機轉變成賺錢的轉機。

↳ 這兩個動作是由同一個行為者（the Royal Cheese Company）完成，兩個動詞都使用主動語態（approved of, adopted），使句子結構平衡。況且，錯誤句子裡第二個分句的主詞很長（a set of . . . profitable opportunities），不適合用被動式。

被動語態的動詞形式

1 be 動詞 + 過去分詞

被動語態是由**助動詞 be 的某一時態形式**（is、am、are、will be、has been 等），加上**主要動詞的過去分詞**所構成的。被動語態可以用於各種時態，以下以 design 為例，說明動詞各種時態的被動用法。

時 態	主 詞	助動詞（單數 / 複數）	過去分詞
簡單現在式	The robot/robots	is/are	designed.
現在完成式	The robot/robots	has been/have been	designed.
現在進行式	The robot/robots	is being/are being	designed.
簡單過去式	The robot/robots	was/were	designed.
過去完成式	The robot/robots	had been/had been	designed.
過去進行式	The robot/robots	was being/were being	designed.
簡單未來式	The robot/robots	will be/will be	designed.
過去未來式	The robot/robots	would be/would be	designed.
未來完成式	The robot/robots	will have been/will have been	designed.

2 被動語態的各種時態

1 簡單現在式：am/is/are + 過去分詞

「簡單現在式被動語態」和「簡單現在式主動語態」的功能一樣，描述永恆不變的事實，一直、經常、重複發生的事，或有時發生以及從未發生的事。

- We are paid twice a month. 我們每個月發兩次薪水。
- According to Mr. Blare, olive oil is often used in preparing healthy food. 根據布雷爾先生所說，橄欖油常用於製作健康食品。

2 現在完成式：has/have + been + 過去分詞

「現在完成式被動語態」和「現在完成式主動語態」的功能一樣，用來談論對現在有影響或與現在有關聯的過去的行為、動作、事件。

- Our sweet old cottage on Lake Gold has been sold.
  我們金湖畔的那棟可愛的舊別墅已經被賣出去了。
- Kay and I have been invited to a surprise birthday party for Sue.
  凱和我受邀參加為蘇準備的驚喜生日派對。

3 現在進行式：is/am/are + being + 過去分詞

「現在進行式被動語態」和「現在進行式主動語態」的功能一樣，用來描述現在正在進行的事。

- "Gus, where's your bus?" "It's being repaired at Mr. Bloom's."
  「加斯，你的巴士在哪裡？」「正在布盧姆先生的車行裡維修。」
- Bob is being interviewed for an EFL teaching job.
  鮑勃正在接受一份 EFL 教學工作的面試。

Job interview

4 簡單過去式：was/were + 過去分詞

「簡單過去式被動語態」和「簡單過去式主動語態」的用法一樣，用來描述已經完成的過去行為、動作和事件。

- John said this computer was not made in Taiwan.
  約翰說這台電腦不是臺灣製造的。
- Nobody was told what had happened to the platinum and gold.
  沒有人被告知那些白金和黃金的下落。

5 過去完成式：had been + 過去分詞

「過去完成式被動語態」和「過去完成式主動語態」的功能一樣，用來表達過去某個時間已經完成的行為動作。

- Last month when I went back to my hometown for a visit, I found out that all the abandoned houses had been torn down.
  上個月，當我回故鄉探望時，我發現所有的廢棄空屋都被夷平了。

6 過去進行式：was/were + being + 過去分詞

「過去進行式被動語態」和「過去進行式主動語態」的功能一樣，用來描述過去某一時刻正在進行的事。

- The suspected serial robber was being chased by Sheriff Daisy Sun, who was wearing a pink cocktail dress and carrying a shotgun.
  連續搶劫嫌疑犯正遭到穿著粉紅色禮服、帶著一把獵槍的警長黛絲·孫所追捕。

7 簡單未來式和過去未來式

簡單未來式：will + be + 過去分詞
過去未來式：would + be + 過去分詞

「未來式被動語態」與「未來式主動語態」的功能一樣，用來描述我們對未來所想的、猜測的、瞭解的事情，或者關於未來所提的問題。

- The highway next to Kay's house will be closed for two days.
  靠近凱的房子的那條公路將被封閉兩天。 → 簡單未來式
- "English will be spoken at this conference," said Trish.
  翠西說：「這次會議要講英語。」 → 簡單未來式（直接引語）

  = Trish said that English would be spoken at the conference.
  翠西說過會議上要講英語。 → 過去未來式（間接引語）

8 未來完成式 ：will + have been + 過去分詞

「未來完成式被動語態」和「未來完成式主動語態」的功能一樣，用來表達一個開始於過去的行為動作，將在未來的某個時刻完成。

- Our huge wind power kite will have been designed by Friday night.
  我們的大型風力發電風箏，會在星期五晚上之前設計出來。

3 不定式和動名詞片語的被動語態

不定式和動名詞片語也可用於被動語態。

» 不定式和動名詞的用法參見 731 頁〈Unit 16 分詞、不定式和動名詞〉。

Active She enjoys taking her children to the Detroit Art Museum.
她喜歡帶她的孩子們去底特律藝術博物館。
↑ 主動:「動詞 + -ing 形式 + 受詞」。

Passive Her children enjoy being taken to the Detroit Art Museum.
她的孩子喜歡被帶到底特律藝術博物館去。
↑ being taken 是被動語態的動名詞片語,作句子動詞 enjoyed 的受詞。

Active After the track meet, Sue's classmates started to admire her.
田徑運動會後,蘇的同學們開始欽佩她了。
↑ 主動:「動詞 + 帶 to 的不定式 + 受詞」。

Passive After the track meet, Sue started to be admired by her classmates. 田徑運動會後,蘇開始受到了同學們的欽佩。
↑ to be admired 是被動語態的不定式片語,作句子動詞 started 的受詞。

- Little Tom really likes to be read to by his mom.
小湯姆很喜歡他的媽媽讀故事給他聽。
↑ to be read to 是被動語態的不定式片語,作句子動詞 likes 的受詞。
- She hates being lectured or criticized by her boss.
她討厭被老闆訓斥或批評。
↑ being lectured or criticized 是被動語態的動名詞片語,作句子動詞 hates 的受詞。
- I am tired of being lectured and criticized by Sue for everything I do.
無論我做什麼都要受到蘇的訓斥和批評,我對此厭煩極了。
↑ being lectured and criticized 是被動語態的動名詞片語,作介系詞 of 的受詞。
- To be elected president of our company is a great honor.
被選為我們公司的董事長是極大的榮譽。
↑ To be elected 是被動語態的不定式片語,作句子的主詞。
- Being elected president of our company means you listen to a lot of voices and make all the tough choices. 被選為我們公司的董事長,意味著要聽取各式各樣的意見,並做出一切棘手的選擇。
↑ Being elected 是被動語態的動名詞片語,作句子的主詞。

· Jenny was the first woman to be elected president of our company.
珍妮是我們公司選出來的第一個女董事長。
↳ to be elected 是被動語態的不定式片語，修飾名詞 woman。

4 情態動詞和使役動詞的被動語態

情態動詞和使役動詞也可以用於被動語態。

1 情態動詞：「must (can, should 等) + be 動詞 + 過去分詞」

· Economic depression cannot be cured by legislative action or executive pronouncement. Economic wounds must be healed by the action of the cells of the economic body—the producers and consumers themselves. (President Herbert Hoover)
經濟蕭條無法透過立法行動或行政公告來醫治。經濟的創傷一定要透過經濟體的基層組織的行動，也就是透過生產者和消費者自己的行動來治療。

2 使役動詞 make：「be 動詞 + made + to」

· She made her Greek students read 175,000 English words per week.
她讓她的希臘學生每星期閱讀 175,000 個英語字彙量。
↳ 主動語態：make + 不定式（不帶 to）

· Her Greek students were made to read 175,000 English words per week. → 被動語態：be made + 不定式（帶 to）

3 使役動詞 let：let 無被動語態形式，要用 allow/permit/give permission 的被動語態代替。

· My uncle let me use his car to learn how to drive.
我的叔叔讓我用他的車學駕駛。
I was allowed to use my uncle's car to learn how to drive.

4 使役動詞 have/get：「have/get + 物 + 過去分詞（含被動意義）」

· I wasn't thrilled to have a tooth filled. 我對補牙一點也不興奮。
How did Lenore get her hand smashed by the door?
蕾諾兒的手是怎麼讓門撞到的？

被動語態的用法

1 動作的執行者

1 何謂「行為者」（agent）？

在被動語態裡，主詞不是動作的執行者，而是動作的承受者。動作的執行者（doer/actor）稱為「行為者」（agent），在被動語態裡通常是未知的或不重要的。在被動語態裡，我們感興趣的是行為、動作本身，而非動作的執行者。

- Thousands of people were killed when the tanks of chemicals were spilled. 那些裝化學品的罐子打翻後，造成了上千人的死亡。
  - ↥ Thousands of people 和 the tanks of chemicals 是動作的承受者。
  - ↥ 這裡強調的是事件本身，而非動作的執行者。
- French is also spoken in the Canadian province of Quebec.
  加拿大的魁北克省也講法語。
  - ↥ French 是行為動作的承受者。
- Professor Herder said, "In the past, a person could be hanged for committing murder." 赫德教授說：「在以前，一個人要是殺了人，可能會被絞死。」
  - ↥ a person 是行為動作的承受者。

- hang 作「懸掛」的意思時，動詞的三態變化為：
  hang—hung—hung
- hang 作「絞死」的意思時，動詞的三態變化為：
  hang—hanged—hanged

2 被動語態如何說明行為者？

在被動語態中，如果要指明動作的執行者，就需要用介系詞 by（不要用 for 和 from）。

- A Singaporean university sophomore told me, "English is spoken by lots of people in Singapore."
  一位新加坡的大二學生告訴我：「在新加坡，很多人講英語。」
  ↳ English 是動作的承受者；people 是行為者。

- Claire and Tom were greatly influenced by their mom.
  克萊兒和湯姆受他們母親的影響很大。

- Jade knows her tuition has been paid by her Uncle Wade.
  潔德知道她的學費已經由韋德叔叔付了。

比較 如果被動句裡面需要交代「動作執行者所使用的工具」，則可用 with。

- Those four satellites will be launched with one rocket.
  那四個衛星將由一個火箭發射。

- Electricity for our house is produced with solar panels. 我們家的電是由太陽能板所產生的。

3 執行者常可以省略。

在被動句中，可以提及動作的執行者，也可以將其省略。

- "My bed was crushed (by Dad's pet gorilla)," complained Ted.
  泰德抱怨說：「我的床被（爸爸的寵物大猩猩）壓壞了。」
  ↳ 如果省略 by Dad's pet gorilla，則只強調床被壓壞了，而不關心是誰壓壞的。

2 及物動詞才有被動結構

只有及物動詞才有被動結構。被動結構的主詞是動作的承受者，**不及物動詞**和**連綴動詞**因為沒有受詞（動作的承受者），因此沒有被動結構。

- They sell root beer floats over there.
  = Root beer floats are sold over there. 那裡有賣冰淇淋漂浮沙士。

⤷ 第一句中的 sell 是及物動詞，接受詞 root beer floats；在第二句的被動結構中，動作承受者 Root beer floats 擔當主詞。

⤷ root beer 是一種清涼飲料，用薑等植物的根部所製成的草本飲品，不含酒精，盛行於美國；root beer floats 則是上面加有冰淇淋。

- **Del sings quite well.** 戴爾歌唱得很好。
  ⤷ sings 在這個句子裡是不及物動詞，沒有受詞，所以沒有被動形式。

- **Joyce sang the national anthem with her beautiful voice.**
  = The national anthem was sung by Joyce with her beautiful voice.
  喬伊絲用她美妙的歌喉唱國歌。
  ⤷ sang 在這個句子裡是及物動詞，可以用於被動語態。

- **This pineapple tastes sweet.** 這鳳梨真甜。
  ⤷ tastes 在這個句子裡是連綴動詞，沒有動作的承受者，所以沒有被動形式。

- **Twenty-nine physicists named Einstein tasted the wine.**
  = The wine was tasted by twenty-nine physicists named Einstein.
  29 位名叫愛因斯坦的物理學家品嚐了這種葡萄酒。
  ⤷ tasted 在這個句子裡是及物動詞，可以用於被動語態。

即使及物動詞後面接有受詞，許多句子還是使用主動語態比較自然。
» 參見 633 頁〈3 不自然的被動結構〉。

Active Meg ate an egg. 梅格吃了一個雞蛋。 → 簡明自然
Passive An egg was eaten by Meg. 一個雞蛋被梅格吃了。 → 不自然

3 不用於被動語態的動詞結構

1 並非所有以及物動詞為主要動詞的句子，都可以使用被動語態。當主動語態的句子中含有特定的**狀態動詞**時，即使是及物動詞，也不能用被動語態。狀態動詞表示狀態而不是動作，在這類動詞中以 have（擁有）最為重要。

✗ **"Some money is had in my purse," stated the nurse.**
✓ **"I have some money in my purse," stated the nurse.**
護士說：「我口袋裡有一些錢。」
⤷ have 表示「擁有」，是及物動詞，但表示狀態而不是動作，不用於被動語態。

✕ Dinner is being had by Mary and Jerry.

✓ Jerry and Mary are having dinner. 傑瑞和瑪麗正在吃晚餐。

↑ have 即使用來描述動作（吃／喝），也不用被動語態。

2 表示「想要」、「喜歡」等意義的動詞，如「want/love/hate + 受詞 + 不定式」，不用被動語態。這些動詞都表狀態，不表示動作。

✕ I am wanted to get a master's degree in education.

✓ My mom wants me to get a master's degree in education.
我媽媽希望我能拿到一個教育碩士學位。

↑ 「want + 受詞 + 不定式」，不用被動語態。

3 含**連綴動詞**的句子，不用被動語態（連綴動詞是表示狀態的動詞）。例如：

- appear 似乎
- become 成為
- taste 嚐起來
- be be 動詞
- seem 似乎

・How can Trish become a first-class user of English?
翠西要如何才能變成一流的英文使用者呢？

↑ become 是狀態動詞，只能用於主動語態中。

4 有些含介系詞的片語動詞，主要用於主動語態。

- agree with 與……一致
- look like 看起來像
- walk into 走進

✕ Amy was agreed with by everyone in the spaceship *Miami*.

✓ Everyone in the spaceship *Miami* agreed with Amy.
在邁阿密號太空船裡，所有人都和艾咪的意見相同。

↑ 含介系詞的片語動詞 agree with 不能用於被動語態。

・Coco walked into the UFO. 可可走進那架幽浮裡。

↑ 含介系詞的片語動詞 walked into 不能用於被動語態。

5 不用被動語態的常見動詞：

- cost 花費
- lack 缺乏
- suit 相配；相稱
- fit（衣服）合身
- resemble 類似
- weigh 有……重量

・That cottage cost us dearly. 那棟別墅花了我們很多錢。

↑ cost 表示「花費」，是狀態動詞，沒有被動形式。

- This shirt doesn't fit Jerry. 那件襯衫傑瑞穿不合身。
  ↳ fit 表「衣服大小合身材」時，雖是及物動詞，但表示狀態，不能用被動語態。
- Midge lacks courage. 米姬欠缺勇氣。
  ↳ lack 表示「缺少」、「不足」，是狀態動詞，沒有被動形式。
- That dress suits me well. 我穿那件洋裝很合適。
  ↳ suit 表示「服裝、樣式、顏色等與某人相配」，是狀態動詞，沒有被動形式。

✗ Ten pounds are weighed by my new baby.
✗ My new baby is weighed ten pounds.
✓ My new baby weighs ten pounds. 我剛出生的寶寶重 10 磅。
  ↳ weigh 表示「稱起來」、「有……重量」，是狀態動詞，沒有被動形式。

上述狀態動詞當中，有一些也可以作行為動詞；作行為動詞時，可以改成被動結構。

- Uncle Wade was fitted with a hearing aid. 韋德叔叔裝了一個助聽器。
  ↳ fit 在這句中指為某人測量，以便提供合身的衣服或合適的設備，通常用於被動語態，意思是「安裝」、「配備」。

4 只能用於被動語態的句型

有些句子只能用於被動語態。含有下面動詞片語的句子，不能用於主動語態。

- be born 出生
- be situated 坐落在……
- be made of 由……材料製成的
- be supposed to 應該

- This old wedding ring is made of gold. 這枚舊結婚戒指是用黃金製的。
- Dee was born in 2003. 蒂出生於 2003 年。
- The cottage built by Jill is situated on a beautiful hill.
  潔兒蓋的那棟別墅坐落在一座美麗的小山丘上。
- I was strongly opposed to going home, but Mom said, "It is late, and Ed is supposed to be in bed."
  我強烈反對回家，但媽媽說：「時間晚了，艾德應該上床睡覺了。」
  ↳ 上述三個例句中的過去分詞 born、situated、supposed，相當於形容詞。

5 同時接兩個受詞的動詞

1 有些動詞（give、lend、promise、send、show、teach、tell、throw 等）可以同時接兩個受詞：一個人（間接受詞）、一個物（直接受詞）。

- **Tom gave his wife Kim the Slim Gym.**
  湯姆把這家瘦身體育館送給了妻子金姆。
  ↳ gave 接了兩個受詞：Kim（間接受詞）和 the Slim Gym（直接受詞）。

2 這類動詞有兩種可行的被動語態結構：

- **The Slim Gym was given to Kim (by Tom).**
  ↳ 需要介系詞 to。
  ↳ The Slim Gym 在主動句中是直接受詞，在被動句中變成了主詞，為動作的承受者。
- **Kim was given the Slim Gym (by Tom).**
  ↳ 這句更自然。Kim 在主動句中是間接受詞，在被動句中成了主詞，為動作的承受者。
  ↳ 在將有兩個受詞的主動句改為被動句時，通常會把間接受詞（人）作為主詞。

有些動詞不能接兩個受詞，這樣的動詞只有一種被動形式，如：

- demonstrate 說明
- introduce 介紹
- report 報告
- explain 解釋
- mention 提及
- suggest 建議

✗ I described Lulu Mom's serious medical problems.
✓ I described Mom's serious medical problems to Lulu.
我向露露描述了媽媽嚴重的健康問題。
↳ 動詞 described 後面不接雙受詞。

✗ Lulu was described Mom's serious medical problems.
✓ Mom's serious medical problems were described to Lulu.
露露被告知了媽媽嚴重的健康問題。
↳ 不能接兩個受詞的動詞，只有一種被動形式。

UNIT

13 直接引語與間接引語

Direct Speech and Indirect Speech

直接引語與間接引語的定義和用法

1 直接引語與間接引語的定義

1 用引號引用人們的原話，稱為**直接引語**；轉述某人說過的話或某人的內心想法，稱為**間接引語**。

2 當直接引語被轉換成間接引語時，要刪除引號。

3 間接引語陳述句中的連接詞 that：

a 在下面一些常見的轉述動詞後面，間接引語裡常省略連接詞 that。

- say 說
- think 想
- agree 同意
- mention 提及
- promise 答應

- **Kay mentioned (that) she'd gone out with you to the movies the other day.** 凱提到幾天前她跟你一起去看過電影。

b 如果 that 子句不緊跟動詞，一般不省略連接詞 that。比較：

- **Jane agreed (that) Bob was the best person for the job.**
  珍承認鮑勃是做這項工作的最佳人選。

- **Jane agreed with Susan and me that Bob was the best person for the job.** 珍同意蘇珊和我的意見，認為鮑勃是做這項工作的最佳人選。
  ↑ 動詞（agreed）和 that 子句被介系詞片語（with Susan and me）分開，不能省略 that。

2 直接引語與間接引語的文法差異

1 代名詞的改變

把直接引語轉換成間接引語時，有時必須改變直接引語裡的代名詞，如：

I 可能改成 he 或 she；my 可能改成 his 或 her；you 可能改成 we、I、us 或 me；your 可能改成 my 或 our。

Direct Bess said, "I am looking for my pink dress."
貝絲說：「我在找我的粉紅色洋裝。」

Indirect Bess said (that) she was looking for her pink dress.
貝絲說她正在找她的粉紅色洋裝。

⤷ 直接引語的第一人稱 I 和 my，在間接引語中變成第三人稱 she 和 her，與主句的主詞 Bess 一致。

Direct Tom complained, "I can't understand her Spanish."
湯姆抱怨說：「我聽不懂她的西班牙語。」

Indirect Tom complained (that) he couldn't understand her Spanish.
湯姆抱怨說，他聽不懂她的西班牙語。

⤷ 直接引語的 I，在間接引語中變成第三人稱 he，與主句的主詞 Tom 一致。
⤷ 直接引語中的 her 在間接引語中不變化，即「第三人稱不變化」。

Direct "The publication of your book may be delayed," explained the editor.「你的著作的出版可能會延誤。」編輯解釋道。

Indirect The editor explained that the publication of my book might be delayed. 編輯解釋說，我的著作的出版可能會延誤。

⤷ 直接引語的第二人稱所有格 your，在間接引語變成第一人稱所有格 my。

Direct I said, "Kim, you look happy and healthy."
我說：「金姆，你看起來幸福又健康。」

Indirect I told Kim that she looked happy and healthy.
我告訴金姆，她看起來幸福又健康。

⤷ 直接引語中的第二人稱主詞 you，在間接引語中變成第三人稱 she，與主句的受詞 Kim（第三人稱）一致。

2 時態的改變

a 在表示**說話**或**報導**的**動詞過去式**（said、stated、reported 等）後面使用間接引語時，有時需要改變原直接引語中的動詞時態。

✗ Ann said she is really happy to meet Dan.
✓ Ann said she was really happy to meet Dan. 安說她真的很高興見到丹。

直接引語	間接引語
➤ 簡單現在式 Kate said, "Henry, you look great." 凱特說：「亨利，你看起來不錯啊。」	→ 簡單過去式 Kate told Henry he looked great. 凱特告訴亨利，他看起來不錯。
➤ 簡單過去式 Henry said, "Jill gave me a ride home." 亨利說：「潔兒送我回家了。」	→ 過去完成式 Henry said Jill had given him a ride home. 亨利說潔兒送他回家了。 ↳ 也可維持簡單過去式（gave）。
➤ 現在進行式 "Dan is surfing the Internet," said Ann. 安說：「丹正在網上搜索資料。」	→ 過去進行式 Ann said Dan was surfing the Internet. 安說丹正在網上搜索資料。
➤ 現在完成式 Glen said, "I have lost my wallet again." 葛倫說：「我又把錢包弄丟了。」	→ 過去完成式 Glen said he had lost his wallet again. 葛倫說他又把錢包丟了。
➤ 現在完成進行式 He asked, "Trish, how long have you been studying Spanish?" 他問：「翠西，你學西班牙語有多久了？」	→ 過去完成進行式 He asked Trish how long she had been studying Spanish. 他問翠西學西班牙語有多長時間了。
➤ 簡單未來式 Ben said, "We'll be late again." 班說：「我們又要遲到了。」	→ 過去未來式 Ben said they would be late again. 班說他們又要遲到了。
➤（情態動詞）will/can/may Kate said, "We may be late." 凱特說：「我們也許會遲到。」	→ would/could/might Kate said they might be late. 凱特說他們也許會遲到。

1 下列時態在間接引語中不改變。

直接引語	間接引語
had arrived	→ had arrived（過去完成式）
had been telling	→ had been telling（過去完成進行式）

- Jane said, "Mike had forgotten to put his seat belt on until I reminded him." 珍說：「直到我提醒，邁克才想到要繫安全帶。」
- Jane said Mike had forgotten to put his seat belt on until she reminded him. 珍說，直到她提醒，邁克才想到要繫安全帶。

2 直接引語中的過去式（如：left, started）不是一定都得改成過去完成式，因為有時改變後會使句子非常不自然，甚至會改變原句的意思。例如：

- Dirk said, "It started snowing heavily when I left work."
德克說：「我下班時，開始下起了大雪。」

✗ Dirk said that it had started snowing heavily when he had left work.
 ↳ 這句不自然，不是道地的英語。

✗ Dirk said that it had started snowing heavily when he left work.
 ↳ 這句雖是正確句，但改變了直接引語的原意，指「開始下大雪」這一動作發生在「下班之前」。

✓ Dirk said that it started snowing heavily when he left work.
德克說，他下班時，開始下起了大雪。

3 轉述動詞是過去式時，如果直接引述句是過去式，間接引述句通常要改為過去完成式。但有時也可以維持過去式。

- Dennis said, "Ann bought more parts for the robot she's building."
Dennis said Ann bought more parts for the robot she's building.
= Dennis said Ann had bought more parts for the robot she's building.
丹尼斯說，安為她正在打造的機器人買了更多的零件。
 ↳ 最後一句用過去完成式，是為了強調「購買」動作發生在「說」動作之前。

b 這類轉述動詞（said、stated、reported 等）如果用在**簡單現在式**（如 say/says）、**未來式**（如 will say）或**現在完成式**（如 have/has said）中，則間接引語句的時態和直接引語句相同。

Direct Ann says, "I live in Japan." 安說：「我住在日本。」
Indirect Ann says she lives in Japan. 安說她住在日本。

Direct Ben says, "We will be late again." 班說：「我們又要遲到了。」
Indirect Ben says they will be late again. 班說他們又要遲到了。

Direct Sue has said, "I will quit dating Ted." 蘇說:「我要停止跟泰德約會。」
Indirect Sue has said she will quit dating Ted. 蘇說她要停止跟泰德約會。

c 如果被轉述的話**永遠是事實**，通常需要保留原講話人的時態。

Direct "The earth always rotates toward the east, and the sun appears to set in the west," Jerry explained to Mary.
Indirect Jerry explained to Mary that the earth always rotates toward the east and the sun appears to set in the west.
傑瑞對瑪麗解釋說，地球總是向東旋轉，太陽看起來就好像由西邊落下。

d 轉述的事件若在被報導或被轉述時**仍是事實**，則轉述人既可以選擇保留原講話人的時態，也可以改變時態。

Direct "I am from Japan," said Ann. 安說：「我是日本人。」
Indirect Ann said she is/was from Japan. 安說她是日本人。
↳ 用現在式 is 是為了強調在轉述的時候，被轉述的事仍然是事實。
↳ 用過去式 was 則是為了在一個句子裡保持時態一致。

Direct "My son Scot does not often come to visit me," Jim complained to Kim.
Indirect Jim complained to Kim that his son Scot does not/did not often go to visit him.
吉姆對金姆抱怨說，他的兒子史考特不常去看他。

↳ 用現在式 does not go 是為強調在轉述的當下，轉述的事情仍是事實。

↳ 用過去式 did not go 則是為了在一個句子裡保持時態一致。轉述這句話時，已經不在 Jim 家，come 改成 go（參見 657 頁〈3 改變其他詞彙〉）。

比較

Direct **"My son Scot does not often come to visit me," Jim complained to Kim a few days ago.**

Indirect **A few days ago Jim complained to Kim that his son Scot did not often go to visit him.**
幾天前吉姆對金姆抱怨說，他的兒子史考特不常去看他。

↳ 如果主句中有一個表示過去的時間副詞（如 yesterday, last week, a few days ago），那麼間接引語裡的時態就要改變成過去式。

e 直接引語中有明確表示**過去時間**的副詞或片語時，則在間接引語中時態不發生變化（簡單過去式 → 簡單過去式；過去進行式 → 過去進行式）。

Direct **Tom said, "I lost my wallet yesterday."**
湯姆說：「我昨天把錢包弄丟了。」

Indirect **Tom said (that) he lost his wallet yesterday.**
湯姆說他昨天把錢包弄丟了。

↳ 不能說 he had lost his wallet yesterday。

f 情態動詞 could, would, should, might, ought to 在間接引語裡**不改變時態**。

Direct **"Sue, I could meet you at the front entrance to the zoo," said Andrew.**
安德魯說：「蘇，我可以在動物園的前門和你碰面。」

Indirect **Andrew told Sue that he could meet her at the front entrance to the zoo.**
安德魯告訴蘇，他可以在動物園的前門和她碰面。

Direct **Trish said, "You should do lots of reading in English.**
翠西說：「你應該大量閱讀英文。」

Indirect **Trish said that I should do lots of reading in English.**
翠西說我應該大量閱讀英文。

g 情態動詞 must 的用法

- **must 表「必須」**：間接引語中用 had to，也可以用 must（不常見）。
- **must 表「推測」**：間接引語中不改變 must（不能改為 had to）。
- **mustn't/must not**：間接引語中不改變否定式 mustn't/must not（不能改為 didn't have to）。

Direct **"You must be home by 10 tonight," said Dad.**
爸爸說：「你一定要在今晚十點以前回到家。」
Indirect **Dad said that I had to/must be home by 10 tonight.**
爸爸說我今晚一定要在十點以前回到家。
↑ 表「必須」。

Direct **"There must be over 100 guests at the party," said Dee.**
蒂說：「聚會上的客人想必有上百個。」
Indirect **Dee said there must be over 100 guests at the party.**
蒂說聚會上的客人想必有上百個。
↑ 表「推測」。

・**"You must not believe everything you read," warned Sue.**
蘇告誡說：「不要盡信所讀。」

✗ **Sue warned me that I did not have to believe everything I read.**
✓ **Sue warned me that I must not believe everything I read.**
蘇告誡我不要盡信所讀。

h 表示「非真實」的**假設語氣**，在間接引語句中**不改變動詞時態**。

Direct **Lily said, "I wish I were taller so that I could be on the basketball team."**
莉莉說：「但願我可以長高一點，這樣我就可以進籃球隊了。」
Indirect **Lily wished she were taller so that she could be on the basketball team.**
莉莉說，但願她可以長高一點，這樣她就可以進籃球隊了。

i 直接引語中含有 since 引導的表示過去時間的副詞子句時，子句中的過去時態不變化。

Direct **Sue Ridge said, "I have traveled to thirty-two countries since I graduated from college."**
蘇·瑞吉說：「我從大學畢業到現在，已經旅遊過 32 個國家了。」

Indirect **Sue Ridge said that she had traveled to thirty-two countries since she graduated from college."**
蘇·瑞吉說，她從大學畢業到現在，已經旅遊過 32 個國家了。
↑ 主句：現在完成式變成過去完成式；since 子句：簡單過去式不改變。

j after 和 when 引導的時間副詞子句裡的過去時態通常不後移，尤其是美式。

Direct **Lily told me, "The knight Sir Lee rode away on his adventurous journey after he put on his helmet."**
莉莉跟我說：「騎士李爵士把頭盔戴上後，便策馬而去，展開他的冒險旅程。」

Indirect **Lily told me that the knight Sir Lee rode away on his adventurous journey after he (had) put on his helmet.**
莉莉跟我說，騎士李爵士戴上頭盔後，便策馬而去，展開他的冒險旅程。
↑ 這裡美式英語用 put；英式英語用 put 或 had put 都可以。子句動作 (had) put on his helmet 在先，主句動作 rode away 在後，因此，主句 rode away 不能改成 had ridden away。
↑ 直接引語中的第三人稱 he 和 his，在間接引語中不變化，即「第三人稱不變化」。

3 改變其他詞彙

a 在表示「說、講」等動詞的過去式（如 said、reported、told）後面，有時需要改變副詞和其他詞彙。因為在轉述的時候，時間、地點、說話者都不同。例如，將某人說過的話向其他人轉述時，也許得改變 here（這裡）、this（這個）、today（今天）、now（現在）這類會有相對變化的字。

直接引語	間接引語
● here 這裡	→ there 那裡
● come 來	→ go 去
● bring 帶來	→ take 帶走
● this 這個	→ that 那個
● these 這些	→ those 那些
● now 現在	→ then 當時
● today/tonight 今天／今晚	→ that day/that night 那天／那晚
● tomorrow 明天	→ the next day; the following day 次日
● next week 下個星期	→ the next week; the following week 下個星期
● yesterday 昨天	→ the day before; the previous day 前一天
● last week 上週	→ the previous week; the week before 上週
● two days ago 兩天前	→ two days before 前兩天

b 轉述同一天所說的話，時間副詞 today、yesterday、tomorrow 等不變。在同一地點轉述，come 和 here 不需要改為 go 和 there。

Direct **Kay said, "I am not working today."** 凱說：「我今天不上班。」

Indirect **Kay said she was not working that day.** 凱說她那天不上班。

↰ 轉述者轉述這句話時，時間已經變化（不是同一天）。

Indirect **Kay said she was/is not working today.** 凱說她今天不上班。

↰ 轉述者在轉述這句話時，時間沒有變化（在同一天，還在今天），時間副詞（today）不變化。用 was not working，是為了保持句子時態一致；用 is not working，是強調時間仍然在今天。

Direct **"The taxi will be here soon," Tom said to June.**
湯姆對茱恩說：「計程車快到這兒了。」

Indirect **Tom told June the taxi would be there soon.**
湯姆告訴茱恩，計程車快到那兒了。

↰ 轉述者轉述這句話時，地點已經變化，不在同一個地點。

Indirect **Tom told June the taxi would be/will be here soon.**

ⓘ 轉述這句話時，時間和地點都沒變（還在同一地方等計程車），表示地點的副詞（here）不變化。在同一時間，動詞時態可變化，也可不變化。用 would be，是為了與主句過去式 told 一致；用 will be，是為了強調轉述時，「等候計程車」這一事實還沒有變。

Direct **Roy said to Kay, "It snowed yesterday."**
羅伊對凱說：「昨天下過雪。」

Indirect **Roy told Kay it had snowed the day before.**
羅伊告訴凱，前一天下過雪。

ⓘ 轉述者轉述這句話時，時間已經變化（不同日）。

Direct **Glen Creek said, "I'll be back next week."**
葛倫·克里克說：「我下星期會回來。」

Indirect **Glen Creek said he would be back the next week, but I never saw him again.**
葛倫·克里克說他下星期會回來，但我從此沒再見過他。

ⓘ 轉述者轉述這句話時，時間已經變化（不同星期）。

Direct **Yesterday Ann said, "I'm going to have spaghetti tomorrow night."**
安昨天說：「我明天晚上要吃義大利麵。」

Indirect **Yesterday Ann said she was/is going to have spaghetti tonight.** 安昨天說，她今天晚上要吃義大利麵。

ⓘ 「昨天說的明天晚上」，轉述這句話時的時間，就是今天。動詞時態可以用 was going，與主句過去式 said 時態保持一致；也可以用 is going，強調轉述時，今晚還沒有來到，「她要吃義大利麵」這一事實還沒有變。

Direct **May said, "Wendy, I hope you will come to my wedding tomorrow."** 梅說：「溫蒂，我希望你明天來參加我的婚禮。」

Indirect **May said she hoped Wendy would go to her wedding the next day.** 梅說，她希望溫蒂隔天去參加她的婚禮。

ⓘ 轉述者轉述這句話時，時間和地點都變了。

ⓘ 如果 tomorrow 是 May 在一星期前提的，那麼那時候的「明天」早就已經過了，tomorrow 這個字就得改成 the following day 或 the next day。

間接命令句與間接疑問句

1 間接命令句（Indirect Commands）

1 間接引語句可用來轉述「提議、建議、命令、意圖」，這類間接引語稱為間接命令句，句型為「**ask/tell 等動詞 + 受詞 + 不定式（帶 to）**」。類似的動詞還有：

- advise 建議
- beg 請求
- command 命令
- compel 強迫
- encourage 鼓勵
- expect 期待
- instruct 指示
- invite 邀請
- order 命令
- persuade 勸說
- recommend 勸告
- remind 提醒
- request 要求
- urge 催促
- warn 提醒

直接引語	間接引語
"Read 25,000 words every day," said Kay. 凱說：「每天要閱讀 25,000 個單字。」	**Kay asked us to read 25,000 words every day.** 凱要我們每天閱讀 25,000 個單字。
Midge said, "Jim, get out of my cottage!" 米姬說：「吉姆，離開我的小屋！」	**Midge told Jim to get out of her cottage.** 米姬要吉姆離開她的小屋。
Sheriff Lisa Sun shouted at the man, "Drop your gun!" 麗莎·孫警長對那個男人大喊：「放下你的槍！」	**Sheriff Lisa Sun ordered the man to drop his gun.** 麗莎·孫警長命令那個男人把槍放下。

"Please don't tell anyone," Kim exclaimed to Sheriff Sun. 金姆對孫警長大呼：「請不要告訴任何人。」	Kim begged Sheriff Sun not to tell anyone. 金姆懇求孫警長不要告訴任何人。（否定句要在 to 前面加 not）
"Sue, you should get a different job," said Bob. 鮑勃說：「蘇，你應該另外找份工作。」	Bob encouraged Sue to get a different job. 鮑勃鼓勵蘇另外找份工作。

2 動詞 say、suggest 的後面不用「受詞 + 不定式」的結構。

✗ Midge suggested my dad to go back to college.

✓ Midge suggested that my dad (should) go back to college.
米姬建議我爸爸回到大學去讀書。

↑ suggested 後面不能接不定式，應該接一個名詞子句，子句裡用「should + 動詞原形」，should 可以省略。

✗ Del said me to tell Jake about the crack in the bell.

✓ Del asked me to tell Jake about the crack in the bell.
戴爾要我告訴傑克，那座鐘有裂縫。

↑ said 後面不用不定式結構，這裡要把 said 改成 asked。

3 直接引語中以 let's 開頭的祈使句表示建議時，間接引語通常用 suggest 加以轉述。

Direct She said, "Let's go window-shopping." 她說：「我們去逛街吧。」

Indirect She suggested that we (should) go window-shopping.
她建議我們去逛街。

4 不定式片語前面的某些動詞不接受詞，這時的間接引語句型為**「動詞 + 不定式（帶 to）」**。這些動詞有：

- agree 同意
- demand 要求
- guarantee 保證
- hope 希望
- offer 願意；提議
- promise 允諾
- propose 打算
- swear 發誓
- threaten 威脅
- volunteer 自願
- vow 發誓

• "I'll give you a ride home," said Ted. 泰德說：「我開車送你回家。」

✗ Ted offered me to give me a ride home.
✓ Ted offered to give me a ride home. 泰德主動提出開車送我回家。

5 間接命令句的否定句，要**直接在 to 前面加上 not**。

Direct "Don't worry," Ted said to Mary. 泰德對瑪麗說：「不要擔心。」
Indirect Ted told Mary not to worry. 泰德要瑪麗不要擔心。

- Del begged me not to tell anyone about it.
  戴爾懇求我不要把那件事告訴任何人。

嚴格來講，應該**盡量不要分離不定式**。動詞不定式的否定式，是在 to 前面加 not，不過在口語中，try to not tell 也許可以被人們接受。這類錯誤因為太過常見，聽起來已經很順耳了，不過在正式用法中，還是盡量不要違反文法規則（try not to break the grammar rule）。

2 間接疑問句（Indirect Questions）

1 **間接疑問句的句型**：間接引語句可以用提問的動詞 ask/inquire/wonder 來轉述問句，稱為間接疑問句。間接疑問句的句型有三種：

- **轉述 yes/no 一般疑問句**：ask/inquire + if/whether 引導的子句
- **轉述 wh- 特殊疑問句**：ask/inquire + wh- 疑問詞（when/where/what/who 等）引導的子句
- **轉述 wh- 特殊疑問句**：ask/inquire + wh- 疑問詞（how/when/where/what 等）+ 不定式（帶 to）

直接引語	間接引語
"Are you Polish?" Andrew asked Trish.「你是波蘭人嗎？」安德魯問翠西。	Andrew asked Trish if/whether she was Polish. 安德魯問翠西是不是波蘭人。
"Is dinner ready, Dad?" asked Jenny 「爸爸，晚飯好了嗎？」珍妮問。	Jenny asked her dad if/whether dinner was ready. 珍妮問她爸爸晚飯好了沒。

"When are you going to Spain?" asked Jane. 珍問:「你何時要去西班牙?」	Jane asked me when I was going to Spain. 珍問我什麼時候去西班牙。
Mom asked, "Why didn't you finish your homework?" 媽媽問:「你的作業為什麼沒寫完?」	Mom asked me why I hadn't finished my homework. = Mom asked me why I didn't finish my homework. 媽媽問我,為什麼我的作業沒寫完。
"How do I get to the airport?" asked Sue. 蘇問:「機場怎麼去?」	Sue asked how to get to the airport. 蘇問去機場怎麼走。
Mary asked, "Where should I park my car?" 瑪麗問:「我應該把我的汽車停在哪裡?」	Mary asked where to park her car. 瑪麗問,她應該把汽車停在哪裡。

2 **間接疑問句的語序**:和直接疑問句不同,而和**陳述句的語序一樣**(主詞 + 動詞)。間接疑問句不用問號,也不加助動詞 do/does/did。

a 在 wh- 或 if/whether 的子句裡,要用陳述句的語序(主詞 + 動詞),連綴動詞和助動詞要置於主詞後。

- Lily asked me, "Who is that guy?" 莉莉問我說:「那個小夥子是誰?」
  ↳ 疑問句語序:連綴動詞 + 主詞

✗ Lily asked me who was that guy?

✓ Lily asked me who that guy was. 莉莉問我那個小夥子是誰。

↳ 在間接疑問句中,要用句號,不要用問號;要用陳述句的語序,即「主詞 + 連綴動詞」(that guy was),而不是疑問句的語序(was that guy)。

Direct Ann asked, "Have you ever been to Afghanistan?"
安問:「你去過阿富汗沒有?」
↳ 疑問句語序:助動詞 have + 主詞 + 過去分詞

Indirect Ann asked me if/whether I had ever been to Afghanistan.
安問我是否去過阿富汗。
↳ 間接疑問句語序:主詞 + 助動詞 had + 過去分詞

Direct Mom asked, "When can you come home?"
媽媽問:「你什麼時候能回家?」
↑ 疑問句語序:情態動詞 + 主詞 + 述語動詞(原形)

Indirect Mom asked me when I could go home.
媽媽問我什麼時候我能回家。
↑ 間接疑問句語序:主詞 + 情態動詞 + 述語動詞(原形)

b 在 wh- 或 if/whether 的子句裡,不要加助動詞 do/does/did。

- Margo asked, "Do you want to go with me to Chicago?"
  瑪歌問:「你想跟我一起去芝加哥嗎?」
  ↑ 疑問句語序:助動詞 do + 主詞 + 述語動詞(原形)

✗ Margo asked me if/whether did I want to go with her to Chicago.
✓ Margo asked me if/whether I wanted to go with her to Chicago.
瑪歌問我是否想跟她一起去芝加哥。
↑ 間接疑問句不加助動詞 did,主詞和述語動詞不倒裝(主詞 + 述語動詞)。

Direct "What on earth do you want for yourself?" asked John.
約翰問:「你自己究竟想得到什麼?」

Indirect John asked me what on earth I wanted for myself.
約翰問我自己究竟想得到什麼。

Direct "What did you say to Lulu?" asked Andrew.
「你跟露露說了些什麼?」安德魯問道。

Indirect Andrew asked what I had said to Lulu.
安德魯問我跟露露說了些什麼。

c 但在轉述**否定疑問句**時,要用助動詞 do/does/did。

Direct "Why don't you want to live in Rome?" asked Sue.
蘇問:「你為什麼不想在羅馬居住?」

Indirect Sue asked me why I didn't want to live in Rome.
蘇問我為什麼我不想在羅馬居住。

UNIT

14 語氣

Mood

肯定陳述句和否定陳述句

動詞的語氣（mood），表示說話者或寫作者對其內容所持的態度。
英文文法包括以下幾類的語氣：

1 陳述語氣（indicative mood）

- a 肯定陳述句（affirmative statement）
- b 否定陳述句（negative statement）
- c 疑問句（question）
- d 感嘆句（exclamation）

2 祈使語氣（imperative mood）

3 假設語氣（subjunctive mood）

1 肯定陳述句（Affirmative Statements）

肯定陳述句陳述事實，並對事實進行肯定。肯定陳述句的動詞不含否定詞。

- **Scot smiles a lot.** 史考特經常微笑。
- **Bing is laughing.** 賓在笑。
- **I know the answer.** 我知道答案。
- **Coco says it looks as if it's going to snow.**
  可可說，看起來好像要下雪了。

2 否定陳述句（Negative Statements）

1 句中若有下列的助動詞或情態動詞，則否定句的構成方式是在這些動詞後面加上 not 或 never：「助動詞或情態助動詞 + not/never」。

- be（am、is 等）
- have/has/had
- must
- will
- would
- can
- could
- shall
- should
- may
- might

- **Liz is not crying, but she knows she is dying.**
  莉茲沒有哭，但她知道自己快死了。

- **You mustn't tell Del about Sue.**
  你決不能把蘇的事告訴戴爾。

- **Pat would never do a terrible thing like that.**
  派特絕對不會做那種壞事。

- **I have never met Jim, nor do I have any desire to meet him.**
  = I have never met Jim, and I have no desire to meet him.
  我從來沒有見過吉姆，也不希望見到他。
  ⮑ 第一句的第二個並列子句用了倒裝句（nor do I）。
  ⮑ 第二句的第一個 have 為助動詞，與過去分詞 met 構成述語，否定詞要 never 放在 have 後面；第二個 have 為述語動詞，表「擁有」，否定詞 no 放在 have 後面（I have no desire to meet him. = I do not have any desire to meet him.）。

2 如果句中沒有助動詞或情態動詞，就要加上助動詞 do、does 或 did，再加否定詞 not 來構成否定句：「do/does/did + not/n't + 原形動詞」。

Affirmative **Coco said it snowed in Tokyo.** 可可說東京下雪了。

Negative **Coco said it didn't snow in Tokyo.** 可可說東京沒下雪。

⮑ 用了助動詞 didn't 後，動詞 snow 就要用原形。

- **She doesn't know the answer.** 她不知道答案。
  ⮑ doesn't + 原形動詞（know）。

3 否定句還有一種構成方式，不是加助動詞 do/does/did 和 not，而是使用下列否定詞（這類詞本身已具有否定意味，不要再加 not 形成雙重否定）：

- nobody 沒有人
- nothing 什麼也沒
- never 從不
- no 不；沒有
- nowhere 沒有什麼地方
- seldom 很少
- rarely 很少
- hardly (= almost not) 幾乎不
- little 少許

✗ Trish has a heavy Polish accent, and I cannot hardly understand her English.

✓ Trish has a heavy Polish accent, and I can hardly understand her English.

✓ Trish has a heavy Polish accent, and I cannot understand her English. 翠西的波蘭口音很重，我聽不懂她講的英語。

↑ hardly 和 not 只能選其一。

✗ Honey West declared, "I haven't no money."

✓ Honey West declared, "I've no money."

杭妮·韋斯特宣稱說：「我沒有錢。」

↑ 不用雙重否定，not 和 no 只選其一。

- Because of her dishonesty, nobody likes Lily.
  由於莉莉不誠實，沒有人喜歡她。
  ↑ 不加助動詞 does 和 not。

- Sue never smokes or listens to sexist jokes.
  蘇從來不抽菸，也不聽性別歧視的笑話。

- There's nowhere for me to go during the snowstorm.
  大雪紛飛之時，我沒地方可去。

- Nothing is more common than unsuccessful people with talent. (President John Calvin Coolidge)
  才智過人而一事無成者，比比皆是。
  ↑ nothing 是否定不定代名詞。

疑問句

疑問句可分為：

1 一般疑問句（General Questions）
2 特殊疑問句（Special Questions）
3 間接疑問句（Indirect Questions）
4 否定疑問句（Negative Questions）
5 附加問句（Question Tags）

1 一般疑問句（General Questions）

需要用 yes 或 no 來回答的疑問句，稱作「**一般疑問句**」，也叫做「**是非疑問句**」（yes-no question），其基本結構為倒裝結構，有以下三種句型。

1 連綴動詞 be + 主詞 + 主詞補語

如果疑問句中的動詞是連綴動詞 be（is/am/are/was/were），則要將 be 動詞放在主詞前面。

- Were you happy when you lived in Honolulu?
  你住在檀香山時很幸福嗎？
- Are Ann and Nan identical twins from Japan?
  安和南是日本來的一對同卵雙胞胎嗎？

2 助動詞 + 主詞 + 主要動詞（原形、現在分詞或過去分詞）

a 如果疑問句中有助動詞或情態動詞（be, have, can, may 等），則要將這些助動詞或情態動詞放在主詞前面，而主要動詞（原形、現在分詞或過去分詞）仍置於主詞後面，不要將整個動詞（助動詞 + 主要動詞）移到主詞前面。

- Kay, can you finish the job today?

  凱，你今天能完成這項工作嗎？

  ↑ 只有情態動詞（can）放在主詞（you）前面，而不是整個動詞（can finish）。

- Have my chicks arrived and survived?

  我的小雞們有活著抵達嗎？

  ↑ 只有助動詞（Have）放在主詞（my chicks）前面，而不是整個動詞（Have arrived and survived）。

- Kate, will the flight be late?

  凱特，班機會誤點嗎？

  ↑ will 是助動詞，出現在主詞（the flight）的前面；不能把整個動詞（will be）放在主詞前。

- Where are President Liz White and her family staying tonight?

  莉茲·懷特總統和她的家人今晚要下榻何處？

  ↑ 助動詞 are 在疑問句中應放在複合主詞 President Liz White and her family 的前面。不能把整個述語（are staying）放在主詞前。

b 如果疑問句中有不止一個助動詞，只把第一個助動詞放在主詞前面。

✕ Will be Mort arrested if he refuses to show up in court?

✓ Will Mort be arrested if he refuses to show up in court?

如果莫特拒絕出庭，會被捕嗎？

↑ 只把第一個助動詞 will 放在主詞 Mort 前面；第二個助動詞 be 與主要動詞 arrested 構成被動式，不要把 be 放在主詞前。

3 助動詞（do/does/did）+ 主詞 + 述語動詞（原形動詞）

句中如果沒有助動詞或情態動詞，則要加上助動詞 do、does 或 did 來構成疑問句。助動詞 do/does/did 要放在主詞前面，主詞後面的主要動詞用原形動詞（即不帶 to 的不定式）。

✕ Did you liked the cowgirl movie you saw with Pearl?

✓ Did you like the cowgirl movie you saw with Pearl?

你喜歡和珀兒一起去看的那部女牛仔電影嗎？

↑ 用助動詞（Did）提問，動詞（like）要用原形。

✗ How much the cottage cost Midge?

✓ How much did the cottage cost Midge?

那棟別墅花了米姬多少錢？

↑ 主詞（the cottage）前面應該有一個助動詞（did）；後面接原形動詞（cost）。

· Why does Kay want to go to the U.S.A.?

凱為什麼想去美國？

↑ 把助動詞（does）放在主詞（Kay）前，原形動詞（want）放在主詞後面。

Statement Brooke knew every story in the book.

布魯克熟悉書中的每一個故事。

Question Did Brooke know every story in the book?

布魯克熟悉書中的每一個故事嗎？

Statement May went shopping yesterday.

梅昨天去購物了。

Question Did May go shopping yesterday?

梅昨天去購物了嗎？

句中如已經有情態動詞、助動詞或連綴動詞 to be，其疑問句就不要再加助動詞 do/does/did，即 do、does、did 不能和其他助動詞或連綴動詞 to be 連用。

✗ Does can Jane pilot a rocket plane?

✗ Does Jane can pilot a rocket plane?

✓ Can Jane pilot a rocket plane?

珍能夠駕駛以火箭為動力的飛機嗎？

↑ 用了情態動詞 can，就不能用助動詞 does。

✗ Do are you and Coco ready to go?

✗ Do you and Coco are ready to go?

✓ Are you and Coco ready to go?

你和可可準備好出發了嗎？

↑ are 是連綴動詞，用了 are，就不能用助動詞 do。

2 特殊疑問句（Special Questions）

用疑問詞（who, what, when, where, why, how, which, whose）來提問的句子就是**特殊疑問句**，也叫做「**wh- 疑問句**」。特殊疑問句有以下三種句型。

1 疑問詞（作主詞）+ 述語動詞（主詞和述語詞序不倒裝）

如果疑問詞 who、which、what、whose 是主詞或主詞的一部分，位於動詞前面時，不需要加助動詞 do/does/did 來構成疑問句，即主詞和動詞的順序不需要做任何改變。

✗ Did who tell that big lie to Sue?

✗ Who did tell that big lie to Sue?

✓ Who told that big lie to Sue?

那個天大的謊言是誰告訴蘇的？

↳ 主詞為疑問詞 who，用陳述句的語序，不要加助動詞 did，
句型為：主詞（Who）+ 述語動詞（told）。

- How many people work for Jenny in her publishing company?
  珍妮的出版社裡有多少人為她工作？
  ↳ 主詞（How many people）+ 動詞（work）

- What makes the world full of fun as it orbits the sun?
  當地球繞著太陽公轉時，是什麼使地球充滿了樂趣？
  ↳ 主詞（What）+ 動詞（makes）

- "Who was at fault?" "It was Jerry and Lily who were at fault."
  「是誰的過錯？」「是傑瑞和莉莉的過錯。」
  ↳ who、what 和 which 作主詞時，即使其所指是複數（Jerry and Lily），
  述語動詞仍使用單數形式（Who was）。
  ↳ 上面的回答句是一個強調句型「it was . . . who/that . . .」。

2 疑問詞（作受詞）+ 助動詞（do/does/did）+ 主詞 + 原形動詞

疑問詞若在句中作受詞，要加助動詞 do/does/did 來構成疑問句。

✗ What more Gus wants from us?

✓ What more does Gus want from us?

加斯還想從我們這裡得到什麼？

↑ What 是動詞 want 的受詞，主詞 Gus 前需要加助動詞 does，主要動詞用原形動詞 want。

- How much did you pay for that man-killer skirt?

你花了多少錢買那件令男人神魂顛倒的裙子？

↑ How much 是動詞 pay 的受詞。

3 疑問詞作主詞與受詞的用法比較

- "What happened to Andrew?"

"I don't know, but something fantastic happened to Bing."

「安德魯發生了什麼事？」「我不知道，不過有一件奇妙的事發生在賓身上。」

↑ What + happened（動詞）

- "What did you see, Sid?"「席德，你看見了什麼？」

"I saw a UFO. "「我看見了一架不明飛行物。」

↑ What + did（助動詞）+ you + see（主要動詞）

- "Who loves Mary besides Gary?"「除了蓋瑞，還有誰愛瑪麗？」

"Jerry also loves Mary."「傑瑞也愛瑪麗。」

↑ Who + loves（動詞）

- "Whom does Mary love?"「瑪麗愛誰呢？」

"Mary loves only herself."「瑪麗只愛她自己。」

↑ Whom+ does（助動詞）+ Mary+ love（主要動詞）

» 參見 11 頁〈Part 2 句子的種類〉。

» 疑問詞的用法參見 89 頁〈Part 5 疑問代名詞〉。

4 疑問句中的從屬子句：主詞和動詞不倒裝

疑問句中若有從屬子句，則子句中的主詞要放在動詞前面，也就是說，疑問句中的從屬子句要用陳述句的語序。

✗ Who do you wish would you marry?
✓ Who do you wish you would marry?
你希望嫁給誰？
→ you would marry 是一個從屬子句；在子句裡，主詞（you）應該放在動詞（would marry）的前面。

✗ How long do you think should I wait for Kate?
✓ How long do you think I should wait for Kate?
你認為我應該等凱特等多久？

3 間接疑問句（Indirect Questions）

對疑問句做間接引述時，間接疑問句中的助動詞（are, have 等）不放在主詞前面，不要加助動詞 do/does/did，也不用問號，即在間接引述的疑問句中，疑問詞後面要用陳述句的語序（疑問詞 + 主詞 + 述語動詞）。

✗ Please let me know when are you going on vacation to your Haitian plantation?
✓ Please let me know when you are going on vacation to your Haitian plantation. 請告訴我你什麼時候要去你在海地的大農場度假。
→ 間接疑問句不要用問號，而且要用陳述句的語序：疑問詞（when）+ 主詞（you）+ 助動詞（are）+ 主要動詞（going）。

✗ How did Fanny solve that problem with the new engine is our company's secret?
✓ How Fanny solved that problem with the new engine is our company's secret.
芬妮如何用新引擎解決了那個問題是我們公司的祕密。
→ 間接疑問句：這裡不是一個疑問句，而是一個陳述句。疑問詞 How 引導一個名詞子句作句子的主詞，子句不用疑問句語序，不需要用助動詞（did/do/does）。

✗ Dr. Harris wanted to know <u>where</u> were the mayor and her family staying in Paris?

✓ Dr. Harris wanted to know <u>where</u> the mayor and her family were staying in Paris. 哈瑞斯博士想知道市長和她家人暫住在巴黎的什麼地方。

ㄴ 間接疑問句：疑問詞 where 引導的名詞子句作 wanted to know 的受詞，子句要用陳述句的語序（主詞 + 述語動詞），不把助動詞 were 置於主詞前。

- **Principal Jerome Day asked the students <u>what</u> they were reading for fun at home.** 傑羅姆．戴校長問學生，他們在家都看什麼書消遣。

» 參見 649 頁〈Unit 13 直接引語與間接引語〉和 359 頁〈Part 6 從屬連接詞或關係代名詞引導名詞子句〉。

4 否定疑問句（Negative Questions）

1 否定疑問句的形式

a 否定疑問句有縮寫與非縮寫（非常正式）兩種構成方式：

縮寫　在主詞前面的助動詞字尾加上 -n't（助動詞 + -n't + 主詞），例如：isn't he、aren't we 等。**縮寫形式更常用**。

非縮寫　在主詞後面加上 not，例如：are you not、is it not 等。

- **Del, aren't you feeling well?**
  = Del, are you not feeling well? 戴爾，你不舒服嗎？

b 如果疑問詞是主詞，句型為「主詞 + 助動詞 + -n't」或「主詞 + 助動詞 + not」。由疑問詞引導的否定疑問句是特殊否定疑問句。

- **Who wouldn't like to be healthy and wealthy?**
  = Who would not like to be healthy and wealthy?
  誰不想又健康又富有？

c 否定疑問句也可以用 never、no、nobody、nothing、nowhere 等否定詞，來取代 not 或 -n't。

- **Why do you never text message me?** 為什麼你從沒給我發過手機簡訊？

2 否定疑問句的用法

a 否定疑問句可用來確認某事的真實性。

- **Dennis, isn't this your cellphone that you were looking for?**
  丹尼斯，這不是你剛才在找的手機嗎？
- **Didn't Daisy get a scholarship from Saint Leo University?**
  黛絲不是獲得了聖利奧大學的獎學金嗎？

b 否定疑問句可用來提出建議、勸說、批評，或表示驚訝。

- **Why don't we go for a swim in Lake Kim?**
  = **Why not go for a swim in Lake Kim?** 我們何不去金姆湖游泳呢？
  ↳ 可以用「Why not + 原形動詞」或「Why don't/doesn't + 主詞 + 原形動詞」提出建議。
- **Can't you keep quiet while your teacher is teaching?**
  老師在上課時，你就不能保持安靜嗎？
  ↳ 提出批評。
- **Why didn't you tell me the truth?** 你為什麼不跟我說真話？
  ↳ 「Why didn't + 主詞 + 原形動詞」不用於提出建議，但可以用來提出批評。
- **Didn't she know who I was?** 她不知道我是誰嗎？
  ↳ 表示驚訝。

c 如何回答否定疑問句？

- **"Don't you want to go out for dinner tonight?"**「你今晚不想出去吃嗎？」
  → **"Yes, I do."**「（不，）我想啊。」 → 願意
  → **"No, I don't."**「（是的，）我不想。」 → 不願意

d 否定疑問句可用作感嘆句。

- **Kay, isn't it a beautiful day!** 凱，今天天氣真好啊！
- **Doesn't little Mabel look adorable!** 小美博真可愛啊！

» 參見 686 頁〈4 否定疑問句形式的感嘆句〉。

附加問句

附加問句是位於句尾的簡短問句，常見於口語中**確認事情的真實性**或**請求同意**，回答用 yes 或 no。附加問句在英式英語中比在美式英語中更常見。

1 附加問句的形式

1. 附加問句由**助動詞**（have、be、do、can 等）和**代名詞**（I、you、he 等）構成。
2. 如果句子裡的動詞是 be 動詞或助動詞，附加問句中就用該動詞。
3. 如果句子裡沒有助動詞，附加問句裡就要用助動詞 do/does/did。
4. **肯定句**後面用**否定附加問句**，**否定句**後面用**肯定附加問句**。**疑問句**後面不要用附加問句。
   - 肯定句 + 否定附加問句
   - 否定句 + 肯定附加問句
5. 否定附加問句通常要用**縮寫**形式（isn't it, aren't you）。

肯定句 + 否定附加問句	否定句 + 肯定附加問句
Andrew, you like sugar and milk in your tea, don't you? 安德魯，你喜歡茶裡加糖和牛奶，對不對？ ㄴ 附加問句的主格代名詞（you）要與前面陳述句的主詞（you）一致；附加問句的時態也要與前面陳述句的時態一致。	**Sue, you don't like sugar and milk in your tea, do you?** 蘇，你不喜歡茶裡加糖和牛奶，對嗎？
Sue, you spoke to the boss about the problem, didn't you? 蘇，你跟老闆說了那個問題，對不對？	**Andrew, you did not speak to the boss about the problem, did you?** 安德魯，你沒有跟老闆說那個問題，對嗎？

肯定句 + 否定附加問句	否定句 + 肯定附加問句
Dee can speak English and Spanish, can't she? 蒂會講英語和西班牙語，對不對？	Sally can't speak English and Spanish, can she? 莎莉不會講英語和西班牙語，對嗎？
Sue, you're a kung fu expert, aren't you? 蘇，你是一名武術專家，是不是？	Andrew, you aren't a kung fu expert, are you? 安德魯，你不是一名武術專家，對嗎？
Claire, there's something wrong, isn't there? 克萊兒，出了一點問題，是不是？ ↳ 陳述句是 there be 句型時，附加疑問句要用「be 動詞 + there」。	Blare, there isn't anything wrong, is there? 布雷爾，沒有出什麼問題，對嗎？
Bing and Kay should quit drinking, shouldn't they? 賓和凱應該戒酒，對不對？	Ben and Ray shouldn't start smoking again, should they? 班和雷不應該又開始抽菸，對嗎？
Jane is happy today, isn't she? 珍今天很開心，不是嗎？ Mom is unhappy today, isn't she? 媽媽今天不開心，對吧？ ↳ 帶有反義前綴的形容詞（如：unhappy, unacceptable, disappointed, discouraged），不是否定詞，而只是原詞的反義詞，所以含有這些字的句子如果沒有否定詞（not、never 等），仍然是肯定句，附加疑問句要用否定形式。	Mike is not happy today, is he? 邁克今天不開心，對嗎？ Lee has nowhere to go, does he? 李沒有地方可以去，對嗎？ ↳ 含有nowhere的句子是否定陳述句，因為 nowhere 是否定詞，其後的附加疑問句要用肯定附加疑問句。 » 參見 679 頁第 8 條。

6 I am 的否定附加問句是「aren't I?」。這種用法主要是英式英語。

✗ I'm still a member of the Mumbai Literary Club, am not I?

✓ I'm still a member of the Mumbai Literary Club, aren't I?

我還是孟買文學俱樂部的成員，是不是？

↳ 否定附加疑問句。

- I'm no longer a member of the Mumbai Literary Club, am I?

我不再是孟買文學俱樂部的成員了，對嗎？

↳ 肯定附加疑問句。

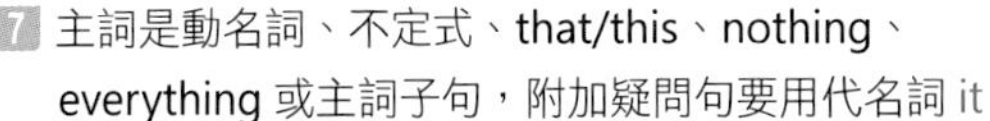

7 主詞是動名詞、不定式、that/this、nothing、everything 或主詞子句，附加疑問句要用代名詞 it。

- Shoveling snow is good exercise, isn't it?
  鏟雪是一種很好的運動，是不是？
- Nothing is as important as your own health, is it?
  沒有什麼比你自己的健康更重要，對嗎？

8 陳述句含有 never、hardly、seldom、scarcely、nowhere、nobody 等表否定意義的字時，屬於否定陳述句，其後的附加疑問句要用肯定附加疑問句。

- Sue has never been to Honolulu, has she?
  蘇從未去過檀香山，對嗎？
  ↳ 否定陳述句 + 肯定附加疑問句（has she）
- There was hardly enough meat for everyone at last night's party, was there? 昨晚聚會的肉幾乎不夠大家吃，對嗎？
  ↳ 陳述句裡含有否定意義的副詞 hardly，其後要用肯定附加疑問句。

9 當陳述句是**並列句**時，附加疑問句的主詞和述語動詞在人稱和數上應**與緊鄰的獨立子句一致**。

- I know Coco Wu is a great pilot, but she crashed two helicopters during her initial flight training in Mexico, didn't she?
  我知道可可．吳是一位了不起的飛行員，不過她在墨西哥進行最初飛行訓練時墜毀了兩架直升飛機，對不對？
  ↳ 這是由 but 連接的並列複合句；第一個獨立子句是由主句和一個受詞子句構成；第二個獨立子句的主詞是 she，述語動詞是簡單過去式（crashed），附加疑問句的主詞也應該是 she，時態也應該是簡單過去式（助動詞 didn't + 主詞）。

10 當陳述句是**複合句**時，附加疑問句的主詞和述語在人稱和數上通常要**與主句保持一致**。

- You think Coco Wu is a great pilot, don't you?
  你認為可可．吳是一位了不起的飛行員，對不對？
  ↳ 這是一個複合句（主句 + 受詞子句），主句主詞是 You，述語動詞是簡單現在式（think），附加疑問句的主詞也應該是 you，時態也應該是簡單現在式。

比較

a「I/We + think/suppose/expect/believe/imagine/guess 等 + 受詞子句」，其附加疑問句要**與子句的主詞和述語動詞一致**。

- I think Coco Wu is a great pilot, isn't she?
  我認為可可·吳是一位了不起的飛行員，對不對？
  ↥ 受詞子句的主詞是 Coco，述語動詞是簡單現在式（is），附加疑問句的主詞要用代名詞 she，動詞也用簡單現在式（isn't）。

b「I/We + don't/didn't + think/suppose/expect/believe/imagine/guess 等 + 受詞子句」，其附加疑問句要用肯定式。

- I don't expect Mary will tell us the truth about her boyfriend Jerry, will she?
  我認為關於她的男朋友傑瑞，瑪麗不會給我們講實情，她會嗎？
  ↥ 動詞 expect 後面的受詞子句的主詞是 Mary，述語動詞是簡單未來式（will tell），附加疑問句的主詞要用代名詞 she，動詞也用簡單未來式（will）。

- I don't think what Dwight said is right, is it?
  我認為杜威特說的話是不正確的，對嗎？
  ↥ think 動詞後的受詞子句的主詞是一個由 what 引導的主詞子句，述語動詞是簡單現在式（is），附加疑問句的主詞要用代名詞 it（陳述句的主詞是子句時，附加疑問句的代名詞要用 it），動詞也用簡單現在式（is）。

2 陳述句是否定句時，附加問句的回答

陳述句是**否定句**時，回答 yes 和 no 的英文和中文的意思剛好相反；其答語 yes 意為「不」，no 則意為「是」。

問句 Dee hasn't arrived home, has she? 蒂還沒有回家，是嗎？
↥ 否定陳述句 + 肯定附加疑問句（has she）。

答一 Yes, she has. → 表達與對方看法不一致的回答：「不，她回來了。」
答二 No, she hasn't. → 表達與對方看法一致的回答：「是的，她還沒有回來。」

3 have 的附加問句

1 動詞 have 作**行為動詞**，表「做某事」時（例如：have a look 瞧一瞧），附加問句要用助動詞 do/does/did。

2 當動詞 have 作**狀態動詞**，表「擁有」時，附加問句可用 do，也可用 have。

- **Aunt Nancy has a nap every afternoon, doesn't she?**
  南茜姑姑每天下午都要睡午覺，是不是？
  ↳ 這句的 has 是行為動詞。

- **Aunt Dee has a new RV, doesn't she?**
  = Aunt Dee has a new RV, hasn't she?
  蒂姑姑有一輛新的露營車，是不是？
  ↳ 這句的 has 是狀態動詞。

a recreational vehicle (an RV)

4 「let's . . . 」的附加問句

1 在 let's 和 let us 後面，附加問句通常用「shall we?」。

- **Dee, let's/let us go out to eat tonight, shall we?**
  蒂，我們今晚出去吃飯，好嗎？

- **Nancy, let's/let us watch a movie tonight, shall we?**
  南茜，我們今晚看電影，好嗎？

- **Let's/Let us get up early tomorrow and see the sunrise, shall we?**
  讓我們明天早上早起床去看日出，好嗎？

2 如果意思是「you let us」時，let us 後面的附加問句也可用「will you?」。

- **Ms. Wu, please let us go back home now, will you?**
  吳老師，請讓我們現在回家吧，好嗎？
  ↳ 這種情境不用 let's，因為動詞 let 的主詞顯然是 you（即 Ms. Wu）。當主詞明顯是指對方（you let us），而受詞 us 並不包括對方時，要用 let us。在這種情境中，附加問句用「will you?」。不過，無論是英式還是美式，這種附加問句（let us . . ., will you?）在實際生活中很少見，即英美人士很少使用這種句型。

3 在考試中究竟要選擇「will you?」還是「shall we?」，這取決於句子的意思。一般在let's/let us後面都是用「shall we?」。除非像上述情況，意思是「you let us」時，才可能用「will you?」。請看下面這道選擇題：

- Let us go, ____________? ⓐ shall we ⓑ will you

上面這句話如果沒有上下文（context），就可以有兩種含意：

① Let us go. = Let's go.（我們走吧。）→ 附加疑問句要選 ⓐ shall we。
② 也可能在請求對方，表示「(You) Let us go.」（你讓我們走吧。）
→ 附加疑問句就可以選 ⓑ will you。

這道題目有歧義，答案不只有一個，設置不合理，是命題中應當避免的。

» 參見 691 頁〈8 Let 引導的祈使句〉。

5 祈使句的附加問句

祈使句也可以加上附加問句，但不具有疑問含意，只是使祈使句變得更加**客氣、委婉**。

1 表「要求、命令、告知」的肯定祈使句，附加問句用「will/won't/would/can/can't/could you?」。

2 表「客氣的請求」或「邀請」的祈使句，附加問句用「won't you?」。

3 否定祈使句後面用「will you?」。

- **Lou, open the door,** would you/will you? 陸，把門打開，好嗎？
- **Andrew, be quiet,** can't you? 安德魯，安靜點，好嗎？
- **Sue, sit down,** won't you? 蘇，請坐下，好嗎？ → 表「客氣的請求」。
- **Please come to my birthday party on Saturday night,** won't you? 請你來參加我星期六晚上的生日會好嗎？ → 表「邀請」。
- **Don't forget Sue and me,** will you? 不要忘了我和蘇，好嗎？
  ↑ 否定祈使句後面一般用「will you?」。

6 肯定句接肯定附加問句的用法

一般說來，當陳述句是肯定句時，附加問句要用否定形式；當陳述句是否定句時，附加問句要用肯定形式。不過，這條規則也有一些例外，如果附加問句並非真正要提問，而只是對前面說過的話的反應時，「肯定句 + 肯定附加問句」也是常見的。當講話者複述他剛聽到的事或剛瞭解的事之後，常加上一個**肯定語氣的附加問句**，用以**確認**或**強調**這件事，並賦予興趣、驚奇、擔心、諷刺等感情色彩。

- **You think Sue is as sweet as honey, do you?**
  你認為蘇像蜂蜜一樣甜，是嗎？
- **It was a terrific banana split, was it?** 這個香蕉聖代真的很棒，對吧？
- **So, that's the new ballet for Brigitte, is it?**
  所以說那是布麗姬要演出的新芭蕾舞囉？
- **Oh! You've made your first million dollars, have you?**
  啊！你賺了你的第一筆百萬美金，是嗎？ → 這句表示驚奇。

Diving Deep Into English 83 簡短的「回應式疑問句」

還有一種簡短的「回應式疑問句」，有以下兩種形式：

a 原句是肯定句時，要以肯定疑問句回覆。

b 原句是否定句時，就以否定疑問句回覆。

Mary: Annie has just announced her engagement.
Jerry: Has she? That's wonderful news!
瑪麗：安妮剛宣佈了她的訂婚。
傑瑞：是嗎？那真是好消息！

Dan: I can't remember my own cellphone number.
Ann: You can't? That's unbelievable! 美式
Ann: Can't you? That's unbelievable! 英式
丹：我記不得我自己的手機號碼。
安：不會吧？真令人難以相信！

感嘆句

對事實表示感嘆的句子就是感嘆句。感嘆句用來表達喜怒哀樂等強烈感情，常以驚嘆號（!）結尾。感嘆句主要有以下四種：

1. what + 名詞（主詞和動詞詞序不倒裝）
2. how + 形容詞 / 副詞 / 句子（主詞和動詞詞序不倒裝）
3. so 和 such
4. 否定疑問句形式的感嘆句

1 what + 名詞（主詞和動詞詞序不倒裝）

1 what + a/an（+ 形容詞）+ 單數可數名詞 +（主詞 + 動詞）

- What a fool I was to believe his lies about loving me!
  我真是個大傻瓜，居然相信他愛我的謊言。
  ↳ What 感嘆句中主詞和動詞結構不倒裝（I + was）。
  ↳ 注意 單數可數名詞前面一定要加不定冠詞 a 或 an。
- What a pretty skirt! 好漂亮的裙子啊！
  ↳ What 引導的感嘆句，有時主詞和述語動詞可省略。這裡省略主詞和連綴動詞（it is）。
- What a great day to play! 這真是一個適合玩耍的好天氣啊！
  ↳ What 引導的感嘆句，還可以接不定式結構。

2 what（+ 形容詞）+ 不可數名詞或複數名詞 +（主詞 + 動詞）

✗ What a beautiful weather it is!
✓ What beautiful weather it is! 天氣真好啊！
  ↳ weather 是不可數名詞，不能與不定冠詞 a 搭配。

- What great news! 這真是好消息啊！

- While stuck in a slow moving stream of cars, Lisa tiredly said, "What heavy traffic!" 麗莎被困在緩慢前行的車流中，疲倦地說：「路上好塞啊！」

比較下列兩種用法：

- What a crazy bunch of fools! 真是一群瘋狂的傻瓜！
  ↳ 這句用了複數名詞，但搭配不定冠詞 a，因為 a bunch of 是固定片語，a 修飾 bunch，而非修飾複數名詞 fools。
- What crazy fools! 真是一些瘋狂的傻瓜！
  ↳ What + 形容詞 + 複數名詞

3 what + 受詞 + 主詞 + 動詞（注意詞序）

- **What a sweet smile that little girl May has today!**
  那個小女孩梅今天笑得好甜啊！
  ↳ a sweet smile 是動詞 has 的受詞，句型為：「What + 受詞（a sweet smile）+ 主詞（that little girl May）+ 動詞（has）」。
- **What a bad attitude Jerry has toward Mary!** 傑瑞對瑪麗的態度真差！
  ↳ 主詞應該在動詞之前。

2 how + 形容詞 / 副詞 / 句子（主詞和動詞詞序不倒裝）

1 how + 形容詞或副詞（+ 主詞 + 動詞）（注意詞序）

✗ How Ann Blues runs fast without her shoes!
✓ How fast Ann Blues runs without her shoes!
安·布魯士光著腳跑得還真快啊！
↳ How + 副詞（fast）+ 主詞（Ann Blues）+ 動詞（runs）

✗ Liz shivered and complained, "How cold is it!"
✓ Liz shivered and complained, "How cold it is!"
莉茲顫抖著抱怨：「好冷啊！」 →How + 形容詞（cold）+ 主詞（it）+ 連綴動詞（is）

- **Ann said, "Oh, how cool!" Then she shared her ice-cream cone with Dan.** 安說：「啊，太酷了！」然後就把她的蛋捲冰淇淋分給丹吃。
  ↳ how + 形容詞（主詞和動詞被省略）

2 how + 句子（= how + 主詞 + 動詞）

✕ Joan, how have you grown!

✓ Joan, how you've grown! 喬恩，你長得真快！

- How I want to visit Mars and then tour a thousand stars!
  我好想參觀火星，然後再周遊上千顆的星星啊！

3 so 和 such

1 so + 形容詞／副詞

- Art is so smart! 亞特真聰明！ → so + 形容詞

- Last night Lily danced so gracefully!
  昨晚莉莉的舞跳得太美了！
  ↑ so + 副詞

2 such a/an（+ 形容詞）+ 單數可數名詞
such（+ 形容詞）+ 不可數名詞／複數名詞

✕ Wendy is a such strong lady!

✓ Wendy is such a strong lady! 溫蒂真是一位強壯的女子！
↑ such + a + 形容詞（strong）+ 單數可數名詞（lady）

- You talk such nonsense! 你真是胡說八道！ → such + 不可數名詞

- Mary and Jerry are such funny people. 瑪麗和傑瑞真是很滑稽的人。
  ↑ such + 複數名詞

4 否定疑問句形式的感嘆句

形式是疑問句（主詞和動詞詞序要倒裝），但實際上是感嘆句，句尾用感嘆號。

- Isn't it surprising news! 這真是驚人的消息啊！

- Hasn't your lovely daughter grown! 你可愛的女兒長得真快啊！

- Wasn't she naughty! 她真是調皮啊！

» 參見 684 頁〈Part 4 感嘆句〉和 675 頁〈4 否定疑問句〉。

祈使語氣

1 祈使語氣用來提供建議、勸告、命令、指示、鼓勵或祝賀。

2 祈使句動詞要用**原形動詞**（即**不帶 to 的不定式**）。

3 祈使句的詞序與陳述句一樣，通常以句號（.）結尾。但如果是強烈命令，可用驚嘆號（!）結尾，像這種情況的命令句既是祈使句，也是感嘆句。

1 祈使句省略主詞 you

祈使句中省略了主詞。事實上，所有祈使句的主詞都是第二人稱代名詞 you（作單數或複數依上下文決定），只是習慣將它省略。

- **(You) Sit down next to Andrew, please.**
  請（你）坐在安德魯旁邊。
- **(You) Go get some cheddar cheese, please.**
  請（你）去買一些巧達起司。
  ↥ go get 是慣用語。

- **(You) Be silent, please. = (You) Please be silent.**
  請不要說話。
  ↥ 祈使句加上 please 會更禮貌。please 可以放在句首，也可以放在句尾；放在句尾時，前面要用逗號與句子分開。

2 點出主詞的祈使句

1. 通常祈使句沒有明確的主詞，如果希望清楚地表明在對誰說話（即祈使句的主詞），可在祈使句前或後面加一個名詞或代名詞來點出主詞，但實際主詞依然是 you。

- Joe, (You) go look for Brook.
  = Go look for Brook, Joe. 喬，去找布魯克。
  ⮤ go look for Brook = go to look for Brook: 口語中常省略 to。

- Mom yelled, "Somebody answer the phone!"
  媽媽叫喊：「誰去接個電話啊！」

- "Nobody move," Roy's mom told all the boys.
  羅伊的媽媽告訴所有的男孩：「誰都不准動。」
  ⮤ Nobody move. = All of you, don't move.

- Everybody, please relax, and I'll see what I can do.
  = All of you, please relax, and I'll see what I can do.
  大家請放輕鬆，我來想想怎麼辦。
  ⮤ 上面三個例句的主詞雖然都是單數第三人稱（Somebody, Nobody, Everybody），但因為這三個句子都是祈使句，所以述語動詞用原形。

2 可以在祈使句前面點出主詞 you（你），表達強烈的勸告或氣憤。

- "You shut up!" Jill screamed at Sue.
  潔兒對蘇大吼：「你閉嘴！」

- You get out of my house! 你滾出我家！

- Sheriff Jill Root ordered the bank robber, "You don't move, or I will shoot!"
  潔兒·茹特警長命令銀行搶劫犯：「你不准動，否則我要開槍了！」

3 肯定祈使句（Affirmative Imperatives）

1 肯定祈使句用原形動詞（即不帶 to 的不定式）。

- Have some green tea. 喝點綠茶吧。
  ⮤ 用原形動詞「have」開頭。

- Get your homework done before you watch TV tonight, please.
  = Please get your homework done before you watch TV tonight.
  今晚做完功課才能看電視。

- Joy told the Asian tourists who came to Iceland, "Enjoy your vacation in our small nation!"
  喬伊告訴來到冰島的亞洲遊客：「在我們這個小國家盡情享受你們的假期吧！」
- Always remember to keep on smiling and not to get grumpy when your path in life gets bumpy.
  永遠要記住，當你人生的道路變得坎坷時，要保持微笑，不要暴躁。
  ↥ 祈使句裡的 always 要置於動詞之前。
- I fear my daughter Ming won't graduate from college, so I often tell her, "Get rolling, won't you?"
  我擔心我的女兒敏大學不能畢業，所以我常對她說：
  「開始用功吧，好嗎？」
  ↥ 祈使句後面可用附加疑問句，以加強語氣。

4 否定祈使句（Negative Imperatives）

否定祈使句以 do not、don't 或 never 開頭。

- Do not do that again! = Don't do that again! 不要再做那種事了！
- Please don't smoke here.
  = Don't smoke here, please. 請不要在這裡抽菸。
  ↥ 否定祈使句也可用 please。

- Never speak to Glen like that again!
  不要再那樣對葛倫講話！
  ↥ 祈使句裡的 never 要置於動詞之前。
- Lily, don't be silly! = Don't be silly, Lily. 莉莉，別傻了！
  ↥ 否定祈使句也可以在句首或句尾加名詞或代名詞，點明主詞，加以強調。
- Don't join the book burners. Don't think you're going to conceal faults by concealing evidence that they ever existed.
  (President Dwight David Eisenhower)
  不要與焚書者為伍。不要以為隱滅催毀的證據，你就可以隱瞞罪過。
  ↥ 第一個祈使句用了縮寫形式 Don't，第二個祈使句也要用縮寫形式，保持風格一致。

5 強調祈使句（Emphatic Imperatives）

強調祈使句用以表達客氣的請求、抱怨、道歉等，句型為「**do + 原形動詞**」，表示「務必要……」。

- Do be **quiet, Sue.** 蘇，請務必保持安靜。
- Do forgive **Andrew. He didn't mean to hurt you.**
  請一定要原諒安德魯，他不是故意要傷害你的。
- **Trish,** do work **hard at your English!** 翠西，請一定要努力學習英語！

6 被動祈使句（Passive Imperatives）

被動祈使句表示「要某人安排，使某事得以完成」，句型為：「**get + 受詞 + 過去分詞**」。

- Get **your hair** cut **before you go for your job interview.**
  在你去做求職面談之前，先去剪頭髮。
- Get **your car** fixed **before you leave for Michigan.**
  去密西根之前，先找人修好你的車。

7 和 and 或 or 連用的祈使句

祈使句後面如果接 and 或 or 引導的並列子句，則此祈使句的意思相當於 if 引導的條件句。

- 祈使句 + or 子句 → 如果不做某事就會……（表示否定條件）
- 祈使句 + and 子句 → 如果做某事就會……（表示肯定條件）

- **Steve, shut up** or **I'll ask you to leave.** 史蒂夫，閉嘴，否則我就要請你離開。
  ↳ 肯定祈使句用在 or 前時，表示否定條件。
  = **Steve, if you** don't shut up, **I'll ask you to leave.**
  史蒂夫，如果你不閉嘴，我就要請你離開。
  ↳ 注意 日常生活中不要常用 shut up，因為這個片語語氣很強，是不禮貌的。

・Please give me one more week, and I'll get my science project done.
請再給我一星期的時間，我就會完成我的科學研究。
↳ 肯定祈使句用在 and 前時，表示肯定條件。

= If you give me one more week, I'll get my science project done.
如果你再給我一星期的時間，我就會完成我的科學研究。

8 Let 引導的祈使句

let 用在祈使句中表達命令、要求、提議。

1 let's/let us 和 let me（第一人稱）

a let us = let's

用第一人稱「let's/let us + 不帶 to 的不定式（即原形動詞）」句型，來為包括講話者自己的一組人提出建議或下達命令。let's 是 let us 的縮寫，通常意思沒有區別，可以互相替換。縮寫形式 let's 在口語中用得比較多一些。

・Let's watch TV tonight with Dee and Dwight.
我們今晚跟蒂和杜威特一起看電視吧。
↳ Let's = Let us。let's 後面要接原形動詞，不能接帶 to 的不定式。

・Let's face it—Henry is not an honest guy.
讓我們面對事實吧，亨利不是一個誠實的傢伙。
↳ Let's = Let us。us 包括講話者（speaker）和聽者（listener/listeners）。

・Let's get started, shall we?
我們開始吧，好嗎？
↳ Let's/Let us 的附加問句是「shall we?」。

・Let us tenderly and kindly cherish, therefore, the means of knowledge. Let us dare to read, think, speak, and write.
(President John Adams)
讓我們溫和而仁慈地珍愛獲取知識的方式。讓我們敢於閱讀、思考、講話和寫作。
↳ 第一個句子用了「Let us tenderly and kindly cherish . . .」，第二個句子就不要用口語形式 let's，保持風格一致。

b Let us ≠ Let's

在有些情況下 let's 和 let us 不能相互替換。如果句中含有第二人稱（you），或者 let 的主詞實際上是第二人稱（you），那麼，let us 中的 us 就只包括說話者的群體（the speaker's group），不包括對方（the listener/the listeners）。這種情境就不用 let's。

- **Fanny and I decided to make an offer to Jane. Fanny said to Jane, "Let us take you on a trip to Spain."** 芬妮和我決定為珍提供一個機會。芬妮對珍說：「讓我們帶著你去西班牙旅行吧。」
  ↳ 句中含有第二人稱（you），這句 us 只包括 Fanny and I，不包括聽者 you（Jane）。

- **Ann and her brother Dan wanted to go to Japan. Ann asked, "Mom, please let us fly to Japan to visit Aunt Nan."**
  安和她的哥哥丹想去日本。安問：「媽媽，請讓我們飛到日本去探望南阿姨。」
  ↳ 這句從上下文可以看出實際主詞是 you（Mom, you let us）。

c「let me + 不帶 to 的不定式」這種句型用來給自己提出指示，意思是「准許我做某事」（allow me to do something）。

- **Let me help you and Sue.** 讓我來幫助你和蘇。

- **Let me see. Did I finish drinking my milk tea?**
  讓我想想，我把奶茶喝完了嗎？
  ↳ 片語 let me see 和 let me think 用得很普遍，表示需要一小段時間來思考某事。

d 在 let's/let us 和 let me 兩種句型中，受格 us/me 是動詞 let 的受詞，同時又是不定式動詞的主詞，即動作執行者。

- **Let's get things done as soon as possible.** 讓我們盡快把事情做完吧。
  ↳ Let's = Let us。
  ↳ us 是動詞 Let 的受詞，也是動詞片語 get things done 的主詞（行為者）。

e let 後接第一人稱代名詞的否定祈使句為 let us not 或 do not let us，口語可簡化為 let's not 或 don't let us。最常用的是 let us not 和 let's not。（do not/don't let us 有可能表達隱含的主詞實際上是第二人稱 you，us 只包括說話者的群體，不包括對方。參見 p.694 的 Note。）

正式
- let us not + 原形動詞
- do not let us + 原形動詞

口語
- let's not + 原形動詞
- don't let us + 原形動詞

- Do not let us/Let us not forget those who have helped us. → 正式
  = Don't let us/Let's not forget those who have helped us. → 口語
  讓我們不要忘記那些幫助過我們的人。

- Let us not say anything to her about it.
  我們不要跟她講這件事。

- Let's not go skiing in this snowstorm.
  我們不要在這場暴風雪裡滑雪。

go skiing

- Let's not invite that playboy Jim to our party.
  我們不要邀請吉姆那個花花公子來參加我們的聚會。

- Let us never negotiate out of fear. But let us never fear to negotiate. (President John Fitzgerald Kennedy)
  讓我們決不要因害怕而談判，但是也讓我們決不要害怕談判。
  ↑ let us never = let us not

2 let 後接第三人稱名詞（或代名詞）的用法

a let 可以跟第三人稱名詞或代名詞搭配，表達提議、請求、要求，或表示警告或威脅。

- "Please let Jerry stay with us for a week," pleaded Mary.
  瑪麗請求說：「拜託讓傑瑞在我們家住一個禮拜嘛。」

- Please let Kim finish her math homework on her own.
  請讓金姆獨立完成她的數學作業。

- "Let the terrorists, wherever they may be, understand that we will not hesitate to defend our world civilization," declared Jill Nation.
  潔兒·納欣宣稱：「無論恐怖分子在哪裡，我們都要讓他們明白，我們會毫不猶豫地捍衛我們的世界文明。」

b let 後接第三人稱的否定祈使句，用 do not let 或 don't let。

- Because Gus was worried about his toys, he requested, "Mom, don't let/do not let May stay with us."
  加斯擔心他的玩具，因此他請求說：「媽媽，不要讓梅住在我們家。」

- My sister Lynne warned me, "Don't let that dog come in."
  = My sister Lynne warned me, "Don't let that dog in."
  我姊姊琳警告我說：「不要讓狗進來。」
  ↳ Don't let 後面也可以接受詞和副詞 in；片語 (don't) let somebody or something in 意思是「（不要）允許（讓）某人或某物進來」。

第一人稱的否定式：
- do not let us/don't let us
- let us not/let's not

第三人稱的否定式：
- do not let/don't let

- "Let us not/Let's not/Do not let us/Don't let us stay here for very long," Kay whispered to Mary.
  凱對瑪麗耳語：「我們不要在這裡待久了。」

- "Do not let us fail in helping that whale," prayed Lulu.
  「不要讓我們的救鯨行動失敗了。」露露祈禱著。
  ↳ 這句話隱含了一個主詞（有可能是 God）。
  ↳ 如果否定祈使句隱含的主詞不屬於句子中 us 所指的一部分，那麼最好用 Do not let us/Don't let us。

- Do not let/Don't let her go out alone. 別讓她獨自出門。
  ↳ 第三人稱否定式。

假設語氣

假設語氣是動詞的一種形式，不是用來陳述一件事實，而是用來表達**願望**、**假設**、**猜測**、**可能性**等。假設語氣用在子句裡有幾種作用：

1. 用來表達**願望**（wish, if only）。
2. if 引導的條件副詞子句，用來表達**與事實相反**的條件（即條件並不存在）。
3. as if 或 as though 引導的方式副詞子句，用來描述**與事實相反的推測**。
4. that 引導的子句，用來表達命令、要求、請求、建議。

1 wish（未能實現的願望）

1 與現在事實不符：wish + 過去式（were/did/could）

a「**wish + 過去式**」用來表達願望與嚮往，而不是表達事實。過去式在這裡並不指過去時間，而是表示「現在不可能發生的事」，是「和現在事實相反的事」，希望現在情況有所改變。

b 用來表示與現在或將來的事實相反的假設語氣中，be 動詞不分人稱和單複數，一律用 were。

» 參見 708 頁〈Diving Deep Into English 85〉。

✗ I wish I am in love again.

✗ I wish I was in love again.

✓ I wish I were in love again. 但願我又談戀愛了。

↳ 與現實不同：子句裡的 were 是假設語氣，意味著「我沒有在談戀愛」。

- Lisa wishes she were married to a robot.
  麗莎希望自己嫁給一個機器人。
  ↳ 現實：Lisa is not married to a robot.

- **Tom wishes he had a sports car.** 湯姆希望擁有一輛跑車。
  ↳ 現實：Tom doesn't have a sports car.
- **I wish Liz could be here right now.** 但願莉茲現在就在這裡。
  ↳ 現實：Liz cannot be here right now.

2 希望未來情況有所改變：wish + could/would + 原形動詞

這個句型用來表達與未來事實相反的事，或表達講話者對目前狀況不滿意，希望未來有所改變。

- **I wish Dee wouldn't keep on interrupting me.**
  但願蒂不要老是打斷我的話。
  ↳ 「wish . . . wouldn't」可以用來抱怨某種情況重複發生。
  ↳ 在 wish 句子裡，主句主詞（I）和子句主詞（Dee）不相同時，常用 would 表達「希望他人改變行為」，尤其當 wish 後面的受詞子句是否定句時。
- **I wish you would stop staring at your computer while I am talking to you.** 我希望當我在跟你講話時，你的眼睛不要盯著你的電腦看。
  ↳ 希望他人改變行為。
- **Sam wishes he could come with us to Rome next week, but he has to stay here and work.**
  山姆但願他下星期可以跟我們一起去羅馬，不過他得留下來工作。
  ↳ 在 wish 句子裡，主句主詞和子句主詞相同時（也就是說希望自己能改變行為），要用 could，不用 would。
- **I wish I could get Louise to quit smoking before she gets a deadly disease.**
  我希望我可以在露易絲得到絕症之前就能夠讓她戒菸。
  ↳ 希望自己能改變未來的狀況。

3 與過去事實相反：wish + 過去完成式（had done）

對自己過去做過或沒做過的事感到後悔或失望，就用「wish + 過去完成式」來表示與過去事實相反的假設語氣。

- **I wish Kay were here now.** 我真希望凱此刻在這裡。
  ↳ 與現在的事實相反。

- I wish Kay had been here yesterday. 我真希望凱昨天在這裡。
  ↳ 與過去的事實相反。

✗ I wish I never told her mother about my brother.
✓ I wish I had never told her mother about my brother.
真希望我沒有跟她媽媽講過我哥哥的事。
↳ had never told 是假設語氣，表示與過去事實相反，意味「我已經說出了這件事」。

- I wish Ruth had told me the truth about my dad.
  要是露絲實話告訴了我有關我爸爸的事，那就好了。
  ↳ 過去事實：Ruth did not tell me the truth about my dad.

- I wish I could have explained that physics problem, but I really didn't understand it myself.
  我希望我當時能解釋那道物理題，但我自己都不懂。
  ↳ 過去事實：I wasn't able to explain that physics problem.

2 if only（與事實相反的願望）

1 if only + 過去式（were/did）：與現在事實相反的願望。

a if only 用來表達我們希望情況有所變化，意思是「要是……就好了」。
b if only 子句可以獨立存在。
c 當 if only 與過去式連用時，表示「現在不可能發生的事」或「與現在事實相反的願望」。過去式在這裡並不意味著過去時間。

✗ If only I am as beautiful as Lily!
✓ If only I were as beautiful as Lily!
如果我像莉莉那樣美就好了！
↳ 與現在事實相反：可惜我不像莉莉那麼美麗。

- If only Jim knew how much I love him.
  如果吉姆知道我有多愛他就好了。
  ↳ 與現在事實相反：可惜吉姆不知道。

2 If only + 過去式（would/could）：與未來事實相反的願望。

- If only Joe would go with me to Norway tomorrow.
  如果喬明天能跟我一起去挪威就好了。
  ꜔ 未來不可能實現的事：Joe will not go with me to Norway tomorrow.
- If only I could go back in time. 如果我能讓時光倒轉就好了。
  ꜔ 未來不可能實現的事：I will not be able to go back in time.
  ꜔ 希望自己能改變未來的事，if only 後面要用 could。

3 If only + 過去完成式（had done）：與過去事實相反的願望。

- If only Glen had called me then.
  如果葛倫那時給我打了電話就好了。
  ꜔ 事實上葛倫那時沒有打電話。
- If only Margo had gone with you to Chicago.
  如果瑪歌跟你一起去了芝加哥就好了。
  ꜔ 事實上瑪歌沒有去芝加哥。
- If only my son could have graduated from college.
  如果我兒子大學畢業就好了。
  ꜔ 過去事實：My son wasn't able to graduate from college.

Diving Deep Into English 84 wish/if only + 無生命的主詞 + would

❶「wish/if only + 無生命的主詞 + would + 原形動詞」：這個句型可以用來對無生命的東西賦予擬人化的描述。

- I wish the snowstorm would stop so that I could go to visit Trish.
  但願這場暴風雪能停下來，這樣我就可以去探望翠西。
  ꜔ 所渴望的變化是有可能的。
- If only the sun would rise soon.
  如果太陽馬上出來就好了。
  ꜔ 未來不可能實現的事：The sun won't rise soon.

❷「wish/if only + 無生命的主詞 + would」結構，不用來表示主詞無法控制的變化或無法改變的過去事實。

✕ I wish electric cars wouldn't be so expensive.

✔ I wish electric cars weren't so expensive.

真希望電動車沒有那麼貴。

↳ 汽車不能控制自身的價格。因此，不能用「wish/if only + 無生命的主詞 + would + 原形動詞」結構。

✕ If only the sun would have been out, our hike would have been more fun.

✔ If only the sun had been out, our hike would have been more fun. 如果當時有太陽就好了，我們的徒步旅行就會更快樂一些。

↳ 過去的事實已經無法改變。因此，不能用「wish/if only + 無生命的主詞 + would have + 過去分詞」結構。

3 if（與事實相反的假設）

1 與現在或未來事實相反的假設

If + 子句主詞 + 過去式 + 主句主詞 + would/might/could/should + 原形動詞

條件子句 主句

a 用 if 表示與現在或未來事實相反，且不真實或不可能發生的事情時，if 子句用動詞過去式，主句用「would/might/could/should + 原形動詞」。這裡的過去式並不指過去時間，而是意味著不真實的、不可能的假設語氣。

b if 子句裡的 be 動詞不分人稱和單複數，一律用 were。

- I was in her position two years ago. 兩年前我就處在她的職位上。
  ↳ 陳述語氣。
- If I were in her position, I would do the same thing.
  假如我處在她的職位上，我會做同樣的事。
  ↳ 假設語氣（與現在事實相反的假設）。
  ↳ were 用在 if 子句裡（不能用 am 或 was），would + do（原形動詞）用在主句裡。

- If I went to Mars, I would take lots of candy bars and sell them to visiting movie stars.
  如果我去火星，我會帶上很多糖果棒，然後賣給來訪的電影明星。
  ↑ 我可能沒希望去火星。（與未來事實相反的假設）

- Scot Link could save a lot of money if he did not smoke or drink.
  如果史考特·林克不抽菸、不喝酒，他就可以存很多錢。
  ↑ 可是他又抽菸又喝酒。（與現在事實相反的假設）
  ↑ if 子句也可以放在主句後面。

- If I were you, I would travel around the world with Sue.
  如果我是你，我就會跟蘇一起環遊世界。
  ↑ 我永遠不可能變成你，「if I were you」是典型的假設句型，用以為他人提供建議。

- If I were Pete, I would marry sweet and petite Mary in a heartbeat.
  如果我是彼特，我就會毫不猶豫地娶可愛嬌小的瑪麗。
  ↑ 我永遠不可能變成 Pete。

Teacher What would you do if a violent ET were attacking the Earth?
Student A I would call Superman for help. He is a good ET.
Student B I would ask all the nations on Earth to cooperate in fighting the ET.

Teacher 假如一個凶暴的外星人要襲擊地球，你該怎麼辦？
Student A 我會打電話向超人求救。超人是一個好的外星人。
Student B 我會要求地球上的所有國家齊心合力來對抗外星人。

ET = extraterrestrial

2 與過去事實相反的假設

If + 子句主詞 + 過去完成式	+	主句主詞 + might/could/should/would have + 過去分詞
條件子句		主句

用 if 表達非真實的過去事件（過去沒有發生的事情）時，if 子句要用過去完成式，在主句用「might/could/should/would have + 過去分詞」。

✕ If Coco was/were my friend a year ago, I would introduce her to my brother Joe.

✓ If Coco had been my friend a year ago, I would have introduced her to my brother Joe.

如果一年前可可是我朋友，我就會把她介紹給我哥哥喬。

↳ 但是一年前可可不是我的朋友，因此我沒有把她介紹給我的哥哥喬。

✕ If Sam would have studied harder, he would have passed the final exam.

✓ If Sam had studied harder, he would have passed the final exam.

假如山姆以前用功一點，他就可以通過期末考試。

↳ 可是山姆以前沒有用功，結果考試沒有及格。

↳ 表示假設語氣的 if 子句裡不用 would，would 用在主句裡。

- If Anna Lace had run a little faster, she could have won that race.

  如果安娜·雷斯跑快一點，她就有可能贏得那場比賽。

  ↳ 但是安娜·雷斯跑得不快，結果沒有贏得那場比賽。

- Jim would not have lost his way if he had followed my advice and taken a map of Boston with him.

  如果吉姆聽我的建議，帶波士頓地圖去，他就不會迷路了。

  ↳ 但吉姆沒聽我的建議，沒有帶波士頓地圖，所以迷路了。

3 省略 if 的倒裝假設語氣

if 條件句中有**助動詞 should、had、were** 時，可**以省略 if**，而將這些字置於句首，構成倒裝假設語氣。（如果條件句中的述語動詞是否定式時，則不能用倒裝假設語氣的結構。）

- Had I studied harder, I would have passed the exam.

  = If I had studied harder, I would have passed the exam.

  我要是更用功些，我考試就會及格了。

- Were you given a chance to be born again, would you want to be born into a different family?

= If you were given a chance to be born again, would you want to be born into a different family?
如果給你一個重新誕生的機會，你想生在不同的家庭嗎？

- Should you be chosen someday to live on the Moon, what would you miss on Earth?
= If you should be chosen someday to live on the Moon, what would you miss on Earth?
如果有一天你被選中去月球上生活，你會懷念地球上的什麼東西？

4 if 的非假設用法

如果 if 子句所表明的條件很可能是事實，那麼動詞就要用陳述語氣動詞，而不要用假設語氣動詞（假設語氣必須用於與事實相反的事）。

- If it is sunny tomorrow, we'll go to the beach with Coco.
如果明天天氣好，我們就要跟可可一起去海灘。
↿ 明天可能會是好天氣。

- If Sue can do it, I can do it too. 如果蘇做得到，我也做得到。
↿ 我有做到的可能性。

- You and Dirk may watch TV if you both have finished your homework.
如果你和德克都把家庭作業做完，就可以看電視。
↿ 可能已經做完功課了。

5 if 的非假設用法與假設用法比較

非假設	假設
If I go to France next year, I'll have to learn French or travel with my sister Lulu. 如果我明年去法國，我就非得學法語不可，不然就要跟我姐姐露露一起去。 ↿ 我明年有可能去法國。	If I had enough money next year, I would go to visit Dan in Pakistan. 假如我明年有足夠的錢，我就要去巴基斯坦找丹。 ↿ 我明年很可能沒有足夠的錢。

If Kay came yesterday, she will not come today. 如果凱昨天來過，她今天就不會來了。 ↑ 凱昨天可能來過。	If Jim had been in the office yesterday, I would have seen him. 假如吉姆昨天在辦公室，我就會看到他。 ↑ 事實上昨天吉姆不在辦公室，我也沒有看見他。

6 非假設和假設混合句

在一個句子中，可以部分為假設，部分為非假設。

- **If I had permitted my failures, or what seemed to me at the time a lack of success, to discourage me, I cannot see any way in which I would ever have made progress.** (President John Calvin Coolidge)
  當初，我要是讓失敗——起碼在當時看起來是不成功——擊潰我的信心，那我現在就不會看到自己的任何進展。
  ↑ 過去事實：I didn't permit failures or a lack of success to discourage me, so I made progress.
  ↑ if 子句用過去完成式（had + permitted），表示與過去事實相反；主句用的是陳述語氣的簡單現在式（I cannot see），陳述一件現在的事實；在主句的形容詞子句裡用「would have + 過去分詞（made）」與 if 子句配合。

7 混合時間假設語氣

當 if 子句和主句所涉及的時間不一樣時，那麼假設語氣就要使用混合句型。

↓ 與過去事實相反（I didn't stay late.）　↓ 與現在事實相反（I don't feel tired.）

If I had stayed late at the office last night, I would feel tired now.

假如我昨晚在辦公室工作到很晚，我現在就會感到很疲倦。

↓ 與過去事實相反（I didn't stay late.）

非混合句

If I had stayed late at the office last night,
I would have finished writing my report. ← 與過去事實相反（I didn't finish writing my report.）

假如我昨晚在辦公室工作到很晚，我就會寫完我的報告。

↱ 與現在事實相反
（Uncle Lee has lung cancer.）

↱ 與過去事實相反 （He did not quit smoking and drinking）

Uncle Lee would not have lung cancer had he quit smoking and drinking.

李叔叔要是有戒菸戒酒，就不會得到肺癌了。

↳ 這是一個倒裝假設句，子句的 if 被省略，助動詞 had 置於主詞 he 之前（had he quit）。

if it were not for、if it had not been for、but for（要不是……）

1 if it were not for 和 if it had not been for

a 與現在或未來事實相反的假設

If it were not for + 名詞或代名詞 + 主句主詞 + would/could + 原形動詞

條件子句 主句

- **If it were not for Dwight, Coco would not go there tonight.**
  如果不是因為杜威特，可可今晚就不會去那裡。
  ↳ 未來事實：因為有杜威特，可可今晚才會去那裡（Coco will go there tonight.）。
- **If it were not for Sue and her sisters, Andrew would not know what to do.**
  如果不是因為蘇和她的姐妹們，安德魯就不會知道該做什麼。
  ↳ 現在事實：因為有蘇和她的姐妹們，安德魯才知道該做什麼（Andrew knows what to do.）。

b 與過去事實相反的假設

If it had not been for + 名詞或代名詞 + 主句主詞 + would/could have + 過去分詞

條件子句 主句

- **If it had not been for the rescue team, I would have drowned.**
  要不是救難隊，我早就淹死了。
  ↳ 是因為有救難隊，我才沒有溺死。

- If it had not been for Pam's help, Scot Pool could not have finished high school.
  要不是因為有潘姆的幫助，史考特·普爾高中都畢不了業。
  ↖ 有潘姆的幫助，史考特已經高中畢業了。

2 but for

片語 but for 可取代「if it were not for」或「if it had not been for」，表示「與事實相反的假設」。

a 與現在或未來事實相反

But for + 名詞或代名詞 + 主句主詞 + would/could + 原形動詞
條件片語　　　主句

- But for Jennifer, I would not go to Alaska.
  要不是為了珍妮佛，我就不會去阿拉斯加州。
  ↖ 未來事實：為了珍妮佛，我會去阿拉斯加州。
- But for her female pilot friends, Jane would not know how to fly a rocket plane.
  要不是她的女飛行員朋友們，珍就不知道該如何駕駛火箭飛機。
  ↖ 現在事實：因為有女飛行員朋友們，珍才知道如何駕駛火箭飛機。

b 與過去事實相反

But for + 名詞或代名詞 + 主句主詞 + would/could have + 過去分詞
條件片語　　　主句

- But for Mary's help, Brook could not have finished writing that book. 要不是因為有瑪麗的幫助，布魯克無法完成那本書的寫作。
  ↖ 因為有瑪麗幫助，布魯克才寫完了那本書。
- But for your bubble gum, the lock on that door would have gotten us into trouble.
  要不是因為有你的泡泡糖，那個門鎖就會給我們帶來麻煩。
  ↖ 因為有你的泡泡糖，所以我們才沒有遇上麻煩。

5 what if、supposing、suppose（假如）

1 what if以及suppose/supposing引導的子句，相當於if引導的條件子句，如果與現在或未來事實相反，子句動詞要用過去式；如果與過去事實相反，子句動詞要用過去完成式。

✕ Supposing you suddenly wake up to find your house on fire, which one thing would you save as you run outside?

✓ Supposing you suddenly woke up to find your house on fire, which one thing would you save as you ran outside?

假設你突然醒來，發現你的房子起火了，當你往屋外逃時，你會救什麼東西走？

↑ 與現在事實不符：Supposing 引導的條件句（過去式）+ 主句（would + 原形動詞）。as 引導的時間副詞子句與前面的條件句一致，用過去式（ran）表示與現在事實不符。

- Suppose you had no need to eat or sleep, how would you spend all your extra time? 假設你不需要吃飯和睡覺，那你會如何度過額外的時間？

↑ 與現在事實不符：Suppose 引導的條件句（過去式）+ 主句（would + 原形動詞）。

✕ What if you are told that you are to move to Mars tomorrow? What will you do?

✓ What if you were told that you were to move to Mars tomorrow? What would you do?

假如你被告知明天就搬去火星，你該怎麼辦？

↑ 從句意上看，這句應該用假設語氣，be 動詞要用 were（與未來事實不符）。

- What if you woke up one morning to discover you had changed bodies with a kangaroo living in a zoo? 要是你有一天早上醒來，發現你的身體變成了一隻住在動物園的袋鼠，那該怎麼樣？

↑ 混合時間假設語氣：what if 子句用過去式，表未來不可能的事（不可能早上醒來發現自己變成袋鼠）；動詞 discover 後面的受詞子句用過去完成式（had changed），表示與過去事實相反（You did not change bodies with a kangaroo.）。

2 what if 以及 suppose/supposing 引導的子句與 if 引導的子句一樣，也可以用陳述語氣的動詞，表示可能發生的現在或將來情況。

- **Supposing Sue is right and I am wrong, what should I do?**
  假如蘇是正確的，而我錯了，我該怎麼辦？
  ↑ Supposing 引導的子句用現在式（Sue is right and I am wrong），表示很可能是現實；主句用 should，不用 would。

6 as if 和 as though（就好像）

1 as if 和 as though 的假設用法

a 描述某件事情，要表達所言不是事實，而是想像的、誇張的，就可用 as if 或 as though 構成假設語氣。

b 依所發生的時間，as if/as though 所引導的方式副詞子句，其假設語氣的結構要隨之變化。

① **子句的動作與主句動作同時發生：**
as if 和 as though 的假設句要使用過去式（be 動詞要用 were）。

- **Sue Lace talks as if she owned the whole place.**
  蘇・勒斯說起話來，好像這整個地方都是她的一樣。
  ↑ 事實：She doesn't own the whole place.

- **The pain was so bad that I felt as if a big needle were being stuck into my left foot.**
  我痛得很厲害，感覺就好像一根大針刺入了我的左腳。
  ↑ 事實：No needle was being stuck into my left foot.

② **子句的動作發生在主句動作之後：**
as if 和 as though 的假設句要使用「were going to, were about to」。

- **When I saw Mark this morning, he looked as if he were going to say something important to me, but he didn't utter a word.**
  今天上午我見到馬克時，他好像要給我說什麼重要的事，但他一句話也沒有說。
  ↑ 子句動詞 were going to 在主句動詞 looked 之後，與過去的未來事實不符。

③ **子句的動作發生在主句動作之前：**
as if 和 as though 的假設句要使用「had + 過去分詞」。

- Joe looks as if he had seen a UFO! 喬看起來好像見到了不明飛行物似的！
  ↑ 事實：He did not see a UFO.
- She is acting as though nothing had happened between her and Brad. 她表現得好像她和布萊德之間什麼事都沒發生過似的。
  ↑ 事實：Something happened between her and Brad.

2 as if/as though 的非假設用法

as if 和 as though 也可以表示「某事看起來是真的」，並且此事確實有可能是真的（亦即所假設的事實有可能發生，並非與事實相反）。

- It looks as if it is going to be a great day for water-skiing on Lake Bear. 看來今天好像是去熊湖滑水的好天氣。
  ↑ 今天確實可能是個好天氣，不用假設語氣。
- Wendy is smiling as though she knows the answer already.
  溫蒂微笑著，好像她已經知道了答案一樣。
  ↑ 溫蒂確實可能已經知道了答案。

Diving Deep Into English 85 假設語氣的 be 動詞，一律用 were

假設語氣裡，不管子句主詞是第幾人稱，也不管子句主詞是單數還是複數，be 動詞一律用過去式 were（不用 was）。

✗ At the party last night, Dee treated her boyfriend Lee Ranger as though he was a stranger.
✓ At the party last night, Dee treated her boyfriend Lee Ranger as though he were a stranger.
昨晚聚會上，蒂對待她的男友李·閏傑就好像他是一個陌生人一樣。
↑ were 是假設語氣，表示與現在事實相反——事實上，她的男友並不是陌生人。

- Claire wishes her boyfriend were a millionaire.
  克萊兒希望她的男朋友是一個百萬富翁。
- If my boyfriend were rich, we wouldn't be in such a mess.
  如果我的男友是個有錢人的話，我們就不用過得這麼狼狽。

7 慣用原形動詞的假設子句

1 表「要求、建議」的動詞後面，要接「原形動詞受詞子句」（base verb clause）

a 用來提出要求、請求、建議、提議等動詞後面的子句，要用原形動詞表達假設語氣。英式常用「should + 原形動詞」，但不能用 would。

b 下面的動詞用在 that 子句前，而 that 子句裡要用原形動詞表示重要性，而且**主句和子句各自要有不同的主詞**。

• advise 勸告；建議	• insist 竭力主張	• recommend 建議；勸告
• ask 要求	• move 提議	• request 要求
• command 命令	• order 命令	• require 要求
• demand 要求	• prefer 寧可；更喜歡	• suggest 建議
• desire 要求	• propose 提議	

這種結構無論主句是現在式（insist/insists）、過去式（insisted）或過去完成式（had insisted），無論子句的主詞是單數或複數（he, they），都應該用**原形動詞**。在英式英語裡，原形動詞前可以加 should。

✗ Lily prefers that John speaks to her face to face.

✓ Lily prefers that John speak to her face to face.

莉莉寧可要約翰親口對她說。

↑ 主句和子句有各自不同的主詞（Lily, John）。

↑ 受詞子句要用原形動詞（speak）的假設語氣。

✗ Doctor Jenny Bush strongly suggested that my husband do not smoke near our baby.

✓ Doctor Jenny Bush strongly suggested that my husband not smoke near our baby.

珍妮·布希醫生強烈建議我的先生不要在我們的小寶貝身旁抽菸。

↑ 助動詞 do 不用在否定式的假設語氣中（不用 do not smoke）。應當將 not 放在原形動詞前面（not smoke）。

- We demand that Kathleen Keating be at the meeting.
  我們要求凱絲琳·基廷出席這次會議。
  ↥ be 是假設語氣。

- I had recommended that Dan read more English storybooks before he went to America.
  我曾建議丹在去美國前應該再多閱讀一些英語故事書。
  ↥ 過去動作 had recommended 發生在另一個過去動作 went 之前，因此用過去完成式。動詞 had recommended 表示「建議」，受詞子句要用原形動詞（read）的假設語氣，也可以用「should + 原形動詞」。

比較

| 美式 | Dee insisted that her boyfriend leave the country immediately.

| 英式 | Dee insisted that her boyfriend should leave the country immediately. 蒂堅持要她的男友立刻離開這個國家。

↥ insist 意為「堅決要求、堅決主張」時，後面接原形動詞的假設語氣子句，英式英語也可以用「should + 原形動詞」。

- I insisted that Professor Brown was wrong.
  我堅持認為布朗教授是錯的。
  ↥ insist 意為「堅持認為」，受詞子句就不能用假設語氣，而用陳述語氣。

2 表要求、建議的名詞後也要接「原形動詞子句」

源自於這類表要求、建議等動詞的名詞，後面的 that 子句也要用原形動詞，構成假設語氣。英式常用「should + 原形動詞」，但不能用 would。例如下列名詞：

- demand 要求
- insistence 竭力主張
- order 命令
- preference 偏好
- proposal 提議
- recommendation 建議
- request 要求
- requirement 要求
- suggestion 建議

✗ The owner's requirement is that everyone in our Paris office is fluent in English.

✓ The owner's requirement is that everyone in our Paris office be fluent in English.

老闆要求我們巴黎營業處的每一個人都得掌握流利的英文。

↑ 在名詞 requirement 和連綴動詞 is 之後的主詞補語子句，動詞要用原形動詞 be，也可以用 should be。

- **Mark Sun followed his friend's recommendation that he (should) drop World Literature 201.**

  馬克·孫聽了朋友的建議，退選「世界文學 201」課程。

  ↑ 在名詞 recommendation 之後的同位語子句，動詞要用原形動詞 drop，或 should drop。

3 某些形容詞後要接「原形動詞子句」

「it is/was important/necessary/desirable . . . + that 子句」的句型，子句裡的動詞也要用原形動詞，而英式常用「should + 原形動詞」，但不能用 would。下述形容詞都是這個用法：

● advisable 明智的	● important 重要的	● required 必須的
● crucial 重要的	● necessary 必要的	● suggested 被提議的
● desirable 令人滿意的	● proposed 被提議的	● urgent 急迫的
● essential 必要的	● recommended 被推薦的	● vital 極重要的

✗ **Lisa said it was important that you came to the meeting on time.**

✓ **Lisa said it was important that you come to the meeting on time.**

麗莎說，你準時去開會，這很重要。

↑ 這句是過去式（said, was），但子句中還是要用原形動詞 come。

- **Dee's mom says it is essential that every child have excellent educational opportunities.**

  = Dee's mom says it is essential for every child to have excellent educational opportunities.

  蒂的媽媽說，每個孩子都應該享有接受優等教育的機會，這很重要。

  ↑ 子句裡的主詞是單數（every child），但動詞應該用原形動詞 have，而不是用簡單現在式的單數動詞 has。

- **It's necessary that the nurse be in the room with the baby.**

  護士有必要與嬰兒一起待在房間。

  ↑ 子句要用原形動詞 be。

8 一些用原形動詞的慣用法

有些固定的表達，要用原形動詞的假設語氣。

- God bless you! 上帝保佑你！
- Heaven forbid! 蒼天不容！（千萬不要這樣！）
- I believe Pat was under pressure at the time. Be that as it may, she shouldn't have yelled at me.
  我相信蓓特當時壓力很大，即使如此，她也不應該對我吼叫。
  ↥ Be that as it may = Although it may be true
- If you can't change my flight reservation, so be it. I'll leave on Sunday. 如果你不能改變我預訂的航班，那就這樣吧，我就在星期天離開。
  ↥ so be it = let it be so = I accept it as it is

- Come what may, I'll get home before Christmas Eve.
  無論發生什麼事，我都要在聖誕節前夕回到家中。
  ↥ Come what may = No matter what happens
- If need be, Erica will buy an RV to travel around America.
  如果需要的話，艾芮卡將買一輛房車，然後周遊美國。
  ↥ If need be = Provided it is necessary

9 it is time that 和 would rather that

1 it is (about/high) time that + 子句主詞 + 過去式（假設語氣）

句型「it is (about/high) time」後面子句的述語動詞用動詞的過去式，表示「**是……的時候了**」。過去式動詞在這個句型裡不表示過去時間，而表示現在或未來。

- It is high time that Roy gave up trying to be a playboy.
  羅伊該放棄想當花花公子的念頭了。

- It is time that Sally went to visit her husband in Italy.
  = It is time for Sally to go to visit her husband in Italy.
  莎莉該去義大利探望她老公了。

2 主句主詞 + would rather + 子句主詞 + 過去式（假設語氣）

如果要表達「某人寧願讓另一個人（不要）做某事」，would rather 後面就要接子句，子句中用動詞的過去式來表示現在或未來要做的事。

注意 主句和子句各自要有不同的主詞。

✗ I would rather you will come on Saturday or Sunday.
✗ I would rather you come on Saturday or Sunday.
✓ I would rather you came on Saturday or Sunday.
我寧願你星期六或星期天來。
↑ would rather 表示「某人寧願另一個人做某事」時，後面的子句不用原形動詞，要用過去式的假設語氣。

- I would rather Ann went to Afghanistan.
  我寧願安去阿富汗。

口語中重音的位置不同，含意也就不同。

- Mr. Sun would rather I called 911.
  宋先生寧願我呼叫 911。
- Mr. Sun would rather I called 911.
  宋先生寧願是我呼叫 911。
  = Mr. Sun does not want to call 911.
  （宋先生不想自己呼叫 911。）

- Mr. Sun would rather I called 911. 宋先生寧願我是打 911 求救。
  = Mr. Sun wants me to call 911, not a neighbor or family member.
  （宋先生寧願我是呼叫 911，而不是去呼叫鄰居或家人。）

比較

主詞 + would rather + 原形動詞	主句主詞 + would rather + 子句主詞 + 過去式
I **would rather** cook **the lunch now.** 我寧願現在就做午飯。	I **would rather** my husband **cooked the lunch now.** 我寧願我丈夫現在就做午飯。
Joe **would rather** not go **climbing tomorrow.** 喬寧可明天不去爬山。	Joe **would rather** you did not go **climbing tomorrow.** 喬寧願你明天不去爬山。

UNIT 15 句子的結構

Sentence Structure

簡單句

1 簡單句的基本句型

1 簡單句內含一個主詞和一個動詞，只包含一個獨立子句（即主句）。

2 簡單句可以有一個複合主詞（一個以上的主詞）、一個複合受詞或一個複合述語動詞（參見 1 頁〈Unit 1 句子〉）。

3 簡單句有以下五種基本句型。

1. 主詞 + 不及物動詞（+ 介系詞片語）
2. 主詞 + 及物動詞 + 受詞（+ 副詞片語）
3. 主詞 + 連綴動詞 + 主詞補語
4. 主詞 + 及物動詞 + 雙受詞（間接受詞和直接受詞）
5. 主詞 + 及物動詞 + 受詞 + 受詞補語

2 句型一：主詞 + 不及物動詞（+ 介系詞片語）

a **主詞**（subject）：是執行動詞動作的人物、動物、地點或事物。主詞可以是一個字、一個片語或一個子句。

b **不及物動詞**（intransitive verb）：後面不接受詞。

- Sue flew above Andrew.
  蘇在安德魯上方飛翔。
- Sue and Andrew dove into the cool pool.
  蘇和安德魯跳進涼爽的游泳池。
  ↑ Sue and Andrew 為複合主詞。

・Mr. Brown sat down. 布朗先生坐了下來。

↑ sat down 為片語動詞。

3 句型二：主詞 + 及物動詞 + 受詞（+ 副詞片語）

a **受詞**（object）：是接受動詞動作的人或物，可以是一個詞、一個片語或一個子句。

b **及物動詞**（transitive verb）：後面要接受詞。

・Bing quit smoking and choking.
賓戒菸了，也不再被菸嗆了。

↑ 動名詞（smoking and choking）作複合受詞。

・Mary loves to water-ski. 瑪麗喜愛滑水。

↑ 不定式（to water-ski）作受詞。

・I did not realize that Amy was so bossy.
我沒有意識到艾咪如此霸道。

↑ 子句（that Amy was so bossy）作受詞。

・Henry married Kay in May.
亨利在五月娶了凱。

↑ 專有名詞 Kay 作動詞 married 的受詞；介系詞片語（in May）作副詞片語（即狀語）。

・Making up a rhyme won't take up too much of my time.
作一首押韻詩不會佔用我太多時間。

↑ Making up a rhyme（動名詞片語）是主詞；too much of my time 是名詞片語作受詞。

4 句型三：主詞 + 連綴動詞 + 主詞補語

主詞補語（subject complement）是用在連綴動詞（appear、be、look、seem 等）後面的名詞、形容詞、動名詞、介系詞片語或不定式片語，用來補充說明主詞的特質、狀態，主詞補語也稱為**表語**（predicative）。

- Dad looked **sad**. 爸爸看起來很傷心。
  ↑ sad 是形容詞作主詞補語。
- I am **in Mumbai**. 我在孟買。
  ↑ in Mumbai 是介系詞片語作主詞補語。

- Her main duty is **to analyze dinosaur bones**.
  她的主要職責是分析恐龍的骨頭。
  ↑ to analyze dinosaur bones 是不定式片語作主詞補語。
- Brook is **a cook**. 布魯克是一個廚師。
  ↑ a cook 是名詞作主詞補語。

5 句型四：主詞 + 及物動詞 + 雙受詞（間接受詞和直接受詞）

a **直接受詞**（direct object）：直接受到動詞行為影響的人或事物，是行為動詞的接受者（指事或物）。

b **間接受詞**（indirect object）：間接受到動詞行為影響的人（有時也指事物），可以是一個名詞或一個代名詞，表明及物動詞所做的行為是為誰而做的（指人）。用作間接受詞的代名詞必須是代名詞的受格形式。

1 主詞 + 及物動詞 + 間接受詞 + 直接受詞（名詞）

- Sally blew Sam **a flying kiss**.
  莎莉給了山姆一個飛吻。
- Kay showed me **the way**. 凱給我指了路。
  ↑ 間接受詞用代名詞的受格形式 me。
- Larry is reading Sherry **a fairy story**.
  賴瑞正在念一個童話故事給雪瑞聽。

- Annie made herself **a bikini**.
  安妮為自己做了一件比基尼泳裝。

2 主詞 + 及物動詞 + 間接受詞 + 直接受詞（疑問詞 + 不定式）

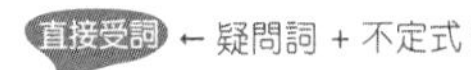

- Sue told Andrew what to do.
  蘇告訴安德魯該做什麼。

- Clive taught me how to drive.
  克萊夫教會了我如何開車。

3 主詞 + 及物動詞 + 直接受詞 + 介系詞（to 或 for）+ 間接受詞

a 直接受詞通常置於間接受詞之後，但有時候也可以把直接受詞置於間接受詞之前。有些動詞如果先接直接受詞，必須再加介系詞 to，才能接間接受詞。這類動詞有：

- bring 帶來
- give 給
- lend 借
- offer 提供
- owe 欠
- pass 遞交
- pay 付
- promise 承諾
- read 閱讀
- recommend 推薦
- sell 賣
- send 寄
- show 展示
- take 拿
- tell 告訴
- throw 丟

- I'll forward Mike's email to you.
  我會把邁克的電子信件轉給你。

- Lily quickly threw the Frisbee to Cindy.
  莉莉迅速地把飛盤扔給辛蒂。

b 有些動詞如果先接直接受詞，必須再加介系詞 for，才能接間接受詞。這類動詞有：

- build 建造
- buy 買
- cook 煮
- do 做
- find 找
- fix 修理
- get 拿
- keep 保有
- knit 織
- make 做
- order 訂購
- prepare 準備

- Jim is going to order some roses for Kim.
  吉姆要為金姆訂購一些玫瑰花。

- Uncle Lee built this sailboat for me.
  李伯父為我造這艘帆船。

6 句型五：主詞 + 及物動詞 + 受詞 + 受詞補語

受詞補語（object complement）跟在直接受詞後面並修飾直接受詞，使受詞意思完整。這樣的受詞和受詞補語又稱為「複合受詞」。受詞補語可以是名詞或形容詞，或是起名詞或形容詞作用的字。

- She called that compromise a fraud.
  她稱這場和解是一場騙局。
  ↥ 名詞 a fraud 作受詞補語。

- I kept the light on. 我讓燈開著。
  ↥ 副詞 on 作受詞補語。（少數副詞可以作受詞補語。）

7 句型六：主詞 + 及物動詞 + 受詞 + 動詞（+ 受詞）

- I heard Joy yell at Del. 我聽到喬伊對戴爾吼叫。
  ↥ 「yell at Del」可看作是受詞（Joy）的補語，也可看作是動詞（heard）的直接受詞。
- Ms. Kay Reed had her students read 25,000 words every day.
  凱·里德女士讓她的學生每天讀 25,000 個單字。
  ↥ every day 是副詞片語。
- She saw a big brown toad crossing the road.
  她看見一隻褐色的大癩蛤蟆正在過馬路。

有些文法家把感官動詞、使役動詞後面的 –ing 形式或不定式看作是**受詞補語**（如上面句型五）。也有些文法家把它們看作是**直接受詞**（如上面句型六），因此通常說「簡單句有五種基本句型」。

並列句和複合句

1 並列句（Compound Sentences）

1 一個**並列句**至少包含兩個獨立子句（即兩個簡單句），由**對等連接詞**（例如 and、but、or、nor、for、so、yet）連接的兩個或兩個以上的簡單句。

2 **獨立子句**：可以獨立存在，互不依賴，並且地位平等。當獨立子句獨立存在時，即成為簡單句。每個子句都包含一個主詞和一個述語動詞。

» 參見 327 頁〈Unit 8 連接詞與並列句和從屬子句〉。

3 在美式英語中，當並列句是由對等連接詞連接起來的兩個獨立子句時，在連接詞前面要加逗號。

Nick's daughter Jan just got her Ph.D. in physics.
獨立子句（簡單句）

She is searching for a job in India, Pakistan, or Iran.
獨立子句（簡單句）

Nick's daughter Jan just got her Ph.D. in physics, and she is searching for a job in India, Pakistan, or Iran.
尼克的女兒簡剛獲得了物理學博士學位，她正在找一份在印度、巴基斯坦或者伊朗的工作。
並列句

↳ 兩個獨立子句（簡單句）用對等連接詞 and 連接，就成為並列句，在 and 前面要加逗號。

- **Kitty, you may stay here with Kay, or you may go with me to the Christmas party.**
綺蒂，你可以跟凱待在這裡，或者你也可以跟我一起去參加聖誕晚會。
↳ 這是一個並列句。兩個獨立子句以對等連接詞 or 連接，or 的前面要加逗號。

- Jim shouted to Kim and her friends, but nobody paid any attention to him. 吉姆對金姆和她朋友喊叫，但沒有人注意他。

- Dirk's new girlfriend didn't dance, nor did she watch the fireworks.
德克新交的女友沒有跳舞，也沒有觀賞煙火。

- Jenny thought she had a good chance to get the job, for her mother was the president of the company.
珍妮認為她得到那份工作的機會很大，因為她的母親就是公司總裁。

2 複合句（Complex Sentences）

1 **複合句**（又稱**主從複合句**）：由一個主句，再加上一個或多個從屬子句所組成。

2 主句包含一個主詞和一個動詞，是句子的主要部分，通常可以單獨表達一個完整的概念（相當於獨立子句）；從屬子句也有主詞和動詞，但不能單獨存在，必須依賴主句才具有明確、完整的意義。

» 參見 327 頁〈Unit 8 連接詞與並列句和從屬子句〉。

- I will go <u>if I am invited by Pam</u>. 如果潘姆邀請我，我就去。
↑ 這是一個複合句，包含一個主句（獨立子句）和一個從屬子句。

- Sunbathing, <u>which is a popular summer pastime,</u> can cause skin cancer.
日光浴雖是很流行的夏季娛樂，卻可能造成皮膚癌。

- Lisa, <u>who used to be a secretary for the mayor,</u> can type 180 words a minute. 曾經當過市長祕書的麗莎，一分鐘可以打 180 個單字。

- Ann can't remember <u>where she parked our van</u>.
安不記得她把我們的廂型車停在哪兒了。
↑ where she parked our van 是名詞子句，是主句動詞 remember 的受詞。

倒裝句

1 何謂倒裝句？

1 英文句子的基本結構是主述結構，倒裝就是將主述結構進行顛倒。如果主述的詞序完全顛倒，就是**完全倒裝**；如果只將助動詞或情態動詞移到主詞前面，叫做**部分倒裝**。

完全倒裝	部分倒裝
Here comes our school bus. 我們的校車來了。	I can't go there, and neither can Joe. 我不能去那裡，喬也不能去。
Outside the door stood four police officers. 門外站著四個警官。	Not a single word did Kay say. 凱一個字也沒有說。

2 **部分倒裝**時，要把助動詞或情態動詞（be、have/had、can 等）置於主詞前；若無這些助動詞和情態動詞，就要用助動詞 do/does/did，並置於主詞前（如上面右欄的第二句）。

2 為了句子結構的需要進行倒裝

1 **一般疑問句**和**特殊疑問句**都需要倒裝。

陳述句（主述結構）	疑問句（部分倒裝結構）
Kay goes to work every weekday. 凱每個工作日都要去上班。	Does Kay go to work every weekday? 凱每個工作日都要去上班嗎？

My kite can fly very high. 我的風箏可以飛得很高。	How high can your kite fly? 你的風箏可以飛得多高?
Nancy has read *The Old Man and the Sea*. 南茜讀過《老人與海》。	Has Nancy read *The Old Man and the Sea*? 南茜讀過《老人與海》嗎?

疑問詞作主詞時，疑問句不倒裝。

- Who wrote this poem? 這首詩是誰作的？

2 在「**there + be**」的結構中，there不是句子的主詞，主詞在be動詞後面。

- **There are 120 large wind generators on this island.**
  在這個島上有**120**個巨大的風力發電機。
  ↑ 主詞 120 large wind generators 在動詞 are 後面。

- **There are lots of good libraries in the U.S.A.**
  在美國有很多好的圖書館。

- **There is no doubt about Joe's honesty.**
  喬是誠實的，這是毫無疑問的。

3 so（也一樣）、neither（也不）、nor（也不）置於句首時，需要部分倒裝。

- **My mom is a bus driver, and so is my Uncle Tom.**
  我媽媽是公車司機，我叔叔湯姆也是。
  ↑ 在並列句中，副詞 so 前面要有連接詞 and。

- **Joe never plays computer games during weekdays, and neither does Coco.** 喬從來不在工作日玩電腦遊戲，可可也是。
  ↑ 在並列句中，副詞 neither 前面要有連接詞 and。

- **I don't believe what you said, nor does Ted.**
  我不相信你的話，泰德也不相信。
  ↑ 在並列句中，nor 本身就是連接詞，不能和另一個連接詞（如 and）一起使用。

- All this will not be finished in the first hundred days. Nor will it be finished in the first thousand days, nor in the life of this administration, nor even perhaps in our lifetime on this planet. But let us begin. (President John Kennedy)
  所有這一切，不會在頭一百天之內完成，也不會在頭一千天之內完成，不會在本屆政府任期之內完成，甚至在我們這一生也可能不會在地球上實現。但是，讓我們開始吧。

- "Jerome has been to Rome twice." "So have I."
  「傑羅姆去過羅馬兩次。」「我也去過兩次。」

- "Erica has never been to North America." "Neither have I."
  「艾芮卡從來沒有去過北美洲。」「我也沒有。」
  ↥ so、neither、nor 置於句首，也可用於簡答倒裝句型。

4 **直接引語**位於句首時，可以用倒裝結構，也可以用主述結構。

- "I'll love you forever," proclaimed Bill. → 倒裝結構
  = "I'll love you forever," Bill proclaimed. → 主述結構
  比爾聲明：「我會永遠愛你。」

- "It's time to go to bed," she said.
  她說：「該睡覺了。」
  ↥ 主詞是人稱代名詞（如 she），必須用主述結構，不能倒裝。

5 地點副詞 there、here 位於句首（主詞必須是名詞）時，需要全部倒裝。

- Here comes my dad's car. 我爸爸的車來了。
- There goes the doorbell. 門鈴響了。
- There he goes. 他走了。 → 主詞是人稱代名詞，就不能用倒裝結構。

6 為了使行文更具文采，某些表示條件和讓步的子句，可以用倒裝句代替 **if 子句**或 **although 子句**。

- If Jean Bur had been in class yesterday, I would have seen her.
  = Had Jean Bur been in class yesterday, I would have seen her.
  假如琴·伯爾昨天來上課了，我就會見到她。
  ↥ 條件子句倒裝是把助動詞（had）置於句首。

✕ Hadn't Jim resigned, we would have fired him.
✓ Had Jim not resigned, we would have fired him.
如果吉姆沒有辭職，我們就會解雇他。
↑ 倒裝的否定句中不用縮寫形式（如：hadn't）。

- If he decides to come/If he should decide to come, please give me a call.
= Should he decide to come, please give me a call.
如果他決定要來，請給我打電話。

- Although he was tall, Paul could not touch the top of the wall.
= Tall as he was, Paul could not touch the top of the wall.
保羅雖然很高，但還是摸不到那堵牆的頂端。
↑ 讓步子句的倒裝是把形容詞置於句首，在形容詞後面用「as + 主詞 + 動詞」。

3 用倒裝句來作強調

為了強調，把一些詞或片語置於句首，句子要全部倒裝。

1 一些**形容詞**和**分詞**等置於句首，句子要全部倒裝。

- Great is the guilt of an unnecessary war. (President John Adams)
發動毫無必要的戰爭，犯下的是滔天大罪。 → 形容詞位於句首。

- Gone are the days when I was free of worry.
= The days when I was free of worry are gone.
我無憂無慮的日子一去不復返了。 → 分詞位於句首。

2 表示**地點**或**方位**的字或片語位於句首（主詞為名詞，而動詞為不及物動詞），句子要用全部倒裝。

注意 主詞是代名詞或動詞為及物動詞，句子不要倒裝。

- My cat Rainbow jumped out of the window. → 非倒裝句
= Out of the window jumped my cat Rainbow.
我的貓「彩虹」從窗戶跳了出去。
↑ 地點副詞片語位於句首，句子用全部倒裝。

- Directly in front of me ran Jim, and I could not pass him. → 倒裝句
  吉姆就在我前面奔跑，而我就無法跑過他。

- Directly in front of me he ran, and I could not pass him. → 非倒裝句
  他就在我前面奔跑，而我就是無法跑過他。
  ↑ 注意 主詞是代名詞（如：he, she, they），句子不用倒裝。

- I opened the window, and in flew a bird.
  我打開窗戶，一隻小鳥飛了進來。
  ↑ 副詞 in 位於句首，句子用全部倒裝。

- Off the coast of North Carolina lie the Barrier Islands.
  堡礁島嶼就坐落在北卡羅來納州海岸那邊。

3 在「so . . . that」的強調句型中，如果把「so + 形容詞／副詞」放在句首，則 so 引導的主句要用部分倒裝。

- I disliked Jim so much that I could not bear to look at him. → 非倒裝句
  = So much did I dislike Jim that I could not bear to look at him. → 倒裝句
  我實在不喜歡吉姆，連看他一眼都受不了。

- So exciting was the computer game that Dirk forgot to do his homework.
  那個電腦遊戲太刺激了，德克竟然忘記了做作業。

4 「such + be 動詞 + 名詞」放在句首，則 such 引導的主句是倒裝句。

- Such is the moment that we've been waiting for.
  這就是我們一直在等待的時刻。

- Such is the popularity of this play that the theater will be filled tonight.
  這齣戲如此受到大眾的喜愛，劇院今晚會爆滿。

5 下列具有**否定**含義的詞或片語位於句首，句子要用**部分倒裝**。

- at no time 在任何時候都不
- in no way 決不
- little 少
- never (before) 從未
- not + 受詞　沒有……
- not once 一次也沒有
- not until 直到……才
- nowhere 任何地方都不……
- on no account 決不
- rarely 很少；難得
- seldom 不常；很少；難得
- under no circumstances 決不

- Never before have I seen Dad so sad.
  我從沒有見過爸爸如此傷心。

- Little does Sam know about politics and economics.
  山姆對政治學和經濟學瞭解甚少。

- Nowhere else have I seen such a beautiful scene.
  我在任何地方都沒有看見過這麼美麗的景色。

- Rarely do I criticize Eli. 我很少批評伊萊。

- On no account should you trust Anna with any of your money.
  任何情況下，你都不要把你的錢託付給安娜。

- Not a single word have I written since I was given that long essay assignment.
  自從我被囑咐完成那篇長論文作業以來，我連一個字都還沒有寫出來。
  ↳ not + 受詞：a single word 是 have written 的受詞。

並不是所有以 not 開頭的句子都要用倒裝句。

- No doubt he refused to go out with Lily. 難怪他拒絕跟莉莉約會。
  ↳ No doubt 開始的句子不用倒裝。
- All the stores are closed, and not one single person can be seen on the street. 所有的商店都關門了，大街上一個人也看不見。
  ↳ 這句不要倒裝，因為 one single person 是句子的主詞，不是受詞。

6 「only + 副詞子句／時間副詞／介系詞片語」（only + if/when/after/later/then/in this way）位於句首，**主句用部分倒裝**，通常用簡單過去式。

- After she had read the first chapter, Coco remembered that she had read the story a long time ago.
  ↑ After 引導的時間副詞子句置於主句前，要用逗號與主句分開，主句不要倒裝。

- Only after she had read the first chapter did Coco remember that she had read the story a long time ago.
  可可讀完了第一章後，才想起她很久以前讀過這個故事。
  ↑ 主句是倒裝（did Coco remember）。
  ↑ Only after 引導的時間副詞子句不要倒裝，不用逗號與倒裝的主句分開。

- By reading extensively for fun, Trish can greatly improve her English.
  藉由大量的趣味閱讀，翠西可以增進她的英文。
  ↑ 非倒裝句

- Only by reading extensively for fun can Trish greatly improve her English. → 倒裝句
  只有靠大量趣味閱讀，翠西才能改進她的英文。
  ↑ 「only + 介系詞片語」位於句首，句子要倒裝。

並不是所有 only 置於句首的句子，都要使用倒裝句。

- Only Mike is allowed to drive that truck.
  只允許邁克駕駛那輛卡車。
  ↑ 「only + 名詞」作句子主詞，句子不能倒裝。

- Only then did I understand why my mother had worked so hard in college. 我在大學時才了解到媽媽為什麼要那麼拚命地工作。
  ↑ 「only + 副詞」位於句首，句子要倒裝。

7 句型「hardly/rarely/scarcely . . . when」和「no sooner . . . than」中的 hardly、rarely、scarcely、no sooner 置於句首，**主句用部分倒裝**，通常用過去完成式。

- No sooner had Coco arrived in Chicago than it began to snow.
  可可剛到芝加哥，就下雪了。

- Hardly had I finished fixing my car when he showed up and asked to borrow it.
  我剛把我的車修好，他就來向我借車。

- Scarcely had I got out of bed when the earthquake occurred. 我剛起床，就發生了地震。

8 句型「not only . . . but also . . .」中的 not only 引導的子句置於句首時要倒裝，but also 引導的子句不要倒裝。

- Not only is Ms. Sun crazy about reading, but her students are also reading extensively for fun.
  不僅是孫老師對閱讀著迷，她的學生也做大量的趣味閱讀。

UNIT

16 分詞、不定式和動名詞

Participles, Infinitives, and Gerunds

分詞

1 分詞的定義（The Participle Defined）

1 分詞可以搭配**助動詞**（be 和 have），構成動詞的各種時態形式，例如：

- are working → 進行式
- have worked → 完成式

2 分詞有兩種：現在分詞和過去分詞。

a **過去分詞**：只有一種形式。例如：
- build 建造 → built

b **現在分詞**：有簡單式和完成式兩種形式，也有主動分詞和被動分詞。例如：

	主動分詞（主動語態）	被動分詞（被動語態）
簡單式	(not) building	(not) being built
完成式	(not) having built	(not) having been built

3 **現在分詞簡單式**：表動作「正在發生」或與述語動詞的動作「同時發生」。

- **Is that crying girl Pearl?** 那位正在哭泣的女孩是珀兒嗎？
  ↳ 現在分詞的主動簡單式 crying 作形容詞，表動作正在發生（that girl is crying）。
- **Being considered the fastest runner in our school, Mike was encouraged to join the track team.**
  由於邁克是學校跑步最快的，他被鼓勵加入田徑隊。
  ↳ 現在分詞的被動簡單式 Being considered 作狀語，與述語動詞的動作同時發生。

4 **現在分詞完成式**：表示動作發生在述語動詞的動作之前。

- **Having said goodnight, Sue went upstairs to say her prayers.**
  道過晚安後，蘇便上樓去禱告。
  ↳ 現在分詞的主動完成式 having said 表示動作發生在述語動詞的動作（went）之前，其主詞（Sue）是現在分詞動作的執行者。

- Not having been invited to Tom's birthday party, Lily felt very unhappy. 因沒有被邀請參加湯姆的生日派對，莉莉感到很不高興。
  ↳ 現在分詞的被動完成式 Not having been invited，表示動作發生在述語動詞的動作（felt）之前，其主詞（Lily）是現在分詞動作的承受者。

2 現在分詞（Present Participles）

1 現在分詞簡單式的形式：以 -ing 結尾。參見 535 頁〈2 現在分詞的構成方式〉。

- advertising 做廣告
- jogging 慢跑
- speaking 說話
- asking 詢問
- kicking 踢
- talking 交談

2 現在分詞與 be 動詞連用：構成進行式，表示現在的狀態或正在進行的動作。

- Is Dan jogging with Ann? 丹正在跟安一起跑步嗎？
  ↳ jogging 與 be 動詞（Is）構成進行式。

3 現在分詞也可以當作**形容詞**，修飾**名詞**，同時具有動詞和形容詞的特徵；現在分詞也可作**副詞**用，修飾**動詞**。現在分詞與主動語態的動詞類似，**具有主動意義**（表示其修飾的詞是動作的**執行者**）。

- a man-eating beast = a beast that eats human beings 食人獸
  ↳ 現在分詞作形容詞，修飾名詞 beast；具有動詞的特徵，含有主動意義。
- a crying baby = a baby that is crying 一個正在哭的嬰兒
  ↳ 現在分詞作形容詞，表示「動作正在進行」，其所修飾的名詞是動作的執行者。

- Is she running after the fluttering butterfly?
  她正跟在那隻振翅飛翔的蝴蝶後面跑嗎？
  ↳ running 與 be 動詞（Is）構成進行式；fluttering 作形容詞，修飾名詞 butterfly。
- Bing walked out talking and laughing. 賓又說又笑地走了出去。
  ↳ 現在分詞 talking 和 laughing 作副詞，修飾動詞片語 walked out。

3 過去分詞（Past Participles）

1 大部分過去分詞的形式：以 -ed 或 -en 結尾（參見 590 頁〈2 規則動詞的過去分詞〉和 904 頁〈附錄 1 不規則動詞表〉）。

- advertised 做廣告
- jogged 慢跑
- seen 看見
- asked 詢問
- kicked 踢
- spoken 談話

2 過去分詞**與助動詞 have 連用**：構成完成式，描述已發生的事。

- **This tooth of mine has rotted beyond repair.** 我這顆牙已經蛀得不能補了。
  ↑ rotted 與助動詞 has 構成現在完成式，描述已經發生的事。

3 過去分詞**與 be 動詞連用**：構成被動語態。

- **The chocolate candy bars were all eaten by the three hungry little green girls from Mars.**
  所有的巧克力糖塊都被那三位來自火星的饑腸轆轆的綠色小女孩吃完了。
  ↑ eaten 與 be 動詞 (were) 構成被動語態。

4 過去分詞可作**形容詞**，修飾**名詞**，具有動詞和形容詞的特徵；過去分詞也可作**副詞**用。大多數過去分詞具有被動意義（表示其修飾的名詞是動作的**接受者**）。

- the beaten path 那條人跡常至的小路
  ↑ 過去分詞 beaten 用作形容詞，修飾名詞 path；有動詞的特徵，表示「被動」。
- a broken heart = a heart that has been broken 一顆破碎的心
- a recently-built cottage → 被修飾的名詞 cottage，是動詞 built 的接受者。
  = a cottage that has recently been built 剛修建的別墅

- **After that incident, she lived alone, forgotten by everyone.**
  那次事件後，她就獨自生活，被所有的人遺忘。
  ↑ 過去分詞片語用作副詞。

5 可以作**形容詞**用的過去分詞多半是**及物動詞**，具有**被動意義**。但有些**不及物動詞**的過去分詞也可作形容詞，用在名詞前面，具有**主動**和**完成**的意義。

- an escaped prisoner 逃跑的囚犯
- a retired professor 退休的教授
- a grown-up son 長大成人的兒子
- a swollen face 腫起來的臉
- my well-read and much-traveled husband
  = my husband who has read and traveled a lot
  我那行萬裡路、讀萬卷書的丈夫
- recently arrived refugees
  = refugees that have arrived recently 剛到達的難民
  ↑ 不及物動詞（arrive）的過去分詞（arrived）用在名詞前，作形容詞，具有主動和完成的意義。

比較

過去分詞 表示動作已完成	現在分詞 表示動作正在進行
developed countries = countries that have developed/ are developed 已開發國家 ↑ 過去分詞 developed 描述已發生的事。	developing countries = countries that are developing 開發中國家 ↑ 現在分詞 developing 描述現在的狀態或行為。
fallen leaves = leaves that have fallen 落葉（已經掉落）	falling leaves = leaves that fall = leaves that are falling 落葉（正在掉落）

Diving Deep Into English 86 比較：-ed 形式的形容詞與 -ing 形式的形容詞

描述某人的感覺是什麼，用 -ed 形式（過去分詞）；要描述引起這種感覺的人、事物、情形、事件，就要用 -ing 形式（現在分詞）。

- a confused teacher 一位感到困惑的老師（被動）
- a confusing teacher 一位令人困惑的老師（主動）

- **Does the short robotic clown seem amusing to you?**
  你覺得那個矮小的機器小丑很有趣嗎？
- **We were amused by the story about how Ann met her husband Dan in Iran.** 我們被安如何在伊朗認識她丈夫丹的故事給逗樂了。

- **Bing said the movie script you wrote about human mating rituals was interesting.** 賓說，你寫的關於人類婚姻儀式的電影腳本很有趣。
- **Mary is interested in the novel you wrote about life and love in the 22nd century.** 瑪麗對你寫的關於 22 世紀的生活和愛情的小說很感興趣。

- **"I am terribly sorry I can't find your file," she said with an embarrassed smile.** 她帶著尷尬的微笑說：「很對不起，我找不到你的檔案。」

» 參見 214 頁〈Part 5 分詞形容詞〉。

4 分詞片語（Participial Phrases）

1 構成：分詞片語包含一個分詞，以及這個分詞的受詞和修飾語（副詞、形容詞、介系詞片語）。由於分詞片語的作用類似子句，有些英國文法家也把分詞片語稱為分詞子句（participle clause）。

- sitting in the corner 坐在角落裡
  ↑ 現在分詞片語：現在分詞（sitting）+ 介系詞片語（in the corner）
- lost in the desert 在沙漠中迷路
  ↑ 過去分詞片語： 過去分詞（lost）+ 介系詞片語（in the desert）
- having lost all my money 丟掉了我所有的錢
  ↑ 完成式分詞片語：現在分詞的完成式（having lost）+ 受詞（all my money）

2 作副詞用的分詞片語：分詞片語作副詞，相當於副詞子句，表原因、條件、結果、時間等。

- **Putting on his helmet, the knight Sir Lee rode away on his adventurous journey.**
  = After he put on his helmet, the knight Sir Lee rode away on his adventurous journey.
  戴上他的頭盔，騎士李爵士騎著馬開始了他的冒險征途。
  ↑ Putting on his helmet 是現在分詞片語作副詞，相當於副詞子句。

- **Encouraged by her initial success, Trish tried to catch another big fish.** 首戰告捷後，翠西很受鼓舞，想再釣一隻大魚。
  ↑ Encouraged by her initial success 是過去分詞片語作副詞，相當於副詞子句。

- **Rob's solar power company has opened a new office in Mexico, creating nine new jobs.**
  羅布的太陽能電力公司在墨西哥成立了新的辦公室，創造了九個新的工作機會。
  ↑ 現在分詞片語 creating nine new jobs 在這裡表示結果，修飾前面整個句子。

- **After nodding his sleepy head, the knight Sir Lee continued to ride his big horse Lady Red.**

睡意正濃的騎士李爵士點了點頭，然後騎著他那匹大馬「紅姑娘」繼續前行。

ℓ 動詞 -ing 形式（如：nodding his sleepy head）可以用在 after、before、when、while、whenever、once、until、on、without、instead of、in spite of、as 這類詞後面。在這種情況下，這些詞後面的 -ing 形式（nodding）為動名詞，整個片語（after nodding his sleepy head）可以被看成是一個省略子句。。

- **Judging from the behavior of Roy, he is not trying to be a playboy.**
  根據羅伊的行為舉止來判斷，他並非想要當花花公子。

  ℓ Judging from . . . 是獨立分詞片語。

  » 分詞片語的用法，也可參見 851 頁〈Unit 20 分詞片語和垂懸結構〉。

3 作形容詞的分詞片語

a 單個分詞作形容詞：置於被修飾的名詞之前。例如：

- a crying baby 一個在哭的寶寶
- a broken heart 一顆破碎的心

b 分詞片語作形容詞：置於被修飾的名詞後面，相當於形容詞子句。

- **In came the first runner Amy, closely followed by the second, Fanny.**
  = In came the first runner Amy, who was closely followed by the second, Fanny. 跑在最前面的是艾咪，緊跟其後的是第二名的芬妮。

  ℓ closely followed by the second, Fanny 是作形容詞用的過去分詞片語，修飾名詞 Amy。分詞片語作形容詞時，相當於形容詞子句。

- **Most of the people invited to his birthday party didn't show up.**
  = Most of the people who had been invited to his birthday party didn't show up. 大部分被邀請來參加他的生日聚會的人，都沒有出席。

  ℓ 過去分詞 invited，表示該動作發生在述語動詞的動作 didn't show up 之前。整個分詞片語相當於一個形容詞子句，修飾 Most of the people。

- **The girl dancing with my brother Jerry is called Cherry.**
  = The girl who is dancing with my brother Jerry is called Cherry.
  正在跟我哥哥傑瑞跳舞的女子叫習麗。

  ℓ dancing with my brother Jerry 是作形容詞用的現在分詞片語，此時，分詞片語相當於形容詞子句。

不定式

1 不定式的形式

1 帶 to 的不定式：一般所說的不定式通常為「to + 原形動詞」（infinitive with "to"）。

- **It's important for your health to get enough beauty sleep every night.** 每晚有足夠的美容覺，對健康很重要。
- **Mike's little sister likes to leap like a frog, play computer games, and sleep.** 邁克的小妹妹喜歡像青蛙一樣跳躍，還喜歡玩電腦遊戲和睡覺。
  ↳ 後面兩個不定式（play 和 sleep）省略了 to，避免重複。
- **Kate would like to have won the chess tournament in Kuwait, but she was too sick to compete.**
  凱特很想在科威特的那場棋賽中獲勝，可是她當時病得很厲害，無法參賽。
  ↳ 這句的不定式完成式（to have won）表示未發生的過去事情。

2 不帶 to 的不定式

a 在一些慣用語中，有些動詞後面直接跟不帶 to 的不定式。

- **Lily made believe that she didn't know me.** 莉莉假裝不認識我。
- **Kay let slip her love affair with Mike yesterday.**
  昨天凱無意中說出了她和邁克的戀愛關係。
- **Ann, you'd better get rolling if you're going to stop in and see Dan.**
  安，如果你要順道拜訪丹，最好現在動身。
  ↳ 「had better (= 'd better) + 原形動詞」用來提建議，had 在這裡不表示過去式。
- **Why not go to the beach on Sunday?** 星期天去海灘，好不好？

- I would rather stay at home than go out into the cold cruel world.
  我寧可待在家，也不願意出門，進入冷酷的世間。

b 一些動詞後面接「**不帶 to 的不定式**」（即原形動詞）：
「動詞 + 受詞 + 原形動詞」。

- make 使……做
- hear 聽見
- see 看見
- help 幫助
- let 讓
- overhear 偶然聽見
- watch 觀看
- feel 感覺

- **Why not let your husband do the dishes?** 為什麼不讓你老公洗碗？
- **Did you see something fly by?** 你有沒有看見什麼東西飛過？
- **Does your English teacher make you read 25,000 English words a day?** 你的英文老師要你們每天閱讀 25,000 個單字嗎？
- **Please help me (to) carry this big monkey back to the zoo.**
  請幫我把這隻大猴子扛回動物園。
  ↑ help 也可以接帶 to 的不定式。

Diving Deep Into English 87 make 等動詞用於被動語態時，要接帶 to 的不定式

make、let、hear、see、watch、feel 等動詞用於**主動**語態時，要接「**不帶 to 的不定式**」（即原形動詞），用於**被動**語態時要接「**帶 to 的不定式**」。

Active **My boss made me work day and night.** 我的老闆逼我日夜工作。
Passive **I was made to work day and night.** 我被迫日夜工作。

Active **I overheard Mary say that she wished she could marry Gary.**
我偶然聽到瑪麗說，她希望能嫁給蓋瑞。
Passive **Mary was overheard to say that she wished she could marry Gary.** 有人聽到瑪麗說，她希望能嫁給蓋瑞。

3 不定式的否定形式：not (+ to) + 原形動詞

✗ Try to not lose your temper over trifles about which you'll soon forget.
✓ Try not to lose your temper over trifles about which you'll soon forget.
不要為那些你很快就會忘得一乾二淨的芝麻小事發脾氣。

- I told you not to call me at home. 我告訴過你不要打電話到家裡來找我。
- Boys, you'd better not make too much noise.
小夥子們，你們最好不要太吵。
- You must learn not to talk about yourself all the time.
你要學會不要老是談論你自己。

4 **不定式搭配 wh- 疑問詞**：不定式有時與 how、what、which、where 等疑問詞連用（不定式置於疑問詞後），接在表示「提問、知道、學習、教導、指示」等意義的動詞或動詞片語之後。

- Coco did not know what to do and where to go.
可可不知道該做什麼、該去哪裡。
↑「wh- 疑問詞 + 不定式片語」，作動詞 know 的受詞。
- Could you please tell Louise Brown where to find the best sauna in town? 請告訴露易絲·布朗在城裡什麼地方能找到最好的桑拿，好嗎？
↑「wh- 疑問詞 + 不定式片語」，作動詞 tell 的直接受詞。
- Have you already told Jenny how many copies to print?
你已經告訴珍妮需要印多少份了嗎？
- Andrew had no idea who to ask about how to complete his task.
要如何才能完成任務，安德魯不知道該問誰。
↑ who 不定式片語置於名詞 idea 的後面，修飾該名詞；how 不定式片語作介系詞 about 的受詞。

5 **「for + 受詞 + 不定式」**：有些詞（動詞、名詞、不定代名詞、形容詞）後面常接「for + 受詞 + 不定式」的句型，即不定式的邏輯主詞與句子的主詞不相同時，不定式主詞用 for 引導。

- Is there any way for Emma to win? 愛瑪有沒有可能贏？
- Our whole village of Beehive is waiting for Clive to arrive.
我們整個蜂窩村的村民都在等待克萊夫的到來。
- For Adam Acts to lose the mayoral election, all you need to do is to report the facts. 要讓亞當·艾克茲在市長選舉中敗選，只需要報導事實就行。
↑ 不定式片語的邏輯主詞是 Adam Acts，句子的主詞是不定代名詞 all。

2 不定式的用法

1 不定式片語表**目的**和**結果**：不定式片語常用來表示一個（群）人做某事的目的，即「為什麼這個（群）人要做此事」。

- **I am writing to thank you for all you have done for my son Paul.**
  我寫信是要感謝你為我兒子保羅所做的一切。

- **Jill went abroad to forget her ex-husband Bill.**
  為了忘記前夫比爾，潔兒出國了。

- **Amy White got up early to have enough time to get to the airport three hours before her flight.**
  艾咪・懷特早早起床，以便有足夠的時間在飛機起飛前三小時到達機場。
  ⤴ to have enough time 是不定式片語表目的，起副詞作用，修飾片語動詞 got up；to get to the airport 是不定式片語起形容詞作用，修飾名詞 time，也稱作名詞補語。

- **I filled my bowl with cereal, only to find out there was no milk in the fridge.** 我把碗倒滿麥片，卻發現冰箱裡沒有牛奶了。
  ⤴ 不定式片語還可表結果，表示「發現意外事情」，常和 only 以及動詞 find、discover、realize 等連用。

2 不定式作形容詞補語

a 不定式片語常用在一些形容詞後面作形容詞補語，在這種情況下，有些文法家把不定式視為修飾形容詞的副詞片語。

- silly to believe 笨到去相信
- easy to understand 容易理解
- sorry to hear 遺憾地聽到
- too hot to work 熱得沒法工作
- old enough to drive 年齡大到能開車

b 不定式（帶 to）常用在下列具有**評論**意味的形容詞後面，表達對某人行為的評論和看法。

- clever 聰明的
- crazy 瘋狂的
- lucky 幸運的
- silly 糊塗的
- smart 精明的
- stupid 愚笨的
- right 正確的
- wise 明智的
- wrong 錯誤的

- You are silly to trust Jenny. 你居然傻到去信任珍妮。
- He was lucky not to have been killed by that thug. → not + 不定式
  他很幸運，沒有被那個惡棍殺死。

c 不定式（帶 to）可用於下列表示**情感**的形容詞後面，表示對某事的感覺。

- afraid 害怕的
- anxious 焦慮的
- content 滿足的
- glad 高興的
- happy 高興的
- hesitant 躊躇的
- pleased 滿意的
- sad 難過的
- shocked 震驚的
- sorry 遺憾的
- surprised 驚訝的
- unhappy 不高興的

- Is Ruth afraid to hear the truth? 露絲怕聽到真相嗎？
- Pam would not be content to just pass the English exam.
  潘姆不會僅僅滿足於英語考試及格。
- Mary was hesitant to tell me about her new boyfriend, Jerry.
  瑪麗遲疑地告訴我她新交了男友，名叫傑瑞。
- My sister is determined to win the next city beauty contest.
  我妹妹下定決心要在下一次的全市選美比賽中獲勝。

d **形容詞修飾不定式**：不定式（帶 to）常成為前面形容詞的修飾對象，這種句型裡的形容詞並不修飾主詞。用於這種情況的形容詞有：

- difficult 艱難的
- easy 容易的
- hard 困難的
- impossible 不可能的
- good 好的
- nice 不錯的
- interesting 有趣的

- Scot, is English easy to learn by reading a lot?
  ↑ easy 修飾後面的不定式 to learn，而不是修飾主詞 English。
  = Scot, is it easy to learn English by reading a lot?
  史考特，靠大量閱讀就可以輕鬆地學會英語嗎？
  ↑ it 是形式主詞，實際主詞不定式片語置於句尾。
- This door is very difficult to open.
  ↑ 形容詞 difficult 修飾其後的不定式，不修飾主詞 this door。
  = It is very difficult to open this door. 這道門很難打開。
  ↑ It 是形式主詞；不定式是實際主詞，置於句尾。

✕ "This mountain is very difficult to climb it," gasped Mary.

✓ "This mountain is very difficult to climb," gasped Mary.

瑪莉喘著氣地說：「這座山真難爬啊。」

↑ very difficult to climb 是主詞 this mountain 的補語，climb 後面不能跟代名詞 it 作受詞，去重複主詞 this mountain。

比較 如果不定式動詞 climb 後面要接受詞（to climb this mountain），就得改變句型，把不定式片語作為主詞：

"To climb this mountain is very difficult," gasped Mary.

↑ 不定式作主詞。

= "It is very difficult to climb this mountain," gasped Mary.

瑪莉喘著氣地說：「這座山爬起來真吃力啊。」

↑ It 是形式主詞；不定式是實際主詞，置於句尾。

e 「too + 形容詞 + 不定式（帶 to）」：表示「太……以至於不能……」。

- Roy is too excited about his new toy jeep to fall asleep.
  = Roy can't fall asleep, because he is too excited about his new toy jeep. 羅伊因為他的新玩具吉普車而興奮得睡不著覺。
  ↑ 這句相當於：羅伊睡不著覺，因為他對他的新玩具吉普車感到太興奮了。
- "It's too hot to walk to work today," groaned sweat-soaked Scot.
  = "I can't walk to work today, because it is too hot," groaned sweat-soaked Scot. 衣服被汗水浸透的史考特咕噥著說：「今天熱得無法走路去上班。」
  ↑ 這句相當於：「今天我無法走路去上班，因為天氣太熱了。」

f 「形容詞 + enough + 不定式（帶 to）」：表示「足夠……而可以……」。

- Mike isn't old enough to drive a motorbike. 邁克年紀太小，不能騎摩托車。
- Is Pat smart enough to figure out that her boyfriend Roy is a playboy? 派特是否夠聰明，能看出她的男友羅伊不過是個花花公子？
- Is she tough enough to handle those six children when they are naughty? 當那六個孩子調皮搗蛋時，她能否夠強悍地來對付他們呢？

注意 不定式還可以作名詞，具有名詞的功能（比如可以作主詞、受詞、主詞補語等）。參見 753 頁〈Part 5 不定式和動名詞的名詞相關用法〉。

動名詞

1 動名詞的定義

1 動名詞以 -ing 為字尾（例如：asking、firing、keeping、running），是具有動詞性質的名詞，具有名詞的所有功能，同時也保留動詞的部分特徵，例如可以接受詞或副詞。

2 一些文法家喜歡稱其為「-ing 形式」（-ing form），而不用術語「動名詞」。

3 動名詞經常與其他一些詞連用，構成動名詞片語，例如：smoking cigarettes（抽菸）。

- Smoking cigarettes is dangerous for you and your family.
  抽菸會危害你和你的家人。
  ↑ Smoking 是動名詞，作句子的主詞（如同名詞），並且接受詞 cigarettes（如同動詞）；Smoking cigarettes 為動名詞片語。

- I hope you enjoy bicycling around Europe this summer.
  希望你今夏的歐洲自行車環遊之旅愉快。
  ↑ bicycling 是動名詞，當作名詞，是動詞 enjoy 的受詞，並且接介系詞片語 around Europe this summer（如同動詞）；bicycling around Europe this summer 則是動名詞片語。

2 動名詞的用法

1 動名詞和動名詞片語實際上是名詞，具有名詞的所有特點，其用法和名詞完全一樣。

a 作主詞或主詞補語

- Being an American politician **can destroy your health and take away your wealth.** 當個美國政治家可能會毀掉你的健康，帶走你的財富。
- Swimming **is my favorite way to keep fit.** → 作主詞
  = My favorite way to keep fit is swimming. → 作主詞補語
  游泳是我最喜歡的健身方式。
- **"**Seeing **is not always** believing,**" noted Scot.**
  斯卡特指出：「眼見並不一定總是為真。」
  ↳ 動名詞 Seeing 作主詞，動名詞 believing 作主詞補語。

b 受詞（動詞或介系詞的受詞）

- **Amy doesn't like** being a politician. 艾咪不喜歡當政治家。
  ↳ being a politician 是動詞 like 的受詞。
- **Dan wrote a humorous book about** being a cook in Japan.
  丹寫了一本關於在日本當廚師的幽默書。
  ↳ being a cook in Japan 是介系詞 about 的受詞。
  » 詳細說明參見 753 頁〈Part 5 不定式和動名詞的名詞相關用法〉。

2 和 No 構成告示語：公告和招牌裡，動名詞前面常與 No 連用。

- NO CAMPING 禁止露營
- NO CYCLING 禁行自行車
- NO DIVING 禁止跳水
- NO DRINKING 禁止喝酒
- NO FEEDING ANIMALS 禁止餵食動物
- NO FISHING 禁止釣魚
- NO PARKING 禁止停車
- NO SMOKING 禁止吸菸
- NO SWIMMING 禁止游泳

3 動名詞可和另外一個名詞連用，構成**複合名詞**，表示此名詞的功能或用途。

- a jogging machine (a machine for jogging) 一台慢跑機（用來慢跑的機器）
- a sewing machine (a machine for sewing) 一台縫紉機（用來縫紉的機器）
- a sleeping bag (a bag for sleeping) 一個睡袋（用來睡覺的袋子）
- a washing machine (a machine for washing) 一台洗衣機（用來洗衣服的機器）
- reading glasses (glasses for reading) 閱讀用的眼鏡（用來閱讀的眼鏡）
- running shoes (shoes for running) 跑步鞋（用來跑步的鞋）

4 區分動名詞與現在分詞

動名詞（構成複合名詞）：表功能	現在分詞（不構成複合名詞）：表動作
● a waiting room (= a room for waiting) 一間等候室（用來等候的房間）	● a waiting train (= a train that is waiting) 一輛等候中的火車（正在等候的火車）
● a sleeping pill (= a pill that aids sleeping) 一粒安眠藥（幫助睡眠的藥丸）	● a sleeping child (= a child that is sleeping) 一個熟睡的孩子（正在睡覺的孩子）

・Please wait for Mary in the waiting room, and don't worry.
請在等候室裡等待瑪麗，不要擔心。

↑「動名詞 + 名詞」構成一個複合名詞。動名詞 waiting 作形容詞，修飾名詞 room，表示 room 的「用途」。

・Is the sleeping baby named Liz? 那個熟睡中的嬰兒叫莉茲嗎？

↑ 分詞當作形容詞，修飾名詞 baby，分詞與名詞之間是主詞和述語關係。

5 動名詞與邏輯主詞的搭配類型

a 動名詞在句中作**主詞**時，其邏輯主詞要用所有格形式（Tom's, Her, My）。

・My refusing to look at any of the sketches Jim had drawn annoyed him. 我拒絕看任何吉姆畫的素描，這惹他生氣了。

b 動名詞作**受詞**時，而句子主詞和動名詞的邏輯主詞不一致，在非正式用語中，動名詞的邏輯主詞可以用名詞的普通格（如：Jerry）或代名詞的受格（如：him, me）；但在正式用語中要用所有格（Jerry's, his, my）。

・Would you mind my working part time for another company?

↑ 代名詞所有格（正式）

= Would you mind me working part time for another company?

↑ 代名詞的受格（非正式） 你介意我在另一家公司兼職嗎？

・Dwight dislikes his wife's working late at night. → 名詞所有格（正式）

= Dwight dislikes his wife working late at night. → 名詞普通格（非正式）

杜威特不喜歡他的夫人夜晚熬夜工作。

↑ 句子主詞（Dwight）和動名詞的邏輯主詞（his wife）不同，動名詞的邏輯主詞用所有格（wife's）和普通格（wife）都可以。

- **Dwight dislikes working late at night.** 杜威特不喜歡夜晚熬夜工作。
  ↑ 句子主詞就是動名詞的邏輯主詞(Dwight dislikes; Dwight working)。

C 在下列情況，動名詞無論作主詞或受詞，其邏輯主詞不能用名詞的所有格。

① 當動名詞之前的名詞為**複數名詞**、**集合名詞**、**抽象名詞**時，該名詞要以普通格出現，而非所有格。

- **Do you remember Steve and his parents visiting us on New Year's Eve?** 你記得史蒂夫和他的父母在除夕時來探望過我們嗎?
  ↑ 邏輯主詞較長，並且含有複數名詞，因此 parents 要用普通格。

- **The noise of car doors being opened and closed can often be heard in the crowded Lake Wood neighborhood.**
  在擁擠的湖木街坊，經常可以聽到汽車開門和關門的噪音。
  ↑ noise 是抽象名詞，並且其後有介系詞片語修飾，因此 noise 要用普通格。

② 當動名詞之前的名詞**被其他詞所修飾時**，該名詞要以普通格出現，而非所有格。

- **I was pleased by Dwight, my ten-year-old son, making supper tonight.** 我很滿意，我十歲的兒子杜威特今晚做了晚餐。
  ↑ 動名詞前的名詞 Dwight 被名詞片語 my ten-year-old son 修飾，Dwight 要用普通格。

③ 動名詞的邏輯主詞是**不定代名詞** someone、anyone 等，該不定代名詞要用普通格。

- **What would you do if you were a police officer and heard someone shouting, "Stop thief!"**
  假如你是一名警官，聽到有人喊叫「抓小偷」，你會怎麼做?

④ **感官動詞**(see、hear 等)之後要用名詞普通格/代名詞的受格，不用所有格。

- **We saw him dancing with Mary in Central Park.**
  我們看見他在中央公園裡和瑪麗跳舞。
  ↑ We 看見的是 him，並不強調看見的動作(dancing)，因此在感官動詞後面要用受格，不用所有格。dancing 是動名詞。
  ↑ 注意 部分文法學家把感官動詞(see、hear 等)後的 -ing 形式視為現在分詞。

不定式和動名詞的動詞特徵

不定式和動名詞都保留了一些動詞的句法特徵，可以接受詞或副詞修飾語，可以與助動詞連用，表達各種時間概念的細微差別，如過去、現在、進行或完成等，也可以有主動式和被動式。

1 不定式的時態和語態

1 不定式的各種形態

時態	主動不定式（主動語態）	被動不定式（被動語態）
簡單式	to fix	to be fixed
進行式	to be fixing	-
完成式	to have fixed	to have been fixed
完成進行式	to have been fixing	-

2 **不定式的簡單式**：根據句意所表達的時間而有所不同，例如：

a 表達一般性的動作（始終如一的事實）

- To dance with you **is my pleasure.** 能跟你跳舞，是我的榮幸。

b 表示其動作與述語動詞的動作同時發生

- **With a grin, Sue Rice whispered, "It's nice** to meet you."
  蘇·賴斯露齒笑著低聲說：「很高興認識你。」

c 表示其動作發生在述語動詞的動作之後

- **Kay and I would like** to visit the moon someday.
  凱和我都想有一天能去參觀月球。

- They are anxious to go back to India. 他們迫不及待想回到印度。

d 表示其**動作**發生在述語動詞的動作之前（通常是表狀態的動詞）

- I am so glad to have you back home. 真高興你回家了。
  ↥ to have you back home 是表狀態的動作，發生在 I am so glad 之前。

3 **不定式的進行式**：表示動作正在進行。

- It's nice to be sitting here with you. 很高興和你坐在這裡。
- The county government seems to be repairing the runways at the airport. 郡政府好像在維修機場跑道。
  ↥ 不定式進行式（to be repairing）與述語動詞（seems）同時，並正在進行。

4 **不定式的完成式**：表動作發生在述語動詞的動作之前，強調動作已經完成。

- It's nice to have met Sue.
  = It's nice that I have met Sue. 很開心能認識蘇。
  ↥ 不定式完成式 to have met 強調動作已經完成，相當於一個完成式子句。
- I'm sorry not to have called you yesterday.
  = I'm sorry that I didn't call you yesterday.
  很抱歉，昨天我沒有給你打電話。
  ↥ 不定式完成式的動作發生在述語動詞 am 之前，相當於簡單過去式。

✗ "To dance with you has been a great honor," declared Andrew.
✓ "To have danced with you has been a great honor," declared Andrew.「和您跳了舞，是莫大的榮幸。」安德魯說道。
↥ 句子的述語動詞是完成式（has been），表示動作發生在過去，而對現在依然有影響。不定式表示過去的動作時，要用不定式完成式。

比較

- "To dance with you is a great honor," declared Andrew.
  「能和您跳舞，真是莫大的榮幸。」安德魯說道。
  ↥ 述語動詞是現在式（始終如一的事實），不定式表達一般性的動作。
- "To dance with you will be a great honor," declared Andrew.
  「能和您跳舞，將是莫大的榮幸。」安德魯說道。
  ↥ 述語動詞是未來式，不定式（to dance）也表示未來的動作。

- "To have danced with you was a great honor," declared Andrew.
「和您跳了舞，真是莫大的榮幸。」安德魯說道。
↑ 述語動詞是過去式（只強調過去的一次跳舞）；不定式完成式表示動作（have danced）發生在動詞（was）之前，並已經完成。

- "To have danced with you is a great honor," declared Andrew.
「能和您跳這舞，真是莫大的榮幸。」安德魯說道。
↑ 述語動詞是現在式（剛跳過舞所說的話）；不定式完成式表示動作（have danced）發生在動詞（is）之前，並已經完成。

5 **不定式的完成進行式**：表示動作發生在述語動詞的動作之前，已經完成，並同時強調動作的持續性。

- I am happy to have been living in Chicago for two years, and I want to stay here after I get my Ph.D.
在芝加哥居住了兩年，我很愉快，希望我拿到博士學位後能繼續留在這裡。
↑ to have been living 在述語動詞（am）之前發生，並強調持續進行到現在。

- It is amazing to have won, and I am truly honored to have been competing with such an elite group of swimmers.
居然贏了，真讓人吃驚。能和這樣一群優秀的游泳者比賽，我感到很榮幸。
↑ to have won 強調動作的完成；to have been competing 強調動作的持續。

6 **不定式的被動式**：當不定式的邏輯主詞是該不定式所表示的動作的承受者時，不定式要用被動形式。不定式的被動形式，只有簡單式和完成式兩種。

✗ My geothermal energy report has to email to Kay by noon today.
✓ My geothermal energy report has to be emailed to Kay by noon today. 我的地熱能報告要在今天中午以前 email 給凱。
↑ 報告不能自動交上去，需要用不定式的簡單被動式。
不定式的邏輯主詞 report 是不定式動作的承受者（email . . . report）。

- To be elected governor might be the long-term political goal of Susan Cole. 當選州長，可能是蘇珊·科爾長期的政治目標。
↑ 不定式的簡單被動式表示未來，其邏輯主詞 Susan Cole 是不定式動作的承受者。

- A man who is good enough to shed his blood for his country is good enough to be given a square deal afterwards.
(President Theodore Roosevelt)

一個能為國家灑熱血的人，一定會得到公正的待遇。

↑ to shed 是簡單主動式，表示其邏輯主詞（A man）是不定式動作的執行者。
to be given 是簡單被動式，表示邏輯主詞（A man）是不定式動作的承受者。

- To have been bitten like that, Mark must have been attacked by a shark. 被咬成這樣，馬克一定是遭到鯊魚的攻擊了。

  ↑ 不定式的完成被動式強調動作已經完成，表示過去發生的事件對現在產生的效果，其邏輯主詞（Mark）是不定式動作的承受者。

2 動名詞的時態和語態

動名詞具有動詞的性質，跟述語動詞一樣，有時態和語態。

1 動名詞的各種動詞形式（與現在分詞的時態和語態形式一樣）

時態	動名詞的主動式（主動語態）	動名詞的被動式（被動語態）
簡單式	fixing	being fixed
完成式	having fixed	having been fixed

2 **動名詞的時態**：和不定式表示的時態一樣，如果動名詞表示一般性動作，或與述語動詞的動作同時發生或之後發生，要用動名詞的簡單式。如果動名詞的動作發生在述語動詞的動作之前時，要用動名詞的完成式。

- Seeing Kay dance a ballet always mesmerizes Ray.
  雷只要看到凱在跳芭蕾舞，就會被迷得團團轉。

  ↑ 動名詞的簡單式 Seeing 表達一般性的動作（習慣）。

- In our seeking for economic and political progress, we all go up or else we all go down. (President Franklin Delano Roosevelt)
  在追求經濟發展和政治進步時，我們一榮俱榮，一損俱損。

  ↑ seeking 是動名詞的簡單式，表示該動作與述語動詞的動作（go）同時發生。

- Midge is thinking of quitting her job and going back to college.
  米姬在考慮辭掉工作，返回大學念書。

  ↑ 動名詞的簡單式 quitting 和 going 所表示的動作，在述語動詞的動作（is thinking of）之後發生。

- Having worked 10 hours on the budget report made me completely exhausted. 做這份預算報告，我工作了十個小時，讓我精疲力竭了。
  ⤴ Having worked 是動名詞的完成式，指發生在述語動詞 made 之前的事。

3 動名詞的語態：和不定式一樣，動名詞也有主動式和被動式。

- Eating chocolate candy bars always makes me happy.
  吃巧克力糖果棒總是讓我感到快樂。
  ⤴ Eating 是動名詞主動簡單式，表示一般性動作（一件始終如一的事實），其邏輯主詞（I）是動作的執行者。

- Jim Wu doesn't like being lied to. 吉姆・吳討厭別人對他撒謊。
  ⤴ being lied to 是動名詞的被動簡單式，表示一般性動作（一件始終如一的事實），其邏輯主詞（Jim Wu）是動作的承受者。

- If you think too much about being re-elected, it is very difficult to be worth re-electing. (President Thomas Woodrow Wilson)
  如果你對再度當選考慮太多，就不要勉為其難了。
  ⤴ being re-elected 是動名詞的被動簡單式，表示在述語動詞的動作（think）之後發生，其邏輯主詞（you）是動作的承受者。

- Being elected governor is not enough for Tom Shaw, because he always wants more.
  對湯姆・蕭來說，當選為州長是不夠的，因為他永遠都不滿足。
  ⤴ 動名詞的被動簡單式（Being elected）表達一般性的動作；其邏輯主詞（Tom Shaw）是動作的承受者。

✗ Being elected governor of California, Coco Wu held a big party at the Blue Hotel in San Francisco.

✓ After having been elected governor of California, Coco Wu held a big party at the Blue Hotel in San Francisco.
  ⤴ having been elected 是動名詞的完成被動式，作介系詞 after 的受詞，整個 After having been elected governor 可以被看成是省略子句。動名詞的完成被動式，表示選舉事件發生在舉辦聚會之前，不能用動名詞的簡單式。

✓ Having been elected governor of California, Coco Wu held a big party at the Blue Hotel in San Francisco.
  可可・吳在當選為加州州長後，在舊金山的布魯飯店舉辦了一場大型的慶宴。
  ⤴ 這句是分詞片語作時間副詞。

不定式和動名詞的名詞相關用法

動名詞和**不定式**都可以當作名詞，具有名詞的功能，可以在句中作主詞、補語、受詞等。

1 不定式或動名詞作主詞

1 像名詞一樣，動名詞和不定式都可以作句子的主詞，不過，動名詞作主詞比不定式作主詞更自然。

- Asking Ms. Lime for help **would be a waste of time.**
  = To ask Ms. Lime for help **would be a waste of time.**
  = It would be a waste of time to ask Ms. Lime for help.
  要萊姆小姐幫忙是浪費時間。
  ↑ 上面第三句用 It 作形式主詞，而實際主詞（不定式片語）後置。

- Smoking (cigarettes) **is bad for your teeth, lungs, and heart.**
  = To smoke (cigarettes) **is bad for your teeth, lungs, and heart.**
  抽菸對你的牙齒、肺部和心臟都沒有好處。

- Being identical twins **was special, because sometimes Bess knew what Tess was going to say before she said it.**
  身為同卵雙胞胎是很特別的，因為有時黛絲還沒開口，貝絲就知道她要說什麼了。

2 **it 作形式主詞**，把實際主詞（動名詞片語或不定式片語）後置。

a 動名詞作主詞後置，常用在下列結構中：

- It is no good . . .（……是無益的）
- It is no use . . .（……是沒有用的）
- It is useless . . .（……是沒有用的）

- It is worth . . .　　　　　（……是值得的）
- It is hardly worth . . .　（……是不太值得的）
- It is a waste of time . . .（……是浪費時間）

・It is no use trying to persuade Gus to go sailing with us.
= Trying to persuade Gus to go sailing with us is no use.
要勸葛斯和我們一起出航，是沒有用的。
↑ 動名詞主詞太長時，用 It 作形式主詞更自然（如上面第一句），使句子保持平衡。

b 不定式作主詞後置，常用在下列結構中：

- It + be 動詞 + 名詞 / 形容詞 / 介系詞片語 + 不定式
- It + 動詞 + 受詞 + 不定式
- It + be 動詞 + 形容詞 + of/for + 名詞 / 代名詞 + 不定式

"It is my plan to reach the top of that ridge before sunset," declared Ann.
← 實際主詞不定式片語後置，結構為「It is + 名詞 + 不定式」。

= "To reach the top of that ridge before sunset is my plan," declared Ann.
← 不定式作主詞

= "Reaching the top of that ridge before sunset is my plan," declared Ann.
← 動名詞作主詞

安宣稱：「我的計畫是在日落前到達山脊頂上。」

It took me five years to get my bachelor's degree because I was working part time.
← 結構為「It + 動詞 + 受詞（間接和直接受詞）+ 不定式」。

因為在做兼職工作，我花了五年時間才拿到了學士學位。

It is easy for me to fall asleep at night.
← 結構為「It is + 形容詞 + for + 代名詞 + 不定式」。

= To fall asleep at night is easy for me.
← 不定式作主詞

= Falling asleep at night is easy for me.
← 動名詞作主詞

我晚上很好入睡。

2 不定式和動名詞作補語

1 不定式和動名詞作主詞補語

a 不定式可以在連綴動詞後作主詞補語，這種用法比不定式作主詞更常見。

Less common　To play ping-pong in the World Cup championship is my favorite fantasy.

Common　My favorite fantasy is to play ping-pong in the World Cup championship.

在世界盃錦標賽打乒乓球是我最大的夢想。

↑ 在第二個句子中，「My favorite fantasy」是主詞，不定式片語「to play ping-pong . . .」是主詞補語。

- One cool judgment is worth a thousand hasty counsels. The thing to do is to supply light and not heat. (President Thomas Woodrow Wilson)
  一個冷靜的判斷，勝過一千個草率的決策。該做的，是提供啟發，而不是衝動。
  ↑ The thing to do 是「名詞 + 不定式」結構，不定式做名詞補語。
  ↑ 不定式片語 to supply 置於連綴動詞 is 後作主詞補語。

b 動名詞也可以作主詞補語。

- Her biggest ambition was getting into Cambridge University.
  = Getting into Cambridge University was her biggest ambition.
  她最大的志向是進入劍橋大學。
  ↑ 動名詞片語在第一個句子中作主詞補語，在第二個句子中作主詞。

c 用不定式或動名詞作主詞補語，意義是一樣的。

- Jenny said her biggest ambition was to get into Yale.
  = Jenny said her biggest ambition was getting into Yale.
  珍妮說，她最大的志向是進耶魯大學。

- His favorite activity is to write romantic poetry.
  = His favorite activity is writing romantic poetry.
  他最喜歡的消遣是寫浪漫派的詩歌。

比較

Sailing my boat *The Sea and Sky* is my favorite hobby. ← 動名詞作主詞

= To sail my boat *The Sea and Sky* is my favorite hobby. ← 不定式作主詞

= My favorite hobby is sailing my boat *The Sea and Sky*. ← 動名詞作主詞補語

= My favorite hobby is to sail my boat *The Sea and Sky*. ← 不定式作主詞補語

= It is my favorite hobby to sail my boat *The Sea and Sky*. 我最喜歡的業餘愛好，是駕駛我的船「大海與天空」。 ← 實際主詞後置

↑ 主詞補語是說明主詞的，通常置於連綴動詞 be 後面。這裡的原句（上面第一和第二句）有連綴動詞 is，因此可以改成動名詞或不定式作主詞補語的句型（上面第三和第四句），也有實際主詞後置的句型（上面最後一句）。

2 不定式作名詞補語和同位語

a 名詞 + 不定式（作名詞補語）：不定式（帶 to）常用在名詞後面作名詞補語，即不定式作修飾名詞的形容詞（或稱定語）。

- Is there any way to ignore May and Kay when they snore?
  有沒有什麼辦法可以對梅和凱的打呼聲置之不理呢？
- We've got things to do and miles to go.
  我們有很多事要做，有很長的路要走。
- Her decision to retire from politics was a surprise to all of us.
  她退出政壇的決定，讓我們所有人都大吃一驚。
- Well, Annie Oakley, you have the right to remain silent and the right to have an attorney.
  好啦，安妮·歐克利，你有權保持沉默，也有權找律師。

- It is common sense to take a method and try it. If it fails, admit it frankly, and try another. But above all, try something. (President Franklin Delano Roosevelt)
  採納一種方法並試一試，這是常識。如果失敗了，就坦率地承認這方法不行，再試其他方法。但最重要的是，要勇於嘗試。

b 有些作名詞補語的不定式後面還有介系詞。這時有以下兩種結構：

名詞 + 不定式 + 介系詞	名詞 + 介系詞 + whom/which + 不定式（書面語）
● 名詞 + to live in	● 名詞 + in + which + to live
● 名詞 + to talk about	● 名詞 + about + whom/which + to talk
● 名詞 + to play with	● 名詞 + with + whom/which + to play

- My little daughter Pam needs a friend to play with.
  = My little daughter Pam needs a friend with whom to play.
  我的小女兒潘姆需要一個朋友和她玩。
- I am looking for a place to live in.
  = I am looking for a place in which to live. 我正在找地方住。

c **代名詞 + 不定式**（作代名詞補語）：不定式（帶 to）常放在下列不定代名詞後面作補語：

● something 某事	● nowhere 無處	● somebody 某人
● anything 任何事	● nothing 沒事	● anybody 任何人

- Would you like something to drink? 你想喝點什麼嗎？
- I am broke and have nowhere to go. 我破產了，哪兒也去不了。
- Claire confessed, "I've got nothing to eat and wear."
  克萊兒坦言：「我沒東西吃，又沒衣服穿。」
- "Isn't there anything else to watch?" Claire Tree muttered as she stared at the TV. 克萊兒·崔瞪著電視機咕噥地說：「還有沒有別的可以看？」

- I believe I shall never be old enough to speak without embarrassment when I have nothing to talk about. (President Abraham Lincoln)

  當我無話可說時，講起話來就無法從容自如。我相信這種情形會一輩子都如此。

  ↳ 形容詞 old 後面要接不定式作補語；
  「不定代名詞（nothing）+ 不定式 + 介系詞」，介系詞不前置。

d **名詞 + 不定式**（作同位語）：同位語對前面的名詞作補充說明。不定式也可以當作名詞的同位語，比較下列兩句的用法：

- Sue says her long cherished wish, to play ping-pong in the World Cup championship, has finally come true.

  蘇說，她嚮往已久的夙願——參加世界盃乒乓球錦標賽——終於實現了。

  ↳ 這句是不定式作同位語。her long cherished wish 就是指 to play ping-pong in the World Cup championship。

- Sue says her wish to play ping-pong in the World Cup championship has finally come true.

  蘇說，她想參加世界盃乒乓球錦標賽的願望終於實現了。

  ↳ 這句是不定式作名詞的補語（或稱定語，修飾或限定名詞），說明她的願望是參加世界盃乒乓球錦標賽。

3 動名詞作介系詞的受詞

1 名詞 / 形容詞 / 動詞 + 介系詞 + 動名詞

a 有些名詞、形容詞、動詞後面常接介系詞，例如：

- the thought of 想到……
- tired of 厭煩……
- talk about 談論……
- thank her for 因……而感謝她

b 這種情況下，介系詞後面應該用動名詞（-ing 形式），而不能用不定式。

- The thought of failing in the bikini contest never entered her head.

  她從沒想過自己會在比基尼泳裝比賽中失敗。

  ↳ 要用「名詞（thought）+ 介系詞（of）+ 動詞 -ing 形式」，
  不能用不定式 thought to fail。

- She is talking about moving her family to Paris.
  她正在談要舉家搬到巴黎的事。
  ⤴ 要用「動詞（is talking）+ 介系詞（about）+ 動詞 -ing 形式」，
  不能用不定式 is talking about to move。

- Excuse me for asking, but how much did you pay for that hard drive? 打擾一下，請問你花了多少錢買那個硬碟驅動器？
  ⤴ 介系詞 for 後面應該接 -ing 形式（asking）。

- Having slept for 10 hours, Ray felt good despite having worked 16 hours the previous day.
  睡了十小時的覺後，雷感覺不錯，儘管前一天他工作了 16 個小時。
  ⤴ 動名詞的完成式 having worked 表示動作發生在述語動詞 felt 之前，其結構為：
  形容詞（good）+ 介系詞（despite）+ 動名詞。
  ⤴ 句首 Having slept for 10 hours 是現在分詞片語，作時間副詞，修飾後面的主句。

2 **「介系詞 to + 動名詞」**的用法（有別於不定式）：to 有時不是不定式，而是介系詞。當 to 作介系詞時，後面要用動詞 -ing 的形式，即動名詞。

- be accustomed to 習慣於
- be devoted to 專心致力於
- be dedicated to 奉獻給
- get around to 抽出時間來做……
- get used to 習慣於
- look forward to 盼望
- object to 對……反對
- take to 開始從事

✗ Are you used to drive on the left side of the road?
✓ Are you used to driving on the left side of the road?
你習慣在左側開車嗎？
⤴ 片語動詞 are used to 中的 to 是介系詞，
後面要接動名詞 driving，不接原形動詞 drive。

- Glen, I look forward to seeing you again. 葛倫，期待再次見到你。
  ⤴ 片語動詞 look forward to 中的 to 是介系詞，要接動名詞（seeing）。

- "I'm half mermaid and prefer swimming to walking," teased Jade.
  潔德揶揄說：「我是半個美人魚，我喜愛游泳勝過散步。」
  ⤴ 動詞片語 prefer . . . to 中的 to 是介系詞，
  後面要接動名詞 walking，不接原形動詞 walk。

- Do you object to working extra hours when we get orders for lots of flowers?
  如果我們接到大量的買花訂單，你會反對加班嗎？
  ↥ 片語動詞 object to 中的 to 是介系詞，
  後面接動名詞 working，不接原形動詞 work。

- Margo took to studying both English and Spanish ten years ago.
  瑪歌十年前就開始學英語和西班牙語了。
  ↥ 在片語動詞 take to（開始從事）裡，to 是介系詞。

3 「before/after/since + **動名詞**」和「before/after/since + **子句**」：
在 before、after、since 等字的後面，可以用動名詞（-ing 形式），
也可以用「主詞 + 動詞」的結構。

a 用動名詞（-ing 形式）：這些字作介系詞用，動名詞為其受詞。

b 用「主詞 + 動詞」：這些字則為連接詞，連接從屬子句。

- Mary always feels happy after talking to Henry.
  = Mary always feels happy after she talks to Henry.
  瑪麗每次跟亨利談過話後，都感到很幸福。
  ↥ 第一句的 after 是介系詞；第二句的 after 是連接詞。

- Ted, you'd better have a glass of milk before going to bed.
  = Ted, you'd better have a glass of milk before you go to bed.
  泰德，你最好在上床睡覺之前喝一杯牛奶。
  ↥ 第一句的 before 是介系詞，第二句的 before 是連接詞。
  ↥ 上述這類用在介系詞（before、after 等）後面的動名詞片語（talking to Henry、going to bed）和介系詞一起，可以看成是分詞片語或省略子句。
  » 參見 736 頁〈4 分詞片語〉。

4 不定式和動名詞可以作動詞的直接受詞

1 動詞後面的直接受詞除了可以用名詞之外，還可以用不定式和動名詞（-ing 形式）。比較：

- Do you like milk tea? = Do you like to drink milk tea?
  = Do you like drinking milk tea? 你喜歡奶茶嗎？
  ↑ 第一句動詞 like 後面接複合名詞作受詞，第二句用不定式片語作 like 的受詞，第三句用動名詞片語作 like 的受詞。

2 「**動詞 + 不定式片語**」：不定式片語可以作動詞的直接受詞。

- Little Sally began to cry. 小莎莉哭了起來。
- Wendy hopes to become an astronaut after she gets her Ph.D.
  溫蒂希望在拿到博士學位後，可以當一名太空人。
- Jake refused to listen to Ruth, because he didn't want to hear the truth. 傑克拒絕聽露絲的話，因為他不想聽實話。
- I don't care much about being wealthy, and I just want to be happy and healthy. 我不太在乎要變得有錢，我只想開心、健康。
- Wisdom consists not so much in knowing what to do in the ultimate as knowing what to do next. (President Herbert Clark Hoover)
  智慧，與其說是在於知道最後該做什麼，不如說在於知道下一步該做什麼。
  ↑ 「疑問詞 + 不定式」可以作動詞或介系詞的受詞。疑問詞後面不接動名詞。
  ↑ 這句的兩個不定式片語 what to do 作動名詞 knowing 的受詞。記住，動名詞有動詞的特徵，可以接受詞。

3 「**動詞 + 動名詞（片語）**」：動名詞或動名詞片語可以作動詞的直接受詞。

- Pat admits that she loves being looked at.
  佩特承認她喜歡別人盯著她看。
- I hate being looked down upon by Kate. 我討厭被凱特瞧不起。
- Wendy has finished reading your book about chocolate candy.
  溫蒂已經讀完你那本關於巧克力糖果的書了。
- Susan wants to practice driving my big truck so she can pass her truck driving road test.
  蘇珊想練習開我的大卡車，這樣她就可以通過路考了。

5 動詞後面接不定式還是動名詞？

哪些動詞後面應該接動名詞，而哪些動詞後面應該接不定式？

✕ Kim and I decided swimming.
✓ Kim and I decided to swim.
金姆和我決定去游泳。
↑ decide 後面要接不定式，不可以接動名詞。

✕ Joy and Bing enjoy to laugh.
✓ Joy and Bing enjoy laughing.
喬伊和賓喜歡笑。
↑ enjoy 後面要接動名詞，不可以接不定式。

- Bing Sun likes to run.
  = Bing Sun likes running.
  賓·森喜歡跑步。
  ↑ 兩句都正確，意思一樣。

- Sally forgot to call her dad.
  莎莉忘了給她爸爸打電話。

- Sally forgot calling her dad.
  莎莉忘了給她爸爸打過電話。
  ↑ 以上兩句都正確，但意義有別。

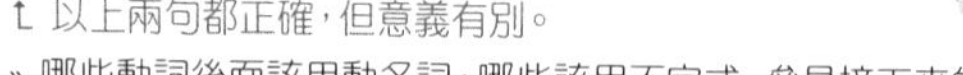

» 哪些動詞後面該用動名詞，哪些該用不定式，參見接下來的說明。

6 動詞 + 不定式（作受詞／動詞補語）

1 下列動詞後面要接不定式作直接受詞，一些文法家稱這種不定式為「不定式補語」或「動詞補語」。動詞補語，即是用來和動詞搭配，以使述語的意義或句法結構更加完整的字或字組。

表格 1 使用「動詞 + 不定式」的動詞

afford 負擔得起	expect 預料	prefer 寧可
agree 同意	fail 失敗	prepare 準備
aim 致力	forget 忘記	pretend 假裝
appear 似乎	get 有機會；有可能	promise 允許；承諾
arrange 安排	go on 繼續下去	propose 計畫；打算
ask 請求	happen 碰巧	refuse 拒絕
attempt 試圖	hate 仇恨	regret 懊悔
beg 請求	help* 幫助	remember 記得
begin 開始	hesitate 猶豫	seem 似乎
can't bear 無法承受	hope 希望	start 開始
care 想要	hurry 趕緊	swear 發誓要
choose 選擇	intend 想要	tend 趨向
claim 聲稱	learn 學習	threaten 威脅
consent 同意	like 喜歡	trouble 費心
continue 繼續	love 熱愛	try 試圖
dare 竟敢	manage 設法做到	undertake 著手做
decide 決定	mean 打算；意圖	volunteer 自願
decline 謝絕	need 需要	wait 等待
demand 要求	neglect 忽視	want* 想要
deserve 應得	offer 願意；試圖	wish* 但願
desire 渴望	plan 計畫	would like 想要

» 標有米字號（* ）的動詞，請參見下頁第 3、4、5 條解說。

- **June promised to be home soon.** 茱恩答應很快就會回家。
- **Kind Tom deserves to live a good life.** 善良的湯姆應該要有好的生活。
- **Mary had agreed to marry Henry, and then she found out he was already married to Sherry.**
  瑪麗已經答應嫁給亨利，但後來她發現亨利已經跟雪瑞結了婚。
- **Mary decided to buy a cute puppy instead of marrying Henry.**
  瑪麗決定不嫁給亨利了，乾脆買一隻可愛的小狗。

2 上述 表格 1 中的藍色字動詞，也可以接動名詞。比較：

- I can't bear to see her suffer like that.
  我不忍心見她如此受罪。
- I can't bear being bossed around by a useless playboy.
  我受不了一個無能的花花公子對我發號施令。
- Mary doesn't like cities. She prefers to live in the countryside.
  = Mary doesn't like cities. She prefers living in the countryside.
  瑪麗不喜歡城市。她寧願在鄉村居住。

  » 參見 771 頁〈12 接動名詞和不定式意義相同的動詞〉
  和 775 頁〈13 接動名詞和不定式意義稍有區別的動詞〉。

3 表格 1 中，有些動詞也可以接子句，例如：

- I wish working were an option.
  我希望可以自由選擇要不要工作。
  ↑ 整個子句 working were an option 是動詞 wish 的受詞。

4 在非正式的英式英語裡，want 後面可接動名詞（-ing 形式），意思是「需要」。

英式 This bill needs paying.
美式 This bill needs to be paid.
英式 This bill wants paying. 這張帳單該繳費了。

5 當動詞 help 用於動詞片語 can't help 裡，後面就要接動名詞，不接不定式，其意思是「忍不住……」、「不禁……」。

- Sue can't help shouting and jumping.
  蘇情不自禁地又喊又跳。

7 動詞 + 受詞 + 不定式（作直接受詞／受詞補語）

1 下列動詞需要先接一個受詞（人），再接一個不定式作直接受詞，也有文法學家稱這類不定式片語為「受詞補語」。

表格 2 **使用「動詞 + 受詞 + 不定式」的動詞**

- advise 建議
- allow 允許
- ask 要求
- (can't) bear（不能）忍受
- beg 請求
- believe 相信
- cause 導致
- challenge 挑戰
- choose 選擇
- command 命令
- convince 說服
- dare 挑逗；激
- encourage 鼓勵
- expect 預期
- forbid 禁止
- force 強迫
- get 說服；使得
- hate 仇恨
- help* 幫助
- hire 雇用
- instruct 指示
- intend 想要
- invite 邀請
- like 喜歡
- love 熱愛
- need 需要
- order 命令
- permit 允許
- persuade 說服
- prefer* 寧可
- prepare 準備
- promise 允諾
- recommend 建議；勸告
- remind 提醒
- request 要求
- require 要求
- show 告知；指出
- teach 教導
- tell 告訴
- tempt* 引誘
- train 訓練
- trouble 麻煩
- trust 信任
- urge 催促
- want 想要
- warn 警告
- wish* 但願
- would like 想要

» 標有米字號（* ）的動詞，請參見下頁第 3、4、5 條解說。

- **Today Ms. Lee allowed <u>us</u> to leave early.** 今天李女士允許我們提早離開。
- **I persuaded <u>Kay</u> to move to the U.S.A.** 我說服凱移居美國。
- **Dr. Sawyer said her parents had wanted <u>her</u> to be a lawyer.**
  索耶醫生說她的父母曾經要她當一名律師。
- **Mr. Bray, the EFL teacher, encouraged <u>his students</u> to read 25,000 words every day.**
  布雷先生是一名 **EFL** 老師，他鼓勵學生每天閱讀 **25,000** 個單字。
  ↑ EFL = English as a Foreign Language 以英語為外國語，
  指「在母語非英文的國家學習或教學英文」。

2 上述 **表格 2** 中的藍色字動詞，也可以直接加不定式，不需要先加受詞，與〈表格 1〉的動詞用法相同。比較：

- want to see you 想見你
- want her to stay 要她留下
- prepare to go to bed 準備上床
- prepare him to stand on his own 使他準備好獨立自主

· Do you wish to sit out on the balcony?
你想坐在外面的陽臺上嗎？

| 英式 | I wish you to go.
| 美式 / 英式 | I wish you would go. 我希望你離開。

3 表格 2 中，有些動詞還可以接動名詞或 that 子句。

· She prefers living in the countryside. 她寧可住在鄉下。
↑ prefer 常接動名詞、不定式或 that 子句（子句裡用原形動詞）。
「prefer + 受詞 + 不定式」結構不常見。

· I wish (that) I had never met Trish. 我希望自己從未遇見過翠西。

4 表格 2 中，動詞 help 有時也可以接原形動詞（不帶 to 的不定式）。
» 參見 738 頁〈2 不帶 to 的不定式〉。

· Can Trish Hammer help me to learn English grammar?
= Can Trish Hammer help me learn English grammar?
翠西·海默能幫我學習英文文法嗎？

5 表格 2 中，動詞 tempt 也可以直接接不定式，不過僅限用於被動語態（be tempted to do something）。比較下面例句：

· Tom is tempted to see if he can get away with it.
湯姆很想看看他是否能逃避責罰。

· What tempted her to steal the diamond ring?
是什麼引誘她去偷那個鑽石戒指？

8 動詞 + 動名詞（作受詞）

1 下列動詞常接動名詞作直接受詞。

表格 3 使用「動詞 + 動名詞」的動詞

- admit 承認
- appreciate 欣賞；感謝
- avoid 避免
- begin 開始
- complete 完成
- consider 考慮
- continue 繼續
- delay 拖延
- deny 否認
- detest 厭惡
- discuss* 討論
- dislike 厭惡
- encourage* 鼓勵
- enjoy 喜歡；享受
- escape 逃避
- excuse 原諒
- face 正視
- fancy 想像
- finish 結束
- forget 忘記
- forgive 原諒
- go (go fishing/swimming) 去（釣魚／游泳）
- hate 仇恨
- imagine 想像
- involve 牽涉
- keep (on) 繼續
- like 喜歡
- love 熱愛
- mention 提到
- mind 介意
- miss 錯過
- postpone 延遲
- practice 練習
- prefer 寧可
- quit 放棄
- recall 回想
- recommend* 建議；勸告
- regret 後悔
- remember 記住
- report* 報告
- resent 怨恨
- resist 抵抗
- risk 冒……的風險
- start 開始
- stop 停止
- suggest 建議
- try 嘗試
- understand 瞭解

» 標有米字號（* ）的動詞，請參見下頁第 3、4、5 條解說。

- **Mary went bowling last night with Gary.**
  瑪麗昨晚跟蓋瑞一起去打保齡球了。
  ↑ 習慣用語是 go bowling，不是 play bowling。

a golf cart

- **I enjoyed talking to Dwight last night.**
  我昨晚跟杜威特聊得很高興。
- **Has Bart finished fixing my golf cart?**
  巴特修好了我的高爾夫球車了嗎？
- **Did I mention meeting Jane last summer in Maine?**
  我提過去年夏天在緬因州見到珍的事嗎？
- **Sue quit smoking and drinking about a week after she met Andrew.**
  蘇認識安德魯大約一星期後就把菸酒戒了。

2 上述 表格 3 中的藍色字動詞，可以接動名詞，也可接不定式作為直接受詞。

» 參見 771 頁〈12 接動名詞和不定式意義相同的動詞〉和 775 頁〈13 接動名詞和不定式意義稍有區別的動詞〉。

3 表格 3 中，動詞 discuss 後面可以接「how/why/whether 等 + 不定式」。

- discuss how to avoid mistakes 討論如何避免犯錯
- discuss doing something 討論做某事

4 表格 3 中，動詞 encourage 和 recommend 也可以接「受詞 + 不定式」。

- encourage/recommend somebody to do something
  鼓勵／建議某人做某事
- encourage/recommend making reservations early
  鼓勵／建議提早預定

5 表格 3 中，動詞 report 也可以接不定式，不過只限於被動語態。

- somebody is reported to do something 報導指出某人做某事
- report hearing a loud noise 報導聽到了一聲巨響

9 動詞 + 受詞 + 動名詞（作受詞）

1 表格 3 中，接動名詞的動詞，有些可以先接受詞（人），再接動名詞當作第二個受詞，如：

- dislike 不喜歡
- like/love 喜歡；愛
- recall 回想
- risk 冒險
- hate 恨
- mind 介意
- regret 後悔
- start 開始
- imagine 想像
- miss 錯過
- resent 怨恨
- stop 停止

・I dislike getting up early on Sunday morning.
我不喜歡星期天一大早就起床。

・Sue dislikes people telling her what to do and what to think.
蘇不喜歡人們告訴她該做什麼、該想什麼。

・She imagined becoming rich and famous. 她幻想致富成名。

- Can you imagine Kate working late at night in her office?
  你能想像凱特在辦公室裡工作到深夜嗎？

2 還有一些動詞在 -ing 形式之前**必須帶有一個受詞**，如：

- catch 偶爾發現
- discover 發現
- feel 感覺
- find 發現
- hear 聽見
- leave 使處於某狀態
- notice 注意到
- observe 注意到
- overhear 無意中聽到
- see 看見
- spot 發現
- watch 觀看

- "I just can't see them winning this basketball game," said Dee with a sigh. 蒂嘆了口氣說：「我無法想像他們會贏這場籃球比賽。」
- Yesterday I caught Andy stealing some candy.
  昨天安迪偷了一些糖果，被我逮到了。

10 動詞片語 + 動名詞（作受詞）

下列動詞片語或片語動詞要接**動名詞**作受詞。

表格 4 動詞片語／片語動詞＋動名詞

- approve of 贊成
- be accustomed to 習慣於
- be better off 景況較佳
- be used to 習慣於
- burst out 突然……起來
- can't help 忍不住
- can't see 無法想像
- can't stand 無法忍受
- count on 依靠
- do not mind 不介意
- feel like 想要
- forget about 忘記
- get through 做完
- give up 放棄
- insist on 強烈要求
- keep on 繼續
- leave off 停止
- look forward to 期待
- object to 反對
- put off 推遲
- think about 考慮
- think of 想到；考慮

- They kept on talking and walking. 他們繼續邊聊邊走。
- Midge is thinking of getting a divorce, quitting her job, and going back to college. 米姬正在考慮離婚，然後把工作辭掉，回大學去讀書。

- She can't help feeling a little jealous about her boyfriend's ex-wife.
  她不禁有點吃男友前妻的醋。
- Susan is not accustomed to dancing with strangers.
  蘇珊不太習慣和陌生人跳舞。

11 「動詞 + 動名詞」或「動詞 + 受詞 + 不定式」的句型

下列的動詞用於主動語態時，如果後面沒有其他受詞，就要接**動名詞**（-ing 形式）；如果還有受詞，受詞後面就用**不定式**。

表格 5 加動名詞或加「受詞 + 不定式」的動詞

● advise 勸告	● encourage 鼓勵	● permit 允許
● allow 允許	● forbid 禁止	● recommend 建議；勸告

✗ Their new rule forbids to kiss in public school.
✓ Their new rule forbids kissing in a public school.
✓ Their new rule forbids people to kiss in a public school.
他們的新規定是禁止人們在公立學校親吻。

- I wouldn't advise taking your car to the ballet, because it's difficult to find a place to park.
  = I wouldn't advise you to take your car to the ballet, because it's difficult to find a place to park.
  我不會建議你開車去看芭蕾舞，因為很難找車位。
- This bank allows making deposits or withdrawals on weekends.
  = This bank allows you to make deposits or withdrawals on weekends.
  這家銀行在週末可以存款或取款。
- I recommend reading this book before you go to India.
  我建議你去印度之前讀讀這本書。
- The travel agency recommended you to book your flight early. → 英式
  = The travel agency recommended that you (should) book your flight early. 旅行社建議你早點訂機票。

↑ 動詞 recommend 後面可以接動名詞，也可以接子句，子句裡用原形動詞（美式）或 should + 原形動詞（英式）。英式還可以用「recommend + 人物 + 不定式」。

- **The police don't permit parking on this street.**
  警方不允許在這條街上停車。

- **We don't permit people to keep dogs in this apartment complex.**
  我們不允許人們在這個綜合公寓設施裡養狗。

動詞 suggest 不能用「動詞 + 受詞 + 不定式」結構。suggest 後面要接 that 子句（子句裡用原形動詞或「should + 原形動詞」）或動詞 -ing 形式。

✗ Mark Day suggests us to go to the park on Sunday.
✓ Mark Day suggests our going to the park on Sunday.
↑ suggest + 代名詞所有格（his, my, our 等）+ 動詞 -ing 形式
✓ Mark Day suggests that we go to the park on Sunday.
馬克‧戴建議我們星期天去公園。
↑ 美式更常用「suggest + that 子句 + 原形動詞」結構。

12 接動名詞和不定式意義相同的動詞

1 下列的動詞可以接不定式，也可以接動詞 -ing 形式，兩者在意思上幾乎沒有區別。

表格 6 接動名詞和不定式意義相同的動詞

attempt 企圖	cease 停止	like 喜歡
begin 開始	continue 繼續	love 熱愛
bother 打擾	hate 憎恨	prefer 偏好
(can't) bear（無法）承受	intend 想要	start 開始

- **When did Joe begin to learn judo?**
  = When did Joe begin learning judo?
  喬是什麼時候開始學柔道的？

- Though she was tired, Sue Flower continued to speak for another hour.
  = Though she was tired, Sue Flower continued speaking for another hour.
  蘇·福勞爾雖然已經很累了，但她還是繼續講了一小時。

- Mitch likes to play volleyball on the beach.
  = Mitch likes playing volleyball on the beach. 米奇喜歡在海灘上打排球。

- I hate to work on weekends.
  = I hate working on weekends. 我討厭在週末工作。

- Do you intend to tell Ann about your plan?
  = Do you intend telling Ann about your plan? 你打算把你的計畫告訴安嗎？

- Claire can't bear to be separated from her robotic doll.
  = Claire can't bear being separated from her robotic doll.
  克萊兒無法忍受和她的機器人娃娃分開。

✗ On Sunday afternoons Kay prefers staying in the church and pray.
✓ On Sunday afternoons Kay prefers staying in the church and praying.
✓ On Sunday afternoons Kay prefers to stay in the church and pray.
星期天下午，凱寧願待在教堂祈禱。

↳ prefer 後面既可以接不定式，也可以接動名詞。句子要用平行結構，要嘛都用動名詞，要嘛都用不定式。但錯誤句用了一個動名詞 staying 和一個是不定式 pray，是不平行結構。

like 後面可以接動名詞，也可以接不定式，意義相同，但其反義詞 dislike 則不一樣。dislike 後面只能接動名詞。

✗ He dislikes to listen to modern music.
✓ He dislikes listening to modern music. 他不喜歡聽現代音樂。

2 like、love、hate、prefer 的美式用法與英式用法對比。

a **談論「樂趣、愛好」**（enjoyment）：like（喜歡）、love（喜愛）、hate（討厭），prefer（比較喜歡），這幾個動詞可以接不定式，也可以接動名詞（-ing 形式）。談論樂趣和愛好時，在美式英語中，兩者意思幾乎沒有區別，而英式英語則常用「like/love + 動名詞」。

| 美式 | Jake's sister Kim likes climbing mountains and swimming in cold lakes.
= Jake's sister Kim likes to climb mountains and swim in cold lakes.

| 英式 | Jake's sister Kim likes climbing mountains and swimming in cold lakes. 傑克的姊姊金姆喜歡爬山和在冰冷的湖裡游泳。

↑ 談論樂趣、愛好。

b **談論「選擇、習慣」**（choices and habits）：無論美式還是英式，談論選擇和習慣時，通常用「like/love + 不定式」。

| 美式/英式 | When Dee is making tea, she likes to add a little bit of coffee. 蒂煮茶的時候喜歡放一點咖啡。

↑ 談論習慣。

c would like/would prefer/would hate/would love 後面要接不定式，不接動名詞。

- "Can I give you a ride?" "I'd prefer to walk, but thanks a lot for your offer of a ride."
「要不要搭我的便車？」「我寧願走路，不過還是要謝謝你，好心讓我搭便車。」
↑ 不能說「I'd prefer walking.」。

- "Do you like dancing/to dance?" asked Sue.
= "Do you enjoy dancing?" asked Sue.
蘇問：「你喜歡跳舞嗎？」
↑ 談論樂趣、愛好。

- "Would you like to dance?" asked Andrew.
= "Do you want to dance?" asked Andrew.
安德魯問：「你想跳舞嗎？」
↑ would like 後面不能接動名詞。

- I like being/to be rich! = I enjoy being rich!
我喜歡富有錢人！

- I'd like to be rich! = I want to be rich! 我想變成有錢人！

比較

① 指「特定場合更喜歡做什麼」時，要用「would prefer + 不定式」，不接動名詞。

✕ "Shall we go out to eat tonight?" "Well, I'd prefer eating at home."
✓ "Shall we go out to eat tonight?" "Well, I'd prefer to eat at home."
「我們今晚去面吃，好嗎？」「這個嘛，我寧願在家吃。」

② 泛指時，用 prefer to do 或 prefer doing。

・She prefers to walk to school.
= She prefers walking to school. 她更喜歡走路去上學。

d begin/start 接不定式或動名詞的用法。

① begin/start 這兩個表示「開始」的動詞，可以接不定式，也可以接動名詞，意義幾乎相同。

② 但是 begin/start 若使用**進行式**（beginning/starting），則後面要用**不定式**，不用動名詞。

③ begin/start 後面如果接**狀態動詞**，如 believe（相信）、understand（理解）、realize（明白）、know（知道）等，也只用**不定式**。

・Joe began to study English two years ago.
= Joe began studying English two years ago.
喬是兩年前開始學英語的。

✕ It's beginning looking like Christmas.
✓ It's beginning to look like Christmas.
已經開始看起來像聖誕節了。
↑ 進行式 is beginning 後面只能接不定式。避免同時使用兩個 -ing 形式。

✕ I have finally begun understanding why Dee doesn't like me.
✓ I have finally begun to understand why Dee doesn't like me.
我終於開始理解安為什麼不喜歡我。
↑ understand 是狀態動詞，跟在 begun 後面不能用 -ing 形式。

13 接動名詞和不定式意義稍有區別的動詞

下列動詞可以接不定式，也可以接動名詞，但意義有區別。

表格 7 接動名詞和不定式意義稍有區別的動詞

• forget 忘記	• need 需要	• stop 停止
• go on 繼續	• regret 後悔；遺憾	• try 嘗試；努力
• mean 意指；打算	• remember 記得	

1 remember（記得）／forget（忘記）

a remember/forget + 不定式：朝未來看，表達仍然待做的事情，或在想起／忘記的當下仍然需要做的事，意思是「記得／忘記要做某事」（with regard to the future）。

b remember/forget + 動名詞：朝過去看，表達某人過去做過事情，意思是「記得／忘記做過某事」（with regard to the past）。

・Sorry, I forgot to tell her about your visit.
= Sorry, I did not remember to tell her about your visit.
對不起，我忘記跟她說你來過。
↑ 我還沒有告訴她，所以我仍然需要告訴她。

・Dirk forgot to do his math homework.
= Dirk didn't remember to do his math homework. 德克忘記做數學作業了。
↑ 德克沒有做他的數學作業，因為他不記得要做作業。

・Dirk forgot doing his physics homework.
= Dirk forgot that he had done his physics homework.
德克忘記他已經做了物理家庭作業。
↑ 德克已經做了物理家庭作業，不過他忘記他已經做了。

・I will never forget visiting the Taj Mahal!
= I will never forget having visited the Taj Mahal!
= I will always remember visiting the Taj Mahal.
= I will always remember having visited the Taj Mahal.

我永遠也不會忘記（我永遠都會記得）參觀泰姬陵的經歷！

↥ 我參觀過泰姬陵。在動詞 forget、remember、regret 等字後面，可以用「having + 過去分詞」結構代替 -ing 形式，意思沒有區別。用動名詞完成式，更清楚表達動作發生在過去，點出時間層次。

2 mean to do（打算）／ mean doing（意味著）

a **mean + 不定式**：打算；意圖（= intend）

b **mean + 動名詞**：意味著；需要（= involve）；某件事以另一件事為結果。

✗ Do you mean going to New York to see Andrew without any money on you?

✓ Do you mean to go to New York to see Andrew without any money on you? 你打算身無分文就去紐約看安德魯嗎？ → 打算；意圖

・My flight will take off at 6 a.m. That means getting up at 3 a.m. so as to have enough time to get to the airport and go through the security check. 我的航班將在早上六點起飛，這就意味著早上三點就要起床，才有足夠的時間去機場並通過安檢。

↥ 牽涉；意味著；需要

3 regret to do（遺憾）／ regret doing（後悔）

a **regret + to tell/inform/say + that 子句**：即將做一件自己感到遺憾的事（with regard to the future）。（regret 接不定式，通常只接 tell、inform、say 這類動詞，用於宣布壞消息。）

b **regret + 動名詞**：涉及過去，後悔做過的某事（with regard to the past）。

・I regret to say that I am unable to help your sister Sue.
很遺憾，我得說我無法幫助你的妹妹蘇。

↥ 宣布一個壞消息。

・I regret saying that I was unable to help your sister Sue
= I regret having said that I was unable to help your sister Sue.
我後悔說過，我無法幫助你的妹妹蘇。

↥ 為過去做過的某件事後悔。此處的 saying 是在動作 regret 之前就已經發生的事。

↥ 這裡也可用動名詞完成式（I regret having said），更明確地表明「說」這個動作發生在過去（點出時間層次）。

- I regret to tell you and Pam that neither of you passed the English exam. 很遺憾地告訴你和潘姆，你們兩個的英語考試都沒有過。

  ↑ 抱歉地告訴對方一個壞消息。

- I regret telling you and Pam that neither of you had passed the English exam.

  = I regret having told you and Pam that neither of you had passed the English exam. 我很後悔，把你和潘姆英語考試不及格的消息告訴了你倆。

  ↑ 動詞 tell 發生在過去（可以用動名詞的簡單式 telling，也可以用動名詞的完成式 having told），子句動詞 pass 發生在動詞 tell 之前，要用過去完成式（had passed），表示「過去的過去」。

4 stop to do（停下來去做……）／ stop doing（停止做……）

a **stop + 不定式**：停止正在做的事，去做另一件事（表示停止做某事的目的）。

b **stop + 動名詞**：停止了做某事（不繼續做）。

- He stopped to say a prayer before he entered the courthouse.
  他停下來祈禱，然後才走進法院大樓。

  ↑ stop to say = stop in order to say（表示目的）

- Amy, stop yelling at me! 艾咪，不要再對我大吼大叫！

- I stopped to smell the roses and enjoy the sunshine.
  我停下來聞玫瑰花，享受陽光。

- I stopped smelling the roses and went into the teahouse.
  我停止了聞玫瑰花，走進茶館。

5 try to do（試圖）／ try doing（試試看）

a **try + 不定式**：努力做某事（make an effort; do something complicated）。

b **try + 動名詞**：試著做某事，看看會有什麼結果（attempt to do something in testing to see what might happen）。

✗ Danny tried to send the architect Nancy Wu two red roses every day, but it didn't have any effect.

✔ Danny tried sending the architect Nancy Wu two red roses every day, but it didn't have any effect.
丹尼每天都試著送建築師南西·吳兩朵紅玫瑰花，但沒有產生任何效果。
↳ 要表示「試看做某事，看看會有什麼結果」，只能用「try + 動名詞」。

- Try drinking some warm milk, and that might stop your hiccups.
試試喝點熱牛奶，也許就不會再打嗝。

- They tried to get the large couch into the room, but the doorway was too small. 他們試著把大沙發搬進房間，可是門道太小，搬不進去。
↳ 表示努力做某事時，通常用「try + 不定式」（但也可以用動名詞）。

6 go on to do（接著做某事）／ go on doing（繼續做某事）

a go on + 不定式：完成某事後，接著做另一件事情，表示行為、動作有變化（start something new）。

b go on + 動名詞：不停地繼續做某事（原本就在做的事）（continue with the same action）。

GIZA

- After the break, Kay went on to tell us about her experiences in Egypt. 休息後，凱接著告訴我們她在埃及的經歷。
↳ 涉及行為、動作變化。

- Despite the snowflakes that began to fall, Mark and I went on playing in the park. 儘管開始落下雪花，我和馬克仍繼續在公園裡玩耍。
↳ 繼續做某事（原本就在公園玩耍，開始下雪後，仍然繼續在公園玩耍）。

7 need to do（需要做某事）／ need doing（某事物需要被……）

a 人 + need + 不定式：need 接不定式，表示「需要」。

b 英式 物 + need + 動名詞：need 接動名詞，具有被動含意。

c 美式 物 + need + 被動不定式：need 接被動不定式，具有被動含意。

- I need to talk to the boss about getting a pay raise.
我需要跟老闆談談加薪。

英式 Your room needs cleaning.
美式 Your room needs to be cleaned. 你的房間需要打掃。
↳ 英式用動名詞表示被動；美式則用不定式的被動式。

8 learn（學）／teach （教）

a **learn/teach + 不定式**：表達學或教的**結果**，意思是「學會 / 教會做某事」（referring to the result of the study）。

b **learn/teach + 動名詞**：表達學習或教學的**內容**（referring to lessons or subjects of study）。

Hong Kong

- **I learned to read Chinese at school, but I learned to speak it while living in Hong Kong.**
  我在學校學會了閱讀中文，但在香港居住時才學會了講中文。
- **Clive taught me (how) to drive.** 克萊夫教會了我開車。
  ↑「teach + 人 + 不定式」=「teach + 人 + how + 不定式」
- **Ann teaches swimming in the summer and ice skating in the winter.**
  安夏天教游泳，冬天教滑冰。

14 感官動詞

下列的動詞可以接**動名詞**（-ing 形式），也可以接**原形動詞**（不帶 to 的不定式），但意義稍有不同。（也有文法家把感官動詞後面的 -ing 形式看成是現在分詞，作受詞補語。）

表格 8 **感官動詞 + 受詞 + V-ing ／感官動詞 + 受詞 + 原形動詞**

feel 感覺	look at 看	overhear 無意中聽到
hear 聽見	notice 注意	see 看見
listen to 聽	observe 看到	watch 觀看

動名詞（-ing 形式）	不帶 to 的不定式（原形動詞）
① 動作在某段時間內不斷重複或發生	動作只發生一次
Mark heard some wild dogs barking most of the night in that nearby park. 馬克昨晚聽見有幾隻野狗在附近的公園叫了大半夜。	**Did you notice that woman spit on the sidewalk?** 你注意到那個女子把痰吐在人行道上了嗎？

動名詞（-ing 形式）	不帶 to 的不定式（原形動詞）
② 只看到或聽到動作的某一部分（不是從頭到尾的全部過程）	聽到或看見動作的整個完成過程（從頭到尾）
As I passed her room, I heard Ann arguing with her boyfriend Dan. 我從安的房間經過時，聽見她在跟她的男友丹爭吵。	**Once I heard Rose play two of Beethoven's concertos.** 有一次我聽到蘿絲彈了兩首貝多芬的協奏曲。
Coco was able to watch the workers building the skyscraper from her office window. 可可能夠從她辦公室的窗戶觀看工人們修建摩天大樓。	**I watched her cross the road and disappear into the forest.** 我望著她過了馬路，然後消失在森林裡。
③ 強調正在進行的活動（非全部過程）	強調整個事件或動作（從頭到尾）
I heard Bing singing. 我聽見賓在唱歌。	**I heard Bing sing.** 我聽見賓唱了歌。
Sue's little son stood nearby and watched her brushing the snow off the car. 蘇的小兒子站在旁邊，望著她把汽車上的雪刷下來。	**I watched Mabel clear the table.** 我望著美博收拾了飯桌。

Diving Deep Into English 88 感官動詞只在主動語態接原形動詞

hear、see、watch 這類感官動詞，只有在**主動**語態裡，才用不帶 to 的不定式（即原形動詞）；如果用**被動**語態，就要接帶 to 的不定式或接 -ing 形式。參見 739 頁〈Diving Deep Into English 87〉。

- **I saw Mark and Anna dance a tango in the park.**
  我看見馬克和安娜在公園跳了一曲探戈舞。→ 主動語態（不用 to）
- **Mark and Anna were seen to dance a tango in the park.**
  有人看見馬克和安娜在公園跳了一曲探戈舞。→ 被動語態（用 to）
- **Mark and Anna were seen dancing a tango in the park.**
  有人看見馬克和安娜在公園跳探戈舞。→ 被動語態可用 -ing 形式。
  ↳ 注意 被動語態更常用 -ing 形式（were seen dancing），比較少用不定式（were seen to dance），因為感官動詞後的被動不定式顯得不太自然。

UNIT

17 標點符號

Punctuation

句號

標點符號用來清楚表達語意和語氣的轉折，就像為讀者設計的交通標誌一樣，帶領讀者穿越語言的條條大道。

1 句尾的句號（Periods）

句號就像公路或大街上的標誌「停」，在你繼續閱讀之前，句號使你完全停下來。句號標示著陳述句、祈使句（一個命令、一個請求等）或一個輕微感嘆句的結束。美國人稱句號為 period，而英國人稱句號為 full stop。

1 **陳述句**要有句號。

- **Good manners are taught and cannot be bought.**
  良好的禮貌是教出來的，不是可以買來的。 → 陳述句

- **I will give Jake a chocolate shake.** 我要給傑克一份巧克力奶昔。 → 陳述句

2 語氣較輕的**祈使句**和**感嘆句**，可以用句號。

- **Ann, watch your step with that foolish young man.**
  安，跟那個愚蠢的年輕男子在一起要小心一點。
  ↑ 語氣輕微的祈使句（不帶強烈語氣）。

- **Erica prayed, "God bless Africa."** 艾芮卡祈禱說：「上帝保佑非洲。」
  ↑ 語氣輕微的感嘆句（指引號裡的句子）。

3 表「**禮貌請求或命令**」的「**疑問句**」，可以用句號：表達請求、建議或命令時，常出於禮貌而採用疑問句的形式，這類疑問句並不需要對方回答 yes 或 no，而是期待對方以行動回應，這類句子可以用句號結尾。也就是說，如果一個疑問句實際上並非用以提問，而只是為了禮貌而用疑

問句形式，那麼就可以用問號，也可以用句號。

- **Would you please email me by Monday if you need another ton of cheese.**
  = Would you please email me by Monday if you need another ton of cheese?
  如果你還需要一噸起司，請在星期一前寄電子郵件給我。

- **May I suggest that you and Amy take your vacation in Miami.**
  = May I suggest that you and Amy take your vacation in Miami?
  我建議你和艾咪到邁阿密去度假。

4 片語和從屬子句置於主句前或主句後，是否用句號？

a 出現在主句前面的片語和從屬子句，不要用句號。

b 出現在主句後面的片語和從屬子句，這個片語和附屬子句的前面（即主句後面）也不加句號，以免產生不完整的句子（sentence fragment）。這些不完整的句子可以是單一個字彙、片語或從屬子句，常被誤當作獨立句子，但實際上卻需要和相鄰的字合併在一起構成完整的句子。

✗ While Rose was sleeping. A rat chewed on her toes.

✓ While Rose was sleeping, a rat chewed on her toes.
  ↑ 從屬子句在主句前，從屬子句後面要用逗號，不用句號。

✗ A rat chewed on Rose's toes. While she was sleeping.

✓ A rat chewed on Rose's toes while she was sleeping.
  蘿絲在睡覺時，有一隻老鼠咬了她的腳趾頭。
  ↑ 從屬子句在主句後，從屬子句前面不用句號。

2 轉述疑問句：句尾要用句號

在間接引語中，疑問句的句尾要用句號，而不是問號。

- **The only question Jan asked was when Dan would come back from Pakistan.** 簡只問了一個問題：丹什麼時候能從巴基斯坦回來。

- **Actually, Lulu knew what to do, the question was how to pay for it.**
  實際上，露露知道要怎麼辦，問題是該怎麼付錢。

3 用於縮寫詞的句號

1 縮寫詞句號的使用原則

a 在**姓名首字母縮寫**（initials）和多數**縮寫詞**（abbreviation）的後面，要用句號。不過，有些縮寫詞的句號和大寫的用法可以有多種變化，例如：p.m.、P.M.、pm 和 PM 都是正確的，只要用法一致就行了（不要在一個句子裡用 p.m.，在下一個句子裡又用 PM）。

b **大寫的縮寫詞**可以省略句號，例如：CNN、CIA、FBI、IRS、NBC、USA。

c 多數**以小寫字母結尾的縮寫詞**通常用句號，例如：Dr.（博士；醫生）、Mr.（先生）、yr.（年）、mo.（月）。

1 以**小寫結尾**的縮寫詞，通常要加句號，但也有些例外，包括一些**計量詞**的縮寫：

- cm = centimeter(s) 公分
- gm = gram(s) 克
- ft = foot, feet 英尺
- mi = mile(s) 英里
- gal = gallon(s) 加侖
- ml = milliliter(s) 毫升
- oz = ounce(s) 盎司
- sq = square 平方
- mpg = miles per gallon 每加侖行駛的英里數
- mph = miles per hour 每小時英里數
- rpm = revolutions per minute 每分鐘轉數

2 **測量單位**的縮寫通常省略句號；無論單複數，縮寫形式都一樣。

- yd = yard = yards 碼

3 在句中，如果英寸的縮寫（in）可能被誤認為是介系詞 in，就需要句號（in.）來區別；如果在句中明顯是表示尺寸，就可以不要句號。

- 8 ft 2 in 八英尺兩英寸

d 含句號的縮寫詞，若位於句尾，則不需另外再加句號，這個句號既代表縮寫，也代表句子結束。

- **We are going to see the antiques that were made on the island of Santorini before 1625 B.C.**
  我們要去參觀西元前 1625 年之前在錫拉島製造的古董。

e 人的名字（first name）或中間名字（middle name），可作首字母縮寫（initial），然後加句號。人名的每個首字母縮寫後面，都要一個句號和一個空格。例如 Anna Marie Bean 這個名字的縮寫要寫成：

✗ A.M. Bean
✓ A. M. Bean
　↳ A 後面的句號，需要和字母 M 之間空一格。
　↳ A. 代表教名的首字母，M. 代表中間名字的首字母，Bean 是姓。

2 對人的尊稱的縮寫

Ms. 女士	這是對女性的尊稱，用於姓氏或姓名之前，可指已婚或未婚婦女。為避免透露婚姻狀況，可用 Ms. 來取代 Miss 或 Mrs.。 ● Ms. White 懷特女士　● Ms. Jane White 珍．懷特女士
Miss 小姐	對未婚女子的尊稱，用於姓氏或姓名之前。
Mrs. 夫人；太太	Mistress 的簡稱，用於已婚女性的丈夫的姓氏之前，或寡婦的已故丈夫的姓氏前。
Mr. 先生	Mister 的簡稱，用於男士的姓氏、姓名或職務之前，例如： ● Mr. Wang 王先生　● Mr. President 總統先生 ▪ Mr. E. B. Kopp and Ms. D. A. Day were married on July 14, 2008, in Tampa, FL, USA. E. B. 卡埔先生和 D. A. 戴女士於西元 2008 年 7 月 14 號在美國佛羅裡達州坦帕市結婚。 ↳ FL（佛羅裡達州）是 Florida 的縮寫；USA 或 U.S.A.（美國）是 United States of America 的縮寫。

尊稱 Ms., Miss, Mrs. 和 Mr. 後面，須接姓氏或整個姓氏和名字，而不能只接名字。比如下面就是常見的錯誤形式：

✗ Ms. Joyce 喬依絲女士 → Ms. 後面不能只接名字 Joyce。
✓ Ms. Brown 布朗女士 → Ms. + 姓氏
✓ Ms. Joyce Brown 喬依絲．布朗女士 → Ms. + 名字 + 姓氏

3 常見縮寫表

A.D./AD	Anno Domini 西元 (after the birth of Christ) ↥ 與日期一起使用。
a.m./am/ A.M./AM	ante meridiem 上午 (before noon) ↥ 如果不會與動詞 am 混淆，就可以縮寫為 am。
Ave.	Avenue 大街；大道
Apr.	April 四月
Aug.	August 八月
B.A./BA	Bachelor of Arts 文學學士
B.C./BC	before Christ 西元前
cm	centimeter(s) 釐米；公分
COD	cash on delivery 貨到付款
dept.	department 部；局；處；科
Dr.	Doctor 醫生；博士
Dr.	Drive 車道
e.g.	for example 例如
etc.	et cetera 等 (and so forth)
Feb.	February 二月
ft	foot; feet 英尺
gm	gram(s) 克
gr	grain(s) 喱；格令 grade 等級 grammar 文法 great 偉大 gross 總量 group 組
i.e.	id est 即；那就是 (that is)

in./in	inch(es) 英寸
IQ	Intelligence Quotient 智商
kg	kilogram(s) 千克；公斤
lb	pound(s) 磅
lit	liter(s) 公升 literature 文學 literary 文學的
Lt./Lt	Lieutenant 中尉
m	meter(s) 公尺 male 男性 manual 手冊 married 已婚 masculine 男性 mile(s) 英里
M.A./MA	Master of Arts 文學碩士
M.D./MD	Doctor of Medicine 醫學博士
memo	memorandum 備忘錄
min/min.	minute(s) 分鐘
min.	minimum 最小數
N.Y./NY	New York 紐約
No./no.	number 號碼 ↥ 小寫 no. 常用於索引。
Ph.D./ PhD	Doctor of Philosophy 博士
p.m./pm/ P.M./PM	post meridiem 下午 (after noon)
St.	Saint 聖…… ↥ 用在人名等之前。
St.	Street 大街

- **Did Ray earn his M.B.A. last year?**
  雷去年獲得商管碩士學位了嗎？
- **Lisa had told me she would meet me at the library before 10 a.m., but she didn't show up till 1 p.m.**
  麗莎告訴我，她會在上午 10 點之前和我在圖書館見面，可是她到下午一點才出現。

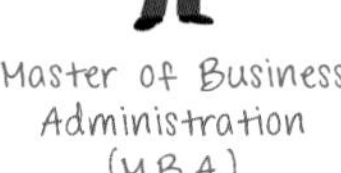

4 小數點、網路和電子郵寄地址

1 **小數點**：整數和小數中間要用句號分開，句號前後不要有空格。

£6.50	6.5 英鎊
€98.5 (= 98.5 EUR)	98.5 歐元
$230.45	230.45 美元
33.33 percent	33.33%

2 **網路**和**電子郵寄地址**：句號在這裡的發音為 dot。

- http://www.bankofbahrain.com
- tomnew@yahoo.com

逗號

1 逗號（Commas）的功能

1 逗號類似公路上的交通標誌「慢」、「暫停再開」；又好比開車時想轉彎，就要先減速，打開方向燈，然後再轉彎。在寫作中，逗號表示「小心」、「慢」、「暫停」，如果你想改變想法，插入別的想法，或對已陳述的觀點或事實加以確認，就要用逗號。

2 逗號可以影響句子的意思，請看下面的例句。

- **The food tasted bad, however Aunt Amy fixed it.**
  不管艾咪姑姑怎麼煮，這食物都很難吃。
- **The food tasted bad; however, Aunt Amy fixed it.**
  這食物不好吃，但艾咪姑姑把它弄好吃了。
  ↑ 第二句表示艾咪姑姑改進了食物的味道。

- **"May," asked Sam, "were you sick yesterday?"**
  「梅，」山姆問：「你昨天生病了嗎？」 → 山姆想知道梅昨天是否生病了。
- **May asked Sam, "Were you sick yesterday?"**
  梅問山姆：「你昨天生病了嗎？」 → 梅想知道山姆昨天是否生病了。

2 逗號的使用規則

1 **三個以上連續的同類字或數字**：一組詞若包含三個或三個以上的項目，就要用逗號將其分開，除非所有的項目都是用 and 或 or 連接的。

✕ It takes time effort and a lot of money to build a space elevator.

✓ It takes time, effort, and a lot of money to build a space elevator.

↳ 這句用兩個逗號和一個 and，將三個複合受詞（一組名詞和名詞片語）分開。

✓ It takes time and effort and a lot of money to build a space elevator. 要建成一座太空電梯，需要時間、精力和大量的金錢。

↳ 這句用兩個 and，把三個複合受詞連接起來。

✕ Mike Mark and I are going sailing on Lake Michigan.

✓ Mike, Mark, and I are going sailing on Lake Michigan.

↳ 這句用兩個逗號和一個 and 分開三個複合主詞（包含名詞和代名詞）。

✓ Mike and Mark and I are going sailing on Lake Michigan.
邁克、馬克和我要在密西根湖上航行。

↳ 這句用兩個 and，來連接三個複合主詞。

✕ I like to take a bus sit up high and watch the world go by.

✓ I like to take a bus, sit up high, and watch the world go by.

↳ 這句用兩個逗號和一個 and 分開三個複合的不定式動詞片語。

✓ I like to take a bus and sit up high and watch the world go by.
我喜歡搭公車，坐在高處上，看著人們從旁經過。

↳ 這句用兩個 and，連接三個複合的不定式動詞片語。

✕ If Sam works hard keeps calm and concentrates then he is likely to pass the exam.

✓ If Sam works hard, keeps calm, and concentrates, then he is likely to pass the exam.

↳ 這句的前兩個逗號用來分開條件子句裡的三個複合的述語動詞，
第三個逗號用來分開條件子句和主句。

✓ If Sam works hard and keeps calm and concentrates, then he is likely to pass the exam.
如果山姆努力學習、保持鎮靜、集中精神，那麼他就有可能通過考試。

↳ 這句用兩個 and，來連接條件子句裡的三個複合動詞，
用一個逗號來分開子句和主句。

Diving Deep Into English 89 and 或 or 的前面，要不要逗號？

❶ 連接三個或三個以上的詞彙時，有些人喜歡省略 and/or 前的逗號，但最好還是保留這個逗號，因為這樣更合乎規範，也使句意更清楚。

- **Please buy a bouquet of yellow, red, pink and white roses for Kay.**
- **Please buy a bouquet of yellow, red, pink, and white roses for Kay.**

請買一束黃色、紅色、粉紅色和白色的玫瑰給凱。

↳ 第一句在 and 前面沒有逗號，意思不是很清楚，包含了兩種意思。一種與第二句的意思一樣，一種卻是指這束花裡其中有一朵花是粉紅和白色混合的。

↳ 應該避免寫出具有兩種含意（double meaning）的句子，第二句在 and 前面有一個逗號，比第一句更清楚。

- **Tom, Midge and I are going to a beach cottage on Cape Cod.**
- **Tom, Midge, and I are going to a beach cottage on Cape Cod.**

湯姆、米姬和我要去科德角的一個海灘別墅。

↳ 第一句可以接受。第二句在 and 前面用了逗號，比第一句好。

❷ 如果 and 只連接兩個字，則不用逗號。

- **Mary and Sherry are going out to buy some lingerie.**

瑪麗和雪麗要出門去買一些女用睡衣。

↳ 只有兩個項目，不要用逗號把它們分開。

2 修飾同一個名詞的形容詞

a 連綴動詞之後的系列形容詞：兩個以上的形容詞，則要用逗號分開。

✗ The socks Ted gave me on my birthday were blue yellow orange or red.

✓ The socks Ted gave me on my birthday were blue, yellow, orange, or red. 在我生日那天，泰德給我的襪子有藍的、黃的、橙的和紅的。

b 名詞之前的系列形容詞：修飾同一個名詞的兩個或兩個以上的形容詞，如果可以用 and 連接，就可以用逗號代替 and；如果不能用 and 連接，就不可以用逗號，因為逗號的作用相當於連接詞 and。亦即，如果第一個形容詞修飾的是「第二個形容詞 + 名詞」（被看成一個整體概念，是複合名詞，即「名詞 + 名詞」），就不用逗號。

- That handsome, brilliant scholar is my brother Sam.
  = That handsome and brilliant scholar is my brother Sam.
  那個英俊瀟灑、才華橫溢的學者，是我的哥哥山姆。
  ⤷ 形容詞 handsome 和 brilliant 都修飾名詞 scholar，逗號相當於 and。

✗ Paul is wearing a white and cotton shirt.
✗ Paul is wearing a white, cotton shirt.
✓ Paul is wearing a white cotton shirt.
保羅穿著一件白色的棉質襯衫。
⤷ cotton 是名詞作形容詞修飾 shirt，構成一個複合名詞（棉質襯衫）；而形容詞 white 修飾整個複合名詞 cotton shirt，因此不要用逗號去分開形容詞 white 和複合名詞 cotton shirt。
⤷ 在修飾語之間（white 是修飾語，cotton 是名詞作修飾語）如果不能用 and 連接，就不要逗號。

✗ They bought a beautiful, spacious, and summer home in Gladstone, Michigan.
✗ They bought a beautiful, spacious, summer home in Gladstone, Michigan.
✓ They bought a beautiful, spacious summer home in Gladstone, Michigan. 他們在密西根的格拉德斯通買了一棟漂亮、寬敞的夏季住所。
⤷ spacious 修飾整個複合名詞 summer home，不要用逗號或 and 把形容詞 spacious 和 summer home 分開。

簡而言之，可以用 and 連接的形容詞，才能用逗號。

- a relaxed, calm, confident manner = a relaxed and calm and confident manner 一種悠閒、冷靜、自信的態度
- an intelligent, hardworking student
  = an intelligent and hardworking student 一位聰明、用功的學生
- an old stone house 一棟老舊的石屋
  ⤷ 不能說 an old and stone house 或 an old, stone house。
- the established Singaporean political system
  · 牢固確立的新加坡政治系統
  ⤷ 不能用 the established and Singaporean and political system 或 the established, Singaporean, political system。

3 **詳細日期和位址**，用逗號：日期和位址的細目，從第二項開始，每一項都要用逗號分隔。

- **Kay and Scot were married on Saturday, July 4, 2010, in Austin, Texas, USA.** 凱和史考特於 2010 年 7 月 4 號星期六，在美國德州的奧斯汀結婚了。

4 **在起介紹作用的成分（前導詞）後面**，要用逗號：位於句首的前導詞或片語後面，要用逗號，與後面的主句主詞和動詞分開。

a 表示**請求**或**命令**的前導詞後面，需要用逗號。

- look 喂，瞧
- you see 你知道

b 表示**評論**的前導詞後面，需要用逗號。

- actually 實際上
- as a matter of fact 事實上
- as you know 如你所知
- by all means 無論如何
- fortunately 幸運地
- happily 幸好
- if possible 如果可能的話
- if necessary 如果需要的話
- in my opinion 依我看來
- no 不是
- obviously 顯然地
- of course 當然
- personally 個人而言
- to tell the truth 說實話
- unfortunately 不幸地
- yes 是

c 在表示**過渡性**的詞語後面，需要用逗號。

- also 而且，再者
- as a result 結果
- as usual 照常，照例
- at any rate 無論如何
- besides 此外
- by the way 順便一提
- for example 例如
- generally speaking 總體而言
- however 然而，但是
- in addition 另外
- in any case 無論如何
- in general 一般地，通常地
- in other words 換句話說
- in the first place 首先
- in the long run 終究，到最後
- moreover 除此之外
- that is to say 也就是說
- therefore 因此
- to sum up 總的說來
- well 呃，這個，好啦，好吧

✗ Look Tess, adversity is the midwife of success.

✓ Look, Tess, adversity is the midwife of success.
瞧，黛絲，逆境促成成功。

- Hi, how are you, Sue! 嗨，你好，蘇！
- Well, that's certainly a happy surprise for Amy.
這個嘛，那對艾咪來說確實是個驚喜。
- In her opinion, you should not eat a big raw onion.
按照她的看法，你不應該吃一個生的大洋蔥。
- Oh, I have been looking for Claire here and there and everywhere.
哦，我一直到處在找克萊兒。
- Hopefully, Emma has learned how to protect herself from that bully.
但願愛瑪已經學會如何保護自己不受那個惡霸欺負。
- By the way, Dee, have you heard anything about Gary's HIV tests?
對了，蒂，你有聽到任何蓋瑞愛滋病毒篩檢的事嗎？
↑ By the way 是表示過渡性的前導詞，後面需逗號；直呼姓名 Dee，後面也要逗號。
» 參見 794 頁〈6 直呼姓名或稱謂，要加逗號〉。

5 **插入成分**的前後，都要使用逗號：當字彙、片語或從屬子句插入句中，打斷了句子從主詞到動詞到受詞（或補語）的連貫性，就要用兩個逗號（一前一後），把這些插入成分與句子分開。

✗ We can deliver this diamond necklace on your wife's birthday if you wish, before noon.

✓ We can deliver this diamond necklace on your wife's birthday, if you wish, before noon. → 插入語位於句中，要用兩個逗號。

✓ We can deliver this diamond necklace on your wife's birthday before noon, if you wish. 如果你希望的話，我們可以在你夫人生日那天的中午之前，把這條鑽石項鍊送去。
↑ 這句 if you wish 位於句尾，則用一個逗號與句子分開。
» 參見 794 頁〈7 句尾的添加成分，要用逗號〉。

- Steve is, no doubt, a straight-A student and a nice guy.
史蒂夫，毫無疑問，是一個高材生，也是一個善良的人。

- It is too late, I guess, to tell him about Kate.
把凱特的事告訴他，我想，已經太遲了。

- Sue, to be honest with you, Roy is a lazy playboy.
蘇，老實告訴你，羅伊是一個懶惰的花花公子。

- To be honest with you, Roy is a lazy playboy.
老實告訴你，羅伊是一個懶惰的花花公子。
↥ To be honest with you 在句首，不是插入成分了，而是起前導作用的不定式片語。

6 **直呼姓名**或**稱謂**，要加逗號。

- Yes, friends, Ruth told you the simple truth.
是啊，朋友們，露絲跟你們說的完全是事實。
↥ 稱謂（friends）在句子的中間位置，所以前後都用逗號。

- I'm telling you, Mr. Sun, I won't be forced to change my beliefs by anyone.
我告訴你，孫先生，誰也不能逼我改變信仰。
↥ 直呼姓名（Mr. Sun）在句子的中間位置，所以前後都用逗號。

- Ms. Day, are you OK? 戴小姐，你還好嗎？

7 **句尾的添加成分**，要用逗號：在句尾順便補充的字、片語或從屬子句，要用逗號和句子分開。

- Deliver this pineapple and double cheese pizza as soon as you can, please. 請盡快把鳳梨雙層起司披薩送來。

- Sally married a man beneath her, but he was a good choice, if my opinion is right. 如果我的看法沒錯，莎莉雖然嫁給了一個地位比她低的男人，卻是一個很好的選擇。

- It's a beautiful day, isn't it? 天氣真好，不是嗎？
↥ 句尾的附加問句要用逗號與句子分開。

8 **不定式片語、分詞片語、介系詞片語**：位於句首，起副詞的作用時，要用逗號和句子分開。

✗ To learn English well **Scot needs to read and listen a lot.**
✓ To learn English well, **Scot needs to read and listen a lot.**
要學好英語，史考特需要大量練習閱讀和聽力。
↳ 逗號把起副詞作用的不定式片語與句子分開。

✗ Exhausted after all the swimming and surfing **Jan and I took a long nap in my van.**
✓ Exhausted after all the swimming and surfing, **Jan and I took a long nap in my van.**
簡和我游泳和衝浪後感到筋疲力盡，於是在箱型車裡睡了個長長的午覺。
↳ 逗號把起副詞作用的過去分詞片語與句子分開。

✗ Seeing Sam Tops again **I felt my heart doing happy flip-flops.**
✓ Seeing Sam Tops again, **I felt my heart doing happy flip-flops.**
再次見到山姆‧塔樸斯，我感覺我的心雀躍不已。
✓ Seeing Sam Tops, **again I felt my heart doing happy flip-flops.**
看見了山姆‧塔樸斯，我感覺我的心又再次雀躍不已。
↳ 第二句和第三句都是用逗號，把起副詞作用的現在分詞片語與句子分開，兩句的逗號位置不同，意思也有細微的區別。

✗ After eating Joyce **always exercises her lovely singing voice.**
✓ After eating, **Joyce always exercises her lovely singing voice.**
吃完飯後，喬伊絲都是要練練她悅耳的歌喉。
↳ 第一句沒有逗號，意思就成了「在吃了喬伊絲之後」，這可嚇人了！

- In response to the many phone calls and emails from Jim, **I finally agreed to move to Miami and work for him.** 吉姆打了許多電話給我，也寫了許多電子信件，我終於同意搬到邁阿密，在吉姆的手下工作。
  ↳ 在比較長的介系詞片語後面，需要使用逗號。
- By the time Sally arrived, **I was getting on the train to New Delhi.**
  當莎莉到達時，我正登上去新德里的火車。
  ↳ 如果介系詞片語含有動詞形式（無論這個介系詞片語長或短），在介系詞片語後面需要使用逗號。

1 當片語是句子的主詞時，就不要用逗號。

- To learn English well requires extensive reading for fun.
  學好英語需要進行大量的趣味閱讀。
  ↳ 不定式片語 To learn English well 是句子的主詞，不需要逗號。
- Eating ice cream always makes me happy.
  吃冰淇淋都會讓我很開心。
  ↳ 動名詞片語 Eating ice cream 是句子的主詞，不需要逗號。

2 如果句子為了強調而使用了倒裝結構，那麼在作副詞的介系詞片語後面就不需要用逗號。

- Out of the window flew the little angel Margo. → 倒裝句
  = The little angel Margo flew out of the window. → 正常順序
  小天使瑪歌從窗戶飛了出去。

Diving Deep Into English 90 介系詞片語搭配逗號的基本規則

❶ 一般說來，**放在句首的介系詞片語**後面要用逗號。

❷ 如果放在句首的介系詞片語**比較短**，**不含動詞形式**（含動詞形式的介系詞片語如 at the time she called、by the time he arrived），**不是轉折語**（轉折語如 as usual、in general、at any rate、in addition、in other words），或**不是獨立的評論用語**（獨立的評論用語如 as a matter of fact、in reality、by all means），那麼這個介系詞片語後面可以用逗號，也可以省略逗號。

- in Taipei 在臺北
- in 2011 在 2011 年
- on Monday morning 在週一上午
- in New York 在紐約

- **In Beijing Claire toured the Great Wall, the Summer Palace, and Tiananmen Square.**
  = In Beijing, Claire toured the Great Wall, the Summer Palace, and Tiananmen Square.
  克萊兒在北京參觀了長城、頤和園和天安門廣場。

9 **同位語**加逗號：當同位語（appositive）用以補充說明前面的名詞或代名詞時，如果對**主詞**作解釋，前後要用逗號和句子分開；如果對**受詞**解釋，前面要用逗號。

✗ Liz my big sister, **is very diligent and intelligent.**

✓ **Liz**, my big sister, **is very diligent and intelligent.**
莉茲，我的大姐，既勤奮又聰明。

- **Have you ever watched** *Romeo and Juliet*, **one of Shakespeare's tragedies?** 莎士比亞的悲劇之一《羅密歐與茱麗葉》，你看過沒有？
  ⮤ *Romeo and Juliet* 是動詞 have watched 的受詞，one of Shakespeare's tragedies 是對前面受詞的補充說明。

如果同位語在句中是**不可缺少的成分**（比如用以限定主詞，而非補充說明），就不需要逗號（在限定性成分周圍都不用逗號）。

- the novelist John Flower 小說家約翰．福勞爾
- William the Conqueror 征服者威廉
- the English teacher Steve Sun 英文老師史蒂夫．孫
- Billy the Younger 小比利

✗ "Shakespeare's play, *Hamlet*, was perhaps written in 1602," noted Ray.

✓ "Shakespeare's play *Hamlet* was perhaps written in 1602," noted Ray.
雷指出：「莎士比亞的戲劇《哈姆雷特》可能寫於 1602 年。」
⮤ 第一句用了兩個逗號，表示莎士比亞只寫了一部戲劇，這當然不是事實。
⮤ 第二句不用逗號，表示《哈姆雷特》是莎士比亞寫的許多戲劇之一，同位語 *Hamlet* 是限定性的，用來限定主詞 play（說明是哪一部戲劇）。

- "My brother Sam is a novelist," said Pam.
  潘姆說：「我兄弟山姆是小說家。」
  ⮤ Sam 是重要的限定語，說明是 Pam 的哪一個兄弟，不加逗號。
- "My youngest brother, Larry, is a novelist," said Mary.
  瑪麗說：「我最小的弟弟賴瑞是小說家。」
  ⮤ Larry 是不重要的修飾語，只補充說明弟弟的名字而已（最小的弟弟一定只有一個），要加逗號。

10 **並列句**要使用逗號和連接詞。

a 由兩個獨立子句（即兩個主句）組成的並列句，常由 and、but、or、nor 或 for、so、yet 連接，在這種情況下，這些連接詞前面要用逗號把兩個獨立子句分開。

b 如果句子包含一個主詞和一個複合述語（複合述語指由連接詞連接起來的兩個述語動詞），就不要用逗號把兩個述語動詞分開。

- Lulu has just received her master's degree in English, and she wants to get a job in Peru.

  = Lulu has just received her master's degree in English and wants to get a job in Peru.

  露露剛拿到英語碩士學位，（她）想在祕魯找一份工作。

  ↥ 第一句是並列句，and 連接兩個獨立子句，需要逗號；第二句是含有複合述語動詞的簡單句，and 連接兩個動詞（has just received, wants），不需要逗號。

- Paul ate breakfast with Kate, or he didn't eat breakfast at all.

  = Paul ate breakfast with Kate or didn't eat breakfast at all.

  保羅如果不是跟凱特一起吃過早餐，就是根本沒吃早餐。

  ↥ 第一句是並列句，需要逗號；第二句是含有複合述語動詞的簡單句，不需要逗號。

c 在獨立子句之間用逗號時，須伴隨一個對等連接詞。

✗ Jill went further up the hill, Jake went down to the beach on Lazy Lake.

✓ Jill went further up the hill, and Jake went down to the beach on Lazy Lake.

✓ Jill went further up the hill. Jake went down to the beach on Lazy Lake.

✓ Jill went further up the hill; Jake went down to the beach on Lazy Lake.

潔兒繼續往山上爬，傑克則下山前往「懶惰湖」湖濱。

↥ 第一句的兩個獨立子句只用逗號而沒有用連接詞來連接，是一個常見的錯誤句。

↥ 第二句是並列句，使用逗號和對等連詞 and；第三句是兩個簡單句，使用句號；第四句用分號把兩個獨立子句分開，就不用連接詞 and。

» 分號的用法參見 807 頁〈Part 4 分號和冒號〉。

d 如果獨立子句很短，則既可以用逗號分開，也可以省略逗號，主要取決於語氣想不想停頓。

- I'm OK but my car is a wreck.
  = I'm OK, but my car is a wreck.
  我還好，不過我的汽車卻成了殘骸。
- Sit down and be quiet.
  = Sit down, and be quiet. 坐下來，保持安靜。

11 從屬子句與主句用逗號分隔。

a 位於句首的從屬子句要用逗號與主句分開，如果逗號被省略或放錯位置，句子的意思就會改變。

✗ After the tiger had eaten John went back home.

↳ had eaten 後面沒有逗號，John 成了動詞 had eaten 的受詞，表示「老虎吃了約翰」。

✓ After the tiger had eaten, John went back home.

老虎用餐後，約翰就回家了。

↳ 使用了逗號把句首的從屬子句和主句分開後，意思就正確了。

✗ While I was cooking Lisa stayed out of the kitchen.

✓ While I was cooking, Lisa stayed out of the kitchen.

我在煮飯時，麗莎待在廚房外。

↳ 第一句沒有逗號，讀者可能會懷疑你是食人族。在煮麗莎嗎？聽起來太恐怖了。

✗ When I am cutting Pam please stay out of the kitchen.

✗ When I am cutting Pam, please stay out of the kitchen.

↳ 「我在切潘姆嗎？」上面兩個錯句也許還會引起我的讀者打電話報警呢！

✓ When I am cutting, Pam, please stay out of the kitchen.

潘姆，我在切東西時，請不要待在廚房裡。

b 位於句尾的從屬子句若為限定性子句，則不加逗號；若為非限定性子句，仍要加逗號與主句分開。

- Before you make your choice, listen to Mona's sweet voice.
  = Listen to Mona's sweet voice before you make your choice.
  在做選擇之前，你應該先聽聽夢娜甜美的聲音。

↳ 第一句 Before 引導的從屬子句位於句首，要用逗號與主句分開；第二句 before 引導的從屬子句位於句尾，這是一個必要的、限定性的從屬子句，所以不需要逗號。

・Because I love Lulu, I am trying my best to help you.
= I am trying my best to help you, because I love Lulu.
因為我愛露露，所以我試著盡力幫助你。
ℓ 第一句 Because 引導的從屬子句位於句首，要用逗號與主句分開；第二句 because 引導的從屬子句位於句尾，這是非限定性子句，對主句作補充說明，需要加逗號。

Diving Deep Into English 91 兩個從屬子句與主句之間逗號的用法

需要用逗號將主句與兩個從屬子句分隔開，但兩個從屬子句之間不需逗號。

✗ Because he had been sick, and because he had not studied hard enough, Sam failed the math exam.

✓ Because he had been sick and because he had not studied hard enough, Sam failed the math exam.
因為生病，也因為不夠用功，山姆的數學考試不及格。
ℓ 兩個 because 引導的從屬子句之間，不需要用逗號。

Diving Deep Into English 92 從屬子句與兩個獨立子句之間的逗號

❶ 由從屬子句和兩個獨立子句組成的句子，若從屬子句位於句首，且同時修飾其後的兩個獨立子句，則兩個獨立子句不要用逗號分開。

✗ Before Sue starts to look for a job, she needs to investigate the job market, and she must prepare her resume and application letter.

✓ Before Sue starts to look for a job, she needs to investigate the job market and she must prepare her resume and application letter.
蘇在開始找工作之前需要調查就業市場，還要準備個人履歷和求職信。
ℓ 用逗號將複合句中由 before 引導的從屬子句與兩個獨立子句（she needs . . . 和 she must . . .）分隔開。
ℓ 錯句中 and 前用了逗號，使得 before 引導的從屬子句似乎只適用於第一個獨立子句（she needs to investigate the job market）。
ℓ 以 before 引導的從屬子句同時修飾其後的兩個獨立子句，因此在連接詞 and 前面不需要逗號。

❷ 如果從屬子句只修飾第一個獨立子句，與第二個獨立子句無關，則在兩個獨立子句之間需要逗號分開。

- **Before Sue starts to look for a job, she needs to investigate the job market, but don't think that's all she needs to do.**
  蘇在開始找工作之前需要調查就業市場，不過，不要以為她只要做這個就夠了。
  ↑ 以 before 引導的從屬子句只修飾第一個獨立子句，與第二個獨立子句無關，因此在連接詞 but 前面要用逗號分開。

12 **引言**加逗號：直接引語句裡的引言，要用逗號與句子的其他成分分開。

- **"Our marriage can be either a hell or a heaven on earth," Sue said to Del.** 蘇對戴爾說：「我們的婚姻不是人間地獄，就會是人間天堂。」
- **Ted winked and said, "Well, Jade, our honeymoon has lasted a good decade."** 泰德眨眨眼說：「這個嘛，潔德，我們的蜜月足足持續了十年之久。」

13 **附加問句**加逗號：附加問句要用逗號與句子的其他成分分開。

- **It's a lovely day, isn't it!** 今天天氣真好啊！
- **Dwight passed the exam, right?** 杜威特通過考試了，對嗎？

14 信函的開頭稱呼語（非正式）和結尾敬辭，要加逗號

- Dear Tom, 親愛的湯姆， → 信函的開頭稱呼語（非正式信函）
- Yours truly, 誠摯地， → 結尾敬辭

如果是正式信函，開頭的稱呼語則要用冒號。

- Dear Ms. Black: 親愛的布萊克女士： → 正式信函

Diving Deep Into English 93 不加逗號的句子成分

❶ 主詞和述語動詞之間，不用逗號分開。

✗ That woman in a whirl, is my sister Pat.

✓ That woman in a whirl is my sister Pat.

那個走路飛快的女子是我的姐姐派特。

❷ 動詞和直接受詞之間，或動詞和補語之間，不用逗號分開。

✗ Jade saw immediately, the mistake she had made.

✓ Jade saw immediately the mistake she had made.

潔德立刻看出了自己犯的錯誤。

✗ My sister is, a military pilot.

✓ My sister is a military pilot. 我的姐姐是軍隊裡的飛行員。

❸ 句中的成對元素（用對等連接詞連接）不用逗號分開。

✗ Jane wants to take her niece Lulu on a trip either to Greece, or to Spain.

✓ Jane wants to take her niece Lulu on a trip either to Greece or to Spain. 珍想帶她的姪女露露去希臘或西班牙旅遊。

❹ 對名詞下定義、起限定作用的從屬子句置於句中，前後都不要逗號，（此為限定成分，不應該放在兩個逗號中間）。比較下面句子：

- Bob says that people who are over fifty have difficulty finding a new job. 鮑勃說，50 歲以上的人要找新工作很困難。

  ↑ who are over fifty 是限定性形容詞子句。

- Fanny Reeds, who is ten, watches TV more than she reads.
  十歲的芬妮·黎茲，她看電視比看書的時間多。

  ↑ who is ten 是非限定性形容詞子句，為補充說明，插入句中時，要加兩個逗號。

問號和驚嘆號

1 問號（Question Marks）

1 問號用來表示句子終了，用在疑問句後面，結束疑問句。

- **Do you have an ID card?** 你有身分證嗎？
- **Who cares?** 誰在乎？
- **Why is Kate often late?** 凱特為什麼常遲到？

2 問號的前後都不加逗號或句號。

✗ "Do you understand the consequences?", Pat asked Sue.
✗ "Do you understand the consequences,?" Pat asked Sue.
✓ "Do you understand the consequences?" Pat asked Sue.
派特問蘇：「你知道後果嗎？」

✗ Dee asked the counselor, "Why me?".
✗ Dee asked the counselor, "Why me.?"
✓ Dee asked the counselor, "Why me?" 蒂問律師：「為什麼是我呢？」

句尾為縮寫詞的疑問句，則要保留縮寫詞的句號，再加問號，這種情況下，問號與句號可以連用。

✗ Are you going to be home by 9 p.m.
✗ Are you going to be home by 9 p.m?
✓ Are you going to be home by 9 p.m.?
你會在晚上九點以前回到家嗎？
↳ 句號只代表縮寫詞，不代表句子的結束。問號才代表句子的結束。

3 不要為了強調而使用一個以上的問號。

✕ Did Sue kick Sid???

✓ Did Sue kick Sid?

蘇踢了席德嗎？

Diving Deep Into English 94 使用句號的疑問句

❶ **客氣的疑問句**：如果疑問句是出於客氣而提出的建議，並不是真正在詢問對方，則可以用問號，也可以用句號。

- **Would you please walk behind Louise.**
  = Would you please walk behind Louise?
  請你走在露易絲後面，好嗎？

❷ **間接問句**：當疑問句是轉述的句子，而不是直接提出的問題，就要用句號，不能用問號。

✕ **Mary asked me if I was going to break up with Larry?**

✓ **Mary asked me if I was going to break up with Larry.**

瑪麗問我，我是否要跟賴瑞分手。

↑ 間接引語的疑問句，句尾不要用問號。

2 驚嘆號（Exclamation Points）

驚嘆號表示突然的、強烈的情感（歡樂、害怕、痛苦、幸福、生氣等），以及強而有力的命令。不要過多地使用驚嘆號，只有要表達真正強烈的情感時才用。美式英語稱驚嘆號為 exclamation point，而英式英語則稱 exclamation mark。

1 **陳述句**和**祈使句**：用驚嘆號表示熱情、驚奇、懷疑、迫切或強烈的情感。

- **Yes, Ben! We have won again!**
  是的，班！我們又贏了！

- **Sit down and shut up, Nick! Now!**
  尼克，坐下，閉嘴！立刻！

- **No! I don't believe Eve!**
  不！我才不相信伊芙呢！

- **"Never!" she screamed at Dee.**
  「絕不！」她對蒂尖叫。

2 疑問句（形式是疑問句，但不用以提問）：可用驚嘆號代替問號，表達強烈的情感。

- **How could Lee do that to me!**
  李怎麼能那樣對我！
  ↑ 這句實際上不是疑問句，而是感嘆句。

3 單一詞彙：驚嘆號用於單一詞彙表示強烈的情感。

- Incredible! 簡直無法相信！
- Awesome! 真是妙極了！
- Lovely! 真是可愛極了！
- Nasty! 真是討厭死了！
- No! 絕對不行！
- Help! 救命啊！

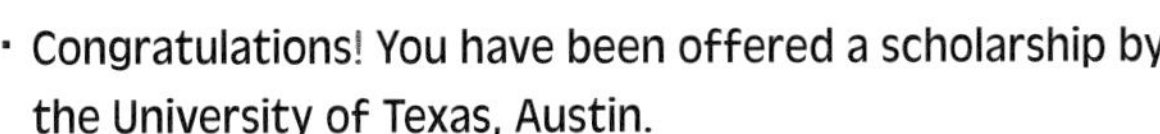

- **Congratulations! You have been offered a scholarship by the University of Texas, Austin.**
  恭喜！你獲得了德州大學奧斯汀分校的獎學金。

4 感嘆詞 oh：可接驚嘆號或逗號，視句子所需的語氣而定。

- **"Oh! What an ugly nightmare!" exclaimed Claire.**
  「噢！多可怕的一場惡夢啊！」克萊兒感嘆說。

- **Oh, did you see how fast the woman police officer arrested Claire's husband for domestic violence?**
  哦，你看見那位女警是多麼迅速地把克萊兒的丈夫以家暴罪名而逮捕了嗎？

5 **驚嘆號**前後不接逗號或句號。

✕ "What a terrible way for a husband to treat a wife,!" exclaimed Pete.
✕ "What a terrible way for a husband to treat a wife!," exclaimed Pete.
✓ "What a terrible way for a husband to treat a wife!" exclaimed Pete.
彼特感嘆地說：「一個丈夫以那樣的方式對待妻子，真是太可怕了。」

✕ Danny remarked, "What a persistent, strong, and polite girl.!"
✕ Danny remarked, "What a persistent, strong, and polite girl!."
✓ Danny remarked, "What a persistent, strong, and polite girl!"
丹尼評論說：「她真是一個有恆心、意志堅強、懂禮貌的女孩啊！」

姓名首字母或縮寫詞後面的句號則可以接感嘆號。

- "The play will start at 7:45 p.m.!" yelled Kay.
  凱喊叫著：「7 點 45 分，戲就要開演了！」
  ↑ 這裡的句號代表縮寫詞，不代表句子的結束。驚嘆號才代表句子的結束。

6 非正式的書面語中，可以連用一個以上的驚嘆號（!!），表達強烈的感嘆；也可以將驚嘆號和問號連用（!?），表達既驚訝又難以置信的語氣。

- "You'll soon have triplets."
  "Triplets!? I can't believe it!"
  「你就快要生三胞胎了。」
  「三胞胎！？真不敢相信！」

分號和冒號

1 分號（Semicolons）

1 分號可用來分開一組詞裡的各個項目：當一組詞的各個項目裡包含了逗號，可以用分號把各個項目分開。

- **By the end of this year, they will open new offices in Tampa, Florida; San Francisco, California; and Ann Arbor, Michigan.** 到年底時，他們就會在佛羅里達的坦帕市、加州的舊金山以及密西根的安阿寶市，開設新營業處。
  ↳ 在州和城市之間已有逗號，要用分號把各個項目分開，而不用逗號。

2 無對等連接詞的兩個獨立子句之間可用分號：並列句裡的獨立子句如果沒有用對等連接詞（and、or、but 等）連接，可用分號將獨立子句分開（分號後面的獨立子句句首不要大寫）。這時若刪除分號，用句號代替，再把第二個獨立子句第一個詞的首字母大寫，就成了兩個完整的簡單句。

- **I struggled for years; prosperity finally came after I started my own business.** 我奮鬥了許多年；我開創了自己的事業後，終於嚐到成功的滋味。
  ↳ 分號後面的獨立子句，首字母不大寫。

- **May played in the beach sand with Ray; they had a great day.**
  = May played in the beach sand with Ray, and they had a great day.
  = May played in the beach sand with Ray. They had a great day.
  梅在沙灘上跟雷玩耍，度過了美好的一天。
  ↳ 第一個例句是由分號分開的兩個獨立子句；第二個例句用逗號分開，並用連接詞 and 連接了兩個獨立子句；第三個例句是兩個完整的簡單句。

3 連接副詞所連接的並列句要用分號：連接副詞是「過渡詞」，連接兩個獨立子句，組成並列句，獨立子句之間要用分號，即連接副詞前面要用分號，後面要用逗號。這類連接副詞或過渡詞有：

- accordingly 因此；於是
- besides 此外
- consequently 結果；因此
- for example 例如
- furthermore 此外
- however 可是；不過
- moreover 並且；此外
- namely 那就是；即
- nevertheless 仍然；不過
- on the contrary 相反地
- otherwise 否則
- that is 那就是；即
- then 那麼；於是
- therefore 因此
- thus 因而
- yet 然而

✗ I felt exhausted, however, I continued writing until I finished the report.

✓ I felt exhausted; however, I continued writing until I finished the report.

✓ I felt exhausted. However, I continued writing until I finished the report.

我感到筋疲力盡，但我還是繼續寫，直到完成了那份報告。

↑ 上面第二句的兩個獨立子句由連接副詞 however 連接，連接副詞的前面要加分號，其後用逗號；第三句是兩個完整的簡單句。

• The dress Bess likes is way too short; besides, it is too sheer.
貝絲喜歡的那件洋裝太短，此外，也太透明了。

• I missed the bus; consequently, I was late for work.
我錯過了公車，結果我上班遲到了。

Diving Deep Into English 95 誤用分號會造成句子不完整

分號除了用來分開一組詞裡的各個項目（比如上面的第 1 條），分號後面必須接一個**沒有連接詞的獨立子句**，否則會造成句子不完整。

✗ Kay shoveled with Ray; and they wondered if the snow would blow all day.

↑ 分號後不能接由連接詞 and 連接的獨立子句。

✗ Kay shoveled with Ray; and wondered if the snow would blow all day.

↑ 分號後面必須接獨立子句，否則會造成不完整的句子。

✓ Kay shoveled with Ray; they wondered if the snow would blow all day.

↑ 分號後面接獨立子句。

✓ Kay shoveled with Ray, and they wondered if the snow would blow all day.

↑ 這句用逗號分開，並由 and 連接兩個獨立子句。

✓ Kay shoveled with Ray. They wondered if the snow would blow all day.

↑ 兩個簡單句，用句號。

凱與雷一起鏟雪，他們想知道會不會整天都飄雪。

2 冒號（Colons）

1 冒號表「**如下所述**」（as follows），表示比較強烈的停頓。冒號用來舉例或列舉，出現在例子、一組詞或列表的前面，也常接在 as follows、thus 或者 for example 等表示「例如」的片語後面。冒號後面的字母通常小寫，除非列舉的是完整的句子或專有名詞，首字母才要大寫。

- **Sam has two tough tasks to finish before he gets his MBA: write a thesis and pass the final written exam.** 山姆在獲得他的商管碩士之前需要完成兩個艱難的任務：寫論文並通過期末筆試。
  ↳ 冒號後面列舉的片語，字母通常小寫。
- **To make a raisin cake, you will need the following items: flour, sugar, butter, eggs, raisins, salt, baking powder, milk, and an oven that is hot.** 要做葡萄乾蛋糕，你需要下列材料：麵粉、糖、奶油、雞蛋、葡萄乾、鹽、烘焙粉、牛奶，以及一個熱烤箱。
- **I only attended three schools: Gladstone Elementary School, Gladstone High School, and Northern Michigan University.** 我只就讀過三所學校：格拉德斯通國小、格拉德斯通高中和北密西根大學。
  ↳ 冒號後面列舉專有名詞，則專有名詞維持大寫。
- **May said the questions would be as follows: Where were you yesterday? For how long were you away? With whom did you spend today?** 梅說那些問題會是：你昨晚在哪裡？你離開了多久？你今天跟誰在一起？
  ↳ 冒號後面列舉完整的句子，句子的首字母應大寫。

2 商務及正式**信函的開頭稱呼語**後面，要用冒號；但在非正式信函中，開頭稱呼語後面則可以用逗號。

Formal Dear Dr. Brown: 親愛的布朗博士：

Informal Dear Mom, 親愛的媽咪，

3 時間的**時**、**分**之間用冒號，冒號前後都不要空格。

- **"The movie will start at 3:30 p.m.!" yelled Jill.** 潔兒喊道：「電影下午三點半開始！」

・**Our work hours are from 9:30 a.m. to 6:30 p.m.**
我們的工作時間是從早上九點半到下午六點半。

4 冒號用在**比例**中代表 to，冒號前後都不要空格。

・**Dr. Ann Sun said, "The ratio of students to teachers is 40:1."**
安‧孫博士說:「學生和老師的比例是四十比一。」

5 **書名**和**副書名**，用冒號分開。

・**You should read the book *Avoiding Strife: How to Behave in Everyday Life*.** 你應該讀一讀《避免衝突:在日常生活中如何舉止得當》這本書。

6 **注釋**中的卷期號和頁碼，用冒號分隔。

- 5:230–235 (= Volume 5, pages 230–235) 第五卷，230 到 235 頁
- Is. 2:4 (= Chapter 2, verse 4 in the Book of Isaiah
  = Isaiah, Chapter 2, verse 4) 以賽亞書第二章第四首

7 在一些短小的**前導詞語**（如：note、remember 或 caution）後面，要用冒號。冒號後面的第一個詞首字母要大寫，因為這些前導詞後面接的是一個完整的獨立子句。

・**Remember: You do not capitalize after a colon if the elements that follow cannot stand alone as a sentence.**
= Remember that you do not capitalize after a colon if the elements that follow cannot stand alone as a sentence. 記住，如果冒號後面的成分不能成為獨立的句子，那麼冒號後面的第一個詞就不要用大寫。

ℓ 上面第二個句子裡的 remember 是句子的主要動詞，後面接一個 that 引導的受詞子句。動詞 remember 在這個句子裡不再是前導詞。在這種情況下，動詞 remember 後面不要用冒號。

8 **互相解釋的句子**，可以用冒號分開：當第二個獨立子句解釋第一個獨立子句，而在兩個子句之間又沒有連接詞或轉折語來連接這兩個獨立了句時，就可以在兩個獨立子句之間用冒號。（這種情況也可以用分號或句號，但不能用逗號。）

- These blue jeans are the best: they are inexpensive, durable, and beautiful.
  = These blue jeans are the best; they are inexpensive, durable, and beautiful.
  = These blue jeans are the best. They are inexpensive, durable, and beautiful. 這些藍色牛仔褲是最好的：它們便宜、耐穿又漂亮。
  ↳ 冒號用於這種情況（對前面的子句進行解釋、說明、詳述）時，後面可以接小寫字母，與分號相同。

Diving Deep Into English 96 必須相連的句子成分，勿用冒號分開

✗ **Nancy Rand, Saint Leo University's representative, has: catalogs, maps, applications, and a friendly attitude.**

✓ **Nancy Rand, Saint Leo University's representative, has catalogs, maps, applications, and a friendly attitude.**

南西·蘭德是聖利奧大學的代表，她有大學概況一覽表、地圖、申請表，以及友善的態度。

↳ catalogs、maps、applications、a friendly attitude 是動詞 has 的受詞，動詞和受詞不能用冒號分開。

✗ **The things I need in my life are: success, love, and a healthy family.**

✓ **The things I need in my life are success, love, and a healthy family.**

在我生活中所需要的東西是：成功、愛情，以及一個健康的家庭。

↳ success、love、a healthy family 是連綴動詞 are 的主詞補語，不能用冒號與連綴動詞 are 分開。

✗ **Their group consists of: Bill, Jill, Ann, Jan, and Dan.**

✓ **Their group consists of Bill, Jill, Ann, Jan, and Dan.**

他們的小組包括比爾、潔兒、安、簡和丹。

↳ Bill、Jill 等是介系詞 of 的受詞，不用冒號分開。

✓ **Their group consists of the following people: Bill, Jill, Ann, Jan, and Dan.** 他們的小組包括下面幾個人：比爾、潔兒、安、簡和丹。

↳ Bill、Jill 等只是對 the following people 作解釋，用冒號分開。

撇號和引號

1 撇號（Apostrophes）

1 撇號（'）加 s：表示所有格（'s），指出物主身分（誰擁有某物）。

- Poland's economy is growing faster than Switzerland's.
  波蘭的經濟成長比瑞士快。

- How frisky is Ann's hog since he met Dan's sow!
  安的公豬自從遇見了丹的母豬後，變得多麼活躍啊！

  ⤷ 注意 在含有 since 的句子裡，主句通常要用現在完成式來談論目前這種情形持續了多久，但有時也可以用現在式或過去式，尤其在上面這種表示「變化」的句子裡。

- Jerry and Mary's frog hopped over the log.
  傑瑞和瑪麗的青蛙跳過了那塊圓木。

2 撇號又叫**省字號**，表示字母的省略。下面列舉一些縮寫詞彙：

• haven't	• hadn't	• isn't	• doesn't	• can't
• hasn't	• aren't	• won't	• didn't	• couldn't

⤷ I'd've（I would have）不是正規用法，應避免使用。

- It's a great night for observing Mars, Jupiter, and the stars.
  今晚是觀察火星、木星和恆星的好天氣。

  ⤷ It's 是 It is 的縮寫；撇號代替了動詞 is 中的 i 字母。

- Fortunately, Jane wasn't on the plane that crashed in Ukraine.
  真幸運，珍不在那架墜毀在烏克蘭的飛機上。

  ⤷ wasn't 是 was not 的縮寫；撇號代替否定詞 not 中的字母 o。

3 撇號加 s（即 's），可表示字母（p, q）、數字（15, 1990）、縮寫詞（M.D., VIP）、單字（but, and）的**複數形式**。

- two VIP's　兩個重要人物
- 1990's　20 世紀 90 年代
- three 5's　三個 5
- lots of CD's and DVD's　很多 CD 和 DVD

· **Joyce got 6 A's on her first semester exams, but she quit school because of her mother's death.**
喬伊絲第一學期的期末考試獲得了六個優等成績，可是她因母親去世而休學了。

· **Liz is studying the hippies of the 1960's who talked a lot about freedom and peace.**
莉茲在研究 20 世紀 60 年代那些大談自由與和平的嬉皮士。

· **Mind your p's and q's.**
= Mind your P's and Q's. 小心謹慎。（注意自己的言行。）

「's」可以表示數字、字母、縮寫詞、單字的複數形式，不過，現代英語傾向於不用撇號，而是直接加 s。

- lots of CDs and DVDs 很多的 CD 和 DVD
- too many "buts" 太多的「可是」
- 1990s 二十世紀九〇年代

2 引號（Quotation Marks）

1 引號用來**引述他人所說的話**：引號用於直接引語，即將他人所說的話原封不動地引述過來。美式英語用雙引號（“ ”），英式英語則用單引號（‘ ’）。

» 參見 816 頁〈Diving Deep Into English 98〉。

· **Clever Jenny proclaimed, "I will love your family forever."**
聰明的珍妮聲明「我會永遠愛你的家人。」

↑ 表示說話的動詞（proclaimed、said 等）位於引言前面時，用逗號與引言分開，不用冒號。

- "Kim, don't let him talk to me like that," screeched Pat.

  「金姆，不要讓他用那種方式跟我講話。」派特尖聲喊叫。

  ↳ 表示說話的動詞（screeched、said、complained 等）和說話者（Pat）若位於引言後，引言的結尾不用句號，要用逗號。如果是疑問句，引言結尾就用問號，是感嘆句，就用感嘆號。

- Jim asked Coco to marry him, and all she said was "No."

  吉姆要可可嫁給他，她只回答了一個字：「不。」

  ↳ 動詞（was）後面不用逗號與引言分開。引言（No.）是一個完整的句子，要大寫。

- "Eve, please be quiet," said Steve sternly, "or you'll be invited to leave." 「伊芙，請安靜，」史蒂夫嚴厲地說：「否則我得請你離開了。」

  ↳ 當引言被中斷（如插入了說話者等），需要繼續引述時，第一個字不大寫，除非這個字剛好是專有名詞或專有形容詞，或繼續引述的句子是新的完整句子，首字母才要大寫。

Diving Deep Into English 97 說話者位置、引語句標點和大小寫

❶ 說話者和表說話的動詞（requested、said、complained 等），可以出現在引言前面，插入引言中間或放在引言的後面。

❷ 當位於引言前面時，一般用逗號與引言分開，不用冒號。

❸ 當位於引言後面時，引言的結尾不用句號，要用逗號（如果是疑問句，引言結尾就用問號；是感嘆句，就用感嘆號）。

❹ 當位於引言中間，中斷引言時，前面的引言要加逗號，後面繼續引語的首字母不要大寫（因為是前述引言的繼續），除非這個詞剛好是專有名詞或專有形容詞，或繼續引述的是新的完整句子，首字母才要大寫。

- Ted said, "Being with Dee is better than watching TV."

  = "Being with Dee is better than watching TV," Ted said.

  = "Being with Dee is better than watching TV," said Ted.

  = "Being with Dee," said Ted, "is better than watching TV."

  = "Being with Dee," Ted said, "is better than watching TV."

  泰德說：「跟蒂在一起，比看電視好。」

  ↳ 說話者（名詞）和表說話的動詞位於引言後面或中間，可以用「名詞 + 動詞」結構（Ted said），也可以用「動詞 + 名詞」倒裝結構（said Ted）。

❺ 當說話者（代名詞）和表示說話的動詞出現在引語句後面或插入引語句中間時，代名詞（I、he、she、it、they、we 等）要放在表示說話的動詞前面。

✗ "I'd really like a diamond bird," answered she.

✗ "I'd really like," answered she, "a diamond bird."

✓ "I'd really like a diamond bird," she answered.

✓ "I'd really like," she answered, "a diamond bird."

✓ She answered, "I'd really like a diamond bird."

她回答說：「我真的想要一隻鑽石鳥。」

↥ 無論說話者和表說話的動詞位於引言前、後或中間，都只能用 she answered，即要用「代名詞 + 動詞」結構。

2 引號可以用於要**強調**的詞彙，或用於具有特殊意義的詞彙或句子。

- I noticed the package was marked "Express."
  我注意到包裹上標著「快遞」。
  ↥ marked、labeled、singed、entitled 等後面的字或片語，要用引號。

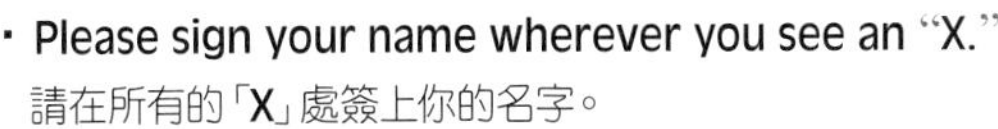

- Please sign your name wherever you see an "X."
  請在所有的「X」處簽上你的名字。

- Ted is cranky today—he must have gotten up "on the wrong side of the bed." 泰德今天很暴躁，想必是早上一起床情緒就不好了。

- Kitty understood that sometimes innocent people were falsely imprisoned in the name of "national security."
  姬蒂明白，有時無辜的人們在「國家安全」的名義下含冤入獄。

- Aunt Lisa fell in love with Uncle Lou's "can do" attitude.
  = Aunt Lisa fell in love with Uncle Lou's can-do attitude.
  麗莎阿姨愛上了陸叔叔「樂觀進取」的態度。
  ↥ can do 是動詞片語，在這裡扮演不同尋常的角色，用作形容詞修飾 attitude，因此需要用引號。用連字號連接的 can-do 作形容詞，就不需要用引號。

3 引號表示**文章名**：下列表示完整的、已發表作品的**部分標題**，要用引號。

a 書籍：章名、篇名、節名、課文名稱、論題題目、條文項目
b 報章雜誌：文章標題和專欄標題
c 單篇文章：論文題目、短詩名、歌名、短篇故事標題、演講題目、會議主題

- John Keats's "Ode to Autumn" → 詩歌名
  約翰．濟慈的詩〈秋賦〉

- Roy Orbison's song "Oh, Pretty Woman" → 歌曲名
  羅伊．歐比森的歌〈哦，美麗女子〉

- **Brook is reading the chapter "Reading Extensively for Fun Is the Most Effective Way to Learn English" in her English textbook.**
  布魯克正在閱讀英語課本裡一篇叫做〈大量趣味閱讀是學好英語最有效的方法〉的章節。

4 電視系列節目或電臺系列節目中的**部分節目名稱**，使用引號（系列節目名稱和電影名稱，則用斜體或底線）。

- **My friend Coco was a guest on *The Space Show* entitled "The Moon Base."**
  我朋友可可曾經是《太空秀》中「月球基地」節目的特別來賓。

Diving Deep Into English 98 美式和英式的引號區別

❶ 英式英語用單引號來引述一段話，而美式英語則用雙引號。

美式 **Liz asked, "Is Mary going jogging with Larry?"**
英式 **Liz asked, 'Is Mary going jogging with Larry?'**
莉茲問：「瑪麗要跟賴瑞一起去慢跑嗎？」

❷ 美式英語中，單引號用於引言中的引言；英式英語中，雙引號用於引言中的引言。

| 美式 | Their new sign reads, "Please endorse your checks, 'Pay to the order of Honshu Barbecue.'"

| 英式 | Their new sign reads, 'Please endorse your checks, "Pay to the order of Honshu Barbecue."'

他們的新告示牌寫著:「請在你的支票上註明:付給杭蘇烤肉公司。」

| 美式 | Amy said, "You declared, 'I'll love you forever.' My memory is accurate, isn't it?"

| 英式 | Amy said, 'You declared, "I'll love you forever." My memory is accurate, isn't it?'

艾咪說:「你聲明過,『我要永遠愛你。』我的記憶正確吧?」

❸ 美式英語中，著名的諺語或格言，因為不是直接引語，不需要引號；英式英語中，則常用引號。

| 美式 | Do you really believe that an apple a day keeps the doctor away? 你真相信一天吃一個蘋果就可以不看醫生了嗎?

| 英式 | Do you understand the saying: 'A little learning is a dangerous thing'? 你明白「一知半解是很危險的」這句格言嗎?

引號和其他標點符號的搭配

1 引號與問號、驚嘆號的搭配

1 問號或驚嘆號如果是**屬於引言**的一部分，要放在引號內。整個句子的句尾只能有一個表結束的標點符號，即使問號或驚嘆號位於引號內，整個句子的句尾也不再用標點符號。

✕ Lee asked, "Who wants to go to the library and study English with Sherry and me"?

✓ Lee asked, "Who wants to go to the library and study English with Sherry and me?"
李問：「誰想跟我和雪瑞一起去圖書館學英語？」
↑ 整個句子並不是疑問句，只有引言才是疑問句，問號要放在引號內。

✕ Sue screamed, "I hate you"!

✕ Sue screamed, "I hate you!".

✓ Sue screamed, "I hate you!" 蘇尖叫：「我恨你！」
↑ 整個句子並不是感嘆句，只有引言才是感嘆句，驚嘆號要放在引號內。
↑ 整個句子的句尾只能有一個代表結束的標點符號，故句號不能和驚嘆號連用。

- With fear in her voice, Joyce asked, "What are you doing here?"
喬伊絲用害怕的口吻問：「你在這裡做什麼？」
↑ 引言的疑問句位於整個陳述句後，問號只適用於引言的疑問句。

- I shouted at the little mouse, "Get out of my house!"
我對著小老鼠喊叫：「滾出我的房子！」
↑ 引言的感嘆句位於整個陳述句的結尾，驚嘆號只適用於引言的感嘆句。

2 問號或驚嘆號若**不屬於引言**的一部分，而是用於整個句子，則放在引號外。

✗ Did you insist, "Not all that glitters is pretty."?

✗ Did you insist, "Not all that glitters is pretty?"

✓ Did you insist, "Not all that glitters is pretty"?

你是否曾堅持「不是所有會閃光的都是漂亮的東西」？

↳ 引言為陳述句，引號內不應該用問號；整個句子才是疑問句，因此問號應該放在引號外，但整個結尾只需要一個結束用的標點符號，句號與問號不能連用。

✗ Stop saying, "Pearl is an ugly girl."!

✗ Stop saying, "Pearl is an ugly girl!"

✓ Stop saying, "Pearl is an ugly girl"!

不要再說「珀兒是個醜女孩」了！

↳ 引言為陳述句，位於整個感嘆句的結尾，驚嘆號適用的是整個句子，應該放在引號外。引號內不需要句號，句號與驚嘆號不能連用。

3 如果引言和整個句子需要**共用一個標點符號**，就共用引號內的標點符號。

✗ Why did Claire ask again and again, "Will Sid be there?"?

✓ Why did Claire ask again and again, "Will Sid be there?"

為什麼克萊兒要一再地問：「席德會在那裡嗎？」

↳ 引用的疑問句位於整個疑問句的結尾，句尾共用引號裡的問號即可。

✗ How Kitty would like to walk into that snotty manager's office and scream, "I quit!"!

✓ How Kitty would like to walk into that snotty manager's office and scream, "I quit!"

姬蒂多麼想走進那個傲慢自大的經理的辦公室，然後大喊道：「我不幹了！」

↳ 引用的感嘆句（I quit）位於整個感嘆句的結尾，句尾共用引號內的驚嘆號即可。

✗ Stop yelling at my pup, "Shut up, mutt!"!

✓ Stop yelling at my pup, "Shut up, mutt!"

↳ 引用的感嘆句位於整個感嘆句的結尾，句尾共用引號內的驚嘆號即可。

✓ Stop yelling "Shut up, mutt!" at my pup!

停止對我的小狗喊叫「笨蛋，閉嘴！」

↳ 注意這句感嘆號的用法，引用的感嘆句置於整個感嘆句的中間，引用的感嘆句要用感嘆號，置於引號內，而整個感嘆句的句尾也要用感嘆號。

總結：問號和驚嘆號（破折號的用法也一樣）如果是屬於引言的一部分，則置於引號內；如果不屬於引言，則置於引號外。

- Did Bing say, "They are going"? 賓說過「他們要走」了嗎？
  ↑ 這句的問號不屬於引言，屬於整個疑問句，置於引號外。
- Did Bing ask, "Are they going?" 賓問過「他們要走了嗎？」
  ↑ 這句的問號既屬於引言，也屬於整個疑問句，只用一個問號，置於引號內。

4 無法共用同一個標點時，**選擇語氣較強的標點符號**：引言位於整個句子的結尾時，不要同時在引號的裡面和外面都使用標點符號，只能擇一使用。當引言與整個句子無法共用同一個標點符號時，應當選用感情色彩較強烈的標點符號。

感情色彩由強到弱排列 驚嘆號 > 問號 > 句號

✕ **Did Kim scream, "Watch him!"?**

✓ **Did Kim scream, "Watch him!"** 金姆是不是尖叫說「提防他」？

↑ 引用的感嘆句位於整個疑問句的結尾，但整個句子的結尾只能有一個表結束的標點，驚嘆號的語氣比問號強烈，因此用驚嘆號。而驚嘆號只適用於引用的感嘆句，因此放在引號內。

✕ **Coco, stop saying, "How should I know?"!**

✓ **Coco, stop saying, "How should I know"!**
可可，不要再說「我怎麼知道」了！

↑ 引言的疑問句位於整個感嘆句的結尾，但驚嘆號的語氣比問號強烈，因此用驚嘆號，不用問號，而驚嘆號適用於整個句子，故放在引號外。

2 引號與逗號、句號的搭配

1 **美式英語**：逗號、句號永遠位於引號內，無論是否屬於引言的一部分。

2 **英式英語**：句號根據不同的情況，而有不同的位置。如果句號結束的是整個句子，要放在引號外；如果句號結束引言，要放在引號內。逗號則一律位於引號外。

| 美式 | The price tag on this Gold & Bold computer is clearly marked "Sold." → 美式：句號永遠位於引號內。
| 英式 | The price tag on this Gold & Bold computer is clearly marked 'Sold'. 這台「金與勇」電腦上清楚標示著「已售出」。
↑ 英式：句號在引號外，因為句號結束的是整個句子。

| 美式 | Pete said, "Let's go out to eat." 美式：句號永遠在引號內。
| 英式 | Pete said, "Let's go out to eat." 彼特說：「我們出去吃飯吧。」
↑ 英式：句號在引號內，因為句號結束的是引言。

| 美式 | "Hard-working," "responsible," and "humorous" are some of the adjectives that can be used to describe Ann.
↑ 美式：逗號位於引號內；連接詞 and、or 等前面通常要用逗號。
| 英式 | 'Hard-working', 'responsible' and 'humorous' are some of the adjectives that can be used to describe Ann.
勤奮、負責、幽默，是可用來描述安的性格的一些形容詞。
↑ 英式：逗號放在引號外面；常省略 and、or 前面的逗號。

3 引號與冒號、分號的搭配

冒號和分號要放在**引號外**。

- **John ordered me to mind my "silly manners"; I told him to get out of my RV.** 約翰命令我留意我「愚蠢的舉止」；我要他離開我的房車。
- **This remark is from an article called "Lily Gives Great Advice to Her Son Andrew": "Before you decide to marry a woman, carefully check out her relationship with her mom, and remember that you are really marrying into a family."** 這句話引自一篇叫作《莉莉為她兒子安德魯提供良好建議》的文章：「你決定娶一個女子之前，仔細查一查她和她媽媽的關係，並記住你實際上是娶進了一個家庭。」

↑ 第一對雙引號表示文章標題；第二對雙引號表示引言，冒號在引號外。
↑ 引言裡 Before 引導的從屬子句只修飾其後的第一個獨立子句，與第二個獨立子句無關，因此這兩個獨立子句之間用逗號分開了。

» 參見 802 頁〈Diving Deep Into English 92〉。

省略號

1 省略號是**三個有間隔的圓點**（. . .），表示有詞彙被省略，尤其是從引言裡省略了詞彙。省略號與前後詞彙之間要空一格，每個圓點之間也要空一格。

注意 英式英文的省略號通常用三個沒有間隔的圓點「...」。

- "Shakespeare," Liz Lime often says, "is considered to be the greatest . . . writer of all time."
  莉茲·萊姆常說：「莎士比亞被視為史上最偉大的……作家。」

2 如果省略的部分位於引言句的句尾，先用省略號（三個有間隔的圓點）表示省略，然後再接一個表示句子結束的標點符號（句號、問號或驚嘆號）。

a 在引言裡，如果省略的部分是在**疑問句的句尾**，省略號與問號之間空一格，第一個圓點與前面的詞彙之間也要空一格。

- Then I asked Coco, "Can you explain why castles have walls that are so high?"

  → Then I asked Coco, "Can you explain why . . . ?"
  於是我問可可：「你可以解釋為什麼……嗎？」
  ↑ 三個圓點代表省略的詞 castles have walls that are so high。

b 在引言裡，如果省略的部分是在**陳述句的句尾**，一共要用四個圓點。最後一個圓點代表句號，前三個圓點代表省略號，四個圓點之間都要有間隔，第一個圓點與前面的詞彙之間也要空一格。

- **Mark told June, "After 2025, we should witness a dramatic change in the transportation costs to and from the Moon, particularly in regard to the cost of shipping helium isotopes back to Earth."**
  馬克告訴茱恩說：「2025 年後，我們可能會目睹往返月球交通費用的巨大變化，尤其是把氦同位素運輸回地球的費用。」

- **Mark told June, "After 2025, we should witness a dramatic change in the transportation costs to and from the Moon . . . ."**
  馬克告訴茱恩說：「2025 年後，我們會目睹往返月球交通費用的巨大變化……」
  ↳ 前三個圓點為省略號，代表省略的詞語。第四個圓點為句號，表示句子的結束。
  ↳ 注意 Moon 後面的逗號也省略了。

3 如果在**句子和句子之間**省略了一個句子或多個句子，則在前面句子句尾的標點符號（句號、驚嘆號、問號）後面再接省略號（三個有空格的圓點）。

- **Liz Lime often says, "Shakespeare is considered to be the greatest British writer of all time. . . . He was great, but not as cute as my boyfriend Paul."**
  莉茲·萊姆常說：「莎士比亞被認為是史上最偉大的英國詩人。……他雖然偉大，但沒有我的男朋友保羅那麼可愛。」
  ↳ time 和第一個圓點之間沒有間格，因為第一個圓點代表句號，表示句子的結束。
  ↳ 後面的三個圓點為省略號，表示省略了一個句子或多個句子，這三個圓點之間要空一格，與第一個表示句號的圓點之間也要空一格。

4 如果引言句尾語氣逐漸變弱，最後停止，則句尾可以單獨用一個省略號（三個有間隔的圓點），以產生一種不確定的效果，或暗示思路的突然中斷。在這種情況下，省略號後面不需要再加句尾的標點符號。

- **I said, "If Joan had only known . . ."** 我說：「要是裘恩知道……」

- **"You could easily have solved the problem by . . . But why talk about it?" sighed Sue.**
  蘇嘆氣說：「你本來可以輕易地靠……解決問題。不過，為什麼要談論這件事呢？」

斜線、破折號和連字號

1 斜線（Slashes/Diagonals）

1 表提供選擇的詞或片語，用斜線分開，斜線與前後的詞都不要有空格。

- Single/Married/Widowed/Divorced 單身／已婚／寡居／離婚
- meet you on Saturday and/or Sunday 週六和／或週日與你見面

2 斜線表示一個人或物具有兩種身分或功能或兩個名稱。

- the owner/manager 主人／經營者 → 兼兩種身分
- an adjective clause/attributive clause 形容詞子句／定語子句 → 兩個名稱

3 斜線用於特定縮寫詞和時間表達。

- m/s (= meters per second) 公尺/秒（每秒……公尺）
- c/o (= care of) 由…… 轉交
- fiscal year 2011/12 2011–2012 年財政年度
- B/L (= bill of lading) 提貨單

4 斜線用於網路和電子郵寄位址中，分開不同的成分。

- http://www.earthfengshui.usa/elt/

2 破折號（Dashes）

1 破折號表**結論**或**解說**：在非正式英語中，破折號可代替冒號或分號，表示後面所接的內容是對前面的總結或解釋。破折號不如冒號和分號正式，但語氣更強烈。（注意 與分號的用法相同，破折號後面的獨立子句不要大寫。）

- **Men were shouting and yelling, women were throwing eggs at the government building, and children were crying—it was very confusing** for lawyer Glen Legs. 男人在大喊大叫，女子在朝著政府大樓丟雞蛋，孩子們在哭泣——葛倫·勒格斯律師被這個景象搞得糊裡糊塗。 → 對前面內容的總結。

- **You lied to me—how can I trust you again?**
  你騙過我——我怎麼可能再相信你？ → 對前面內容的總結。

- **My arrangement with my husband is a simple one—he is responsible for taking care of the housework and I make our money as a dentist.**
  我與我丈夫的安排很簡單——他負責家務，我當牙醫掙錢。
  ↑ 破折號代替冒號，後面的獨立子句對前面的獨立子句進行說明或解釋。

2 破折號表強調

a 破折號表**強調**：破折號可以代替逗號，來對並列句中的第二個獨立子句作強調。

- **The story I told you is true—and you know it!**
  = The story I told you is true, and you know it!
  我告訴你的事是真的——這一點你是知道的。

b 破折號**分開要強調的詞**：破折號可分開需要強調的詞彙或需要重申的詞彙。

- **I'm not going to miss this opportunity—the opportunity of a lifetime!** 我不會錯過這次的機會——這可是一生都難得的機會啊！
  ↑ 為了強調而重複 opportunity。

- **Swimming—that's what she lives for.** 游泳——那就是她生活中的享受。
  ↑ 強調 swimming。

- **At Dan and Ann's wedding reception, the singers—and the food—were superb.** 在丹和安的婚禮宴會上，歌手——還有食物——都是一流的。
  ↑ 要強調的成分「and the food」置於句中，用兩個破折號。

3 破折號表**停頓**：句子停頓且被非限定性的片語或從屬子句打斷，可用破折號或逗號；句子被打斷後又繼續，可用一對破折號或一對逗號。用破折號分開被打斷的成分時，逗號就要省略。兩者只用其一。

✗ **Dan saw his girlfriend's sons, —all four of them—, standing in front of her van.**

✔ Dan saw his girlfriend's sons—all four of them—standing in front of her van.

✔ Dan saw his girlfriend's sons, all four of them, standing in front of her van. 丹看見女友的四個兒子全都站在她的廂型車前面。

4 破折號用在**表概括性**的詞彙前：如果 these、they 或 all 概括前面的系列詞彙，並在句子中作主詞時，那麼在這幾個概括性詞彙的前面使用破折號。

- China, India, and Vietnam—all are important new markets for our company.

  = China, India, and Vietnam are all important new markets for our company. 中國、印度和越南——這些都是我們公司重要的新市場。

  ↳ 第二句中的 all 不是主詞，不用破折號。

破折號與前後的字母沒有間格。

✗ I do the hard work — you get the credit!

✔ I do the hard work—you get the credit!
我努力工作，功勞卻屬於你。

↳ 這句的破折號代替分號，用在兩個獨立子句之間。

3 連字號（Hyphens）

1 連字號用來連接兩個或兩個以上的字彙，成為複合詞。

- deep-hatred 深仇大恨
- high-tech 高科技
- husband-to-be 未婚夫
- old-fashioned 過時的
- once-in-a-lifetime 千載難逢
- mother-in-law 岳母；婆婆

2 連字號連接詞頭和專有名詞，成為複合詞。

- pro-Russian 親俄的
- pre-Raphaelite 前拉斐爾派之畫家或作家

3 連字號用以拼寫從 21 到 99 的複合數詞（compound number）。

- twenty-five 25
- thirty-two 32
- forty-six 46
- fifty-four 54
- sixty-three 63
- ninety-one 91

斜體和圓括號

1 斜體（Italics）

1 在電子設備列印的文字裡，斜體字表示書籍、報紙、雜誌、劇本、長詩、電影名稱；在書寫或打字機列印的文字裡，用底線表示。

- an article in *The Times* = an article in The Times《時代雜誌》的一篇文章
- Shakespeare's *Hamlet* = Shakespeare's Hamlet 莎士比亞的《哈姆雷特》
- the movie *True Lies* = the movie True Lies 電影《真實謊言》

2 斜體字用於強調或給詞彙下定義（也可以用底線表示）。

- Do you know the origin of the word *sinister*?
  = Do you know the origin of the word sinister?
  你知道 sinister 這個詞的來源嗎？

- I'm not going there—*you* are.
  = I'm not going there—you are. 要去那裡的人是你，我不去。

2 圓括號（Parentheses）

1 圓括號可用於分隔句中的額外訊息或評語。比較下列兩種括號的英文名稱：

a 圓括號「( )」：美式英文稱圓括號為 parentheses，英式稱為 brackets。

b 方括號「[ ]」：美式稱方括號為 brackets，英式稱為 square brackets。

- Trish thinks that modern music (i.e., anything written after 1900) is rubbish. 翠西認為，現代音樂（凡是寫於 1900 年以後的音樂）是垃圾。
  ↑ 提供額外的資訊。
- I merely said I was unhappy with (not strongly opposed to) your suggestion that we move to Chicago.
  我只是說過，我對你說我們搬去芝加哥的提議不太高興（而非強烈反對）。
  ↑ 進一步解釋。
- Please come to visit us (we are less than 20 miles from the airport) whenever you come to Tampa.
  你隨時到坦帕，請一定來探望我們（我們離機場還不到二十英里）。
  ↑ 括號裡即使是一個完整的句子，也不需要大寫。

2 圓括號還可用於交叉參照。

- The article an is used before vowel sounds (see Unit 4).
  冠詞 an 用在母音前面（參見第四單元）。
  ↑ 參考內容被視為句子的一部分。
  = The article an is used before vowel sounds. (See Unit 4.)
  冠詞 an 用在母音前面。（參見第四單元。）
  ↑ 參考內容被視為獨立的句子。

3 圓括號可以區別並分隔表示順序的號碼或字母。

✗ Jenny says she has the following objectives: 1) to find a well-paid job, 2) marry a good man, 3) have five children, and 4) enjoy her grandchildren in her old age.

✓ Jenny says she has the following objectives: (1) to find a well-paid job, (2) marry a good man, (3) have five children, and (4) enjoy her grandchildren in her old age.

珍妮說她有如下目標：(1) 找到高薪的工作；(2) 嫁給一個好男人；(3) 生五個孩子；(4) 年老時享受弄孫的樂趣。
↑ 單括弧（single closing parenthesis）只用在提綱裡（outline）。

UNIT

18 首字母大寫

Capitalization

基本規則

1 句子開頭的字母要大寫

句子開頭的第一個字母，要大寫。直接引語的引言，第一個字母也要大寫。

- **Silently and slowly, Ms. White began to write.**
  懷特女士默默地、慢慢地開始寫了起來。
  ↑ S 為句子裡的第一個字母，要大寫。
- **Pop shouted, "Stop!"** 爸爸喊著：「停下來！」
  ↑ P 是句子裡的第一個字母，S 是直接引語裡的第一個字母，所以都要大寫。

如果引言被中斷，第二段引言的第一個詞不大寫，除非那個詞是專有名詞或專有形容詞，或是新句子的開始。

- "My wife, Joy," he said, "loves to smile and enjoy life."
  「我的妻子喬伊，」他說：「喜歡笑，很享受生活。」

2 I（我）永遠要大寫

- **Dee and I love *The Old Man and the Sea*.** 蒂和我喜歡《老人與海》這本書。
- **Must I read this old story about gold?**
  我一定要讀那則關於黃金的古老故事嗎？

3 表示星期、月分、節日或假日的字首字母要大寫

表示星期、月分、節日或假日的字，被視為專有名詞，故首字母要大寫。

- **Why is Thanksgiving Day on the fourth Thursday in November?**
  為什麼感恩節是在 11 月的第四個星期四呢？
- **Does Labor Day in America fall on the first Monday in September?**
  美國的勞動節是在九月的第一個星期一嗎？

以下是一些美國的國定假日：

- the Fourth of July 美國國慶日 = Independence Day
- Thanksgiving Day 感恩節
- Christmas Day 聖誕節
- New Year's Day 新年
- Labor Day 勞動節
- Martin Luther King Day 馬丁・路德・金紀念日
- Memorial Day 陣亡將士紀念日
- Presidents' Day 總統紀念日
- Veterans Day 退伍軍人節

4 專有名詞（及縮寫）和專有形容詞首字母要大寫

1 除了表示星期、月分和節日的專有名詞要大寫外，其餘專有名詞和形容詞也需要大寫。專有名詞的詳細說明參見 20 頁〈2 專有名詞〉；專有形容詞的詳細說明參見 206 頁〈2 專有形容詞〉。

a 特定人名

- Uncle Dan 丹叔叔
- Barbie Bard 芭比・巴德

b 與人名結合的稱謂

- Professor Barbie Bard 芭比・巴德教授
- Dr. Rose Reed 蘿絲・里德博士

c 國籍、種族及語言

- Polish 波蘭語；波蘭人
- Native Americans 美洲印第安人
- Chinese 中文；中國人
- Japanese 日語；日本人

d 地名（洲、國家、地區、島嶼、大街、河流、海洋等）

- South America 南美洲
- Canada 加拿大
- New York 紐約
- Third Street 第三大街
- Washington and Tenth Streets 華盛頓街和第十街
- the Atlantic and Pacific Oceans 大西洋和太平洋

  ↑ 街名、海洋、河流名等，即使是複數，也要大寫 Streets、Oceans。

e 政府機構和政黨

- the Supreme Court 最高法院
- the Republican Party 共和黨

f 建築物、大橋名稱等

- the Great Wall 長城
- the Golden Gate Bridge 金門大橋

g 公共團體、企業

- Harvard University 哈佛大學
- General Motors 通用汽車公司

h 宗教

- Buddhism 佛教
- Christianity 基督教
- Muslim/Moslem 穆斯林

・**Aunt Coco and Uncle Joe live in Toronto, Ontario.**
可可姑姑和喬姑丈住在安大略的多倫多。

・**Does your American friend Clive live in Tampa, Florida, near U.S. Interstate Highway 75?**
你的美國朋友克萊夫住在佛羅里達州坦帕市，美國 **75** 號州際高速公路附近嗎？

・**On the way up the mountain, the old Indonesian woman met two FBI agents—Mary and Jerry.** 在上山的路上，那位印尼老太婆遇見了兩位聯邦調查局的特務人員——瑪麗和傑瑞。

・**Trish is trilingual; she speaks three languages: Russian, Spanish, and English.** 翠西能講三種語言：俄文、西班牙文和英文。

2 專有名詞、縮寫詞和首字母縮略詞表

- British Literature 402　英國文學 402（特定的課程）
- CA　加州
- *Gone With the Wind*　《飄》（書名）
- Michigan State University　密西根州立大學
- Ms. Tess Crown　黛絲・克朗女士
- Saint Luke's Hospital　聖路加醫院
- Maple St.　楓樹街
- the 2012 Olympics　2012 年奧運會

- the Bronze Age 青銅器時代
- the Dark Ages/the Middle Ages 中世紀
- the Victorian Era 維多利亞時代
- the Christian Era 西元；基督紀元
- the Roaring Twenties 怒吼的二十世紀二〇年代
- UNESCO 聯合國教科文組織
- U.S./US/U.S.A./USA 美國

3 非專有名詞、不用大寫的片語

- the space age 太空時代
- the colonial times/the colonial period 殖民地時期
- the age of the computer 電腦時代
- during the twenties 二〇年代期間

4 類似 the space age、the atomic age 這樣表示當今「時代」的片語，如果與大寫的、表示古老「時代」的片語（比如：the Bronze Age, the Dark Ages）用在一起時，就需要改成大寫。

- **Love stories have been popular from the Bronze Age through the Space Age.** 從青銅時代到太空時代，愛情故事一直都很受歡迎。

5 重要的事件和文件的首字母要大寫

- World War II 第二次世界大戰
- the Great Depression 大蕭條時期
- the Renaissance 文藝復興
- the Gettysburg Address 蓋茨堡演說

- **Clive's dad says the American Civil War cost a lot of lives.** 克萊夫的爸爸說，美國內戰造成很多人喪生。
- **Tess White can recite the Gettysburg Address.** 黛絲·懷特可以背誦蓋茨堡演說。
- **Erika carefully studied the Constitution of the United States of America.** 艾芮卡仔細地研究了美國憲法。

6 標題裡重要詞彙的首字母要大寫

1 完整的作品標題，重要詞彙的首字母要大寫。這類作品包括書籍、雜誌、報紙、電影、戲劇、歌曲、畫作、雕刻和詩歌等。

- *Something Wicked This Way Comes* is a fantastic book.
  《邪惡之事朝這裡來了》是一本很棒的書。
- Is *The New York Times* the best newspaper in the world?
  《紐約時報》是世界上最好的報紙嗎？
- Last night they watched *Hamlet*. 昨晚他們看了《哈姆雷特》。

NOTE 已經發表的作品題目（書名、雜誌名、戲劇名、長詩歌名、電影名）出現在句子或片語裡，要用**斜體**或**底線**，而文章、短詩歌、短篇故事、電視節目和電臺節目的題目則用**引號**（“ ”）。

Diving Deep Into English 99 標題裡次要詞彙的首字母是否要大寫？

❶ 標題裡的介系詞如果少於四個字母（of、for、in 等），首字母不需要大寫；如果是四個或四個以上字母的介系詞（about、from 等），首字母就要大寫。

❷ 標題裡的短小的連接詞（and、or、but 等）不要大寫。

❸ 標題裡的冠詞 a、an 和 the 不大寫；冠詞位於標題的開頭時，若屬於標題的一部分，就要大寫；若不是，就不大寫。

- Every day she reads ten articles in *The New York Times* on the Internet. 她每天要上網閱讀十篇《紐約時報》的文章。
  ↑ The 是標題的一部分。
- Erica has read the first six volumes of the *Encyclopaedia Britannica*. 艾芮卡已經讀了《大英百科全書》的前六卷。
  ↑ the 不是標題的一部分。

❹ 不過，當冠詞、較短小的介系詞以及較短小的連接詞出現在標題的最前面或最後時，需要大寫。

- Did you read my new book *A Love to Be Proud Of*
  你讀了我的新書《一個值得驕傲的心上人》嗎？

❺ 較短小的介系詞（in, on, up）與較長的介系詞（from, down, between）連用時，標題裡的這些短小的介系詞要大寫。

- Sailing Up and Down the Mississippi River 在密西西比河上下航行

7 詩歌的每一行首字母都要大寫

Crybaby, crybaby,	愛哭的寶貝兒，愛哭的寶貝兒，
Wipe your little eyes.	擦乾你的小眼睛。
Go and ask your mommy	去找你的媽咪，
For two small pies.	討兩個小派餅。

8 信件稱呼語與結尾敬辭首字母要大寫

- Dear Mr. Hess: 親愛的赫斯先生：（稱呼語）
- Yours truly, 真摯的，（結尾敬辭）

9 表次序的名詞首字母要大寫

如果名詞後面接有數字或字母，用以表示次序，則名詞的第一個字母要大寫。

Act 1 第一幕	Column A A 欄	Platform 3 第三月臺
Appendix 3 附錄三	Exercise 10 練習十	Policy 34564382 第 34564382 號保單
Article 8 第八篇	Exhibit C 展覽場 C	Purchase Order 888 第 888 號採購訂單
Book IV 第四部	Figure 5 圖解五	Section 4 第四項
Building 7 七號大樓	Flight 88 八十八號班機	Table 8 表格八
Chapter 24 第 24 章	Item 53D 第 53D 條目	Unit 9 第九單元
Chart 4 圖表四	Lesson 38 第 38 課	Volume II 第二冊
Check 45 第 45 號支票	Model B4-2 型號 B4-2	
Class 7 第七班	Part Five 第五節	

後面接阿拉伯數字表次序的詞彙，通常首字母要大寫，但 line、note、page、paragraph、size、verse 不要大寫。例如：

- line 2 第二行
- page 478 第 478 頁
- size 6 尺碼六
- note 7 注釋七
- paragraph 3 第三段
- step 5 第五步

10 東南西北的大小寫

1 下列表示**某地方人**的名詞，首字母要大寫。

- Northerner 北方人；北部人
- Westerner 西歐人；美國西部居民
- Southerner 南方人；南部人
- Easterner 東部人；美國東部居民

2 若 north、south、east、west 和衍生詞 northern、southern、eastern、western 指的是**某個明確的地區、區域**，或是**某地區人們的政治、社會或文化活動及特徵**，或是**某個專有名詞不可或缺的部分**，那麼這些字就要大寫，因為它們實際上已經成為專有名詞，以 west 為例：

a the West 常用大寫，指西方、西半球、歐美、西方各國或美國西部。

b West（作形容詞）常用大寫，指某地區、國家、大陸的西部，例如 West Africa（西非）。

- in the East 在東方（中國、日本等）
- the Middle East 中東
- the Far East 遠東
- the East Coast（美國）東海岸
- down South 南部各州；南方
- the Deep South（美國）南方腹地
- the South Pole 南極
- the Southern vote 南部的投票結果（指政治活動）
- the Southeast（美國）東南部

- the West 歐美國家；西方國家
- the Midwest（美國）中西部
- the West Coast（美國）西岸
- Western science and technology 西方科技
- up North 北部各州；北方
- the Far North 北極地帶
- the North Pole 北極
- Northern accent 北部口音（文化特徵）

3 當這些字僅僅是指**方向**（direction）、**一般的位置**（general location）或是**某地區的氣候**（the climate of a region）時，就不要大寫。

- **"Which way is west?" asked Kay.** 凱問：「哪一個方向是西邊？」
  ↑ 指方向，不大寫。

- **They built a cottage in the south of France.**
  他們在法國的南部修建了一棟別墅。 → 指位置，不大寫。

4 northern、southern、eastern、western 這幾個形容詞，如果出現在地名前面，就不要大寫，因為這時只是表明在某地區內的大致位置而已；如果這些字是地名（專有名詞）的一部分，那麼就要大寫。

在地名前	地名的一部分
● northern Tokyo = northern part of Tokyo 東京的北部	● Northern Ireland 北愛爾蘭 （Northern 是地名的一部分）
● southern Europe 歐洲南部	● Southern Sporades 南斯波拉提群島 （Southern 是地名的一部分）
● northeastern Europe 歐洲東北部	● Western Europe 西歐 （Western 是地名的一部分）
● eastern New York State 紐約州的東部	● Eastern Europe 東歐 （Eastern 是地名的一部分）

- **Sometimes the acidity of rain in northern North America and Europe can be similar to that of vinegar.**
  有時候在北美洲的北部和歐洲，雨的酸味和醋的酸味很相似。

- **On a cold, gusty wind blowing hard from the northeast, the fairy Louise glided through the air toward the Southern Sporades.** 仙女露易絲乘著從東北方刮來的寒冷狂風，在空中滑行，朝著南斯波拉提群島奔來。

5 方位詞（東南西北）的大小寫比較

區域或地區	大致位置或方向
● on the East Side 在東區（紐約市曼哈頓區）	● on the east side of the house/village/river/mountain 在房子／村子／河流／山脈的東邊

• Eastern civilization 東方文明	• the eastern half of Alberta （加拿大）亞伯達省的東半部
• on the West Coast 在西海岸	• the west coast of Canada borders on the Pacific Ocean 加拿大在太平洋邊界的西海岸線 （只指海岸線地帶）
• Western Australia 西澳	• western Ontario 安大略省的西部
• in the South 在南部	• in the southern part of France/Germany/India/Iraq 在法國／德國／印度／伊拉克的南邊
• Northern hospitality 北方人的好客（指特徵）	• northern temperatures 北部的氣溫（指該地區的氣候）

- **Drive north on Highway 75.**
  在 75 號公路上朝北行駛。 → 方向
- **I have a cottage in the south of Michigan.**
  我在密西根的南邊有一棟別墅。 → 大致位置
- **She is moving to Boston after five years in the West.**
  她在西部住了五年，要搬到波士頓去了。 → 區域

- **The Southern counties of Florida voted against Proposition 4.**
  佛羅里達州的南部各郡投票否決「提議 4」。 → 政治活動
- **The flood in Florida is expected to continue in the southern counties.**
  佛羅里達的洪水可能會在南部各郡繼續氾濫。 → 氣候
- **Most of our customers are in the southern counties of Florida.**
  我們大部分的客戶都住在佛羅里達州的南部各郡。 → 大致位置

特殊情況

1 常見的組織名稱

1 如果作者或說話者是某組織的成員，那麼提到自己所屬的組織名稱時，通常都要大寫。

2 如果作者或說話者不是這個組織的成員，那麼一般不用大寫，除非作者或說話者要特別強調這個組織的名稱。

3 組織名稱前如果有代名詞所有格 its、our、your 等修飾，不需要大寫。下列為一些常見的組織名稱：

- the physics department 物理系
- board of directors 董事會
- advertising department 廣告部
- finance committee 財政委員會

✗ I am calling about the position that is currently open in your Apartment Managing Department.

✓ I am calling about the position that is currently open in your apartment managing department.
我打電話來是為了詢問你們公寓管理部目前的職缺。
↳ 說話者是局外人，而且 apartment managing department 前有代名詞 your 修飾，因此在書寫這句話時不能大寫。

- "We have 14 teachers in the Physics Department," stated Lee.
李說：「我們物理系有 14 位教師。」
↳ 很顯然 Lee 屬於物理系。

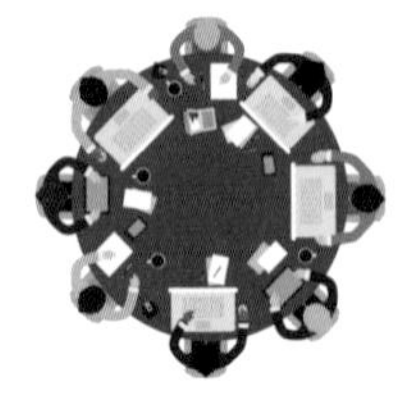

- **According to June West,** the Advertising Department **will meet this Thursday at noon.**
  據茱恩·韋斯特說，廣告部這星期四中午要開會。
  ↥ 局內人使用的風格（大寫）。
- **Kitty will meet you at seven tonight in** the advertising department **of Earth & Mars before the party starts for Jill.**
  今晚在為潔兒舉辦的晚會開始之前，姬蒂晚上七點要在「地球與火星公司」的廣告部與你見面。
  ↥ 局外人使用的風格（小寫）。

2 行星及其他太空實體的名稱

1 小行星、衛星、行星、恆星和星座的名稱，需要大寫。

小行星 asteroid	• Ceres 穀神星 • Pallas 小惑星 • Pallas 智神星
衛星 moon	• Deimos 戰神次子星 • Titan 土衛六（土星最大的衛星） • Ganymede 木衛三（木星最大的衛星） • the Moon 月球
行星 planet	• Mercury 水星 • Mars 火星 • Uranus 天王星 • Venus 金星 • Jupiter 木星 • Neptune 海王星 • Earth 地球 • Saturn 土星 • Pluto 冥王星
恆星 star	• Polaris/the North Star 北極星 • the Sun 太陽 • Regulus 軒轅十四（獅子座最亮的恆星）
星座 constellation	• the Big Dipper 大熊星座的北斗七星 • Leo 獅子座 • Sagittarius 人馬座 • Aquarius 寶瓶星座 • Virgo 處女座

2 一般而言，the sun（太陽）、the moon（月亮）、the earth（大地，指 land）不要大寫，但如果 sun、moon 和 earth，與別的大寫行星或恆星並列使用，與天文學有關時，則需要大寫。

3 有些文法學家認為，當 Earth 指行星（planet）而非土地時，通常要大寫，甚至省略定冠詞 the（尤其是在片語 on Earth 中），與沒有 the 的 Mars（火星）、Venus（金星）等行星用法一致。

✕ Why does the Sun seem to rise in the east and set in the west?
✓ Why does the sun seem to rise in the east and set in the west?
太陽為什麼看起來像是從東方升起、在西方落下呢？ → 這裡的 sun 不要大寫。

- It's another wonderful night,　又一個良宵美夜，
The stars are bright,　月兒可見星燦爛。
And the moon is in sight.　請你沉沉入夢鄉，
Please sleep tight,　莫讓臭蟲給咬到。
And don't let the bedbugs bite.

↑ 由於別的行星也有 moon（衛星），因此 moon 通常會用冠詞或其他限定詞修飾；the moon 表示地球獨一無二的衛星，也就是月亮。

- Art has gone to the ends of the earth to look for his childhood sweetheart. 亞特走遍天涯海角尋找他兒時的心上人。
↑ 這裡的 earth（不大寫），指我們居住的土地（land）。

- The thousands of asteroids that orbit the Sun between the orbits of Mars and Jupiter are great places to do mining. 在火星和木星的運行軌道之間，有成千個小行星圍繞太陽運行著，它們是採礦的好地方。
↑ 當 Sun 與大寫的 Mars 和 Jupiter 等行星相關聯時，就要大寫。

- The Moon orbits the Earth, and the Earth orbits the Sun.
月球繞著地球運行，而地球繞著太陽運行。
↑ 與天文學有關，可以大寫 Moon、Earth、Sun。

3 學科、研究領域及特定課程名稱

1 一般而言，學科或研究領域的名稱不用大寫，但當這些名稱裡有專有名詞或專有形容詞時，就用大寫。

學科名稱（普通名詞）

- biology 生物學
- math 數學
- chemistry 化學
- philosophy 哲學
- history 史學

學科名稱（專有名詞）

- English 英語
- Latin 拉丁語
- Chinese 中文
- Russian 俄語
- German 德語

✕ Mona likes to study Biology and Psychology.

✓ Mona likes to study biology and psychology.

夢娜喜歡研究生物學和心理學。

2 **特定的課程名稱**被視為專有名詞，因此要大寫。（課程：美英式語用 class，英式英語用 course。）

學科	特定的課程
• American literature 美國文學	• American Literature 103 美國文學 103
• biology 生物學	• Biology 201 生物學 201
• physics 物理學	• Physics 101 物理學 101
	↳ 在美國，學科名稱後面的數字代表特定課程的號碼，號碼小的課程通常是大學低年級課程。

- Dr. Day's American Literature 103 meets at 8 a.m. on Mondays.
  戴博士的「美國文學 103」，每週一早上八點上課。

4 父母、爺爺等的稱謂

1 家人的稱呼前面，如果有**所有格**修飾（如 my、Paul's 等），則不要大寫。

✕ Scot Sawyer says his Dad is a lawyer.

✓ Scot Sawyer says his dad is a lawyer.

史考特·索耶說，他的爸爸是律師。

- My sweet mom never forgets to say hi or goodbye.
  我可愛的媽媽從不會忘記說「你好」或是「再見」。

2 家人稱謂若**獨立存在**，或後面接**人名**或**姓氏**時，就要大寫，當作專有名詞。

- Then Mom told me, "Next month, I'm going to marry Tom."
  接著媽媽告訴我：「下個月我要跟湯姆結婚。」
  ↳ 獨立存在。
- Does Aunt Ann like to work in Japan? 安姑姑喜歡在日本工作嗎？
  ↳ 後面接有教名 Ann。

・**Does** Grandma Sun **love to run?** 孫奶奶喜歡跑步嗎？

↑ 後面接有姓氏 Sun。

1 Aunt 和 Uncle 後面要接名字，不接姓氏；
Grandma 和 Grandpa 後面，要接姓氏，不接名字。

2 美式英語的口語中，慣用 mom 和 pop/dad；
英式英語的口語中，慣用 mum 和 dad。

5 姑叔、堂表親的稱謂

1 uncle、aunt、cousin 和人名連用時，常大寫，即使前面有所有格修飾也可以大寫。

・**I hope Mary likes** my Uncle Jerry.

我希望瑪麗喜歡我的傑瑞叔叔。

↑ Uncle Jerry 整個看作一個單位，視為專有名詞。

・My Cousin Kay **may come to visit me at the end of May.**

我的凱堂妹五月底可能會來找我。

↑ 這裡把 Cousin Kay 視為專有名詞。

2 如果只是在描述親戚關係，而不是把這個稱謂當作專有名詞，當有所有格修飾時，就不需要大寫 uncle、aunt 或 cousin。

・My cousin Ray **may go to Norway at the end of May.**

我的堂哥雷五月底可能要去挪威了。

↑ 在這裡只強調此人為 Ray，cousin 只是補充說明親戚關係。

・**It's fun to camp in Yellowstone National Park with** my uncle Andrew.

和我的叔叔安德魯一起去黃石國家公園露營，很好玩的。

↑ 這裡的 uncle 只是表示親戚關係。

UNIT

19 平行結構

Parallel Structure

Part 1

Definition and Use of Parallel Structure

平行結構的定義與用法

1 由**逗號**或**連接詞**分開的系列片語，須具相同的文法形式，這就是平行結構。

2 平行結構指在一個目錄標題、清單或句子中，要用同一種文法結構和同一種詞性，所有的成分都是對等的（例如形容詞與形容詞平行、不定式與不定式平行、獨立子句與獨立子句平行），這樣文筆就會優雅、有邏輯。

✗ **That movie about a chess tournament was** long, boring, **and** without a plot.

✓ **That movie about a chess tournament was** long, boring, **and** plotless. 那部講國際象棋比賽的電影，冗長、無聊，又沒有情節。

↑ 連綴動詞（was）+ 形容詞（long, boring, plotless）。

✗ **I enjoy competing in** sleeping **and** to eat.

✓ **I enjoy competing in** sleeping **and** eating.
我喜歡參加睡覺和吃飯的比賽。

↑ 介系詞（in）+ 動名詞（sleeping, eating）。

✗ **Jake's symptoms were** fever, dizziness, **and** his head hurt.

✓ **Jake's symptoms were** fever, dizziness, **and** headaches.
傑克的症狀是發燒、頭暈、頭痛。

↑ 連綴動詞（were）+ 名詞（fever, dizziness, headaches）。

✗ **Kay Monroe wants to** play the piano, dance the tango, **and** singing songs on Broadway.

✓ **Kay Monroe wants** to play the piano, dance the tango, **and** sing songs on Broadway. 凱·門羅想在百老匯彈鋼琴、跳探戈和唱歌。

↑ 動詞（wants）+ 不定式（to play, dance, sing）；不定式符號 to 出現過一次，後面就可以省略。

✗ **Jenny prepared her AIDS speech on the train, and it was presented during the huge conference that was held on the Internet.**

ㄴ 非平行結構：在兩個獨立子句中，前者用主動語態，後者用被動語態。但動詞 prepared 和 presented 的行為者是同一個人（Jenny），應該只用主動語態。

✓ **Jenny prepared her AIDS speech on the train, and she presented it during the huge conference that was held on the Internet.**

ㄴ 為平行結構：兩個獨立子句都使用主動語態（Jenny prepared . . ., and she presented . . .）。

✓ **Jenny prepared her AIDS speech on the train and presented it during the huge conference that was held on the Internet.** 珍妮在火車上準備討論愛滋病的講稿，然後在那場隆重的網路會議期間進行了演講。

ㄴ 為平行結構的簡單句：主詞 + 動詞（prepared, presented）。

✗ **Jan grabbed my keys, jumped in, and speeding off in my van.**

ㄴ 非平行結構：and 連接兩個述語動詞和一個現在分詞片語。

✓ **Jan grabbed my keys, jumped in, and sped off in my van.**
簡抓了我的鑰匙跳了進去，然後加速開走了我的廂型車。

ㄴ 為平行結構：由 and 連接三個述語動詞。

✗ **Clive wants to make a lot of money, buy a big house and a lot of stock, and he wants to retire at the age of forty-five.**

ㄴ 非平行結構：因為有兩個不定式片語（make a lot of money, buy a big house . . . stock）和一個獨立子句（he wants . . . of forty-five），而這個子句的述語動詞（wants）與前面子句的述語動詞一樣。要避免用這類重複的句型：Clive wants to . . ., and he wants to . . .。

✓ **Clive wants to make a lot of money, buy a big house and a lot of stock, and retire at the age of forty-five.**
克萊夫想賺很多錢，買一棟大房子和許多股票，然後在 **45** 歲時退休。

ㄴ 為平行結構：有三個不定式片語。

✗ **Last weekend, Paul and I visited the National Museum, the Summer Palace, and took a trip to the Great Wall.**

ㄴ 有兩種不同形式的片語：the National Museum（名詞片語）、the Summer Palace（名詞片語）和 took a trip（動詞片語），所以不是平行結構。

✓ **Last weekend, Paul and I visited the National Museum, the Summer Palace, and the Great Wall.**

上星期，保羅和我參觀了國家博物館、頤和園和長城。

↑ 為平行結構：因為三個片語都是名詞片語。

✔ **Last weekend, Paul and I visited** the National Museum **and** the Summer Palace**, and then we took a trip to** the Great Wall**.**

上星期，保羅和我參觀了國家博物館和頤和園，然後我們去了長城。

↑ 有兩個平行結構：(1) the National Museum 和 the Summer Palace 是兩個名詞片語作動詞 visited 的受詞；(2) Paul and I visited . . . 和 and then we took . . . 是兩個由 and 連接起來的並列子句。

- **John F. Kennedy showed his gallantry when he said, "**Ask not what **your country can do for you;** ask what **you can do for your country."**

  約翰·甘迺迪表現出他的勇氣，說道：「不要問你的國家能為你做什麼，問問你自己能為你的國家做什麼。」

  ↑ 引語是由分號連接兩個「ask + 受詞子句」的簡單句，構成一個並列句。

- **Let every nation know, whether it wishes us well or ill, that we shall** pay **any price,** bear **any burden,** meet **any hardship,** support **any friend, [and]** oppose **any foe to assure the survival and the success of liberty.** (President John F. Kennedy) 讓所有的國家都知道，無論是祝福還是詛咒我們的國家，為保障自由的生存和成功，我們願意付出任何代價，承受任何重任，迎接任何艱難困苦，支持任何朋友，反對任何敵人。

  ↑ 為平行結構，由五個動詞片語構成，分別以 pay、bear、meet、support 和 oppose 引導。

NOTE

1. 一般而言，當列舉兩個以上的**字**、**片語**、**獨立子句**時，應在每個詞、片語、子句之間加逗號，在最後兩項之間加對等連接詞 and、or、but 等。學生在書面語和口語中一定要遵守這條規則。
2. 但在一些名人名言中，有時也省略了最後兩項之間的連接詞。如上面的例句，就在最後一個動詞（oppose）前面省略了連接詞 and。這種省略通常出現於下面三種情況：(1) 子句很短且句型相同；(2) 語調從容、流暢且是會話體；(3) 句子押韻的需要。又如：

- We cannot dedicate, we cannot consecrate, we cannot hallow this ground. (Abraham Lincoln)

  這塊土地我們不能夠奉獻，不能夠聖化，不能夠神化。

須使用平行結構的成對連接詞

除了連接詞 and 和 or，下列成對連接詞也應該用平行結構，兩組連接詞後面接的片語或詞彙在詞性上必須相同，一邊用什麼詞性，另一邊就要用相同的詞性。

- not only . . . but also 不但……而且
- both . . . and 既……又
- either . . . or 不是……就是
- neither . . . nor 既不……也不
- whether . . . or 是……抑或

✗ Scot Mist is not only gifted as a poet but also as a pianist.

↳ 非平行結構:「not only + 形容詞(gifted)」、「but also + 介系詞(as)」。

✓ Scot Mist is gifted not only as a poet but also as a pianist.

史考特·密斯特不僅有詩人的天賦,還有鋼琴家的天賦。

↳ 為平行結構:「not only + as」、「but also + as」。

✗ Sam is either late or I am early.

↳ 語意不清楚,文法也不正確,either 的位置放錯了,是不平行結構:「either + 形容詞」、「or + 獨立子句」。

✓ Either Sam is late or I am early.

不是山姆遲到,就是我早到。

↳ 為平行結構:「Either + 獨立子句」、「or + 獨立子句」。

- I have a hunch Jan can both kick and punch.

我有一種直覺,簡會打拳,也會踢腿。

↳ 為平行結構:「both + 動詞(kick)」、「and + 動詞(punch)」。

- I want to find a smart girlfriend who neither smokes nor drinks.
  我想找一個不抽菸、不喝酒的聰明女朋友。
  ⮤ 為平行結構：「neither + 動詞（smokes）」、「nor + 動詞（drinks）」。

neither nor

- His wife not only has beautiful eyes but also is wise.
  他的妻子不僅有一雙漂亮的眼睛，而且還很聰明伶俐。
  ⮤ 為平行結構：「not only + 動詞（has）」、「but also + 動詞（is）」。

- It doesn't matter to Kay whether you go or stay.
  你要走還是要留下，對凱來說都無所謂。
  ⮤ 為平行結構：「whether + 子句（you go）」、「or + 子句（you stay）」。
  ⮤ or 後面的 you 可以省略，避免重複。

UNIT

20 分詞片語和垂懸結構

Participial Phrases and the Dangling Construction

分詞片語／分詞子句

1 分詞片語和句子共用一個主詞

1 現在分詞以 -ing 結尾，過去分詞通常以 -ed 或 -en 結尾。

» 參見 732 頁〈Part 1 分詞〉。

- talking 談 → talked
- speaking 說 → spoken

2 分詞可以與其他字結合，構成類似從屬子句的結構，例如：

- having lost my job 失去了我的工作
- rejected by all her friends 被她所有的朋友拋棄

3 美國文法學家把這種類似從屬子句的結構稱為「分詞片語」，而英國文法學家則稱為「分詞子句」。分詞片語在句中可以起到形容詞或副詞的作用。

» 參見 736 頁〈4 分詞片語〉。

4 **分詞片語的主詞必須與句子的主詞一致**，只有當句子裡的兩個行為動作共有同一個主詞的時候，才能用分詞片語。如果分詞片語的主詞與句子的主詞不一致，就必須刪除分詞片語，使用另一種句型，或者改變句子的主詞。

✗ Advancing across the desert, **the hot sun burned Henry and Mary.**

↳ 這句的主詞是 the hot sun，如果這個主詞也是動作 Advancing 的執行者，那麼就成了 the hot sun was advancing across the desert（火辣辣的太陽在穿過沙漠），就不合邏輯了。

✓ Advancing across the desert, **Henry and Mary were burned by the hot sun.**

✓ **Henry and Mary,** advancing across the desert, **were burned by the hot sun.**

↳ 上兩句的兩個動作（穿越過、被曬傷），為同一個主詞，所以可以用分詞片語。

✓ While advancing across the desert, **Henry and Mary were burned by the hot sun.**

↳ 把分詞片語與 while 用在一起，主詞仍然用 Henry and Mary。

✔ The hot sun burned Henry and Mary as they advanced across the desert. 亨利和瑪麗穿過沙漠時，被火辣辣的太陽曬傷了。

ℓ 也可以用副詞子句來代替分詞片語。

✘ Completely exhausted, Linda's books fell to the floor.

ℓ Completely exhausted 的主詞不可能是 Linda's books，書怎麼可能累壞了？人（Linda）才可能累壞了。因此，句子的主詞應該改成 Linda。

✔ Completely exhausted, Linda let her books fall to the floor.
琳達累壞了，她讓書都掉落到地板上了。

✘ Will the customer be charged for the entire order of CDs when only shipping a partial order?

ℓ customer 不是 shipping a partial order 的主詞，因為裝運貨物的不會是顧客。

✔ Will the customer be charged for the entire order of CDs when only a partial order is shipped?
如果只運送部分光碟，顧客要付全部訂單的價錢嗎？

ℓ 把 shipping a partial order 改為 when 引導的副詞子句，並使用不同的主詞。

- While standing on top of the huge balloon that was drifting over the English Channel, Joe saw a UFO.
當站在大氣球頂，飄過英吉利海峽時，喬看見了一個不明飛行物。

- Seeing the furious look on the robber's face, Jim kept moving forward to protect the unknown girl.
吉姆看到強盜臉上的憤怒後，仍然繼續向前走，要去保護那個陌生女子。

» 參見 855 頁〈Part 2 垂懸結構和避免垂懸結構的方法〉。

2 獨立分詞片語不需與句子主詞相關聯

一般來說，分詞片語和句子共用一個主詞，不過，有些慣用的分詞片語並不遵守這條規則。這些慣用語稱為**獨立分詞片語**。這類獨立分詞片語有：

- assuming the worst 做最壞的打算
- broadly speaking 大體來說
- generally speaking 一般來說
- concerning 關於
- considering everything 從各方面考慮
- strictly speaking 嚴格來說

- given the conditions 在……條件之下
- judging from 根據……來判斷
- taking everything into consideration 考慮到各方面

- Generally speaking, **Sally loves swimming in warm weather and tickling her husband with a feather.**
  一般來說，莎莉喜歡在溫暖的天氣下游泳，還喜歡用羽毛給丈夫搔癢。
  ↑ 獨立分詞片語 generally speaking 不需要與句子的主詞（Sally）相關聯。

- Considering everything, **Mary really isn't suitable for Gary.**
  從各方面考慮，瑪麗並不適合蓋瑞。

3 允許分詞主詞與句子主詞不一致的句型

當主要句子的主詞為 it，或主要句子是 there is/are 的句型時，可以允許分詞的主詞和句子的主詞不一致，這種用法很自然。

- Having so little time, there was **not much that Sue could do to help her boyfriend Andrew.** →
  ↑ 句子的主詞是 there was 後的代名詞 much，而分詞的邏輯主詞是 Sue。
  蘇的時間實在很少，她幾乎做不了什麼來幫助男朋友安德魯。

- Having grown **up in Sichuan,** it**'s not surprising that Louise loves to eat red peppers.**
  ↑ 句子的主詞是代名詞 it，而分詞的邏輯主詞是 Louise。
  = Louise grew **up in Sichuan,** so it**'s not surprising that she loves to eat red peppers.** 露易絲在四川長大，所以她喜歡吃紅辣椒一點也不意外。

4 分詞片語也可以有自己的主詞（即分詞獨立主格結構）

有時候分詞可以有自己的主詞，與句子的主詞沒有關聯。

- Weather permitting, **the giant rocket will be pulled to its launch site as scheduled.** 如果天氣允許，這架巨型火箭將如期發射。
  ↑ 分詞的主詞是 Weather，而句子的主詞是 the giant rocket。

- **With** my parents gone **most of the year, our big house is often empty.** 我父母常年在外地，我們家的大房子經常空著。
  ↑ 分詞主詞是 my parents，句子主詞是 our big house。
  分詞片語前面還可以有介系詞（with）。

垂懸結構和避免垂懸結構的方法

1 何謂垂懸結構？

1 一個字或一組詞在句中如果放錯位置，修飾了不該修飾的成分，就稱為**垂懸結構**。垂懸結構與句中的其他成分之間缺乏明確的句法連接，這種錯誤常在報紙、雜誌、網路新聞、電臺或電視新聞裡出現。

2 規則：修飾語應緊靠其所修飾的成分，否則就會出現垂懸結構。

2 垂懸結構與正確用法的對照說明

1 介系詞片語

✗ At the age of 53, the baby adopted gave Kate Erickson lots of fun.

↳ baby 和介系詞片語 At the age of 53 緊靠在一起，即介系詞片語「在 53 歲時」修飾句子的主詞「嬰兒」，難道嬰兒有 53 歲嗎？所以介系詞片語在句中的位置錯了，像這樣就是垂懸結構。

✓ **The baby, adopted when Kate Erickson was 53, gave her lots of fun.** 凱特·埃瑞克森在 53 歲時收養的這個嬰兒為她帶來了很多歡樂。

✗ Like Wendy, Nancy's new car cost a lot.

↳ Wendy 與 Nancy's new car 緊靠在一起，就成了介系詞片語 Like Wendy 修飾主詞 Nancy's new car，「人」與「車」比較，意思是「南西的新車和溫蒂一樣貴」。有人買了溫蒂嗎？南西的車像溫蒂嗎？當然不是！

✓ **Like Wendy, Nancy paid a lot for her new car.**
跟溫蒂一樣，南西也花了很多錢買她的新車。

↳ 用 Nancy 作主詞，與 Wendy 緊靠在一起，介系詞片語 Like Wendy 就修飾了主詞 Nancy，將 Nancy（人）與 Wendy（人）相比較。

✔ Like Wendy's, Nancy's new car cost a lot.
跟溫蒂的車一樣，南西的新車也花了很多錢。

ℓ 如果要以 Nancy's new car 作主詞，那就要把 Like Wendy 改成 Like Wendy's（= Like Wendy's new car），將「車」和「車」相比較。

✘ They reported that John Yu, a Malaysian rock star, had died on the six o'clock news.

ℓ on the six o'clock news 緊靠動詞 had died，意味著約翰·余在六點的新聞報導中去世。

✔ They reported on the six o'clock news that John Yu, a Malaysian rock star, had died.

✔ On the six o'clock news, they reported that John Yu, a Malaysian rock star, had died.
六點鐘的新聞報導說，約翰·余這位馬來西亞的搖滾樂明星去世了。

ℓ 應當把 on the six o'clock news 靠近 They reported，或是移動到句首，兩種結構都用來修飾動詞 reported，表示何時報導的新聞。

2 分詞片語

✘ While eating ice cream and talking, Kate's cellphone began to vibrate.

✔ While Kate was eating ice cream and talking, her cellphone began to vibrate.
凱特正在一邊吃冰淇淋一邊聊天時，她的手機開始振動起來。

ℓ 正在吃冰淇淋的不是手機，而是凱特。

» 參見 852 頁〈Part 1 分詞片語 / 分詞子句〉。

Unclear Lee ran up to Lily breathing heavily.

ℓ 是誰上氣不接下氣？Lee 在跑步，是 Lee 上氣不接下氣，但句中的 breathing heavily 靠近 Lily，好像是 Lily 上氣不接下氣。雖然文法好像沒有錯，但這樣的句子不自然、不清楚。

Clear Breathing heavily, Lee ran up to Lily.
李上氣不接下氣地朝莉莉跑去。

ℓ 分詞片語位於句首時，分詞片語的主詞應該與句子主詞一致（兩個主詞都是 Lee），這句明確指明是 Lee 上氣不接下氣，意思符合邏輯，文法也正確。

Clear **Lee ran up to Lily** who was breathing heavily.

李朝著上氣不接下氣的莉莉跑去。

↑ 如果要明確表達是 Lily 上氣不接下氣，最好改用形容詞子句。

如果給上面第一個不自然的例句加一個逗號，把分詞片語與前面的句子分開，是否就成了正確的句子？

- Lee ran up to Lily, breathing heavily. 李跑向莉莉，氣喘噓噓的。

從句型結構上看，因為有了逗號，分詞片語不是修飾其前面 Lily，而是修飾句子的主詞 Lee，分詞片語和句子共用一個主詞（Lee）。文法上這看起來似乎是正確的，但這種句型不是道地的英語，看起來還是不自然的、不清楚的。既然跑步的是 Lee，分詞片語 breathing heavily 就需要靠近 Lee，才不會產生歧義。

如果口頭上講這句話，聽者看不到逗號，就會因此感到疑惑。無論是口語還是書面語，都應該避免用一些文法正確但意思含混、不道地的句子。

3 形容詞片語

Unclear So quiet and small, **you'll never know the android Claire is there!**

↑ So quiet and small 修飾緊跟在逗號後面的 you，你很安靜、很微小嗎？從句子要表達的意思來看，顯然是指機器人克萊兒 so quiet and small。

Clear Because the android Claire **is so quiet and small, you'll never know she's there!**

因為機器人克萊兒是那麼地安靜、微小，你永遠都不會知道她就在那裡！

✗ Upset and sad, this tiny tropical island was used as a place for Daisy Lover to rest and recover.

✓ Upset and sad, Daisy Lover used this tiny tropical island as a place to rest and recover.

✓ Daisy Lover was upset and sad, and she used this tiny tropical island as a place to rest and recover.

黛絲·拉維既苦惱又傷心，便利用這個熱帶小島當作她休息和康復的地方。

✓ Whenever Daisy Lover was upset and sad, she used this tiny tropical island as a place to rest and recover.

每當苦惱、傷心的時候，黛絲·拉維就利用這個熱帶小島當作她休息和康復的地方。

↳ Upset and sad 修飾緊跟在逗號後面的詞。第一個句子卻錯誤地把 this tiny tropical island 靠近形容詞片語 Upset and sad，這個熱帶小島苦惱、傷心嗎？當然不是，是人（Daisy）苦惱傷心，因此應該把 Daisy 靠近形容詞片語 Upset and sad（第二句）；第三句和第四句也是正確的，只是使用不同的句型表達了大體上相同的意思。

4 不定式片語

✗ To avoid any errors when you communicate, all danglers need getting rid of.

↳ 靠近不定式片語的主詞是 all danglers，這個主詞是述語動詞 need 的主詞（行為者），同時也是不定式片語的主詞。其結果表達出來的意思是「所有垂懸結構要避免溝通上的失誤」。不對！是人們要避免溝通上的失誤。

✓ To avoid any errors when you communicate, you need to get rid of all danglers. 為避免溝通上的錯誤，你需要擺脫所有的垂懸結構。

↳ 不能讓以不定式片語開始的句子垂懸。句首的不定式片語必須與動作的行為者（句子的主詞）有關聯。這句用 you（人）作主詞，語意就合乎邏輯了。

✗ To achieve fluency in English, all of Sue Mills' reading skills must be further developed.

✓ To achieve fluency in English, Sue Mills must further develop all of her reading skills.

為了提高英語的流暢度，蘇．米爾斯一定要全面地進一步增進閱讀技巧。

↳ 第一句表達的意思是「閱讀技巧為了英語流暢必須進一步提高」。需要達到英語流暢的是蘇本人，而不是她的閱讀技巧，所以應該把動作的行為者 Sue Mills 靠近句首的不定式片語。

5 副詞

Unclear **You will appreciate the advice Sue gives you years from now.**

↳ 副詞片語 years from now 靠近名詞片語 the advice Sue gives you。從結構上看，是指「你會感激數年後蘇要給你的建議」。而從意思看，應該指「從現在起數年後，你會感激蘇給你的建議。」因此，這句具有雙重含意。副詞片語的位置放錯了，修飾了不該修飾的成分，是一個垂懸副詞片語結構或錯位的副詞片語。

Clear **Years from now you will appreciate the advice Sue gives you.**
數年後，你會感激蘇給你的建議。

Unclear **Emma's supervisor reminds the FBI agents often to wear their bulletproof vests.**

↳ 副詞 often 是修飾前面動詞 reminds，還是修飾後面不定式動詞 wear 呢？語意不清楚。

Clear **Emma's supervisor often reminds the FBI agents to wear their bulletproof vests.**
愛瑪的老闆常常提醒聯邦調查局的特務人員們要穿防彈衣。

a bulletproof vest

↳ 一定要把副詞與其所修飾的動詞連在一起。often 緊靠動詞 reminds，就清楚地表明要修飾的是 reminds。

6 形容詞子句

✗ **Kitty gave some clothes to a charity that she did not need any more.**
✓ **Kitty gave some clothes that she did not need any more to a charity.**
姬蒂把一些她不再需要的衣服給了一家慈善機構。

↳ 上面錯誤句子中的形容詞子句 ，that she did not need any more 放在名詞 charity 後面，意思是「她不再需要的慈善機構」。應該把形容詞子句放在名詞 clothes 後面，意思就清楚了。

3 可以垂懸的片語

1 獨立分詞片語可以垂懸：修飾語不應垂懸，應緊靠其所修飾的成分。不過這條規則也有些例外。一些習慣用語雖然不修飾句子中的任何成分，卻可以在句首垂懸（甚至慣用垂懸結構），我們稱這些慣用語為獨立分詞片語。
» 參見 852 頁〈Part 1 分詞片語 / 分詞子句〉。

- Generally speaking, **in the Northern Hemisphere birds move south when winter comes, and so do reindeer herds.**
  一般說來，北半球的冬天來臨時，小鳥就往南遷移，馴鹿群也一樣。
  ↥ 雖然 birds 和 reindeer herds 不是動詞 speaking 的行為者，但這是正確的句子。

- Judging from **her facial expressions, Annie was quite upset.**
  從她的臉部表情來看，安妮很難過。
  ↥ 雖然 Annie 不是動詞 Judging 的行為者，但這是一個正確的句子。

2 其他可以垂懸的片語

- after all 畢竟
- on the whole 總之
- to be frank 坦白說
- in the long run 長遠來看
- contrary to popular belief 與公眾信仰相反
- in the final analysis 歸根究底
- to tell you the truth 老實說

- In the long run, **this project is not much fun.**
  長遠來看，這個計畫沒有什麼樂趣。

- On the whole, **Jean has dug the best hole to hide in.**
  總之，琴挖的洞最便於藏身。

- To be frank, **he still can't drive the tank.**
  坦白說，他還是不會駕駛那輛坦克。

UNIT

21 重疊詞和累贅修飾語

Doublet Phrases and Unnecessary Modifiers

重疊詞與累贅修飾語的定義

1 避免同義重複

1 所謂的重疊詞，就是使用多餘的字來重複同樣的意義。要想寫出文筆優美的作品，就應該避免使用多餘的重疊詞和修飾語。

2 一些動詞和副詞的意思相同。比如動詞 advance 意思是「向前」，副詞 forward 的意思也是「向前」，如果 advance 和 forward 用在一起就成了重疊詞。

» 參見 280 頁〈Part 3 不應使用副詞的情況〉。

✗ **Mary and Jerry, your wedding plan is entirely complete. I'm sure everyone will have a wonderful time.**

✓ **Mary and Jerry, your wedding plan is complete. I'm sure everyone will have a wonderful time.**
瑪麗和傑瑞，你們的婚禮計畫很完善，我相信大家都會度過一個愉快的時光。

↑ complete 的前面不需要用 entirely 來修飾，因為 complete 本身就有「完全」的意思。

✗ **Jane is a widow woman from Bahrain.**

✓ **Jane is a widow from Bahrain.** 珍是一位來自巴林的寡婦。

↑ 寡婦一定是女子，不需要在後面加個 woman 來修飾。

✗ **Two and plus two are four.**

↑ and 或 plus 擇一即可，不能兩個同時使用。

✓ **Two and two are/is four.**

✓ **Two plus two is four.** 2 加 2 等於 4。

↑ 注意 如果主詞是 two and two，述語動詞可用複數（are），也可用單數（is）；如果主詞是 two plus two，則述語動詞只能用單數（is）。

Informal The truck accident that killed Gus and Paul last night should be a lesson to each and every one of us. Never drink and drive if you want to get somewhere alive!

Formal The truck accident that killed Gus and Paul last night should be a lesson to every one of us. Never drink and drive if you want to get somewhere alive!

Formal The truck accident that killed Gus and Paul last night should be a lesson to us all/all of us. Never drink and drive if you want to get somewhere alive!

昨晚造成加斯和保羅死亡的貨車車禍，對我們大家來說都是一個教訓。如果你想活著到達某處，就不要酒後開車。

↳ 在口語中，有些人為了強調而常用 each and every。但在書面語中應該避免同時使用 each 和 every。

2 避免使用過時的隱喻、慣用語和明喻

在正式書面語中，還應該避免使用過時的隱喻（metaphor）、慣用語（idiom），或是索然無味的明喻（insipid simile）。學生常誤以為這些用法可以為語言增色，隨時都想抓住機會在商務會話、報告、電子信函、傳真或商務信件中使用，卻不知道也許已經過時，或因使用過度而變得索然無味了。以下詞語在非正式語中可以使用，但在書面語中應該避免。

- it's a catch-22 左右為難的處境
- it's a breath of fresh air 像一絲清新空氣一樣
- a piece of cake 輕而易舉
- a pain in the butt/neck 令人討厭的事
- as busy as a bee 像蜜蜂一樣忙碌
- as strong as an ox 像牛一樣強壯
- as slippery as an eel 像鰻魚一樣溜滑

as strong as an ox

如何避免重疊詞和累贅修飾語

以下刪除線的部分是重疊詞，應刪除；或累贅的修飾語、過時的詞語，應換用別的詞彙。

- ~~actual~~ truth 事實（或用 actuality）
- ~~added~~ bonus 額外津貼；獎金
- ~~advance~~ planning 計畫；規畫
- ~~advance~~ warning 警告
- advance ~~forward~~ 前進（或用 move forward）
- ~~and~~ etc. 等等
- ~~and~~ plus 加上
- and ~~plus~~ 加上，及
- any ~~and all~~ 任何
- ~~any and~~ all 所有
- anything ~~and everything~~ 任何事
- ~~anything and~~ everything 所有事
- at that ~~point in~~ time 當時（或用 then）
- at the present ~~time~~ 現在（或用 at this time/now/today）
- ~~bad egg~~（過時的用語）→ brute/villain 壞人
- basic ~~and fundamental~~ 基本的
- ~~basic and~~ fundamental 基本的（或用 primary/essential）
- because ~~why~~ 因為
- ~~because~~ why 為什麼
- big ~~in size~~ 大的
- blue ~~in color~~ 藍色
- ~~call your attention to the fact that~~（累贅詞語）→ remind you 提醒你
- collaborate ~~together~~ 合作
- contemporary writers ~~of today~~ 當代作家
- continue ~~on~~ 繼續
- cooperate ~~together~~ 合作
- currently ~~at this time~~ 目前
- ~~currently~~ at this time 目前
- each ~~and every~~ 每一個
- ~~each and~~ every 每一個
- end ~~result~~ 結果
- ~~end~~ result 結果
- ~~entirely~~ complete 完整的
- exact ~~same~~ 精確的

- ~~exact~~ same 一樣的
- first ~~and foremost~~ 第一的
- ~~first and~~ foremost 最早的
- ~~free~~ gift 禮物
- ~~fundamental~~ basis 基礎
- ~~future~~ ahead 向前
- ~~get back on your feet~~
  （使用過度的用語）
  → gain strength/get better/heal/improve/recover 恢復健康；改善
- ~~honest~~ truth 事實
- ~~important~~ essentials 要點
- in ~~the year~~ 2032 在 2032 年
- ~~in spite of the fact that~~（累贅詞語）
  → though/although 雖然
- join ~~together~~ 連接
- ~~joint~~ cooperation 合作
- long ~~in length~~ 長的
- mix ~~together~~ 混合
- ~~more~~ better 更好的
- ~~most~~ ideal 理想的
- ~~most~~ perfect 完美的
- ~~one of the~~ only 唯一的
- ~~owing to the fact that~~（累贅詞語）
  → since/because 既然；因為
- ~~past~~ history 歷史
- raise ~~up~~ 提高
- repeat ~~again~~ 重複
- retreat back 撤退
- return ~~back~~ to 回到
- round ~~in shape~~ 圓的
- rules ~~and regulations~~ 規則
- ~~rules and~~ regulations 規則
- share ~~in common~~ 分享
- share ~~together~~ 分享
- sufficient ~~enough~~ 足夠的
- ~~sufficient~~ enough 足夠的
- ~~the question as to~~ whether 是否
- ~~there is~~ no doubt ~~but that~~ 無疑地
- ~~true~~ fact 事實
- two ~~in number~~ 兩個
- ~~the reason is~~ because 因為
  （或用 the reason is that）
- ~~unexpected~~ surprise 驚奇
- used for fuel ~~purposes~~ 做燃料用
- ~~very~~ excellent/delightful/brilliant
  優秀的／令人愉快的／有才華的
- ~~very~~ unique 獨特的
- ~~wealthy~~ millionaire 百萬富翁
- west ~~in direction~~ 西邊
- widow ~~woman~~ 寡婦
- yearly ~~annual~~ 每年的 / 一年的
- ~~yearly~~ annual 每年的 / 一年的
- 5:30 p.m. ~~in the afternoon~~
  下午五點半
- 5:30 ~~p.m.~~ in the afternoon
  下午五點半
- 8:30 p.m. ~~at night~~ 晚上八點半
- 8:30 ~~p.m.~~ at night 晚上八點半

UNIT

22 主詞和述語一致

Subject-Verb Agreement

主詞和述語一致的基本原則

1 動詞應該與主詞的人稱（第一人稱、第二人稱或第三人稱）和數量（單數或複數）一致。

2 單數主詞要用單數動詞，複數主詞要用複數動詞。

3 代名詞 you 是一個例外，無論是單數還是複數的 you（你；你們），都接複數動詞。

- **My brother is an engineer in Jordan, and my sisters are doctors in Afghanistan.**
  我哥哥在約旦當工程師，我的姐妹們在阿富汗當醫生。
  ↑ 第三人稱單數主詞（My brother）和單數動詞（is）連用；複數主詞（my sisters）和複數動詞（are）連用。

- **Are you both willing to travel with us?**
  你們兩個都願意跟我們去旅行嗎？

- **You alone are willing to travel with us.**
  只有你一個人願意跟我們去旅行。
  ↑ 第一句中的 you 為第二人稱複數主詞，第二句中的 You 為第二人稱單數主詞，動詞都用複數形式（are）。

- **Victory has a thousand fathers, but defeat is an orphan.**
  (President John Fitzgerald Kennedy)
  成功有一千個父親，但失敗是一個孤兒。
  ↑ 不可數名詞（victory, defeat）與單數動詞（has, is）搭配。

- **Dee loves tea, and her mom and dad love coffee.**
  蒂愛喝茶，她的媽媽和爸爸愛喝咖啡。
  ↳ 第三人稱單數主詞 Dee 接一個以 -s 結尾的單數動詞（loves）。複合主詞（her mom and dad）是複數，動詞用複數形式 love。

My big brother Pete loves any chocolate treat,
And my little sister Dorete is so neat and petite.
They both love to eat meat and wheat,
But never ever smell their stinky feet!

大哥彼特任何巧克力餐都愛，
可愛小妹朵芮特靈巧又嬌小。
肉和小麥他們兩個人都愛吃，
但自己的臭腳丫從來都不聞。

Diving Deep Into English 100 不規則形式的名詞

❶ 有些名詞形式上是單數，但意義是複數，作主詞時，要用複數動詞。參見 25 頁〈6 集合名詞應當搭配單數動詞還是複數動詞〉。

- people 人們
- police 警方
- cattle 家畜；牲口

- **The police are searching for a terrorist from Greece.**
  員警在搜索一個來自希臘的恐怖分子。

❷ 當 youth（泛指年輕人）作主詞時，動詞通常用複數，但也可以用單數。

- **Are the youth of America inspired and motivated?**
  = Is the youth of America inspired and motivated?
  美國的年輕人有熱忱、有積極性嗎？

連接詞連接的主詞

1 由 and 連接的複合主詞（compound subject）接動詞的複數形式

用對等連接詞 and 或 both . . . and 連接的複合主詞／並列主詞（一個以上的主詞）要接動詞的複數形式。

and 連接的複合主詞 + 複數動詞

✗ A cup of tea and a glass of milk often helps me to wake up.

✓ A cup of tea and a glass of milk often help me to wake up.
一杯茶再加一杯牛奶，通常有助於讓我清醒過來。
↳ 複合主詞（A cup of tea and a glass of milk）+ 複數動詞（help）

- Both Coco and Kay are Brazilians, and they want to visit their brother Joe in Tokyo.
可可和凱是巴西人，他們想去東京探望他們的兄弟喬。
↳ 複數動詞（are, want）與複合主詞（Coco and Kay）和複數代名詞（they）一致。

- My manner of living is plain and I do not mean to be put out of it. A glass of wine and a bit of mutton are always ready. (President George Washington)
我的生活方式很簡樸，我也不打算改變這種生活方式。
一杯葡萄酒和一點羊肉總是現成的。

2 以 and 連接卻用單數動詞的主詞

1 如果由 and 連接的兩個或多個主詞指同一個人或事物，就要用單數動詞。

and 連接的複合主詞(被當為一個整體)+ 單數動詞

- **Our secretary and treasurer is Mary Flower.**
  我們的祕書兼會計是瑪麗·福勞爾。
  ↳ Our secretary and treasurer 指同一個人(兼任祕書和會計)。

- **Bacon and eggs was the best brunch for hungry Meg.**
  對飢餓的梅格來說,培根蛋是最好的早午餐。
  ↳ Bacon and eggs 是一個整體單位,指醃燻肉加蛋,一種固定的食物搭配。

- **A horse and carriage was what they bought right after their marriage.** 他們婚後立刻買了一輛馬車。
  ↳ A horse and carriage 是一個整體單位。

- **Peace and friendship with all mankind is our wisest policy, and I wish we may be permitted to pursue it.**
  (President Thomas Jefferson)
  實現全人類的和平與友誼是我們最明智的政策。
  我希望允許我們為之奮鬥。
  ↳ 雖然名詞 Peace 和 friendship 由 and 連接,但 Peace and friendship with all mankind 被看成一個整體(全人類的和平與友誼),而不是兩個分開的個體(全人類的和平或全人類的友誼),因此要用單數動詞 is,而後面用單數代名詞 it 來代替。

2 and 連接的兩個或多個主詞的前面若有 each、every、many a/many an 這些修飾語,就要用單數動詞。

every、each 等修飾的複合主詞 + 單數動詞

- **Ruth Gold asked why every computer, printer, and fax machine was marked "Sold."**
  露絲·戈爾德問,為什麼每一台電腦、印表機、傳真機都標上了「已售」字樣。

- **"Yes, many a woman and man has joined the US Navy, because it offers lots of meat with gravy," agreed Ann.**
  安同意說:「是的,許多男男女女加入了美國海軍,因為海軍提供很多多汁的肉。」

3 由 or、nor 以及成對連接詞連接的複合主詞

1 如果主詞是由連接詞 either . . . or、neither . . . nor、or 或 nor 連接的兩個或兩個以上的**單數詞**（名詞或代名詞），則主詞仍為單數，要用**單數動詞**。

✗ Are Tom or Kay **going to do shopping today?**
✓ Is Tom or Kay **going to do shopping today?**
今天是湯姆還是凱要去購物？
↑ 由 or 連接的兩個單數名詞作主詞，動詞用單數。

✗ Neither Mom nor Uncle Tom are **able to help Mabel.**
✓ Neither Mom nor Uncle Tom is **able to help Mabel.**
媽媽或湯姆叔叔都無法幫助美博。
↑ 由 neither . . . nor 連接的複合主詞包含兩個單數名詞，因此動詞用單數。

2 如果這些連接詞連接兩個或多個**複數詞**，主詞就是複數，**動詞也用複數**。

- Neither **her** dogs nor **her** hogs are **able to help Mabel set the table.**
無論是她的那些狗還是那些豬，都無法幫助美博擺好飯桌上的碗筷。
↑ 由 neither . . . nor 連接的複合主詞包含兩個複數名詞，因此動詞用複數。

3 如果這些連接詞連接的是一個**單數詞**和一個**複數詞**，動詞的單複數則與**靠近動詞的主詞一致**。最好的用法是把**複數詞靠近動詞**，用複數動詞，這樣聽起來也比較自然。

Acceptable Neither **the other family** members nor Mom is **able to help Mabel clean the stable.**
↑ 主詞的第一部分是複數詞（members），第二部分是單數詞（Mom），既然單數名詞靠近動詞，動詞就應該用單數。

Better Neither Mom nor **the other family** members are **able to help Mabel clean the stable.**
無論是媽媽還是其他家庭成員，都無法幫助美博清洗馬廄。
↑ 主詞的第一部分是單數詞（Mom），第二部分是複數詞（members），既然複數名詞靠近動詞，動詞就應該用複數。這一句比上一句更自然。

單數主詞與修飾語；there be 句型的主詞與動詞

1 單數主詞與修飾語

1 accompanied by、along with、as well as 和 with 等插入成分，和 and 的意思類似，但在用法上與 and 不同。當 with、as well as、in addition to、except 等組成的片語**插入在單數主詞和動詞之間**時，句子的述語動詞用**單數**，並要用雙逗號將這些片語與主詞分開。

2 插入成分只是修飾語或附加說明，句子的動詞修飾的仍是主詞本身，要與主詞一致，而不是與伴隨片語或修飾語一致。主詞是單數，就用單數動詞；主詞是複數，就用複數動詞。用於附加說明的插入成分有：

- accompanied by 伴隨
- along with 與……一起
- as well as 也
- besides 除……之外（還）
- except 除……之外
- in addition to 除……之外（還）
- including 包括
- not + 否定主詞 是……，而不是……
- not even 甚至不
- plus 加上
- rather than 而不是
- together with/with 一起

主詞與修飾語無關

✗ The mayor, as well as her sister Susan, are going to jail.

✓ The mayor, as well as her sister Susan, is going to jail.

↳ 主詞是單數（The mayor），as well as 引導的片語不是主詞的一部分，只是對主詞的補充，所以動詞也仍然是單數（is）。

✓ The mayor and her sister Susan are going to jail.

市長和她的妹妹蘇珊要進監獄了。

↳ 由 and 連接的複合主詞（The mayor and her sister）要用複數動詞（are）。

- Aunt Wendy, along with her dog Arty, is coming to your going-away party.
  = Aunt Wendy and her dog Arty are coming to your going-away party. 溫蒂姑姑和她的狗亞提都要來參加你的告別聚會。

- President Jan Johnson, accompanied by her advisors, is visiting Japan. 簡·詹森總統由她的顧問陪同，要去訪問日本。
- President Jan Johnson and her advisors are visiting Japan.
  簡·詹森總統和她的顧問要去訪問日本。

- No one, not even the president of our company, knows what to buy for Jenny. 沒有任何人，甚至連公司的董事長都不知道該為珍妮買什麼東西。
  ↳ not even . . . 是插入成分，主詞是單數代名詞 No one，動詞也要用單數 knows。

2 there is/was + 單數主詞；there are/were + 複數主詞

there be 句型中的主詞不是 there，而是位於動詞（is/are/was/were）後面的詞或片語，因此 there be 句型中的動詞要與其後作主詞的第一個名詞或代名詞的數一致（這個名詞或代名詞必須是主詞，才能與前面的動詞的數一致，而不可以是修飾語的一部分）。

- There is no doubt that reading is healthy fun for everyone.
  毫無疑問，閱讀對每個人來說都是有益於健康的娛樂。
  ↳ 單數主詞 doubt 搭配單數動詞 is。
- A long time ago, there were three poor sisters, Dee, Amy, and Alice, and they had one apple tree.
  很久以前，有三個窮姐妹，蒂、艾咪和艾麗絲，她們有一棵蘋果樹。
  ↳ 複數主詞 sisters 搭配複數動詞 were。
- If there is anything that a man can do well, I say let him do it. Give him a chance. (President Abraham Lincoln)
  人若有一技之長，我說就讓他發揮吧，給他一次機會。
  ↳ 單數動詞 is 與單數主詞（不定代詞 anything）一致。

- There are blessed intervals when I forget by one means or another that I am President of the United States. (President Thomas Wilson)
只有我設法忘記自己是美國總統的時候，才感到有片刻的幸福。
⤷ 複數動詞 are 與複數主詞 intervals 一致。

- I am persuaded there is among the mass of our people a fund of wisdom, integrity, and humanity which will preserve their happiness in a tolerable measure. (President John Adams) 我相信，我們的人民大眾富於智慧、誠實和博愛，這些特質將在一定程度上維護他們的幸福。
⤷ 雖然 there be 句型後面先接複數名詞 people，但這個複數名詞是介系詞 among 引導的修飾片語的一個部分，動詞不與修飾語一致，而應該與主詞一致。把修飾片語刪除後，就清楚單數名詞 fund 才是 there is 的主詞（there is a fund of）。

3 there is/are（或 there was/were）與複合主詞的搭配

1 由 and 連接的複合主詞

當主詞包括一系列單數名詞，或單數和複數名詞混合在一起，而**第一個名詞是單數**時，儘管整體主詞是複數，但用單數動詞 there is 通常比用複數動詞 there are 更符合語言習慣。

- There is a pear and an apple on the chest for Claire.
五斗櫃上有一顆梨和一顆蘋果，是給克萊兒的。
⤷ 動詞後面的第一個名詞是 a pear（單數名詞），因此動詞用單數（is），符合 there be 句型的基本規則：動詞的單複數與緊隨其後的主詞一致。
- There are a pear and an apple on the chest for Claire.
⤷ 主詞被視為一個複合主詞（a pear and an apple），因此動詞用複數（are）。
⤷ 這句雖然文法正確，但很不自然，生活中很少使用。

Idiomatic There is a pear and three apples on the chest for Claire.
⤷ 符合慣用法：there be 句型中的動詞單複數配合後面的第一個名詞。

Better There is a pear plus three apples on the chest for Claire.
五斗櫃上有一顆梨和三顆蘋果，是給克萊兒的。
⤷ 把連接詞 and 改成介系詞 plus，主詞就成了單數的 a pear，動詞自然是單數 is。而介系詞 plus 引導的片語只是插入的說明成分，並不影響主詞和動詞的單複數。

Better There are three apples and a pear on the chest for Claire.
五斗櫃上有三顆蘋果和一顆梨，是給克萊兒的。
↥ 當主詞是由 and 連接起來的一系列名詞時（包括單數和複數），最好把複數名詞放在前面，緊接在動詞之後，理所當然使用複數動詞（are），這樣不僅文法正確，聽起來也比較自然。

2 由 neither . . . nor、either . . . or 等成對連接詞連接的複合主詞

there be 的單複數要與靠近動詞的主詞一致，即 be 動詞後面的第一個名詞是單數，動詞要用單數，第一個名詞是複數，動詞就用複數。由 neither . . . nor、either . . . or、not only . . . but also 等成對連接詞連接的兩個主詞，動詞應該與 neither、either、not only 後面的主詞的數一致，即第一個主詞。

a 成對連接詞連接**兩個單數主詞**，要用**單數動詞**；連接**兩個複數主詞**，要用**複數動詞**。

- There is neither an elementary school nor a middle school in this poor village. 在這個貧窮的村子裡，沒有一所小學，也沒有一所中學。
  ↥ neither . . . nor 連接的兩個單數名詞，要用單數動詞。
- There are neither hotel rooms nor motel rooms available for rent in our town on this holiday.
  在這個節日裡，我們鎮上的飯店房間和汽車旅館房間全都租出去了。
  ↥ neither . . . nor 連接的兩個複數名詞，要用複數動詞。

b 成對連接詞連接一個單數主詞和一個複數主詞時，there be 動詞要與後面的第一個主詞的數一致。

- There is neither central air conditioning nor electric fans in any of the rooms in this hotel. 在這個飯店的所有房間裡，既沒有空調，也沒有電扇。
  ↥ 第一個名詞是單數（central air conditioning），動詞要用單數（is）。
- There were neither shops nor a swimming pool in the hotel we stayed in last night. 我們昨晚住的那個飯店，沒有商店也沒有游泳池。
  ↥ were 與最近的複數主詞一致（shops）。

動詞與作主詞的不定代名詞一致

當不定代名詞作主詞時，動詞必須與主詞的數（單數或複數）一致。

» 參見 104 頁〈Part 8 不定代名詞〉。

1 永遠是單數的不定代名詞

1 下面的不定代名詞永遠是單數，要用單數動詞：

- another 另一個
- anybody 任何人
- anyone 任何人
- any one of 任何一個
- anything 任何事
- each 每個
- each one 每一個
- either 任何一個
- everybody 每個人
- everyone 每個人
- every one of 每一個
- everything 每件事
- little 沒有多少
- many a 許多
- much 許多
- one 一個
- neither 沒有一個
- no one 沒有人
- nobody 沒有人
- nothing 沒什麼
- somebody 某人
- something 某事
- someone 某人

everyone 和 everybody 表示「人人、大家」，容易被錯誤地作複數使用，然而，這兩個代名詞永遠是單數，只與單數動詞連用。

- **Something tells Bing he has picked the wrong song to sing.**
  有一種感覺告訴賓，他選錯了要唱的歌曲。
- **Everyone is interested in his funny story about how Liz got into showbiz.** 大家對於他那關於莉茲如何進入演藝圈的有趣故事都很感興趣。

- Is everybody here? 大家都到了嗎？
- **Daisy admits that she might have made some kind of parenting error, because each of her four boys is a little terror.** 黛絲承認她教育子女的方式可能不當，因為她的四個兒子都是令人討厭的小傢伙。
  ↑ 雖然出現複數名詞 boys，但主詞 each 是單數，因此在正式用語中要用單數動詞。

1 each 後面常接帶有**複數名詞**的介系詞片語（each of the CDs, each of her four boys），這時 each 仍然是單數，要與單數動詞搭配。

2 但在非正式用語中，也有人用複數動詞搭配「each of + 複數名詞」。注意 在商務信函、學術報告、考試中，一定要用正式文體。

3 each 跟在複數主詞的後面時，動詞要用複數，因為這時 each 不是主詞。

- Joyce and Louise each have to get their homework done, and then they can read for fun. 喬伊絲和露易絲兩人都需要把自己的家庭作業完成，然後就可以愉快地閱讀了。
  ↑ 主詞是 Joyce and Louise，而不是 each。

2 如果 each、every、many a 或者 many an 位於一個由 and 連接的複合主詞前面，動詞仍然應該是**單數**。

each, every, etc. + 複合主詞 + 單數動詞

- **Every teacher and student has been practicing what to do in case there is a fire.** 所有師生都在練習萬一發生了火災該怎麼辦。
  » 參見 870 頁〈2 以 and 連接卻用單數動詞的主詞〉。

3 當兩個不定代名詞（anyone、nobody、everything 等）被 and 連接起來，並作句子的複合主詞時，要用**單數**動詞。

- **Nobody and nothing is going to stop Liz from marrying Andrew.**
  沒有任何人和事可以阻止莉茲嫁給安德魯。

4 代名詞 one 的用法

a one of + 複數詞（名詞／代名詞） + 單數動詞

用單數動詞搭配 one of 或 one of the 片語，因為主詞是單數代名詞 one。

- One of the reasons I like school is that I love to play basketball in the gym with my classmates.
  我愛上學的原因之一，是我喜歡在體育館裡跟同學們一起打籃球。
  ↑ 這句的主詞不是 reasons（複數），而是 one（單數），所以動詞應用單數。

- One of you is going to have to tell Sue the truth about Ruth.
  你們之中有一個人得把露絲的事，實話實說地告訴蘇。

- One of us has to tell Gus about the flat tire on the bus.
  我們之間需要有一個人告訴加斯，那輛公車有一個輪胎壞了。
  ↑ 這句的主詞不是 us（複數），而是 one（單數），所以動詞應用單數。

b more than one + 單數名詞 + 單數動詞

「more than one + 單數名詞」是單數片語，作主詞時，要用單數動詞。

- Lily said, "More than one child is too much work and responsibility."
  莉莉說：「撫養不只一個孩子，不僅太辛苦，而且責任也太大。」

- More than one student has complained about the food in the school cafeteria. 不只一個學生抱怨過學校餐廳的伙食。

c one or more/one or two + 複數名詞 + 複數動詞

「one or more + 複數名詞」及「one or two + 複數名詞」是複數片語，作主詞時，要用複數動詞。

- One or more vehicles are parked illegally in front of the school every night.
  每天晚上都有一輛或多輛車非法地停在學校前面。

- One or two bananas a day are enough for me.
  我一天吃一、兩根香蕉就足夠了。

2 永遠是複數的不定代名詞

下面的不定代名詞永遠是複數含義，用作主詞或作限定詞修飾主詞時，述語動詞用複數。

- both 兩者都
- few 少數
- many 許多
- others 其他人／物
- several 一些

- Both of my sisters-in-law are from Pakistan.
  我的兩個嫂子都是巴基斯坦人。

- Several of my friends are Pakistani astronomers.
  我的朋友中有好幾個都是巴基斯坦的天文學家。

3 既是單數也是複數的不定代名詞

1 有一些不定代名詞（all, any, most, more, none, some, such），可以與單數或複數動詞搭配，根據所指的名詞數量而定。選擇動詞搭配這類不定代名詞時，要特別注意此代名詞所指的是複數可數名詞還是不可數名詞。

- all/any/most/more/none/some/such + 複數可數名詞 + 複數動詞
- all/any/most/more/none/some/such + 不可數名詞 + 單數動詞

- Dad said, "Some of the beef has gone bad."
  爸爸說：「有些牛肉已經壞掉了。」
  ↥ 不可數名詞（beef）+ 單數動詞

- Some of our chickens are missing. 我們的一些雞不見了。
  ↥ 複數名詞（chickens）+ 複數動詞

- Such is life. 人生就是這樣。
  ↥ 單數動詞（is）+ 不可數名詞（life）；這是倒裝句，動詞在主詞前。

- "Be happy." Such were his last words. 「快樂吧。」這就是他最後說的話。
  ↥ 複數動詞（were）+ 複數名詞（words）；這是倒裝句，動詞在主詞前。

- Oh, dear, none of our food is here.
  哎喲，天啊，我們的食物都不在這裡。
  ↥ 不可數名詞（food）+ 單數動詞

  General usage None of us are called Gus.

Formal usage None of us is called Gus. 我們沒有人的名字是叫葛斯的。

↑ 複數代名詞（us）+ 複數動詞（are）。這是現代英語的常用法。

↑ 不過，在「none of + 複數名詞」的結構中，傳統用法是用單數動詞（is）。因為主詞是 none，而 none 應該是單數。

» 參見 104 頁〈Part 8 不定代名詞〉。

- None of my children have done their homework.
  = None of my children has done his or her homework.
  我的孩子沒有一個做了家庭作業。

Diving Deep Into English 101 neither of/either of + 複數名詞

「neither of/either of + 複數名詞」作主詞時，在非正式文體裡，尤其是在疑問句中，可用**複數動詞**。在正式文體中（如商務信函、學術報告、考試），要用**單數動詞**。

- either of + 複數名詞 + 單數動詞（正式）
  + 複數動詞（非正式，主要用於疑問句中）
- neither of + 複數名詞 + 單數動詞（正式）
  + 複數動詞（非正式，主要用於疑問句中）

- Have either of you ever been to Honolulu?
  ↑ 非正式（正式文體要避免使用複數動詞）
- Has either of you ever been to Honolulu? → 正式
  你們兩人中有任何一個人去過檀香山嗎？
- Neither of her daughters is diligent or intelligent.
  她的兩個女兒都不勤奮，也不聰明。
  ↑ 非疑問句中，只能用單數動詞。
- "What do you think of Penny and Jenny?"
  "Neither is as trustworthy as Liz."
  「你對潘妮和珍妮的看法如何？」「她們兩個都不像莉茲那樣可靠。」
  ↑ Neither 作主詞，只能接單數動詞。

形容詞子句的動詞要與先行詞一致

1 單數先行詞搭配單數動詞，複數先行詞搭配複數動詞

形容詞子句（即關係子句）的動詞，要與先行詞的單複數一致。先行詞指形容詞子句所修飾的詞，或指關係代名詞所用來代替的詞。

關係代名詞 who、which、that 既可以看作單數，也可以看作複數，應根據其所指的名詞（即先行詞）是單數還是複數來決定。

- **He is the economist** who is **doing consulting work for our company.**
  他是為我們公司承接諮詢業務的經濟學家。
  ↳ who 用來代替單數名詞 economist，who 後面就應該用單數動詞。

- **Jenny is one of the four women** who are **managing our company.**
  珍妮是主管我們公司的四個女子之一。
  ↳ who 用來代替複數名詞 women，who 後面就應該用複數動詞。

- **If a free society cannot help the many** who are **poor, it cannot save the few** who are **rich.** (President John Fitzgerald Kennedy)
  如果一個自由社會不能幫助眾多的窮人，它就不能留住少數的富人。
  ↳ 形容詞子句的複數動詞 are 與複數先行詞 many 和 few 一致。

- **It is not the salary but the job itself** that has **attracted Bob.**
  吸引鮑勃的不是薪水，而是工作本身。
  ↳ 形容詞子句的單數動詞 has 與單數先行詞 job 一致。

2 比較 one of . . . who, the only one of . . . who, only one of . . . who

a one of . . . who + 複數動詞（其中一個）

- Is Lily one of those people who often go to work early?
  莉莉屬於那些總是早早就去上班的人之一嗎？
  ↑ who 用來代替複數名詞 people，who 後面用複數動詞。

b the only one of . . . who + 單數動詞（其中唯一一個）

c only one of . . . who + 複數動詞（不只一個）

- Jane is the only one of my classmates who has visited Spain. 在我同學中，只有珍去西班牙旅遊過。
  ↑ 在 one of . . . who/that/which 結構中，如果 one 之前有 the only，那麼，關係代名詞 who、that、which 後面的動詞就一定要用單數。

- Jane is only one of my classmates who have visited Spain.
  在我同學中，珍只不過是去西班牙旅遊過的同學之一。
  ↑ 這裡用複數動詞 have，因為不只 Jane 一人去過西班牙，還有其他同學去過。在 one of . . . who/that/which 結構中，如果 one 之前有 only，那麼，關係代詞 who、that、which 後面的動詞就要用複數。

- Sue King is the only one of my students who loves reading.
  在我的學生中，只有蘇．金喜歡閱讀。

- Sue King is only one of my students who love reading.
  在我的學生中，蘇．金只不過是喜歡閱讀的學生之一。

以 -s 結尾和以 -ics 結尾的名詞

1 以 -s 結尾的名詞

1 形式是複數、意義是單數的單數名詞：一些以 -s 結尾的詞看起來像複數名詞，意思卻是單數，要用單數動詞。

» 參見 46 頁〈2 形式為複數、意義為單數的不可數名詞〉。

- **The news about the war is very bad and sad.**
  關於這場戰爭的消息很不好，令人傷心。
- **Do you think billiards is an interesting game?**
  你覺得撞球是一種有趣的遊戲嗎？

2 形式是複數、意義是單數的複數名詞

a 有些名詞形式上是複數，在意義上卻是單數，但因含有「一對」的意思，被看成複數名詞，要用複數動詞。

» 參見 48 頁〈3 形式為複數、意義為單數的複數名詞〉。

- glasses 眼鏡
- pants 褲子
- scissors 剪刀

- **Your glasses were in my glove compartment, not in your apartment.**
  你的眼鏡在我汽車儀器板上放雜物的架子裡，不在你的公寓裡。
- **Your pants are blue, and they are not in my closet.**
  你的褲子是藍色的，不在我的衣櫃裡。
  ↳ pants 意義上是單數（指一件褲子），但被看成是複數名詞，動詞要用複數，用代名詞替代時，要用複數代名詞。

b 當這些名詞與片語 a pair of/this pair of 連用時，則必須用單數動詞，這種情形下，pair 才是句子的主詞。

- This pair of scissors is getting dull. 這把剪刀快變得不鋒利了。

- A pair of green jeans is hanging on the door, and Theodore is snoring on the floor.
  門上掛了一件綠色牛仔褲，希歐多爾正躺在地板上鼾聲大作。

- Your new scissors are in your car's glove compartment, not in your apartment.
  = Your new pair of scissors is in your car's glove compartment, not in your apartment.
  你的新剪刀沒有在你的公寓裡，而是放在你車上的置物箱裡。

3 表示單一物品的複數名詞：有些名詞表示單一物品，卻永遠用複數形式，作主詞時，述語動詞要用複數。

» 參見 49 頁〈4 表示單一物品的複數名詞〉。

- belongings 財產
- earnings 收入；收益
- goods 商品；貨物
- grounds 基礎；庭院
- odds 機會；成功的可能性
- quarters 住處
- riches/assets 財富；資產
- savings 存款；積蓄
- thanks 感謝
- winnings 獎金

- Most of her assets were wiped out when the tsunami hit the coast.
  她大部分的財產都在海嘯襲擊沿海地區時被毀了。
  ↳ assets 意為「資產、財產」，表示單一物品，卻永遠是複數名詞，作主詞時，述語動詞要用複數。

- The odds are high that our rocket ship will crash on Mars.
  我們的火箭飛船墜毀在火星上的可能性很高。
  ↳ odds 指「幾率、可能性」，作主詞時，要搭配複數動詞。

4 形式是複數、單複數同形的可數名詞：有些名詞以 -s 結尾，但單數和複數同形，單數名詞作主詞時，要用單數動詞；複數名詞作主詞時，用複數動詞。

- a crossroads 一個十字路口 → two crossroads 兩個十字路口
- a means 一個方法 → two means 兩個方法
- a series 一套；一系列 → two series 兩套；兩個系列
- this species 這種物種 → many species 多種品種

- Is there a quicker means of getting information than using Wikipedia on the Internet?
  要獲得資訊，有沒有一個比使用網路維基百科更快捷的方法？
  ↳ means (= method)「方法、手段、工具」，means 的單數和複數結尾都是 s。
  這句的 means 是單數，動詞用單數 Is。
- There are several means of solving this problem.
  解決這個問題有好幾種方法。
  ↳ 這句的 means 是複數，動詞用複數形式 are。

2 以 -ics 結尾的名詞

許多以 -ics 結尾的名詞，可以與單數動詞或複數動詞搭配，這取決於這些名詞的含意。如果指的是一門**學科**，就是**單數**（如：politics 政治學），搭配單數動詞；如果指的是**特性或行為活動**，就是**複數**名詞（如：politics 政治信仰），搭配複數動詞。

- economics 經濟學；經濟情況
- linguistics 語言學
- mathematics 數學；數學運算
- physics 物理學
- politics 政治學；政見
- statistics 統計學；統計資料

- Jake said, "Economics is fun, but politics is a headache."
  傑克說：「經濟學有趣，但政治學卻令人頭痛。」
  ↳ economics 為學科名稱（a course of study）。
- The economics of mining gold on the moon in the future are very interesting and exciting.
  未來在月球上開採黃金的經濟前景很有趣，令人興奮。
  ↳ economics 表示經濟狀況（the economic aspects）。

- Statistics is the only course which gives Jake a headache.
  統計學是唯一讓傑克頭疼的學科。
  ↳ statistics 指「統計學」，是單數，動詞用單數。
- The statistics indicate that those who are wise rarely tell or believe lies. 統計資料表明，聰明的人很少撒謊，也很少相信謊言。
  ↳ statistics 指「統計資料」，是複數，動詞用複數。

» 參見 47 頁〈Diving Deep Into English 6〉。

表示分數的片語；算術的總和與乘積

1 表示分數的片語

1 表示分數的片語（half of 等）有時用作單數，有時用作複數，須根據上下文的意思來判斷。如果介系詞 of 後面的名詞是單數，動詞就用單數；如果是複數，動詞就用複數。

- half of 二分之一
- two-thirds of 三分之二
- a majority of 大部分
- a part of 一部分
- a percentage of 比例；部分
- the rest of 其餘

· A high percentage of our younger population is attending school outside our nation.
年輕人口中，有很大一部分的人在國外讀書。
↑ 單數名詞（population）+ 單數動詞（is attending）

· I'm sure a high percentage of our students work part time.
我確定大部分的學生都在打工。
↑ 複數名詞（students）+ 複數動詞（work）

· According to Jane, three-fifths of our city has been flooded by the huge hurricane. 據珍說，我們城市有五分之三被這場颶風淹沒了。
↑ 單數名詞（city）+ 單數動詞（has been flooded）

· Two-fifths of our soldiers were killed by friendly fire.
有五分之二的士兵，是被友軍的炮火誤殺的。
↑ 複數名詞（soldiers）+ 複數動詞（were killed）

2 在 percent（或 %）之後，用動詞的單數形式；在「percent of + 單數名詞」之後用單數動詞，在「percent of + 複數名詞」之後用複數動詞。

✗ 5% is my commission for arranging your vacation.

↑ 數字位於句首時，一般要用英文拼寫，不要用阿拉伯數字。
數字用英文 five，符號「%」也要用英文拼寫出來。

✗ Five percent are my commission for arranging your vacation.

✓ Five percent is my commission for arranging your vacation.
我為你安排假期要收取 5% 的佣金。

↑ percent 後面要接單數動詞（is）。

- Twenty percent of the apartments need major repairs.
那些公寓房有 20% 需要大修理。

- Twenty percent of the water has evaporated.
那水已經有 20% 蒸發了。

3 「one + and + 分數」作主詞時，述語動詞通常用複數動詞，但如果被看成是一個整體，就要用單數動詞。

- One and a half hours have been wasted in watching this foolish movie. 已經浪費了一個半小時看這部愚蠢的影片 。
↑ 分開的個體（一小時和半小時）

- One and a half hours is not enough for me to learn how to drive.
要學會如何駕駛，一個半小時是不夠的。
↑ 一個整體單位（一段時間）

- One and a half cups of tea is enough for me. 一杯半茶足夠我喝了。
↑ 一個整體單位（一個總數）

比較 One and a half years have passed since I last saw Jim.
= A year and a half has passed since I last saw Jim.
自從我上次見到吉姆，已經過去了一年半了。
↑ 如果「one + and + 分數」的結構前面是由不定冠詞 a/an 取代 one，動詞要用單數。

2 算術的總和與乘積

表達加、減、乘、除運算時，主詞通常是用**單數**形式，須搭配單數述語動詞。

1 **加法：用介系詞 plus 或連接詞 and。**在談論加法時，用 plus 是比較正規的用法。

Formal Three plus three is six.
= Three plus three equals six.

← 句子的單數主詞 Three 不會因 plus 引導的介系詞片語，而改變成複數。

Informal Three and three are/is six.
= Three and three equal/equals six.
3 加 3 等於 6。(3 + 3 = 6)

← 主詞由 and 連接的兩個數字（Three 和 three）構成，述語動詞可以用複數（are 或 equal），也可以用單數（is 或 equals）。

2 減法：用介系詞 minus 或 from。

Formal Eight minus three is five.
= Eight minus three equals five.
8 減 3 等於 5。(8 – 3 = 5)

← minus 和 from 都是介系詞，不是連接詞。

Informal Three from eight is five.
從 8 裡面減去 3 就等於 5。
= Three from eight leaves five.
從 8 裡面減去 3 還剩下 5。

3 乘法：用過去分詞片語 multiplied by 或介系詞 times。

Formal Three multiplied by five is fifteen.
= Three multiplied by five equals fifteen.

← times (= multiplied by) 是介系詞。

Informal Three times five is fifteen.
3 乘 5 等於 15。(3 × 5 = 15)

4 除法：用過去分詞片語 divided by 或介系詞 into。

Formal Eight divided by four is two.
= Eight divided by four equals two.

Informal Four into eight goes two times.
8 除以 4 等於 2。(8 ÷ 4 = 2)

表總數的數字；集合名詞和外來語複數名詞

1 表總數的數字

1 代表一個總數或**一個整體**單位的數字，要看作單數，用**單數動詞**。亦即，以**時間**、**金錢**、**距離**、**重量**的測量（measurements of time, money, distance, weight）作主詞時，通常接單數動詞。

✗ Eight hours of sleep are enough for Kate.

✓ Eight hours of sleep is enough for Kate.
八小時的睡眠，對凱特來說就足夠了。
↑ 時間 Eight hours 代表一個整體單位或一個總數，要接單數動詞。

- Eight hundred kilometers is not too far to travel by car.
開汽車旅行，八百公里的距離不算太遠。 → 一段距離

- A million dollars is a lot of money to hide under your bed.
把一百萬美金藏在你的床下，那可是一大筆錢啊。 → 一筆金錢

2 注意 上面這些主詞如果用來表示**一系列個體單位**，一些分開的數目（a group of individual components, a number of individual units），就要接**複數動詞**。比較下面兩句：

- Ten million dollars have been spent repairing the Italian cruise ship the *Royal Olympian*. 修理義大利巡航船「皇家奧林匹斯」已經耗費了一千萬美金。
↑ 一系列個體單位（一百萬、兩百萬、三百萬……）

- The one thousand dollars his dad gave him was spent in a week.
他爸爸給他的那一千元美金，他在一個星期內就花光了。
↑ 一個總數

» 參見 26 頁〈9 表達數目的集合名詞，是單數還是複數？〉。

2 集合名詞

1 代表的動物和事物的集合名詞（參見 912 頁〈附錄 3 集合名詞表〉）

- an army of ants 一大群螞蟻
- a bed of flowers 一花壇的花兒
- a block of houses 一街區房屋

2 代表人的集合名詞

- air force 空軍
- audience 觀眾
- band 樂團
- class 班級
- club 俱樂部
- college 大學
- committee 委員會
- company 公司
- department 科系、部門、局
- family 家庭
- gang 一幫
- government 政府
- public 公眾
- school 學校
- staff（全體）職員
- team 隊

3 集合名詞常作**單數**。如果這個集合名詞所代表的團體被看成是**一個整體**在活動，動詞就用單數。

- **When the people fear their government, there is tyranny; when the government fears the people, there is liberty.**
  (President Thomas Jefferson)
  當人民畏懼政府，暴政當道橫行；當政府害怕人民，自由鼓舞人心。
  ↑ people 要接複數動詞；government 要接單數動詞。

- **Our committee has announced its decision to fund the wind power farm.**
  我們的委員會已經宣布，決定要為風力發電廠提供資金。
  ↑ 集合名詞 committee 搭配單數動詞 has 和單數所有格代名詞 its。

the wind power farm

4 如果團體的成員被看成是**分開**、**個別地**活動，就有複數意義，在這種情況下，英式要用複數動詞，而美式常用 members 作主詞。不過，集合名詞與複數動詞連用常顯得很不自然，應儘量避免，尤其是在美式英語中。因此，如果想表達團體成員的個別行動，就在集合名詞的前面加上片語 the members of the 或 individuals in the，來表示個別行動的團體成員。

» 參見 24 頁〈4 集合名詞〉。

- the members of the/our/your . . . ……裡的成員
- individuals in the/our/your . . . ……裡的個人

| 英式 | Del, I hope your family are all well.

| 美式 | Del, I hope your family is well.

戴爾，我希望你全家人都好。

↑ 英式英語可以用 family 指家庭中的成員，可用複數動詞；美式英語則把 family 看成是一個整體單位，用單數動詞。

| 美式 / 英式 | Del replied, "I also hope all the members of your family are well."

= Del replied, "I also hope all your family members are well."

= Del replied, "I also hope everyone in your family is well."

戴爾回答說：「我也希望你全家人都好。」

↑ 美式常用 members 來指家庭中的成員，動詞用複數。英式也可以用 members 來指家庭中的成員。

| 英式 | Our teaching staff are going to laugh a lot when Lily demonstrates how she improves her creativity.

| 美式 | Our teaching staff is going to laugh a lot when Lily demonstrates how she improves her creativity.

| 美式 / 英式 | The members of our teaching staff are going to laugh a lot when Lily demonstrates how she improves her creativity.

當莉莉展示她是如何提高創造力時，我們的教學員工將歡笑不停。

| 英式 | The loud crowd are begging for rain from a huge wet cloud.

| 美式 | The loud crowd is begging for rain from a huge wet cloud.

那群喧鬧的人群，正在祈求從一大片濕雲中降下雨來。

3 外來語複數名詞

1 一些外來語名詞的複數結尾與英文不同。這些字如果是複數名詞（例如 criteria, parentheses）並作主詞時，要接複數動詞。

- **No criteria have been set in advance for judging a student's dance.**
  判斷一個學生舞姿的標準還沒有提前確定下來。
  ⮤ criteria 是 criterion 的複數形式。

- **"The level two exercise identifies where parentheses are needed," explained Sue.** 蘇解釋說：「二級練習題鑑定何處需要括號。」
  ⮤ 「括號」的英文：單數是 parenthesis，複數是 parentheses。
  ⮤ 括號要成對使用，因此應該用複數 parentheses，接複數動詞 are。
  ⮤ 比較單數的用法：
  * The closing parenthesis is missing. 後面的括號不見了。

2 data 指「**訊息**」（information）時，是單數名詞，接單數動詞；指個別的「**資料、數據**」（individual facts, statistics, or items of information）時，是複數名詞，接複數動詞。

- **The data gathered by the nine robotic explorers on the Moon are now being compared and analyzed online.**
  由月球上的九個機器探索者收集的資料，目前正在網路上比較和分析。
  ⮤ 正在進行比較（now being compared）的東西不可能是單數，
  因此這裡指「資料、數據」，是複數名詞 data，接複數動詞 are。

- **Lots of data about that rocket engine is available on the Internet.**
  關於那個火箭發動機，從網路上可以獲得大量的資訊。
  ⮤ data 指「信息」(information) 時，是單數名詞，接單數動詞。

- **Additional data is available from the president of our company.**
  從公司的總裁那裡可以獲得額外的資訊。
  ⮤ data = information

肯定和否定的主詞

如果句子有一個肯定的主詞和一個否定的主詞（是……而不是……），而其中一個是複數，另一個是單數，那麼**動詞的數應該與肯定主詞的數一致**；要用雙逗號把否定主詞分開，但如果否定主詞前面有連接詞 and 或 but，就不用逗號分開。

- **The English department members, not the chair, have decided not to work this summer.**

  = The English department members and not the chair have decided not to work this summer.

  是英文系的成員，而不是委員會主席決定今年夏天不工作。

  ↑ 複數動詞（have decided）與複數肯定主詞（The English department members）一致；否定主詞是一個插入語，沒有連接詞 and 或 but，要用雙逗號把否定主詞分開；反之，就不要用逗號。

- **The English department, not the chair, has decided not to work this summer.**

  = The English department and not the chair has decided not to work this summer.

  是英文系，而不是委員會主席來決定今年夏天不工作。

  ↑ 單數動詞（has decided）與單數肯定主詞（The English department）一致。

- **"It is not our citizens but the President who decides this type of issue," Liz said to Scot.**

  莉茲對史考特說：「對這種事有決定權的是總統，而不是公民。」

  ↑ 單數動詞（decides）與單數肯定主詞（the President）一致。

  ↑ 句型是「It is not . . . but . . . who」。

- "It is our citizens, not the President, who decide this type of issue," Scot explained to Liz.

  ⤷ 複數動詞（decide）與複數肯定主詞（citizens）一致。
  這句沒有 but 或 and 連接，需要雙逗號分開肯定主詞和否定主詞。

  = "It is our citizens and not the President who decide this type of issue," Scot explained to Liz.

  ⤷ 句型是「It is . . . and not . . . who」。

  = "It is not the President but our citizens who decide this type of issue," Scot explained to Liz.

  史考特對莉茲對解釋說：「對這種事有決定權的是公民，而不是總統。」

  ⤷ 句型是「It is not . . . but . . . who」。
  ⤷ 第二句和第三句用了連接詞 but 和 and，就不需要再用逗號。

- It was the personality of the manager Jane Bees, not her ideas, that has provoked her employees to complain.

  = It was the personality of the manager Jane Bees and not her ideas that has provoked her employees to complain.

  引起員工抱怨的原因，是因為經理珍·比斯的人品，而不是她的觀念。

  ⤷ 單數動詞（has provoked）與單數肯定主詞（personality）一致；
  第一句的否定主詞用雙逗號分開，第二句的否定主詞前有連接詞 and，
  就不用逗號，句型是「It was . . . and not . . . that」。

- It was not the personality of the manager Jane Bees but her ideas that have provoked her employees to complain.

  引起員工抱怨的原因是因為經理珍·比斯的觀念，而不是她的人品。

  ⤷ 複數動詞（have provoked）與複數肯定主詞（ideas）一致；
  有 but 連接，不需要逗號分開肯定主詞和否定主詞。
  句型是「It was not . . . but . . . that」。

地理名稱、出版物名稱、片語或名詞子句作主詞

1 地理名稱、書報雜誌名稱、片語或名詞子句與單數動詞搭配

地理名稱、書報雜誌等出版物名稱、片語或名詞子句在句中作主詞時，動詞要用單數。地理名稱或書名、雜誌名即使形式上是複數，如果指的是一個整體，仍應視為單數，用單數動詞。

- The Philippines is the first stop on our journey.
  菲律賓是我們旅程中的第一站。
  ↑ 地理名稱：the Philippines 的形式雖是複數，但指一個整體（國家）。

- Good Manners is a funny new book written by our friends Sue and Andrew.
  《彬彬有禮》是我們的朋友蘇和安德魯寫的一本有趣的新書。
  ↑ 書名作主詞。

- Riding in a horse and carriage is a good way to start a happy marriage.
  乘坐馬車，是展開一段幸福婚姻的好方式。
  ↑ 動名詞片語作主詞。

- Whether you want to go or not is no longer important now.
  無論你想不想去，現在都已經不重要了。
  ↑ Whether 引導的名詞子句作主詞，要用單數動詞。

- Whatever Kay said and did was OK with Sid.
  = Anything (that) Kay said and did was OK with Sid.
  凡是凱所說的和做的，席德都覺得不錯。
  ↑ Whatever 引導的名詞子句作主詞，要用單數動詞。

- That a peasant may become king does not render the kingdom democratic. (President Thomas Woodrow Wilson)
  一個農夫可能會當上國王，但不能使王國變得民主起來。
  ↑ That 引導的名詞子句作主詞，動詞用單數。

2 what 引導的主詞子句，須根據語意來決定其單複數

1 當 what 引導主詞子句，而 what 是子句動詞的**受詞**時，主句動詞用單數還是複數，主要取決於補語是單數還是複數。主句裡的補語是單數，主句動詞總是用單數；主句裡的補語是複數，主句動詞常用複數。

- What I want is just some sweet chocolate from Pete.
  我想要的，不過是彼特給我一些甜甜的巧克力。
  ↑ What 是子句動詞 want 的受詞，What 引導的子句指的是不可數名詞 chocolate，即主句的補語是單數，因此主句動詞應該用單數（is）。

- What I want are some movies starring Jackie Chen.
  我想要的是幾部由成龍主演的電影。
  ↑ What 子句指複數名詞 movies，即主句的補語是複數，動詞用複數（are）。

比較 含連綴動詞的句子，動詞要與主詞一致，不與主詞補語一致。

- Cellphones are the only product our company makes.
  手機是我們公司生產的唯一產品。
  ↑ 動詞要與複數主詞一致（Cellphones），不與單數主詞補語（the only product）一致。

2 當 what 引導主詞子句，而 what 是子句的**主詞**時

a what 子句的動詞和主句的補語都是複數或都是單數，主句的動詞通常要與子句的動詞和主句的補語一致。

- What drives me crazy is Dan's bad attitude.
  讓我發瘋的，是丹惡劣的態度。
  ↑ What 引導主詞子句，在子句中作主詞。子句的動詞（drives）和主句的補語（attitude）都是單數，主句的動詞要用單數（is）。

- What give away Aunt Linda's age are her bad feet.
  洩漏琳達姨媽的年齡，是她兩個不好用的腳。
  ↥ What 是子句裡的主詞，引導一個主詞子句。子句的動詞和主句的補語都是複數（give, bad feet），主句的動詞也用複數（are）。

b 如果主句的補語是複數，而 what 子句的動詞是單數，主句的動詞可以與子句的動詞一致，用單數，也可以與補語一致，用複數，但表達的意思有點不同。

- What gives away Tom's poverty are his bad teeth.
  洩漏湯姆的貧窮，是他那些壞牙齒。

- What gives away Tom's poverty is his bad teeth.
  洩漏湯姆的貧窮的，是他那口壞牙齒。
  ↥ 當 What 子句的動詞是單數（gives），而主句的補語是複數（bad teeth），主句的動詞可以是複數（are），也可以是單數（is）。用單數 is，把 bad teeth 看成是一個整體；用複數 are，把 bad teeth 看成是一個個分開的個體。

- What drives me crazy is her angry glances.
  讓我發瘋的，是她憤怒的目光。
  ↥ 把「angry glances」看成是一個整體。

- What drives me crazy are her angry glances.
  讓我發瘋的，是她那些憤怒的目光。
  ↥ 把「angry glances」看成是一個個分開的個體（一個又一個憤怒的目光）。

c 主句的補語若有兩個或多個名詞，如果這些名詞都是不可數名詞（單數），主句的動詞和子句的動詞通常應該用單數；如果這些名詞都是複數，主句的動詞和子句的動詞通常用複數。

- What pleases Ann's brothers is her honesty and willingness to help others. 使安的兄弟們感到滿意的，是安的誠實，以及樂意幫助他人。
  ↥ 補語是兩個單數名詞（honesty, willingness），動詞都用單數（pleases, is）。

- When you enter Pat's room, what catch your attention are her four rats and two cats.
  一進入派特的房間，抓住你的注意力的，是她的四隻老鼠和兩隻貓。
  ↥ 補語是兩個複數名詞（rats, cats），動詞都用複數（catch, are）。

d 主句的補語有兩個或多個名詞，單數或複數動詞的選擇偶爾會表達不同的意義。

- What excite Ms. Flower most are money and power.
  ↑ 金錢和權力是兩個分開的目標，子句和主句都用複數動詞。

- What excites Ms. Flower most is money and power.
  使福勞爾女士最激動的，是金錢和權力。
  ↑ 金錢和權力被看成是一個整體，子句和主句都用單數動詞。

3 當 what 引導受詞子句，而 what 是子句動詞的主詞時

what 子句的動詞要與子句的補語一致，補語是單數名詞或片語，what 子句的動詞用單數；補語是複數名詞或片語，what 子句的動詞用複數。

- I see what seems to be a cold and stormy sea.
  我看見的似乎是一個寒冷、狂暴的大海。
  ↑ what 引導受詞子句，整個子句是述語動詞 see 的受詞。what 是受詞子句裡的主詞，子句的動詞和子句的補語要一致，補語是單數名詞片語（a cold and stormy sea），子句動詞也用單數（seems）。

- Alice often makes what seem to be gestures of forgiveness.
  艾麗絲常常做出一些好像是寬恕的示意。
  ↑ what 引導受詞子句，整個子句是述語動詞 makes 的受詞。what 是受詞子句裡的主詞，子句的動詞和子句的補語要一致，補語是複數名詞（gestures），子句動詞也用複數（seem）。

the number/a number; the couple/a couple; the + 形容詞；倒裝句

1 the number/a number

- the number of → 意為「……的數量」，具有單數意義，作主詞時要接單數動詞。
- a number of → 意為「許多的，大量的」，具有複數意義，作主詞時要接複數動詞。

✗ The number of students in my biology class are twenty.
✓ The number of students in my biology class is twenty.
我的生物學班上有二十名學生。

· Kate noticed a large number of her classmates were late.
凱特注意到有許多同學遲到了。

· The number of smiles Kay gives to me is increasing every day.
凱對我微笑的次數與日俱增。

· Quite a number of those bold pink blouses have been sold.
那些鮮豔的粉紅色上衣已經賣出很多件了。

「the total of/a total of + 複數名詞」的用法也一樣：
- the total of + 複數名詞 + 單數動詞
- a total of + 複數名詞 + 複數動詞

2 the couple/a couple

couple 如果指**兩個個體**（two individuals），就是複數，動詞用複數；
如果 couple 指**一個整體**（a whole），就是單數，動詞用單數。

1 the couple 指「夫妻、配偶」，通常被看成是一個整體，後面接單數動詞。

- **Kate has noticed that the young couple next door often stays up late.** 凱特察覺隔壁那對年輕夫婦常熬夜。
- **A nice British couple has moved in next door to Lenore.**
  一對友善的英國夫婦搬進蕾諾兒的隔壁。
  ↑ 這裡 nice British couple 前面雖然有 a，但仍然要接一個單數動詞，因為一對夫妻（a married couple）是一個整體（a whole）。

比較

- **The couple have moved into their new apartment.**
  那對夫妻已經搬進他們的新公寓裡了。
  ↑ 一般來說，the couple 作主詞時，要用單數動詞。但這句的 The couple 後面要用複數動詞（have）搭配複數代名詞所有格（their），這樣聽上去更自然，更符合語言習慣。

2 「a couple of + 複數名詞」指兩個個體，意思是「幾個、兩個」（= a few of; two of），接複數動詞。

- **Lenore did not notice that a couple of her friends were standing near the door.**
  蕾諾兒沒有注意到她的幾個朋友正站在門邊。

比較

- **A couple of weeks is all I need to prepare for that accounting exam.**
  我只需要兩週的時間來準備會計考試。
  ↑ 指一整段時間，用單數動詞。

3 the + 形容詞 + 複數動詞

有些形容詞與 the 連用（the + adjective），變成了含複數意義的名詞，用來指所有具有那種特性的人或某個國家的民族。「the + 形容詞」作主詞時，動詞要用複數。

» 參見 204 頁〈4 「the + 形容詞」的用法〉。

✗ "The rich gets richer and the poor gets poorer," complained Mitch.

✓ "The rich get richer and the poor get poorer," complained Mitch.
米奇抱怨說：「富人越來越富有，而窮人越來越貧苦。」

4 倒裝句子：動詞的數與修飾語無關

當句子是倒裝句時，即主詞和述語動詞順序顛倒（主詞在述語動詞後面），動詞要與主詞一致，不與句首的修飾語一致。

- Behind that door wait Pat and Kate. 派特和凱特在門後等待著。
  ↑ 主詞是由 and 連接起來的並列主詞／複合主詞（Pat and Kate），動詞要用複數。

- Behind that door waits Pat. 派特在門後等待著。
  ↑ 動詞後面的主詞是單數名詞（Pat），動詞要用單數。

- Outside were the three horses I had learned to ride. → 倒裝句
  = The three horses I had learned to ride were outside. → 主述結構
  我已經學會騎的那三匹馬就在外面。
  ↑ 主詞是複數 the three horses，述語動詞要與複數主詞一致，而與句首的修飾副詞 Outside 無關。

- On the top of the mountain stands an old temple.
  → 倒裝句
  = An old temple stands on the top of the mountain.
  → 主述結構
  那座山的山頂上座落著一間古剎。

附錄

Appendixes

不規則動詞表

ⓐ 以下詞序由左至右為：原形 → 過去式 → 過去分詞
ⓑ ★表示三態同形。
★表示有三態同形和不同形兩種寫法，若意思不同，以編號①②標示。
ⓒ † 表示具有兩種變化形式且表示不同意義，並以編號①②標示。

(be) am	→ was	→ been	be 動詞 am
(be) are	→ were	→ been	be 動詞 are
arise	→ arose	→ arisen	升起；產生
awake	→ awoke/awaked	→ awoken/awaked	喚醒；醒來
babysit	→ babysat	→ babysat	當臨時保姆
bear †*	→ ① bore	→ borne	承受；生（孩子）
	→ ② bore	→ born	誕生；生（孩子）
beat	→ beat	→ beaten	打；擊
become	→ became	→ become	變成；成為
begin	→ began	→ begun	開始
bend	→ bent	→ bent	彎曲；轉彎
bet ★	→ bet	→ bet	打賭 ◈ 過去式和過去分詞，英式也用 betted。
bid ★	→ ① bid	→ bid	喊價；出價
	→ ② bade/bid	→ bidden/bid	〔古〕致意；吩咐
bind	→ bound	→ bound	捆；綁
bite	→ bit	→ bitten	咬；啃
bless	→ blessed/blest	→ blessed/blest	為……祝福
bleed	→ bled	→ bled	流血
blow	→ blew	→ blown	吹；刮
break	→ broke	→ broken	打破；折斷
breed	→ bred	→ bred	使繁殖；產生
bring	→ brought	→ brought	帶來；拿來
broadcast ★	→ broadcast	→ broadcast	廣播；播放
build	→ built	→ built	建築；建造

* **a** bear 表「生（孩子）」時，後面若無 by，被動語態中的過去分詞用 born。

- She was born into a poor family. 她出生在一個貧窮的家庭裡。
- Have any children been born at the South Pole? 有沒有在南極出生的孩子？

b bear 表示「生（孩子）」時，主動語態的句子要用過去分詞 borne（常與助動詞 have/had 連用）；也用於被動語態，但需要與介系詞 by 連用：

- She has borne three children. 她生了三個孩子。
- The baby borne by her last year is dead. 她去年生的孩子已經死了。

burn	→ burned/burnt	→ burned/burnt	燃燒；著火 ◈ 過去式和過去分詞 burnt 主要為英式用法。
burst ★	→ burst	→ burst	爆炸；破裂
buy	→ bought	→ bought	買
catch	→ caught	→ caught	接住；抓住
choose	→ chose	→ chosen	選擇；挑選
come	→ came	→ come	來
cost ☆	→ ① cost	→ cost	花費
	→ ② costed	→ costed	〔商〕估計成本
cut ★	→ cut	→ cut	切；割
deal	→ dealt	→ dealt	處理；對付
dig	→ dug	→ dug	掘(土)；挖(洞)
dive	→ dived/dove	→ dived	潛水 ◈ 美式英語的過去式可用 dove。
do	→ did	→ done	做
draw	→ drew	→ drawn	畫
dream	→ dreamed/dreamt	→ dreamed/dreamt	做夢 ◈ 過去式和過去分詞 dreamt 主要為英式用法。
drink	→ drank	→ drunk	飲；喝 ◈ 過去分詞 drunken 只放在名詞前面作形容詞。
drive	→ drove	→ driven	駕駛(汽車等)
eat	→ ate	→ eaten	吃；喝
fall	→ fell	→ fallen	落下；降落
feed	→ fed	→ fed	餵養；飼養
feel	→ felt	→ felt	摸；觸；感覺
fight	→ fought	→ fought	打架；打仗
find	→ found	→ found	找到；發現
fit ☆	→ fitted/fit	→ fitted/fit	① (衣服)合身；② 適合於；③ 安裝，配備(此意可用於被動) ◈ 美式英語的過去式和過去分詞通常用 fit，被動語態用 fitted。
fly	→ ① flew	→ flown	飛；駕駛(飛機)
	→ ② flied	→ flied	〔美〕(棒球)打高飛球
forbid	→ forbade/forbad	→ forbidden	禁止
forecast ☆	→ forecast/forecasted	→ forecast/forecasted	預測；預報
foresee	→ foresaw	→ foreseen	預見；預知
forget	→ forgot	→ forgotten/forgot	忘記 ◈ 美式英語中，過去分詞有時用 forgot。
forgive	→ forgave	→ forgiven	原諒
freeze	→ froze	→ frozen	結冰
get	→ got	→ got/gotten	獲得 ◈ 美式英語中，過去分詞用 gotten；英式英語用 got。

give	→ gave	→ given	給
go	→ went	→ gone	走
grow	→ grew	→ grown	成長
hang †	→ ① hanged	→ hanged	絞死；吊死
	→ ② hung	→ hung	懸掛
have (has)	→ had	→ had	擁有
hear	→ heard	→ heard	聽見
hide	→ hid	→ hidden	隱藏
hit ★	→ hit	→ hit	打
hold	→ held	→ held	握著；舉行
hurt ★	→ hurt	→ hurt	使受傷；疼痛
input ★	→ input/inputted	→ input/inputted	輸入 ◈ 過去式與過去分詞 inputted 為英式英語，但不常用。
(be) is	→ was	→ been	be 動詞 is
keep	→ kept	→ kept	保持；存放
kneel	→ knelt/kneeled	→ knelt/kneeled	跪著 ◈ 美式英語中，過去式和過去分詞也用 kneeled。
knit ★	→ ① knit	→ knit	使接合 ◈ 如：a closely knit community
	→ ② knitted	→ knitted	編織
know	→ knew	→ known	知道
label	→ labeled/labelled	→ labeled/labelled	貼標籤 ◈ 過去式和過去分詞 labelled 主要為英式用法。
lay	→ laid	→ laid	放；鋪設
lead	→ led	→ led	引導
lean	→ leaned/leant	→ leaned/leant	傾斜 ◈ 過去式和過去分詞 leant 主要為英式用法。
leap	→ leaped/leapt	→ leaped/leapt	跳躍 ◈ 過去式和過去分詞 leapt 主要為英式用法。
learn	→ learned/learnt	→ learned/learnt	學習 ◈ 過去式和過去分詞 learnt 主要為英式用法。
leave	→ left	→ left	離開；留給
lend	→ lent	→ lent	借給
let ★	→ let	→ let	允許；讓
lie	→ lay	→ lain	躺
light	→ lit/lighted	→ lit/lighted	照亮
lose	→ lost	→ lost	失去；輸掉
make	→ made	→ made	製造
mean	→ meant	→ meant	意指；意味
meet	→ met	→ met	遇見；認識
mislead	→ misled	→ misled	誤導
mistake	→ mistook	→ mistaken	弄錯；誤解

misunderstand	→ misunderstood	→ misunderstood	誤會；曲解
mow	→ mowed	→ mowed/mown	割（草等）
output ★	→ output	→ output	生產；輸出
overcast ★	→ overcast	→ overcast	（雲等）遮蔽
overcome	→ overcame	→ overcome	戰勝；克服
overdraw	→ overdrew	→ overdrawn	透支；誇張
overhear	→ overheard	→ overheard	偷聽；偶然聽到
oversleep	→ overslept	→ overslept	睡過頭
overtake	→ overtook	→ overtaken	超過；趕上
overthrow	→ overthrew	→ overthrown	推翻
pay	→ paid	→ paid	支付
plead	→ pleaded/pled	→ pleaded/pled	辯護；請求 ◈ 美式英語中，過去式和過去分詞也用 pled。
proofread ★	→ proofread	→ proofread	校對 ◈ 三態同形，但過去式和過去分詞與原形動詞的發音不一樣。
prove	→ proved	→ proved/proven	證明 ◈ 過去分詞 proven 主要為美式用法。
put ★	→ put	→ put	放
quit ★	→ quit/quitted	→ quit/quitted	離開；放棄；辭職 ◈ 過去式和過去分詞 quitted 主要為英式用法。
read ★	→ read	→ read	閱讀 ◈ 三態同形，但過去式和過去分詞與原形動詞的發音不一樣。
retell	→ retold	→ retold	再講；重述
rethink	→ rethought	→ rethought	重新考慮
rewrite	→ rewrote	→ rewritten	重寫
rid ★	→ rid/ridded	→ rid/ridded	使免除
ride	→ rode	→ ridden	乘坐
ring †	→ 1 rang	→ rung	按（鈴）；搖（鈴）
	→ 2 ringed	→ ringed	成環形；包圍
rise	→ rose	→ risen	上升
run	→ ran	→ run	跑
saw	→ sawed	→ sawed/sawn	鋸開 ◈ 過去分詞 sawn 主要為英式用法。
say	→ said	→ said	說
see	→ saw	→ seen	看見；會見
seek	→ sought	→ sought	尋找
sell	→ sold	→ sold	銷售
send	→ sent	→ sent	發送
set ★	→ set	→ set	放置
sew	→ sewed	→ sewed/sewn	縫合

shake	→ shook	→ shaken	搖
shave	→ shaved	→ shaved/shaven	刮臉
shine †	→ ① shone	→ shone	發光；出眾
	→ ② shined	→ shined	擦亮
shrink	→ shrank/shrunk	→ shrunk/shrunken	收縮
shoe	→ shod/shoed	→ shod/shoed	給馬釘蹄鐵；給……穿鞋
shoot	→ shot	→ shot	發射；射擊
show	→ showed	→ shown/showed	顯示 ⊙ 過去分詞偶爾用 showed。
shut ★	→ shut	→ shut	關上
sing	→ sang	→ sung	唱
sink	→ sank/sunk	→ sunk	下沉 ⊙ 過去式偶爾用 sunk。
sit	→ sat	→ sat	坐
sleep	→ slept	→ slept	睡覺
slide	→ slid	→ slid	滑動
smell	→ smelled/smelt	→ smelled/smelt	嗅；聞 ⊙ 過去式和過去分詞 smelt 主要為英式用法。
sow	→ sowed	→ sowed/sown	播種
speak	→ spoke	→ spoken	説話
speed	→ speeded/sped	→ speeded/sped	迅速前進
spell	→ spelled/spelt	→ spelled/spelt	拼寫 ⊙ 過去式和過去分詞 spelt 主要為英式用法。
spend	→ spent	→ spent	花錢；花時間；花精力
spill	→ spilled/spilt	→ spilled/spilt	溢出 ⊙ 過去式和過去分詞 spilt 主要為英式用法。
spin	→ spun	→ spun	紡紗；旋轉
spit ★	→ spit/spat	→ spit/spat	吐（唾液等） ⊙ 過去式和過去分詞 spat 主要為英式用法。
split ★	→ split	→ split	劈開；劃分
spoil	→ spoiled/spoilt	→ spoiled/spoilt	寵壞 ⊙ 過去式和過去分詞 spoilt 主要為英式用法。
spoon-feed	→ spoon-fed	→ spoon-fed	用湯匙餵食；溺愛
spotlight †	→ ① spotlit	→ spotlit	聚光照明
	→ ② spotlit/spotlighted	→ spotlit/spotlighted	聚集目光焦點；使公眾注意
spread ★	→ spread	→ spread	使伸展
spring	→ sprang/sprung	→ sprung	跳；躍 ⊙ 美式英語的過去式也用 sprung。
stand	→ stood	→ stood	站立
steal	→ stole	→ stolen	竊取
stick	→ stuck	→ stuck	釘住；粘住；刺入
sting	→ stung	→ stung	刺；叮
stride	→ strode	→ stridden	邁大步走

strike	→ struck	→ struck/stricken	攻擊 ◈ 美式英語的過去分詞也用 stricken，表示受疾病侵襲。
string	→ strung	→ strung	用線綁、串；伸展
strive	→ strove/strived	→ striven/strived	努力 ◈ 過去式和過去分詞 strived 不太常用。
swear	→ swore	→ sworn	發誓
sweat ★	→ sweat/sweated	→ sweat/sweated	出汗
sweep	→ swept	→ swept	清掃
swell	→ swelled	→ swollen/swelled	腫起；(使)膨脹
swim	→ swam	→ swum	游泳
swing	→ swung	→ swung	搖擺
take	→ took	→ taken	拿走
teach	→ taught	→ taught	講授
tear	→ tore	→ torn	撕開
telecast ★	→ telecast	→ telecast	電視廣播
tell	→ told	→ told	告訴
think	→ thought	→ thought	思索
throw	→ threw	→ thrown	投；擲
thrust ★	→ thrust	→ thrust	刺；用力推
unbend	→ unbent	→ unbent	弄直
unbind	→ unbound	→ unbound	解開
underbid ★	→ underbid	→ underbid	出價低於
understand	→ understood	→ understood	理解
undo	→ undid	→ undone	解開；取消
unwind	→ unwound	→ unwound	解開
uphold	→ upheld	→ upheld	舉起
upset ★	→ upset	→ upset	弄翻；使心煩意亂
wake	→ woke/waked	→ woken/waked	醒來 ◈ 過去式和過去分詞 waked 主要用於口語。
wear	→ wore	→ worn	穿著
weave †	→ 1 wove	→ woven	編織；使交織
	→ 2 weaved	→ weaved	搖晃著前進
wed ★	→ wedded/wed	→ wedded/wed	結婚
weep	→ wept	→ wept	哭泣
wet ★	→ wet/wetted	→ wet/wetted	淋濕
win	→ won	→ won	獲勝
wind †	→ 1 wound	→ wound	轉動；蜿蜒；上(發條)
	→ 2 winded	→ winded	使喘氣
withdraw	→ withdrew	→ withdrawn	取消；撤退
withhold	→ withheld	→ withheld	阻擋；保留；隱瞞
withstand	→ withstood	→ withstood	抵擋；反抗
write	→ wrote	→ written	寫

專有名詞表

1 星期

Sunday 星期天（一週的第一天）
Monday 星期一
Tuesday 星期二
Wednesday 星期三
Thursday 星期四
Friday 星期五
Saturday 星期六

2 月分

January 一月
February 二月
March 三月
April 四月
May 五月
June 六月
July 七月
August 八月
September 九月
October 十月
November 十一月
December 十二月

3 節慶日

Children's Day 兒童節
Christmas 聖誕節
the Dragon Boat Festival 端午節
Easter 復活節
Halloween 萬聖節
Independence Day（美國）獨立紀念日
the Mid-Autumn Festival 中秋節
Mother's Day 母親節
New Year's Day 元旦
the Spring Festival 春節
Thanksgiving Day 感恩節

4 書名

the Bible 《聖經》
Hamlet 《哈姆雷特》
War and Peace《戰爭與和平》
the New Testament 《新約》

5 人名

Abraham Lincoln 亞伯拉罕·林肯
Aladdin 阿拉丁
Albert Einstein 阿爾伯特·愛因斯坦
Beethoven 貝多芬
Cinderella 灰姑娘
Harry Potter 哈利·波特
Larry 賴瑞
Mother Teresa 德蕾莎修女
Robin Hood 羅賓漢
Robinson Crusoe 魯賓遜
Santa Claus 聖誕老人
Snow White 白雪公主
Vicky 薇姬

6 著名勝地及建築物

the Eiffel Tower 艾菲爾鐵塔
the Grand Canyon 大峽谷
the Great Wall of China 長城
the Statue of Liberty 自由女神像
the Summer Palace 頤和園
the Sydney Opera House 雪梨歌劇院
the Taj Mahal 泰姬陵

7 國名／民族名

America/Americans 美國（人）
Australia/Australians 澳洲（人）
Britain/British 英國（人）
Canada/Canadians 加拿大（人）
China/Chinese 中國（人）
Egypt/Egyptians 埃及（人）
France/French 法國（人）
Germany/Germans 德國（人）
Italy/Italians 義大利（人）
Japan/Japanese 日本（人）
Korea/Koreans 韓國（人）
Malaysia/Malaysians 馬來西亞（人）
Spain/Spaniards 西班牙（人）

8 城市名

Bangkok 曼谷
Beijing 北京
Berlin 柏林
Cairo 開羅
Jakarta 雅加達
London 倫敦
Madrid 馬德里
New Delhi 新德里
Paris 巴黎
Rome 羅馬
Seoul 首爾
Taipei 臺北
Tokyo 東京
Toronto 多倫多
Washington, D.C. 華盛頓特區

9 州名／省名

〔美國〕
Alaska 阿拉斯加州
Arizona 亞利桑那州
Florida 佛羅里達州
Michigan 密西根州
Oregon 俄勒崗州

〔加拿大〕
Ontario 安大略省
Quebec 魁北克省

10 山川湖海名

the Pacific Ocean 太平洋
Lake Michigan 密西根湖
Niagara Falls 尼加拉瀑布
the Mediterranean Sea 地中海
the Yangtze River 長江
Mount Qomolangma 珠穆朗瑪峰
↳ Mount 就等於 mountain，縮寫為 Mt.，常為專有名詞的一部分，又如：Mount Fuji（富士山）。
the Himalayas 喜馬拉雅山脈
the Alps 阿爾卑斯山脈
↳ 海、洋、河流、山脈的名稱前，常加 the。

集合名詞表

集合名詞是團體或集體的名稱。

academy (of scholars) 學院
agenda (of tasks) 事項；議程
air force 空軍
armada (of ships) 艦隊
army (of ants/caterpillars/frogs/soldiers) 軍隊；大批（如：螞蟻／毛毛蟲／青蛙／士兵）
association (of professionals/intellectuals) 協會、社團（如：專業人員協會／知識份子協會）
audience (of listeners/watchers) 視聽眾、讀者群（如：聽眾／觀眾）
band (of angels/gorillas/musicians/robbers/thieves)
　樂團；一群、一夥（如：一群天使／一群大猩猩／一群音樂家／一夥強盜／一夥小偷）
bank (of lights/seats/snow) 一排、一堆（如：一排燈光／一排座位／一堆雪）
bed (of flowers/vegetables) 可生長植物的一塊土地（如：一塊花圃／一塊菜園）
block (of houses/stamps/shares) 一塊、一組、大宗（如：一排房子／一套郵票／大宗股票）
board (of managers) 委員會、董事會；局、部
bundle (of clothes/sticks/nerve cells/money)
　捆；大批（如：一捆衣服／一捆棍子／許多神經細胞／一大筆錢）
cast (of actors) 班底；演員陣容
chain (of events/islands/mountains) 一連串、一系列（如：事件／島嶼／山脈）
chest (of drawers) 箱、櫃（如：五斗櫃）
choir (of singers/dancers) 聖樂團、表演團體（如：合唱團、歌舞團）
chorus (of singers/dancers) 合唱隊伍（如：合唱團、歌舞團）
class (of students) 班級
clergy 神職人員
club (of members) 俱樂部；會、社
collection (of art/books/coins/stamps)
　大量；聚集；收藏品（如：藝術收藏品／藏書／收藏硬幣／集郵）
college (an association of academics/individuals) 學院；學院的全體師生；團體
colony (of ants/artists/writers)〔生〕集群、群體；聚居人群（如：螞蟻群／一群藝術家／一群作家）
committee (of people) 委員會（如：人民委員會）
commission 委員會

company (of firefighters/soldiers/workers)
公司;合夥者;一隊;(軍)連(如:消防隊/連隊/一群工人)

congress (of representatives/delegates) 代表大會;國會(如:國會議員/大會代表)

corporation 股份有限公司

corps (formed of diplomats/marines)
(經專門訓練或有特種使命的)隊、組、團(如:外交團/海軍陸戰隊)

council (of advisors) 顧問委員會

couple (of newlyweds) 一對;夫婦(如:新婚夫婦)

counsel (of lawyers) 議事機構、委員會、理事會(如:律師委員會)

crew (of sailors) 全體船員、全體機員、一組工作人員

crowd (of spectators/workers/robots) 人群(如:一群觀眾/一群工人/一群機器人)

culture (of bacteria) 人工培養;養殖;培養菌

deck (of cards) 一副(如:紙牌)

department (of police officers) 大學系所;(行政或企業等)部門、局、司、處、科(如:警察局)

dozen 許多;一打

drove (of cattle)(被驅趕的或向前走動的)畜群(如:牛群)

enemy 敵軍;仇敵

faculty (of teachers) 全體教職員(如:全體教師)

family (of languages/people) 家庭;家族(如:語族/家族)

firm (of partners/doctors) 公司;工作集體(如:一組合夥人/一組醫生)

fleet (of ships/cars) 船隊、機隊、車隊(如:船隊/車隊)

flock (of sheep/birds/believers/tourists)
(飛禽、畜牧、人等的)群(如:羊群/鳥群/一群信仰者/一群觀光者)

flood (of complaints/emotion/anger/light/tears/words/ideas/money)
一大批、大量(如:許多抱怨/百感交集/大發雷霆/大片明亮的光線/淚如泉湧/滔滔不絕/大量的見解/財源滾滾)

furniture 傢俱

galaxy (of stars)(尤指出色的人或燦爛的事物)一群(如:恒星團)

government 政府

group (of people/things) 群、組(如:一組人/一組東西)

grove (of trees) 小樹林、果林、果園(如:樹叢)

heap (of parts/tires/coal/stones) 一堆(如:零件/輪胎/煤/石頭)

herd (of buffalo/cows/reindeer) 畜群、牧群(如:一群水牛/一群乳牛/一群馴鹿)

hive (of bees/people)(蜂或人的)群體(如:蜂群/熙攘喧鬧的人群)

host (of angels/friends) 一大群人、許多(如:一大群天使/一大群朋友)

huddle (of football players/lawyers/people) 〔美式足球〕賽前隊員列隊;(雜亂的)一團、一群
(如:美式足球賽前隊員列隊/混亂的律師群/雜亂的人群)

jury 陪審團；（競賽等的）評審委員會

kind（動、植物等的）類、族

knot (of toads) 一小群、一小隊（如：一小群癩蛤蟆）

legion (of veterans/soldiers/admirers)
軍隊；大量（如：眾多的退伍軍人／眾多的士兵／一大批愛慕者）

league (of teams/nations/women voters)
聯合會；同盟、聯盟（如：聯隊／同盟國／婦女投票者聯盟）

legislature (of individuals responsible to make laws) 立法機關

line (of people/robots/tanks/vehicles) 列、排（如：人／機器人／坦克／車輛）

litter (of kittens/piglets/puppies) 一窩（如：小貓／小豬／小狗）

lot（商品等）一批；某一類的人；多數；全部

majority (of the people) 多數人

mass (of soldiers/children) 眾多、群（如：一大群士兵／一大群孩子）

ministry（政府的）部；全體閣員

minority (of the people) 少數人

mob (of violent fanatics)〔貶〕烏合之眾；人群（如：一群極端狂熱份子）

multitude (of believers/followers) 民眾；一大群人（如：許多信仰者／許多信徒）

nation (of citizens) 國民

navy 海軍

nest (of birds/criminals/insects/mice/snakes/spies)
一窩、一群（如：一窩小鳥／一夥罪犯／一群昆蟲／一窩老鼠／一群蛇／一夥間諜）

network (of computers) 電腦網路

(the) number (of people) 總數；數量（如：人數）

orchestra (of musicians) 管弦樂隊

pack (of wolves/dogs/hounds/lies/gum)
（野獸、飛機等的）一群、一隊；一幫〔貶義〕；一堆、大量；一包、盒、箱、袋（如：一群狼／一群狗／一群獵犬／一派謊言／一盒口香糖）

panel (of experts/participants) 專門小組（如：一組專家／一組參與者）

party (of diners/fishermen/people)
政黨；（共同工作或活動的）一夥人、一行人（如：一群用餐者／一群漁夫／一群人）

parliament (of representatives) 議會、國會（如：議會代表）

patch (of carrots/clover/flowers)
一小塊土地（如：一小塊胡蘿蔔地／一小塊苜蓿園／一小塊花園）

people (of China/India/Japan/Berlin/Moscow)
人們；國民、民族（如：中國人／印度人／日本人／柏林人／莫斯科人）

pile (of rocks/stones/sand/things/work/money)

一堆、大量（如：一堆岩石／一堆石頭／一堆沙／一堆東西／大量的工作／大筆錢）
police 員警
portfolio (of pictures/stock/work)
代表作選輯；全部有價證券（如：代表畫集／全部有價證券／代表作品集）
press 新聞界、記者們、通訊社、報刊
pride (of lions) 群（如：獅群）
public 公眾、大眾、群眾
range (of mountains) 一系列；排、行（如：山脈）
school (of fish/porpoises)（水族）群（如：魚群／一群海豚）
series (of baseball games) 連續、系列；連續比賽（如：連續棒球比賽）
set (of dishes/knives/teeth) 一套、一副（如：一組盤子／一副刀／一副牙齒）
shelf (of books) 架子上的東西（如：一書架的書）
shock (of hair/wheat) 一堆（如：一頭亂髮／一堆麥子）
society 社會；俱樂部；社團、協會
spread (of cattle/horses/food)（廣闊的）一片區域（如：大牧牛場／大牧馬場／豐盛的宴席）
squad (of cheerleaders/police officers)（軍）班；小隊、小組（如：啦啦隊／一隊員警）
stack (of pancakes/waffles/books/paper)
一堆、一疊（如：一疊薄煎餅／一疊鬆餅／一疊書／一疊紙）
staff (of employees)（全體）工作人員（如：員工）
string (of beads/ponies) 一串、一行、一列（如：一串珠子／一列小馬）
suburbia 郊外居民
swarm (of bees/flies/reporters) 一大群、一大批（如：一大群蜜蜂／一大群蒼蠅／一大批記者）
team (of athletes/horses/mules) 隊、組、班；群（如：一隊運動員／一群馬／一群騾子）
total 總數
tribe (of natives) 一幫、一夥；部落（如：原住民部落）
trio (of musicians/singers) 三個一組、三件一套；三重唱（如：三重奏音樂家／三重唱歌手）
troop (of baboons/kangaroos/police officers/scouts/soldiers)
軍隊；大量、許多、一群（如：一群狒狒／一群袋鼠／一隊員警／一隊偵察兵／一隊士兵）
troupe (of actors/performers/singers) 劇團、戲班子；一班、一團（演員／表演者／歌手）
union (of artists/actors/workers/scientists)
協會、社團；工會（如：藝術家協會／演員協會／工人工會／科學家協會）
wave (of emotion/insects/water)
浪潮；情緒高漲；活動高潮（如：一股情感／一群昆蟲／一波水浪）
wealth (of information) 大量（如：大量的資訊）

複合名詞表

① 在「名詞 + 名詞」結構裡，第一個名詞修飾或描述第二個名詞，類似形容詞的作用。
② 除了「名詞 + 名詞」結構，還有其他的複合名詞結構。例如：以 up 結尾的複合名詞（warm-up），以 out 結尾的複合名詞（lookout），以 away 結尾的複合名詞（runaway）。
③ 一些有連字號和沒有連字號的複合名詞，很接近動詞片語，例如：follow-up、takeoff、go-between。
④ 有些複合名詞是由兩個或多個字合在一起構成，有些由兩個或多個字分開所構成，還有些是由連字號所連接。

A

air-conditioning 空調設備
airfreight 貨物空運（費）
airline 飛機航線
airmail 航空郵件
airplane 飛機
airport bus 機場巴士
airport 機場
anchor person 主播
apple juice 蘋果汁
applesauce 蘋果醬
armchair 扶手椅
army officer 軍官

B

backbone 脊骨
background 背景
backpack（登山、遠足用的）背包
ballroom 舞廳
bank rate（中央銀行的）貼現率；銀行利率
bankbook 銀行存摺
baseball 棒球
basketball 籃球
bathroom 洗手間
bedroom 臥室
birdhouse 鳥籠
book review 書評
bookcase 書櫃
bookshelf 書架
bookstore 書店
boyfriend 男朋友
brainstorm 突來的靈感
bus driver 公車司機
bus stop 公車站
businessman 商人；實業家
businessperson 商人；實業家
businesswoman 女企業家
buttermilk 酪乳

C

campfire 營火
can opener 開罐器
car door 車門
cash flow 現金流
cashbook 現金出納帳簿
chalkboard 黑板
check mark 打勾符號，「✓」號
check-in 投宿登記手續，驗票並領取登機卡
checklist 核對用的清單；投票人名冊
check-out/checkout（商店等）收銀檯；（旅館等）結帳離開的時間

checkup 核對；身體檢查
chicken soup 雞湯
chocolate cake 巧克力蛋糕
chocolate shake 巧克力奶昔
classmate 同班同學
clipboard 寫字夾板
coffee cup 咖啡杯
cookbook 食譜
copyright 版權
court order 法院指令
court-martial 軍事法庭
courtroom 法庭
cowboy 牛仔
cowgirl 女牛仔
cross section 橫斷面
cross-reference 互相參照
crossroad 十字路口
cupcake 杯形蛋糕

D——

daughter-in-law 媳婦
daydream 白日夢
daylight 日光
daytime 白天
doorbell 門鈴
doorknob 球形門把

E——

earring 耳環
earthquake 地震
earthworm 蚯蚓
eye shadow 眼影
eyeball 眼球
eyelid 眼瞼
eye-opener 令人大開眼界的事物
eyewitness 證人

F——

father-in-law 岳父；公公
fingernail 手指甲
firefighter 消防隊員
fireplace 壁爐
firewood 木柴
foot brake 腳剎車
football 英 足球；美 美式足球
footnote（註在本頁下方的）註腳
footprint 腳印；足跡

G——

girlfriend 女朋友
good-bye/goodbye 再見
goodwill 善意
grapefruit 葡萄柚

H——

hand brake 手剎車
handbag 手提包
handbill 傳單
handcuff 手銬
history book 歷史書
homeowner 自己擁有住房者／屋主
horse race 賽馬

I——

ice cream 冰淇淋
iceberg 冰山

J——

job hunter 求職者
job lot 整批雜貨
jobholder 有固定工作的人
job-hopper 常換工作的人

K——

keyboard 鍵盤
keyhole 鎖眼

L——

landlord 房東
lifeboat 救生艇

lifeline 救生索；重要航線
lifespan 壽命
lifestyle 生活方式
light bulb 燈泡
lighthouse 燈塔
lightweight 輕量級選手
light-year 光年
lipstick 口紅
lunchtime 午餐時間

M

master plan 總平面圖
masterpiece 傑作
mineral water 礦泉水
money market 金融市場
moneylender 放債人
moneymaker 會賺錢的人；能賺錢的工作
moonlight 月光
mother-in-law 岳母；婆婆
motorcycle 摩托車
mountain climber 登山者

N

newspaper 報紙
nightgown 女用睡袍
nose ring 鼻環
notebook 筆記本

O

oatmeal 燕麥片
office manager 辦公室主管
oil well 油井
olive oil 橄欖油

P

pancake 薄煎餅
paper clip 迴紋針
paper plate 紙盤
paperback 平裝本
paperwork 文書工作
pea soup 豌豆濃湯
peanut 花生
pinball 彈鋼珠遊戲
plastic fork 塑膠叉
pocket money 零用錢
pocketbook 女用手提包；錢包；袖珍本
ponytail 馬尾辮
postage stamp 郵票
postcard 明信片
postcode 郵遞區號
postman 郵差

R

railroad 鐵路
rainbow 彩虹
raincoat 雨衣
Rollerblades 直排輪溜冰鞋
roller-skates/roller skates 四輪溜冰鞋
roommate 室友

S

sailboat 帆船
sales tax 營業稅
salespeople 店員
school board 教育委員會
schoolchild 學童
schoolteacher 教師
seacoast 海岸
seafood 海鮮
seaport 海港
seashell 貝殼
sheep dog 牧羊犬
shoe shop 鞋店
shoelace 鞋帶
showbiz 演藝界；娛樂圈
showcase 玻璃陳列櫃
side effect 副作用

sidekick 共犯
sideline 邊線；兼職
skateboard 滑板
sleeping pill 安眠藥（片）
snowball 雪球
snowboard 滑雪板
snowflake 雪花
snowman 雪人（男）
snowplow 除雪機
snowshoe 雪鞋
snowstorm 暴風雪
snowwoman 雪人（女）
spotlight 聚光燈
stakeholder 賭金保管人
starfish 海星
stepbrother 異父異母兄弟
stepfather 繼父
stepmother 繼母
stepsister 異父異母姐妹
stick figure 人物線條畫
stone wall 石牆
strawberry 草莓
suitcase 手提箱
sunflower 向日葵
sunlight 日光
swimsuit 游泳衣
swordfish 箭魚

T——

tail end 末端
tailcoat 燕尾服
taillight（車）尾燈
teammate 隊友
textbook 教科書
thunderstorm 大雷雨
ticket office 售票亭
time deposit 定期存款
timeline 時間計畫表
timeout/time-out 比賽暫停
time-saver 省時工具
timeshare 分時享用度假別墅的所有權
timetable 時刻表
toenail 腳趾甲
tomato juice 番茄汁
toothbrush 牙刷
toothpaste 牙膏
trade name 商品命名
trademark 商標
trade-off 交易
turtleneck 高領毛衣

V——

vacuum cleaner 吸塵器
vacuum tube 真空管
vegetable soup 蔬菜湯
vineyard 葡萄園
voicemail 語音信箱
voiceprint 聲紋

W——

wastebasket 廢紙簍
water power 水力
watermelon 西瓜
waterproof 防水材料
weatherman 氣象播報員
weatherperson 氣象播報員
weekend 週末
wheelchair 輪椅
windmill 風車
windshield 擋風玻璃
woodland 森林地帶
work force 勞動力
workload 工作量
wristwatch 手錶

不可數名詞表

1 抽象名詞

anger 生氣
attention 注意力
beauty 美麗
courage 膽量
good 利益
honesty 誠實
integrity 正直
intelligence 智慧
kindness 仁慈
literacy 讀寫能力；識字
love 熱愛
lust 欲望
peace 和平
poise 鎮定
sadness 悲哀
wealth 財富

2 同類物品總稱

clothing 衣服
equipment 配備
furniture 傢俱
garbage 垃圾
jewelry 珠寶
machinery 機器
mail 郵件
silverware 銀器

3 氣體、水汽、煙霧

air 空氣
carbon dioxide 二氧化碳
carbon monoxide 一氧化碳
hydrogen 氫
nitrogen 氮
oxygen 氧氣
pollution 污染
↥ 可以是氣體、液體或固體。
scent 氣味
smog 煙霧
↥ = a noxious mixture of fog and smoke
smoke 煙
steam 蒸氣

4 液體

beer 啤酒
blood 血
coffee 咖啡
cologne 古龍水
gasoline 汽油
juice 果汁
kerosene 煤油
ketchup 番茄醬
milk 牛奶
oil 油
paint 油漆
perfume 香水
pop 含氣飲料
saliva 唾液
shampoo 洗髮精
soda 蘇打水；汽水
soup 湯
soy sauce 醬油
syrup 糖漿
tea 茶
urine 尿
vinegar 醋
water 水
wine 酒

5 小顆粒物品

corn 穀粒；玉米
dirt 灰塵；泥
dust 灰塵
flour 麵粉
grass 青草
pepper 胡椒粉
rice 稻；米
rye 裸麥
salt 鹽
sand 沙
sugar 糖
wheat 小麥

6 柔軟物質

bacon 培根
beef 牛肉
bread 麵包
butter 奶油
chicken (meat) 雞肉
↑ 指「雞肉」時，是不可數名詞；指「(餵養的)雞」時，可數。
↑ 複數形：chickens
chocolate 巧克力
↑ 指「巧克力」時，不可數；指「巧克力糖」時，可數。
↑ 複數形：chocolates
cloth 布料
cotton 棉
ham 火腿
ice cream 冰淇淋
jam 果醬
jelly 果凍
leather 皮革
meat 肉
mud 泥漿
paper 紙
↑ paper 指「紙」時，不可數；指「報紙；考卷」時，可數。
↑ 複數形：papers
pork 豬肉
seafood 海鮮
silk 絲綢
skin 皮膚
snow 雪
soap 肥皂
toast 吐司
tofu 豆腐
toilet paper 衛生紙
toothpaste 牙膏
wool 羊毛

7 固體

aluminum 鋁
copper 銅
glass 玻璃
↑ 指「玻璃」時，不可數；指「杯子」時，可數。
↑ 複數形：glasses
gold 金
ice 冰
iron 鐵
↑ ron 指「鐵」時，不可數；指「高爾夫球杆」和「熨斗」時，可數。
↑ 複數形 irons 也指「鐐銬」。
plastic 塑膠
platinum 白金
plutonium 鈽
silver 銀
steel 鋼
uranium 鈾
wax 蠟
wood 木頭

8 其他各種不可數名詞

advice 勸告
damage 損害
evidence 證據
fun 樂趣
geography 地理學
geometry 幾何學
help 幫助
history 歷史
homework 家庭作業
ignorance 無知
information 資訊
knowledge 知識
land 陸地；田地
leisure 閒暇
mass 團；塊
momentum 動量
money 錢
music 音樂
news 新聞
patience 耐心
permission 允許
poetry 詩
poverty 貧窮
progress 前進
psychology 心理學
scenery 風景
sex 性
slang 俚語
sleep 睡眠
vogue 時尚

美式英語和英式英語對照表

A 美英單字拼法對照表

美式		英式	
1 -or	→	-our	
armor	→	armour	盔甲
color	→	colour	顏色
colored	→	coloured	有顏色的
colorful	→	colourful	色彩鮮豔的
colorless	→	colourless	無色的
coloring	→	colouring	顏料
favor	→	favour	贊同
favorable	→	favourable	贊同的
flavor	→	flavour	味道
harbor	→	harbour	港灣
honor	→	honour	榮譽
honorable	→	honourable	高尚的
humor	→	humour	幽默
humorous	→	humourous	幽默的
labor	→	labour	勞動
laborer	→	labourer	勞工
neighbor	→	neighbour	鄰居
neighborhood	→	neighbourhood	附近
neighboring	→	neighbouring	附近的
neighborly	→	neighbourly	和睦的
odor	→	odour	氣味
rumor	→	rumour	謠言
tumor	→	tumour	腫瘤

2 -er	→	-re	
center	→	centre	中心
kilometer	→	kilometre	公里
liter	→	litre	公升
meter	→	metre	米；公尺
theater	→	theatre	電影院；劇院

3 -se	→	-ce	
defense	→	defence	防護
license	→	licence	執照
offense	→	offence	冒犯

4 -ce	→	-se	
practice	→	practise (v.)	實行

5 -l	→	-ll	
canceling/ canceled	→	cancelling/ cancelled	取消
counseling	→	counselling	商議
counselor	→	counsellor	顧問
jewelry	→	jewellery ↑ 英式不僅有兩個「ll」，還多了一個 e。	珠寶
marvelous	→	marvellous	令人驚嘆的
traveler	→	traveller	旅行者
traveling/ traveled	→	travelling/ travelled	旅行
woolen	→	woollen	羊毛製品

6 -ll → -l

fulfill	→ fulfil	實現
install	→ instal	安裝
skillful	→ skilful	熟練的

7 -ze → -se

analyze	→ analyse	分析
apologize	→ apologise	道歉
authorize	→ authorise	授權
characterize	→ characterise	以……為特徵
criticize	→ criticise	批評
emphasize	→ emphasise	強調
minimize	→ minimise	最小化
organize	→ organise	組織
organizer	→ organiser	組織者
realize	→ realise	實現
recognize	→ recognise	認出
specialize	→ specialise	專攻
summarize	→ summarise	總結

8 -za → -sa

organizational	→ organisational	組織的
privatization	→ privatisation	私有化

9 -m → -mme

gram	→ gramme	公克
program	→ programme	節目單；方案

10 其他

airplane	→ aeroplane	飛機
aluminum	→ aluminium	鋁
check	→ cheque	檢查；支票
encyclopedia	→ encyclopaedia	百科全書
gray	→ grey	灰色的
gypsy	→ gipsy	吉普賽人
judgment	→ judgement	審判
plow	→ plough	犁
specialty	→ speciality	專長
sulfur	→ sulphur	硫磺
tire	→ tyre	輪胎
whiskey	→ whisky	威士忌酒

B 美英用語對照表

美式	英式	
airport/small airport	aerodrome	（小）飛機場
apartment	flat	公寓
area code	dialing code	（電話）區域號碼
attorney/lawyer	barrister/solicitor	律師
automobile/auto/car	motorcar	汽車
baby carriage/baby buggy	pram	嬰兒車
baggage	luggage	行李
baggage room	left luggage office	行李寄放處
bathing suit	bathing costume	泳衣
balcony	gallery	（劇院）樓座
bathrobe	dressing gown	浴袍
bathroom/restroom/john	lavatory/toilet/water closet/WC	盥洗室
business suit	lounge suit	西裝
busy	engaged	（電話）占線
cab/taxi	taxi	出租車
call collect	reverse the charges	受話方付費
can (of beans)	tin (of beans)	罐頭（如：一罐豆子）
candy	sweets	糖果
candy store	sweet shop	糖果店
check/bill	bill	（餐廳的）帳單
city/municipal government	corporation	市政府
congress	parliament	議會
cookie	biscuit	（甜的）餅乾
county	shire	（行政區）郡
cracker	biscuit	（不甜的）餅乾
connect	put through	接通（電話）
corn	maize	玉蜀黍；玉米
crib	cot	兒童床
crazy	mad	發瘋的
cuffs (on pants)	turn-ups (on trousers)	褲腳的翻邊
diaper	nappy	尿布
deck	pack	一副（紙牌）
doctor's office	doctor's surgery	診所
do the dishes	wash up	洗碗
don't need to	needn't/don't need to	不需要做……
driver's license	driving licence	駕照

美式	英式	
downtown	centre	市中心
dress	frock	洋裝
drugstore/pharmacy	chemist's	藥房
druggist/pharmacist	chemist	藥劑師
dumb/stupid	stupid	愚蠢的
elevator	lift	電梯
eggplant	aubergine	茄子
eraser	rubber/eraser	橡皮擦
faculty	staff	全體教職員
fair	exhibition	展覽會
fall/autumn	autumn	秋天
faucet/tap	tap	水龍頭
first floor, second floor . . .	ground floor, first floor . . .	一樓、二樓
flashlight	torch	手電筒
flat tire	flat tyre/puncture	爆胎
freeway/thruway/throughway/ expressway/interstate/ superhighway/turnpike	motorway/main road	公路
French fries	chips	薯條
front desk	reception	（旅館）接待處
garbage can/ash can/trash can	dustbin/rubbish bin	垃圾桶
gas/gasoline	petrol	汽油
gear shift	gear lever	排檔桿
grade	class/form	（學校的）年級
grades	marks	成績
graduates	school leavers	畢業生
grain/wheat/oats	corn	穀物
hamburger	mince	碎牛肉
hardware store	ironmonger	五金店
hood of a car	bonnet of a car	汽車的車蓋
intersection	crossroads	十字路口
janitor	caretaker/porter	門房
rent/rental	let/letting	租金
legal holiday	bank holiday	法定假日
line	queue	行列；長隊
liquor	spirits	烈酒
liquor store/package store	off-license/wine merchant	小酒店
living room	sitting room/lounge/living room	客廳
locomotive	engine	火車頭

美式	英式	
long distance/long-distance call	trunk call	長途電話
low marshy land	fen	沼澤
mad/angry	angry	生氣的
mail	post	郵件
mail box/mail drop	pillar box	郵箱；郵筒
mean	nasty	脾氣不好的
median strip/divider	centre reservation	中央分車道
monkey wrench	spanner	扳手
movie/film	film	電影
mutual fund	unit trust	合股投資公司；共同基金
nurse	sister/nurse	護士
one-way ticket	single ticket	單程票
orchestra seats	stalls	（劇場）正廳前座區
pants	trousers	褲子
pass	overtake	超車
pavement	road surface	路面
penny	pence	便士；一分
perfume	scent	香味
period	full stop	句號
person-to-person call	personal call	指名通話
pitcher	jug	大水罐
pocketbook/purse	handbag	女用手提包
pot holders	oven cloth	隔熱布
potato chips	crisps	炸洋芋片
principal	headmaster/mistress	校長
private school (fee-charging school)	public school	私立學校
public school	state school	公立學校
radio	wireless	無線電
railroad	railway	鐵路
raincoat	mackintosh/macintosh	雨衣
raise in salary	rise in salary	加薪
realtor	estate agent	房地產經紀人
recess/break	break	學校假期；下課時間
rent	hire/let	租借
rest room/restroom	public toilet/WC	公共廁所
review	revise	（為了考試）複習
round-trip ticket	return ticket	來回票
run	stand for	競選（公職）
salesclerk/salesperson	shop assistant	店員

美式	英式	
Santa Claus	Father Christmas	聖誕老人
schedule	timetable	時刻表
second floor	first floor	二樓
sedan	saloon	轎車
semester（一年兩學期）	term（一年三學期）	學期
shorts	pants ↥ 英式 pants 指短褲，也指內褲（= underpants）；而美式 pants 指長褲。	短褲
shot	jab	注射
sidewalk	pavement/footpath	人行道
sink	basin	水槽；洗臉盆
slingshot	catapult	彈弓
sneakers (= sports shoes)	trainers	運動鞋
soccer	football	足球
stingy	mean	吝嗇的
store/shop	shop	商店
stove	cooker	爐灶
subdivision	housing estate	住宅區
subway	underground/tube	地鐵
suspenders	braces	吊褲帶
take a bath/a shower	have a bath/a shower	洗澡／淋浴
taxes	rates/ratings	稅金
television/TV	television/telly	電視（telly 為英式口語）
time payment/installment	hire purchase	分期付款
traffic circle	roundabout	（道路）圓環
trailer	caravan	拖車；居住車
truck	lorry	卡車
trunk of a car	boot of a car	後車箱
underclothing/underwear	smalls	內衣褲
undershirt	vest	汗衫；內衣
vacation	holiday	假期
vacuum cleaner	hoover	吸塵器
valley	dale	溪谷
vest	waistcoat	背心
wait	await/wait	等待
wash cloth	face flannel	洗臉毛巾
water heater	geyser	（瓦斯）熱水器
windshield	windscreen	（汽車）擋風玻璃
zero	nought	零
zipper	zip	拉鍊

C 介系詞和小品詞（包括某些副詞、冠詞、連接詞等）的區別

美式	英式	
different from/than	different from/to	不同的
check something (out)	check something	檢查
do something over/again	do something again	再做一次
live on Tenth Street	live in Tenth Street	住在第十街
on a team	in a team	在隊伍中
on the weekend/ on weekends	at the weekend/ at weekends	在週末
Monday through Friday	Monday to Friday	星期一到星期五
to/in the hospital	to/in hospital	去／在醫院

7 美國的州、領地及首府

	州名	縮寫	中文	首府	中文
1	Alabama	AL	阿拉巴馬州	Montgomery	蒙哥馬利
2	Alaska	AK	阿拉斯加州	Juneau	朱諾
3	Arizona	AZ	亞利桑那州	Phoenix	鳳凰城
4	Arkansas	AR	阿肯色州	Little Rock	小石城
5	California	CA	加利福尼亞州	Sacramento	薩克拉門托
6	Colorado	CO	科羅拉多州	Denver	丹佛
7	Connecticut	CT	康乃狄克州	Hartford	哈特福特
8	Delaware	DE	德拉瓦州	Dover	多佛
9	Florida	FL	佛羅里達州	Tallahassee	達拉哈西
10	Georgia	GA	喬治亞州	Atlanta	亞特蘭大
11	Hawaii	HI	夏威夷州	Honolulu	檀香山
12	Idaho	ID	愛達荷州	Boise	博伊西
13	Illinois	IL	伊利諾伊州	Springfield	斯普林菲爾德
14	Indiana	IN	印第安那州	Indianapolis	印第安諾波利斯
15	Iowa	IA	愛荷華州	Des Moines	得梅因
16	Kansas	KS	堪薩斯州	Topeka	托皮卡

17	Kentucky	KY	肯塔基州	Frankfort	法蘭克福
18	Louisiana	LA	路易斯安那州	Baton Rouge	巴吞魯日
19	Maine	ME	緬因州	Augusta	奧古斯塔
20	Maryland	MD	馬里蘭州	Annapolis	安納波利斯
21	Massachusetts	MA	麻薩諸塞州	Boston	波士頓
22	Michigan	MI	密西根州	Lansing	蘭辛
23	Minnesota	MN	明尼蘇達州	St. Paul	聖保羅
24	Mississippi	MS	密西西比州	Jackson	傑克遜
25	Missouri	MO	密蘇里州	Jefferson City	傑斐遜城
26	Montana	MT	蒙大拿州	Helena	海倫娜
27	Nebraska	NE	內布拉斯加州	Lincoln	林肯
28	Nevada	NV	內華達州	Carson City	卡森城
29	New Hampshire	NH	新罕布什爾州	Concord	康科特
30	New Jersey	NJ	紐澤西州	Trenton	特倫頓
31	New Mexico	NM	新墨西哥州	Santa Fe	聖菲
32	New York	NY	紐約州	Albany	奧爾巴尼
33	North Carolina	NC	北卡羅來納州	Raleigh	羅利
34	North Dakota	ND	北達科他州	Bismarck	俾斯麥
35	Ohio	OH	俄亥俄州	Columbus	哥倫布
36	Oklahoma	OK	奧克拉荷馬州	Oklahoma City	俄克拉何馬市
37	Oregon	OR	俄勒岡州	Salem	賽勒姆
38	Pennsylvania	PA	賓夕法尼亞州	Harrisburg	哈里斯堡
39	Rhode Island	RI	羅德島州	Providence	普羅維登斯
40	South Carolina	SC	南卡羅來納州	Columbia	哥倫比亞
41	South Dakota	SD	南達科他州	Pierre	皮爾
42	Tennessee	TN	田納西州	Nashville	納什維爾
43	Texas	TX	德克薩斯州	Austin	奧斯汀
44	Utah	UT	猶他州	Salt Lake City	鹽湖城
45	Vermont	VT	佛蒙特州	Montpelier	蒙彼利埃
46	Virginia	VA	維吉尼亞州	Richmond	里士滿
47	Washington	WA	華盛頓州	Olympia	奧林匹亞
48	West Virginia	WV	西維吉尼亞州	Charleston	查爾斯頓
49	Wisconsin	WI	威斯康辛州	Madison	麥迪森
50	Wyoming	WY	懷俄明州	Cheyenne	夏延
51	District of Columbia	DC	哥倫比亞特區	Washington	華盛頓
52	Guam	GU	關島	Agana	阿加尼亞
53	Puerto Rico	PR	波多黎各	San Juan	聖胡安
54	Virgin Islands	VI	維爾京群島	Charlotte Amalie	夏洛特阿馬利亞

索引

Indexes

Diving Deep Into English 索引

英文索引

中文索引

國家圖書館出版品預行編目資料

英文文法全書（彩色二版）/ Dennis Le Boeuf & 景黎明著 二版. 一[臺北市]：寂天文化，2018.04印刷 面；公分.

ISBN 978-986-318-260-3 (20K平裝)
ISBN 978-986-318-388-4 (32K平裝)
ISBN 978-986-318-437-9 (20K精裝)
ISBN 978-986-318-555-0 (25K精裝)
ISBN 978-986-318-681-6 (25K平裝)

1. 英語 2. 語法

805.16 107004758

作者 _ Dennis Le Boeuf & 景黎明
校對 _ 陳慧莉 & 歐寶妮
編輯 _ 安卡斯
製程管理 _ 洪巧玲
出版者 _ 寂天文化事業股份有限公司
電話 _ +886-2-2365-9739
傳真 _ +886-2-2365-9835
網址 _ www.icosmos.com.tw
讀者服務 _ onlineservice@icosmos.com.tw
出版日期 _ 2018年9月 二版再刷（320205）

郵撥帳號 _ 1998620-0 寂天文化事業股份有限公司
訂購金額600（含）元以上郵資免費
訂購金額600元以下者，請外加郵資65元
若有破損，請寄回更換